Sequel to the Janaforma Trilogy

The
PERMEABLE WEB
of
TIME

Sequel to the Janaforma Trilogy

The
PERMEABLE WEB
of
TIME

Martha Fawcett

JANAFORMA PRESS

Davidsonville. Maryland

Text copyright © 2014 Martha Fawcett

Janaforma Press

Davidsonville, Maryland

www.marthafawcett.com

Cover image by Duncan Long

Library of Congress Control Number:
2014942912

ISBN: 978-0-9890636-5-4

Printed in U.S.A.

First Edition

DEDICATION

To Penelope, my daughter, an artist of life that creates beauty everywhere she goes

CONTENTS

ONE

We look out from *The Mother*, our home.
We live in her and she lives through us,
yet we are blind before her unflinching eye.
In us, she is a bit of mist before time,
a sound that began with strange rumblings
shortly after midnight.
What can we know of our passions that she holds tenderly between her teeth?
What sense can decipher the depths of her glorious creation?
What spiral dance she might perform within the possibility of our lives
remains her darkest mystery.

Pulled from her lemniscate,
she held me suspended between dimensions,
the place where I always need to decide.
I made a jump
and found myself passing through the Library of All Creation,
a place where words begin to form the faltering definition of our lives.
We wrestled there, she and I, on the edge of awareness—
I to create logic
and she to hide again as drifting mist.
My face reflected only angelic innocence,
yet my denial was my forgetfulness,
my bony head struggling endlessly to be born.

****

The approaching hand smelled clean, like lavender. It was Elay. She was

1

my creator and child just as I was her creator and child. We were a continuum, indistinguishable life seeding a universe. "*Saannte,*" she whispered. Her breath was immaculate perfume, heady bergamot to be exact. How real was my choice when her perfume was a sensory trail luring me back to life? My focus stayed soft as I bathed in the soft theta waves cruising through my brain. No need to come back from meditation too soon, no need to rush anything at all. The orbit of the ship, *La Ventana,* curved and brought the light from the star Chesaray nearer. The sudden intense light prodded me to open my eyes. Through thready eyelashes, I watched Elay move across the garden and perch upon a stone settee. She was beautiful, vital, my greatest supporter, too direct with her opinions and a complete enigma to me. She appeared softer than usual. Dressed in a clingy silk blouse—a gossamer flowered-happening of sky-blue—she had pinned a white gardenia to the inner-cuff of her sleeve. Her skirt seemed to be made of tiny sweeps of green and brown. Blues, jungle greens, hot desert browns, earthy tans—the colors of life worlds, were her favorite shades. "Where's your Vanguard uniform?" I wondered aloud. She did not answer, but laid a hand on the settee as a silent invitation to join her. Elay was a Regression* graduate many times over and realized with utter certainty that I was her *febr* (lifegiver parent) in my previous life. Was this a problem between us? It always was a problem when we framed our relationship within the narrow context of one life. Now in the glow of the ship's afternoon garden, I sensed a gap between us a light-year wide. As always, this particular gap threw me into a tizzy, a state of emotional regression, where I automatically became her problem child.

Elay's focus remained one-pointed, her questioning eyes suggesting and probing. Over lunch, a week earlier, I told her my personal life was none of her concern and she politely did not mention the topic again until the dessert arrived. Now I went to sit next to her on the settee where she said, "You're so precious to me." Her tone seemed too controlled, too prudent for her normal shoot-from-the-hip style.

"What's up, *mebr*?" (lifebearer parent)

She lifted her left hand until it sat poised in front of her face. "Do you know the genetic planning and love that went into the making of just one of your hands?" She twisted her arm precisely, letting her gardenia-decorated wrist fall in a gentle spiral.

Should I have returned the reminder and asked, do you realize the genetic planning that went into your eyes, to make sure they were the correct shade of Janaforma blue-green? Instead, I consented to her parental fussing. Meditation had restore my patience and I was almost ready to

---

*Regression is a drug that opens memory to the knowledge of past lives. Many Janaforma believe in the power of Regression and a Janaforma adolescent usually take the drug for the first time when reaching the age of 18 bio-years.

admit I had parched places inside me that needed replenishing. My loneliness spilled into a pool of nostalgia, making me feel as if I was an exile, an outsider peering through a window into a cozy room. I remembered a childhood of comfort and love, a time when arms held me and I knew I was safe. Nostalgia made the yearning worse and all of me responded. Searching and craving, I plucked a pleasant memory from experience and devoured it as only a gourmand of love can do.

****

I had stopped by The Quasar to get a drink before going to bed. The Quasar is a hole-in-the-wall club down on Q-deck. Its dark ambience masks its peeling facade, the results of too many slipshod paint jobs by a string of inattentive owners. A lack of tourists make The Quasar a popular hangout with Vanguard Scouts who drop by after their shifts, to mellow out in the club's insouciant atmosphere. When the parties get going, music and patrons spill out onto the public walkway in casual disarray.

The hour was late and the ship deep into night mode. The music drifting out of The Quasar sounded lush, refined, and jazzy. Listening for a moment, the music turned misty before taking an impulsive leap into new and unexplored realms. One of the musicians was Bejan, my *fra* (consort parent). I went inside and Bejan was playing keyboards with a couple of *cis* (her/his) pals on the small stage next to the bar. They were, what Bejan called, "surfing the time threads." Just then, Bejan was chilling, letting Weegan Zu explore some smoky-colored theme with his muted, brass horn. The scene made me smile. Weegan was evoking some faraway sounds, plumbing the depths like only a Tyrowsian musician can do.

I was avoiding Bejan and not seen *cim* (him/her) in several cycles. *Ce* (he/she) never was as direct as Elay; but lately, even the reticent Bejan could not help mentioning that I was ignoring my gifts. *Ce* waved and I went over to say hello. *Cis* curly locks hung loose and relaxed around *cis* shoulders. "Want to sit in?" *ce* asked. "I'll let you play my new keyboard," and *ce* laid down a few chords in the deeper register. Sometimes we dabbled with improvisation within the security of family gatherings. Besides being famous for *cis* aromatherapy work on the Regression drug, Bejan was a string of famous musicians and composers in several past lives. Family modesty keeps me from mentioning who they were, but some were truly great.

"You think I'm ready to go public?" I asked.

"Let's give it a whirl," Bejan said with a wink.

"Could I sing instead?"

"Since when do you sing?"

"Remember a tune called, 'Nobody Does Me Like You Do'?" The foolish urge felt like a whim that jumped into me. Bejan started exploring the keyboard and a few seconds later, plucked my requested tune from thin air. Bejan's genius possessed the ability to perform tiny miracles such as this—creative stunts that flared out from the fiery center of *cis* collective mind. *Cis* fingers relaxed on the keys and Weegan Zu stepped in to fill the void with a series of seamless improvisations.

The lyrics to "Nobody Does Me Like You Do" already were singing in my head. For the last three cycles, the song had been driving me crazy. Three thousand years earlier, on the world of Aeternus, I heard the tune for the first time; now it seemed stuck on continuous replay and trying to tell me something I did not understand. I needed to dig the memory out, to expose the emotional trauma it was causing me. Bejan did a few gymnastic runs over the keyboard and the melody began germinating seeds of emotion from another life. Half-scared about what began to happen, I still did nothing to change my trajectory. Instead, I closed my eyes and let go. While memories pulled me backward through time, music was my tether. My mind uncoiled like wire released from a spool and with a definite snap, half my mind found itself on Aeternus Complex, three thousand years earlier.

****

"It-took-me-some--to-recognize-the-feelin'. But-I-know-tonight-I-don't-need-no-clues. 'Cause-you're-on-my-mind-from-morning—through, 'til-evening. Nobody-does-me-like-you-do. I-chased-after-dreams-that-never-came-to-nothin'. And-tried-being-free, but-the-nights-were-so-blue. It's-easy-to-see-that-I'm lost-without-your-lovin'. Nobody-does-like-you-do." Suspicions turned to utter certainty and I knew Cle was in communion with my psychic hawk, Ezek*. "Mister-Moonlight, shine-your-light-on-down. Spread-those-tender-feelings-aaall-around. Every-moment-I-spend-by-your-side. Love-begins-to-make-me crazy—one-more-time. I've-made-up-my-mind-got-myself-together. Just-say-you'll-be-mine, and-we'll-stick-like-glue. I-got-this-feelin'-and-it's-true. Baby, nobody-does-me-like-you-do." The synthesis got hotter and the connection sizzled with energy. "Oh-rock-me-easy-when-the-day-is-done. Wrap-me-in-your-passion-all-night-long. Every-moment, I-spend-by-your-side, love-begins to make me CRAZY—ONE-MORE-TIME! YOU'RE-MY-LIFE! 'Till-the-eeeeend**."

The music climaxed and spread me out through the centuries. Then, now, and in the future, Cle and I are one throughout time. *Cis* voice scatted around the melody for the next twenty-two bars, while Bejan let the music drift. Like the gentle sipping of tiny waves against land, the alchemy slowed and settled. Finally, the higher notes of the keyboard tinkled, tiny bells from a sacrosanct place where sound and silence meet.

The unexpected applause broke my spell. A bevy of consorts were hanging around the stage and I leaned over the edge and gave the closest one a kiss. Weegan Zu shouted, "Terrific, Sante! Your new talent has real

---

*Ezek: from "ezekalmende" meaning "higher vision"; language origin, Mescale.
**"Nobody Does Me Like You Do," Rod Temperton, Human, planet Earth.

flare." A tear or two trailed down his pale cheek. Weegan Zu was a hypersensitive Tyrowsian, an artiste. His small pink eyes managed to get teary-eyed over every love song.

Bejan appeared astounded and suggested, "We should do this more often."

"It wasn't me, *Fra*."

Cis enthusiasm quickly sank into kindness. "Want to talk about it?"

"Not really, my only intention was to come in here and get a drink. My singing was a fluke." Bejan shook *cis* head and was on the verge of lecturing me, but changed *cis* mind. Ezek, my psychic hawk, wanted to probe a bit more, but the rest of me did not feel like working that hard. Giving Bejan a kiss on the forehead, I jumped down off the small stage to go get my drink.

****

A cluster of Vanguard Scouts stood around the bar and the usual crowd was in residence. I scarcely recognized Xana. Her hair was hot pink and she sported rainbow-colored adhesion lenses. One throaty, "Love your new gig, Sante," and I knew it was Xana. On a one-to-one basis, she was spontaneous and adventurous, exactly what I needed when the past waterlogged my mind. She sashayed over to where I sat and draped her luscious, perfumed arms around my neck. "Say nothing, just give me a kiss," she said in her own special way. Happy to oblige, we kissed and her smell, beneath the lingering traces of perfume on her collar and sleeves, came through like champagne and caviar. She was slightly drunk and ripe for picking. Three years earlier, Xana and I indulged in a prolonged affair, but no matter how we tried, we could never get the feelings between us beyond our lust. The sexual heat between us was so intense that the affair lingered on for nearly a year. "You look grouchy," she said.

"I never look grouchy," I snapped.

"Right! An artist never indulges in baser emotions, such as common irritability. The artist drifts in romantic sentiment and makes everyone else grouchy instead." I insisted that we kiss again in a truce. Once I sipped champagne mixed with her personal juices and the mere memory of it still had the power to arouse me. It did not take Xana long to focus on my desires and she suggested, "Let's go somewhere and work on your grouchiness together." Her offer was getting me started and I knew I needed to make another choice.

Cle had wired me, but now I lied and said, "I'm too tired."

"When are you going to stop playing Saint Sante? Throw off your sackcloth and ashes. Let's enjoy life. Do you think you're going to be this gorgeous forever?"

"Come on Xana, have some pity on this particular fool."

She focused on me for a few seconds and said, "You're getting rigid. Do you know what happens when rigidity sets in on lifegivers?" I expected her to say we wasted away as lonely ghosts, but she said, "Savvy doolies* come along and make them into poets. Come on!" she now insisted. "Let's not sit here and torture the past together. I'm going to perform an altruistic act for once in my life and introduce you to the Vanguard's latest addition, the *très fabliaux,* Miro Rugen." In one minute flat, Xana filled me in on the gossip concerning her new team leader. "Scuttlebutt says Miro has connections to Tyrowsian wealth that's bought *cim* an up-front position in the Vanguard. No bullshit, Sante, this kid has my psychic antennae doing handsprings. Mark my words, Commander Miro is going straight to the top in the Vanguard." Xana exhaled hot air across her rainbow-colored fingernails, making the colors turn vibrant. She giggled before adding, "Tokla, in Operations, told me they were going to put extra security blocks on the thrusters, just to make sure there's no impromptu misfiring when Commander Hot Pants visits the bridge."

I glanced around, looking for the new Vanguard talent. When I first laid eyes on Miro Rugen, *ce* terrified me because I knew *ce* could take me down. *Ce* was young, not more than twenty bio-years. Xana introduced us and Rugen went into *cis* routine. "Just arrived from Uropae," *ce* effused, in the staccato language of those still excited with life. "I'm Commander Brooke's replacement." Whoever Rugen was, *ce* enjoyed impressive connections. *Ce* joined the Vanguard, not as a lowly scout, but as a flight commander on the captain's shift. *Ce* oozed—mostly with enthusiasm. *Ce* talked about *cis* career with an eager sense of dedication. *Cis* professional biography seemed especially important to *cim,* suggesting *ce* believed *cis* life held the same thrill for everyone else as it did for *cim.* A graduate of the elite Cerribeame Academy on Calypso, *cis* training had brainwashed *cim* into believing that *ce* was prepared for life's contingencies. My skin began to crawl when *ce* told me the Cerribeame taught *cim* everything *ce* knew about flying vitasphere spacecraft. My repulsion for the Cerribeame went back centuries. In my last life, the methodical savagery of the Cerribeame had kidnapped Cle— tortured and stripped *cis* mind clean as a desert bone. For me, this was too much to reconcile, let alone forgive. Logic suggested that we lived in a new age and the Cerribeame ceased killing the moment the Regression drug opened their minds. Regardless, my heart ached for my beloved Cle and the misery *ce* suffered at the hands of the sadistic Cerribeame Guard.

Rugen talked-the-talk of the Vanguard and *cis* personal charisma managed to congregate a small entourage of potential devotees around *cim.* As if *ce* were the personal stanchion of eternity, *ce* declared, "It's up to the Vanguard to make sure the shape of time remains undisturbed." Several of *cis* peers toasted *cis* assumption with handy, beer glasses, while the old timers looked down into their drinks and grimaced. I listened politely and

*"narcissistic consort"; language origin, Mescale, Janaforma slang.

decided not to mention that I created the Vanguard Scouts in my last lifetime and their primary responsibility was to protect *La Ventana* and its people.

Miro Rugen was one-hundred-percent authentic consort. The thoughtfulness *ce* exhibited in *cis* meticulous cosmetics and the tailored attention to *cis* Vanguard uniform all were overt consort affectations. *Cis enewetak** was jaw dropping. *Ce* was too damn handsome and too beautiful, all at the same time. The way *ce* leaned against the bar suggested *ce* was strong, while underneath waited a universe of tender softness. Rugen neither flaunted nor concealed *cis* sexuality; but it was there, like a subtle smile of confidence coming up from *cis* depths. *Cis* champagne-toned hair hung scandalously free and was as copious as a lion's mane. In time and with the right partners, Miro Rugen would be The Wizard commanding the mind of some constrained lifegiver. Gradually I became aware that *ce* was attracted to me. *Ce* encouraged me to gaze into *cis* lake-blue eyes, doing a gravitational interlock on me, as if *ce* expected me to stay in *cis* orbit. "Love your sexy witch eyes," *ce* flirted with me, using the personal tense in Mescale. "You have the psychic talent to go with those eyes?"

"Maybe," I offered. That Rugen was talking about my eyes in personal-tense Mescale suggested that *ce* was seeking greater intimacy. Beyond the obvious, only a foolish prophet might declare how far *ce* wanted to go with the affair. My many truncated love affairs left me skittish. Consorts I had avoided for four years, while Xana finally left me drained and impotent. Now I fought what I felt and ran for cover. I made excuses to myself on the social level. *Miro Rugen is a brilliant young star. Ce will need to be polished, loved, and eternally embraced. Cis life will be public, nauseatingly wholesome, especially as a Vanguard Scout.* For sure, I was too neurotic for the young, heroic Rugen with my deep, incestuous secrets. My resistance decided to put this particular consort on the dark side of a nameless moon and pretend not to care. Besides, I felt pressure to hurry-up and decide and that alone made me want to say no. Four predatory lifegivers and three ovulating lifebearers waited inside the cluster of *cis* admirers for the pubescent Rugen to give one of them an encouraging glance.

Rugen continued to flatter me with *cis* attention. "Want to dance? I sing too."

My ego was basking, declaring I still looked good, while thoughts of holding *cim* in my arms almost left me breathless. *It's just a dance, not a commitment*, I rationalized. "Let's do it," I agreed. We waltzed over to the anti-gravity chamber and *ce* insisted that I lead. I tried and then *ce* wrapped *cis* legs around mine and pulled me into a dizzying spin. Rugen definitely was a space jockey who knew how to control our every move inside the

---

*"an attractive balance between male and female"; language origin, Mescale.

dance chamber. And *ce* wasn't shy. *Ce* slipped *cis* hands around my waist and pulled me so close that I became lost in *cis* perfume that was built around the foundation of frankincense, the upper notes of forget-me-knot flowers, and the stratospheric essence of *tartan ratu*. Several delightful whiffs later, I sneezed all over *cis* meticulous black shirt and found myself apologizing. Then my curiosity prodded me to ask, "I can understand about *ratu* and frankincense, but why forget-me-knots?"

Rugen's Mescale slipped into the personal tense again, *cis* accent in that language declaring *ce* spent at least one life on the Ivory Coast of Euterpe. "It was the whimsy of the aromatherapist. *Ce* said my eyes were the color of blue forget-me-knots in a previous life."

"By any chance was that whimsical aromatherapist named Bejan?"

"Yes! Is that a problem?"

"Bejan is my *fra*."

"Oh really? How about that! *La Ventana* is turning out to be a small world. Everyone seems to be related to everyone else." Part of me wanted to escape. My righteousness wanted someone to reverse the gravity switch on the wall so I could watch Rugen, like a leaking balloon, slowly drift to the floor. Instead, *ce* gazed all dreamy-eyed at me, eager to play the kind of consort games that make lifegivers into funnels and think about giving themselves away. Holy Mother! The obsession to die in someone is as innate feeling in most lifegivers. The obsession causes them to commit, to fuel the future, to spread their love out to a lifebearer, a family, a Community, and beyond.

Rugen was clever, making up new lyrics to old familiar tunes. *Cis* voice was a light immature baritone, singing, "You-make-me-feel-like-a-saffroneke. So-tell-me-what-words-I-might-speak-that-will-return-you-to-me." The Mescale word *"saffroneke,"* I had not heard in centuries At one time, the Island Worlds of Gathos was home to many professional courtesans who called themselves *"Les Saffroneke."* In subsequent centuries, the prestige of the word diminished, becoming more generic, meaning any high-classed pleasure prince or prostitute.

"You're a lousy poet," I teased and when *ce* laughed—I knew I could fall in love with *cim*. *Cis* warm breath smelled like fragrant lemon thyme from the ship's garden. Bejan had sensually programmed Rugen for me. Knowing that, you can bet I felt torn in two. Part of me entertained a desperate urge to take Rugen somewhere and lose my urgency in *cis* groin and another part resented that *ce* came with an endorsement from one of my parents.

I needed to be with someone again, but I refused to fake it. My only refuge was love and I was honor-bound to respect it. Passion created me through a thoughtful act of creation and I could no longer fall down on my knees before any ready and willing consort, no matter how potent the onslaught of *cis* advance. All I needed to say was yes and I knew Rugen was mine. My decision-maker remained befuddled and I fumbled and lingered a bit longer. I struggled to extract some face-saving response from myself, to save my withering ego from yet another disgrace, but words failed me. I excused myself and fled The Quasar without saying goodbye to anyone.

****

I wandered around the ship, mainly on D-deck, where the half-light of night mode and the scent of orange blossoms, from the trees along the main promenade, gave me time to ponder. Alone in the dark, I felt free enough to admit that I needed what Rugen was offering. I heard whispers ending with, "—need a picture too? It lasts longer." An indignant voice, from the darkness, flamed my shame. I saw nothing, but felt guilty nonetheless. Who and what were shaming me? Was it merely the past or was it love itself pointing a finger at my loneliness?

When I arrived home, I resorted to magic. I had no inspiration to write a new book, so was playing with tarot cards. Belinda, Bejan's *mebr*, gave the cards to me on my sixteenth birthcycle. That was eleven years ago, yet I could still smell traces of her perfume, Essence of Salamander, on the silk scarf. When she gave the cards to me, she said, "I hope these cards help you become the psychic magician you were born to be."

Bejan chided her when she said that, telling her, "Psychic skills are the frosting on the cake, not the cake."

Stripping the scarf away from the cards, I ignored ritual or respect in their handling. "Okay, give me your heraldic advice," I challenged. "Give me a card for Miro Rugen." Then I pulled a single card from the deck and flipped it over. The Ace of Coins lay inert on the tabletop, but its message wiggled like a lure. The Ace of Coins is a symbol for material wealth. Xana had hinted that Rugen possessed connections to Tyrowsian wealth. The ace, the beginning, suggested Rugen and I were just getting started. I turned toward my multidex and requested, "Bibliodexteritas? Tell me the divinatory meaning of the Ace of Coins in the Trinity Witch tarot."

The answer was already waiting on the tip of its simulated tongue. "The divinatory meaning of the Ace of Coins in the Trinity Witch tarot is perfect contentment, joy, ecstasy, and lively intelligence."

"If a lifegiver pulled this card for a potential consort, should the lifegiver consider the consort favorably?"

"Go get *cim*!" hummed the Bibliodexteritas.

****

While Elay and I sat in the garden together, the light had dimmed again. "I'm pressed for time," she said.

The situation called for a small white lie. "I'm sorry, I was deep in meditation."

Elay turned impatient. When she did, she always hit the psychic mark with annoying accuracy. "Is that right? Well this meditation wears skimpy black undershorts." That statement woke me up and I became meek with guilt over my wandering mind. Elay smiled indulgently, but it still felt parental. "You're as stubborn as I once was. Let it happen, cherub. Your future is bright."

Sitting there in her perfect, blue blouse, Elay was a compelling image of hope. If anyone could make me believe in the future, it was Elay. She was one of the greatest souls I ever met. She was tireless and fanatically faithful to her family. She managed to raise three distinctly different children, while keeping two consorts and a lifegiver in love with her for thirty years. At the same time, without a doubt, she was one of the finest Vanguard Scouts on *La Ventana*. Elay was a committed player, but despite my undying love for her, she bugged me. "I need you to do me a favor," she said.

"Why can't You-Know-Who do it?" Two months earlier, I told Elay, "Never mention You-Know-Who's name in my presence again." Since then, she pussyfooted around topics concerning You-Know-Who in an attempt to honor my foolish request. My avoidance of speaking the name of You-Know-Who was my feeble attempt at evasion. You-Know-Who is Nova. Genetically, Nova is my *febr*, my lifegiver parent, but Nova is much more to me. Now Elay came down with a no-nonsense singularity of purpose. "Michael, Bejan, and I need to take a short trip to Aeternus and Nova will be busy with the Executive Gathering while we're gone. So are you available to do this favor for me or not?"

"Depends on what it is."

She turned abrupt. "Evose is on his way here."

"Uncle Evose?" A childhood image of Evose popped into my mind. He was nine, awkward, and homely. His lips were too full and his nose cut out from his forehead in a wedge. His dense black hair was bushy and possessed a tendency to frizz into wavy coils. As a child, I frequently accused him of recharging his hair through electrical outlets. He was brassy, a bit of a smart aleck, which I realize now was an act of bravado.

Because our genetic connections are convoluted, the proper relationship between Evose and me is difficult to describe. Bejan is Belinda's oldest offspring, the consequence of Belinda impregnating herself with a DNA concoction left by two Janaforma geneticists, who lived three hundred years ago. The preferred story, inside our family, is that when Belinda tried to use the stored DNA for impregnation, the essence was weak. At this critical juncture, Bogwa, of the Damarian species, came into the procreative picture and supplied an "extra boost of lifegiver energy"—whatever that may be—to get the pregnancy "to take" in Belinda. To accomplish the impregnation, Bogwa became Belinda's lover. Shortly afterward, Belinda and Bogwa took my maternal *bramma* (lifebearer grandparent), Estrella, into their relationship. Eventually, Bogwa ended up doing the same favor for Estrella, when she was trying to create Elay from genetic material I left in my previous life. Bogwa, Belinda, and Estrella formed a bonded family and Estrella gave birth to another daughter, named Hope, while Belinda gave birth to a daughter named Bellanna. Several years later, Bogwa and Belinda conceived another child they named Evose. Despite Evose's exotic mix of genes, his sex was male.

"Do you think you could meet Evose at the landing portal?" Elay asked.

"When?"

"He should be here sometime in the next eleven hours. I don't want him landing and finding no one to meet him."

"Why? Evose is a big boy. He can find his way around *The Mother* without a tour guide."

The pitch of her voice went up an entire octave. "It's a matter of courtesy and you know it."

"No need to shout. I'll take care of your problem. Do you want me to take him out to dinner too?"

"Basically, I would like you to be nice—like Bejan."

I give up! I thought. I was not going into the subject of Bejan's altruism just as I was not going into the subject of You-Know-Who.

"Other than being annoyed with me, how are you doing?" she probed. "Have you started a new book yet?"

"I don't want to talk about it."

"Your dry spell will pass. Besides, your reputation is secure. *Visions of The Wall* received excellent reviews from critics."

"That shows how little you know about writing. Who cares about *Visions of The Wall?* I need to be writing now."

She wanted to say, *then do it*, but changed her mind. She tried to hide her cresting thoughts, but with me, it was useless. I could read her easier than I could read myself. She was thinking, *why can't Sante find someone to love so I can stop worrying about* lim *(him/her)?*

I answered her unstated thought. "We both know that Nova wants me to be a loner this time around."

"That's self-pitying crap," she shot back. "The last thing Nova wants is for you to be alone."

In all honesty, I do not blame Elay, Bejan, or even Nova for my depression. If anything, they've sought to help me in too many ways. In this life, my childhood was close to idyllic. I received love, praise, and copious attention from all my parents. Around puberty, new past-life memories surfaced and I began to withdraw from my family and then from myself. For years, I harbored a feeling of shame for the physical lust I felt for my own *febr* (lifegiver parent). I began seeking answers from a long list of authorities and professional therapists in an effort to escape my pain. Therapy did not work for me because no therapist could explain away my lust. By then, my psyche was raw, and I felt ashamed down to my last intimate and indiscreet thought.

My beloved *fra*, Michael, came to my rescue and saved me from total self-destruction. One cycle when I was feeling particularly morose, Michael reminded me, "No one has the right to define you, including you." *Cis* words were ordinary and offered in an offhanded manner; but *ce* said the right words, at the right time, That's Michael's genius. *Ce* is one of the most appropriate creatures I've ever met. *Ce* let me know that defining was limiting; and if I could stay open to new possibilities, I would be okay in my own unique way.

I leaned over and gave Elay a kiss on the cheek and another waft of her lavender-scented aura hit me. "Please reconsider taking Regression," she suggested again. "It does have a settling effect. Think about it, Sante. This time, honestly think about it."

I dispensed with her Regression suggestion by agreeing with her. "I'll think about." When we stood up, I noticed a few streaks of white hidden in her pale blonde hair. Elay, the incarnation of Venus, was beginning to show her age.

"I need to get going," she reminded me. "The shuttle to Aeternus leaves in an hour." We embraced and she wanted to say, this separation between Nova and you is unnatural, but instead said, "Remember, I love you, my cherub."

****

In some ways, I do not need Regression because I already remember large chunks of my past lives. The phenomenon is rare, but it is happening more often as children are born to Regression graduates. While my parents might feel this talent is another of my gifts, I fear what additional Regression therapy might demand of me. As a child, my intrinsic past-life memories became casual tools I exploited to shock my parents. When I reached puberty, those same past-life memories of Nova came down like an avalanche and crushed my spontaneity, pride, and joy.

In the domain of physical existence, biological evolution has its prickly points—genetic predisposition, birth, disease, aging, and death, to name the top five. However, in the game of karmic evolution, farce, and ironic situations of paradox are involved. In this absurd impasse, I know Nova is my soul mate. For some crazy and unknown reason, we chose to be inside bodies at the same time and like all bodies, we participate in a society of absurd convention dedicated to the contradictions of societal rectitude and personal lust. Every essential truth within me understands that Nova is my connection to eternity, but beyond Nova, I remain an atheist. I've attempted to refocus my attention, away from Nova. I've spent hundreds of hours scanning Unalix, for leads to Cle and our lifebearer, Hibernia. Unalix has a huge database, containing the genetic and past-life chronologies of Regression graduates; but for me, every clue has terminated in a dead-end and I no longer believe I will find Cle or Hibernia alive, at least not in this lifetime.

Still, my yearning for unfettered connection forces me to entertain strange and foolish questions and sometimes I manage to scare myself. Like—did I willingly leave my cosmic love connections or did they abandon me? What if none of us has a choice where we are born and we are randomly tossed out on the beaches of alien dimensions? Might we truly die in these alien places, burn into nonexistence under the scorching heat of insentient stars?

I recognize my frustration and struggle to accept this life as the gift my parents claim. Perhaps my discomfort is a remnant of impatience to be part of a greater game, even a deeply embedded memory of some perfect state this life has eclipsed from my complete memory. If this is true, I'm not alone. In times past, all sentient-life proclaimed their disillusionment with this dimension, viewing third-dimensional life as a teetering steppingstone to the great beyond. Sentient minds focused on transcendence spawned theories and conjectures that filled this universe with centuries of confusion, hate, and religious fervor.

For the Janaforma, the closest analogy to any religion is the Regression drug. Regression graduates not only become privy to their personal past lives, but tune into a new frequency that takes each person to the core of truth. This new frequency of knowing has allowed reverence for this life to recover. The restoration of memory keeps peace in this universe and has allowed time for the reseeding of damaged minds and worlds. This metaphorical reseeding is a slow process, a process that requires a new sense of dedication to living. Out of a new sense of surrender to our obvious impermanence, we are proud to be alive in the third dimension, a dimension that fits the living-of-life like a glove.

****

If the third dimension fits the myriad expressions of life, then the fourth dimension seems to fit nothing. Every culture in the Orion Spur has legends concerning the plausibility of a fourth dimension. For centuries, psychics have hinted at its nature, suggesting the fourth dimension is a region where trickery and illusion abound, a place capable of losing wandering tourists for an eternity. Then, in SY2603 (space year), the Ganat Cerribeame inadvertently pierced a thinning membrane between this dimension and the next. It became apparent that something bizarre occurred when five Cerribeame rifters winked out of existence as they flew through this unexplored area of space. Four of those five rifters never returned. Their disappearance has evoked scientific controversy for hundreds of years, yet we know little about this region of space except it is strange, inhospitable, and approachable only on its own terms. No one knows who found the courage to follow those four lost rifters into that permeable breach, all we know is some bold Ganat did and lived to tell the tale on this side again. It did not take the Cerribeame long to notice the time twisting involved when crossing back and forth. Unfortunately, the Cerribeame failed to apply this discovery to any peaceful purpose. Instead, they used their newfound ability to jump time as a means to initiate surprise strikes on unsuspecting spacecraft in this dimension.

Then, fifty years ago, cosmologists at the Pacific Institute of Berkeley, California, Earth, issued a benchmark document entitled, Third-Dimensional Existence and The Dangers of The Fourth Dimension that postulates, "From the viewpoint of this reality, the entire fourth dimension exists as a buffer between our existence and all others. The fourth dimension wraps around the third as an elastic band, holding third-dimensional time together." Previous models of our universe, which envisioned its shape as flat, like a piece of paper, or curved, like a saddle, fell into disfavor and the catenoid shape became the ideal silhouette in everyone's mind. The borderworld, or "corridor" between the third and fourth dimensions became known as, "hyperspace*." That this theory emanates from the prestigious Pacific Institute carries significant political influence and has lured us into a false sense of security. Most people believe that the fourth dimension is a literal cosmic safety shield holding the third dimension together.

The Orion Spur Council responded to the "danger signals" alluded to by the Pacific Institute, by installing and enforcing its infamous Interdiction 151 that bans "all exploration of the fourth dimension by unauthorized individuals," and enforces the ban with severe penalties for "anyone caught trying to enter hyperspace without official sanction.**" The Orion Alliance supports Interdiction 151 by using the Vanguard Scouts to police the corridor where the only known fourth dimensional door shimmers and eludes us as The Great Unsolvable Mystery of physical reality. However dangerous the fourth dimension might be, Interdiction 151 has a growing number of critics. Two of the most outspoken detractors are Elay and Michael, who have made lifting this ban their personal mission in life. While a few radical fringe elements seem capricious and hell-bent on self-destruction in a suicidal plunge into the fourth dimension, Elay and Michael's resolve comes from a meticulous consideration for the dangers of the fourth. Michael insists that the Orion Alliance ruling committee is exaggerating fourth dimension dangers. Michael has made more jumps into the fourth dimension than anyone alive and is a respected, fourth-dimensional authority with the Janaforma people. Michael and Elay have offered illuminating seminars on the subject of the fourth dimension for the

---

*Maxwell Masters, Ph. D. "Third Dimensional Existence and The Dangers of The Fourth Dimension," Journal of Cosmic Science (San Francisco, California: Atlas Publishing Inc., Spring, 5552, p.343).
**Congressional Letter of The Orion Arm Alliance, Interdiction 151, 5524 p. 2189.

past twenty-five years. According to Michael, "Hyperspace is a realm of illusion, dominated by bands of distorting energies that possess the ability to cleave time from space. Streaming from the third dimension and into the fourth, enormous energy strands, or time threads, the length of galaxies can forsake unwary travelers in endless phantasms of confusion." Even Michael gets a peculiar expression of respect in *cis* eyes when *ce* talks about the creatures inhabiting the borderworld just inside the fourth dimension.

Michael says, "The *graeymlins* are ten times the size of great white whales. The barbed tail of a *graeymlin* possesses the ability to whip the time threads into illusory cosmic foam. This phenomenon can cause terminal confusion for anyone from this dimension; however, *graeymlin* behavior is a natural phenomenon and must be respected for its mighty force."

Michael describes the *manatees* that inhabit the upper regions of the fourth dimension as, "sirens," whose particular genius takes the form of exposing one's will to the "quintessential, aboriginal heart." I once asked what *ce* meant by that enigmatic statement and *ce* told me "*Manatees* propose The Ultimate Challenge to invaders from the third."

"What is The Ultimate Challenge?"

"You don't know until you get there," said Michael. And what lies beyond the *manatees*? Michael says, "As far as we know, it's a one-way door." Absolutely no one from the third dimension has penetrated beyond the *manatees* and lived to tell the tale. Meanwhile, *The Mother* drifts in magnetic concert to The Door, which Orion law forbids us to open. The Vanguard Scouts act as the assigned sentinels, perhaps even the equivalent of fourth-dimensional *manatees* on this side. For the past twenty-five years, the Vanguard—who refer to hyperspace as the River Styx—have been carefully patrolling this strange space and know more about its quirky nature than anyone else alive.

TWO

It only took a modicum of my energy to check the multidex and see what time the Earth shuttle was due. It was a year since I had been near any of the shuttle bays. Little reason existed for me to frequent these places since I rarely traveled. In my last life, I visited thousands of planets, several new regions of space, and now it seemed apparent that every place is different, yet the same. Despite my lethargy and boredom, as I attempted to gaze into the starry infinitude, a longing to go flying haunted me. Had I forsaken my sense of adventure, stranded part of myself somewhere without any means of traveling onward? Space travel still was the obvious metaphor for possibility; yet, here I lingered, living my latest life, in the same physical predicament as my last. Why had my soul returned to spend another life on *The Mother*? I knew my reasons had nothing to do with honor or choice. I was here because of Nova.

Three thousand years ago, Maria Ventana Clidmore, the wife of Waber Clidmore, christened this great starship, *La Ventana*." Waber Clidmore and Brian Kinsey, a team of space explorers persuaded a bunch of young rebels—me among them—to fly to the far regions of Pegasus and back. It took generations to complete the mission, 354SY in total. As far as I know, *La Ventana* is the one expedition to travel that far from its point of origin and send an expedition home to tell the tale of what's waiting on the periphery of this galaxy. Now, *La Ventana* was stuck and responsible for tracking the whims of an elusive door to another dimension. Not only was *La Ventana* floating like a ship in dry-dock, but an intricate network of space structures were clamped to her hull. Everyone refers to *La Ventana* as *The Mother*, but these words mean little to those not part of The Great

Voyage. Vanguard Scouts began calling *La Ventana The Mother* because we loved this ship with a passion reserved for what we held sacred. *The Mother, My Mother,* was the original thrill, the authentic adventure, and she alone prowled physical space and took us along to show us the sights. In my last life, I once enjoyed the pleasure of captaining her. She responded to my hands inside her control gloves and turned direction on my every whim. Now, *The Mother* is a sorry excuse for what she once was. I'm ashamed of what we've allowed her to become—an imprisoned bird, waiting to die inside a cage. Her engines have not sung in years. The only sound coming from her is the hum of the ventilation system as it reprocesses spent air. It's humiliating for her to languish in disuse and heartbreaking for me to watch.

The structures annexed to *The Mother's* hull obstructed the narrow windows of the landing bay. Irrational as it may sound, the situation felt suffocating. My authentic vision felt trapped behind a multi-framed perspective. If I wanted to view a space-side scene, I needed to go to the courtesy viewer, peer at an image of reality broken down into energy that is transferred into a facsimile called a hologram. To my eyes, the image was reduced and somewhat flat and the shadows mostly distorted. *The Mother's* telescopic sensors demonstrated the ability to catch light images ten thousand light years away on infinity focus and if Engineering calibrated the sensors correctly, I could read the printed registry on the hull of an approaching ship. It was ancient technology, another reminder of *The Mother's age.* However inadequate the ship's technology, it still was easier than clipping on a *vitarattha** and stepping off into open space. Space navigation from inside a *vitarattha* still took more courage than most individuals could muster. People who approached space capriciously, still died regularly. I went to the closest interactive membrane and the message— "Speak slowly and clearly," flickered across the screen, in the languages of Mescale, Tyrowsian, and Universal.

"Show approach of Earth shuttle on upper northeast point," I requested. The viewer projected a utility grade hologram of the Earth shuttle as it began its final curving approach. "Maximize view." The ship was *The Ohio* and the licensing registry read "MIS N CLE." I had no idea what "MIS N CLE" meant in relationship to *The Ohio*; I only knew what "MIS N CLE" meant to me. It was just one more synchronistic jarring, a prodding reminder of a previous life. I waited for the ship to dock. On cue, *The Mother* opened her steadfast metal pincers and clamped the Earth shuttle to the under-curve of *The Mother's* hull, the place the Vanguard called, "The Armpit."

*Vitarattha meaning, "future life protector." *Vitarattha* technology was invented by Jana Kerisa and further developed by *La Ventana's* Vanguard Scouts. In its present form, a *vitarattha* acts as a life-sustainable energy field around a scout when in open space. Its power source usually is integrated with their uniforms. Language origin, Cuneate and Universal.

Five minutes later, the airlocks hissed opened and out poured a stream of weary commuters and a tour of bewildered, but colorfully dressed tourists. Some tourists invading *The Mother* were here merely to gawk at what they considered Janaforma peculiarities. Because *La Ventana* is a place of limited space, private lives often spill into public view. Sometimes *The Mother* is overflowing with Janaforma passion that comes in waves, like seasons on planets. A few weeks earlier, during one of those waves, unauthorized photographers, equipped with concealed camera equipment, boarded *The Mother* and filmed the personal love-play of some of *The Mother's* citizenry. Bootleggers sold the sacred sexual interactions of Janaforma triads as prurient entertainment to the media. In response, for the first time the ship's Gatherings were talking about regulation.

****

I made my way through the crowd of arriving strangers in search of a familiar face. Then I saw him—Evose. To me, our mutual family marks were as obvious as leopard spots. Calling his name, he glanced my way and smiled. "Sante?" he shouted in return. We embraced and the long spirals of his shiny, black hair spilled around his shoulders. His smell was uncorrupted. No perfume screened his deeper odors. He was one hundred percent natural Earth, the mingled scent of sunlight upon sea and soil. I traveled like a gull along a gray coast on that scent and it took me to Hibernia. I fell in love with her the moment I saw her glow. From a distance, her aura was the color of pale coral light and up-close, she could be either fuchsia or a pointed red. She was an exquisite miracle no genetic artist could ever duplicate. As my lover, she once explained the conjunction between Earth and the senses in intimate detail to me. "Earthiness," she said, "is the embodiment of living on the planet Earth." In her case, earthiness meant a sensual connection to the physicality of her world. My mind lingered on that sweet and saucy Irish girl that smelled of heather and lavender perfume.

Evose pulled back and we studied each other from arm's length. Emotion flooded me with memories—childhood scenes when he was seven and I was ten. Indisputably, Evose now was an adult. Tall and thin, like Bogwa, Evose's taunt mahogany skin appeared polished. His face had filled in and his too big nose and lips appeared manly and assured. The moment I saw him, I saw Belinda in his eyes. Time and her influence had rendered him uniquely attractive and with Belinda as a parent, he probably knew how to charm the pants off anybody he took a fancy to.

Evose wore some elaborate cosmetics, his attention to enhancing his physical assets well considered. Pale yellow rouge highlighted his cheekbones and black kohl traced his dark eyes. "How long has it been since we've seen each other?" he asked.

"In Earthtime —fourteen years, two months and twelve days."

His smile erupted into a laugh making him more handsome. "You always were good at time calculations."

"It's a useless skill."

"I'm sorry I missed Estella's birthday celebration. I heard you were there."

I began showing off. "Yes, that was three years, twenty-one cycles ago." His expression slipped into sober sincerity. Three years before, everyone questioned why Evose stayed away when Estrella was dying. What was more important than a birthday celebration for his dying step-*mebr*, who affectionately called him, "Terrif?"

"Your eyes sure have developed," Evose said.

As Gathosians age, the rutilates in their eyes grow more pronounced. It's the Gathosian equivalent of Human men getting more hair on their chests when they reach maturity. What Evose actually meant was I had developed the psychic skills involved with Gathosian eyes. I told him that his eyes were darker and more dramatic than mine while he insisted mine possessed more golden shafts of light. It was flattery all around. "My eyes are the same genetic code as Bejan's," I confessed. "*Ce* says eyes such as ours make us appear as if we are halfway to someplace else."

Evose laughed again and out of nowhere, I began confusing him with Miro Rugen. Maybe it's because they both mentioned my eyes. True, Evose did not communicate in personal-tense Mescale, but in broad, Earth Universal. On the verge of dismissing his remark about my eyes, he raised the stakes and touched my hair. He did it easily too, as if we already were intimate. "You have Nova's beautiful hair," he said. "What's the genetic code for that particular shade?"

"Apricot blonde 201.34. It's an easy, genetic trait to encode if the parents are so inclined." My hand went up to meet his, near my hair. "Please, if you don't mind."

"I'm sorry; I forgot. I should know better by now." He pulled back and I felt self-consciously awkward. He seemed to be a bigger version of the child I remembered. He intrigued me and I decided to peer deeper into his eyes the first chance he allowed me access.

Diverting attention away from myself, I told him, "You have Belinda's good looks." Then Ezek, my psychic hawk, began squawking and I felt myself turn a dozen shades of embarrassed red and turned practical concerning Evose's luggage.

We collected his belongings and I escorted him to family quarters. He told me the eighty-two hour trip from Earth left him feeling "jumpy and fried thin." Jumpy and fried thin is Earth slang for the stress to the circadian rhythms that space travel causes. For some it's more difficult than for others. For natural planet-dwellers, reduced gravity and light, along with the radical time changes, can cause intestinal upset and spiking internal body temperatures. I offered to allow Evose time to rest; but he insisted that with a shower and a half-hour inside our family's reorientation unit that he would be as good as new.

****

I waited in the sitting area while he bathed and put in time in the reorientation unit. "Family quarters," as Elay insisted on calling our family apartment, was located along the starboard flank of *The Mother* in the Southern Annex. My family moved to the Southern Annex when I was five bio-years old. Elay and Bejan decided that my siblings, Una and Senon, and I needed separate sleeprooms. I considered taking Evose to The Quasar for dinner, but Ezek, who was on the alert, said, *take him to the Paragon Cafe, where it's quiet and cozy and he can mellow out.*

An hour later, at the Paragon, Evose peeked over his menu and asked, "Would you like to share a bottle of wine with me?" This is the first time I consciously realized my sexual attraction for him.

I was honest and told him, "My genetics does not handle alcohol very well." Then my sexually repressed voice put its tongue in my ear and whispered, *go ahead Sante. Evose is family; you can trust him.* I attempted to guide our conversation into the delicacies of Mescale. In Mescale, any romantic intentions Evose entertained would be clearer. Unfortunately, his Mescale was limited and our conversation remained stranded in stark Universal. By then, my belly felt warm and my lips tasted of wine.

In many ways, Evose proved to be a typical Earthling. I saw it, but my initial attraction for him skipped over his aggressive approach toward conversation. We ordered dinner and he seemed to care so little about what he ate that he said, "I'll have whatever you're having." Evose was focused on me and he asked, "So, what do you do?" I knew all too well that Humans talked this way to each other and I knew what he meant, but the Janaforma people considered casual questions such as this as rude. Evose was on my native turf so I felt that I had a right to balk. I willingly would tell him anything about myself, but I refused to allow him to pigeonhole me by my profession. I was on the verge of getting snippy with him when he said—"When I talked to Elay last week, I think she mentioned that you were a writer. What do you write?"

"I write fiction. I also write articles for the Bibliodexteritas and have a monthly commentary in *La Ventana Review*."

"Fiction? Ain't no such critter," he challenged. He looked pleased with himself as if he had won the first round and he helped himself to a piece of bread from the basket as a reward.

"That's your subjective opinion, Evose. In my opinion, all writing is fiction because we can never overcome subjectivity. Writers put a few awkward thumbs into the universal pie and if they're lucky, might pull out a plum or two. Beyond that, writing is mostly fantasy."

20

Evose did not challenge my assertions regarding subjectivity nor did he even want to discuss the topic further. As we danced toward some unknown point, I grew more suspicious than flattered. "With your background and talents, what made you want to become a writer?" he asked.

"I'm not a major player and never have been. I'm merely an observer with a good memory."

"So who were you in your past lives?"

This question stopped me short. In the context of casual conversation, Janaforma consider this question blatantly rude and nosy. Evose still was pouring plenty of energy in my direction and my ego was basking. With the help of the wine, my guard came down more. I remembered a life I regarded as minor, and decided to share a bit of its content to add to our conversational soup. "One time, on Earth, in their 17th century, I was a model for the Italian baroque artist Caravaggio." Evose never heard of Caravaggio so I quickly moved on. "I reincarnated three times during the matriarchal genocide in Europe merely because I was pissed. I remember the physical layout of Northern France so well, I can still map the underground tunnels we dug to survive. In total, I worked in the political underground for almost two hundred years. At the end of my last life, I figured I was done manifesting; but as you can see, I've returned for some vague reason I have yet to discover."

"Your eyes have an overload of Gathosian fire. Does it come from seeing too much?"

My desire broke out of prison and asked, "I've seen a lot, but never enough. Would you care to look more deeply into my eyes?" I gazed into his black rutilated windows, toward his soul, going only as far as he would allow me to go. Our eyes met and mine asked for acceptance. *Okay*, I thought. *Invite me in.*

Instead, he asked, "In which life did you first meet Nova?"

I felt as if someone had emerged from the dark and stabbed me in the back. I told him flat out, "My relationship with Nova is not open for discussion." Since he already was rude with me, I decided to be rude too. "What do you do to earn a living, Evose?"

He was not insulted; in fact, he was glad that I asked. He seemed to relax for the first time. I had finally found his happy place where he could wax eloquently with minimal input from me. "No job description exists for what I do," he said. "Sometimes I joke and call myself a soul-fragment archaeologist. I retrieve soul fragments, you know, split-offs that have been trapped for centuries in denial."

I was feeling silly from the wine and mocked him. "And I am a cheese-maker from Hattonia!"

This time, Evose did not laugh, but swallowed a lump in his throat.

Then he rubbed the palms of his hands together and the gesture made a strange scratching sound, similar to the shuffling of brittle leaves. "I'm totally serious," Evose assured me.

****

Evose no longer was a brassy smart aleck, yet he still seemed tone deaf and socially obtuse. My sexual attraction for him caused me to be concerned about the nervous wire jumping around inside him and I started thinking, *you could soothe that nervous wire with your love.* A couple of evocative clouds drifted through my mind and then I liked all kinds of subtle qualities about him. His teeth were very white. His cheekbones were high, while the shadows at the corners of his eyes were real. His hands were large and powerful, yet beautiful. Then I leaned back in my chair, sipped my wine, and entertained a dream of mutual seduction. "Tell me, how do you retrieve a soul fragment?" I asked.

"Very carefully," he replied. "Fragments can get testy."

I was struggling to concentrate, but most of me still wanted to laugh. "Where do these fragments come from?"

Evose took a gulp of wine and sat down his glass. He held his large masterful hands in an expressive way, as if poised to give an orchestral downbeat. "If you're interested, I'll need to start at the beginning—by explaining the actual constitution of an oversoul's* reality."

I made a strained face, telling him that I did not feel like listening to his philosophical version of reality on an empty stomach. "That subject might take the rest of our lives," I said.

"Not really. I can explain the oversoul's constitution in twenty minutes."

I knew then that I was doomed. "Okay, you have my full attention until my entrée arrives."

Evose held up four long fingers. "In the beginning, every oversoul divided itself into four separate selves in order to more efficiently explore reality—body-self, feeling-self, mind-self, and finally, the will or generator."

Some of Evose's theories correlated with certain principles Simon Forma used to create the Janaforma, yet Evose's theory sounded too glib to be true. "You make these soul components sound as if they are entities possessing independent lives, instead of dimensions of one personality. Next, you'll be telling me they have picnics on Mount Olympus on sunny afternoons."

"They are separate entities. You take your existence and freewill for granted. Why can't other components of your soul enjoy the same rights? In truth, each part of our soul needs freewill to function. Originally, the four soul parts were reciprocal. Their perfect empathy provided each part an assured feeling of wholeness, a secure place within the united self."

*Bibliodexteritas defines, "oversoul" as "The unity of knowledge and love directed through sentient will."; language origin, Universal.

My skepticism was probably showing and I could see Evose pulling back and puffing up his chest in defense. "It's an interesting concept," I began to say and Evose interrupted me to say that what he was describing was not a concept, but unbridled truth. "Are you involved with a Trinity Witch cult on New Delphi?" I was aware that my question sounded more like an accusation.

Evose again scratched the palms of his hands, making the energy crackle between them. "No, I'm not; my knowledge comes directly from The Great Mother."

"I beg your pardon?"

"The Great Mother," he said more carefully. "It's the energy that pervades each and every animate and inanimate thing of this universe. The greater purpose of this energy is still unknown because The Great Mother does not communicate through our logical brain, but we do know her energy acts as a sort of proto-language that saturates this universe."

"Your idea is not new, Evose. Everyone who spends any length of time in space is aware of this pervading energy. It's become anthropomorphized in certain circles. Depending on your attitude toward life, some regard this energy as an annoying imp while others view the energy as a beneficent feminine presence. Where it comes from, nobody knows, yet we all know the energy exists. The Janaforma call it *Mebr* or The Mother. Many Orion cultures see this energy as a caretaker, a fertility goddess that is living and dying right along with us."

"Yes, the Janaforma call it *Mebr*. On Earth, many call it God or Goddess, but I still call it the Great Mother because that's what Kulupans call it and that's what I called it long before this cycle of existence began."

"Are you implying that you have memories older than this universe?"

He never hesitated and gave me an unequivocal, "Yes."

"I'm sorry, Evose. I know Regression is close to a miracle drug and I can see that you believe everything you are saying, but you need better evidence before anyone here on *La Ventana* is going to believe you have memories that predate the creation of this universe."

He laughed gently and said, "I remember because my memory has no blocks, as yours still does. I remember why the last cycle of existence failed and I know the same issues are causing our demise this time."

"Why did the last cycle of existence fail, Evose?"

"It failed because of a clash between freedom and denial and the same thing is happening again."

****

With the movement of his left hand, Evose drew a lemniscate in the air. "In the beginning, freewill was meant to be a lubricant between soul parts, the play within a limited range of action, so parts might mesh to greater advantage. Instead, freewill has allowed layers of distortion to form. Many

23

of these parts are disenfranchised, paranoid, narcissistic and in some cases, psychotic. They believe they are the one and only self. Imagine the head, heart, or gut within the physical body declaring they are separate, independent, and complete entities unto themselves. What might happen if your pinkie finger entertained the pomposity to declare itself independent master of the body?" The more Evose talked about soul fragments, the more excited he grew. "Unbalancing builds a repository of inexpressibility within each part that eventually cannot be contained. In other words, when the inexpressibility becomes thick—kind of like a black sludge overcoat—it splits and produces a shadow self to handle the burden. These shadow selves possess the ability to act and interact like original selves, although their range of mobility is somewhat reduced and their movement is slower. Because shadow selves work from limited self-resources, they quickly become dysfunctional and, in due course, another shadow splits off from its parent. Billions of shadow selves exist, denied parts, waiting to be united with their original selves."

"You make it sound like internal cloning," I offered in jest.

"I've never heard it stated quite like that, but you have the idea. It's like cloning from a clone and we both know what happens when one clones from a clone—genetic drift. This shadow drifting has progressed to a critical stage in the third dimension. Parts are replicating themselves like rabbits and in some cases, the locked-up energy has exhausted all potential for growth."

"Where are these denied parts?"

"Everywhere, but of course, one must be educated to see them. Dimensions coinciding with the third allow them to slip through all the time. Old energy loops always attract soul fragments. On Earth, I've seen fragments slip through Himalayan mountain peaks and emerge from caves in Brazil. I've seen thousands walk on the Ionian Sea off the Western Coast of Greece. Once, I found a lost fragment under a rock just south of Detroit, Michigan."

"Are you talking about ghosts?"

"Ghosts are different. It takes a mighty shadow force, almost a relentless cause for an archetype to manifest a ghost." Prickles ran up my arms. "Ghosts are societies unto themselves, accumulated denial, conglomerates of chipped-off parts. Ghosts may be whole armies gone down in defeat from Earth's Middle Ages, all witches ever burned alive, all children who ever starved of hunger and neglect."

"Isn't Regression addressing the denial in the third dimension?"

"Regression has allowed us to make peace with our conscious past lives. I'm talking about our unconscious past lives."

I stared down at the white tablecloth and played with a breadcrumb between my thumb and forefinger. "So who's guilty of this self-abandonment?" Ezek was screaming, *it must be you, 'cause it sure isn't me!*

"Most of us."

"If you're telling the truth, why cushion it?"

"What do you mean, Sante?"

"Because who might express enough unanimity of spirit to know for certain that they had not abandoned parts of themselves somewhere along the way?"

"All right then, let's do be honest—everyone."

"How can you be sure you don't have another metaphoric plum on the end of your thumb, one more elastic band theory?"

Evose reached across the table and snatched my thumb, then wiggled it back and forth, as if manipulating a joystick. "No, Sante. We have no elastic bands, thumbs or plums. I am talking about the whole pie. I've proven it, not once, but thousands of times."

I gazed down at his hand on mine and one of my inner voices began chattering like a perturbed monkey. My ego was making some radical assumptions that I yearned to believe, such as, *he wants you too. He's reaching out for physical contact.* I felt dreamy from the wine when I said, "Tell me, my dear Evose. How have you proven it?" His eyelids fluttered and he appeared so attractive to me that I wanted to lean across the table and kiss him. I wanted to hold him and tell him everything was going to be okay.

"It's a bit complicated," he admitted.

The waiter brought our food and I ignored mine. "I'm interested, Evose, honestly. How do you retrieve denied soul fragments?"

He started to eat, but I began trying to bore a psychic hole through him without his permission. The wine made me careless and I became as obvious as a hot consort looking for a handy bedmate. He dropped his fork and it chattered against his plate when he realized my intent. At that instant, a barrier came down between us like a dark curtain. "Don't try to probe me, Sante. I'm just as psychic as you are."

"Is it special Kulupan knowledge that allows you to retrieve these lost parts?"

Evose assumed a serious expression. "I'm attempting to protect you. Certain knowledge can be a burden."

My head felt woozy and Evose resembled an out-of-focus hologram. "You're a tease. I thought your intention was to spark my curiosity."

"Soul retrieval is sober and confidential work—ten times more dangerous than the Vanguard making their silly patrols along the corridor. I can see what would happen if I told you. My information would end up in one of your novels and we'd have a bunch of tally-ho amateurs destroying the reality of the third dimension."

I became ridiculously rhetorical. "I guess you think it's impossible for me to keep a secret."

He stared at me as if I was crazy. "I do know you lack the personal audacity to push me into a psychic corner over the matter."

I laughed, but mostly at myself. I felt light-headed and had trouble putting my thoughts together. "I have more audacity than you might imagine. Are you aware that I'm sexually attracted to you?"

Unimpressed with my confession, he shrugged. "I sensed your attraction as soon as we sat down at this table. Listen Sante, you're obviously handsome, but I'm not attracted to you."

My wine induced aspirations turned to vinegar in my mouth. A cynical mood took hold and I felt sick to my stomach and blamed the wine. Then, Evose started acting the typical Earthling again. "What are you in this life, a lifegiver or a consort?"

He still wanted to define me and I responded by acting peevish. "For your information, asking whether I'm a lifegiver or a consort is considered rude unless you are seriously interested in making a sexual connection."

He possessed the impudence to ask, "Why?"

"Because the minor notes of my Tyrowsian genes suggest you are asking so you can compartmentalize me, put me in a box, and believe you know who I am."

"I don't do such things."

"You just did. You already made up your mind that I can't be trusted. When we met, you led me on by touching my hair and now you're asking if I am a lifegiver or a consort. What do you care which sex I am when you feel no sexual attraction for me? If you're as psychic as you claim, you wouldn't need to ask, you would know in your guts that I am a lifegiver."

Evose was as level as a Kansas landscape. "Why are you so reactive? You made a pass and I told you I couldn't reciprocate. What could be simpler? I'm not offended—why are you? Oh, now I see the problem. You're not accustomed to being turned down."

A mountain of silence rose up between us. "Obviously, I've drunk too much wine." I apologized and tried to cover my sexual yearnings by staring at my pasta that was congealing on my plate.

"No big deal," he said. What he considered "no big deal," was the yearning of my soul. The awkward silence continued as he tried to decide what to say next. "I'm committed to someone else," he finally decided. Evose took a locket from under his shirt and pressed a small red arrow on one end. A holograph of a Human female appeared in the air between us. The holographic quality was poor and all I could see was the fuzzy image of a woman with dark hair. "May I introduce Iris?"

"How do you do," I said.

"This locket is my treasured possession. A Tibetan artisan made the gold case and Atlas Holographic & Sound created the holo. Their engineers fitted the locket with a program that allows me to refine the image as I go along."

"You could simply upload a better picture."

Evose crossed his arms over his chest before saying, "I can't. This is all I have left. Iris is dead. She was murdered. This wasn't an ordinary murder; it was bigger. The negative forces came and took her away."

My shock was real. "What negative forces?"

Our eyes went deep into each other. This time, his eyes held no subterfuge and I knew what he would say next. "The soul fragments, of course."

"How do you know soul fragments took her?"

His mood shifted into impatience and the wall came up again. "All evidence points to that conclusion. She left no trace or clues. It's as if she winked out of existence. I know how shadows operate. Evil has a strong charge. It goes for the tenderness, the path of least resistance. Despite their receptive beauty, why do you think roses keep their thorns? Iris was a rose who gave up her thorns of immunity to help me. Each breath is dangerous territory in that vulnerable state." Evose appeared astonished by his own statement. "She was incredibility psychic. No one could coax fearful fragments from their hiding places as she could." The mere thought of Iris affected Evose so deeply that he reached across the table and held my hand. "I'm here on *The Mother* to ask for help. Last week I spoke to the Orion Spur Council in Noble City and, after giving me exactly twenty minutes of their scheduled time, they labeled me a Regression kook and turned me down flat. Now, I intend to go in front of a Janaforma Gathering." He leaned forward and his voice held a new imperative edge. "If the citizens of *The Mother* agree to support my purpose with the Council—"

"To do what?"

"To go back in time and prevent Iris' death."

Was Evose suffering from mental impairment? "You must be crazy," I said. "The best minds alive believe it's suicidal to the present to tamper with the past. What do you think *La Ventana* is doing here in the corridor? The Vanguard's entire purpose is to prevent anyone from trying to alter time."

Evose pushed his food around with a fork before shoving the plate to one side. "I've heard that nonsense my whole life. That's what the Council told me too. It's a lie coming from restricted minds and directed against our souls. Besides, this is bigger than the death of one person. Can't you see what's happened? This is an affront to the integrity of the third dimension. We've come too far to allow renegade soul fragments to destroy what we've accomplished."

****

Neither of us had eaten much food so Evose said, "Let's get out of this place." I hated the waste, so I insisted we take our dinners with us, in two, small square boxes, to eat later. We walked around the ship for a while and finally ended up at The Quasar. It was late in the cycle again. Evose ordered a Calypso brew and I had my usual, a glass of iced tea. I spotted Rugen a couple of minutes after we sat down at the bar. It was dark in The Quasar and the shifting light-beams from the ceiling played off the heads and faces of the dancers. One beam touched Rugen for a couple of seconds, splaying pink and green swirling patterns across *cis* face. *Ce* was dancing with a lifegiver named Tolt and a goddess named Raven. I knew Tolt and Raven well. They were on the prowl for a consort. The trio swept past me on their way from the dance chamber. My eyes met Rugen's for only an instant, but it was enough time for me to fall in love with *cim*. Then *ce* deliberately took Tolt's arm and my imagination jabbed me with a few graphic imaginings of their probable lovemaking.

Evose and I finally made it back to family quarters and I was only a little drunk by then. "Come in and we'll talk?" he said. "I won't be able to sleep for a while because of the time difference."

We went inside. Ambience controls responded and the sitting area began glowing with soft amber light while soft music played in the background. Nova was out, probably at an Executive Gathering. The quiet within these rooms seemed an odd contrast to my childhood memories. Once Elay, Bejan, Michael, Nova, my siblings, Una and Senon, and all the people that gravitated around our busy lives, filled these rooms with their vitality and joy. Ten years had slipped by since Senon launched *lis* separate life with a consort and lifebearer. Senon was a technical genius, our family's success story.

Una was complex and serious. When she interacted with others, she could be either extremely tender or direct. In my mind, she combined the finest genetic qualities of Elay and Michael. Una possessed Elay's will and Michael's incredible sense of timing and *cis* dead calm in every crisis. I've seen Una hold her child Renée—who has a penchant for getting hysterical and sobbing—until she becomes utterly peaceful and serene. Yet, Una can be brutal, fierce, and can cut like a sword. Professionally, she works as a Shardasko defense instructor. Her body is lean, muscular, and appears to be molded of steel. On her own time, she serves as a psychic counselor and her whole demeanor changes and she takes on soft rosy glow. Her psychic visions are different than mine. Most of the time, I know what a person is going to say before they say it. The pending unspoken, shot with highly charged emotions, is easy for me to read. When I'm with people I know well, I can read even their subtle thoughts and emotions if I stay perfectly calm and they do not block me. If someone blocks me, I try to stay respectful and do not push. However, Una sees far-reaching and cataclysmic possibilities that can make your hair stand on end. Her unexplainable gift, I can only imagine as a psychic multidex sitting inside her head. Impending catastrophes, she sees quite well. She never says an event will happen. Instead, she makes statements such as, "That's the way time is pointing." Once, when Una was being utterly frank, she said, "People enjoy their personal ignorance." Her obvious cynicism makes her exceptionally quiet and she refuses to talk about her visions unless she's convinced the individual sincerely wants to know. Then, her insights come out as tidal waves of revelation. Frankly, not many people can deal with her directness for long, especially if they possess a shred of arrogance and continue to flaunt it in her presence.

The terminally ill trust Una. They come to her in droves and she advises them concerning their impending deaths. Many Janaforma, in the twelve and thirteen age-range, are beginning to remember meeting Una in past lives. In previous lives, many decided, with her help, to reincarnate and what issues their next life might address. Una considers these adolescent Janaforma, *The Mother's* hope for the future, a confirmation that this side of creation is becoming an equal partner in existence with the great unknown.

Una lives with her child Renée in a different part of the ship and I rarely see her unless we make a concerted effort to get together. Every time I think of her chosen life, I know her path is difficult. Una is only twenty-nine bio-years old and Renée is thirteen. Una lives without a lifegiver or consort. When I asked her why, she said, "My stark simplicity scares all potential mates away."

****

Evose and I sat in opposite chairs in our family's quarters and I offered to make a pot of tea. He said, "Relax, I've had enough to drink," and he crossed his right leg over his knee in a pose Earthmen favor.

I had another annoying hunch and this one hinted that Evose wanted some kind of favor from me. The situation felt like a setup, a waiting snare he blithely expected me to enter. We had destroyed social niceties between us hours earlier, so I asked, "What do you want from me, Evose?" He half-smiled and he was the most attractive in that state of questioning irony. If I possibly could, I decided to give him what he wanted. My sexual attraction for him had not waned, despite his rebuff.

"You are extremely psychic," he said. This was not flattery, but an acknowledgement of fact. "However, I see your psychic skills are not so strong that you know what I need. It's simple enough, I want you to help me with the Gathering."

I was disappointed that he wanted a favor so mundane. "You have the wrong Janaforma. It's been five years since I've been to a Gathering. I hate Gatherings; that's where Nova wastes *lis* time and efforts."

Evose again reached for my hand and I allowed him to hold it for a moment. "I say this with as much sincere respect as I can muster, I know who you are and I know the details of your past lives as if we are soul mates. Please, Sante, I would like to open myself a bit more, so I might gain your trust."

"I'm confused; I've been waiting for you to open up since we sat down to dinner. Now you are going to let me read you simply because you want my help with a Gathering?"

His purpose was not seduction, but a frank invitation to communicate information on the psychic level. I did not hesitate and entered Evose through his eyes. My look was so complete that I fell through him—through a distance as deep, dark, and mysterious as the fourth dimension itself. I flushed hot and scared from the sudden vertigo of the sensation. I've peered into hundreds of individuals; and usually, shadows create ghost-like impressions that lead the psychic observer to insights about who that soul was in previous lives. My sister Una, above all, held more ghost-like impressions than any individual I ever encountered. However, with Evose, I found only empty space. It felt spooky and I wanted to know why. "Where's your genetic and karmic legacy?" I asked.

"My genetic and karmic legacies are insentient vehicles. I maintain a bit of ego to face others. My real name is Sirushi." When I heard that name, prickles of gooseflesh washed over my arms. I silently studied Evose for clues, but was incapable of reading him in the dark he was throwing up before me. "That confused expression on your face tells me you do not understand. You want to wrap meaning around what you just experienced."

"Who wouldn't?"

"Again, we must start at the beginning," he said, "Eons ago, another universe gave birth to a group of spirits. We were unique because we lacked any imprinting that bound us to our original state or dimension. Our potential was toward possibility without actually becoming anything. If we possessed any singularity of purpose, it was toward wandering. We had no sense of identity, but did have a rudimentary method of communication that kept us together. As we drifted away from our point of origin, a greater attraction grew up amongst us that produced extraordinary changes. We realized that we were greater together than we were alone, yet we lacked any notion of a purpose. For eons, we wandered through dimensions accumulating many unlinkable impressions. Then in 5532, we found ourselves inside the third dimension and sensed the pleasures of physical reality. We knew desire and climaxed together in an unprecedented way. For a brief time, we became as real as any third-dimensional beings could be. Our brief and tentative manifestation near the Ta'haja System attracted the Janaforma, who stopped to investigate what phenomenon we might be. By observing us, this alien concern suffused us with more energy, but we quickly learned one of the primary rules of this universe. Energy is not free. In fact, the Janaforma energy was encoded with third-dimensional genome maps, which meant, if we used this energy to enhance our tenuous physicality, we would be limited to the genome maps within that energy.

Despite the limitations, we experienced a great deal of desire through this energy and decided to take the bait and taste this physical existence. The rest is, as we have learned to call it, 'our story through time.' The Janaforma invited us aboard *The Mother* and made us feel as if we were a part of this creation. The Janaforma gave us strength to manifest stronger bodies and afforded us an outlet for our potential for the first time in our long existence. Despite the generous energy infusion from our new friends, it was difficult to maintain actual bodies at all times. Mehiel and I decided to give as much energy as we could to Bogwa so he could display an authentic, interactive body. Only when Bogwa became sexually active did we decide, with Belinda and Estrella's cooperation, that it might be possible to create bodies for Mehiel and me to live inside."

"What about the story I've heard my whole life that you, Bogwa, and Mehiel were Damarians who were persecuted for your philosophical beliefs?"

"Pure fabrication. In the beginning, we did not think the Janaforma would believe the truth."

My astonishment was fueling my curiosity and I asked, "So is this your first life as a Human?"

"I think of it as my second. I am forever Sirushi, but I am taking a side trip as Evose, the child of Bogwa and Belinda."

"So who is Mehiel now?"

"Mehiel is now living as my sister Hope."

"I've never heard any of this before. Is it a secret?"

"We do not broadcast our facts. I'm telling you because I want to be honest with you so that you will be honest with me."

"Honest? I've admitted that I'm sexually attracted to you. You won't even share how you retrieve lost soul parts with me."

"This is not a game, Sante. When I said retrieving lost soul parts was dangerous, I wasn't lying." Evose turned intense and demanding. "Tell me. Who are you?" he asked again.

Since we were struggling to speak Universal, I asked him if he minded if I went directly into his mind to clarify what he was asking. He gave me partial access and I did not have far to go. "You want me to tell you that I am the original Sante? Okay, I'm the original Sante—so what?"

He sighed as if he won a major battle with me. "I know you want to keep a low profile in this life, but this is your time to come out of hiding and use your gifts."

"And what gifts might those be?"

"Your psychic gifts, of course. Plus, you possess a unique connection to Cle that no other being in existence can ever claim. I heard that you are able to channel Cle's soul so *ce* is able to speak through you."

"Who told you such nonsense?" Evose ignored my question and again blocked my probing, but I was sure Bejan had a hand in betraying me.

"This may be a second chance for Simon Forma's finest creations to finally make a difference in this dimension."

Evose was referring to a discovery I made in my last life while working to decipher Simon Forma's journals. Forma created a process to influence his creations down through several biological generations. Through a time-release process in our DNA, certain individuals were empowered by compulsions to act in certain ways that Forma hoped might initiate evolutionary change into society. Cle was supposed to be Simon Forma's understanding creation and I—yes, neurotic little me—was supposed to be Forma's incarnation of love. Simon Forma never understood while he was alive that his soul would tag him and expect him to become his own future creation, Nova.

THREE

For a dream to reach fruition, many elements must meet at the crossroad. If we miss a connection, dreams change. It's useless to mumble how different life could be if we had a second chance because this universe is in constant motion and nothing ever remains the same. In my last life, I missed an opportunity that will never again come. I carry the grief of losing Cle and Nova too soon. Whom can we blame for our failures? We can blame everything and everyone, including ourselves. I blame my ignorance, cowardice, and lack of patience and I blame the historical times Nova, Cle, and I lived in and the conservative resistance of society. I even blame my oversoul for the lack of support that could have nourished our luck and timing a bit more. From the perspective of this life, it seems uncanny that those lives unfolded in the way they did. Circumstances doomed us to defeat on the very eve of our flowering. In Nova's last life, *ce* was murdered and shortly afterward, the Ganat Cerribeame kidnapped Cle and stripped *cis* mind away. So many obstacles we encountered seemed so purposeful that I became paranoid and saw assassins everywhere. I was bitter and wept my life away for the two lost lives it was my destiny to bridge. My own direct experience told me, *I do not believe in second chances.*

Evose insisted, "Even as we speak, Cle is demanding a second chance. Let *cim* speak through you. *Ce* possesses the charisma and leadership to motivate the Gathering. Only The Number One Janaforma will be able to get the Orion Alliance to lift Interdiction 151."

Hearing Cle called The Number One Janaforma aroused my yearning. Feelings of irritation quickly followed as if someone was attempting to wake me and all I wanted to do was sleep. "Let me state this as simply as possible. I will never, ever, invoke Cle for a Gathering or any other public display."

"Are you sure?" Evose asked. "I've heard Cle enjoys singing at The Quasar lately."

"That's play, not what you're talking about. The Cle you seek died over three hundred years ago in *The Mother's* time and over three thousand years ago in Orion Spur time. The Cerribeame destroyed more than Cle; they scarred *cis* soul. That's the hideous part about mindstripping, its ability to reach back and destroy veins of genius certain individuals carry through lives. If you truly are Sirushi, you must know mindstripping is capable of raping the memory of souls."

"You're carrying a grudge against the Cerribeame for what they did to Cle."

"I feel the loss for what never can be recreated. I think I channel my oversoul quite clearly and I do not leave split-offs or parts of myself lingering as soul fragments. My oversoul is frustrated with the destruction of genius it incarnates in this dimension that is ignored and systematically destroyed by cruelty, ignorance, and mediocrity. Any oversoul worth its ectoplasm would be."

"I hear your frustration," said Evose. He scratched a spot behind his ear. "But you've made a fundamental error. Nothing is ever lost. Cle's genius retreated deeply into the oversoul. At any second, Cle's oversoul deems appropriate, it can and will release Cle's genius. Maybe the oversoul will reincarnate the historical Cle. Wouldn't *ce* be a sight for sore eyes?"

"That's absurd."

"Cle was the most eloquent and inspirational leader the Janaforma ever produced. I believe *ce* is attempting to return at this critical time in history to inspire the Janaforma to its next level of evolution."

"Your belief is built upon sand. The historical Cle is passé, no longer apropos for this time. The tugging I feel is from the memory of our great love. Besides, I do not believe in linear reincarnation."

"That's a dumb statement, Sante. How can you sit there and tell me you are the original Sante, but don't believe in linear reincarnation? You're Sante to your core and nobody can be you, but you. So let Cle speak through you and I know *ce* will rise to the occasion with the right words."

I stood up with the intention of leaving. "Listen Evose, you have space distortions and I've drunk too much wine. Whatever the truth, we're not going to reach it in these states."

"Please stay, just a while longer. Tell me about Cle. What does *ce* say to you? What are *cis* thoughts and visions for the future?"

"Haven't you been listening to me? Cle has no visions. What do you want? Do you need a soothing bedtime story before we retire to our cold, separate beds."

"Can you tell me a bedtime story about Cle?"

"Sure thing, Evose. This is one my favorites. I call it The Muse of Eloquence and Truth."

****

Once upon a distant time, on the planet Earth, in the city of Athens a marvelous child was born. He was so beautiful that his parents named him Candidus, meaning, 'shining white.' He was a young soul, young enough that the clouds of karmic illusion did not shadow his vision. His wise and devoted father recognized his son's potential and Candidus was educated by the leading scholars of the day. He was only twenty-three when he became an outspoken voice around Athens. His fire made him a persuasive speaker and he was a relentless debater. He was popular, especially with the Athenian youth, who dubbed him The Muse of Eloquence and Truth. Then he met Socrates. Socrates managed to change Candidus, but it was an extremely slow process. Socrates explained that no real advancement was possible until one awakens and faces the *daimon*, the mystical inner voice, within the self. Socrates believed that the improvement of the collective was impossible unless every individual awoke to his or her inner truth first. At the time, Candidus lived under the erroneous belief that he was capable of inspiring the hearts of listeners with the mere sound of his voice. He argued with Socrates about this fact. Candidus proclaimed, with a certain amount of youthful arrogance, that he knew he was right. After all, he possessed proof that he was. Hundreds of Athenian young men already followed him and were fervently willing to listen to him articulate for hours concerning his philosophical beliefs. Socrates was unimpressed and advised Candidus that if he continued speaking out in public places that it might bring about his demise."

"Candidus believed he enjoyed all rights of a legal citizen. Despite faith in his own invincibility, the state arrested him and dispatched him to Mycenae Prison. Mycenae was already a city in ruin, but the Cyclopean Walls still stood and the place was used as a penal colony for dissidents who were an embarrassment to the enlightened Greek State. Candidus was in exile at Mycenae until his spirit broke. It took a while. He died at the age of thirty-six a forgotten man. Despite his failure, the karmic inclination of his soul demanded that he speak truth. In subsequent lives, he became a teacher, a historical scholar specializing in Greek philosophy. He was a Buddhist monk in Tibet and then Northern China. She spent several lives as a Trinity priestess on the Gathosian planet Numidia where she was an accomplished poet. Then on the planet Ravenna, late one soft and drowsy afternoon, the long dead Candidus used the vehicle of a future life to made peace with his *daimon*. When the soul incarnated on Aeternus as Jana Cle the wispy bits of old karma that hounded *cim* through the centuries, again, surfaced. Cle was a genius, but had *ce* developed the patience and humility to work toward collective evolution? Again, *cis* eloquence emerged to tackle his karmic burden. Pressured by supporters, Cle became a spokesperson for social justice with the Tyrowsian government. I watched as *ce* gave *cis* eloquence away to thousands. *Cis* punishment came through the Cerribeame Guard. Only after the Cerribeame humiliated *cim* by stripping *cis* mind did Jana Cle realize the foolhardiness and waste of time it was to approach change on a societal level. You see? That's what it took. Cle needed to fall that far in that many lifetimes to touch the truth. With only the shreds of *cis* great mind left, *ce* realized that transformation was valid only when we approach it on an individual basis. Not only did Cle get it, so did every other Janaforma alive. Understand this simple fact, Evose; Cle's eloquence never moved the Janaforma people. It was *cis* failure and our collective shame over *cis* failure that moved us to action. The Janaforma knew they could no longer allow Cle to carry the banner of evolution for the rest of us. "We Are One," is not a logo or a talking point for the Janaforma. We Are One is a commitment to the truth that each of us is responsible. And that's the end of my story, except to say that when Cle speaks to me, it's as a precious memory of our love."

****

"Is that story true?" Evose asked.

"You tell me. About an hour ago, you told me that no such animal as fiction exists."

"I think you're channeling Cle, but don't even realize you are doing it."

I shook my head in frustration. "You are the most incredibly stubborn person I've ever met."

"And so are you," he returned. "I guess you think you've written all those novels by yourself?"

"What are you implying?"

"I've read everything you published. Cle's influence permeates your work. Your sappy romanticism is definitely you; but everything else, including your eloquence, is pure Cle."

"I guess I'm nothing more than Cle's scribe in your mind."

"I think you're good at what you do; but if Cle actually reached all those realizations with *cis* mind stripped away, then *ce* must be wiser now. If you could let *cim* speak, through you, to the Gathering, it would be a perfect blending of your talents." My psychic skills saw Nova emerge from Evose's mind and I wanted to bolt for the door. "Nova suggested a slim chance existed that I could get you to channel Cle to the Gathering." I was flabbergasted into silence over Nova's audacity. My thoughts were spinning and I was dizzy with speculation from my mind. Nova put Evose hot on my trail, just as Bejan sensually programmed Miro Rugen to seduce me. Why was my family manipulating me?

"You seem shocked." I could sense Evose probing and immediately blocked him. "What's wrong between you and Nova?" he asked

"Just as you don't discuss the process of soul-fragment retrieval, I don't discuss Nova. Besides, Nova and I rarely see each other."

"That is totally and completely impossible," said Evose. "Whom do you think you are talking to? I'm Sirushi. I was present when you and Nova joined on the planet Lemira Jha."

"I have no idea what you're talking about. I've never been to the planet Lemira Jha in any of my lifetimes. *La Ventana* visited Lemira Jha between my lives."

Evose appeared confused. "What is it with you, Sante? Sometimes you act as if you are pre-Regression."

"I haven't taken Regression. I've always remembered my past lives."

"Ah! So, you're one of those. With your natural talent and Regression onboard, you would be capable of remembering astounding details from the past. Nova and Bejan must have explained that progressive use of Regression by the psychically gifted unfolds the space between lives."

"I've heard that my whole life."

Evose's large, dark eyes twinkled with their golden shafts of light. "So what are you waiting for? Isn't it time you claimed your portion of the truth for the rest of us?"

I stood up. "I'm tired, Evose. I've drunk too much wine and told you your bedtime story and have no energy left to discuss the obscure subject of my portion of the truth."

Evose followed me to the door. Then, he deliberately touched me, putting his hands on my forearms. I understood what he was trying to do. He wanted intimacy without sexual contact. It was impossible for me to give him my intimacy without sexual contact as it was for him to consider me a potential lover. It was an authentic impasse. I closed my eyes and took a deep breath in an effort to restrain my yearning. "If you are afraid to take Regression, I'll hold you through it," he offered. "I guarantee no harm will come to you."

Out came my preprogrammed reply. "I refuse to alter the natural flow of my life with Regression."

Evose did not challenge me on this excuse and I was grateful. "Even if you do not want to take Regression, think about helping me with the Gathering. It will give your life and Cle's spirit renewed purpose."

****

I walked home slowly and when I arrived, I decided to pick a tarot card for Evose. I needed a clue in the dust he was kicking up inside my mind. This time, I acquiesced to the ritual of lighting a candle and a stick of *ratu* incense before shuffling the cards and holding them to my forehead. Then I pulled out the Three of Swords. In the Trinity Witch deck, this particular card shows three swords piercing a rose in full bloom. The rose appears to be weeping blood, while overhead, ominous clouds release a pelting rain. I turned to the multidex and again asked the Bibliodexteritas to do my work. "Reference divinatory meaning of the Three of Swords in the Trinity Witch Tarot."

The multidex pulled up some informative illustrations of the Three of Swords telling me, "This card can relate to an anxiety-filled three-sided relationship that can explode. A separation may result from a quarrel, an upheaval in the family, or an impending rupture." The card seemed on the mark, but I was suspicious. Was the card predicting Evose's influence or mirroring my greatest fears?

I tried to sleep afterwards, but the wine was compelling my well-trained mind to react. The wine caused a silly dispersion inside me of a dozen different voices, all with personal agendas and each discussing their separate problems without my input. Chief among them was my undirected love presenting me with images of Evose, seductive angles of Miro Rugen, and past-life memories of *You-Know-Who*. I definitely ignored Evose, skirted around *You-Know-Who,* and concentrated all my efforts on Miro Rugen, managing to undress *cim* in fifteen delicious and different ways. I moaned, groaned, and touched myself in a tender way and finally pumped on my engorged physical outlet. I experienced only a moment of expansiveness as the energy pulsated along my neural pathways and drained me of my energy from my third chakra downward. It was biological relief. I enjoyed neither heart nor soul release, making me feel nothing but sleepy. My higher energy stayed locked away in some place as far away as Mycenae. What a life, when an incarnation of love has no place to put *lis* love except in *lis* own hand. Tapping the controller on the side of my bed, I went to zero gravity. Still, sleep came so slowly that I saw it coming. It took me down into eternal darkness, to a place where no verbal language has ever been.

****

Inspiration awoke me from sleep. For seven months, I had waited for an idea to surface, some clue that might jumpstart a new book. Now I was appropriately excited. My idea was sketchy, but the crucial words were emerging long before I opened my eyes. I tapped the gravity controller and the bedcovers fell toward the floor. Wasting no time, I opened a new program where I typed, *The Permeable Web of Time,* followed by, "I sensed an approaching hand; it smelled clean, like lavender." As soon as I wrote these words, they owned me. A new door opened just a crack and it was enough to peak my curiosity about what may lie on the other side. Writing experience taught me that if I focused and followed the clues, like footprints in the sand, those clues led home to a complete story. Then I knew this new book wanted me to write it as nonfiction. Unmasked honesty of that sort was risky and my guts felt queasy with apprehension. Fiction afforded me a façade, at least an illusion of façade. If I used my real life as book fodder, was I any better than a tourist who came aboard *The Mother*, took pictures, and sold them to the media? Despite the implications involved in my decision, my compulsion to write nonfiction seemed my only path forward. I salved my shaky conscience with the vague notion that if the book were too revelatory, I simply could change a few names and release the book as fiction.

Three hours later, I emerged from my writing trance and felt happy for the first time in months. I had a solid beginning, although the book already seemed lopsided. Why did I waste so many words on the naughty image of Miro Rugen? Where was that subject headed? I knew that I needed to trust my instincts, allow them to lead, especially where I was afraid to go. Occasionally, themes popped up that needed editing, but more often than not, rogue material turned into star systems of meaning that solved the puzzle of the book. Still my lingering reflections on Rugen annoyed me and I regarded them as I did masturbating one too many times.

Much of new inspiration I owed to Evose, but I did not intend to thank him just yet. His dour comment, "If I told you, it might end up in one of your novels," still was fresh in my mind. Truth is, Evose initiated a chain-reaction inside me—caused some foggy abstractions to come into focus. My impulse was to rush over to family quarters and pester Evose to tell me more about the fourth dimension and the trapped soul fragments. For Evose, it was the middle of the night and he probably was sleeping. A montage of sleeping Evose-images drifted through my mind as Ezek took flight. A moment later, half of me was in the guest sleeproom at my family's quarters.

The room was dark, but I could see the outline of Evose's body sprawled across the bed. He was sleeping with full gravity, like a typical Earthling. One of his long, lean legs protruded from under a tan-colored blanket. Hovering over him, I slowly matched my breathing to his. Mentally, I peeled back the covers to expose his nakedness. He stirred and scratched himself across his chest. The scratching drew my attention to a fine sprinkle of red bumps around his waist and groin. He shifted, pulling the blanket over his leg and I withdrew, afraid he might catch me. *You need to go over there*, said Ezek. I did not give in to Ezek's suggestion for another hour. Instead, I ate my leftover pasta from The Quasar and drank a cup of tea before giving in to the urge.

****

I let myself into family's quarters and was surprised to see Evose and Nova huddled together in conversation. Evose was wearing a robe and Nova was dressed in a pair of loose shorts and an old shirt. The shirt bore the faded imprint of *The Mother's* elliptical profile zooming through the stars. As always, Nova attracted my senses like a magnet. My eyes caressed *lim* while my nose sought the pleasure of *lis* familiar scent. As always, the bottom notes of *lis* perfume were woodsy aromatic, a predominance of sage with hints of lavender and lime. Top notes of rose crowned the concoction like a luscious cherry. Naturally, Bejan created Nova's perfume and *le* wore it to please *lis* physical lover. Nova cared little about perfume because *lis* nose was not set up to appreciate finer scents. Drawing closer, I could smell the peppermint mouthwash *le* used minutes before and the unique smell of *lis* sweat. Side by side, on the table, sat two cups of jasmine-scented tea and I knew in a moment, *lis* breath would smell like tea. "You're up early," I said. "I came over to make breakfast for you both."

"A dream awoke me prematurely," said Evose. "Nova was helping me decipher the symbols." I knew what Evose dreamt. In the dream, he was a soul fragment caught in some dark, obscure dimension.

"Where have you been hiding lately?" Nova asked me.

I had not seen Nova for 32 cycles. Again, this was deliberate. This last time, my love for *lim* had turned demanding and I knew I needed to take a sabbatical or my frustration and anger would cause me to say something, I later would regret. "Elay and I had lunch last week. Didn't she tell you? I told her to say 'hi.'"

Nova is a handsome lifegiver. *Lis* shoulders are wide and comfortable, perfect for weary heads. *Lis* long, apricot-blonde hair, the same color as mine, usually hangs free and trails down *lis* back. *Lis* eyes are a mesmerizing turquoise blue. Clarity and compassion sit within *lis* eyes, which definitely are Janaforma eyes and mark *lim* as a Simon Forma creation. Right now, blonde stubble covered *lis* cheeks and chin making *lim* appear a bit scruffy. It was obvious that *le* was playing bachelor and not shaved since Elay, Bejan, and Michael left for Aeternus. I noticed the tiny lines at the outside corners of *lis* eyes were deepening and I flailed myself for not returning sooner. My fear of losing *lim*, of limited time, made me experience a chill of desperation and further provoked my need to be with *lim* constantly.

Nova's eyes were boring a hole through me. I felt trapped between *lis* innate knowledge of my foibles and my own foolishness. Then someone rang the attention signal at the front door and I was eager to volunteer. "I'll get it," I said.

I went to the door and opened it. Standing there, looking sober-faced as a Tyrowsian judge, was Miro Rugen and another Vanguard Scout named Solange. Seeing Rugen again, I flushed hot, especially since *ce* was the focus of my latest linguistic drool. For a tiny moment, I wanted to drift off in *cis* fabulous lake-blue eyes; then Ezek squawked, *pay attention, fool! I smell death.*

Rugen said, "I'm so sorry, but this is an official visit."

"*Ce* had not yet said it, but for me the moment was over. All I needed to hear were the words to make it real. "Say it!" I pleaded.

"Is Nova here?" asked Rugen.

I glanced over my shoulder and saw Nova and Evose getting up from the sofa and walking toward us. They appeared to be moving in slow motion, struggling through a dimension as dense as syrup. It seemed to take an eternity for them to cross the room. Nova was speaking words that sounded like—"*Wh-aaat-issss-iiii-it?*"

I snapped like a shocked spring and clawing and groping, I went inside Rugen's mind for details. I brushed right past *cis* discomfort, which was asking, *why did I volunteer for this assignment?*

Solange's thoughts crowded out Rugen's with, *this time I definitely am going to retire.*

The two stepped more deeply into the room and now Nova snapped too. "What's wrong?" *le* demanded.

Then started a speech that began with, "I'm sorry to inform you—" Rugen's voice seemed to contract, to become so constrained that I struggled to hear *cis* actual words. "The bridge just received word—from Aeternus Space Command—something, as yet unknown, destroyed the shuttle headed for *The Mother.*" A protracted silence sucked all the air out of the room, but an anticipatory "and" hung in the air—that tenuous "and" that clings to hope against all odds. As the survivors waited for the messenger to complete *cis* deadly missive, the messenger seemed stuck for the proper words. Rugen appeared miserable and I empathized with *cis* quandary. *Ce* longed to say something comforting and hopeful, or at least neutral. Finally, *ce* decided upon, "I'm sorry; Aeternus Space Command has found no survivors."

At that instant, I shut down my independent grief and my entire consciousness melded into Nova. *Le* did not ask me to support *lim*; my response was automatic and natural as breathing. I allowed myself to experience the full excruciating agony of what *le* felt. Nova reached out to *lis* three mates, demanding they answer, but the silence was overwhelmingly empty. "Elay," Nova moaned. *Le* inhaled only once before *lis* aura faded to pale gray. Then, *le* began to topple like an ancient Greek pillar in an earthquake. Evose managed to catch Nova before *lis* head hit the floor. Drawing *lim*self into a fetal position, *le* lay there, frozen in complete catatonia with *lis* turquoise-colored eyes fixed on eternity.

****

"I'll call a doctor," said Solange.

"No!" I insisted. "I will care for *lim*. I'm the only one who can."

Rugen opened *cis* mouth to argue with me, but Evose put his hand on Rugen's shoulder and said, "It's okay. Sante knows what *le* is doing."

Evose was wrong. I had no idea what I was doing. Regardless, I began giving orders. Solange carried Nova into *lis* sleeproom and put *lim* on the bed. "Now all of you get out and leave us alone," I said.

Everyone left except Evose. "Don't let *lim* die," he said. "We need *lim*." At that instant, I despised Evose, despised him for his intervention into my private relationships with first Cle and now Nova.

"Fuck you," I returned without hesitation, which managed to rid me of Evose too.

I climbed into bed with Nova and yanked the blanket up to our necks to preserve *lis* body heat. The bedclothes smelled of Elay's lavender perfume and I wanted to shriek with despair, but could not spare the energy. Instead, I began pouring the cumulative skills of lifetimes into saving Nova. Crisis turned me into a super-efficient savior and simultaneously, I was reducing the room's gravity to zero; wrapping myself around *lis* back so our major energy vortexes aligned; while another part of me was gingerly picking my way through the stinging briars growing up around *lis* mind.

My sanity already was gone. One more step and I was inside Nova's internal apocalypse with *lim*. Getting in was easy, while courage to stay took all my stamina. *Lis* traumatized senses were in a state of stupidity. *Le* looked like one of the shellshock victims I treated as a doctor in the Belgium trenches of Earth's First World War and reminded me of Cle, when I found *cim* in Herzayzen Prison. I fought to focus on each unfolding moment, but the agony was so intense that I kept slipping into a previous life where I died by evisceration.

Then death began dragging us both from the security of the third dimension and into a dimension without time or demarcation. Time plodded away in the third dimension, but I was not there. Minutes? Hours? Time lost all meaning. Struggling to be an open channel, I felt my every block and chasm. I was a flawed conduit, unprepared for this grisly task. Without question, I gave Nova every life-giving force I had; but *le* continued slipping toward physical death. I refused to stop loving *lim* and prepared to die too. "Stay," I whispered. *Come back*, I prayed. My tears soaked and anointed *lim*, yet *le* remained fixed upon a distant shore.

I heard a voice that sounded like Bejan. The voice was sweet and melodious and its gentility was pristine as morning in the garden. *When you are in need, ask simply, and don't decorate it*, ce *said.*

What do you mean?

We want to carve words into icons, fashion words into incantations to do our miracles for us. Utter a sound—any sound, before our soul imbues sound with passion, sound is an empty vessel. Prayers do not travel through sound; they travel through desire.

Was I talking to myself, admitting I was helpless? *Show me the way*, Fra. *Let Nova go.*

Wiser parts of me knew that I was involved in a useless struggle. I had strong C3 genetic programming in my head that was screaming warnings and telling me my motives were selfish and I was in jeopardy of destroying my integrity. Torn between integrity and desire, I began to shutter from the strain of being pulled in two directions. Then, from the depths of Nova's own despair, *le* reached out to me and spoke my true name. *Le* pressed me to *lis* heart and told me, "*ejesay epay**."

I released *lim*, tamping down my desire, just as I always did. Yet, this time I felt like a powder keg with a lit fuse. Then, when *le* leaned forward to kiss me goodbye—at *lis* most vulnerable moment—when *lis* lips were upon mine, I took our combined energy and sent it up through the crown of *lis* head.

****

Nova was still alive, yet I was terrified to sleep, afraid that *le* might slip away. Lying so close to *lim* my head began tingling with wild and colorful visions of strange scooped out spaces, canyons carved from wind. The visions vanished and my inner scope rained needles of light upon me. For a moment, I thought I might be dying instead. During the struggle, I had offered my life in trade. Then my mind leapt and I was swinging like a pendulum, hanging above a strange and gorgeous world I knew to be the paradise of Lemira Jha.

The setting was late afternoon and Nova and Sirushi were camping on a high mesa. Nova was clad in a short white sarong and several strands of colorful crystals hung around *lis* neck. *Le* was younger and exquisitely handsome. *Le* knelt and placed ten white candles on the ground in a pentagram formation. Meanwhile, Sirushi busied himself with positioning rose quartz crystals between the candles in strategic places. "Are you sure Sante will come?" asked Nova.

"Have faith," returned Sirushi. "Sante will come."

Sirushi was right. In truth, I was already waiting for Nova to enter the right frame of mind so that I could join with *lim*. They sat down cross-legged and began to pray, asking me to manifest before them. Nova went to considerable trouble to prepare an elaborate ceremony. The crystals and candles were merely tokens of *lis* sincerity. In *lis* naiveté, *le* did not comprehend that no need existed for decoration between us.

Don't decorate it, Bejan said again.

Barely was there a need to ask, but Nova did ask me to enter life through *lim*. I wanted *lim* to know that wherever *le* might go, I would follow. *Le* doubted that and me—often. *Lis* eyes scanned the most ethereal, esoteric, and remote byways of creation for my spiritual presence, while all the while I sat like sweat upon *lis* brow. I flew into *lim* so swiftly that I knocked *lim* backward on the parched and dusty earth of the mesa top. And in this sacred time of joining, no symbol could fashion, decorate, or provoke us to question the validity of our eternal love. We burned like rose and frankincense incense into the ash of our essential selves and together, we laughed at every indiscretion of the past.

****

*"ejesay epay" meaning "My love will be fulfilled only in you."; language origin, Mescale.

My attention went to red alert and I sensed the touch of an impending hand. My eyelids blinked and an electric shockwave of hope bolted through me. *Was it Elay? Was I emerging from a prolonged nightmare?* No, it was the somber figure of Una hovering over Nova and me.

"*Febr* is all right for the time being," said Una. "Take a break and I'll stay with *lim* for a while."

Stumbling out of bed, I snatched my clothing and struggled to the edge of the doorway. "Sante?" Una called. Her voice was sober, brave, and distant. "Heads up, I see trouble brewing on the horizon."

The instant I stepped into normal gravity, my nausea struck like a hammer. Vague sounds of conversation and muffled sobs drifted toward me from the sitting area. The mourners were arriving. I managed to stagger to the closest toilet where I began vomiting up my life—gagging my misery into the waiting porcelain bowl of cool indifference. I felt vacuous, inside-and-out with agony, yet life was demanding the contents of my guts. "Why?" Despite my millenniums of lives, I continued to ask the most stupid of questions. After a while, I grew cold and began to shiver, only half-aware that I pissed my pants from the pressure of my intense retching. I huddled there, frozen on the floor and every time I attempted to move, I became violently sick to my stomach. I loathed wallowing in my own filth, but could not pick myself up.

My body was wedged between the toilet and wall. Somebody pushed against the door and against my legs. Perhaps I spoke. I know I thought, *go away and let me die in peace*. I managed to glance up and initially did not recognize who was standing there. I focused with every bit of my feeble concentration to remember the face. "Go away," I said. Rugen said something about helping me and began trying to prop me up. My bones were crackers, my muscles mush. I was an old rag someone wiped out the toilet with.

"Lots of people are arriving out in the sitting area," *ce* said. "Would you like to come to my place where you can clean up and avoid the crowd for awhile?"

"Uh huh," I managed to say.

"Wait here." *Ce* returned a moment later, draped a blanket around my shoulders, and helped me to stand. We escaped through a side entrance, near the kitchen. It was early in the cycle and the halls and byways still deserted. I possess no memory of what happened next. All I remember is Rugen opened the door to *cis* apartment and I went inside and collapsed to my knees on the floor. Then *ce* was helping me undress in the bathroom as the tub filled with hot water. *Ce* asked me questions—meaningless questions—questions the Vanguard always ask in a crisis to determine a person's emotional state. "Do you know where you are? Do you know who I am? Do you want me to stay with you or leave?"

"Leave," I said.

"I'll let your family know where you are so they don't worry," and then *ce* left me alone in *cis* bathroom. A cobalt-blue bottle of bath perfume sat on the edge of the tub. I pulled out the stopper and smelled it. The scent was the one Rugen wore that night in The Quasar. The bottle bore one of Bejan's aromatherapy labels. I dumped the entire contents into the bathwater and got in, allowing the mingled essence of frankincense, forget-me knots, and *tartan ratu* to fill the humid air. Steamy white heat filled space and time and I wondered if Ganats longed for their original "Heat" every time they took a bath. I slipped deeper into the Ganat "Heat" and my mind refused to work at all.

****

"They are dead." I heard a voice speaking and it was my own. Never again would Elay sit amid the pink hawthorn flowers in her blue blouse or Bejan play keyboards in The Quasar or Michael tell stories about the fourth dimension in the Gathering." Life hurts when death tears up our rulebook. Long ago, in the adolescence of my soul, I entertained a naïve assumption that lives were strategies I could play out; but I learned the hard way that living destroys our most precious plans. In time, my body self—whom this life's parents named Sante—would learn to accept *lis* latest loss. Ten thousand times, I had climbed up from grief. Only this time, the experiment offered a fresh twist. A new dread filled me with horror that Nova might cast me away for what I had just done. I squandered every life, committed ignorant sins for which I was eternally ashamed, but never had I taken my impudence this far. I was certain Nova would never forgive me for destroying *lis* will with my love.

Rugen came to the bathroom door and opened it. "I've brought you some toiletries and a bathrobe," *ce* said and then *ce* came fully into the room and managed to put *cis* fingertips in the water. "The water is cold," *ce* said. "Let me help you get out and into some dry clothes."

"I'm not completely insane. I remember how to get out of a bathtub and put on clothing."

"I'm sorry. I'll leave you alone." Rugen had called me back to persistent reality, made me aware the water was getting chilly. I hated the demands of my body self. Where were my reciprocal selves that Evose insisted were real? They certainly did not stick around for the discomfort of the body; but I was here and my body was demanding its prosaic comforts, wanting to be warm, clean, and secure. I climbed out of the tub and my knees were trembling. I went through a routine that soothed my body into silence, drying myself, brushing my teeth, combing my damp and tangled hair smooth. I put on Rugen's robe and stared at myself in the mirror. I was the sad soldier that somehow survived the battle.

****

Attempting to be brave, I knew I was a sham, but the illusion gave me courage to venture forth from the security of Rugen's bathroom. Instinct led me. I opened a door that led to a room I knew to be a sleeproom. Its styling was Janaforma in its simplicity, yet it was elegant in its monochromatic ambiance. The furniture was high-quality lacquerware, made according to Tyrowsian standards by Tyrowsian artisans. I headed toward a door opposite from the bathroom and walked down five short steps to a landing. It was Rugen's *neipanin* (mediation area). Sitting on a black lacquerware altar was a golden incense burner meant to hold the beautiful coils of burning fragrance that can energize a room with their vibrant scent. I went down a few more steps and around another corner and found a sitting area, the food center, and Rugen *cim*self. "I'm making hot tea—do you want some?" *ce* asked.

My body self said, "okay." It even possessed the audacity to declare that it was hungry. "My stomach feels empty," I added. "Do you have a few crackers?"

"Sure, and I can make you some of my special healing soup."

Fumbling for polite words to smooth over my feelings of awkwardness, I said, "Your apartment is beautifully decorated."

Rugen appeared a bit embarrassed. "I hope it is not too much. By the way, I disposed of your clothing. Feel free to take whatever you need from my wardrobe upstairs."

"Thank you for rescuing me. I—in my last life—I was a scout too. I understand about duty. Going to someone's door with that kind of news is the hardest part of the job."

"I didn't do it because of duty," *ce* assured me.

Ezek flew up and whispered in my ear, *Rugen knows you are the original Sante. Someone in the Vanguard told cim shortly after ce arrived on* The Mother. *You're a curiosity—a tourist attraction pointed out right along with the bronze statue of Clidmore and Kinsey that sits in the middle of the memorial gardens.*

Rugen served me a bowl of clear soup in a beautiful porcelain bowl, with a matching porcelain spoon. It was miso soup with a few pea pods, bits of fresh herbs, and star-shaped pasta floating around in the broth. "I'm sorry, but I must leave you alone," *ce* was telling me, "I have an appointment that's important for me to keep."

"I don't need a babysitter. Besides, responsibilities await me too."

"I'm not suggesting you should leave. I would like you to stay as long as you want. It's quiet here and no one will disturb you."

"Why the special kindness, Rugen? I have no influence with the Vanguard. I can't help your career, if that's what you are thinking."

Rugen's tone remained neutral, yet *ce* gave me a cold stare. "Do you have any reason to consider me dishonorable?"

"Of course not."

"For your information, I did not apply for the position of flight commander on the captain's shift. The Gathering courted me to accept this assignment."

"Who told you that I am the original Sante?"

"At least a dozen people. If you're serious about keeping your identity secret, perhaps you could start by changing your name."

"What's going on between us, Rugen?"

Cis eyes caught mine for a second, yet my fear of disappointment stopped me from taking a good look. The minute trembling of Rugen's bottom lip verified that *cis* emotions lay invested in a matter pertaining to me. "I believe a past-life connection exists between us?" *ce* said with incredible confidence. "Do I seem the least bit familiar to you?"

"I'm sorry, but no."

Rugen swallowed hard and appeared embarrassed. It was obvious that *ce* entertained a well-fed ego. "Whatever the truth, it's not far away. My appointment is to take Regression."

"It won't make any difference," I assured *cim*.

"It will to me," and *ce* walked away and went upstairs. When *ce* returned a few minutes later, *ce* was wearing brown tweed pants and a loose jacket. *Cis* clothing displayed a Tyrowsian bias, just as the furnishings in *cis* apartment did. Rugen hesitated a moment before walking out the door and told me again to make myself at home. I sensed apprehension looming within *cim* about what lay ahead. If it were another time, I would have been reciprocally generous and kind enough to want to hold *cim* through the Regression experience; but in my present state, it was impossible. We both knew I was too exhausted for a Regression session. "I'll see you in a few hours," *ce* assured me and *ce* walked out the door.

FOUR

Rugen was the perfect distraction for my grief. I was reluctant to relinquish the comfort of that distraction just yet. I was ill and every muscle in my body ached as if spirit demons had sucked marrow from my bones. With no effort, I saw myself drying up like a mummy. Exhaustion almost detached me from caring and I decided to go upstairs and take advantage of Rugen's comfortable sleeproom. On my way upstairs, the attention signal at the door sounded. I cursed and decided to ignore the intrusion, but the signal continued to wail like the exigency siren on the bridge. I checked the door monitor to see if my suspicions were correct. I activated the intercom, and yelled, "Go away, Evose."

"I'm not going away, so you might as well open the door," he yelled back. I opened the door so he would stop shouting and the instant the door opened, he flew into Rugen's apartment and demanded, "Come home."

The tone of his voice felt like sandpaper against my grief and angry tears welled up in my eyes. "Go back to wherever you came from and leave me alone."

Evose scratched the side of his neck and told me, "Elay, Bejan, and Michael, decided to help in the best way they could. They died to give us a chance." If it's possible, I disliked him more. I despised his detached logic, his reduction of my family to sacrifices for the bungling of the living. I wondered why I thought him attractive a few hours earlier, when he looked so foolish to me now. "Just a few hours ago, you told me the death of one individual was not sufficient reason to go back in time and attempt to correct inequities." "Over three hundred people died on that Aeternus shuttle. How much inequity does it take to move you? Elay, Michael, and

Bejan are dead, your own parents. How can you hide out here amidst this obvious bourgeois setting, dressed in that silly silk robe, when you know you possess the power to make a difference?"

Thoughts of ejecting Evose physically from Rugen's apartment ran through my mind. I wanted to strike him with a Shardasko blow or perhaps boot him out the door with a precise backward spin-kick to the temple. I restrained all my primitive urges and instead whirled around inside my anger, making myself sick again.

"The destruction of the shuttle from Aeternus was not an accident. Soul fragments are getting desperate. They saw an opportunity for reintegration and made a quick jump into this dimension."

"That's preposterous."

"Wait! You'll soon see the face of preposterous. In a few hours, the scientific data will show that The Door has widened. The future does not need to unfold this way. However, there is a point—a Rubicon will be crossed and it will be impossible to turn back."

"Trying to change the past is not going to save the future."

"You're wrong. We can travel into the fourth dimension, enter time anywhere we choose, and the future certainly will be different."

"If you actually believe that—then do it. Go back in time, save your woman, but leave me out of your equation."

"I need your help more than ever."

"No you don't. You're the great Sirushi. I'm certain you make regular trips to the fourth dimension without the support of technology or the encumbrance of a genetic legacy. Even if you now have a body and are concerned about official sanction from the Orion Spur Alliance—why involve me? You possess the stellar likes of Bogwa and Belinda to support your unholy cause—get their help."

Evose admitted, "I can go to the fourth dimension." He also admitted his trips were psychic projections, an advanced form of astral trekking. "I cannot travel into history without technical support. I need a ship; specifically a vitasphere would fit the bill rather nicely. Help me, Sante. Be the conduit for Nova's will and let Cle speak to the Gathering through you. You alone can make this happen."

"Get it through your thick head, Evose, Cle is dead and *cis* essence is with our oversoul. Cle has no connection to the nonsense of this time. As far as Nova is concerned, *lis* life is dangling by a thread. What do you think happened when I threw you out of *lis* sleeproom? In order to keep *lim* alive, I destroyed *lis* will to die. What do you think that did to the love between us? I sullied our connection with my betrayal."

"How?"

"At *lis* most vulnerable moment, I joined my energy to *lis*."

"That was not a betrayal; it was clever way to save *lim*."

"It wasn't clever; it was stupid. I violated *lis* will. Go home, Evose. You're an innocent living your second life and too naïve to realize you're not going to win."

Evose's voice sank into thoughtfulness. "I'd rather be naïve than cynical like you. You're a waste, Jana Sante of The Mother. Nova gave you extraordinary gifts as an enticement to enter life, yet you ignore your talents because you want to punish Nova. At least I'm a committed player. My purpose is to build a bridge between the living and their soul fragments. You may think me naïve, but I'm smart enough to know that love is the only power strong enough to hold that bridge together."

Love's memory sang as a faraway songbird. *"Set-me-as-a-seal-upon-your-heart-as-seal-upon-your-arm; for-love-is-as-strong-as-death."* On the cycle Cle died, Hibernia placed Cle's armlet upon my arm and spoke those words. *Hibernia? Are you tormenting me too?* Such sweet words were an antithesis to my sour mood. I felt ill. Nausea came up again and I responded by shutting down. "For me, it's over," I told Evose. "The love I carried found nowhere to go, so it died. The death knell sounded a couple of hours ago in Nova's sleeproom."

"You're over dramatic and always have been. Nova would not have put *lis* love in you, if *le* didn't think you could handle it."

"You and Bogwa might have your emotions cleanly separated, but that's not the way it works for the Janaforma. Nova is a complete person with *lis* own mind, body, and feelings, just as I am."

"Fine, then even more reason to believe your love is safe. Love is the only tool capable of supporting positive evolutionary change. This universe has staggered at many critical times. Your great Orion Spur civilizations have perverted wisdom, suffocated understanding, and murdered will, but never has this universe been without love. Love is the fulcrum of this universe and cannot give up."

"That's archetypal malarkey, not my grinding reality."

"I know you're stunned over the loss of your family. I too was stunned when I lost Iris, but think about this. Archetypal metaphor is not malarkey; it's the starting material of all reality." He peered at me and attempted to read me, but I blocked him. Then he asked, "Why haven't you asked me how Nova is doing? Have you stopping caring about *lim* too?"

"How is *le?*"

"Thanks to you, *le* is going to live. Come home, please. Nova will need you to administer to *lis* physical and emotional needs. No one can comfort *lim* as you do."

"Absolutely not; I've interfered for the last time in Nova's lives."

Evose scratched under his chin. "All right, take your selfish holiday from responsibility; but believe me, quite soon, circumstances will force you to come to your senses. When you do, please realize your delay makes you responsible for the deaths of millions of incarnate beings and the suffering of billions of soul fragments. Sit with that on your immortal soul for a while and see how you feel."

****

After I managed to rid myself of Evose, I dragged myself upstairs and crawled into bed. I didn't even adjust the gravity terminator. The moment I sank into that wonderful downy bed, I was asleep. My unconsciousness did not last long because I woke up inside a high-pitched dream.

Cle and I are officers in the Orion Spur Space Security Corps. Our commanding officer has delayed our promotions to be involved in a month-long rescue operation in an area of space known as the Headwater Planets of Gathos. Relentless meteor barrage is destroying the planet Sutcay Tay. Cle and I have been on the surface of this world for almost two days and not slept in nine space cycles. We could go for long periods without sleep only because second generation Janaforma were bio-designed to endure long periods of sleeplessness. Despite my genetics, I am nearly psychotic with exhaustion and I see victims on both sides of my eyes. Torrential rain is falling, yet I feel dry inside. Cle and I are living on the stimulant, Aminoply. My cheeks burn with sweat and my throat clogs with pent-up fear; but all this must be stuffed down for expression at another time because the winds of destruction are blowing lives into the cosmic sea and it's our duty to respond.

Cle and I are trying to rescue three children from the roof of their home. Before we can get them to safety, we see an old woman trapped inside her roofless house. My psychic gear is keeping us alive and I see the wall of water coming before it reaches us. "Lift off!" I'm screaming over the sound of the hammering rain. "The Tartha dam just broke."

"We can't leave her," Cle screams back. We hate each other in these critical moments. The stark cruelty of our lives has worn us down and made us impatient with each other. Cle and I need to work as a team; instead, our differences make us fight.

"We can't make ship with that much weight," I say.

Cle makes a decision without me and tosses our one spare vitarattha *to the old woman, putting the rest of us in the position of trying to make it up to the ship inside one* vitarattha. *"You reckless asshole!" I scream.*

My eyes blink open and Rugen is standing over me. Tears are dripping off *cis* chin and one had plopped on my face. "Who am I?" *ce* demanded.

"I don't know," I stuttered.

Rugen reached down, grabbed my crotch through the thin blanket, and squeezed. *Ce* was not hurting me, but I gasped in anticipation that *ce* might. "I said—who am I?" *ce* repeated.

I defied *cim*, despite the fact that *ce* held my favorite conduit for pleasure in *cis* hands. "I don't care who you are and even less about who you've been."

Rugen released me, flicking *cis* fingers in the air as if I irked *cim* to the end of *cis* patience. "Your renown psychic abilities are worth shit!" *ce* said.

****

Afraid what my psychic-self was suggesting, I sat up in bed, but refused

51

to listen even to myself. Rugen perched gingerly on the edge of the bed and we silently peered into each other's eyes, first in amazement and then total recognition. Then Rugen began pouring *cim*self out like the floodwaters of Sutcay Tay. *Cis* lake-blue eyes turned misty with fresh memories released from *cis* Regression trip. "I was the first officer on *Aeternus One* for almost two years when I walked into its tiny garden and saw the ship's new medical officer sitting on a stone bench. When I got closer, I noticed tears stained *lis* eyes so I thought it inappropriate to disturb *lim*. Months later, *le* would confide that *le* was weeping for *lis* consort who abandoned *lim* because they were genetically incompatible. Two cycles later, I was on a mission and injured my leg." Rugen was methodical in *cis* torture and pointed to the exact spot on *cis* left leg where *ce* injured *cim*self in *cis* last life. "I went to the clinic to get medical attention and waited in a small cubicle for a doctor to attend my wound. By the way, in this life, I've been plagued with visions and dreams of a bloodstained white sleeve my entire life. During Regression, I saw that bloodstained sleeve in lucid detail. You apologized about the bloodstain, telling me you did not have time to change. I understood—so many wounded, dying, and dead."

"Amidst all that misery, you were an immaculate vision to me. Your skin was pale and flawless; your hair plaited in one long braid that hung down your back. When you leaned over me, to examine my wound, your braid slipped over your shoulder and accidentally brushed the back of my left hand. Then you took a scalpel and casually slit my pant leg up to my knee." Rugen smiled with the memory as *ce* wiped a tear from under *cis* eye. "My parents raised me to be strong and independent. I was the senior officer on the prestigious flagship of the fleet. Teachers, mentors, and peers endorsed my pride and I believed my destiny was to command a starship. Pride made me rigid about maintaining control, yet the instant your hair touched the back of my hand, all I wanted to do was surrender to you. I played innocent and told you I would be delighted to introduce you to some of our compatriot officers and you agreed to meet me in the officer's lounge after your shift. I arrived early and amused myself by talking to some of my friends. I was impatient and kept watching the door. You were late in coming and I worried that you changed your mind."

"I was delayed by an emergency," I said.

"When you came through that closely watched door, you were wearing a dark blue, silk shirt. Your hair was hanging loose and wavy around your face. A good omen, I thought. We made eye contact; but you did not join me as I expected. Instead, you went to the bar and waited for me to come to you. It took me about thirty seconds to get over there and sit down. You were neither dominant nor shy and I was surprised a few minutes later when you said—"

"I would like to hold you in my arms," I interjected into *cis* story. I was riding the crest with *cim*, the moment in our last life when we knew we were going to connect.

"And my exact words in return were, 'If you hold me, you will have to make love to me.'"

I was breathless, aware that my mouth was hanging open. "I thought you were with our oversoul."

"Obviously, I'm here."

I anticipated an emotional response within myself, a lifting of my spirit, but felt only terrified. It was difficult for me to accept that Cle was now Rugen. Cle's body was bigger and more rugged than Rugen, while this new-edition Cle still was young and untested. However, the more I put the clues together, the more I realized the truth was sitting right there on the edge of the bed.

Rugen went to the bottom line with me. "Connect with me, Sante, Connect with me and together we will illuminate the universe with the golden light of our mutual outpourings. Love me, as only you can, and no doubt will be left in any corner of your mind about who I am." Holy Mother! Rugen was even beginning to talk like Cle. Rugen assumed a great deal at that moment. *Ce* reached behind *cis* head and released *cis* beautiful hair from the confines of a clip, hoping the gesture would arouse me. *Ce* shook *cis* head so the freed abundance of *cis* hair cascaded down, all the way to *cis* waist. This well-known gesture of Janaforma seduction left me two narrow choices. I needed to respond fully or pull away. Rugen combed *cis* hair with *cis* open fingers as *ce* offered *cim*self up as a banquet for my pleasure. The energetic magnet of *cis* aura drew me forward and I began fondling *cis* hair. I was teetering between intense lust and frozen fear. "I want to do this right," *ce* whispered.

Doing it right meant we needed to go through a bathing ritual, and then, we would need to sit in meditation for hours. Only then, might we be free to consummate the physical part. "I don't have the energy to do it right," I replied.

"Then the hell with doing it right; we'll do it right later."

Ce made me smile. "I don't know if I can do it at all. Three years ago, I began having sexual problems. Since then, I've been unable to make love to anyone but myself."

"I hear it's like roller-skating," *ce* offered.

"You mean once you know how you never forget?

"Not exactly, I was thinking more along the lines—if you can't stand up, you better skate with a pillow tied to your ass." We laughed and it helped break the tension. Rugen turned serious again. "Don't be afraid, Sante. I'm a modest dilettante myself." *Ce* was bold enough to begin undressing, yet *ce* was self-conscious about doing it. *Ce* removed *cis* shirt and placed it on the end of the bed as if the shirt was *cis* prize possession. *Ce* had strong, lean biceps and tight pectorals from *cis* rigorous Vanguard training. *Ce* shivered and *cis* small bud-like nipples went erect. "I'd be afraid if this was happening with anyone other than you." *Ce* sat on the edge of the bed again and took off *cis* shoes, placing them in precise side-by-side position. *Ce* pulled off *cis* socks and tucked them, one by one, inside *cis* shoes. "I'm a little nervous," *ce* admitted; but *ce* managed to take off *cis* pants and drop them on the floor. *Ce* shyly left on *cis* skimpy black underwear, then picked up the covers, and slipped into bed next to me. "Please be gentle," *ce* whispered. "I'm still a virgin."

"I promise." I reached over and tapped the gravity terminator on the side of the bed and we floated up slowly, side by side, not touching, just gazing into each other's eyes. I was not fully in my body, but outside myself watching what was happening in perfect amazement.

We moved closer and I needed to dip down into baser emotions to ignite my physical passion. The dewy heat of *cis* body was eager; the honey of *cis* lips offered kisses and the silk of *cis* skin found mine and brushed against my chest and legs. *Ce* encouraged me to do whatever I wanted and I carefully explored and appreciated *cim* from head to toe. I even put my fingers inside *cis* mouth and touched the place from which absolute eloquence spoke. Rugen turned braver. Gripping my shoulders, *ce* pulled me down so I could savor the exquisite taste of *cis* sexual excitement. *Cis* mingled female/male elixir tasted like golden light upon my tongue and exploded my senses with the perfect madness of desire. An essential gear shifted in me and the affair turned hot, bittersweet, primal, salty, and finally unquestionable. I wanted nothing but to make each love moment last forever with *cim*.

"I offer you my undivided surrender," *ce* whispered with such complete sincerity that I wept. *Cis* words unlocked my heart and stripped away my confusion. Rugen was a Janaforma consort. *Cis* genetic programming declared *cis* sexual identity with utter triumph at that moment. In *cis* surrender, *ce* unlocked me from my prison too. I was a lifegiver and that meant I could pretend to the universe with absolute swagger that I was dominant over Rugen, but the truth was simple. Rugen took sexual possession of me. Before we were through, *ce* would surround me and bring me to the ground of surrender too. Through *cim*, again my well would be effulgent. No words can explain, limit, or confine the love *ce* unleashed from my heart.

****

If Simon Forma encoded my genes with information that made me an incarnation of love, then I assume he endowed me with special talents in that area. One of my talents is—lovers cannot fool me and, of course, I cannot fool myself. Once I embrace a lover, focus must be mutual and complete. If that fails to happen, then deception on some level exists.

Rugen was present in every moment with me and I felt confident that this new body held the essence of Cle. The Regression drug opened an enormous portal to past-life memories and as hours passed, *ce* grew more fully into *cis* authentic self. Rugen opened *cis* love to me on all levels and I was all too happy to bore down into *cis* receptive tenderness and drown in my own passion. In return, Rugen requested my candor. I decided to give it to *cim* and we began dancing with complete honesty. The comfort of the warm, love-soaked bed embraced us with our mutual perfume. Our intimacy did not stop Rugen from burning through the passion to uncover what *ce* needed to know. The first subject *ce* asked me about was Nova. I hesitated only because Nova was a complicated topic. "I have a right to know," Rugen reminded me. In our last life, Cle tolerated my unrequited passion for Nova our entire lives. Of course, that life was pre-Regression and I never realized, beyond a rudimentary level, what our soul's aspirations might be.

I leveled my voice and declared, "This Nova is the same Nova I loved in my last life."

"I'm not surprised," Rugen said.

"That doesn't shock you? Then how about this? Roughly three thousand years ago, Nova went by the name Simon Forma."

Rugen receded into *cim*self a little. "Holy Mother!" *ce* murmured in amazement. "And you have no doubts?"

"Absolutely no doubts whatsoever. A bond exists between Nova and me and I've come to learn, in this life, that the bond is unbreakable. It makes no difference if we are together or apart; my attachment never wavers. Life put us in this absurd situation as parent and child, yet I want to be *lis* intimate lover. I know it's sounds absurd, but I will not lie here and invent falsehoods to hide my true feelings."

"After I told Nova about the space accident, what did you do with *lim* in the sleeproom?" Shame made me avert my eyes. Again, it was a struggle to admit the truth. I don't know how I managed to say the actual words, but I told Rugen the complete, unadulterated raw story.

"Love defies convention with its generosity and is not bound by space or time," *ce* assured me.

Cis words already seemed stitched to my heart, hanging like a needlework sampler inside my soul. During those moments, my love for Rugen was extravagant and attentive. I loved *cim* now for all the times I knew *cim* in other lives. I saw *cim* as Cle, the Number One Janaforma, who carried the legacy of Candidus, The Muse of Eloquence and Truth. I had worshiped her as Helena, the wise and poetic, as Patrice who wore the mask of actor and clown. He was my passionate Edward, my aide de camp. I adored her as Maria, the patient Odessa, and the elegant Serene who died by my side in those terrible places where brutal tyrants murdered us for our belief in sisterhood. I knew this soul to be my understanding, a vital incandescence within my core.

****

"There's more we need to discuss," I told Rugen. "How much do you know about three beings who called themselves Bogwa, Sirushi, and Mehiel?"

"The Vanguard has dossiers on all three, which I've read, but not scrutinized."

"As soon as I was sure Nova was not going to die, a strange vision began unrolling in my mind. I saw Bogwa, Sirushi, and Mehiel, and they were playing a leading role."

"What did you see?"

"About thirty years ago, before I was born, Nova went to Earth on a mission. The Cerribeame Guard kidnapped *lim* and when Bogwa, Sirushi and Mehiel appeared, Sirushi whisked Nova away to the planet Lemira Jha. According to everyone involved in the mission, Nova was gone only eight hours, but Nova claims that *le* remained on Lemira Jha for eight years. Sometime during this eight year period, I appeared on the scene."

Rugen waited a long time to speak, "Tell me, Sante, what happened between you and Nova on Lemira Jha?"

"Nova asked me to incarnate again and I am bargaining about something I want or need. By then, Nova was a Regression graduate many times over and knew *le* was Simon Forma. Perhaps I told *lim* I needed *lim* to create a body for me that might serve my special needs. At that meeting, I did know cosmic details beyond Nova's grasp."

Rugen urged me onward, deeper into the vision. "What could you possibly know that was not available Nova?"

"I knew that Nova and I are one. Wherever *le* goes, I follow; and sometimes, wherever I go, *le* follows."

"So where does that leave me?"

"My immortal soul remembers you. It tells me you were there in the beginning with me. If you are not Nova's soul mate, then you and I will be exclusive with each other." A stronger bond developed between us. The result was what Elay hoped the Regression drug might do for me. Within my heart, Rugen's understanding calmed the jagged surface of my needy passion. We stripped our eyes naked and peered hard into each other. Rugen was a glorious sight, *cis* energetic emanation a pure white mass of energy possessing a million tendrils of light. "Do you know why you've reincarnated this time?" I asked.

"I don't remember—not yet; but I must have returned for you and perhaps even Nova. I'm going to take Regression again so I can see the entire picture."

"I've never taken Regression." Despite all I did remember, Rugen began to insist I take Regression and that I take it with *cim* and, hopefully, with Nova. I attempted to explain my apprehension regarding Regression in a dozen different ways. None of my usual excuses made sense to Rugen, including my favorite rationalization, "I refuse to alter the natural flow of my life."

Rugen laughed and *cis* laugh possessed an indulgent edge. I could read *cim* and *ce* was thinking, *do you expect me to believe that flimsy excuse?* Rugen assumed one of Cle's favorite expressions—the questioning stare, which possessed the ability to reduce university professors to inarticulate freshmen. Then *ce* made one simple statement that cut my "natural flow" pretext to the ground, "You're afraid of the truth."

That one simple statement destroyed the facade between Nova and my heart. A profusion of fresh past-life memories flooded my mind and dared to consume me. "Do you have any idea, the least inkling, how difficult it is to be this close to *lim*, yet so far away? Can you comprehend the depth of my longing to hold *lim* in my arms? Long ago, we exchanged our fire, our complete passion. Regression will awaken more memories of unrequited lives with *lim*, stir my anger, and expose my failure to hold *lim* in even one life." I began to sob, but I wanted to shriek over my unrequited feelings. "Three years ago, we had a horrible argument," I admitted. "Nova demanded I take Regression and I said some hateful things."

"Such as?"

"I accused *lim* of wasting this life, of debauchery with two consorts and a lifebearer, while I had no one to love."

"Nova may be many things, but you are going to have a difficult time convincing me that *le* is a debaucher."

"I admit it; it was a mean-spirited remark. I'm a big disappointment to my family, a waste of their genetic spunk."

"I don't believe that," said Rugen. "Nova did a damn good job creating you. Matter of fact, I think someone finally captured the real you."

Rugen made me smile. "I do feel more grounded in this body. Unfortunately, grounding makes me want to fuck more. My life has been holy hell for the past three years. Where were you three years ago?"

"Three years ago I was fifteen years old?"

"Right! That would have been awkward."

"This is perfect!" said Rugen. "I wouldn't change a moment."

We kissed and snuggled for a while until the passion came up to a simmer. "My hunger for you is as great as my hunger is for Nova," I assured *cim*.

"I remember your hunger," said Rugen. "All you want to do is get into a lover's vast creative space and have your own way."

"That's right. For instance, right now, I want to get inside you and have a wild sexual affair with your transcendence. Let me in and I'll show you how I can pull your transcendence down into the third dimension." Rugen wrapped *cis body* around mine and took delight in my hunger. Afterward, my heart raced from the orgasm when *ce* confessed, "The moment Xana introduced me to you, I knew we had been lovers before. Then, when you held me in the dance chamber, gears began shifting in my mind, and I've been in this weird psychic state ever since."

The bizarre events of the last few days had psyched me too. My greatest fear now involved what Evose wanted from Cle, via me. In no life did Rugen possess my psychic abilities. *Ce* did not need psychic abilities with *cis* obvious genius. *Cis* genius was so expansive that people mistook his intelligence for psychic insight. Cle kindled the kind of mind capable of making logical links between the most remote topics with incredible ease. Once *ce* made that link, *ce* could expound for hours explaining the connection to the rest of us.

"This weirdness is not weirdness for its own sake," said Rugen. "This weirdness is an opportunity."

"What kind of opportunity?" I dared to ask.

"What else, but to take evolution to greater heights in this dimension?"

The notion of that task made me shrink with inadequacy. "I was afraid you'd say something far-flung such as that." I began mind mapping and connected previous mistakes with future predictions. I saw Cle sacrificing *cim*self under the guise of helping society, and wondered if Rugen was capable of the same kind of fervor. "By now, I hope you realize how fragile life is. I cannot live through your death another time, cannot see you destroyed by lies. Please, this time, try to feel what I am feeling. Every time you and Nova leave me alone, you leave me bruised, battered, and hanging by my fingernails. Hibernia and I were devastated when we discovered you in Herzayzen Prison. Understand this Miro Rugen; I will not support your martyrdom this time around."

"I have no intention of being a martyr," Rugen assured me.

Another vision of Cle in Herzayzen Prison blasted through my memory. "Do you know what I wanted to do when we found you at Herzayzen? I wanted to put you out of your misery. If Hibernia hadn't stopped me, I would have done it."

"Are you trying to shock me? I know you can kill, but you're a liar when you say you wanted to kill me."

"Hibernia begged your case."

"I know you had a painful time accepting me as that shattered mind and disfigured body. You tried to convince yourself that I was somebody else because you could not stand to think of me so reduced; but Sante, my love, it was always me. It was my opportunity to learn that my assumptions were capable of reducing my understanding to idiocy. This time, I swear, we will work together. We will make changes from the inside out, just as you advised me to do twelve thousand years ago. I will use this opportunity wisely, I swear."

"Wouldn't you rather go away to someplace safe, away from The Door, and live a quiet life?"

"Sante, where is safety except in ourselves?"

"Some geographical locations are safer than others. We could buy land on a small, remote planet and spend our days gardening and our nights making love."

"We're not farmers. We're Janaforma and we have a responsibility to greater Community."

"Then how do you see our lives unfolding? What is our great mission this time around?"

"You know me, I always have plans, but this time, I'd like to skip the great mission part. I want plenty of time to be with you and build a life together."

Laying my hands upon *cis* chest, I felt the strength of *cis* commitment to life, the poignant legacy of *cis* burden. "That's good because certain people already are setting traps for you."

"Traps for me? Who?"

"After Nova collapsed, I assume Evose introduced himself."

"He did."

"About thirty years ago, Evose went by the name Siruchi."

"You're kidding! Evose is The Siruchi that rescued Nova and took *lim* to Lemira Jha?"

I nodded yes. "Evose arrived aboard *The Mother,* just a few hours ago. He wants the Gathering to give him a vitasphere, so he can go back in time. He believes soul fragments in the fourth dimension are exacerbating the dimensional split, which we all know is inevitable. He's predicting that within a few hours, The Door will widen again and this will prove he is right. His story is sketchy and involves a woman from the past with whom he was able to establish a psychic link."

"What kind of psychic link?"

"He refuses to explain what they were doing—says it's for my protection. Evose claims that soul fragments kidnapped this woman. He wants to go back to an earlier time, before the event happened, to save her, and believes this action will disburse the soul fragments. He came to me with the ridiculous notion that I could channel you, as Cle, and you could speak to the Gathering and convince them to support his cause."

I could see the wheels spinning in Rugen's head and some of them were on the verge of catching fire. "Is Evose mentally impaired in some way?"

"No, he is sane, that's what scares me."

Rugen smiled. "Then I'll simply tell him no and that will put an end to it."

"I don't want you to underestimate the seriousness of the pressure Evose can exert on you."

"It's okay, Sante. To me, Evose is just another one of your crazy family members. For now, let's put them all in the closet because I have a mission we can accomplish right here in this sleeproom."

****

We stopped talking because our physical parts kept demanding attention from the reciprocal parts in the other. "Come on, let's do it right," *ce* coaxed. *Ce* reached over and hit the gravity button and we came down and settled into the bed. We decided to take a shower; then *ce* took me by the hand and led me down to *cis neipanin* on the landing. We lit a coiled snake of *tartan ratu* incense and sat facing each other with our bellies glued together. My psychic feelers wrapped around *cim* like arms and *ce* allowed me to explore *cis* internal darkness with my love. We were quiet and focused as our energy rose as one.

Afterward, I tried to sleep in *cis* bed, but it was difficult to do more than nod off. I did not want to sleep and miss being with *cim,* even for a moment. I wanted to gaze at *cis* angelic innocence as *ce* slept in my arms, to fuse the image of *cis* new face in my memory, and savor the exotic scents oozing from *cis* body. *Cis* clean, young face tucked itself into the space between my chin and shoulder and, as if in a dream, *cis* thoughts peeked through the dim light of the sleeproom. "Help me, my love," *ce* whispered. "Share your psychic insights with me about possible futures and I will try to put my understanding around your words." In the hushed glow of amber light, we became two whispering voices, sharing our most intimate thoughts.

In the sacred moments that followed, hope lifted its head within me and I could almost believe that Rugen and I emanated from the same oversoul. With my whole heart I wished it were true and if wishing can make dreams come true, then nothing would be truer for me. Suspended, as I was, within the rosy glow of *cis* body, new visions fell upon me like gentle rain. They were not past life or future visions, but visions from beyond that I never knew until now. A veil parted within Rugen and *ce* showed me a thousand golden cords that connected *cim* to a definite feminine force. *Ce* was incontestable perfection. How could I not want to claim some small part of *cis* obvious perfection as my own? "You're more beautiful than you can ever imagine," I told *cim*.

****

Rugen began telling me about *cis* present life. It was a veritable revelation to say the least. "My biological parents were born here on *The Mother* and worked as Regression advocates. They immigrated to the planet Uropae about twenty years ago and I was born there. I was five weeks old when they died in a space accident on one of their frequent jaunts to

Sasaybin, one of Uropae's moons. A Tyrowsian couple named Miro Kayya and Ceff quickly adopted me. Kayya and Ceff already were Regression postgraduates and well known in the Executive Gathering from their previous incarnations as Kerisa, Reyneldi, and Dyne. I'm eager to introduce you to Kayya and Ceff. They personify the ideal of perfect soul mates. When I was a child I would go to their laboratories and they would show me the holographic models of their paradigmatic spacecraft. I was three when I saw the first prototype for a vitasphere. Ceff would lift me up and I would perch on her shoulders as she explained how a vitasphere worked. I remember the day she told me, 'Vitaspheres will make Cerribeame rifters obsolete.' I was an impressionable eight-year-old mind when they christened the first vitasphere as it came rolling off the line in their assembly plant. Flying became my passion. All I ever wanted to do was become a vitasphere pilot. Kayya and Ceff respected my dream and laid the way for me. I was eleven when I soloed and graduated from the Cerribeame Academy at fifteen."

"I'm impressed with your accomplishments."

"I was hot!" Rugen smiled with pride. "Ceff and Kayya believe that vitasphere technology at Trans-Miro is just getting started. If production goes according to our hopes and plans, we will have a new generation vitasphere in about a year."

"Are Ceff and Kayya grooming you to take over Trans-Miro?"

"They better be!" Rugen smiled sweetly. "I'm their only child."

"So gaining permission from the Gathering would be merely a formality for you."

The smile dropped off Rugen's face and *ce* appeared alarmed. "I told you, I'm not getting involved with Evose. I do think we should do our homework—discover as much background information as possible on him and his two cohorts—just so we know what we might be up against." Rugen turned practical and told me that *ce* needed to be on duty in a short time. "Where are you going to be?" *ce* asked.

"I need to go see my family."

"Do you want my help in any way?"

"I'm okay; you gave me the strength to do what I need to do."

Cis shyness was gone and *ce* deliberately climbed over me to get out of bed. It was a way of teasing me with *cis* body. It worked too and I managed to grab *cim* in a few strategic hot spots before *ce* escaped. *Cis* clothing, which *ce* had arranged so precisely, now lay strewn around the room. *Ce* bent over to retrieve the scattered pieces, then stood there for one priceless moment showing me *cis* flawless backside. My mind snapped an indelible picture of the kabalistic wonder that presented itself to me. *Cis* pearly flesh glowed in the dim sleeproom light. *Cis* long disheveled hair cascaded over *cis* lithe back, ending in suggestive curls that drew my attention to *cis* daring little ass that was as inviting as two firm apples. Like Eve, I helped myself to the knowledge, the wonder therein, and gave it a gentle bite. "May I have a token to take with me?" I begged. No use pretending otherwise, I was the lovesick troubadour.

We showered again. Afterward, Rugen gazed at our twin images reflected in the bathroom mirror. "We look great together," ce said pushing some damp strands of hair off cis forehead. The gesture flexed the impressive biceps of cis right arm, making me go semi-erect with renewed lust. Ce noticed and responded by singing a few bars of "Nobody Does Me like You Do."

I asked, "Are you still able to mimic voices?" In several of cis past lives, ce possessed an uncanny talent to duplicate people's voices with incredible accuracy. As Cle, not only could ce mimic peoples' voices; but ce also possessed a facility to speak hundreds of different languages.

My words boomeranged from Rugen's mouth sounding like me. "Are you still able to mimic people's voices?" ce asked.

"Is that what I sound like?"

Cis face lit up with an amazed expression. "And that's what you looked like when I told you I was Cle."

"Cle used to tease me by imitating my voice and putting the most outrageous statements into my mouth."

Rugen grabbed me and pulled me close. Ce was a powerful lover. At the height of our lovemaking, I allowed cim to take complete control of me. Now cis voice became mine and ce said, "How is this for outrageous? This time, I swear, I will never let you go."

My heart was pounding with excitement. Rugen held my complete amazement and admiration. Despite remembering cis lives, through pain and failure, ce was able to speak of hope and the future. I desperately needed cis youth and enthusiasm, to bring me up from the grief of losing my family and living a life deprived of Nova.

We went downstairs, ate toast, and drank tea before parting. We planned to meet later. Then ce went to the multidex and programmed the security system to accept my palm print. "Now my place is your place too," ce said. We kissed one last time and I was already planning our next orgy in my mind.

FIVE

The nightmare at family's quarters was ongoing. The sitting area was jammed with thirty to forty sad-faced mourners. Some people appeared trapped there for eons. By no means, did I recognize all these folks; many were complete strangers to me. Evose was nowhere in sight and I wondered what mischief he might be plotting and with whom. The moment I arrived, I was the focus of attention. I felt as if I walked on stage and it was my cue to emote the critical line, but had forgotten the plot. Ezek cruised around the room and picked up random thoughts drifting through their minds.

I wonder how le is handling it.

Le *looks well despite what's happened. How's that possible?*

Le *should have been here sooner for Nova.*

I employed the uncommon, "good morning," to shatter the false silence. It seemed to be a room dominated by deaf mutes and I asked, "Can anybody tell me where the remnants of my family are located?"

I recognized one of Elay's closest friends. Laurel came over to speak to me in a hushed tone, as if what she was saying was a secret. "Una went down to Landing Bay 10," said Laurel. "She went to meet family members coming in from Earth. Senon is in charge of caring for Nova."

I walked down the short hall to Nova's sleeproom. It was a long walk. Inside, the gravity was set at about ninety percent, just enough to take pressure off the physical body. Inside, the light was dim. "Senon?" I called softly.

Senon gave me a hand signal and then floated over to the door and stepped outside. *Le* looked like Michael—tall, lanky, and perennially youthful. We put our arms around each other and cried. I thought about parroting some clichés about death that I used in several previous lives, but words seemed particularly meaningless now. Besides Senon was angry and I did not want to make *lim* anymore upset. Anger was coming off *lim* like steam off hot concrete. The problem was Senon entertained a logical bias that always needed to make sense of life's absurdities. The whites of his eyes were fiery red from crying. "It's not fair," *le* said. "Why does spiritual essence go home in glory, while the fragile ego and the body get shoved into the cosmic recycling bin?"

I shrugged instead of talking about the ego's projected illusions or about the body being the vehicle for spirit. It was too esoteric. Senon was not into vague esoteric concepts. Senon was into life and *lis* body and *le* felt the cosmic insult to the parts of the self not invited to the party in the afterlife. *Le* wiped *lis* eyes and sniffed back some tears. "I don't care if they weren't perfect. I want them back, exactly as they were."

"Would you be willing to violate the order of time to get them back?"

Senon was a genius on the pickup. "You mean use the fourth dimension to abrogate time?"

"Yeah."

Le sighed. "Thank heaven it's a temptation I don't have to face."

"How's *Febr*?"

"As stubborn as ever. *Le* refuses to talk to anyone, except to say, 'Get out of my sleeproom and leave me alone.' I'm glad you're here. Maybe you can thaw *lim* a little."

"I will need uninterrupted time to try."

"Don't worry; I'll keep everybody at bay."

****

I went inside the darkened sleeproom and my mind shifted into a surprising state of mind, one I remembered, but had not employed in centuries. It was an instinctive state where I became the stalker. *Nova* was lying on *lis* left side, with *lis* eyes closed, about a meter above the bed. *Le* was a total wreck. *Le* looked old and dry for the first time in this life. *Lis* face was white with grief and the stubble on *lis* face had grown into a scruffy beard. I drew closer and noticed *lis* body smelled like tar baking in an equatorial sun. A nasty sore on *lis* bottom lip was just beginning to scab over where *le* had bitten *lim*self during our ordeal. I tapped the gravity controller and brought *lim* down by increments. Gradually, the blanket and Nova settled into the position of normal gravity. *Le* sensed me, but took *lis* time in opening *lis* eyes. I decided to perform a quick diagnosis, taking *lis* pulses along *lis* wrists and they still were scattered and weak. I touched a few points on *lis* arms, and a spot between *lis* nose and cheek. *Lis* body woke up and *le* started to cough. The cough sounded dry and hacking, and *lis* breath smelled as if *lis* stomach was empty. *Le* had an energetic tangle in *lis* guts that *le* needed to work out during meditation or it would kill *lim*. The knot in *lim* did not worry me because Nova was an energy expert. If given the chance, *le* would clear the tangle in *lim*self. *Le* squinted, but it took *lim* five more minutes to focus.

Then I knew our time had arrived. We were eye to eye and truth up against truth. I felt the unexpressed emotion between us, the weight of eons, but kept my grief to myself. If I possessed any genius, it was my ability to permeate my every word with feeling; but I played fair and attached no emotion to my statement. "There is no truth for me other than my love for you is eternal," I told *lim*.

I seemed to wait another lifetime for *lim* to speak. "I'm sorry I've failed you so many times," *le* replied. *Lis* declaration held no emotion either. *Le* harbored no anger, as I feared. Fear was my projection.

"You haven't failed me because it isn't over between us."

Nova rolled over and gazed up at the ceiling. *Le* laughed for about three seconds. "You are such a pain—in my heart." I put my hand on the center of *lis* chest and poured my energy into *lim*. *Le* submitted to it and stared straight-ahead, playing my helpless patient. "Right before you arrived, I had a dream," *le* confessed. "In it, you're a toddler; and as always, you managed to amaze me with your precocity. I said to Elay, 'Look! Sante is walking. We will need to make sure we put the dangerous stuff up high.' The scene changed again and you came into my study. You were a perfect prodigy, not more than fourteen months old." Tears spilled over Nova's eyes. "You gazed at me with complete equanimity and demanded, 'Who am I?' For some strange reason, I told you, 'Your proper name is Victoria, but the family calls you Vicky.' Your face assumed an expression of childish defiance and you told me, 'You're wrong, *Febr*. My name is Victory.' I ran to get Elay, to tell her our small miracle was talking in complete sentences. I tried to get you to repeat your linguistic trick; but instead, you stared at Elay with complete confidence, as if I was the crazy one for believing you spoke a moment earlier."

"Then the scene changed and this time I was sitting behind the wheel of a land car. You sat beside me and Una was in the backseat. We were stuck in a traffic jam waiting for the light to change so we could drive across the intersection. I said to Una, 'Quick, make sure Sante is wearing *lis* safety belt. Put yours on too, so we can all be safe.'" More tears flooded Nova's eyes. "Then the light changed and it was time to drive across the intersection and something goes terribly wrong—wrong with the traffic signals. They're jammed and everything seems to be happening at once. Pedestrians are stepping into the street; two crazy women in their car are cutting across the lanes—all confused and half-blind. I activated the alert signal on the steering column in an attempt to get them to snap out of their senile trance, but circumstances forced me to veer left to avoid an accident. I'm sure I've hit something. I stop, get out, and notice the bumper is only slightly damaged, but now I've lost you and Una. 'Where are my children?' I scream. Nobody answers me. I force myself to look inside the car where I find your body on the front floor. It's crumpled, discarded like a carapace that's grown too small. I took your precious remains and draped them across my arms. I am filled with so much grief that I cannot bring myself to look behind the seat, to see what I've done to Una. I know this entire dilemma is my fault and ask, 'Why did I strap my precious children into this ridiculous contraption that tore them apart? Why did I insist that they buckle themselves between a force that impels and restrains at the same time?'"

"You didn't strap me into this life, Nova. I returned here of my freewill. My soul wants to be with you. I always want to be where you are. I remember now that you summoned my spirit to Lemira Jha and sacred alchemy passed between us that brought me to life. See me! Feel me and know I am truly here, just as I always am. I will never leave you—how could I?" I touched Nova's cheek and an intense vibration passed between us. It was the shuddering of utter bliss. "You are my divinity."

Lis voice dipped low. "That's a job that should be made redundant."

I dared to smile and could feel *lim* relax for the first time. "So you've decided to stick around for a little more time?"

"Do I have a choice? It was a shock to my ego to learn that you are a more powerful force than I am."

I thought of Rugen and quoted *cim*. "Love defies convention with its generosity and is not bound by space or time.'"

"Very eloquent. I guess you've proven that is true." We held hands and those moments remain precious to me. "Sante, I want to make things right between us; no more impelling and restraining, but for now, I need a few hours to untangle my core."

"Your chances are limitless with me."

"That's very generous of you. Evose told me a few hours ago that you did not believe in second chances. When I heard that, it scared me."

"Evose is not my soul mate."

"Are you sure? If we all are One—aren't soul mates erroneous?"

"We may be all One, but I'm never going to fully realize it unless I am one with you first. Only one person can make me walk away from you and that's you. Tell me you no longer want a relationship with me and I swear, Nova, I will never trouble you again. Love does not stay where it is not wanted."

Nova squeezed my hands tighter. "Sante, you are my definition of love. If I lost you, I would lose myself."

I relaxed too, but I knew this was not a sprint, it was a marathon and I decided it was time to clear the air. "Do you remember what happened after you fainted out in the sitting area?"

"Yes. I tried to leave life and you tethered me here with the strength of your love." *Le* looked slightly amused. "When you were an infant, a chunk of bread became stuck in your throat. I needed to put my fingers into your gooey little mouth and pull it out before you choked to death. You were pissed with me when I did it and bit me with your sharp little baby teeth. Regardless, I did not stop and ask, 'pardon me, do I have permission to save your life?' I just did it because it is what I needed to do."

"Thank you. I've been extremely worried about that."

"You should be more worried about the future and that unknown phenomenon that destroyed the Aeternus shuttle."

"Do you have any ideas about what it could be?"

"A few."

"Was it an accident?"

"I don't believe in accidents. So far, they've found no trace of bodies in the debris field, which is extremely suspicious. Furthermore, Elay, Michael, and Bejan had to know, at some point that the risk was a strong possibility. What I don't understand is how they kept the truth from me. I grant them one margin. Perhaps they encountered a threat so powerful and so urgently dangerous that as enlightened beings they were compelled to face it."

A horrible shiver went through me. I imagined winged Hermes, the god of travel and the protector of sacrifices, sailing across the heavens with his lyre poised against his chest. Those siren strings could trick the consciousness of gods and the incarnate alike. Maybe it was just a matter of time until the trickster came through The Door and the denial from all time came spilling out into this creation. Had the willing souls of Bejan, Elay, and Michael sacrificed their lives to plug the dam? Whatever the truth, it seemed to be waiting just a few light years beyond *The Mother*. I knew it; Nova knew it; and certainly, Evose knew it too.

****

Nova climbed out of bed, shaved, showered, and brushed *lis* teeth. *Le* asked me to go out to the food center and get *lis* nutrient capsules that *le* kept refrigerated. After swallowing a handful of *lis* favorite green capsules and drinking about a liter of water, it was amazing how much better *le* appeared. "I'd appreciate it if you would stay for a while longer," *le* said. "I want to discuss some topics with you that I've been putting off for far too long."

I assured *lim*, "Antares couldn't drag me away." The telepathy between us was spooky. The instant I thought, *I need to tell lim about Rugen—*

Nova said, "And we definitely need to discuss Cle." Nova still was not ready to face the mourners. "Please, do me a favor before we get started? Go out to the sitting area and tell those people that I appreciate their support, but I need some privacy right now." I went out to the sitting area to make a short announcement, only this time Evose was present. The atmosphere was not quite as somber as before. It was agitated, something Evose was stirring up. I ignored him and politely told the crowd that Nova needed privacy. Then Evose stepped forward and began ripping my reality apart for a second time.

"My predictions are starting to manifest in this dimension," he said. "The bridge announced a few minutes ago that two vitaspheres were destroyed out in the corridor."

My mind shot to Rugen and I was halfway to insanity with panic. "You're lying!" I said and the room went from quiet to stone silent.

Evose stared at me as if his vindication was imminent. "And you're unstable," he replied. "Your frequent emotional outbursts make you highly unpredictable."

I suppressed my emotions only to convince Evose that I fit his definition of stable and trustworthy. The suppression caused a sudden rigidity in my energy body that I would need to purge in meditation. The rigidity inside me began to stockpile adrenaline in my physical body and fear in my mind. My emotions produced a story in me, exactly as I produced a new novel. My story was Nova's dream and I was strapped inside a vehicle that impels and restrains at the same time. "Tell me!" I demanded.

"Commanders Solange and Xana Capsun are dead. Commander Miro Rugen lives to tell the tale."

No! Not Xana. "Was Commander Miro injured?"

"I hear your new lover is just fine."

****

I left Evose standing in the middle of the sitting room wondering when my next emotional outburst might occur. My spirit reached the bridge before I did. I did not ask Captain Issed's permission to walk onto *lis* bridge—I just did it. Behavior such as this, I still got away with because of who I was in my previous life. Rugen was the only person that mattered to me. The moment I saw *cim*, I parroted every cliché that popped into my head. "Thank the Divine Mother you're safe," came out of me at least twice. To silence me, Rugen took my hand and discreetly held it. Captain Issed zeroed in on my bridge presence about thirty seconds after I arrived.

"You finished with me, Captain Issed?" Rugen was eager to take my emotional histrionics somewhere safe, so I could vent.

"It's my duty to call a Gathering," Issed told Rugen. "Dismissed and stay available."

Nova once called Captain Issed, "the insipid Captain Issed." It was obvious that Issed was methodical. *Le* sometimes communicated with people in weary monotones. *Lis* body posture was odd, and *le* held *lis* shoulders too tight and high. I thought of *lim* as a stork perched on a pillion, afraid that *le* might get *lis* feet wet. I cannot say *le* inspired much confidence. The bridge's Prime-I multidex was programmed to hold the ship in a tight orbit around The Door. *La Ventana* had not flown one independent meter under Issed's command. This was not *lis* fault; it was the fault of the Gathering.

Issed received a customary little salute off the side of Rugen's top lip. "Permission to leave the bridge?" *ce* asked. Issed nodded *lis* approval and Rugen and I slipped away.

Outside, in the corridor, in the darkest corner we could find, Rugen and I held each other. There was a slight trembling in *cis* body, a nervous static from holding *cis* emotions in check for so long. "You're breathing so hard, you sound as if you are going to faint," *ce* told me.

"I've been breathless since Evose told me that two vitaspheres were destroyed out in the corridor." Because of the accident, the area around the bridge was a hotbed of activity. We pulled our hair forward to cover the sides of our faces and I leaned my elbow against the wall to hide us from prying eyes. "Spill it!" I demanded. Rugen attempted to look away and I pulled *cis* chin around, forcing *cim* to gaze into my eyes. It gave *cim* no chance to put any filters between us.

Rugen managed to surprise me with, "I was supposed to die with Xana and Solange."

I was halfway to crazy again. "Don't ever say that." I was too loud again and people coming and going to the bridge glanced our way.

"I have no choice," *ce* said. "I need to take Regression again. All the stops must be opened for me."

"It's too soon, Rugen. Your life is in turmoil and mine is in grief. I'm not ready to handle unresolved problems from past lives when I can't get a grip on the present. Now tell me, what happened out in the corridor?"

Rugen had experienced something awesome that shook *cis* well trained cool. "It came from deep fourth, honing in on the two lead vitaspheres, swallowing them like two snack crackers." Rugen caught *cis* breath and swallowed hard. "It was black, blacker than starless space—if that's possible. I don't know what to call it—maybe a fast-moving endoplasmic cloud." *Cis* voice turned quieter and raspier at the same time. "This is all between you and me—promise?"

"You have my word."

"Whatever it was, it gave me an eerie feeling, just from being in its proximity. It possessed a black aura, a presence that provoked feelings of inevitability inside me. It seemed to know where it was going and nothing in our Mother's universe was going to stop it. It whizzed right past me, leaving a strange sensation of—" Rugen shuttered. "Icy wind. You know the feeling when a door opens or slams shut from strange pressures. At first, I thought the *manatees* had found a hallucination to make me afraid or I was experiencing a high-pitched nightmare and still was asleep in bed."

"How did you get back to *The Mother*?"

Rugen shrugged. "I can't remember." Suspicious and afraid, Rugen peeked over my arm. *Ce* lowered *cis* voice and put *cis* lips closer to my ear. "Even before we hit space, we started having problems. When I arrived for my shift, as usual, I checked all three vitaspheres. They were operating within normal parameters. Then right before we launched for the corridor, the system initiators on Xana's multidex went haywire. Communications coming through ship-to-ship systems were jammed with interference. Bridge consensus decided the disturbance was drifting in from around The Door. Whatever it was, it scrambled communications coming from the bridge."

I thought again about the symbol in Nova's dream, about crossed-signals, and wondered if it was a telepathic warning *le* picked up and included in *lis* dream.

"Despite our problems, Xana's B-drive kept telling us that all systems were operational. We had clear visuals with space and could see with our naked eyes that this was untrue. A Martian transport had just left *The Mother* and was crossing our launch path. Anyway, we monkeyed around for a solid fifteen minutes—tried rebooting. It was obvious that we needed to shut down and slap in a new relay network application. This particular application takes five minutes to install and thirty seconds more to integrate; still, we needed a tandem presence in the corridor, so I told Xana to fly lead, and I would stay behind to complete repairs and we would rendezvous at our second tangent point."

"Why do you believe you were supposed to die?"

"Because it was my duty to fly point." I wanted to tell Rugen that *cis* conclusion was illogical and *cis* heroics out of proportion. Instead, I tried to respect *cis* predicament and promised that I would be *cis* ardent supporter. The tension broke loose in *cim* and *ce* said in full voice, "Let's go home."

I sighed with frustration and remembered my promise to Nova. "We can't." I attempted to explain, in the best way I could, what was going on with Nova.

"Okay. Let's go there instead," Rugen said. The soul that enlivens Rugen is the most unselfish consciousness in my universe. Our lives always presented problems and challenges; but this soul was my closest confidante, treating my problems and desires with compassion and loving tenderness, no matter what was going on with *cim*.

****

By the time we arrived at family quarters, it was clear of mourners. Only Senon and Evose remained. Nova had emerged from *lis* sleeproom and was eating scrambled protoplex and toast. I was not gone more than forty minutes, but it was enough time to make *lim* suspicious. Nova knew I would not leave unless it was an emergency. Furthermore, I was certain

Evose informed *lim* that I went off the deep-end when told about the destruction of the vitaspheres.

Nova glanced my way and started sifting through me for clues. I surrendered to *lis* probing because I planned to tell *lim* about Rugen at the first opportunity. Nova said nothing immediately, but took *lis* time and finished chewing *lis* toast. Then *le* methodically wiped *lis* hands on a napkin and pointed a finger at Rugen and then me. "Okay. It makes no difference which one of you goes first, but one of you please do me the courtesy of verifying my suspicions, which are suggesting some definite conclusions."

"Only in private," I said.

Evose called the spirit of will "a generator." Will was a dynamo, a force that knew how to get what it wanted, one way or another. The problem with "will" was the one-way-or-another part. If "will" has surrendered to its oversoul, then it can be a force of incredible beauty, a transparent strength, a Buddha, a Baybairn, a Christ. Nothing is more charismatic than pure will channeled through love. The problem for will people, and it is ongoing, is ego has a ravenous appetite for willpower. Ego comes to the dinner table of "will" with a hearty appetite and if allowed, stays until the bones are clean. When ego controls will, distortions abound. Distorted will, in mild stages of ego control can be irritated, sarcastic, critical, impatient, and arrogant. It is the impolite autocrat at the dinner table. Strongly distorted will can be decisively cruel, it can murder, rape, and pillage. Down through time, will has done all these things and more.

I felt sorry for Nova and the burden *le* carried. *Le* was an angel, who, eons ago, surrendered *lis* will to *lis* oversoul, but Nova was alive in a body and that made it difficult. All bodies possess egos; and in most cases, the ego and body are great pals. Legends abound about Jesus of Nazareth, Siddhartha Gautama, and Baybairn the Elder—that these individuals transcended ego. Who can claim with true authority that these historical individuals surpassed ego as Evose claimed he had done? Dare I believe that Jesus of Nazareth might have enjoyed getting his feet anointed with oil by Mary Magdalene? Why does the *Ganat Book of Prayer* tell us that only the flattery of potential lovers can elevate the ardor of Baybairn the Elder? Legends are aggregates of nebulous meaning. Legends can shame us and make us feel inadequate when interpreted by demanding egos. In my life as a Janaforma, saints of the third dimension were plentiful. I knew many personally and every one possessed an ego. These saints took pride in their bodies and the needs of their bodies. They enjoyed making love, wore stunning clothing, and owned beautiful possessions. They wanted people to love them and they wanted to love in return. They were compassionate, humble, searching, and honest. Even the most energetic eventually tired; and when they did, sometimes they got pissed off about the gap between what they wanted and what they were getting. Despite their flaws, I knew for sure that authentic saints always do their homework. My psychic eye strained to see the soul fragments of the Janaforma people and what I saw instead was authentic integrated life. Just as I did, our oversoul adored Nova. I knew enough to realize my puny longings could not generate the kind of unselfish feelings I possessed for this great soul. In truth, it was our oversoul's love, burning through me, which fueled my love for Nova. Now, Nova's ego nudged *lim*. *Move over*, it suggested. *Let me handle this.* Nova nodded to Evose and he left without a word. Even Senon offered to leave, but Nova told *lim* to stay.

"Okay. Let's have it," demanded Nova. Yeah, *lis* ego was soaring.

Rugen put *cis* arm around me. "Allow me," *ce* offered. "I am Cle."

"Eternal *hataeasta!*" swore Senon.

Surprise struck Nova dumb and *lis* ego ran for shelter. What *le* saw across *lis* flashing supersensory billboard was that Rugen and I were lovers, not that Rugen was Cle. For a second, *le* looked as if *le* might collapse again and *le* looked to me to confirm it.

"There's no doubt in either my mind or my groin," I said.

"Excuse me," *le* said weakly. "This changes everything," and *le* stood up and left the room.

After a discreet silence, Senon cleared *lis* throat. "Una will be here shortly with the others. If you want, I will hold down the fort, while you and Rugen talk with Nova."

I thanked Senon and asked *lim* for another favor. "Don't tell anybody that Rugen is Cle, especially Evose."

"You got it," Senon promised

****

Rugen and I followed Nova. *Le* had gone into Bejan's study. When Rugen opened the door, Nova turned around and asked, "Would you please take off your shoes before coming in here?" The room was full of Bejan's possessions—books and stacks of music spools, *cis* collection of musical instruments, an icon of Bellawand, *cis* favorite Trinity Witch saint. Bellawand was dark, like Bejan, and her white wings appeared soft as *cis* tender heart. A dozen aromatherapy bottles sat on *cis* desk waiting for clients to pick them up. Near the space window was *cis* altar. It featured a cluster of crystals and a now wilted bouquet of scarlet roses.

Nova stood by the window staring out at the stars. Space was tranquil. The heavens were pristine in their eternal order and revealed no hint of impending danger anywhere. "Bejan was one of the most compassionate souls I ever met," said Nova. *Le* went to the altar and removed one of the fading roses from the vase. *Le* plucked two petals from the flower and blessed them with a kiss before handing a petal to each of us. Despite *lis* grief, Nova appeared powerful. *Le* was a handsome demigod in *lis* prime. How *le* managed to pull *lim*self together, to this degree, in such a short time, was a mystery to me. Nova gazed at Rugen with intense fascination. "That you returned to life and found Sante at this critical time is a foreshadowing of what is possible for the three of us. Like this rose, our oversoul is in full bloom within us. Nova extended *lis* right hand with the palm facing upward. Then *le* shook the fading rose and the petals fell away from the stem. A few sat as willing sacrifices in *lis* open hand waiting for *lis* careful crush. *Le* did not disappoint. An instant of rose scent permeated the air as *le* closed *lis* hand around the petals. "I am soaked in illumination, a truth that sits visibly in my right hand. My Rugen, my creation of understanding, you are my own."

Rugen was amazed. "Then *I am* your soul mate too?"

"To deny you would be true sin," said Nova. "I do not want to go home with any shred of arrogance clinging to my soul. I want to be an equal partner with love and understanding. It's time to own my special evil that has attempted to reclaim me through my children. The sins of the fathers and all that rubbish—there's a shred of truth in that old saying." Beads of sweat appeared on Nova's brow and *lis* whole body winced. *Le* was trying to remember something remote that *le* struggled to put into words. "I need to go back, way back to the beginning to try to touch it," *le* admitted. "I have played many games through time. In this universe, my consciousness was born in a nebular simoom. There was no plan—just hubris and a burning desire to create something rare and exquisite. Incarnations were difficult, muddy pools of half-conscious reality. I stacked them, one upon the next, returning each one to our oversoul as foolishness and despair. My karmic disposition strangled me with the most horrific of mortal sins—willful ignorance. So, I was given a chance—one chance. I drank an infusion of brilliance, an elixir from divinity's own breast; and suddenly, I was alive in a body so physically weak, I could not touch the universe I yearned to embrace. I was mortally afflicted, so handicapped and removed from my vision of perfection that people turned away with revulsion rather than look upon me. Everything and everyone in my life told me I was unwanted. Talk of euthanasia circulated around me, of mercifully allowing me to starve to death, suggestions that I was costing the state too much money and rumors that I might be an incarnation of Satan. I had no mother or father to nurture me, no champion to defend my rights. I had no name. I called myself Simon for the simoom that birthed my soul and took Forma as my surname from the Forma Foundling Home that was my physical shelter. I was barely alive, but I was alive enough to believe what my world told me about myself—that my sins had saddled me with a horrible karmic burden. How could I understand, with my limited mind, that I was not cursed, but finally blessed? The exact tools that I needed to create my vision already were mine, yet I lived as though damned. I failed miserably at living. I seethed with hatred, vowing that I would get even with a god who afflicted me with deformity and disease." Sweat poured down the sides of Nova's face. "I pushed hard, but found nothing to push against except myself—my anger, my inadequacies and illusions. I found no consciousness, out there, where I could disgorge my rage. Deep in self-loathing, I attempted to kill myself, but I did not die. However, I was shattered into a million pieces. My own vultures came to feast on my bloodied and bruised corpse. They stripped me to the bone and dragged me to the edge of new reality—a reality that demanded I become a true martyr, a witness to my own inner truth.

I had lived many lives as an ouroboros; yet, amazingly, love was still with me. I learned about love in a new way and through it, I began to create. Love was the one authentic inspiration of any of my lives. I created you my precious children and your angelic presence lifted me into a palace of utter bliss. You made this universe my playground." Nova staggered a bit. This time we merely needed to steady *lim*. "You have far surpassed my original vision of a beautiful mind." Nova reached out and touched Rugen's cheek.

"I need to ask something important," said Rugen.

"Ask it. Ask it eloquently, as only you can. Breathe new understanding into me, my perfect child."

"I'm sorry. Eloquence escapes me at this moment; besides, I believe it should be asked simply."

"Yes, as Bejan would say, 'Why decorate it?'"

"Are you suggesting that you've outgrown Simon Forma and now want to be just Nova?"

"Yes! Simon Forma's overcoat is inappropriate for where I'm headed. Now what I want to do is to set you both free." I began to cry and Nova asked, "What's wrong, Sante?"

"Just an hour ago, you told me you wanted to get it right with me."

"Setting you free is the beginning of getting it right. Your dependency on me is an illusion. I might have created your original bodies, but in actuality, you have created yourselves. How do I know? You both have become greater than I ever thought possible."

Rugen touched me in an effort to restrain me. "How can you free us before you've truly embraced us?" *ce* asked.

"Don't do this," I begged. "You're talking as if you are a detached god. Maybe, cosmically, you are a god; but dammit, you are also alive in that body you created for yourself. Have a little respect for your present life."

Nova confounded me. *Le* looked pleased over my angst. "Don't you understand, Sante? Once, that statement could come only from me, but you said it, just now, exactly as you did. You said it with Cle's wisdom and my steely sense of purpose. Don't get me wrong; I'm not quitting life. This time I'm going to embrace it, but I need to stop playing god to you and Rugen. I have too much to learn and too little time left to entertain ridiculous notions about my omnipotence over my creations. I refuse to be the exclusive father, mother, child, will, or god. Instead, I want the freedom to be all those things and more. Sante, of all my creations, you are my most intimate ally. I fashioned the original Sante after that inextinguishable love that lifted me from the depths of Hell, but you have become so much more. Selfishly, I've kept you by my side longer than any other soul. We even had a stint as lovers."

I surprised myself. I was so angry that I wanted to shake *lim* and awaken *lim* to the memory of my loss. "That's right! We experienced a stint as lovers; you never embraced me with the love and commitment that I embraced you. You haven't changed. You're still trying to avoid feeling anything. For too many lifetimes, you forced me to carry our passion as my exclusive burden. Yes, please, do come down off your godly pedestal; but when you do, come down in the gap where you left me." Three years ago, when we argued, I had come close to saying these things. Now Rugen was by my side and *ce* gave me *cis* strength to speak my truth.

The rise and fall of new voices drifted in from the sitting area. Then someone opened the study door, just a crack, and we were startled. It was Belinda. "May I come in?" she asked.

Nova masked the tension among us with a façade of normalcy. "Hello Belinda," *le* said carefully. "Would you please excuse us for a few minutes more? We're right in the middle of something important."

"Okay, sweetheart," she said, and she let the door close again.

"Let's not keep the others waiting," said Nova.

"I'm not done," I insisted.

As if on cue, Rugen's spot speaker sounded on *cis* belt. "My Gathering will take place in two hours," *ce* said.

"Please?" coaxed Nova. *Le* embraced me and kissed me on the cheek. *Le* was good at getting *lis* own way by performing gestures such as this. "I promise, we will figure this out, but right now I am at the limit of what I can handle."

I let Nova go, but I grieved over it. When would come our next opportunity? When would come the right words or my courage to face *lim* again? Love hated acquiescing to will's convention, but it did. Love laced itself over and went outside to meet the mourners. There, love poured itself out like water, spreading itself thin with words of condolence.

****

This time we found seven people in the sitting area, my *bramma* (lifebearer grandparent) Belinda, my siblings Senon and Una, and Una's child Renée. Seeing Bogwa, Evose, and Hope together almost seemed historic because this was the first time I knew their identity. Evose seemed to be the extrovert in his soul group, the nervous talker. He reminded me of a jittery bird recently released from its cage—too much freedom and no knowledge about where to fly. "Now maybe the Gathering will listen," he was telling Bogwa. Apparently, Evose's request to speak publicly was put on the backlog for review because he was not a citizen of *La Ventana.*

"I'm no longer a citizen either," Bogwa told Evose. "I enjoy no special influence with the Gathering." This was untrue. Although Bogwa was no longer a citizen, he was a living legend with considerable power aboard *The Mother.* Bogwa made the rounds with personal words for each of us. He said some comforting things and some odd things too, such as, "Elay's whole life, she was impatient to go home to her oversoul." I admired Bogwa for reasons beyond family connections. He always demonstrated a special kindness and an evenhanded respect for people and situations. If such a thing as egoless incarnation existed, perhaps Bogwa had attained it.

Bogwa and I had not seen each other since Estrella's memorial service, three years earlier, but his appearance had not changed. He was a powerful-looking creature. His body was graceful, thin, and sinewy and his complexion was dark mahogany and his black hair long and secured in a ponytail. His nose was broad and flat and his lips perfectly symmetrical and his best feature. His entire eyeballs were black, like the eyes of Ganats, but Bogwa's eyes were not as large. I don't know why he chose to appear as he did because he admitted a long time ago that this façade was a calculated decision on his part. People frequently accused Bogwa of being a shapeshifter and when I was a child, I asked him, "If you're a shapeshifter can you change into a frog?"

His eyes twinkled when he asked, "Do I look like a frog to you?"

"A little bit," I said.

Bogwa laughed with delight and slapped his knee. "Now I get it! Elay has been reading you *The Princess and the Frog* again.

"True," I admitted and I stared hard at Bogwa. "Can't you at least turn green? I've seen lizards in the garden that can turn green."

"I'm sorry to disappoint you, Sante, but I can't change myself into a frog or turn green. I do possess some flexibility to slightly modify my appearance within a narrow range of possibilities, but that's all." Bogwa was never showy about his talents to "slightly modify" his appearance and as long as I can remember, he never changed. A few years ago, Elay asked why he did not assume a more mature appearance to match his aging wives and he quipped, "Belinda and Estrella enjoy the notion of having a lover who looks half their age."

Hope and I said a brief hello, kissing each other on either side of the forehead in the Janaforma manner. When Hope was Mehiel, she was the most reclusive of the three; and in this life, she was still shy. Her skin was the color of cinnamon and her face perfectly proportioned. As Mehiel, she had been a prose writer. In this life, Hope was a poet and I knew she worked as a teacher of young children. I've read everything she ever published, both as Mehiel and as Hope. Mehiel's prose was strong and filled with the awe of an alien lifeform seeing this universe through new eyes and telling us what she saw. I learned many new ways of enjoying my senses from Mehiel's books, especially from the volume entitled *The Wonder of It All*. In it, Mehiel describes how the sudden sensation of color upon the eyes affected her, the ability of sound to evoke different moods, the pleasure of the kinesthetic in the wind and rain. Her fresh perspective and incredible wit and humor allowed us to appreciate this universe anew through her perspective. Now, as Hope, her writing was timid. I was not sure what was driving her deeper into her protective shell; but her poetry had turned into a lament, a cry for help.

> I climbed inside a teacup, no bigger than a cap.
> Everything was in there, so I prepared to take a nap.
> I've been there now, so steeping long
> in dreamy little repose,
> that I can no longer extrapolate
> or dare interpose.

Hope Bogwa

As the old saying goes, "Saturday's child must work hard for a living." Belinda definitely was Saturday's child. She was complex and worked at keeping an illusion going around her that masked her identity. In some ways, Belinda was the most elusive person in the room. She was a lover, like me, that much I knew for sure. She enjoyed many physical lovers in every one of her lives. She told Nova, "Not even my own death could keep me away. It's very difficult to be this old and see incarnations such as Elay and Michael, and my beloved Bejan take a leap into the arms of eternity. It makes me feel as if I'm a plodder. The natural order of life is disturbed when children die first."

If Bogwa entertained any weaknesses, it was for the dark and lovely Belinda. His devotion to her was complete. He never displayed any overt neglect of Estrella. Bogwa always treated his mates with complete respect. His grief seemed genuine when Estrella died; nevertheless, my psychic senses told me that Belinda owned Bogwa's passion. The littlest things do give people away. Bogwa always called Belinda, "darling," while he called Estrella, "Estrella." I used to wonder about this as a child because, then, I always preferred Estrella. Now, as a sexually voracious adult, I too prefer Belinda.

Belinda has been a Trinity Witch many times in her past lives. She commands the psychic powers fueled by the New Delphi Crystal and that's saying a lot. Her powers put her into the category of legend. Despite her divine connections, she can act ditsy. Her powers are authentic. She can see across dimensions and can predict the inclinations of time, exactly as Una can. I have great respect for Belinda because she still is incarnating into this dimension on a persistent basis. Belinda was eighty-two bio-years old. In many ways, she was a female Bejan without *cis* balanced temperament. Even at this moment, despite her grief, she exuded sensuality. She was a hungry lover's dream, with a dark cascade of hair that was slick as raven's feathers. Her hands were exquisite and she usually wore a different ring on each of her dainty digits. She favored emeralds and pearls, but she also wore diamonds and occasionally rubies. Her waist was hourglass shapely and she dressed in form-fitted clothing to accentuate her curves and voluptuous butt.

In many ways, Estrella was Belinda's opposite. In Estrella's later years, her long hair was white and she wore it loose and spilling around her shoulders. As a child, I remember her holding me and rocking me to sleep. I would squirm around on her comfortable lap until I found that special space, a universe of peace between her warm breasts. Once she invited me to exchange gazes. She never told me what she saw in me, but with my special psychic vision, I knew she carried many souls around inside her, just as Una did. Estrella was a kaleidoscopic wonder, changing from minute to minute, as first this one and then the next emerged to experience life in a new way. As her years accumulated, life seemed to make her wider and more inviting. Memories of her reminded me of Earth's knurled olive-tree trunks that grow around the Mediterranean Sea. After these olive trees die, their trunks remain standing as memorials to their lives. Estrella had departed, but her beauty and warmth lived on as a tribute to her life.

****

Una brought Renée to see Nova. This was the first time since "the accident" that Renée had seen Nova. "Renée begged me to come," said Una. "She wanted to see you with her own eyes and make sure you were safe." In many ways, Renée seemed younger than her thirteen years. It was difficult to believe she was only five years younger than Rugen. She was tiny with classic blonde-hair and a cherubic face. She was sensuous and sensitive, a disciple and a martyr for love. She climbed onto Nova's lap and patted *lis* cheeks with her delicate little hands. "I love you *lefebr* (lifegiver grandparent) from the bottom of my heart," said Renée.

"I love you too, little cherub," returned Nova.

"What happened to your lip? It looks kind of sick."

"I accidentally bit myself."

"Because you're sad?"

"Yes, because I'm sad."

"You're silly," Renée said in her little bird voice. "You know *bramma* and *cefras* (lifebearer and consort grandparents) are just playing hide-and-seek behind the *manatees*. They'll all be back when the game is over."

Nova's eyes clouded with tears and *le* bit *lis* damaged lip. "I can't believe what a beautiful and intelligent cherub you've become."

Renée put her hands over her face. "I told *Cefra* Bejan that *ce* was acting silly because *ce* is not hiding very well."

"What do you mean, sweetie?"

"I had a scary dream and *Cefra* Bejan came into my sleeproom and sang me a pretty song to make me feel better. That's when *ce* told me they were all playing hide-and-seek. I hope you don't mind, but I told *Cefra* Bejan that I loved *cim* best."

"That's perfectly all right."

Renée assumed a thoughtful expression filled with childish innocence. "I love you best too, *Lefebr*."

We ten souls joined forces at this crucial time to comfort each other. No matter our past or transgressions—together, out of love, we transcended our isolated pettiness and became better than we were alone. No words seemed necessary among us. After a short bit of embracing and greetings, we moved into intentional silence. It was a courtesy not only to each mourner, but also to the dead. We hoped that the dead might speak through someone present and silence gave that possibility a chance. Then, nobody suggested it, but everyone sat in a circle and we held hands. "By the way," said Nova, "If any of you are wondering why Rugen is here. Rugen is Sante's new mate and that means Rugen is now part of this family and very special to me."

"How special?" Belinda asked.

"I'm Cle," said Rugen. A few people gasped and Evose's jaw dropped dramatically. What would Evose do with this new information? Despite my fears, I respected Rugen for coming out with the truth the way *ce* did. Now *ce* could handle Evose without me as an intermediary.

"Welcome back to life," said Belinda.

Despite Nova's recent retirement from playing the part of exclusive will, *le* invoked *lis* authority for Rugen's sake. "I know from experience that each of you can be tight-lipped when needed. Too many avatars, aboard this ship, can see almost anything at a psychic glance, so we need to hold this information close. It is not up to us to divulge Rugen's truth; only *ce* has the right to do it, if and when *ce* feels ready." Nova glanced at *lis* watch. "I would like to sit in quiet meditation with you for many more hours; but unfortunately, Rugen is expected to face a Gathering in a short time. I intend to be present to support *cim*, to make sure our Number One Janaforma is not turned into the sacrificial lamb, this time round."

One by one, they each said, "We'll be there too."

SIX

Rugen and I took a quick detour and stopped at *cis* apartment so *ce* could change into *cis* uniform. I waited in the sitting area so I could take notes on what was happening for my book. Rugen was not gone long when I glanced up and *ce* came walking down the stairs appearing stiff and formal. To me, *ce* looked seductive dressed in *cis* formal, black uniform with its tight mandarin collar; but I knew *ce* was feeling constrained and pressured over facing a Gathering. I was proud of *cim* and our new relationship for a bunch of romantic notions. If I had not wanted to protect *cis* identity, I might have posted a silly note on the general multidex shouting, "I'M THE LUCKIEST LIFEGIVER ALIVE. CLE HAS RETURNED AND WE'RE TOGETHER AGAIN!" "You look sexy," I said.

"So do you," *ce* returned, "especially wearing my pants." *Ce* touched my cheek with the back of *cis* hand in a loving gesture and said, "As soon as we can, let's go somewhere private and enjoy a proper honeymoon."

"My imagination is already there," I said.

"Right now, duty calls." Where Rugen was concerned, the word "duty" gave me the shivers. I longed to direct *cis* attention away from duty and onto building a life with me; however, that seemed impossible, considering the latest turn of events.

Many types of Gatherings occur on *La Ventana*. Most Gatherings are informal and focus on personal and community enhancement. Each operates independently with its own rules. Gathering precepts were confusing for Evose, who was still waiting to get the scheduling committee's approval to speak. Rugen's Gathering was an official event because two Vanguard Scouts died while on active duty. Turnout was expected to be large and it was being held in The Pavilion, the biggest arena onship. A few rules regulated this type of Gathering that did not apply for informal events. To gain admittance, a person needed to be a genuine citizen aboard *La Ventana* and if one wanted to add an official voice, that person needed to register at the speaker's podium right before the event began. Live proceedings were available over the multidex, but if anyone wanted to question or challenge Rugen, they needed to be physically present. *La Ventana's* citizenry decided a long time ago that questioning from the privacy of a remote multidex was unacceptable.

We arrived at The Pavilion about fifteen minutes before the start of the proceedings. The crowds assembled at several doors were filing past security scanners. A couple of times a small buzzer sounded and Security would escort the person or persons away. Minor problems persisted concerning tourists at Gatherings. Inside, activity around the podium was less than I anticipated. This was a good sign and meant the crowd wanted to hear what Rugen had to say rather than challenge *cim*.

Eight of us were present to support Rugen. We marched right in, with no questions asked, and occupied several seats down front. The rules of citizenship did not apply for Belinda, Bogwa, and their Earth contingent because the person facing the Gathering had twenty reserved seats for family or friends, no matter who they were or where their citizenship emanated. A moment after we arrived, eight members of Rugen's Vanguard team joined us. *Ce* went over and spoke to them, then came back, and sat between Nova and me. "I'm going to be fine," *ce* assured us. "The Vanguard stands with me."

I was unsure. My feelings surrounding this Gathering reminded me of similar situations in past lives. Starting all the way back in Athens, Rugen possessed an inclination to get involved with trials and trial-like events. Each time, there was a common thread. He/she/*ce* would be flying high, a leader, a motivational orator, a person on the cutting-edge of thought and social change. Then something questionable would occur and despite all good intentions, Rugen would be unable to extricate *cim*self from the problem. My fear surrounding this situation was proportional. I was not as fatalistic as when Candidus faced the Athens jury, as terrified as when Serene was brought before the Spanish Inquisition, or as pessimistic as when the Aeternus Council of Three destroyed Cle. Still, I was skittish.

Nova held a prestigious position as a senior adviser in the Executive Gathering. Ordinarily, *le* would sit opposite along with *lis* peers. Because of obvious conflict of interest, Nova had forfeited *lis* seat for this specific Gathering and *lis* opinion held no authority except *lis* own. *Le* leaned toward Rugen and whispered, "Rex Clidmore will be in charge. *Ce* is fair and will not allow anyone to bully you."

Nova spotted Michael's parents and they stopped and said a brief hello.

Mercy and Kebir were the pale remnants of this once great Janaforma triad. Their consort Lyfe died two years earlier. Lyfe's death broke the fragile Kebir; and what Michael's death was doing to their waning constitutions, I could only imagine. At this moment, Kebir seemed reduced to nothing more than a dove over *lis* beloved Mercy. Nova embraced them and tears filled all their eyes. The grief made a lump as large as a goose egg stick in my throat. With great difficulty, I held myself in check so I could channel my support to Rugen for what *ce* needed to face in the next few minutes. Nova asked Rugen's permission to include Mercy and Kebir in the last two seats in our reserved section and, of course, Rugen said, "Yes," making a point to get up and tell them, "I appreciate your support."

Members of the Executive Gathering drifted in by twos and threes. Somewhere in the middle, Rex arrived. Rex was slightly older than Nova, near sixty bio-years. *Ce* was dressed in black from head to toe and wore one gold earring in *cis* left ear. The earring was a copy of the icon painted on the outer hull of *La Ventana*, the symbol that stood for loyalty, altruism, self-sacrifice, and Community. Every Vanguard uniform that dated back to our earliest cycles sported that embossed symbol and highlighted the Janaforma raison d'être. However, each of us fell short in the areas of loyalty, altruism, and self-sacrifice, the Janaforma Community considered the Gathering holy ground. Here, our intentions were to aspire to our highest selves and to these sacred principles.

****

The name Rex suited this soul well. Rex exuded authority and everyone knew *ce* was a leader. Rex was not arrogant about *cis* status; *ce* merely was comfortable with the understanding that *ce* earned every gram of respect that came *cis* way. Nova did not have hundreds of casual friends as Elay had; Nova had a few intimate allies. At the top of the list was Rex. It was a strange alliance between two powerful will personalities. Thirty years prior, Rex and Nova were co-captains of *La Ventana* and during that time, it was common knowledge that these two had frequent and serious encounters with Cerribeame rifters. When they got together, they still talked about the time Nova possessed the temerity to hide *The Mother* behind a moon or how Rex managed to outrun a Cerribeame rifter. To listen to them talk about their term as co-captions, one might get the impression they flew *The Mother* around the heavens as if she were a cruiser instead of a starship.

Nova and Rex had taken the Regression drug together and telepathy activated itself between them whenever they were in close proximity. Rex dropped some items on the speaker's podium and glanced our way. Nova stood up to greet Rex and they engaged in a couple of minutes of intense conversation.

Rex's last minute advice to Rugen was, "Make a careful statement of the truth and tell what happened only from your perspective. Answer all questions patiently, directly, and as clearly as possible. If you tell your truth, you have nothing to fear. Besides, I'm here to make sure everyone plays nicely." A chime sounded and Rex went to *cis* place behind the speaker's podium. The room was already quiet, but Rex said, "We will observe three minutes of silence for Commanders Jana Solange and Xana Capsun."

****

Rex held the controls and it reminded me of the moment when the outer bulkhead opens on a spaceship. When those doors open, there is nothing to do except step forward into the vast permeable web of time. Rex's voice came out as clear authority. "It's my honor to introduce Commander Miro Rugen, Vanguard team leader on the captain's shift, who accepted this position on *La Ventana* thirty-one cycles ago. Captain Issed requested that I convene this Gathering to allow Commander Miro an opportunity to present and explain *cis* perspective concerning the tragic events surrounding the deaths of Commanders Solange and Capsun. After Commander Miro's finishes his initial statement, *ce* will answer questions and comments from the gallery. I'm certain we all know the rules, but please allow me to remind you that questions and comments must pertain to the topic before us, i.e. the accident in the corridor and the deaths of Commanders Solange and Capsun. Commander Miro, your Gathering awaits."

Rugen gave my hand a final squeeze and went to the speaker's podium. *Ce* took *cis* time and glanced around. *Cis* eyes lingered on me for a moment and I read *cim* clearly; *hold me in your love.* "I would like to offer my heartfelt condolences to the families and friends of Commander Capsun and Commander Solange—" Rugen caught *cis* breath and swallowed hard. "Thank you, Admiral Clidmore, the Executive Gathering, Captain Issed and my fellow citizens for this opportunity to face a Janaforma Gathering and offer my firsthand perspective on what happened in the corridor between dimensions." Rugen hesitated an exceptionally long time, which highlighted some uncomfortable scuffling in the auditorium. "Thirty-one cycles ago, when I came aboard *La Ventana*, Captain Issed told me that *le* offered Commander Solange the prestigious position as *lis* first officer; but Solange refused the promotion in order to remain in the Vanguard as my mentor. This was an enormous personal gift to me and I acknowledge it. I was able to learn from Commander Solange's vast experience. *Ce* fostered my introduction into the Vanguard and made my transition nearly seamless. My time with Commanders Solange and Capsun was short, yet I regard them as family."

Rugen hesitated again and I knew *cis* timing was off.

"To fill you in on my background, I earned Alpha Accreditation when I was thirteen bio-years old. Shortly afterward, I began making solo excursions into the fourth dimension and quickly advanced to senior

83

instructor at the Cerribeame Academy on Ruean. As a senior instructor, I completed fifteen hundred trips into the corridor of the fourth dimension and am well acquainted with fourth dimensional phenomena and what I observed, approximately six space-hours ago, does not correspond to anything I ever witnessed before from *graeymlin* or *manatee* emanations."

The gallery rumbled with comments and Rugen waited for the noise to abate. Then *ce* told *cis* story almost the way *ce* told it to me, except now, *ce* added the flourishes of technical detail. Rugen seemed more comfortable in the measuring realm, as if mentioning times, positions, and procedures made the tragedy less tumultuous. "When I arrived for my shift, I personally checked all three vitaspheres and they were operating within normal parameters. Then right before we launched, system initiators on Commander Xana's vitasphere, began functioning erratically. *La Ventana's* bridge told us a surge of electromagnetic radiation was drifting in from the Kalalangla Asteroid Belt, but the corridor was calm and clear. Senior bridge staff advised us to proceed and gave us a three-minute window to execute our launch. I had clear visuals of space and could see that a Martian transport had just left *The Mother* and would be directly in our launch path. I advised the bridge of the disparity and ordered a fifteen-minute delay in our launch. I knew we needed to shut down and install a new relay network. Usually, it takes about five minutes to install and thirty seconds more to integrate, but I know how to complete the entire process in less than four minutes. The bridge was reminding me that we had no presence in the corridor, so I ordered Commander Xana to take my vitasphere and fly point and I would rendezvous with her and Commander Solange at the second tangent point.

"They launched and roughly, four minutes later, I did the same. I was closing on the second tangent point when I started experiencing communication interference with the bridge and the other two vitaspheres. A few seconds later, the new relay network, which I had just installed, burned out. Through my eyepiece, I still had clear visuals on both my screens and could see that I was closing in on Commander Solange's lead position. In this situation, it's standard-operating procedure to allow the team leader to assume point in the triad. Instead, Commander Solange increased speed and widened the gap, while Capsun shadowed Solange's starboard lead by approximately ten degrees. Approximately five seconds later, I observed an optical disturbance off portside of my vitasphere coming from what I believe was deep fourth. The phenomena appeared black, blacker than empty space and gyrated in a clockwise motion—something like a cosmic typhoon or small black hole. My main tracking screen informed me the phenomenon was twenty-two kilometers long and approximately nine kilometers at its widest point. It showed cunning and an ability to track and anticipate the movement of the vitaspheres. I assume

Solange and Capsun noticed the same behavior because they instantly switched to multidex control, to take advantage of random evasive maneuvers—" Someone began sobbing in the audience. Rugen hesitated and glanced up toward the gallery. "—Which proved woefully inadequate in response to the powerful and overwhelming presence of this unknown force."

Rugen took a deep breath and I could see the tension accumulating in *cis* face. "Many of you present are well-acquainted with the dangers of space, but only vitasphere pilots experience the quirky dangers of the fourth dimension and realize the enormous risk in patrolling an area of space riddled with dimensional fissures. The Vanguard works to minimize susceptibility to illusion by practicing self-discipline, rigorous Shardasko training, a team approach to all situations, and by relying on scientific instrumentation to advise us of situations and probable time lapses. Nevertheless, sentient life, at least sentient life born into third-dimensional space, is susceptible to distortions in the corridor and fourth dimension. The reason I point this out again is because what I observed and what Commanders Solange and Capsun observed, might have been radically disparate. I estimate the lapse time, between my initial sighting of the disturbance and when it stuck the two vitaspheres, to be approximately twenty seconds. However, my ship's instrumentation recorded the same time —and this is approximate because of the curvature of the corridor—as 33 space years." That statement caused an audible stir. "That concludes my prepared remarks, but I will remain and respond to your comments and answer all questions from the gallery."

****

Six people filed down to the gallery podium and waited for their turn to speak. I was nervous, but proceedings continued to go smoothly. It was obvious people wanted more details and Rugen patiently supplied all the minutiae that each person needed to hear. Then a woman, about sixty bio-years of age, approached the podium. The woman was a stranger, but I knew it was Xana's *mebr*. I had seen her picture in Xana's sleeproom. "Is it standard procedure to trade vitaspheres?" she asked Rugen.

"No," *ce* admitted. "It's not standard procedure to trade vitaspheres. Pilots develop a familiarity and intimacy with a particular craft."

"Then why did you trade vitaspheres?" she asked. "When the corridor is already fraught with dangers and illusion, why disadvantage a pilot by ordering that person to fly an unfamiliar ship?"

Rugen became even more formal. *Ce* addressed Xana's *mebr* with the universal term, "madam." If Cle had been standing there, *ce* would have softened; *ce* might have leaned forward across the podium or emerged from behind the podium to minimize the distance between this grieving *mebr* and *cim*self. Cle, at least, would have asked her name so *ce* could address her personally. It got worse. "A Vanguard Scout is weaned on danger and it's part of our job to make decisions concerning risky situations and to minimize those risks," said Rugen. "All vitaspheres aboard *La Ventana* are technically compatible and every scout is capable of flying every vitasphere. I can only state that someone was needed in hyperspace and I made the decision that Solange and Capsun should go."

All this was true—but why did it sound so stilted coming from Rugen? I moved forward and rested my elbows on my knees in order to send my love *cis* way. It was the closest I could get to *cim* without getting up and embracing *cim*.

"As a team leader, I take my responsibility seriously," *ce* said. "I wish I could offer a reasonable excuse, an explanation that made sense about what went awry. No hard rules govern this ever-shifting space and most of the time we need to make it up as we go along. I'm fallible and will never know what would have happened if we had not traded vitaspheres."

"I didn't mean to suggest you made an error in judgment," said Xana's *mebr*. I know the hazards the Vanguard faces because I worked on the bridge for twenty years and realize the pressures are intense. Please understand me too. Xana was my only child. Yes, she knew the dangers of being a vitasphere pilot and she accepted them. I did not. How could I? How could I feel comfortable knowing my child was constantly in harm's way? I thought perhaps you could tell me something that made sense. I understand nothing can change what's happened, but to lose Xana, in this strange way, with no reasonable explanation makes the loss worse."

The silence of grief flooded the auditorium. Rugen seemed uncomfortable with public grief and stood there looking like a gawky unprepared child. If I saw it, so did many others. I questioned it and felt a deception, not from my senses, but from Rugen's. How much did *ce* really remember about *cis* past lives? A single Regression trip never gives a person the complete picture. Rugen remembered that *ce* was Cle, but did *ce* remember those subtle emotions that made up Cle's wisdom? Where was the passionate Candidus in the eighteen-year-old Janaforma consort that grew up rich and graduated from the Cerribeame Academy at fifteen? Where was Rugen's empathy with *cis* past lives?

Only now did I see how young my shining star truly was. Rugen was just getting started and *ce* was damn scared. At eighteen, *ce* never tried to face the challenge of the crowd. I adored this soul. It was exciting meeting *cim* at this tender age and I was flattered to be *cis* first lover. To me, *ce* was one of the most exquisite souls in creation. *Ce* lived lives where *cis* eloquence and compassion moved millions and now *ce* was a nervous eighteen-year old consort, acting gawky inside *cis* body.

Life is ironic and tutorial all at the same time and the lessons come fast and furious for individuals keen enough to catch them. Rex, the master of *cis* own body and mind, got up to help. "Maybe I can assist on this important point," *ce* said and *ce* put an arm around Rugen's shoulder in a parental way. "As most of you know, I was co-captain about seventeen years ago, back when *The Mother* was experiencing a few glitches with the Cerribeame. I can categorically state that it makes no difference which vitaspheres, shuttles, pulsars, and cruisers a scout flies. We do switch planes, and often, because routine breeds complacency. Commander Miro was not acting in any way outside standard operating procedures to send Commander Capsun out in another vessel."

One more person waited at the gallery podium. Rex stood next to Rugen for the remainder. It was the Tyrowsian, Weegan Zu, Bejan's musician friend. He wanted to know, "Do you think there's a connection between this accident and the destruction of the Aeternus shuttle that occurred three cycles ago?" That question caused a definite commotion and a rumble of comments moved through the crowd. I glanced down the row at Evose and it was obvious that he could scarcely contain himself.

"I'm sorry," said Rugen. "I cannot comment on that investigation. I am not involved in it and have no special information pertaining to the particulars*."

After the Gathering, I sighed with relief. My sigh was for more than this event; the sigh was for all the lifetimes when trials, hearings, and inquiries distorted my soul mate's lives into tragedy. It was ironic. Rugen had never come through an ordeal with so little eloquence in *cis* corner and still been absolved of guilt. In my eyes, it was a miracle, maybe not for Rugen, but for our Janaforma Culture. I possessed new respect for the process of the Gathering. They were not witch-hunts or excuses to pin blame on someone. Gatherings were forums for acknowledging problems that affected our Community.

****

My relief was short lived. As Rex was declaring Rugen stainless, the blacker-than-black phenomenon was pursuing three vitaspheres from the second shift. This time there were no survivors. However inadequate Rugen's descriptions were, *ce* was the one person alive who saw the unknown and lived to describe it. Forty minutes later, the unknown broke through The Door and entered the third dimension. Whatever the intentions of the phenomenon, it passed within meters of *La Ventana*. When it happened, the ship trembled as if struck by a solar flare and almost thirty-five seconds of total hysteria ensued. No damage befell the main part of the ship; but several annexed sections tore free, allowing open space to obliterate ordered matter. One of those sections was the Southern Annex that contained our family's quarters. Fortunately, for our family, no one was home at the time.

*Rugen's comments from the official transcripts of *cis* Gathering, SY5715.

Several hundred people were dead and survivors were appropriately terrorized. What we considered stable reality was in jeopardy. Four hundred twenty-three annex residents and five experienced Vanguard pilots, presumably, were dead. Financial loss was yet inestimable, but expected to be catastrophic. Five vitaspheres, valued at twenty-three million credits each, were gone without a trace. And if the disappearance of the Aeternus shuttle was part of the equation, three hundred fifty-three more people were victims of a phenomenon nobody could describe except Rugen.

Within hours, a Gathering convened to discuss moving *La Ventana* back from the edge of the corridor and into safer space. Belinda and Evose vetoed the idea of attending. Bogwa was unhappy about their decision and the three exchanged some heated and angry words. "This time no restrictions apply to our attending," Bogwa pointed out. "We could speak and get the support we need."

Belinda was heading in the opposite direction. "Why go to a Gathering merely to see if they will help us convince the Orion Spur Council?" she asked. "We no longer have the luxury of time. I propose we handle this problem directly and as quickly as possible."

Nova was uncomfortable about the idea of bypassing the Gathering and *le* asked, "How can we trust our exclusive opinions on critical decisions involving the third dimension and know we are doing the right thing?"

The problem for Rugen and me was identical. We lacked critical information to determine where we stood. We needed facts, and if not facts, a few dramatic clues. When Rugen asked my opinion, I said, "We should stick around. I think we can learn more here."

Nova and the Earth contingent had no place to stay since the destruction of the Southern Annex. Hospitality was quickly abundant, from Una, Senon, and several close friends of the family. Again, Belinda had a different agenda, which involved Rugen, and *cis* place. At first, the incident seemed innocent. Not until later, did I realize that one of the greatest witches in the third dimension had manipulated Rugen into a corner.

Belinda managed to appear helpless, exhausted, and seductive. She had just glossed her lips and reddened her rouge a bit before fluttering around Rugen like a colorful and fragile butterfly. "You look so darling in your formal uniform," she told *cim*. She brushed a speck of lint off *cis* shoulder so she could touch *cim*. "I'm so exhausted from my trip. I was wondering if we could impose on your hospitality a bit longer. Could Bogwa and I stay in your apartment until the memorial service?"

Her acting was careless and thin and if I were the casting agent, I would have given her the hook. This time, Rugen didn't check with me first and *ce* followed Belinda like a lamb. "You're welcome to use my place for as long as you want," *ce* told her.

Belinda moved into Rugen's apartment and promptly found enough energy to invite Evose and Nova there for a powwow. Since Rugen assured me that *cis* place was now mine, I took it upon myself to also ask Hope if she would like to join us for lunch.

A psychic premonition, concerning our miniature gathering, kept bugging me. I sensed all kinds of walls going up around information people knew, but still did not want to share. "What's the use of blocking information at this point?" Rugen asked. Regardless, there was blocking and more intrigue was going on at Rugen's place than in the whole Tyrowsian stock market.

Rugen and I made cucumber-cheese sandwiches and tea for everyone. Evose wasted no time and began needling Rugen with, "We know who your parents are. They must have a spare vitasphere sitting around that they wouldn't miss. If I could borrow it, then I could go back in time and repair this rupture and then we could return to whatever we were doing, before this crisis occurred." This was the first time I heard Evose use the word "rupture," but it wouldn't be the last. The Bibliodexteritas had used the word "rupture," in conjunction with the Three of Swords. I wanted to ask Evose more about his association with this word, but the atmosphere turned heated.

Rugen was sitting on one of the stools, in the eating area, and reminded me of the shining Candidus with just a hint of Cle thrown in for good measure. "What you want me to do is illegal," *ce* told Evose. "If I break any law, it must be in defense of a greater truth than that law upholds. Therefore, I can't consider helping you unless you are completely honest with me about everything pertaining to this mission."

Evose's stupid reply was, "Your problem is you listen to too much gossip from your new lover."

Rugen remained undaunted. "Your attempts at deflection are not clever. Tell me Evose; to start with, how do you retrieve soul fragments?" Evose scratched the side of his neck, bringing my attention to the fact that his nervous rash was all the way up to his chin. I felt sorry about that part. The pressure everyone was exerting on him was a veritable force. It was psychic and a lot more.

"Yeah, how do you retrieve soul fragments?" asked an elfish little voice. It was Hope and her question surprised me.

I searched Nova's eyes for clues and *le* raised *lis* eyebrows and gave me a half-amused expression as if to say, *oh well, here it comes.*

****

Evose was in the spotlight and he sighed and scratched in frustration; but he backed up and began telling the whole story about soul fragments that he told me three cycles earlier. Somewhere in the middle, all hell broke loose. "Of all the colossal audacity!" It was Hope again and her voice was seething with agitation. "How did you manage to keep this information from me?"

Evose acted surprised and said, "I didn't think you were interested in soul fragments. You always have your head buried in a book or are writing a poem."

The cold rage in Hope was enough to chill the room. "I'm offended. Your endless search for new possibilities is destroying the hope I have struggled to manifest in this dimension."

"Wait a minute," interrupted Bogwa. "That's untrue. Evose is trying to keep your hope alive."

"How would you know?" she asked. "I manifest our hope—not you. All you two are interested in are your endless possibilities without ever asking whether your possibilities are appropriate or not. I want to know exactly what you're doing, especially in the realm of retrieving soul fragments."

Evose and Bogwa were exchanging telepathic messages that sounded like a series of erratic clicks—but I could not splice into its frequency because I was excited and they were communicating very fast. Bogwa definitely was agitated, but on the surface, he appeared perfectly calm. "That's not a subject I'm at liberty to discuss," said Evose. "It's too dangerous. Anyway, it's no longer important how we retrieved soul fragments because we are never going to do it again. What's important is I get a vitasphere so I can go back in time and mend this rupture."

"Well you won't get a vitasphere through me," said Rugen. "You want me to break the law, jeopardize the fabric of time, and dishonor my immortal soul without understanding the motivation behind my behavior? Why should I risk everything sacred to me when you are still hiding information from me?"

"I've hidden nothing," said Evose.

"Then tell me how you retrieve soul fragments."

Evose was cornered, but held his ground. "Knowing how I do it will make you more vulnerable to soul fragments. It makes it easier for them to pull you into the darkness with them."

"Excuse me," said Belinda. "I'll explain how we did it."

All eyes shot to Belinda who glanced toward Bogwa for support. Bogwa placed a hand on Belinda's shoulder and I think he wanted to stop her. Then Hope interceded with a threat. "You better allow her to speak or I will withdraw my support from you." Astoundingly, Bogwa backed down.

"Wow!" I thought. Hope was not as timid as I first imagined.

"Do you know anything about ancient Tibetan Buddhism?" Belinda asked.

"Please *mebr*, reconsider?" begged Evose.

Evose and Belinda indulged in a telepathic conversation that, this time, was crystal clear. *We made a few mistakes, now let's own up to the consequences,* communicated Belinda. "I might get some of the details wrong," she told us, "but this is the way we pieced together the clues and what motivated us to act as we did. Tibetan Buddhists have long possessed metaphysical insight into the afterlife or state of the soul between lives. Buddhists call these states, 'the bardos.' In the ancient Tibetan language, *bar* means 'between' and *do* means 'two.' Together, *bardo* means 'transition' or 'gap.' An integral part of Tibetan Buddhist philosophy is how and why we return to life. Buddhists believe that near the end of a soul's journey through the *bardo* of becoming, a soul becomes mesmerized, even seduced into reincarnating into another life. Bogwa, Evose and I know the *bardo* is more than metaphor; the *bardo* also is dimensional space."

The surface appeared calm, but the undercurrent was deadly. Hope was glaring, first at Evose and then Bogwa and she put her hands over her mouth to stop herself from speaking. Finally, Nova and I were staring at each other as if our eyes were dueling laser beams because a memory was beginning to surface within me that concerned *lim*.

Belinda said, "Tibetan Buddhists believe that an evolved soul will be able to negotiate parents of their choice from the *bardo* of becoming; but unfortunately, most poor souls do not have the luxury of choosing. As souls hover near life, they miss having a body and become entranced by seeing individuals indulging—let's say—indulging in the pleasures of life."

"You mean sex?" asked Rugen.

"Aaah, primarily," admitted Belinda.

At that instant, illumination seized me. The scene became vividness itself, the power of midday entering a dark cave. What I saw, at first, confused me, then entranced me, and finally made me explode with anger. *That's why I was on Lemira Jha!* The rutilates in my eyes became weapons and Nova had no power to withstand my psychic assault. I noticed then that *le* had bitten *lis* bottom lip open again.

Rugen whispered in my ear. "What's wrong?"

I was experiencing a vision of Lemira Jha. Nova and Sirushi are atop a high mesa and I see them as clearly as I see them sitting across the room. They are engaged in calculated sexual intercourse. "You invoked my spirit, seduced it, and took it hostage," I said to Nova. "Why didn't you tell me? You've had every opportunity to tell me. I incarnated too early. That's why I'm nine years older than Rugen."

Nova covered *lis* face with *lis* hands, just as Evose and Hope did a moment earlier. "I felt lost on Lemira Jha," *le* confessed. "I was thirty light years from anyone remotely resembling myself and alone most of the time. One time, when Sirushi appeared, he told me about the division of the soul parts—said I could call for help from these parts and they would hear me. I remembered you then in your full glory. You were my love and all I ever wanted. And when you answered my plea you came to me and I understood you in a way only a creator can understand *lis* own creation."

I stood up and walked over to where *le* sat, to help myself to what I thought I deserved, an explanation coming from within *lis* depths. *Le* did not rebuff me as I expected; instead, *le* pulled me down, until we were face to face. "Be patient," *le* whispered in my ear. "I going to give you everything you want, very soon." My heart flooded with penned up emotion and I instantly forgave *lim*. I loved *lim* so much that I would have laughed at a million-year detour to be by *lis* side in a loving relationship.

"Well!" laughed Belinda. "The acting out of true love is always a fascinating sideshow. I would enjoy being a fly on the wall when Nova gives Sante everything *le* wants; but right now, let's get back to the subject of retrieving soul fragments. Evose was not kidding when he said the method for soul fragment retrieval was dangerous. It is. If you want to know how we do it, the knowledge has a price. To begin with, never again will you be able to enjoy the private spontaneity of sex." Belinda hesitated and glanced around the room at her captive audience.

"This is nonsense," barked Hope. "Get on with it. We're all adults here." Hope twisted her head and deliberately smiled at Rugen with such a wide-eyed expression, it seemed as if she just woke up.

My new and fragile relationship with Rugen was vital to me and I did not want to jeopardize our future together in any way. *No way!* I thought. The only thing I enjoyed about my life was making love to Rugen. Rugen agreed with me and told Belinda, "Feel free to use this place for as long as you want, but I'm leaving and I expect Sante will be going with me."

"Stay put," said Belinda and she pointed a red-lacquered nail at Rugen, "Sante may go, but you are going nowhere. It's time to put our cards on the table. We need a vitasphere and we need your expertise as a pilot, to fly it backward in time."

"If you think I'm compromising everything I've worked for to do something I don't even believe in doing—you're deranged," said Rugen.

Belinda turned even more direct. "Listen sweetheart, if you don't cooperate with us, there ain't gonna be no more third dimensional relationships. Besides, I did not say you would have to give up your relationship with Sante, I merely said that never again will you be able to enjoy the private spontaneity of sex."

"And what is that double-talk nonsense supposed to mean?"

"Let's all calm down," said Nova. "Please believe me, Rugen, you have nothing to fear. I know because I know what Belinda is going to say."

"Believe you? Why?" exploded Rugen. "Frankly, I distrust you after what you've done to Sante in our last two lifetimes. I might have died and left *lim* alone, but you deserted *lim* and moved in next door just to torture *lim*. Do you know what you are to me? You are me dropping a brick on my own toe. I'm glad you set me free because I don't need you to tinker around in my life and make major decisions concerning my future, especially when we have so little personal involvement with each other."

Thoughts of fragmented souls drifted through my mind and I knew this was one way to create our own. "Wait a minute," I said. "You can't cut Nova away from your life. We've all made mistakes, but we have healed and prospered because of our commitments to each other."

Rugen's frustration with the situation, and with me, boiled to the surface. "That's absolute trash, Sante. Love and forgiveness taints everything for you. I will not submit to abuse from anyone and most especially if that person claims to be my soul mate. Wake up. How many times will you allow Nova to use you and then walk away before you find the courage to walk away from *him?*"

"I will never walk away from Nova," I said.

Rugen sighed. It was a sigh of surrender before *ce* finished. *Ce* knew my commitment to Nova was impervious. "Can't we, for once, reach beyond our genetic programming?" asked Rugen. "Must I always understand and must you always love?" Rugen turned to Nova. "I would like to extend my understanding to you, but the way things stand between us, it's impossible. Just as Sante cannot walk away from you, I cannot walk away from Sante. So go ahead, tell us, Nova. Bottom line—and do not give me any bullshit because I recognize bullshit the minute it comes out of someone's mouth. Why will this new knowledge destroy the private spontaneity of sex for Sante and me?"

"Because after you know, your perspective on having children will be so dramatically changed that you might decide that you do not want to have children," said Nova.

"Thank you," said Rugen. "Then, I guess, Sante and I need to talk in private."

****

Rugen and I left everyone, including Nova, and went upstairs. We sat on the end of the bed as the silence lingered. "How much do you actually remember about Hibernia?" *ce* asked me.

"I remember a great deal."

Rugen smiled. "She came through clearly during my Regression trip. Do you remember our holiday on Wonder World right before we met her?"

"Sorry, I don't recall that part."

"On Wonder World, we drifted into a place called Future Pavilion, thinking we would be able to see prototypes of new spacecraft. Instead, we ran into a bunch of gypsies and fortunetellers. We were in high spirits and you convinced me that we should allow a Trinity Witch to read our tarot. It was your romantic notion that she read our tarot cards as if we were one person. The witch told us that within five cycles we would encounter a special person who would be able to chart a course for us that would change our lives. Then, five cycles later, we rescued Hibernia from that stranded space taxi."

"I remember that I yearned to have a child with you and Hibernia," I said.

"That's why we are sitting here right now, Sante. I remember your needs. Tell me, what do you want this time around? Does our brief journey give us time to include the blind navigation of a lifebearer? Shall we attempt to fill the future with the laughter of children? What do you honestly need, my love? Tell me now, not in a dozen years when we can't turn back."

Rugen's demand almost felt official, as if *ce* planned to hold me to my declaration. Silence lingered again until I was able to say, "Unless we find Hibernia, I plan to concentrate all my love on you."

"What about Nova?"

"Nova is a non-starter and I can't see that changing any time soon."

"In my opinion, Nova is selfish son-of-a bitch."

It hurt when Rugen said that, it hurt as much as if *ce* said it about me. "Nova is doing the best *le* can and that's better than I'm doing in several ways."

"Nova is lucky to have a soul mate as loyal as you."

"It has nothing to do with luck."

"I said Nova is lucky," Rugen declared more firmly. "I'm lucky to have you too; but right now, I'm feeling scared and manipulated. My life feels particularly ominous at this moment." Rugen closed *cis* eyes. "I can't remember asking for this scenario; but if I did, do you think I might have the option of changing my mind? Would our oversoul respond if I begged, 'Please, give me something less impossible to do than to go back in time."

We embraced and I thought *nothing could ever destroy my love for you.* I assured Rugen of that and *ce* closed *cis* eyes and rested *cis* forehead on my shoulder.

****

A couple of minutes later, we went downstairs to hear what we were dying to hear, but were afraid to find out. Rugen expected a direct answer from Nova and *ce* stood in the middle of the room demanding it. "Okay Nova, as you can see, Sante and I are still here; so tell us why this new knowledge will destroy our perspective on having children."

Nova was reciprocally direct. "Because you'll realize the true connection between sex and death. Sex and death are like this." *Nova* made a gesture with *lis* hands that Humans use. *Lis* gesture meant sexual intercourse. "The sex act is the most powerful act of life and death. That's why so many taboos exist around sex and death in Human and Tyrowsian cultures. Through the sex act, incarnate life has the ability to call souls into third-dimensional existence. It's not all black and white. Variances exist. Some incarnate life has weak and distorted energy and their ability to attract new life is limited. And spirits do have dissimilar efficacy in their ability to respond and resist. The truth is, no sex act is ever private. Spirits are always watching for the possibility of integration. In a way, they cannot help themselves. When the possibility for procreation is present, there is no hiding for any of us."

Belinda was right. What a sobering and impotent notion that was. What I considered my private sex was fodder for soul voyeurism.

Rugen let go a little sigh. "Okay, what else?"

The undercurrent surged and Ezek told me, *they're trying to decide who is going to reveal the next part. Yeah, I got it. It will be Evose.*

"Allow me," said Evose. "After all, I'm the one who caused this rupture in the first place." Rugen settled down in a chair and I sat down on its arm. It was the perfect spot for me to keep an eye on Nova. Evose told us, "Three years ago, I went to an area of Asia the natives still call Tibet. My purpose was to study meditation with a Buddhist monk named Naljorpa Rinpoche. Rinpoche eventually told me about the *bardo* states and I told him about the soul fragments that Bogwa and I knew existed in—what we called, up to that time—'peripheral metaphysical dimensions.' We protected Hope from this new knowledge about soul fragments because we thought it detrimental to her spirit, to subject her to negativity of this magnitude so early in her first manifestation."

"Well I hope you realize that you were off the mark concerning that one too," snarled Hope.

"You are fragile," insisted Evose.

Hope turned snippy. "Not as fragile as you're about to become," she predicted. Evose scratched his neck and I noticed that it was raw. "When Rinpoche told me about the *bardo* of becoming, it was as if someone removed a mask from my eyes and I could see for the first time. What I saw was that peripheral, metaphysical dimensions and the *bardo* were the same space. Three months later, I attended a lecture in San Francisco, California and heard Isek Wellstein, the noted hyper-dimensional physicist, speak on the reality of the fourth dimension. That's when everything came together rather dramatically. The truth was obvious. Metaphysics, religion, and science were looking at the same phenomenal space and calling it different names. Peripheral metaphysical dimensions, the *bardo* of becoming and the corridor of the fourth dimension were identical."

"Mother of Creation!" Hope exclaimed.

Evose said, "That knowledge changed everything. For the first time, Bogwa and I knew that we could pinpoint soul fragments with scientific accuracy. We could direct our minds toward specific energetic space and know with certainty that we were on target. Together, we sat down in meditation and were flooded with the consciousness of soul fragments yearning for reunification with their original parts. The willing, we helped first. Vast numbers were spinning inside their own hysterical illusions and calling it Hell. At first, all we could do was lull them into meditative silence. We experienced moderate success using this process. Some advanced so far that for the first time they could hear their oversoul's poetic beacon from beyond the fourth dimension. This confirmed for us that the ability to listen and the ability to believe in the continuity of consciousness are of primary importance to a soul. At this point, we decided to take Belinda into our confidence because she knew more about incarnate existence than either of us. We told her everything and—"

"Please, let me tell this part," said Belinda.

A telepathic warning sailed right across the room—*be careful in what you say.* The warning came from Bogwa.

Belinda dismissed his suggestion with an offhand flip of the wrist. "When they told me what they were doing, I was eager to get involved because I had a few ideas that I wanted to explore. I thought, if it's true—that souls are seduced into life through watching incarnate beings during the sex act—then soul fragments might be rebirthed into this dimension through a gentle indulgence in some backdoor witch tricks."

Claiming that backdoor witch tricks were a "gentle indulgence" is like saying, "I had a mild case of the plague." Witch practices of the backdoor variety were iconoclastic dances through the macabre, their aim and purpose to confront the resistant pressures of fear and disgust in initiates. Backdoor witches seek out taboos, the impure substances of whatever society they live in and indulge in nefarious rituals to violate and therefore transcend accepted convention. It takes great will and inviolable honor to take the backdoor approach to freedom. Most souls get lost along the way.

A hint of incredulity surfaced in Rugen's voice. "You were seducing soul fragments with sex magic?"

"Yes," said Belinda, "and it was a whopping success. We captivated split-offs with startling visuals and once we had their attention, we were able to redirect them to their source. We experienced our greatest success in clearing the corridor of soul fragments in this time."

"Then what's happening out in the corridor?" Rugen asked.

Evose spoke up. "Soul fragments, from all times, are congregating where the openings are the largest and thinnest. That's here and now."

This information was not a revelation. I don't know what planet dwellers or politicians on Nobelium believe, but out in space, anybody with common sense knows The Door is a euphemism for a rip in the dimensional threads. The original cause of this rupture is not known, but we do know that certain spacecraft can do damage to delicate dimensional threads. Considering all the theories about why this dimensional breach is happening and what's causing it, no one ever thought it possible that our own denial was beating down The Door to get to us.

SEVEN

"We were ambitious," Belinda was saying. "We attempted to clear as many soul fragments as possible from all previous times and we did that by employing a rather unusual method. Through psychic vision, I traveled outside this time and scanned along the timeline until I found one of my previous incarnations. Once I saw myself in the past, I was able to connect with those previous emanations through deep meditation and their dreams. In those times when they—or me, depending on how you look at it—were most open, I channeled the entire problem and what I was trying to do to solve it. It was amazing. Within three months, I possessed an entire army of my previous incarnations who grasped the entire problem and were my willing allies."

"We thought we were on the right track," said Bogwa. "Everything was going so smoothly—we only wanted to help mend the rupture, I swear!"

While Bogwa and Evose were stewing in their shame, Belinda told us, "I decided to allow Bogwa and Evose the opportunity to indulge in sexual communion with my previous emanations."

"You mean Evose was performing ritualistic sex with your former incarnations?" asked Hope.

"Something like that," admitted Belinda.

"It's not something like that; it's exactly like that," said Hope.

"How is this even possible?" asked Rugen.

"It's possible through creative visualization," Belinda admitted. "We methodically worked our way backward in time. Unfortunately, the farther back we traveled, the more tenuous and distorted our connections became."

I remembered the holographic locket Evose showed me at the Paragon Cafe. That fuzzy picture was actually Belinda in a previous incarnation. I wondered if Evose was my shadow twin. The oedipal implications of what he, Belinda, and Bogwa were doing, were mindboggling. "A crisis came in the year 2015," Evose admitted. "I was doing an exercise with an incarnation named Iris when something happened—I'm not sure what. She lost concentration for a moment, or was distracted or maybe the pressure from the great number of split-offs, in that time, swamped her. Whatever the problem, a rupture occurred just like the rupture that is beginning to happen in this time."

"Do you have any physical proof whatsoever?" Rugen asked.

Bogwa appeared serious in a way I had never seen him before. "We have many, many indications that a split in the universe is imminent. If you don't believe me, ask Una. As far as Iris is concerned, I have confirmation that she was taken by the denial into the fourth dimension and we can substantiate this fact through historical databanks. Iris exists in Earth's records until July of 2015. Beyond that date no databanks show that she ever lived."

"Many people slip through historical records unnoticed," I said.

"There's more," said Bogwa. "2015, 2020, and 2025, we begin to see huge chunks of history missing. Major events, we all believe happened, are lost because the time threads can no longer hold the pattern of time together." Bogwa concentrated all his attention on Rugen. "A small possibility exists that this rupture can still be averted if Evose can interrupt the meditative connection early enough."

"You can't be sure of that prediction," said Nova.

"That's true," Bogwa admitted. He looked toward Hope. "I do know that without mending the rupture, a strong possibility exists that these two ruptures, the one in 2015 and the one here, in 5603, will accumulate enough energy to tear this dimension in two. If we allow this rupture to happen, then hell will be our ordinary reality and everything we know as beauty and truth will be a vague dream. Evose turned to Rugen. "Now, are you going to help me or sit back and watch this universe be destroyed by denial?"

"Do I have a choice?" asked Rugen. That great karmic hook, again, snagged *cim*—that hook that destroyed *cim* and made me watch as it happened. This time, Rugen did not glance my way or ask what I thought. I forgave *cim* just as I forgave Nova. I tried to understand, although my understanding fell grossly short of *cis*. What I did not understand, I covered with my love for *cim*. Perhaps it was too painful to again offer *cim*self as a sacrifice and gaze into the eyes of a soul mate at the same time.

"I believe it's why you incarnated this time," said Belinda.

"I'll go to the Gathering immediately," said Rugen.

"We don't have enough time to go through a Gathering," Belinda insisted.

A full-blown argument erupted with shouting and a few irrational accusations on both sides. We decided to take a vote. Nova, Rugen, and I favored taking the issue to the Gathering. Belinda, Bogwa, Evose, and surprisingly, Hope voted to circumvent the Gathering. "I'm sorry," said Hope. "If we go through a Gathering, divisive factions will arise and the loudest voices will be the ones who believe we should fire up *La Ventana's* engines and head for the Perseus Arm. If we can delay this rupture, we will buy ourselves at least five more years in this area of space. We can save a lot of soul fragments in that time."

Rugen let out a deep sigh. "Okay. I'll call my parents and tell them to send their fastest cruiser. It will take roughly thirty-six hours to get a ship here and the same amount of time to fly to Uropae. It'll take a few more days to prepare a vitasphere; then, we'll do it. My one stipulation is I will not attempt this mission unless Sante accompanies me."

"Absolutely not!" said Evose. "Your lover is excess baggage."

"Let's get one straight, Evose. I'm heading this mission not you." Rugen turned to me and addressed me for the first time since deciding that *ce* was going to sacrifice *cis* life. "Will you be my co-pilot, Sante?"

This was different. Maybe the old karmic hook had not caught us. Despite my feelings for Nova, I knew I needed to say yes immediately. "Sure, I wasn't planning to do anything special with the rest of my life." Suddenly, it was sealed. Evose, Rugen, and I would attempt to go back in time so Evose would have a chance to mend the rupture.

****

While Rugen went to see Captain Issed to request a leave of absence, Nova and I had lunch in the main cafeteria. "I've never been able to figure out why the tea tastes better here than anywhere else on the ship," said Nova. Words seemed so compressed between us that one wrong word might tip the balance and destroy the illusion of normalcy we cultivated between us.

"This tea tastes like generic cardboard," I said. "Michael knew how to make a great pot of tea." Nova glanced away, into a memory. "I'm sorry," I told *lim*. "I didn't mean—I never want to cause you pain."

"I'm not sure of many things, Sante, but I'm sure any pain I've experienced is my fault. You, on the other hand, have saved my life so many times and in so many places that I've lost count. When I returned from Le Mira Jha, with you inside me, I already knew I wanted to create a body for you. Bejan warned me that putting you inside a body might re-ignite the passion between us. I thought that making you a lifegiver and the fact that you were my biological child would be enough to dampen the passion between us, but I was fooling myself. I know that now. Our love is eternal."

"Can you make me believe it this time?"

"Let me try. For starters, I've decided to go with you and Rugen to Uropae."

"Thank you. Are you well enough?"

"I'm not well, but I'm well enough. Let me go see Rex and make sure that *ce* can cover for me in the Executive Gathering. I'll call you afterward."

****

When we arrived at Rugen's apartment, Hope was not talking to Bogwa, Evose was arguing with Hope and Belinda was attempting to make peace with all three. The tension seemed to be ricocheting off the walls so Rugen and I abandoned *cis* place and went to my apartment. Nova called me a short time later and complained about the noisy commotion still going on between Hope and Bogwa. Nova was an introvert. Despite *lis* three marriage-partners and active life in Gatherings, *le* needed private space and time. This life steered *lis* destiny away from solitude. Still, if *le* could not indulge *lis* need for a soothing retreat, at this grief-filled time, then *le* would withdraw even more. If Rugen's place was my place, my place certainly was *cis*. We communicated through a couple of private signals and I understood that it was okay to invite Nova. "Please come," I said.

Nova arrived an hour later and asked, "Have you been out—seen what's happening? People are leaving the ship in droves." We had seen the exodus. Byways were busy and the tourists already gone. In the special Gathering we all missed, the majority of the citizenry decided that *The Mother's* position in space was in peril and she needed to widen her orbit around The Door. Despite the Gathering's resolution, *The Mother* would not attempt to fire her engines, but await tug ships from the Hattonian Hub, that could tow *La Ventana* to safer space. I watched the highlights of the Gathering's debate on the multidex and Captain Issed, who referred to *lim*self, not as caption of *La Ventana* but as, "the logistic head on the bridge," was the first to suggest towing *The Mother* as the "safest option."

Afterward, I tried to explain to Nova and Rugen the déjà vu that fueled my foreboding. "Hibernia and I lived through the destruction of Aeternus. The state was detached and watched from their perches as rumors turned into insanity and finally social collapse. Even after they kidnapped Cle and subjected *cim* to the savagery of the Cerribeame Guard, the Janaforma stayed and helped turn the crisis around."

"Yet Aeternus did die," Rugen reminded us."

"Hibernia and I made the decision that we needed to leave if we had any chance of helping you."

"You and Hibernia made the right decision," said Nova. "I've lived through social collapse twice, once on Hattonia and again on Delta Urbana. Both planets recovered, but went through centuries of dark ages when the majority of the population went underground. On Delta Urbana, where the scarcity myth was promoted as reality, the middleclass ran away and deserted their cities to vermin. Millions lived on the outskirts, waiting for the end to come, while their society rotted away at its core. On Hattonia, it was pure denial. Hattonia pumped so much toxic waste into their atmosphere that children were dying from ancient diseases such as measles, malaria, and amoebic dysentery. As Simon Forma, I invented a mask with a simple algae filter that children could wear to protect their lungs." Nova appeared glum, biting *lis* newly damaged lip. "It took the sight of children playing orbitball in masks to bring Hattonia back from the edge of catastrophe."

"This time I feel as if I'm one of the deserters," said Rugen. "I just told Captain Issed that I was optioning my first leave of absence."

"What did Issed say?" asked Nova.

"Nothing."

"Issed should have questioned it. A captain should be intimate with *lis* directs. Of course, you could have told Issed that it was personal; but the captain should give directs the opportunity to confide in *lim*."

I pointed out, "Issed is on the dull side. *Le* thinks *The Mother* is too old to take for a spin."

Nova tried not to smile. "Picking on Issed is one thing, but please spare *The Mother*. She has a few reserves and modifications that might surprise you. Over the years, she has done some evolving herself and I would pit her against the finest vessels in her class.

"Do you really think it's possible to strip away the annexed frou-frou and move her?" Rugen asked.

"I do," said Nova. "Strip away the annexed leeches and Rex could fly this ship. If called for, Rex could hide *The Mother* inside a hatbox. *Ce* is one of the finest captains we ever had on the bridge. When we served together, I had tremendous respect for *cim*. *Ce* never forgot that *ce* controlled the fate of thousands."

"Did your tremendous respect veer toward the passionate?" I asked.

Nova appeared surprised and then coy. "What makes you ask me such a bizarre question?"

"It's psychic. I feel a strong energy connection between you two."

"Well, the energy connection you're sensing is not sexual. When we were shift commanders, Rex and I played some cruel power games. I went through a lot of emotional maturation during that period and thankfully realized how much our games were hurting other people. When I came back from Lemira Jha, with your soul inside me, you zeroed in on Rex like a laser beam and wanted me to connect sexually with *cim*. In fact, you wanted me to make love to almost every person I met. For a time, Elay, Michael, and Bejan thought I had turned into a sex addict."

I snickered. "You need to have strong will to be a devotee of love."

Rugen used the opportunity to put more pressure on Nova. "Sante tells me you are going to Uropae with us. Did *le* also mention that I'm looking forward to having an open relationship with you?"

"Yes, but I am slightly surprised. In the past few hours, I haven't been sure where our relationship stood."

"Now you know how I've felt for my last two lifetimes," said Rugen. "It's your move, Nova."

****

My apartment is tiny with one sleeproom, which I offered to Nova. Instead, *le* insisted on sleeping on the sofa, in the sitting area, where no gravity controller existed. "This is fine," he insisted. "In fact, I've spent too much time in gravity-free space lately and feel physically weak." I covered the sofa with a clean sheet and gave *lim* a couple of pillows and a blanket. *Le* sat down and I gave *lim* a deliberate wise-guy stare and asked, "Want me to tuck you in?"

"No, I want you to go to bed and pretend I'm not here."

No way was that going to happen. I went to bed with Rugen, but couldn't sleep. One wall away was Nova. Completely awake, I lay there thinking about the possibility of a time rupture. Two hours later, Rugen whispered, "I guess you're not sleeping either. I'm going to get up and meditate."

I waited a few minutes and then decided to get up and work on my book. Tiptoeing out to the sitting area, I noticed that Nova was sleeping on *lis* side, facing the back of the sofa. *Le* looked uncomfortable because the sofa was too short for *lis* body. I opened the multidex file holding the manuscript and wrote the beginning of chapter seven. After the first couple of pages, I reread the pages making a few changes along the way. I was tired and inefficient and the reality of the deteriorating situation on *The Mother* was edging out my delight over writing a new book. I thought again of dumping the project. I had proven my basic assumption concerning writing. No such thing as a non-fiction existed. Putting actual life events into a book format condensed and distorted reality. It was just another way to make life into one more spectacular disaster for the amusement of the bored. I reread where Evose told me about the soul fragments. The words I wrote were a composite of what Evose said. My words reflected my direct bias, and my bias hid under the illusion that I was a good witness.

Moreover, all the personal details I was revealing made me feel ill at ease and exposed. Why was I struggling to legitimize my passionate feelings for Nova with strangers? A memory banged back and forth in my overtired and sluggish mind. The memory was of a therapist I consulted when I was in my early twenties. I had sat in her office and read her thoughts as if she were speaking. *This one is stubborn, a cynical case, possessed with an over-active libido and a lifegiver fixation.* After my encounter with Doctor Samantha Stone, I treasured my cynicism. For almost three years, I never talked to anyone about my feelings; instead, I encrypted my passion and stored it in books. At the same time, I indulged in a series of short and shattering sexual affairs, all shot with cynicism on both sides. These affairs always left me confused, emotionally battered, and abandoned. I shared in the demise of every relationship, no matter how brief, played games with my life and the lives of my lover's as they played games with me. The games always were bits of truth or dare, standoffs over who would bolt and run away first. Now, for the first time in a long time, I felt secure enough to consider letting my cynicism go. I glanced over at Nova, expecting to see *lim* asleep; but instead, *le* was lying there staring at me. "You should write it," *le* said.

"Are you reading my mind?"

Nova blinked. "I need a distraction from the back-breaking pain this sofa is causing me." *Le* sat up and rubbed the small of *lis* back with *lis* hands.

"You want to read my new book? You're in it."

"I'm always in it," *le* yawned. "Have you made me the villain or the hero this time around?"

"I made you part of me."

"I thought you said this book was fiction."

"Actually, I didn't say. You better read it." I quick copied the six plus chapters onto a spool and slipped it into a bookscreen. You can bet, I was nervous. "It's a little different than what I usually write."

"How so?"

"I'm unsure. Maybe you can explain it to me."

"Will you sit with me while I indulge?" I plopped down beside *lim* on the sofa and *lis* arm encircled my back and gave me a tender squeeze. "Would you massage my back a little?" *le* asked. "My lower back hurts." I did not presume to remind *lim* that *lis* pain came from *lis* desire that *le* cut off from me. *Le* already knew that; instead, I lovingly rubbed *lis* back. I handed *lim* the bookscreen and *le* took the transmitter off the side and slipped the separate membranes into *lis* ears. "I hope it's set for slow," *le* said. "And set the pitch of your voice down a tad." I adjusted the bookscreen for *lim*. *Le* closed *lis* eyes and listened for a moment. "That's better," *le* said sounding a bit dreamy. *Le* squirmed and turned *lis* back toward me, knowing that I would accommodate *lim*. It did not take long for *The Permeable Web of Time* to ensnare *lim*. I interrupted *lim* only to ask if *lis* back felt better. "Thanks, I know you're tired," and then *le* invited me to snuggle inside the circle of *lis* arm.

"I've missed you so much," I told *lim*. "It feels good being close to you again." *Le* stroked my hair. For me, this was therapeutic heaven. When I was a child, *le* let me snuggle with *lim*. *Le* would read to me or sometimes read to *lim*self. I loved to wallow in *lis* familiar scent. Nova's scent told me my world was safe and it was okay to fall asleep against the safety of *lis* chest. I wanted that type of assurance from *lim* now. I wanted *lim* to hold me and will the madness of our universe away. I wanted to honor *lim* in the same way *le* honored me, but I could give *lim* nothing *le* didn't already have. I wasn't even clever enough to tell *lim*, in a new way, how special *le* was to me. *Le* hugged me again and I drifted off to sleep, inside the comfort of *lis* embracing arm.

****

Awakening later, I glanced across the room. Rugen and Nova were sitting in the eating area drinking tea and eating breakfast rolls. "What's the time?" I asked.

"Relax," said Rugen. "We have plenty of time. I just received a call from Clione, captain of our cruiser. The ship is in stack-back and will not be able to land for another three hours. All thirty landing portals are being used by exiting craft."

The bookscreen was turned off and sitting on the table next to the sofa. I did not want to pressure Nova, so I went about my business and fixed myself a cup of tea. When I joined them at the table, Nova asked, "May we talk about your new book?" My heart spiked, despite my anticipation. Our eyes met and danced together for a moment. "I love it. I think it might even be better than *Visions of The Wall*. Are you going to publish it as fiction or non-fiction?"

"I don't want to embarrass anyone including myself. I'm going to change a few names and publish the book as fiction, but for right now, I need to call things and people by their own names."

"I understand."

"Thank you, Nova, Your opinion is important to me."

"I never told you this before, Sante, but when Bejan, Elay, Michael, and I were planning your creation, it took us two years to formulate your DNA. We already knew you were a powerful soul with unique genius and we wanted to give you as many gifts as possible so you would possess all the options you needed to evolve. We imagined you working with Bejan on the Regression drug, becoming a healer again, or perhaps working as a leader in the Vanguard Scouts. If you wanted, you could have become a musician. We never guessed that you would use your genius to become a writer. You have proven to us, once again, that you refuse definition. You are a love creation, but you are the most powerful love creation I've ever met because you love truth more than you love either Rugen or me."

"That's not true, Nova. Rugen and you mean everything to me and if I needed to lie to protect you, I would do it in an instant."

"I'm not talking about telling lies to protect someone you love; I'm talking about the ability to love truth so much that you are willing to throw your views on the funeral pyre, if they prove false." Nova tapped the bookscreen. "You're not afraid to write the truth and Truth knows it."

"I know what you're going to say, Nova, and my answer is no. I don't want that kind of responsibility."

"This book is your opportunity. Truth is patient. It waits for the right vehicle to deliver its punch. If not you, then who? I know this, Sante: the truth will be written, if not by you, by someone, somewhere, in some way. The truth is written on the walls of heaven."

****

Una stopped by my apartment with Renée to say goodbye. She and Renée each carried a small piece of luggage. Una had decided to go to New Delphi and explained, "New Delphi is the safest place to be until the crisis clears." Nova was surprised and questioned her decision. "My decision to go to New Delphi is not clear cut," Una admitted. "As I understand the problem, I possess two options. I can stay and attempt to use my energetic presence to protect *The Mother* or I can go to New Delphi and protect Renée and help direct New Delphi's energy toward this area of space. I love *The Mother* as much as I love anyone, but the energy channeled from New Delphi is what can save this universe."

"Okay, go for it!" Nova told her. "It seemed that you've thought it though so what can I do but respect your choice?"

Una's calm wrapped around Renée like a cozy blanket, yet Renée's peaceful veneer seemed tenuous as the stability between the dimensions. "*Lefebr?*" she said to Nova. "If we have to stay on New Delphi, will you promise to come and visit me?" Her request was serious and seductive with childish innocence.

The lifegiver part of Nova was a genius with children and *le* became tender with Renée now. "Sit down with me on Sante's backbreaking sofa so we can enjoy a quiet talk," *le* suggested. Renée snuggled in like a typical lover, resting the side of her head on Nova's arm. She stared off into space looking like an overtired infant on the verge of falling asleep. "I tell you what, Renée. I might not be able to come as you see me now, but I can come to you in a different way. Do you know how to focus your mind?"

"Yes *lefebr. Mebr* taught me how to focus my mind toward The Great Mother. Do I focus on you as I focus on the Mother of Creation?"

"If you focus toward The Mother, I'll hear you because I ride around in The Mother's apron pocket, just like a little mouse." Nova tickled Renée under the chin and she giggled. "I will be able to hear you from the Mother's apron pocket. Please remember that anytime you feel lonely, afraid, and need courage to go on, I will be there as The Mother's little mouse. One more thing, don't ever forget that you are a Janaforma, a child of Truth. Truth knows the depths of your soul, from Eden to Armageddon. Everything you are is perfection. Do you understand?"

"No," said Renée.

"You will," said Nova.

"I'm sorry," said Una. "We should get going."

"Una, may I talk to you in private for a moment?" I asked.

Una glanced at her thumbnail watch and said, "Renée, would you go see if Sante has any ice cream bars in *his* refrigerator? If you find them, bring me one too."

"What do you think is happening?" Rugen asked her. "Is this rupture real or a figment of Evose's imagination? I want to know the truth no matter how awful it is."

"I don't know the truth," said Una. "The truth changes from moment to moment. I only know about veins of possibility."

"Then tell us about the vein of possibility that could lead to this rupture," said Rugen.

Una was so explicit that her prediction came out as a naked embarrassment to us. "Nothing is new and nothing is different in this crisis," she said. "An actual crevasse, or gap, runs along the timeline, between the third and fourth dimension, which grows ever more critical as we move forward in time. Incarnate life fuels this hellish chasm with its denial. This crevasse leads to cataclysm and always has. At irregular intervals, pressure inside the gap reaches critical mass and something must happen to alleviate the pain and suffering inside. In the past, conjunction points, or opportunities for reconciliation, occurred when gatherings of great altruistic oversouls entered this space and willingly offered their bliss and energy in an attempt to reintegrate our denial. Through their grace, not ours, this dimension continues to survive. Denial creates its own demons inside these illusions. Bent toward cataclysm, denial indulges in pathetic games while greater souls relinquish their own evolution to nurse our denial with their hope. These souls need and want to move into their greater evolution. Energetically, the situation is causing a pressure upon us to respond, to become responsible and equal players with other dimensions. We need to know the rules and abide by them. The rules are not a mystery and are identical in every dimension. Every soul in every dimension must exercise conscious responsibility for its accepted freedom. The third dimension will soon reach another rare opportunity for assimilation of its denial. Will we be successful or will our efforts be too little too late? I think we have a slim chance, but if we can do enough, soon enough, with enough humility of purpose, then life will continue. If we cannot heal this rupture then a time of revelation will come when all greater spirits and evolved souls will move away from the third dimension. If that happens, all those left behind will know all hope is gone. Then they will feel the full and dismal rush of their denial. No comfort will exist and time will be short. In that time of dead calm and no sound, the rupture will reach critical mass and open a hole in the antimatter. No one can say anything about what may happen beyond that point."

Nova opened *lis* arms to Una and they embraced. Tears were wetting Una's lashes and trailing down her cheeks. I realized then that I never saw her cry before, even as a child. "I will never let you go from my heart," she promised. She embraced us all one by one. "Take care of *Febr*," she told me. "Renée?" Una called. "Did you find those ice cream bars yet?"

Renée popped around the corner and one ice cream bar was in her mouth and the other one she pulled out from behind her back, "Found them!" she giggled.

Nobody suggested this was the end; but I was convinced that I would never see Una again in this life. After they departed, Nova grew unusually quiet. *Le* did not cry, despite the wrenching poignancy of losing two more individuals that *le* adored. I felt as if Nova was asking me to cry for *lim* and I obliged. *Le* put *lis* arms around me and held me as I sobbed against *lis* chest. After a while, *le* spoke quietly saying, "A few hours ago, I told you that I wanted the freedom to feel and be more than I was. I hope I am not being arrogant in my assumption, but I think I'm beginning to feel your longing. I'm beginning to sense not only the expansiveness of love, but the burden it carries too."

Time turned short in my mind. Not enough time remained to prepare a memorial service for Elay, Bejan, and Michael or even enough time to say adieu to friends. Not having a memorial service was difficult for Nova. Despite *lis* introversion, *le* needed to express *lis* emotional grief over losing *lis* mates, but *le* never mentioned *lis* disappointment to Rugen or me. "Thank you for coming with us," I told *lim* again.

"It's not a matter of thank you," *le* said. "I would come with you no matter what. I mean that, Sante—no matter what."

We turned our attention toward Uropae. I packed a few personal belongings, my microdex so I could work on my book, and my tarot cards. "Better pack warm clothing," advised Rugen. "It's late autumn in our region of Uropae." Time seemed more important now that a strong probability existed that little time remained. I took a tiny watch, which I rarely wore, and pasted it on my left thumbnail. Rugen asked me if *ce* could read my book, so I gave *cim* a copy along with my psychic confessions, *Visions of the Wall*, my love confessions, *Mother's Garden*, and my cynical confessions, *Sleepwalk*.

****

We met the others down in Shuttle Bay 22. Evose seemed ill as if he was coming down with the flu. He told us that his rash was disturbing his sleep. I hung onto Rugen and my insecurity was childlike about leaving *The Mother*, as if losing sight of her, even for an instant, I might lose her for good. Because of the large volume of space traffic in stack-back position, landing control informed us that we had a six-minute window to board and launch.

Once the cruiser landed, flight control would permit no one to leave the ship and it would be our responsibility to hop aboard as soon as the airlock opened.

Only Senon came down to see us off. *Lis* mates were tending to their families and pressure to leave *La Ventana* was building from those families. I assumed Senon had a business appointment because *le* was carrying *lis* small microdex that sometimes looked as if it grew out of *lis* arm. *Le* reminded me of no one but *lim*self as *le* stood there struggling to contain *lis* pain. The tattered remnants of *lis* family were leaving *lim* behind. Nova was worried about Senon and *lis* mates, but Senon was adamant about *lis* intentions. "I'm staying on *The Mother* no matter what," *le* told us.

"Please do not say, 'no matter what,'" said Nova. "Don't put your life and the lives of your family in jeopardy for any reason you might interpret as noble. You're a young soul. You have lots of growing to do. Live and protect your mates." Nova smiled, yet sadness now seemed a permanent part of *lis* every expression. "You know *The Mother* doesn't expect young souls to act like fools—leave that to old fools such as me."

"You'll never be a fool to me," said Senon.

When Senon and I embraced, *le* seemed to metamorphose into Michael again. It seemed strange. Michael had been athletic—tall, lean, and incredibly tough, the body of a warrior. Senon, on the other hand, spent most of *lis* time sitting on *lis* backside in front of a multidex. Senon reminded me of Bejan, tender and sentimental. I asked Senon, "Could you please do me a favor?" *Le* tenderly reminded me that I asked *lim* for many favors in the past. "You're very organized and I'm not," I admitted. "When we were kids, you were the one who always had clean socks."

"Yeah, and you always were borrowing mine,' *le* teased me. "I'm still waiting to get those socks back. I have twenty-eight socks at home with missing mates."

"I own twenty-eight orphan socks myself."

"There you go!" *le* chuckled. "If we could get our single socks together—" Senon stared at the docking doors that soon would snap open.

"Did Nova tell you where we're going beyond Uropae?" I asked.

"We talked," *le* said seriously. "You said you needed a favor?" *le* reminded me.

I gave Senon the spool I had slipped inside my pocket before leaving my apartment. "It's a new book I'm working on. I call it *The Permeable Web of Time*."

"I can't wait to read it. Do you want me to release it?"

"No, it's not finished yet. I need to change the names of some of the characters, but I wanted you to have a copy just in case—"

"What's it about?"

"It's hard to say. I'm going to attempt to write as much as I can before we leave—"

"Leave for the past?" asked Senon.

"Yeah. I will try to send you the chapters as I finish them and any changes I decide to make for as long as I can."

"I'll take care of it," *le* promised. "By the way, I have a present for you too." Senon stared at Nova in a studied way. "This belongs with Sante," *le* said. "I trust *lim* to handle it with the sensitivity it needs."

"Yes!" Nova agreed. "It definitely belongs with Sante."

Senon handed me the microdex *le* was holding. I took it, but Senon's hands remained poised on the case as if *le* was reluctant to let it go. "In some ways, this is my brain child," *le* explained. "It's a sentient multidex program, a project I've worked on for many years. It can get inside any multidex and grease the circuits, so to speak. I figured you might need this kind of technology where you're going. It's important you treat this program with a great deal of respect. Let it work at its own pace and make sure it always has access to its home." *Le* patted the top of the microdex case.

"Are you sure you trust this technology with me?"

Senon smiled. Behind the smile lingered subtle countercurrents of anguish, irony, and inevitability. "The decision for it to go with you was not mine, but made by the program itself. One last thing, it understands about your ability to turn it off. If you need to turn it off, remind it that you will always turn it on again—that it cannot die."

"I will care for it as if it were my own child." Only then did Senon take *lis* hands away from the case. We embraced, kissing each other on opposite sides of the forehead.

The doors opened on *The Mother* and then a second set belonging to the cruiser. Senon's voice was soaked in reverence. "My heart and the heart of *The Mother* go with you, Sante."

Rugen squeezed my hand. "We must go." Bogwa, Evose, and Belinda boarded. Nova embraced Senon again and then I saw Nova's eyes scanning the open space of the landing bay. Nova was the last to board the cruiser.

****

The cruiser left *The Mother* ninety seconds after the doors squeezed shut. While Rugen went to check in with the captain, a super-efficient steward came by and whisked Bogwa, Belinda, Evose, and Hope off to their respective quarters. Our cruiser pilot—whoever that was—was steady at quarter-speed because of all the space traffic in the area. Nova and I stood by a portal and stared out toward the elliptical profile of *The Mother*. Neither of us said a word; we just watched *The Mother* slip away and into the darkness of space. Rugen said, "I want to introduce you to Captain Clione." I was surprised, maybe even a bit horrified, when we stepped on the bridge and I discovered Captain Clione and the entire crew were Ganats. My life was in the hands of the descendants of the Ganat Cerribeame. My repulsion was entirely mine because Rugen was completely at ease. Rugen might have reincarnated precisely to fly that vitasphere backward in time, but along the way, *ce* learned *cis* lessons and made *cis* peace with Ganats.

Karmic evolution sometimes is a delicate dance through sequential opportunities that all hinge on acceptance. Case in point, Rugen. *Ce* could have entertained a life of total hatred for Ganats. After all, they tortured and frustrated *cis* entire purpose when *ce* was Cle. Instead, *ce* forgave Ganats and they taught *cim* how to fly vitaspheres in this life. It was perfect karmic justice. What destroys us must then teach us; and if we accept what we once feared, then we fly free.

****

Captain Clione was the size of a Janaforma child of about nine or ten bio-years of age. Like all Ganats, she was gray. Her skin was like velvet, with those typical huge eyes that engulf everything and give nothing away. Ganat eyes are so bewildering, consuming, and unexplainable, writers and poets have written about them for the last twenty centuries.

> "When the mysteries of space are no more,
> Ganats will swallow the darkness with their eyes,
> and nobody will know we were ever there."

> *Inside the Darkness*; Delhi Blake; writer; Fifth Age of Cipher-
> Cycle of Naught; species, Ganat;

Rugen introduced us and we went through a few formalities. Captain Clione gestured as if she wanted me to lean toward her. Rugen said, "Captain Clione would like to extend an honor and greet you in the Janaforma tradition. I acquiesced and Clione kissed me, on either side of my forehead. I never touched a Ganat before nor had one touched me. I was surprised. Her skin felt cool and soft. Being who I am, her touch gave me sensual pleasure and I thought it might be enjoyable to touch her again. I was socially obliged to return the gesture, which I did, and then she went through the same ritual with Nova.

"Welcome," she said resting the fingertips of her furry paws together. The gesture created a small pyramid or temple in front of her and I'm unsure if it was a personal mannerism or a symbolic gesture on her part. Clione was a small queen, very sure of herself. "It was a pleasure to join with *The Mother* even for a moment," she nodded. "I'm sorry I had no opportunity to step aboard. My body feels warmth for the Janaforma and what they contributed to the restoration of my home world of Calypso."

"Thank you for your hospitality," replied Nova.

Clione continued to nod. "Before we docked, I spoke with Rugen via multidex and *ce* tells me your trip to Uropae is urgent. In fifteen minutes, we will catch maximum speed and be completely underway. While you're aboard, my crew is at your disposal and ready to make you feel comfortable. We've outfitted your quarters in a way I hope will be acceptable for the Janaforma and are prepared to serve food to your liking."

"As usual, I'm sure everything will be excellent," said Rugen. Clione extended further courtesies to Rugen. "It would be an additional honor for you to take the helm."

"Thank you, but I feel completely at ease in your hands," *ce* returned.

She nodded again. Only my psychic skills could tell that she was happy with this response. Her face was typically Ganat—expressionless.

I know Clione was being kind, but I still felt uneasy. I kept thinking about the Cerribeame stripping Cle's mind. To me, Ganats seemed more alien than other sentient beings. They cared nothing for the physical refinements that Humans and especially Tyrowsians considered important. What other species considered comfortable surroundings, Ganats rejected. Their dress resembled clothing primitive nomads wore in the past. The fabric was rough, basic brown, and without individual distinction. Ganats did not sleep in either beds or reduced gravity chambers. They preferred to sleep in nests made of fur plucked from their bodies, like a squirrel or rabbit.

Ganat females, of the Cerribeame tribe, were purported to be able to move fast, some even faster than Shardasko Warriors. When the Ganat Cerribeame were out murdering and mindstripping thirty years ago, only Vanguard Scouts trained as Shardasko Warriors had a chance against the Cerribeame. Whatever natural fighting skills Ganats possessed, I saw none now. The fastest any of them moved was to make sure we had clean towels and extra pillows. In some ways, I think the Janaforma were as alien to Ganats as they were to us. They knew Janaforma family units were triads, but could not distinguish our sexes and the ship's steward ended up escorting Rugen, Nova, and me to one small suite of rooms. Just as Clione promised, our quarters were perfect. The sleeproom contained one outfitted bed just about the size a triad would need.

****

Nova was annoyed and asked Rugen, "Did you arrange this?"

Rugen was indignant and formal about defending *cis* honor. "I told them we needed four suites, not three." Rugen left and returned ten minutes later. "Well, we do have a slight problem," *ce* admitted.

"How slight?" Nova asked.

"How do you feel about sleeping in a traditional fur nest?"

"That sounds—unsanitary," said Nova.

I started howling with laughter and said, "I'm willing to give it a try."

Nova managed to appear abused and Rugen said, "I apologize to you both. This is entirely my fault. I told them we had six people, but forgot to mention, we were not two triads. Anyway, the bottom line is three beds exist on this ship. One is in Bogwa and Belinda's room, another is in Evose and Hope's room, and the last one is here."

"You must stay with us," I said. "I'll sleep on the sofa this time and you can sleep with Rugen."

"Nobody is going to sleep on anymore sofas," said Nova. "The three of us can sleep together. Sante, you can sleep between Rugen and me."

A spontaneous fantasy engorged my mind with a banquet of seduction scenarios, but sleep is exactly what Nova had in mind. I wanted to push the situation, but held myself in check because pushing any further would have bordered on sexual abuse.

Nova suggested we wear clothing to bed. I had not worn clothing to bed since I moved away from my parent's home and, along with everything else, this too felt odd. When it was time to go to sleep, we reduced the gravity and I did drift off almost immediately. Then I began experiencing a dream in which I'm promoting a romance between Rugen and Nova. I want this affair so much that I trick Nova into sleeping with Rugen. The next part is somewhat confusing. For a while, we are jumping from bed to bed as if we're actors in a rowdy, slapstick comedy. At some point, we end up in a fur nest and are giggling because it tickles and then I watch as Nova makes love to Rugen

Something awoke me and I could feel the dampness on my clothing between my legs. Rugen was sleeping wrapped around me and *cis* eighteen-year-old penis was ready for action and poking my hip. Nova was sleeping with *lis* back toward me and *lis* butt was comfortably wedged against my back. It was cozy, perfect for those who are intimate. However, this setup quickly became torture for me. I thought about screaming, *I refuse to endure this any longer*. Instead, I stirred, just a little and Rugen shifted a little too. I reached down and put my fingers into the evidence of *cis* excitement and *cis* penis cooperated by popping out of *cis* underwear like a released spring. I squeezed *cis* penis together with mine. That woke *cim* up and then *cis* hand was down there too. A moment later, Nova got up and went to the toilet. *Le* stayed there an exceptionally long time. I wanted *lim* to come back, but *le* didn't. I was very aroused and notions of *lim* watching made me more excited. Rugen and I masturbated each other to climax.

****

Later, I awoke and glanced across the darkened room to where Rugen and Nova sat in meditation. I decided to take a shower and join them. We sat there for several hours and in those hours I began to unwind the snarls in my emotional body. My grief gave way to fear and I knew that despite my cavalier agreement to make this trip, I was afraid to go. I attempted to face my fear by feeling it, but my mind still wanted a logical reason why I had agreed to this crazy venture. My mind wanted the Infinite to be a kindly old consciousness that directed all life with the evenhandedness of one of *The Mother's* Gatherings; but when I sank down into the silence within me all I could hear was The Mother crying from the darkness—*why are you destroying my creation?*

How had we failed creation and ourselves? With only three-tenths of our galaxy explored, creation was too young to die. A generation ago, we were optimistic when Bejan released the music of enlightenment. We believed the solution to the problems of our universe lie in the Regression drug. Bejan, Elay, Michael, and the other pioneers of Regression therapy, devoted their lives to the belief that Regression was The Panacea, yet here we were again, back on the edge of Armageddon. Why was Regression not enough?

I had witnessed the historical holographs and been alive for much of the misery myself. We left a dangerous legacy for ourselves in the future. Our personal denial had become society's denial and been interpreted into Orion Spur law. In our time, we were wrong to block The Door. In truth, space travel was a paradox, a safe illusion that we created for ourselves. The very thing we thought was protecting the third dimension was helping to destroy it.

****

I came down into the needs of my body and felt healthy, sensual, and extremely alive. "I'm hungry," I said. Rugen called the kitchen and ordered food. About a half-hour later, food came on a pushcart. It was delicious, fresh, and made especially for us. It did not possess the genetic drift taste that food from replicators has. We indulged in a hardy meal. "As soon as we finished, Nova suggested, "We should meet with the others as soon as possible, so we can begin to lay out a strategy."

"Let's hold off on that for a while longer," said Rugen. Something was up with Rugen and it was popping up like *cis* eighteen-year-old penis. *This is a good time to talk about greater connection, ce* thought. Rugen's approach to life is different than mine. This time, I hoped *ce* would skip the logic and stick to *cis* consort charms, which were obvious and abundant. Just as Nova was coming home to us, I didn't want Rugen to scare Nova away. Still, Rugen was hot on the topic of connecting with Nova and *ce* persisted. "Before we meet with the others, could we please talk about our connecting situation, which still has no real resolution?" *ce* asked.

"Maybe we should talk about this in private first," I suggested.

"I'm sorry, my love; but not this time," said Rugen. "I don't want to give you a chance to siphon off the pressure I feel over this matter. Besides, you're afraid of pushing Nova because you're afraid of losing *lim*. I think you should realize that by not pushing *lim*, you're losing yourself."

"I don't need pushing," said Nova.

"We'll see about that," said Rugen, "because I'm going to push you." Nova turned quiet. The willful one was ready to listen to understanding. "First of all, I'm sorry I told Sante that *le* should leave you and I'm sorry I said you were me dropping a brick on my toe. When I was Cle, I tolerated this repressed passion between you and Sante; however, as Rugen, I reject the pseudo-security of the status quo. I want to know where I stand with you and the only way I'm ever going to know the truth is if we connect on every level."

"I know that," conceded Nova. "When the time is right, I'm going to give you and Sante everything you want."

"And when is this magical right-time going to be?" Rugen asked.

"I don't know yet," admitted Nova.

"You have to know, We have little time left to be together." Rugen had Nova by the metaphorical throat and Rugen was not about to let go. I was impressed; still, I preferred to operate through love. "If you are going to start talking about your physical age or any other social convention, then you're talking nonsense. You may know a lot about eternity, but you still have plenty to learn about this dimension. You want completion in eternity; you can't have it until you transcend imposed convention here."

"I know it's my responsibility to make the first move," said Nova, " but I need a stronger bridge for my journey." Now Nova was talking to me. "I know this has been a source of pain between us for a long time, but if we could take Regression together, I know it will help. Regression will enable us to respond to each other with more sensitivity."

"You want more sensitivity from me?" I asked.

"Yeah, more sensitivity; can you handle being that exposed with me?"

I felt as if I was falling over a cliff. I was going down, down with inevitability. "Okay, I'll do it," I promised. "I'll take Regression."

EIGHT

We eased into greater intimacy, spending time meditating, sleeping, and innocent embracing. I had started a new meditation, when I heard a sharp rapping at our cabin door. I knew it was Hope. Rugen went to answer the door and roused me with, "Hope says she needs to speak with you." The moment I saw her, I noticed her anxiety. She reminded me of Elay the last time I saw her alive in the ship's garden. No sooner did I think *Elay* than Hope said, "Elay once told me you have skills as a healer. I was wondering if you might come and examine Evose's rash. It's grown worse since we've left *The Mother.*"

"Why doesn't Bogwa heal Evose's rash?" Rugen asked. "Bogwa could dump it in the fourth dimension."

"At the moment, Bogwa and I are estranged and incommunicado," said Hope. "We have agreed to be polite to each other in public, but I no longer understand his mind. A very long time ago, we made a pact that we would play by the rules of each universe we entered. Of late, this promise seems to mean nothing to Bogwa."

"Why doesn't your anger extend to Evose?" asked Rugen.

"Because Evose is as naïve as I am," said Hope. "The difference between Evose and me is—I know I'm naïve about the ways of this universe and he does not."

"Can you be naïve if you know that you are?" challenged Rugen.

Hope's eyebrows arched with thoughtfulness. "Acknowledging one's naiveté might be the saving grace between conceit and humility. Compared to Bogwa and Evose, I'm reserved in my interactions; but at least I'm willing to admit that I have plenty to learn about living in a body. Anyway,

I'm here because of Evose. Do you know a salve or powder that might help his rash?"

We brought no medications with us, just as we brought no Regression drug, so I offered to do some energy work on Evose. Rugen volunteered to help and Nova said, "I'll get dressed and be along in a couple of minutes too."

We went to their room, located a dozen steps down the narrow passageway. Inside, the lights were dim and Hope called out, "Evose? I've brought Sante to examine your rash. May I turn on the light?" As soon as the lights came up, I remember glancing at the tiny watch pasted on my thumbnail and thinking, *we're more than halfway to Uropae.*

Evose groaned and said, "Light hurts!" His voice sounded rough and tinny, reminding me of two pieces of metal scraping against each other. Then Hope switched on a second light, above the bed. Evose's arms rose to shield his eyes from the sudden glare of the lamp, but instead flailed in confused patterns above his head. I walked into the room considering myself a healer. I had firsthand memories of the medical horrors of the past. A thick, blistered rash covered the backs of his hands and arms. I moved closer to him and he smelled putrid, as if he were rotting away. I remembered this odor too. It was the perfume of battlefields where the injured lay dying from unattended wounds and in plague-infested hospitals where the dead waited for the brave to bury them. I touched Evose and he cried out in agony. This I remembered too—when it hurt too much to be touched. I became gentle, not touching him at all. I felt the energy field around his body, the hot and cold spots, allowing my intuition to lead. Evose managed to tell me the pain was not on his skin but—"It hurts, down deep in my bones, in what holds me together."

Hope stood stiff at the end of the bed. She was fragile and tense with worry. "His rash turned worse about a half hour ago," she explained.

Rugen put an arm around her and assured her "Sante and I are going to figure this out." Rugen glanced my way with—*okay, Sante. Figure it out.*

I retracted the bedcovers to get a closer look at Evose's body. Around his midsection were splotches of degenerative purpura. Blood was seeping from his blood vessels and collecting just under his skin. On his hipbones and thighs were large pustules. The skin in the creases between his legs appeared necrotic. His condition was analogous to the necrosis-causing diseases, I had seen on the third-world planets of the Gathos System. His rapid deterioration suggested that he might have a super-infection. He needed serious drugs and quickly. Perhaps somewhere in the Hattonia Hub they had an antibiotic that could cure him, but out here, in the far reaches of Daleth Sector, little hope existed that I could find such a cure. I placed my hands a few millimeters distance from his face. He had a raging fever. Rugen took Hope by the arm and the three of us stepped outside their room. "Evose doesn't have a simple rash," Rugen explained. "His condition is critical. If he doesn't get proper medical attention, he is going to die. Go to the captain and see if a doctor is aboard."

"I better ask Bogwa first," she said.

Rugen practically screamed, "Forget Bogwa. Evose needs a doctor. Go!"

I stepped back inside the room a second time. "Light—burning," groaned Evose. I dimmed the light.

"Can you hear me?" I whispered.

"Yeah" he said. "This time the pain is pretty bad."

"I'll try to help you with the pain, but I will need to touch you." He agreed and I gently took his pulses along his wrists. They were erratic."

As he lay there, his head began to thrash from side to side. "I'm coming," he muttered and then he fell into unconsciousness.

Nova knocked on the door and entered. "I just saw Hope screeching down the hall in the opposite direction," *le* said. "What's going on?" Nova took one look at Evose and knew the situation was grave. Hope returned a couple minutes later and was breathless from running. "The captain says—no doctor is aboard, but I brought a medical kit from the kitchen. Maybe you can find something in it that will help."

****

The communicator on the multidex bleeped. It was Captain Clione and she wanted to know what kind of medical emergency we had. Zeroing in on Nova, I said, "Would you please handle the captain? Hope, go get Bogwa and Belinda and tell them Evose is critically ill." I glanced at the watch on my thumbnail. Six minutes had elapsed since Rugen and I first entered the room.

Evose woke up and started gagging. I needed to touch him to prevent him from choking, yet he screamed in agony at the slightest touch of a hand. "Don't worry," he croaked. "I'll be okay."

Rugen grabbed the medical kit that Hope brought into the room and dumped the contents on the end of the bed. The kit contained a few cartridges of a mild analgesic inhalant, some antiseptic, and a few bandages. "Give me that analgesic," I said to Rugen. Working fast, I peeled the red safety tabs off the twin cylinders. "I'm going to give you something for the pain," I told Evose.

Evose gasped as soon as I released the medicine into his nostrils and then his chest caved inward. "You win," he rattled, and he slipped into unconsciousness again. I continued to hold Evose's wrists and take his pulses. They were faint, waning, and sometimes not there. His body was dying. Everything was happening in a series of quick linear bursts of actions and reactions—miniature explosions of activity, yet nothing made sense. Hope returned with Belinda. When Belinda saw Evose, she ran to fetch Bogwa. She was gone less than thirty seconds. Sometime during those thirty

117

seconds, Evose's heart stopped beating. I glanced at my watch to begin timing the steps of cardio-resuscitation and realized only eight minutes had elapsed since I walked into the room with the assumption that Evose was suffering with a skin rash.

Bogwa arrived wearing nothing but undershorts yet Belinda was urging him to, "Hurry! It's serious this time."

****

When Bogwa walked into the room, he was different than I ever saw him before. He was neither scared nor sad, but highly alert. "Get out of my way," he said to me. I ignored him, going on with my cardio-resuscitation routine. He tapped me on the shoulder rather hard, telling me, "You're making matters worse. If you don't stop, you're going to kill him." I moved aside and Bogwa sat down on the bed. His attitude became intimate and probing. I was sure he was trying to excite a memory feeling because Bogwa and Evose were like two magnets getting closer and closer. Belinda stopped sobbing long enough to watch in complete amazement and then Hope came through the wide open door and shouted, "Stop!"

Bogwa turned and glared at her. His pointed expression was that of an angry god giving the evil eye. "Stay out of this!" he roared from his distant hill. Evose's body began to heave as if a mountain were rising beneath it. Did I imagine what happened next? Did I blink or did Evose and Bogwa disappear for a second? It was as if two magnets finally clicked together—and flash, flash, flash! It happened three times. I glanced around the room and everything seemed the same. Where was the illusion, in the flash or now? I checked my thumbnail watch. Twelve minutes had elapsed in what I observed to be three quick flashes.

Evose groaned and his groaning brought my attention back to the elapsing moments. My senses seemed shattered and unsure of reality. Clearly, Evose was metamorphosing toward healing, but I felt no trust in the reality of what I was seeing. I peered at Nova and then Rugen, seeing the astonishment in their eyes. I kept checking my watch, observing each second vanish into the past. To me, the truth was undeniable. Twelve minutes of reality had vanished without a trace or memory.

"This is wrong," drifted in through my concentration filters. Hope was speaking. Bogwa abruptly stood up, but was awkward and stiff. His appearance was stoical and he looked like an ancient, tribal chief, facing certain defeat. Then, as if someone sawed him in half, he collapsed to his knees. A second later, he went all the way to the floor. Everyone rushed to his rescue and now I was taking Bogwa's pulses too. He was barely alive. Admittedly, I was in an altered state. My consciousness was up on the ceiling watching everyone move around the room. They all seemed as alien as black ants, racing around on a square meter of dusty earth. There in my altered state, I wondered why ants were so involved in their programmed agendas that they never noticed the looming foot. I actually stood there and speculated about ants, but never saw the paradox, the ghastly humor in its meaning. What within the genetic disposition of ants made them into efficient pallbearers? Why, in the face of anthill Armageddon, did the omega ant continue carrying the dead to the preordained graveyard until the last ant dropped dead? Why were we all perfunctory and unexceptional in a crisis?

Knowing this, I continued to take Bogwa's pulses. They were weak. The multidex began bleeping again and Rugen possessed enough sense to answer the call. I barely heard *cim* talking to Captain Clione—telling her the emergency was a false alarm. "Evose is a planet dweller," said Rugen, "and he merely experienced an upset stomach from space sickness.' After *ce* talked to the captain, Rugen explained that if communicable diseases were suspected, we would be quarantined for an indefinite period.

Belinda put a pillow under Bogwa's head and covered him with a blanket. I reexamined Evose. The rash was already returning, but now was a fine sprinkle across his torso and similar to what I saw when I projected my mind into his sleeproom a few cycles earlier. We waited. Whatever was happening was way beyond my understanding. It took another eight minutes for Evose and Bogwa to begin emerging from unconsciousness, but they did emerge. Bogwa opened his eyes and glanced around. The first thing he demanded to know was, "Were drugs administered to Evose?" I admitted that I dosed Evose with the analgesic.

"Well, don't ever do that again," he barked. "Analgesics are toxic to us."

"Why?" Rugen demanded.

"Give me a moment to breathe," replied Bogwa and he picked himself up on shaky elbows. He eventually managed to get up with Belinda's assistance. "My darling," he said in that special way he spoke only to her. He kissed her on the cheek and asked her, "What would I ever do without your help? Help me over to Evose and let's be quick about it." Belinda glanced around at the rest of us and said, "All of you, keep your distance."

There they were, Belinda and Bogwa. They were born into two different universes and were as different as night and day. She was tiny and voluptuous and he was a string bean, yet they had been together for so long that their roots had wrapped around each other and neither one of them knew where they started or the other ended. They were icons from the Age of Regression, yet they were beginning to show their age.

Bogwa hovered over Evose with outstretched arms, encompassing his soul mate and son in a hands-on clamp. This time, whatever Bogwa did, his actions were enough to remove the remainder of the rash from his son's body. Seconds later, Evose's eyes fluttered open and they were clear, bright, and innocent. With obvious fatigue, Bogwa sat backward on the floor and embraced his knees. He refused to look at us, but instead stared at the floor.

"I guess you all have questions," he eventually said. "If you give me a chance, I will attempt to be candid. Let's go to another cabin so Evose can rest."

"I'll stay with Evose," said Hope.

"No!" said Bogwa. "Evose will be fine. Come with us. I want to see how tough you really are; plus, I don't want you to accuse me of leaving you out of anything, ever again."

****

We walked down the hall to Bogwa and Belinda's room. Bogwa sat on the edge of the bed, next to Belinda, as she massaged his neck. "Can we keep this brief?" she begged. "These kinds of things are exhausting for him."

"What do you mean by 'these kind of things'?" asked Rugen.

"I'm fine," Bogwa insisted. "Go ahead, ask whatever you need to know."

"How come analgesics are toxic to you and deadly plagues are not?" asked Rugen.

Bogwa sighed as if he were about to recite a boring litany. "Anything that deadens response is poisonous to us."

"What's wrong with Evose?" I asked.

Belinda turned annoyed as if we were a pack of morons. "What do you think is wrong with him?" she wailed. "He's processing denial that this dimension doesn't want to take responsibility for."

"We shouldn't be doing this," said Hope.

Bogwa was still irked with her, but too exhausted to demonstrate his full irritation. "What do you suggest we do instead? Let Evose die?"

"If that's what's supposed to happen, then we should let it happen," said Hope.

"For a person who chose hope for her name, you seem to lack compassion for your own cause," said Bogwa. "Beyond that, may I remind you that Evose is your soul mate and brother? Evose is my soul mate too and now he is my son; I'm not going to let him die when I have the power to save him."

"Please dear, don't get so excited," said Belinda.

I could see Hope gritting her teeth as she struggled to reconcile her loyalty to her soul mates and her integrity. "Everything here is supposed to die," she said.

"Not this way!" said Bogwa.

"Who are you to make that decision?" she asked.

Bogwa turned quieter and a lot stiffer. "I guess I can make that decision, if I have the power to make it."

"How many times has this happened to Evose before?" asked Nova.

"Six times," admitted Bogwa. "But this was a very close call."

"What about the lost time?" I asked.

"I don't know what you're talking about," said Bogwa.

"Right before Evose started to heal, I glanced at my watch. Then something happened, a kind of flashing and I glanced at my watch again and twelve minutes had elapsed."

Bogwa still insisted, "I didn't notice anything."

He's lying! Ezek said. The smoothness of what I imagined to be reality continued to wrinkle into greater and greater doubts. How could an individual I once believed was the most holy man in all creation, tell me a bald-faced lie? "Did anyone else notice the time loss?" I asked. Everyone looked innocent except Nova. Then Nova gave me a private look with a message and I knew he would tell me in private.

"Have we all been exposed to this deadly plague?" asked Rugen.

"Bogwa hesitated and glanced around the room. "At the onset, everyone thinks they are strong enough to know the truth, but no one thinks about the responsibility that comes along with truth."

"Why don't you let us worry about our responsibility?" said Rugen.

"Okay," said Bogwa. "The truth is all yours. The voices of eternity are interested only in willing sacrifices; however now that you know such a need exists, your oversoul will ask you to make these sacrifices." Bogwa was correct. No sooner did the truth reveal itself than the highest sources of my soul requested that I make similar sacrifices. I suddenly saw the fuzzy gap in myself with greater clarity. My ego was parading around as a clown— wearing a costume of love—without truly being love. How had I failed? I did not take Regression when offered the chance.

"Please?" Belinda said after a moment. "Let Bogwa rest. We can talk more about these matters later."

What else could I ask if Bogwa did not want to discuss the missing time? Many questions remained unanswered, but I felt inarticulate and confused and suggestions about being a willing sacrifice pecked away at me. As we left their room, I felt as if life was moving too fast. I had no time to stand back and make thoughtful decisions. I wondered again about my purpose for reincarnating. Did I reincarnate to be with Nova or had my ego projected that notion too? In complete honesty, did Nova need me? I was the one who needed Nova and I was the one demanding the commitment through physical bonding. Why was I alive if not to help Nova and how does an incarnation of love act as a willing sacrifice? In the next few minutes, I concluded that I knew nothing, not even myself. I related only to my inadequacies and my distance from surrender.

Rugen asked Hope if she wanted to come back to our room and talk and she said, "I want to stay with Evose and make sure he is going to be okay. Thanks, both of you, for trying to help. You probably think I'm heartless, but I'm not. I'm merely careful. Sometimes I don't think Bogwa realizes how fragile Evose and I are in this dimension.

****

Nova and I returned to our room while Rugen went to see the captain and make sure we would have no problems landing. The moment our cabin door closed, Nova asked, "Have you noticed that Rugen is sexually attracted to Hope?"

"I've noticed, what about it? It's not a serious attraction."

"You should honor Rugen's attractions as much as *ce* honors yours."

I emerged from my reverie about willing sacrifices, Evose, and the missing time by millimeters. "Give me a clue, Nova. What are we talking about now?"

"I'm attempting to help you face those things still hidden in your dark corners."

"Hope is not an issue between Rugen and me."

"Maybe she should be."

"Why? To take the pressure off you?"

Nova hesitated and it gave me a chance to catch *lis* thoughts. *Le* was going to say, *I love you;* but instead said, "Don't be foolish! You're a writer, yet it's incredible that you still can be so literal. Think! What is the direction of refined hope?" I struggled to concentrate on what *le* was saying; but part of my mind remained occupied by the time loss and by my oversoul demanding that I become a willing sacrifice. "You seem confused," *le* noticed. "Answer me. Define the direction of refined hope."

My body was shaking and I felt stupid. "I don't even know what you mean by refined hope." An inner tension, an anxiety bordering on anger, filled my body and made me rigid and unresponsive. "Why are you pressuring me?"

"Sorry," *le* smirked. "I guess I'm not an advanced lover like you."

Nova was taunting me, calling me out. I knew that now. "I'm not worried about Hope; but if you are, why don't you ask Rugen about *cis* feelings for her?"

"I intend to," said Nova.

An intense longing drained me of my self-control. If Nova and I could have made love, I was positive I could give *lim* everything *le* wanted. My hands went behind my head and released my hair from its restraints. Draping my hair over my shoulders, my voice was an interloper asking, "Do you find me the least bit attractive?"

"Attraction is a weak word to describe what I feel for you," said Nova.

Rugen came through the door and told us, "I took care of the situation with the captain." Then *ce* noticed my hair down and the seductive vibration I was giving off. "Damn!" *ce* exclaimed. "I was gone no more than five minutes. How did you get this far without me?"

"It means nothing," and I retied my hair.

"Sure! And *The Mother* is a banana cream pie." Rugen took off *cis* shoes and flopped down on the bed.

I went to the washroom to brush my teeth. I felt confused and slow as a snail. Why did I take down my hair? Why was I setting myself up as a foolish target so Nova could shoot me down? *You're trying to force the love into the physical and short-circuit your growth,* said Ezek. Was I?

The washroom door stood open and I overheard Nova and Rugen chatting. Their talk was banter, a game I was too raw to play; but their casual exchange meant something more. "I noticed you're sexually attracted to Hope," said Nova.

I stopped brushing my teeth and listened. "She's beautiful and soulful," said Rugen. "I find her restraint as sexy as Sante's overt sexuality."

"Are you serious about her?"

"Serious enough that I would not engage her in an affair. Sante and I just found each other and for me, that's enough."

Everything turned quiet. That was it? What was I supposed to understand? I emerged from the washroom and was almost breathless with anticipation when I asked Rugen? "What is the direction of refined hope?"

To my amazement, *ce* actually possessed the right answer. "Absolute trust," *ce* said. "It's precious as unconditional love."

****

As we came into range of Uropae, we emerged from our separate rooms. Evose's rosy glow of health had evaporated and he appeared fragile and thin; however, no visible rash showed on the exposed parts of his body. Bogwa and Belinda were supporting Evose. Not that they were holding him up, but they were hovering and never quite out of sight. Rugen and I were standing near a space portal, waiting for Uropae to come into view, when I felt Evose focusing on me. "Before we land, we need to talk," he said and he nodded toward Rugen, "—privately, if you don't mind?"

"Sure thing," said Rugen and *ce* walked away.

"I merely wanted to thank you for coming to my rescue when I was ill," said Evose.

"Forget it; besides, if it wasn't for Bogwa's intervention, I might have killed you."

"Your intentions were honest. You had no way of knowing analgesics were harmful to me."

It was quiet between us as I tore away the mask worn by my intentions. I turned around and faced him squarely. He looked so pathetic to me now, so different from the vibrant soul I greeted in *The Mother's* landing bay a few cycles earlier. My empathy softened me and I was standing in his shoes. "I've been a physician and healer for many lifetimes," I said. "I should know that what is medicine for some might be toxic for others. I acted too quickly and made too many assumptions."

"Did you think if I were dead that it might spare Rugen from undertaking this dangerous mission?"

"You've certainly tested my patience, Evose; nevertheless, if I turned myself inside out, I find no desire in me to see you dead. Your initial rejection stung, especially when you were trying to manipulate me; but I've let that go. I realize now that we have different ways of operating. I feel things and then through my feelings, I explore their intellectual validity. This system works for me—you should try it sometime. As a physician and healer, I've given away more compassion to strangers than you were willing to expend on me to win me over to your cause."

Evose hesitated and I knew what was coming next. "I did not want this conversation to turn into another debate. I'm attempting to clear the air between us before we begin this mission."

"I am clearing the air."

"To me, it sounds as if you are still angry."

"That's because you've never seen me angry."

Evose waved his hands around in a short spastic gesture. "Okay, I get your point, Sante. I'm sorry I offended you in so many ways. Now may we move on?"

"Sure! Just remember this, Evose. Love owns this dimension and the beings of this dimension and you will never succeed here, either in the past or in the present, unless you find a stable reference point through love."

"I've spoken to Bogwa about your faith in love. Bogwa carries my love. He has made me understand I was clumsy in my interactions with you and Rugen. I recognize our situation might be more compatible if the physical could have sparked between us; but I'm not interested in sexual connections or relationships. Please try to understand my viewpoint. I feel desperate and responsible for this rupture and that's all I have room for in my life."

"I share your current angst and sense of urgency. I promise, I will try not to accentuate the enormous differences between us or our diverse approach to life, but Rugen and I expect to be equal partners with you in this venture."

Evose went internal and a new sadness showed on his face. "I know! I can't do this alone." A few tears dropped onto his high cheekbones and slid down the gully around his nose. "I have this fear concerning Iris. I've been foolish and careless concerning her safety and now I feel as if I'm running out of time. I don't have all the answers, but I do know Iris is the linchpin in this impending rupture. If she goes, the entire universe will go."

"You are not as lost as you might imagine," I said.

He tried to mask his misery with a wisp of a smile. "Your resiliency is so amazing to me. If I could understand your resiliency—" I felt a need to catch him, a foreboding fear that he might fall into that vast gap between us. He cried and leaned forward, putting his head upon my shoulder. I embraced him gently and detected a nervous stutter inside his body. It was strange as if his internal clock were skipping beats and within those missing beats he was already gone. As a healer, I knew that nervous stutter was my archenemy, a signal that my healing skills were dust in the wind.

****

Rugen arrived to save me. "We are coming in range of Uropae," *ce* said. I went with *cim* to another portal, in the cruiser's main lounge, so *ce* could show me the local sights as we approached *cis* native world. *Ce* was excited about "coming home," despite the grim circumstances surrounding our reasons for coming. It was important to *cim* that we were together when Uropae first came into view. "Keep watching there," *ce* said pointing to a spot.

We watched as our ship made a wide left-angle correction and then Uropae eclipsed all other views. "She's exquisite," I said. "Just what I need to heal my grief."

Uropae was twice the size of Hattonia and four times the size of Earth; but unlike Hattonia, the landmass of Uropae covered only one-eighth of the surface. Landmasses appeared like delicate green necklaces trailing around the planet's sapphire-blue surface.

Rugen kept pointing to geographical features through that narrow portal as *ce* blessed me with *cis* encyclopedic knowledge of *cis* home world. "Planetary ethnologists consider Uropae prime-virgin because of her pristine condition," *ce* said. "Her fragile topography has made heavy colonization impossible. It's a blessing for the native flora and fauna; but talk abounds that the rich jewelight deposits under her oceans make her a valuable commodity." *Cis* face contorted into a frown. "I hate when a planet is worth more torn apart than in its entirety."

"What do you call those two moons hanging so close to Uropae's equator?" I asked.

My question made Rugen smile. "The tan one is Gophpa*. It has no atmosphere. The blue-green one is my favorite place in creation, Sasaybin. "Sasaybin—" Rugen said again. *Ce* allowed the word to slip over *cis* tongue as if *ce* enjoyed saying it. "—is a planetoid of dense, green jungles and virgin waters where trees rise like cathedrals into the skies." He smiled with a memory. "Sasaybin dresses herself as carefully as a bride with no sentient help whatsoever." I lost myself in a fantasy. Rugen and I would bathe in a lagoon of transparent beauty while the passionate rhythm of the jungle stirred our hearts. We would fill our nights with lovemaking and spend several hours each day merely weaving flowers through each other's hair. "Conjunction comes in only eight days," Rugen was saying. "Too bad

*Gophpa meaning "torchlight" or "lantern"; language origin Cuneate

we'll miss that too."

"What happens during Conjunction?" I asked.

"Every one hundred twenty-eight days, Gophpa passes between Uropae and Sasaybin and from the surface of Uropae, Gophpa appears as a blood-orange spot on the surface of Sasaybin." Rugen's voice went dreamy. "The nighttime sky turns a translucent green and the last time it occurred, the clouds turned bright orange. Everyone goes to the beaches and enjoys bonfires made of dried peat and powerful local herbs. There's music everywhere, feasting, and the seductive ambiance of dancing in Gopha's moonlight."

I felt Rugen's lingering loneliness at that moment, that existential bit of *cim* that *ce* bore without me. *Ce* had gone to the beaches during Conjunction; but always went home alone. I longed to erase all *cis* memories of Conjunction loneliness; but knew no way to fix what already happened. No matter what Evose declared about time travel, he had not convinced me that it was possible. How could I return to the moment when Rugen wandered the beaches, meet *cim*, and then heal *cis* loneliness with my love? My love for Rugen wanted to delete *cis* every lonely sigh and rewrite our existence into a conjoint erotic novel. While making changes, this time I would scald every heart inside creation with tender passion. All light would be brighter in my revised story of reality. Open moonlight would be a florid fuchsia and every corner a darker scarlet. My whole objective to rewriting history would be to celebrate love in a place where I could love Rugen forever. The End.

****

A half-hour later, we landed on Space Station 41, which was a hundred kilometers above Uropae's surface. Because of the delay in leaving *La Ventana,* we wasted no time in thanking Captain Clione and departing. SS 41 was cold, bleak, and dull with a retractable atmosphere that exhaled when planes landed and inhaled as soon as planes departed. Colors there were hesitant shades of gray and nobody lived here except a dozen mobile robots. Rugen's parents kept several spacecraft housed on SS 41 to transport cargo and personnel to the Uropae surface for their company's business. *Cis* parents had made sure a sleek little cruiser was available and ready for our use. The ship was so new, the interior smelled factory fresh. We were on and off SS 41 in just under fifteen minutes. Rugen went to the cockpit to check in with Uropae flight control, while the rest of us found seats. I was sitting aft, with the others, when Rugen's voice came over the intercom asking me to go up front and serve as co-pilot. "I don't fly much anymore," I tried to tell everyone.

"What if Rugen needs your help on The Big Trip?" asked Nova. Nova tapped me on the shoulder and said. "Come on, I'll sit in the jump seat and talk you through it." I went forward to see if I could remember anything about flying reentry craft. Ten minutes later, we were cutting through Uropae's atmosphere toward the planet surface and I was flying.

"Go ahead, take us in," Rugen told me.

"Come on Sante!" coaxed Nova. "You flew *The Mother*—you certainly can land this little cruiser."

I reminded them, "That was in my last life and out in space, not inside gravity where the slightest error can amount to disaster."

"Posh!" returned Nova. "Stop your niggling and do it!"

Ten minutes later, I was landing the cruiser on the surface of Uropae at a spaceport called Jejune's Gateway. "It was as smooth as glass," complimented Rugen. As usual, *ce* was generous.

I heard some cheering from the rear of the plane. "Hooray! We're still alive!" someone yelled.

"Ignore them," smiled my loyal Rugen. "None of them could fly a paper airplane across a room."

That was not exactly true. Bogwa had been a Vanguard Scout with Elay. She once told me, "No one was better than Bogwa."

Where we landed, we were a million kilometers from nowhere, yet everything seemed perfectly civilized. A few people were milling around—some Tyrowsians and a few Ganats—but no one took note of our landing. It was late autumn and the weather was chilly. As soon as we deplaned, Rugen waved toward two people standing just behind the safety line who were—no surprise—Kayya and Ceff. They rushed toward Rugen and embraced *cim* and the three of them cried with happiness.

Both Kayya and Ceff had chalk white skin, but that's where their physical similarities ended. Kayya was reedy and tall for a Tyrowsian. Her eyes were the color of dusty lavender and her long white hair was highlighted with purple streaks. Ceff was shorter and exceptionally robust, especially for a Tyrowsian female. Her eyes were the color of pink marbles and she wore her long hair in a sensible ponytail. Like most Tyrowsians, they dressed in beautiful attire. Kayya wore a short skirt of buttery yellow and Ceff wore a flawless pair of gray silk pants. These two souls were important for reasons far beyond being Rugen's adoptive parents. In their previous lives, as Janaforma, they invented the *vitarattha* and that meant they touched the lives of everyone who worked in space. The *vitarattha* opened space just as the Regression drug opened memory. The *vitarattha* made it possible to penetrate space minus the confines of a bulky spacesuit with the safety and confidence of stepping outside on a pleasant autumn afternoon.

"You look so wonderful!" exclaimed Kayya and her misty lavender eyes shed tears of happiness. She pulled back and examined Rugen from arm's length. "I can't believe it! You've actually grown taller in the last couple of months."

"Rugen has matured!" said Ceff. "Don't bother denying it, Rugen. I can see it in your eyes. You've lost your virginity." That was Rugen's cue to introduce me. "You're so handsome!" Ceff said. She called me a "heartbreaker" and I knew she meant it as a compliment. "Where did you get your fabulous Gathosian eyes?"

"My *fra*, Bejan, was part Gathosian," I explained. "My eyes are a genetic copy of *cis.*" I attempted to discover who was who in this life and Kayya let go some typical Tyrowsian titter, claiming Kerisa was "manifesting heavily" in them both and it was Kerisa's influence that caused them to be female. "But which one of you is Dyne and which is Reyneldi?"

"Why both!" Ceff shrugged. "We were re-mixed and concentrated by our oversoul."

Dispensing with that question, Kayya said, "Rugen, you must take Sante to Sasaybin to see the statue."

They looked as if a mysterious collusion was developing among them; then Rugen turned sober and said, "This time we'll not have time to go to Sasaybin."

"But you must!" Ceff insisted. "It's as obvious as kismet."

Rugen put her off with, "We'll talk about the statue later."

****

When Nova told Kayya and Ceff that *le* was Simon Forma, they cried. Tears flooded Nova's eyes too because Dyne, Kerisa, and Reyneldi were original Janaforma creations. As Simon Forma, he died shortly before they were born. "I cannot tell you, in words, what this means to me, to meet you in the flesh," Nova told them. "To have great souls, such as you, honor my creations with their lives, is a blessing from the highest sources."

Ceff's hot pink eyes turned glassy with tears. "I feel equally blessed," she said. "To meet the creator of such refined bodies is an honor. I always swore that if I ever met the reincarnation of Simon Forma wandering this universe, I would ask one question. Tell me Nova, what was your master plan for creating the Janaforma?"

I was hanging on the edge of myself with curiosity. Why did I never think to ask Nova this simple question? Nova smiled and *lis* smile was beautiful and when *le* spoke, *lis* voice was velvet with humility. "The initial idea for creating the Janaforma came in a flash, but it took a great deal of scientific discrimination in the planning stage to define what I considered genetic superiority. It was a given that the Janaforma would need to be physically superior to endure the rigors of space work, but it was my personal bias that decided to make them beautiful. Your brains were superior and your adaptability quotients were off the scale. As Simon Forma, I realized that adaptability would help the Janaforma adjust quickly to new technologies and facilitate their interactions with alien cultures; but adaptability turned out to be more important than I realized. Adaptability became the springboard to the Janaforma's rapid evolution. As Simon

Forma, I prayed a lot. I learned how to pray from the nuns at Saint Hildegard's Church. Once the genetic formulas were combined and developing in their nativity vats, I prayed that purity would inhabit my creations. Meeting you now, I see that you heard my prayers and honored me with your lives."

"My dear creator," said Kayya. "You are the star in the diadem of *hataeasta.*"

"That goes double for me," said Ceff. This was the highest compliment a Tyrowsian could bestow on another person. For Tyrowsians, that said it all.

NINE

We collected our few pieces of luggage and Kayya and Ceff took us to a nearby hovercraft. Ten minutes later, we were landing at Iona. Iona was an island estate. Its magnificence was classical Tyrowsian. Classical Tyrowsian architecture uses geodesic units. The largest structure usually sits front and center with several *binnies* (literally, "children" Cuneate) clustered around.

I knew Kayya and Ceff were wealthy, but Iona was far more than I expected. The gardens were elaborate and the surrounding sea the same color as Rugen's eyes. When I first saw the house and grounds from the air, I asked *cim*, "Did you ever think of incarnating as someone poor for a change, just to get the feel for what it might be like?"

The inside of the house was equally impressive. We settled into sleeprooms that were exquisite with luxury and then gathered in the library for lunch. The library was my idea of heaven and featured a generous balcony running around the perimeter. The walls were inland wood-panels between scroll-edged moldings and the ceiling featured a domed skylight made of stained glass. An impressive collection of paper books covered the walls of the upper tier. On floor level, hundreds of scientific books and holospools on genetic enhancement, engineering, and quantum physics lined the shelves. I also found books on Tyrowsian and Ganat philosophy, a handful of books on mysticism and The Occult, poetry by Rainer Maria Rilke, Dulce Cœur, and Jana Pierette. I counted thirty-three books Kayya and Ceff had published on *vitarattha* and vitasphere technology. Like any egotistical writer, I was searching for my books. They owned a copy of *Visions of The Wall*, but none of my others.

To take the chill off the room, Rugen built a fire with real wooden logs in an authentic fireplace. "Please dear, don't make it too large," cautioned Ceff. "I can't stand it when it gets too hot in here."

"Yes mother," Rugen said obediently. It was odd seeing a fireplace in a Tyrowsian home because Tyrowsians preferred cooler temperatures. Rugen explained that *cis* mothers had several heating systems installed throughout the house because they wanted Rugen to be comfortable as a child and they worried about the Ganat servants and their children who were always in and out.

Despite the lovely ambience of Iona, the next few hours were intense. Shortly after building the fire, Rugen went to the massive, carved doors, which separated the library from the front foyer, and shut them. Ceff and Kayya already suspected something was awry. Rugen had told them, via multidex, that a critical situation concerning vitaspheres existed out in the corridor. That's as much as *ce* dared reveal over an open multidex. Now *ce* got ready to break their hearts. When Rugen closed the library doors, Kayya's face fell into a serious expression and she asked, "What's the matter, dear?"

Most of us played interactive roles in explaining the situation; however, Bogwa and Hope were almost silent. Hope's silence was understandable. Her soul mates kept her in the dark about soul-fragment retrieval, but Bogwa's silence seemed more like a terminal case of resignation. Evose appeared to be healthy and was back to being his typical outspoken self. He plunged forward, and for the third time, I sat through his recital concerning soul fragments—how he retrieved them and what happened to Belinda in her previous incarnation as Iris. Ceff and Kayya were unimpressed and admitted, "we already know about soul fragments." However, they reacted with—in their own words— "righteous indignation!" when they heard about the impending rupture that Evose had initiated. "Tell me, Evose," demanded Ceff. "What gives you the right to come into this dimension and begin altering the flow of reality with your interference?"

Bogwa at last spoke up and he was riled. "That accusation is harsh and unfair. Our intentions were of the highest order. Besides, who are you to judge? Look at your manifestations. Trans-Miro Technologies manufactured most of the spacecraft that is destroying the time threads in this area of space."

Ceff's white face blanched whiter. "When we found out which spacecraft were damaging the time threads, we stopped manufacturing them. Period. Now we take extraordinary precautions to make certain Trans-Miro spacecraft does no damage to time threads. *Fisetuss!*" she swore. "Why am I defending our actions with you? Our research is public record. You can't make that claim about what you're doing."

"Wait a minute," said Nova. "We've always known that a strong probability exists that a rupture could occur in this area of space. Knowing that, can't we all admit the obvious? The time threads are damaged. We don't know what's going on in the fourth dimension, but we know the third dimension is governed by time, which we seem to be running out of."

"Thank you," said Belinda. "Even when we know the consequences, see how easy it is to slip into a state of denial?" Ceff and Kayya responded with a quick apology too, but I noticed they continued to feel no real connection to Bogwa or Evose. Ceff and Kayya did have faith in Nova. Nova realized this and started playing a larger role in our discussion. Only now, did I see the powerful force *le* could be. Nova knew how to direct us toward our goal without overwhelming the rest of us. *Le* understood that the ability to lead without force was the highest refinement of will.

Kayya began to sob and Ceff was distressed in her efforts to console Kayya. "*Vitaspheres* are not why we reincarnated," said Kayya. "We incarnated to nurture Rugen's greater evolution. She cursed. "*Hataeasta* takes us low with this unseen variable. Why must we sacrifice our only child? I will go on the mission myself rather than sacrifice *cim*." Nova reminded her that *le* was sacrificing me to the mission as Bogwa and Belinda were sacrificing Evose.

Belinda spoke up and assured them that if they stopped Rugen from piloting the vitasphere that they would be perverting *cis* purpose for reincarnating. It was almost enough and then Rugen pushed Kayya and Ceff over the edge. "Please?" *ce* begged them. "Don't make this harder than it already is. I've decided to attempt this mission and I humbly ask that you respect my decision to go."

****

Despite our enormous doubts, we all pretended that it was possible to go back in time. Some of us were more sold on the notion than others. Even Evose admitted, "Our chances for returning to this time are slim."

Ceff was a scientist and she reminded him, "Your margin is slim to nonexistent,"

According to Kayya, "If any margin exists, it will come from your vitasphere operating at optimum efficiency."

Ceff swore they needed two weeks to equip a vitasphere that she would feel "borderline comfortable" about releasing to us.

"That's too long," insisted Belinda.

After a bit of negotiating, we all agreed to gamble an additional three days to allow Kayya and Ceff to outfit a vitasphere especially for us. Kayya and Ceff wanted to spend the next three days with Rugen. *Ce* went off somewhere with them and came back about an hour later to tell me, "I have some great news, Sante. It seems we will have time to go to Sasaybin." Rugen immediately turned into Miss Efficient. In a whirlwind of activity, *ce* had servants packing food, clothing, and provisions, enough to last three days. Meanwhile, Ceff and Kayya supplied us with enough Regression drug to regress the entire population of Uropae for the next two years.

Nova balked a bit. "Maybe you and Sante should go ahead and enjoy your honeymoon and I'll come later."

"Impossible!" insisted Rugen. "My place on Sasaybin is remote and impossible to find."

Nova explained. "I'm not trying to be difficult, merely considerate."

Rugen agreed that Nova was the most considerate of individuals. "You must realize you're integral to this honeymoon," said Rugen. "Do you need a special invitation?"

"That would be a lovely first gesture," admitted Nova. Rugen responded by kneeling in front of Nova as a humble consort. Nova was embarrassed and huffed, "You certainly don't have to go that far."

"Shut up," said Rugen. "You asked for it." Granted, it was a performance, a combination of consort and Tyrowsian flamboyance with a big dose of total sincerity thrown in for good measure. "Please come?" Rugen begged. "Come and I promise that Sasaybin will tantalize you with her beauty." Rugen pressed *cim*self against Nova's leg and smiled up at *lim* with full and appropriate consort submission.

Nova put *lis* hand under Rugen's chin and stroked *cis* throat. It was as obvious as daylight that Rugen's display was arousing Nova and he leaned over and kissed Rugen on the cheek. "Say yes," I said.

"Yes," said Nova.

****

Two hours later, our cruiser pierced Sasaybin's atmosphere and leveled off. Clearly, we were approaching a world where sentient life was a footnote. "About a half-dozen ornithologists and entomologists do research here at any one time," Rugen mentioned. "Sasaybin has only one permanent resident, an old Ganat that lives alone about five hundred kilometers from here. Counting us, the population, right now, is probably around ten."

Nova had that faraway look of someone experiencing a past-life memory when he said, "This place is perfect. I can feel it. Sasaybin has no static. We have three days to achieve alignment so the less static, the easier it will be for us to make every connection."

"Is that what we are doing—aligning?" asked Rugen.

"Yeah!" said Nova and *le* added, "In three days we're going to know each other in ways we can't now imagine."

We landed at a place that was nothing more than a clearing in a tropical rainforest. The leaves on the trees were an intense and succulent green and seemed to be as big as elephant's ears. A warm rain was falling. Nova insisted rain was an excellent omen, a blessing from the consciousness of Sasaybin for our arrival. We brought a hovercraft with us to travel inside the atmosphere to Rugen's place, which *ce* explained was a short eight-

133

minute-hop across the rainforest. Nova and I wanted to go outside and stretch our legs while Rugen backed the hovercraft off the rear of the shuttle. We stepped outside and Rugen warned, "Don't go far. It might be dangerous."

Nova froze in *lis* footsteps. "How dangerous?"

"Think wild and dangerous animals with teeth as long as your thumb."

As if on cue, a resounding "yawk, yawk, yawk," came from nearby. I jumped and let out a loud explicative. My reaction made Rugen collapse in peals of laughter. "Look over there," *ce* pointed. On a tree, about eight meters away, sat an enormous bird. It was black and possessed a gigantic orange-colored beak, almost the length of its body.

"Does that surviving pterodactyl eat meat?" asked Nova.

Rugen wiped tears of laughter from *cis* eyes. "It's a female birn-birn. She eats only fish, but don't go far. Other creatures out there aren't so tame."

Nova made a silly face. "Damn! Maybe we should have put up with the static and checked into a nice hotel on Uropae."

"No, my place is perfect," insisted Rugen. The birn-birn was the solitary indignant that came out to greet us, but I could hear the chatter of abundant life hidden in the lush fecundity. It was flirting, arguing, and calling to its loved ones to return to the burrow and nest.

****

From the air, Rugen's place first appeared as a primitive dwelling with a large deck attached to one end. The entire structure sat on enormous support poles that elevated the living space to a height of about twenty meters off the ground. Rugen landed the hovercraft on the deck and when we deplaned, we found ourselves standing among the upper limbs of the forest trees. The ground sloped down to the west where there was an open view to the sky. While Nova and I carried provisions inside, Rugen slid down a rope to ground level and connected the solar energy-collectors to the household current. I stood by the railing and watched as *ce* shinnied back up the rope. While hanging by one hand, *ce* blew me a kiss with the other. "Be careful," I yelled.

"Relax," *ce* sang like a bird. "I'm fine." I pulled *cim* up to safety and helped *cim* brush the cobwebs off *cis* shoulders and legs. "We need to be careful with our energy consumption," *ce* explained. "Some of the cells need a recharge since I've last been here. We have enough power to refrigerate our perishables and run some electrical fans, but beyond that, we'll not have many conveniences."

Sasaybin was hot and humid. By the time we finished carrying everything inside, sweat poured off our faces and down our bodies. Rugen took us on a quick tour as we helped open windows to cool the interior. Rugen's place was primitive; but as always—where and when Rugen was creating—very lovely. The ceilings were high and vaulted to facilitate air circulation. The huge screened windows throughout enhanced the sensation of being one with this world. We found one sleeproom, a combination sitting and eating area, a bath, and toilet cubicle. Up a stairway was a screened loft that cleared the tree canopy, which Rugen used as a *neipanin*. The décor throughout was light and breezy with simple furniture woven from sturdy reeds. We brought plenty of pillows, sheets, towels and a few blankets with us and now we scattered them around to make the rough furniture a bit more comfortable. "This place is perfect," said Nova.

I was uncertain about what was going to happen here on Sasaybin. However successful our "alignment," might be, right attitude needed to direct the experience. Right attitude meant we needed to relax and enjoy ourselves, yet we also needed to be serious. We knew of only one way to find the balance between relaxation and seriousness and that was through meditation. Nothing could be rushed or faked and we needed to start at the beginning. We bathed and put on clean, loose-fitting clothing and went upstairs to the *neipanin* where Rugen lit a wand of sweet incense. We assumed positions a bit different for this meditation. We usually did not touch each other while meditating, but this time we sat in a tight circle allowing our knees to have gentle contact. Rugen was to my left and Nova sat to my right. Rugen joined *cis* palms together and bowed toward Nova, telling *lim*, "I acknowledge you as my soul mate and surrender to your greater will."

Nova replied, "Thank you for inviting me here, into your sanctum sanctorum." *Le* joined *lis* palms and bowed *lis* head toward Rugen. "I acknowledge you as my soul mate and surrender to your genius of understanding." Then Nova turned to me and said, "I acknowledge you as my soul mate and surrender to your love."

I bowed my head to Rugen and told *cim*, "My precious angel, I acknowledge you as my soul mate and surrender to your understanding."

The remaining commitment needed to come from me and go to Nova and I felt as if I was about to utter the most important words of my many lives. I took my time and they waited until I said, "My beloved Nova, we are one. I surrender to your will."

We moved deeper into the meditation and greater silence gathered around us and sheltered us from the teeming life. Nova opened as the primary channel and *lis* energy was clean and elegant. It came directly through my right knee where it nourished me and dined upon my love. I did not hold onto the energy, but allowed it to flow through me and into Rugen. When it came around the second time, I had fresh resolve and knowledge of myself. As the energy moved through me, I scoured myself for any bit of resistance, perversion, or distortion that might sour the milky purity of this great energy. That took time and infinite patience and I could not fake the process. However long it took, I would sit there and reclaim my shadows and answer the questions within myself. Only then did I have the privilege to emerge into the infinite and join my soul mates. Nova and Rugen were doing the same.

****

As committed soul mates, we were quiet and gentle with each other. No words clouded our purpose. We put a few blankets and pillows down on the floor to make it a bit more comfortable for our Regression trip. We wanted to continue giving ourselves away to each other and did not hesitate. Nova showed me how to insert the ampoule of Regression into Rugen's nose. I waited for Rugen's permission. "Do it," *ce* said and I pressed the release valve.

Nova did not give me a chance to panic although the instant Rugen breathed in, *ce* was gone, dead, no longer in *cis* body, and that gave me a moment of doubt. Nova put an ampoule of Regression up my virgin nose. *Le* was holding me so tightly I did not know if I could inhale. "I'm not going to run away," I promised.

Nova said something in an ancient tongue, "*I oou jadjoy hoidpa,*" but I did not know what *le* meant. Then Regression took me and I was vaguely aware that, an instant later, Nova administered *lis* own medicine. Then Regression laid me open to the truth. I know; they know; we all know the truth.

****

Hearing is acute as it melds with other senses to become burnished matter. I can see! I'm floating in an expanse of vague grays. Something is tinkering with my DNA, continually probing me—quick flashes, fluid lives, and watery deaths.

Inside life, I squat inside a dark cave. My exquisite sense of smell appreciates the mingled odors of blood, earth, and smoke: it's home. I am giving birth and groan because it hurts, but the pain vanishes as soon as I hold the newborn in my arms. Instinct arises like spiritual insight, as I put the newborn to my breast. A blue-eyed man of enormous physical stature watches from nearby while he tends a great blazing fire in the mouth of the cave. He is dressed in the wooly hide of an animal and singing incantations of praise to the Great Mother of Creation for his first child. "I oou jadjoy hoidpa," he sings, which means, "I and thou! Great praise to Her!" The man is Nova; the female child I hold is Rugen. Snap!

In another life, my village is burning and marauding barbarians from somewhere I've learned to call "Nort" are upon us. The invaders are barbarians and their clothing is made of metal. I smell their stink as they slash and burn. Terror rules, life or death, do or die, fight or flight! Nova is dead; his throat cut a moment before. I flee—heart hammering against my breathless lungs. A fragile newborn clings to my flabby breast. The child ceased crying days before. It has known my dried breast for days and now is starving. This child stands for legions of others that carelessly stepped into life. This is her first foray as a Human, but she will die this morning along with me. A wooden spear, as thick as the Mongolian warrior's arm that threw it, pierces my chest. Snap! I'm dead, but cannot leave the soul of the infant, the one who came for an innocent taste of life but now must go home in thirst.

I carry fear and unresolved pain into my next life as a female. I'm angry, smart, and out-spoken and have told more than one man that he is an ignorant waste. I'm an army of one as the women of this time stay locked in their prisons and lend me no support. Men call me witch and spit in my face, but they think of me while they fuck their wives. A posse of men arrives at my cottage door and we argue about some herbs I've given to one of their wives. Soon others come and take me away to put me to "the test." I feel inescapable terror now. My cowardly torturers blind me with the hot blade of a sword to hide their shame before my eyes. They call my eyes wonton and full of the devil as they take my sight. My eyes are blue and reflect their cruelty. They want me to betray others, but eviscerate me before I can. Snap! Again, I linger with the body and watch as the crowd of men chant, "Kita, the devil's whore, is finally dead!" I turn away, but the men cheer and drink as ravenous vultures consume my naked entrails.

"Remember!"

I sense a vast openness now, a space I cannot see with physical eyes. I know my name is Chwang and my home is Northern China. My life is quiet, ordered, simple, and direct. I've been blind since birth. "It's karmic blindness," say the elders of the village, "something caused in her previous life." My blindness helps me develop my other senses and I earn my way as a healer with my intuitive skills. Snap!

Dust chokes my throat and the smell of the street fills my nostrils. I'm a man, a slave. The mistress of the house has sent me to the agora to barter for fruit; but I hear great commotion and see crowds of excited people standing around. "What's happening?" I ask a passerby.

"The Muse of Eloquence and Truth is about to speak," he says. I push through the crowd and see him. Candidus! He is a blonde demigod. I try to get closer to hear his words.

"All we have are our actions and our freewill to express them," he tells the crowd. His words fill me with new ideas and hope. He makes me feel strong about myself and tells me that I have the power within myself to recognize truth when I hear it. He talks about honor in all that we do, whether we are freeman or slave. And he introduces me to an idea he calls Community. Love pours out of my heart for Candidus; but when he glances my way, I lower my eyes in shame. I do not want him to see my lust when I'm a lowly slave.

The next day, in late morning, I'm on my way home from the agora. I walk past a small inn near the Piraean Gate and see him sitting in the courtyard with his favored companions, eating the midday meal. His disciples are men and a couple of women, and even a freed slave. I recognize the woman Rachael, another Babylonian like me—free only because a Greek took her as wife. I know the master will punish me—whip me when I return home late with the lemons and pears; still, I stop and go inside. The greasy-looking innkeeper, with the goiter on his neck, stops me. "What's a Babylonian goat doing off his chain?" he sneers my way.

I give him a well-practiced look of total submission. "I have a delivery from the agora for one of your customers." Holding up the basket of fruit, he waves me to come ahead.

Despite my fear, I push on, going through a low doorway to the courtyard where he sits. The mere sight of his profile makes me feel warm inside my heart. The right side of his face is smiling because Rachel just said something clever. He takes a long draw of wine from his tin cup and sets it, just so, on the table. I approach, but he does not notice me until I kneel by his side. I stare at his dusty feet, laced up with sandals because I'm afraid to look up, afraid that he will see my lust. Desire floods me with delusions of grandeur. My dream is to make love to him and have his eloquence tell me how it feels. I need to find the courage to look at him and I summon my nerve and do. His eyes are waiting—two orbs of blue perfection. "I want to be your disciple," I stutter. "If you let me be your disciple in the same truth and honor that you speak of in public, then, I will love you. I am slave, yet no one can enslave my love. Say yes, and I will follow you freely with my heart, no matter who enslaves my body."

His friends laugh and he looks embarrassed, but he does not push me away. He touches my forehead and says, "Perhaps I should become your disciple." He asks my name.

"I have no name; but my master calls me fool."

"Get up," he tells me. "Your name from now on will be Victory."

He looks serious and then turns abruptly away. When he turns back, he says, "Go now, leave me alone. This may be a public place, but I'm in a private mood."

I'm devastated and feel humiliated and when I get up the fruit spills to the floor. I slink away in total defeat. I know now that a slave has an ego, however battered. Later, I enjoy the stinging blows of the master's whip. I howl in confused irony as I reach orgasm as he beats me. He locks me in the earthy smelling root cellar for the night—a taste of death for the body. I sit in the pitch darkness and plan suicide. I will steal a knife from the kitchen, cut my wrists, then throw myself into the sea for good measure; or I will get a vial of poison from the witches. "I want out!" I scream, but have made no sound.

Long past eventide, past the time when upright citizens might call unannounced, Candidus comes to the master's door alone. He flatters the master with words and flatters me by paying too much. It becomes legal as money and documents change hands.

Outside in the darkness, I stand before this demigod smelling of sweat, blood, semen, and body filth. "What am I going to do with you?" he asks.

Near midnight, we arrive at his villa on a hill above Athens. I feel heavy with sleep and no longer care that I am filthy. I am content to be by his side as he instructs me to be silent and still. His elaborate kindness is foreign to me for I was born a slave and all my masters were incarnations of twisted will. I'm smart enough to recognize that Candidus is different. My sensitivity, hidden away for protection, comes out to dance in the moonlight of the Greek hillsides.

Crickets sing love songs from their niches along the walls that surround his elaborate house. His rich mansion sits with other rich mansions in a special section of the city. He shows me the way through the rear courtyard and a few servants rush out to greet us, but he tells them, "Go back to bed." Water splashes in a small nearby fountain as we stand together in the darkness. "We meet as two men on equal ground," he tells me. Then he moves farther away so I can barely see him in the sweet summer darkness. "Sometimes, at night, I'm afraid," he admits. "You are free, Victory; but I invite you to spend the night with me in any way you feel appropriate."

"I want to make love to you," I tell him.

He makes me take a bath before I do. He helps me. Afterward, he puts an unguent on the cuts my previous master inflicted on my back and dabs perfume behind my ears and on my neck. He makes it clear to me in nonverbal ways that he wants me to run the show. While we are making love, I make a critical jump in my mind. Laughing inside myself, I realize my love for him has made me a slave again in short order.

The next morning, he slips a golden ring on my finger, a clear symbol of freedom for a freed slave. I wonder how many times he has done this before and with how many different men. I ask him about it and he sighs and looks away in shame. "I'm different," I tell him. "I will not leave you as the others have. Let me stay with you, Candidus. I'm the one you've been looking for and I'm the one that can take you directly through passion's doorway—I swear."

After that, we never leave each other. They allow me to go with him to Mycenae after his arrest. I act as his public slave even in exile. I do not own his mind; I know that. He keeps his mind away from me in the daytime. At night, together we discharge the poison from our souls through acts of desperate passion. I adore him on every level; I love him most in those areas I do not understand. Snap!

My name is Chosoray and I am a Shardasko Warrior. Life is clear and cold on this Gathosian world. Vision is rich ocher, burnt sienna, and gold by the light of oil lamps. My robe is dark scarlet and permeated with the scent of incense. I hear the scraping of brass cymbals calling me, clanging sounds, and the chanting of brothers catches my ear. "Oui, waaaaaaaaay Oiu Chosrje. OOOOOOOO. Oui. Waaaaaaaay. We recite together,

"Without understanding, I cannot comply.
Without a master, I am without mind or talent.
Without love, there is no ritual or compassion.
Without awakening, there is no reality.
Without intuitive enlightenment, nothing is found.

I am understanding and compliance.
I am master with talent and mind.
I am love in ritual and compassion.
I am the awakened one.
I am reality.
I am intuitive enlightenment.
I am and everything is found."

Snap! I sit as a hawk on my master's gloved hand. He gets drunk and calls me "Ezek," while I watch the world for him. Sometimes he leans forward and strokes the side of my feathered head with his gloved finger. Then he calls me "the light of his soul." He is my roost until adventure calls me to flight. Then I show off for him, fly higher, do *wingovers. I am an acrobat held in his trust. Between us, all our love lies in that trust. His morals are not my morals, yet I trust him to decide. He has taught me to fly off and invade people's chambers. I sift through their jewelry sorting the worthless trinkets from the jewels, bringing back what's of true value to him. Snap!*

My name is Sante, a genetically engineered C3 Janaforma lifegiver. I'm fifteen bio-years old and Nova is sixteen. We already know how we feel about each other, but we both are virgins. We go on a camping trip together to Hattonia with the express purpose of consummating our love. Nova excites me with some well-chosen love patter and then we masturbated each other until we shoot our loads. We eat a meal of vegetables toasted on the ends of sticks as we sit by the fire and admit to each other how lucky we are to be in love.

"Remember!" insists my oversoul.

"Let's leave it at that," I say, but the power of Regression burns the forgetfulness away and reveals the pain. Nova is leaving me now, deserting me because our genetic makeup is too close to guarantee healthy children. My begging cim *to stay drives* cim *farther away. "I hate you!" I tell* cim. *"Once you told me that you had been hunting me for centuries and now you tell me you're leaving me because of genetic incompatibility."*

"Remember!" says my oversoul.

I returned to my body and found myself in intimate contact, lying between Nova and Rugen. "Don't move," cautioned Nova. "Rugen is still in process."

"How long?" I whispered.

"About four minutes, the process time afterward was about fifty minutes?"

"Four minutes?" It seemed almost as long as the first time I lived through it. I stared out through the large screened windows. My physical eyes sought patterns, but there were none. Vision was lost in the tangle of rainforest shadows. Each of us moves within our infinite darkness, aware and unaware.

****

I heard the rain stop, anticipated the last fragile drip-drop before it splashed against the roof. Afterward, the late afternoon went pianissimo and crept closer, nestling in at the corners of our dwelling. Rugen emerged from *cis* Regression trip and rolled over on *cis* back, *cis* limbs opening like a flower. Golden wands of light seeped through the screens and fell across *cis* angelic face. Even now, *ce* was heroically handsome. *Ce* sighed, *cis* voice but a whisper, "By what gesture could you ever know the depth of my total devotion to you?" *ce* asked.

Despite the heat, the three of us moved closer. An aperitif of what might come moved through my mind. *To make love, in love, was all I ever wanted.* We were high on spirit and it was as intoxicating as any drug. We wanted to make physical love, but all we could do was embrace. We eased our minds down into our bodies and indulged in a simple meal of bread, cheese, and fresh fruit. We drank a bottle of sparkling *lume* wine. Nova poured the garnet-colored effervescence into three stemmed glasses and lifted *lis* in a toast to our reunion. "My personal integration would be incomplete without all you've given me," *le* said. *Lis* remark was so simple that I almost missed the importance of what *le* meant; however, Ezek began screeching in alarm. "You both have completed me," said Nova. "Now I plan to open my personal integration and include you both. I want this more than anything I ever wanted before." With that, Nova tapped *lis* wineglass with ours and we drank.

I had a difficult time swallowing. "What will happen if you open your personal integration to us?" I asked.

"We will be one," said Nova.

"You mean you'll die?" asked Rugen.

Nova's mouth crinkled into an ironic smile. "You think you can trick me with that koan? My head will not fit through that harness anymore. Anyway, I want to talk about something more exciting than biological death. We began to eat and it was a meal like no other. Rugen was ravenous and full of questions while the lump in my throat kept me mostly quiet. As Nova spoke *le* became a concentration of *lis* true self, accompanied by the most light-hearted mood I ever witnessed in *lim*. "I am very proud of you both!" *le* exclaimed. "Do you know the greatest virtue you hold in common—your ability to go on incarnating despite the frustration of your driving purpose?" Nova laughed and *lis* laugh was that of a born lover, not an incarnation of will.

"So you experienced every moment of our Regression trips?" I asked.

"Every moment," Nova assured us. Realizing that Nova could get inside me and experience my reality, I felt naked in a new way.

"I'm not proud of some of my lives," I admitted.

"Nonsense!" Nova exclaimed. "You're brave, curious, and experimental. With that kind of energy, you are bound to get into a bit of trouble."

"I sensed something vague from my Regression trip," said Rugen, "something that's still confusing me. I feel as if I have a stronger connection to Sante than I do to you. Does that mean I'm a soul-fragment of Sante and Sante is a soul fragment of you?"

"Your conclusion is wrong and it's my fault," said Nova. "Sante was on target when *le* said I had not embraced *lim* with the same intensity *le* embraced me. I'm down off my pedestal and I intend to keep coming down until we embrace on every level. Your perceptions happened as they did because my will was coming to you partly through Sante. You are a soul fragment, but not exclusively of Sante or exclusively of me. We each are soul fragments of our oversoul. Even our oversoul is a fragment; but please understand, our creation was not an accident. We were created consciously, for exploration, love, and enhanced perspective."

"You magnanimity sounds like the voice of our oversoul," said Rugen.

"Occasionally, I take it upon myself to speak for the whole; however, assuming the ultimate perspective has a cost to my personal self."

"Are you talking about the destruction of the ego?" asked Rugen.

Nova admitted, "The destruction of the ego is just the beginning."

Rugen admitted, "My ego has destroyed me, not once but several times."

The ominous feeling that this integration would cost Nova *lis* physical life grew stronger. Fear of losing *lim* joined the conjunction of my senses and told me Nova was walking on a dangerous edge. I was hungry to know truths too, but did not want to lose the physical Nova in the process. "Without an ego, I think we'd all be rather dull," I said. "Bejan once told me the ego was like an aggressive garden shrub that needed regular pruning to keep it within bounds, but we tolerate the shrub because it's a beautiful addition to the garden. I think *ce* was right." I thought it was a safe topic to keep talking about Bejan, so I asked, "Can you tell me why I have such a strong connection to Bejan? Since *cis* death, I sometimes hear *cim* speaking to me, especially in my dreams."

"You're both love emanations," said Nova. "Your interactions with *cis* soul, were, are, and will continue to be for mutual evolution." Nova laughed with total delight. "Love did its post-graduate work in Bejan. It will be fascinating to see what Love has in store for you."

"I experienced a few Regression memories of Bejan too," said Rugen. "But I had stronger memories of Michael, which is strange because I barely knew *cim* in this life."

"Your energy vibrations match Michael's and again the lessons, were, are, and will be for mutual evolution."

"Who dominates your Regression trips?" I asked Nova.

"My strongest memories are of you and Elay. My energy vibrations match Elay's and our interactions were, are, and will be for enhanced will. It's natural for our most significant memories to be of soul mates, no matter who or what we might remember; however, what each of us believes to be our exclusive memories may actually be memories from our own soul mates. When a life dies, it is shared in a soul banquet where the memories of the life are shared and the karmic burdens are dispersed to newly developing lives for resolution."

"So we come into this life with our own karma plus a karmic burden from soul mates?" asked Rugen.

"Yes," said Nova. "In my humble opinion, being able to participate in this soul banquet between our lives is the greatest moment in the soul's evolution. To compare it to anything I can describe with words, is inadequate."

"Try," insisted Rugen.

Nova laughed. "It's impossible I tell you. The best I can do is paste a few inadequate analogies over the process and therefore cloud its absolute glory."

"I want to hear your analogies," Rugen declared.

Nova stared at Rugen with the tender expression of a sensitive lover. "You want poetry, not the truth."

"Don't leave us hanging," urged Rugen. "Give us a few clues."

Nova shrugged and reeled off, "Okay, its rapture is ten thousand times better than any sexual orgasm you've ever experienced. It's stepping out into space minus a *vitarattha* and living through the adventure. It's rose petals falling away from the stem. It's the dark and the light becoming one. As Renée suggested, it's like playing hide-and-seek and finally being found." Nova hesitated and *lis* voice turned delicate. "Truly, it is this moment here, with you now." *Le* went back to nonchalant. "Sorry, that's the best I can do."

"I want to hear more about this soul banquet," Rugen urged.

"When an oversoul incarnates a soul, it comes into existence with a wealth of inherent knowledge," said Nova. "This knowledge is conscious, emotional, intuitive, and spiritual. The soul can participate fully in the banquet because the ego-personality is unmasked as the illusion it is. From our incarnate perspective, we have a tendency to judge experience as good or bad; but from the perspective of our oversoul, everything has value."

"What about linear reincarnation?" Rugen asked. "Evose told Sante that an oversoul can reincarnate a particular soul—for example the historical Cle—anytime it wants."

"I respectfully declare that Evose is incorrect. Beings are as complex as a universe and are rare works of art. We will never see the historical Cle walking around in this time, just as we will never see another Dulce Cœur, Albert Einstein, or Leonardo di Vinci. Every soul is born with unique gifts; however, these gifts are in raw, undeveloped forms. It's our responsibility to use these gifts and develop them into tools. These tools will help solve the riddles of our lives. Cœur, Einstein, and di Vinci did have something in common that many of us lack and that is an unquenchable curiosity. When curiosity takes our potential and leads us into the realm of possibility, the brain makes new connections."

"I asked because I'm the only one, as far as I know, that believes *ce* was the historical Cle," Rugen said.

"I must admit you possess more Cle patterning than anyone I've ever seen before. Cle brands your soul, but you are not Cle. You are an ensemble of reciprocity with the memories of Cle that was refined by our oversoul. I believe that if it were possible to reincarnate someone into a historical identity that it would be redundant, boring, and stagnant, a true state of death. We know that third dimensional creation is unique, unrepeatable, and evolving, yet soul groups create new lives based upon established templates, or guidelines. Cle's life was great and regarded as a treasure within our soul group. Your soul has chosen to reincarnate again through this Cle template and the more you do this, the more persistent that template becomes within you."

"Can you tell us anything new about Evose?" asked Rugen. "Is he processing denial from the fourth dimension as Belinda's claims?"

"What's in the greatest is mirrored in the smallest," said Nova. "Or, Evose is mirroring the rupture between the dimensions in himself."

Rugen admitted, "Something about Evose and Belinda continue to annoy me. They act as if they have a monopoly on the truth and have nothing left to learn. Is Belinda as enlightened as she claims?"

"You should examine your annoyance concerning Belinda and attempt to understand why she seems troublesome to you. Your irritation means she offers you a lesson that you need to learn. Pay attention and you will find out what it is; ignore it and you will miss a valuable opportunity. Belinda is a bodhisattva, but so are Kayya, Ceff, and Una. Bodhisattva means that within one incarnation, the oversoul is manifesting an entourage of refined will, love, and wisdom. The amalgamated soul of the bodhisattva, of course, has the choice to reincarnate and devote itself to helping others reach integration. However, when the bodhisattva reincarnates, with that mission in mind, it might take ten thousand years and fifty thousand more incarnations to complete its mission. A chance exists that the bodhisattva might lose its way. Perhaps Belinda became so involved with her goal, she neglected parts of herself along the way. It's lamentable for any person to believe they have arrived at a point of absolute perfection where it's unnecessary to scrutinize motivation. The bodhisattva needs to be especially vigilant or fall from grace."

I finally decided to mention the missing time and get Nova's views.

"Ah yes!" *le* exclaimed. "It's incredible that you noticed. You never flinch—do you, Sante? Hope was correct when she said Bogwa was not playing by the rules of this universe. The problem started about thirty years ago when he did something that, in retrospect, maybe he should not have done. Aeternus lay in ruin then. It was nothing but pieces of junk floating around out in space. Elay led a mission to Aeternus to see if she could recover its multidex core. The team managed to locate the core, but while they still had boots on the ground, Aeternus started breaking apart." Nova sighed and bit *lis* lip. "Elay fell down a deep crevasse on Aeternus. She died down in that chasm and Bogwa found her and brought her back to life. She was pregnant with Una at the time and Michael, Bejan, and I loved her so much that we were afraid to question the propriety or immorality of the action. We were grateful to get her back."

"So that's why Bogwa said Elay was always impatient to go home."

Nova looked sad for a moment. "She experienced many close calls in the Vanguard."

"What was supposed to happen instead?" asked Rugen.

Nova shrugged. "I don't know. The only reality I know is she lived and we enjoyed a life together. Is it real? I hope so. Anyway, to answer Sante's specific question about the missing time, Bogwa made a jump between the time threads. He stepped out of this universe, went out into the corridor between the third and fourth dimension, and removed the denial or soul fragments clinging to Evose. He left them there and then came back to this universe. The only problem with doing that is he cannot separate either Evose or himself from the equation. Every time he removes denial from Evose, he also removes parts of Evose and therefore parts of himself. In other words, parts of Evose and Bogwa and Hope are now out in the corridor too."

****

Rugen was thoughtful. "If we are one, then the separation of the soul from its fragments must be an illusion too."

"You're correct," said Nova. "However, we can disregard the difficult and uncomfortable quite easily. We know a million ways to ignore the truth."

Rugen seemed on a roll and said, "Tell me more, Nova. How do you know these things? To me, it seems as if you are important to our oversoul in a special way. Why were you trusted with more knowledge than we were? The genius to create the Janaforma was yours alone. Why?"

Nova smiled. "I adore you Candidus. Your fifth chakra is brilliant and demanding. Understand, I am not criticizing you; actually, it's quite stimulating being in your presence. I always try to be articulate, but it's impossible to explain because truth is beyond the scope of our current language. Nevertheless, I will try my best. If you know me, then you know yourselves. As you first sensed me as your will, I sensed you as my mind and passion. We came from a vast universe before time, but I know no name I can attribute to this vastness. My earliest awareness is of my will consciousness, the oldest part of us. Sante awoke and joined me, but we did not come here straightaway, even though Sante was quickening my passion to explore. We waited until you awoke too and brought forth our greater consciousness. When the intermingling of will, understanding, and passion were complete, we were three separate souls and had one purpose—to evolve. We incarnated here to explore the greater depths of love and understanding through the freedom of our own will. It has been one hell of a struggle; but that is our only mission. After eons of testing, I'm certain you will agree when I say, we did our best to realize and complete ourselves."

"What about our pending trip to the past?" Rugen asked. "Are we undertaking a fool's mission?"

Nova smiled softly. "We're always undertaking the fool's mission."

"You know what I mean," insisted Rugen.

Nova apologized. "I am not the kind of psychic Una and Sante are."

"What kind of psychic are you?" I asked.

Nova was completely candid. "People have a difficult time deceiving me when I step back and become their witness."

"What does your witness tell you about Evose?" asked Rugen. "I don't know if I want to attempt this mission with Evose. I'm a Vanguard Scout. Scouts might go on fool's missions, but we do not go with people we do not trust."

"Mark my words," said Nova. "Evose will not be able to make this trip. He is too ill. Hope will go with you."

Le had said it! *Le* was not going with us. Nova's actual physical presence was the most precious thing in my universe and I was going to lose *lim* again, this time in just a few hours. "Hope!" Rugen exclaimed. "She's a hothouse flower. She can't fly or navigate."

I felt as if Nova had slapped me. "I don't think I can handle being separated from you again," I said.

"Can you name what will make it right?" asked Nova.

"I don't know." It was quiet amongst us as Nova continued staring at me, asking me with an enigmatic expression to explain. We were so close, yet I wanted to be closer. Something in me responded to my frustration. I wanted to tear off the few clothes I was wearing and run naked through the rainforest, to feel the primitive satisfaction of innocent abandon. "I need to make physical love with you," I said. This was always my solution to the neediness in me that never went away.

Nova leaned across the small table and kissed me between the eyes. *Lis* will at that moment was the strength of Atlas holding up my entire existence. "Continue to open up to me, Sante, and I will heal this wanting inside you—I swear!" *Le* rose from *lis* chair, leaned over me, and gave me a gentle hug. "I swear."

I tried to explain my need so Rugen might understand and Nova could sooth my need away. "It must be my frailty, my clinging."

"It is not clinging!" said Nova. "It's *watarie*." Perhaps the Cuneate word did come closer to explaining what I felt. What is *watarie*? It is the tugging of our heartstrings when faced with the fleeting moment. It's feeling the loss of what even our oversoul cannot recreate. *Watarie* was the reaction of our soul to the truth that there is nothing we can hang onto and accepting it with its full pain and glory.

> In twilight mist of autumn,
> one golden leaf silently drifts to earth.

Watarie Scents, Kale Ranpa; poet; 10:27-11:33; Tyrowsian, Pybatium.

TEN

Rugen began to ask more questions about Hope and then Nova stopped *cim* short. "Please! For the time being, let's allow the future to handle itself. I want to come back to the here and now so the three of us can create something beautiful that we can cherish." The three of us came down into the practical. We cleaned the dishes and stored the unused portions of food away in a safe place. Afterward, we spent time on the deck looking across the treetops and listening to the chatter of exuberant life in the jungle beyond.

The chronos god of Sasaybin was alien to me; but the natural rhythms of the day/night cycles were familiar. Evening came gradually, leaking its inky darkness into the light, stirring in the most unimaginable shades of indigo and green. It was a gentle nudge, a reminder that our first day on this small world was nearly complete. It was here during the last moments of twilight that our physical honeymoon began and it was a honeymoon beyond my wildest dreams. It was useless to pretend we were virgin lovers. Playing coy brought no satisfaction to my greater soul. We did not need Regression to tell us we already had expressed our love for each other in every way incarnate beings could make love. Now, it was inappropriate to put on self-conscious masks with soul mates. We came out of hiding and were beyond the sexual limits of man, woman, child, master, or slave. We were total lovers.

Sasaybin entertained us, sang us passionate ragas to set the mood. We gradually allowed ourselves to come into gentle contact. No dominance, no construct, no grasping desire, no goal to our lovemaking impeded this all-night affair. Our hearts were beating, our breaths moving and our love juices flowing. All senses were awake and keen with desire. In that perfumed atmosphere of freedom, our oversoul descended into our presence as an answered prayer. Our surrender to greater and greater intimacy came naturally. We gave everything away and everything returned to us in exponential bursts of joy. When the final organism took us, the air around us was tinged pink with delight.

Awe filled Rugen's voice when *ce* whispered, "What we could not do alone, we did together." We had brought our oversoul into physical matter with our complete surrender. The greater consciousness shattered our sense of solitude. What name would this consciousness wear before us but Love? Through Love, I was Rugen, Nova, and truly myself. I realized my most intimate self within my lovers. I fell asleep in that knowledge and slept for almost ten hours with no memory of dreams.

****

In the morning, I awoke in a pool of my own sweat. "Get up," Nova was saying. "Rugen wants to take us on an adventure." After breakfast, we climbed aboard the hovercraft and flew to a new location about twenty-five minutes away. Rugen was secretive about where we were going and contagious childish-delight made *cim* appear even younger. "It's a surprise, my bonding gift to you both," *ce* insisted. I played along and soothed Ezek so as not to ruin the fun.

We landed in a clearing and I was not sure how Rugen could find *cis* way around on a planet that seemed to be one confusing entanglement of vegetative life. We climbed out at the new location and it looked exactly like where we lifted off. Rugen retrieved a bamboo stick, about a meter long, from the rear of the plane and explained, "Just in case we meet any wild animals along the trail."

"Don't you have a stungun?" asked Nova.

"We don't need fancy gadgets," Rugen said. Vanguard Scouts were the epitome of fancy gadgets, yet Rugen was relying on a bamboo stick to scare the predators away. It was steaming hot and insects kept buzzing around our heads. We did resort to a bit of advanced technology in this area. Rugen produced a can of insect repellant and sprayed us from head to toe. Whatever the formula, the insects kept their distance, which was about an intimate two centimeters from my face.

We found a narrow trail that needed clearing in spots. Our hiking was slow because of the intense heat. To me, everything about this place was new and alien. The enormous trees were daunting and supported tiny ecosystems along their craggy trunks and branches. Vines wandered here and there until they found a sunny spot, where they would open their huge umbrella leaves. Some fifteen minutes later, Rugen stopped along the trail and made some obvious noise by rapping *cis* bamboo stick on the side of a tree. It made a clunking reverberation that sang through the rainforest. Then *ce* cupped *cis* mouth and yelled, "Tanicos come!" Rugen explained,

"We must wait here until the signal comes that we might draw nearer."

Ezek was eager so I allowed him to reach out a short distance away. Ezek sensed magnificence, transcendent frolic, and the animation of the mundane by the spirit of total divinity. Something big was about to happen and it all felt good to Ezek.

Everything went silent. Even the birds in the trees took a respite from their songs. A moment later, a huge parrot-like bird, with green plumage came swooping down from the treetops and dove straight for our heads. Nova and I instinctively ducked and began to retreat. "It's okay!" shouted Rugen. The large bird landed on Rugen's shoulder and managed to knock *cim* off balance for a moment. The bird was at least a meter tall and possessed a lethal-looking curved beak. Its talons alone were almost the diameter of one of my fingers. "Tanicos, tell your master that Rugen is here."

"Go away!" Tanicos squawked.

"Tell your master that Rugen is here with *cis* soul mates," Rugen insisted.

"Go away!" Tanicos said again. This time the bird flapped its wings in agitation and Rugen protected *cis* eyes with *cis* hand.

"Go tell your master that Rugen is here with potential heat."

"I will go tell my master that three fools just arrived to eat his jhap biscuits," said Tanicos and the bird flew off like a loaded space tanker.

The unruffled Rugen was enjoying our confusion. "Close your mouth," *ce* told me, "You're going to swallow a bug."

"What was that?" asked Nova.

"Tanicos is merely part of the show," said Rugen. In the distance, I heard the deep gonging of a bell. "We're being invited to come ahead." We hiked a short distance and approached an opening in the vegetation. In the center sat a rough weather-beaten dwelling with a couple of tiny windows near its middle. A simple stairway ran up one side. As far as dwellings go, this one lacked any semblance of grace, beauty, or style. It was crude, a square box sitting on several massive poles to raise the structure off the jungle floor.

"Who disturbs my immersion in Heat!" thundered a voice from above. I glanced up and an enormous head with an equally enormous face peered back from one of the tiny windows.

"Greetings," shouted Rugen.

With that, the head let loose the thunderous laugh of a giant. The laugh rolled down from above like a boulder and was so loud I expected wildlife to scatter and maybe even tree limbs to fall. "Do my *premis* and *yant** lose their will?" the creature bellowed. "Do my eyes grow dim

---

*Premis and *yant* meaning, "penis and testicles."; language origin, E'tof.

with age?"

"Of course not!" returned Rugen. "You are forever young."

"Impossible!" boomed the voice. "The last time you were here your *premis* was as skinny as a twig."

"I'm all grown up!" exclaimed Rugen.

The large bear-like body emerged before us by carefully descending the short staircase. The way it moved, I thought it might be old or even sick. When it reached the ground, it said, "What a total delight, Rugen! Seeing you again brings back my fire." The creature seemed to be on surer footing on the ground. Up close, it was easy to see that it was Ganat, with large black eyes, expressionless face, and heavy jowls. This Ganat was huge, muscular and lumbering, seeming to be the antithesis of the fast-moving Cerribeame. It was male and wore no clothing. His body nap was course and hung in long gray fringes, especially around the groin. The lengthy pubic fringe was not long enough to conceal his large genitalia.

"I would like to present the two hundred twenty-sixth incarnation of Baybairn," said Rugen proudly. "These are my soul mates, Nova and Sante."

What a planetoid! What a honeymoon! What a life! What might happen next? Would we discover Gautama under the Bodhi tree?

"Ah!" exclaimed Baybairn and his voice went kitten soft. "You finally made the ultimate connection. Congratulations, Rugen." Baybairn peered at first Nova and then me—examining us. "Oh! What a warm moment! What a light filled moment!" he sang. "Truly, my senses burn with pleasure. By *Pym*!* We will remember these moments on Sasaybin. We must celebrate this blessed reunion. Of course, my little bird, Rugen, has brought you to see the statue. The statue moves for some. Come inside my *prat* (humble structure). I'll warm some goat's milk and together we will imagine perfection."

Despite his expressionless face, his delight was obvious. I thought, perhaps, that I saw an expression of joy in his huge black eyes. There was sorrow around his eyes, where the flesh hung in generous folds. Bright pink tinged the folds as if he just finished crying over something extremely poignant. It was clearly *watarie*.

We went upstairs and into a square room. It was beastly hot inside—no fans. Amazingly, the place was bug free. *Did insects respect the sacred space of the two hundred twenty-sixth incarnation of Baybairn?* The *prat* was all one room and the ceiling was flat. Despite the crude exterior, the interior was beautiful. The walls and floor were highly polished hardwood. The room had no furniture and nothing hung from any wall. Baybairn's huge fur nest sat in one corner. Ganat nests are heirlooms handed down through generations

*Pym is the Ganat caretaker of memory; language origin, E'tof.

and woven of fur plucked from their lower bellies. Each generation adds another layer of fur to the sacred nest. Nova might have considered sleeping in a nest "unsanitary," but I think it might be sensual to sleep in an ancestral nest.

The focal point in Baybairn's home was a low circular stone hearth. A lively wood fire burned inside a cast-iron brassier. An inverted funnel chimney hovered above and went out through the center of the roof. Close by sat a simple three-legged stool that held a blue glazed vase with some cooking equipment, a pitcher, and several tin boxes.

I felt woozy from the heat, yet Baybairn insisted we sit near the fire and warm ourselves. For me, it was already a question of endurance. This place and Baybairn were special to Rugen, so for *cis* sake, I sat down on the bare floor and endured the heat. I knew Ganats preferred warmer temperatures, but the heat inside this dwelling seemed dangerous for the Janaforma species. I know I sounded ridiculous when I asked, "How do you tolerate so much heat?"

Baybairn laughed and patted me on my sweaty arm. "By going right into the middle of it," he said. He squatted before the fire, with his huge penis resting on the floor between his legs. He stoked the embers and added another piece of wood. I noticed after a moment that what he was doing seemed ceremonial. His actions were reverent, but completely natural.

****

Baybairn sat an old and battered cooking pan on the red-hot brassier. He poured fermented milk from a clay pitcher into the ready pan and the milk plopped out in coagulated globs. The milk, which was the consistency of thick yogurt, had bits of yellow fat that sizzled when it hit the pan. Baybairn was not afraid of the fire and took the side of the pan, with his huge bearish paw, and gave it a rough shake to distribute the clotted milk and fat. Then, he opened some tin boxes and helped himself to bits of their contents. As soon as he was finished with each one, he resealed it. From one he ladled a huge dollop of dripping honey and from the next a broken piece of cinnamon stick. He took a small whisk made of irregular grass strands and used it to stir the concoction. From the last tin, he extracted a small pinch of blue-colored powder and included it—stirring it all around. I wanted to ask about the powder, but was unsure whether my inquiries might be considered impolite by Ganat standards. Rugen seemed to understand what was happening and I trusted him. When the drink was finished, Baybairn poured it into a large clay cylinder and proceeded to taste the concoction. "Hum," he said and then he passed it to Rugen along with the whisk.

Rugen took the whisk, stirred it thoughtfully, and then drank. "Excellent batch!" *ce* proclaimed and then *ce* passed the clay cylinder to Nova who did the same.

When Nova handed the cylinder to me, the last thing I wanted was a container of hot fatty milk, yet I drank it because I did not want to hurt Baybairn's feelings. The initial taste was complicated—gamy, sour, sweet, spicy, smoky, and slightly grassy. The middle taste was rich and fatty. The aftertaste was flowery, something I connected to the blue powder. I began to drift away on that flowery taste; then I heard laughter and it startled me. "Ganats have only one rule," said Baybairn. "Do not fall into malaise when you sit in the goat milk circle." Then Nova handed me the cylinder a second time.

"Maybe I've had enough," I said.

Rugen quickly reminded me, "It's impolite to waste what Baybairn has prepared for us."

Just as quickly, I reversed myself. "On the other hand, maybe I'm just getting started."

"That's the spirit!" boomed Baybairn. "We've haven't yet begun the course of jhap biscuits. Jhap biscuits bring up the ardor, engorge the *premis*, and make it into a lively snake that can please many, many lovers." He reached between his legs and hefted his substantial testicles to show me what I might aspire to on a steady diet of jhap biscuits and goat's milk. "I fuel my ardor on jhap biscuits in the winter. Without jhap, there would be no new Ganats."

"Sante is very romantic," said Rugen. "*Le* has no problems engorging *lis premis*."

Baybairn roared with insinuative laughter. "*Le* may have ardor, but without jhap biscuits, *le* will never have the stamina. Look at *lim* stuffed into those clothes, despite the fact that *le* is suffocating. *Le* would rather sit inside *lis* manufactured shell than come out and be dressed in nature like me."

I felt unsure, oafish, and stupid and I asked, "Should I remove my clothing?"

Baybairn doubled over with laughter and then Nova was handing me the cylinder a third time. I drank and caught myself thinking—*this is delicious!* I felt a surge of spontaneity. "I look around your home and it reminds me of my roots, my beginnings in a cave with Nova," I told Baybairn. "I feel at home here," and I wasn't hot anymore. I stared at Nova. *Le* was silent, steady, and the most beautiful soul in creation to me.

Come here, le seemed to say to me with *lis* eyes. *Inhibition is immersion in illusion.*

I scooted closer to *lim* and *le* took one of my hands and held it. *Lis* eyes were the bluest blue in all creation, the tender expression of *lis* divine heart. "The firelight is in your eyes," I said.

"The firelight is in your eyes," *le* echoed. "I guess that makes us equals." In that moment, the impossible happened. I was inside Nova looking back at me. My soul gasped in surprise. Sante was a construct, an empty shell. In Nova, it was vast beyond my imagination. *Le* was an alien landscape of exquisite beauty. *Go back, le* said immediately. *Do not desert your body. It will happen the other way around, but now the pathway is open, truly open, and it will never again grow shut.* Snap! I was back inside my body, inside Sante.

****

Nova and I stared at each other and then *le* said, "I certainly want to try those jhap biscuits."

"That's because you are a real baybairn!" exclaimed Baybairn and he proceeded to prepare the jhap biscuits with much the same ingredients that he used to make the drink. Into a wooden bowl, he dumped flour. This time he ground the cinnamon into a powder between two flat stones. He wet the solution with goat's milk, making sure to include plenty of the buttery parts before adding a dollop of honey. Then he tossed in a large pinch of blue powder. The concoction was the consistency of bread dough. He dumped it into the same pan that he used for the milk and flattened it with his hand. After a couple of minutes, it started to bubble on top and he managed to reach into the pan and flip the biscuit with his bare hands. When both sides had browned, he divided it into four equal portions, and gave a part to each of us.

Rugen grinned with amused delight. "Bon appétit!" *ce* said flexing *cis* eyebrows. Then *ce* popped part of the biscuit into *cis* mouth. I started to eat my portion and when I did, I lost track of Rugen, then Nova, and finally a sense of the room. Strangely, Baybairn was still sitting before me as a great silent mountain of flesh. I gazed into his eyes. The red of his eye sockets was empathy itself. I trusted him totally, yet he spoke about resistance and trust. *To resist is foolishness*, he said.

I heard a loud roar in my head and I let go. The sound swallowed me and took me inside the black consciousness of Baybairn's eyes. There I became a bobbing cork in the ocean of his blood—caught in the moving tide of a harmonic rhythm. The beating of his heart propelled me, sweeping me through his sacred being. Knowing that he cared for endless souls within himself, I was humbled. Within Baybairn, the heart never lost its dream. His godly contact with reality was natural, intimate, multi-sensual, and real. He said two simple words to me that changed my life. "Direct experience."

I have no idea how I got there, but found myself standing by one of the windows in Baybairn's house. It was as if my consciousness opened on a scene with me already in it. I stood there and wept for my past loneliness and for the wonders of this universe I would never see. Visions pierced my heart, every one real before my physical eyes. The scent of life filled my sensitive nose, telling me life smelled thick and rich, like goat's milk. Sound? No sound ever played in heaven equal to the sounds of Sasaybin when the silence and music became one. I felt a huge paw on my shoulder. "Let's go outside and touch the day," said Baybairn. His voice was the sweetest voice in creation.

"I apologize for going off by myself," I said.

"You are never by yourself. That is the greatest illusion of all."

"I understand."

"You do? Good for you! I don't and perhaps I never will." In one great burst of happiness, Baybairn let go a robust laugh that shook the timbers of the dwelling.

Afterward, when Rugen and I spoke about those moments with Baybairn, we realized our experiences were different. Rugen told me that *ce* experienced the most profound connections in Baybairn's presence. "Yes," I agreed, but it was not the same and we both knew it.

What was the experience like for Nova? "I will not say," *le* told us. "I can't describe it; but I will give it to you in its entirety in the natural unfolding of our commitment."

The four of us went downstairs with Baybairn leading the way. Again he was clumsy on the stairs as if they were a convention he never could grow accustomed to. I knew now that he was old. We talked for a while about ordinary things. Baybairn asked about Ceff and Kayya, and Rugen explained how physically difficult it was for them to visit because of the heat on Sasaybin. "Thank them again for this beautiful refuge," said Baybairn.

Baybairn placed his hairy paw on Rugen's shoulder. "If you want to show the statue to Sante and Nova, then you should get started. Darkness comes quickly on Sasaybin. Besides, it's time for my nap. I must store my strength, like a seed, for next year's mating."

We said goodbye and *watarie* filled those moments. After we left, I thought again of the bird that came and landed on Rugen's shoulder. I wondered why I did not see Tanicos with Baybairn. "Baybairn is evasive when people ask him about Tanicos," said Rugen. "Baybairn once told me that we can search for Tanicos, but we will never find him until Tanicos begins searching for us."

****

We hiked down another trail that Rugen promised would lead to the statue. This one seemed well trod and I assumed Baybairn used it often. Not more than a half-kilometer away, we came to another tiny clearing. A forcefield protected this spot and I was surprised to see sophisticated technology after Rugen's insistence on keeping everything primitive. *Ce* explained that the forcefield was there to protect the statue from the natural elements that certainly would destroy it in such a hot, damp climate as Sasaybin. The deactivation switch sat inside a clear plastic box on a simple wooden stake. Rugen reached inside the box and deactivated the forcefield so we could move closer.

I laughed when I saw the statue because it took me back to my life with The *Enfant Terrible*. "It's not supposed to be funny," said Rugen defensively. "Some people claim the statue moves for them."

"When it moves, does it jerk itself off?" I asked with an irreverence that was appropriate only in my mind. I laughed because the statue was of me in a previous life. Michelangelo Merisi, better known as Caravaggio, had sculpted it. I assumed nobody realized the sculpture was by Caravaggio because he did not sign it. As ribald as Merisi could be—what he considered artistic failure still embarrassed him. Merisi was a painter, not a sculptor; but he wanted to try something different and I was his handy child slave. He said, "I want to recreate you as you truly are in third dimensional form." He was naïve enough, in that ancient life, to imagine he could do it, especially in stone. He called the statue, "Barueco," meaning "irregularly shaped pearl."

I was a ten-year-old child when Merisi hired me to catch fireflies for him. At twelve, he took me on as his apprentice. In a previous life, I had been the French monk Bastion and died with unresolved sexual frustration, which Merisi helped me vent. I stood for the sculpture when I was sixteen and Merisi posed me in all my natural glory—with wings! I was holding a long spear and a small shield. He instructed me to stand with my right foot thrust dramatically forward and my shoulders at an angle that made me appear haughty and proud. I was The Holy Virgin, the triumphant Archangel Michael, but still my seductive self. The look on my face was one of absolute piety. Merisi accomplished that tiny miracle by performing fellatio on me until my expression captured the correct transcendent appeal. Naturally, The Church declared the statue blasphemy. I stared at my old self and the memory was so complete I could still hear the marble chipping away and Merisi screaming *keep your chin up you little bastard*. I stood there and told my soul mates what I remembered.

"After hearing that, I'm never going to feel the same way about this sculpture," said Rugen. "But when I saw it, I fell in love with it—had to have it! Just like when I saw you."

"Where did you get it?" asked Nova.

"I bought it, from an agent on Earth when The Vatican was forced to sell many of their art treasures."

I laughed again. "You mean The Vatican recanted about what they considered blasphemy?"

Rugen shrugged. "Whatever their regard for 'Barueco,' they charged me a fortune. The government of Uropae considers it an irreplaceable art treasure. People make pilgrimages here to see it and lately I've been thinking about moving the statue back to Uropae to preserve Baybairn's privacy. The main reason I have not done that is he takes pride in his independence—the fact that he takes care of 'Barueco' in exchange for perpetuity rights to this land."

I took a closer look at my previous self now chiseled into stone. Seeing it through Rugen's eyes, instead of Merisi's, I could see what I missed long ago. "You were wrong Merisi. It's a great work of art." The sculpture was sitting on a large circular stone that was not part of the original piece. Rugen said no one knew why the base was added; but it obviously originated from a later period. Carved around the base was trailing ivy and words written in Italian. The words started where my stone toe pointed forward. I walked around the base, appreciating myself from all angles, as Rugen read the inscription to us. "*Amore tutto sopporta, tutto crede, tutto spera, tutto sopporta. L'amore non manca mai.*"

I knew the words were essential to me because I literally was standing before a chipped-off part of myself from the past. "What does that mean?" asked Nova.

Rugen said, "Love bears all things, believes all things, hopes all things, endures all things. Love never fails."

****

It was late in the day when we returned to Rugen's dwelling. We enjoyed a light supper and gravitated to the upper deck where we watched the twinkling stars freckle and splatter across the cobalt sky. In space, the absolute heart-breaking clarity to starlight can be blinding. Stars can be fifty million light-years distance, yet one can swear a flexed elbow might move them around. Here on Sasaybin, stars became glittering crystals, rare treasures found in distant streams. Life was cozy and private on this small world and it was difficult to imagine the consequences of our behavior here could affect the fate of the universe. Somewhere in the nearby vegetation, some unknown creature cooed with pleasure. In six weeks time, she would birth a nest of bald little nestlings that someday would birth nestlings of their own. She was where she belonged and doing her part to seed and feed her world with the diversity of precious life.

Nova wrapped *lis* arms around Rugen and the back of Rugen's head was resting on Nova's shoulder. Together they gazed up at the stars. "Look!" Rugen said and pointed toward a small falling meteorite, "It's a teardrop of light." Seeing them now, as lovers, made me feel complete. No longer did I need to channel Nova's will to Rugen or Rugen's understanding to Nova. Their connection was direct and powerful and each time they made love, they took me into their bliss. I pulled myself out of my personal reverie and joined them. Nova pressed me with, "Do you remember when I said that it was a shock to learn you are a more powerful force than I am?" I assured *lim* that I did. "You temper my every mood, my every response," *le* confided.

"Everything feels perfect this evening," Rugen said and *cis* voice held a reverent tone.

"Thank you for bringing me home," said Nova. *Lis* aura was so ecstatic and vibrant that it was glowing with perfect equilibrium. "By the starlight of this lovely Sasaybin evening, we will celebrate," *le* declared.

Did my greater soul always know this perfect moment would come? I had nothing left to rehearse or analyze. My past-life melodrama felt like false intensity acted out on a stage. Nova gave me so much power that night that I delighted in the nuance of our every embrace. The celebration was not tame, but wild. Love always surpasses the stage and becomes a testament to our highest virtues. Our spontaneous ingenuity reached levels of genius that kept me in profound and delighted wonder for hours.

On the morning of our third and final day, we arose early. We did a bit of exploring. Rugen flew the hovercraft around the entire planet. We stopped by a tiny lake, which had no name. It seemed perfect that the lake was nameless because naming it might have limited the perfection of the scene. Here, in nameless paradise, happiness was truly possible.

A gentle feeder stream sat at one end of the lake, nourishing it from an underground source. We spied some huge paw prints in the moist and squishy earth and Nova was thrilled. *Le* knelt and touched them with reverence. "It's a Sasaybin panther," Rugen said. "One comes here at dawn to drink sometimes. She's sable brown and has yellow eyes as bright as flames."

"How do you know it's female?" asked Nova.

"She moves like a female," said Rugen and *ce* showed us what *ce* meant by sashaying back and forth a couple of times and exaggerating the swinging of *cis* hips. *Ce* was a funny mimic and made us laugh.

It was so beautiful by that nameless lake that it humbled my imagination with its authenticity. Rugen said it was safe to swim, so we indulged in the clear, tepid water. The water was buoyant, as we lay back and relaxed by floating on the top. Afterward, we made love and ate lunch at the same time. We indulged in the simplest, silliest, and most romantic pleasures. Rugen showed us how *ce* could throw grapes in the air and catch them in *cis* mouth. Nova insisted *le* could top that and showed us how *le* could juggle four apples at the same time. I told Rugen, "Elay taught Nova how to juggle."

It was a little past midday and I could sense a subtle shift in each of our moods. We returned to the dwelling, packed, and tidied the premises. All we needed to do was close the windows and shut down the solar generator below. We went out on the deck and took a final look at the beauty of Sasaybin. The urge within us wanted to make physical love. We did not act upon this urge because we all agreed that it was too desperate and disrespectful to love to rush the act to completion. Instead, we said goodbye to paradise, our honeymoon, and returned to Uropae.

****

Uropae was stark and chilly after the heat and humidity of Sasaybin. Kayya met us when we walked in the front door and told us that Evose had suffered another episode of what I was beginning to think of as, Willing Sacrifice plague. Kayya was alarmed since neither Belinda nor Bogwa had allowed her to call for medical assistance. "Evose collapsed at dinner last evening," said Kayya. "He fell forward, right into his plate. He scared the daylights out of everyone." Kayya appeared tired and on the verge of tears as she embraced Rugen. "I've been thinking and thinking some more and— I'm having serious second thoughts about this crazy venture."

Rugen sighed. "Where's Ceff?"

"Still at the facility. We want the vitasphere to be as flawless as we can make it. We've been in constant communication over what to do and frankly, I've not slept since you left. Last night, I almost decided to fly to Sasaybin to talk to you. Instead, I called Ceff and she advised me to let you enjoy your honeymoon. But now that you're here—please Rugen, are you listening to me? Let's go into the library and talk."

"If you want," *ce* said, "but it will change nothing. I've already committed, given my word." Rugen leaned into me and I understood *ce* needed Nova and I present to support *cim*. The four of us went into the library and this time, Kayya closed the doors. Nova and I sat, but Rugen feigned a stubborn stance and stood staring out the window with *cis* back toward us. "It's freezing in here," *ce* complained. *Ce* brushed *cis* arms as if a bit of friction could make the cold go away.

"Build a fire if you're cold," Kayya said.

Rugen growled, "It's too much trouble." We were away three days, yet I could see Uropae was fast moving toward winter. The rich orange, red, and gold were gone, replaced with quiet browns and dry grays. "Was there a storm while we were gone?" *ce* asked.

"Yes," said Kayya. "As you can see, the storm took down most of the leaves." Her tone changed and she sounded almost impatient. "Rugen, please sit. I can't talk to your back."

"Mother, please? Don't make this harder than it already is."

"Things need to be said between us. I can't let you fly off into oblivion and pretend you are going to return in a few hours. You need to consider the ramifications, the problems that may arise."

"If we sat here for the rest of our lives, we could never discuss all the ramifications connected with this venture," said Rugen.

Kayya persisted. "A way must exist to mend this rupture without the three of you sacrificing your lives. Together, we can find a better way. If we approached the problem rationally, step by step, I know there's a solution." It was obvious the same archetypal vibration that moved Rugen also moved Kayya. Rugen knew our venture into the past was ill planned; yet, Kayya expected *cim* to defend it. Kayya already was crying. Not all the understanding in creation could stop a Tyrowsian from getting effusive when it involved someone they adored. "I would be remiss if I didn't mention just a few of the reasons you should not attempt this crazy scheme," she said.

Rugen flopped down on an overstuffed chair. "If it makes you feel better, go right ahead," *ce* told her.

"The very least that can happen is you will be discovered in this time, prosecuted, and condemned as a time-traitor."

"That's not going to happen. I'm Janaforma and a Vanguard Scout and no Janaforma would ever turn me over to Orion justice."

"If you actually clear The Door, some evidence suggests that when you approach the year of your physical birth the passage will grow too narrow and you will die. Pacific Institute scientists believe this barrier cannot be crossed by the physical body, let alone by a mechanical spaceship."

"That's nonsense," snipped Rugen. "I don't believe anything coming out of the Pacific Institute. That's as stupid as their elastic-band theory."

"What about time itself?" asked Kayya. "Science is in the dark ages in its attempts to determine the time ratios and differentials. We have no idea how long it will take a vitasphere to travel backward to the year 2015. What will happen to your soul if it takes lifetimes?"

"Mother, I'm not stupid. I've done the math. The longer we're in the fourth dimension, the faster we will go. Trans-Miro's big Prime I multidex projects the trip will take roughly twenty-two hours tops."

"Rugen, we don't know that you will go faster as you go back in time; that's conjecture based upon unproven theories. Even if the trip takes only twenty-two hours, no vitasphere pilot has ever been able to concentrate the full focus of the mind for that length of time. Please, take me with you. It's the one logical solution if you expect to survive."

"Absolutely not," said Rugen.

"Why not?"

"Because it feels totally wrong to me."

"It feels wrong? What's gotten into you?"

"Sante has gotten in me and I'm going nowhere without *lim*."

"Okay," said Kayya. "You, Sante, and I will make the trip. Evose is too sick to go anyway."

Rugen did not mention that Nova already told us that Hope would be our traveling companion. "I'm sorry, Kayya, maybe you should have created a larger vitasphere, but you didn't. While I admit your technical skill and knowledge would be invaluable, I know no way to conceal your alien appearance on the Earth of 2015. Furthermore, you know nothing about Trinity Witches or about this Human female, Iris."

Kayya sighed. "Perhaps I would be more of a liability than an asset, but a real danger exists, which we have not discussed. Some of the newest

Prime I multidexes project that if we try to go backward in time, our memory and soul will return to previous reference points in the past. Think long and hard about whether you want to subject yourself to another mind-stripping and become amnesic to all you know."

"None of these things are going to happen," said Nova.

"How do you know?" Kayya demanded.

"I know because I have a plan to protect them."

Kayya stared at Nova with an expression of disbelief. "I have great respect for you, Nova; but even you don't have the kind of insight to know for certain that this mission is possible."

"It is risky," admitted Nova. "But I believe in Rugen and Sante. I believe in them so completely that I am willing to bet my soul, from its alpha to its omega, to support their journey."

"How are you going to do that?" she demanded.

"How I do it is a private matter between my soul mates and me."

Kayya appeared frustrated. "How am I to believe you if you won't share specifics?"

Nova's sudden equanimity scared me. "When I created the Janaforma, I put my own 3C gene into them. You took advantage of the opportunity and manifested through the lives of Kerisa, Dyne, and Reyneldi. Now you are Tyrowsian and that's okay with me, but your genius is using knowledge that came directly from Simon Forma. I would hope that you could find a measure of respect for Simon and what he gave you and take me at my word. If not, eventually I will be vindicated by truth itself." Then *le* got up and left the library.

****

My heart was beating so fast, I could hear it in my ears. I was terrified of many things at that moment, but mostly I was terrified of losing Nova's physical presence. I jumped up and followed *lim*. "Wait," I called.

Le was halfway down a side hallway that led to an outside garden. *Le* turned and smiled at me. A moment before, *le* was irritated with Kayya, even cold. Now his expression was one of fragility. I was tongue-tied because I felt like Kayya. I needed something from *lim* to help me believe. "I'm sorry," I said. "I'm experiencing that feeling again as if you were slipping away from me. I'm so sorry to pressure you about it. I love you; that's all I wanted to say."

Le uttered my name with complete tenderness at that moment. "Sante, would you mind if I had a few minutes by myself?"

I started to weep. "I'm so sorry, Nova. Forgive me for interrupted your solitude."

"There is nothing to forgive; you've done nothing wrong. I wanted to go somewhere and gather my thoughts. Give me a kiss," *le* said. We kissed, but it was dry and without passion.

I was horrible to Nova in those brief moments. I pressed *lim* harder. "Will you come right back?" I made *lim* swear.

"Right back," *le* promised.

"Stay warm." I pulled the sweater Rugen gave *lim* up around *lis* neck and buttoned it. I let *lim* go then and went back to Rugen in the library. Kayya was still talking about the dangers and I felt as if I possessed no more patience to listen. "I'm going to go lie down for a while," I interrupted.

"I'll be right along," Rugen promised.

I did not go lie down. Instead, I went for a walk outside, a very fast walk. At some point, it turned into a run, even a dash. I went in the opposite direction from Nova so I did not run into *lim*. When I returned, I discovered that I had worried everyone. Nova was there—safe. "I'm sorry," I said; and then I sneezed.

"This is not a good time to get sick," said Rugen. Nova started fussing over me and insisted that I go take a hot bath. I figured that I caused enough problems, so I was very obedient. As I was emerging from the bath, Nova came to tell me Ceff had returned and the vitasphere was ready.

"This is it!" Nova said. "We're going to go down to the library and Evose will announce that he cannot make the trip and Hope will go instead." *Le* waited for me and we went down to the library together.

The moment I caught sight of Evose, my inner voice blurted out, *holy shit!* He was hoary, gaunt, and stiff. His hair was falling out. He was sitting in a chair with pillows tucked in around him. Belinda was on one side and Bogwa was on the other. "I'm going to be fine," Evose again insisted.

Bogwa was his new usual self—subdued. I was beginning to think of him in this way instead of the way I knew him when I was a child, which was open, wise, funny, and strong. Hope was missing without explanation. Belinda was the one constant, although she was not wearing her usual green attire. She wore white, a color I never saw her wear before, in any lifetime. As usual, she was animated. We all tried to be sensitive about Evose, so we sat and listened to what Belinda wanted to say. She reiterated many of the things we already knew, before telling us that they decided amongst themselves that she, Belinda, was going back in time with Rugen and me, not Evose.

Rugen went ballistic and said, "Like hell you are!" *Ce* jumped up from *cis* overstuffed chair and *ce* did not raise *cis* hands, but they were clenched into fists.

"Rugen!" admonished Ceff. "Let's try to be civil with each other."

Belinda was cool. "No! Let's let it go and see where it flies!" she returned in a challenge. It was an old expression from the Island World of Gathos. It meant she was willing to debate Rugen on the issue.

"You're on," challenged Rugen.

Nova and I stared at each other and *le* raised *lis* eyebrows in amusement.

I was not as blithe as Nova and I sat down and put my face in my hands. I hated life on this level. I hated the posturing involved in debates and I hated sitting through balderdash. To me, debating was as primitive, constrained, and ridiculous as fencing with swords.

Belinda was a skilled debater, although she was not of the same ilk as Rugen. She was a lover, like me. A lover's idea of winning any argument is to seduce the opponent. Granted, Belinda was way ahead of me in this area. She was integrated with her will and understanding and had been for centuries. She probably possessed the power to channel Socrates and get him to debate Rugen. What I hated most about debating was its stark duality. While Belinda and Rugen were going at each other, the rest of us were supposed to be silent and allow Belinda and Rugen to argue their differences. After they finished, perhaps one of them would concede. Only then, would the rest of us have a chance to contribute.

Belinda stood. "One rule—I expect to have my complete say. So don't interrupt me and I will not interrupt you."

"Agreed," said Rugen. "Who will go first?"

"Let's draw cards," Belinda suggested. "I have cards with me. I'll go get them."

"This is bullshit," I said as soon as she was gone. "You're the pilot of this vitasphere; it's your right to tell her no."

Evose managed to tell Rugen, "You've just been outwitted by the best. Happened to me once too!" Despite Evose's deteriorating condition, his frankness finally was beginning to show through.

ELEVEN

Belinda was a Trinity Witch and all Trinity Witches were adepts in handling cards. Physical incarnations of Trinity Witches had used the Trinity tarot deck to their advantage for the last six thousand years. Naturally, what Belinda brought back from her sleeproom was her special deck of cards. A wispy bit of green silk lay twisted around the cards, which she laid aside. Ezek told me the cards were old and that, with methodical proficiency, Belinda's previous incarnations arranged to secret those cards in special places so each new incarnation always knew where to find them. They were exquisite and stamped with gold on their edges. If I believed in magic, I would say that deck possessed special alchemy.

Rugen and Belinda went through more balderdash, which was a waste of time. Finally, Belinda suggested that the first one to pull the Wheel of Fortune card would decide who would go first in the debate.

I had been doing my tarot homework over the past few weeks and had a hunch that Belinda chose the Wheel of Fortune as a symbolic gesture. It was a subtle yet calculated statement about what would follow. The Wheel represents random luck; but on a deeper level represents the fluctuation of the personal within the spiritual. Deeper still, The Wheel demands honor from the one who accepts the card. I knew then that the cards already revealed to Belinda that she was not going back in time with us. It would be as Nova predicted. Hope was going with us; yet Belinda wanted to go through this charade for some purpose I did not understand.

Since it was Belinda's deck, she agreed to let Rugen select a card first. Rugen began to draw the card and then *ce* gazed up at her with an innocent expression and asked— "Would you mind if Sante plucked my card—just for good luck?"

"Sure," agreed Belinda and she walked over to me and fanned the cards out before me. "Go ahead," she said. "It's your move, hotshot."

I pulled the card out and said, "I love *cim*," and then I handed the card to Rugen. Ce turned it over and it was the Wheel of Fortune.

"I'm impressed," Belinda conceded. "You've come a long way."

"Ladies first," Rugen nodded. That was the last time Rugen alluded to etiquette. With the words that came out of *cis* mouth during that debate, it was difficult to believe that *ce* was my tender lover a few hours before.

****

"I will not waste time, because we have no time left to waste," said Belinda. "Bottom line, I do not want to go on this journey, but I must. As you can see, Evose is incapable of going and Bogwa is under tremendous strain to keep the balance between Hope and Evose. I was involved almost from the beginning and know more about Iris than anyone. She is part of my past and I will know how to deal with her. That's important because nobody knows how much time we have left."

"Where's Hope?" asked Rugen.

Belinda huffed. "That's not a debating point; that's a question."

"Sorry," said Rugen. "Would you mind answering it anyway?"

"Hope is resting. Some of the problems are swinging in her direction."

Bogwa added. "I asked Hope to rest for us. By doing that, it takes some of the pressure off Evose and me. She agreed to do that."

"You're not supposed to speak or interrupt," Belinda chided Bogwa. "We're debating my right to go back in time."

"Are you sure you are not keeping Hope isolated so she no longer is a disagreeable variable?" asked Rugen.

"That's not debating issues," exploded Belinda. "That's a ludicrous accusation. I consider Hope as much my child, as Evose. Estrella gave Hope life, but I witnessed her conception, applauded it, and helped deliver Hope into this life. I nursed Hope at my breast and I feel a special responsibility to Estrella to protect her child from harm. Estrella named Hope for what she is—our hope for the future. I have tried to protect her at all cost, even at the cost of two very dear incarnations to me—Bogwa and Evose. Why are you questioning and challenging me in such a rude manner? Why do you feel this hostile prejudice for me, when all I ever wanted to do is help?"

"It is not prejudice," said Rugen.

"It's prejudice if your reasoning is shoddy," countered Belinda.

"You're right, but my reasoning is on target and you know it. On the other hand, your reasoning is emotional, spastically unsound, and aimed for the heart. Let's stick to the facts and I'll omit any discussion about the probable outcome of this venture if you were to accompany us into the past. Which points do you want to debate first, Belinda? Should we talk about your carelessness or your lack of judgment in initiating this problem in the first place? No? Well then, let's skip over the obvious and talk about your conceit. To you, all these things might be minor issues; but they reveal an accumulation of missteps, the very essence of who you are. Bogwa, Sirushi, and Mehiel came into this universe because they were attracted to the Janaforma. In this case, the attraction was hope and possibility in the Janaforma people. For some reason, these three souls are now involved with you. Please elucidate why they were attracted to you and away from what brought them into this universe in the first place? What do you offer that they cannot get from the Janaforma? Whatever it is, it's obvious that your carelessness found fertility in their naïveté and taken root."

"I resent those accusations," said Belinda.

"And I find you careless and your approach to life self-serving," said Rugen. "Perhaps most people would not understand the ramifications of going back in time and meeting themselves, but you're not ordinary—are you Belinda? You are well versed in metaphysics and realize that it's a perfect way for you to go into the past, transmit all your knowledge from the present to a previous incarnation so you could make an evolutionary leap before you are ready. Well, perhaps that idea is a bit too farfetched; too bizarre to comprehend that someone as evolved as you, could be that cunning."

Belinda was crying, yet her voice never lost control. "I cannot believe someone as evolved as you claim to be, would accuse me of such premeditated evil. I'm a bodhisattva. I renounced my right to bliss in order to absorb the sting of people such as you—people who accuse others of terrible things without a shred of evidence. You treat me with contempt, yet I died for you many times. Look to your own denial. Where were you when the government agents buried me alive on Gathos? You were living as a rich Hectarian monk in a temple. You never lifted a finger when I was murdered. When and wherever I incarnate, I incarnate among the poor who need my help. Where do you incarnate? Look around you, Rugen; you can answer that question without my help. I always find you with the stink of wealth and privilege around you, while the rest of us suffer for your attachment to these trinkets and toys. Yet, I have helped you in every way I can. Where is the truth of your Regression memories, Rugen? I gave the fruit of my womb, my beloved Bejan so I could help develop the Regression drug. I had as much to do with the refinement of Regression as your precious Sante. I attempted to help Bogwa, Evose, and Hope despite the fact that I needed to do no more after I delivered Bejan into this life. Yet, I stayed and gave life to Bellanna and Evose. Look at my beautiful child now. Look at what's happened to him." Belinda began to sob. "You can see with your own eyes that he is incapable of making this journey. Now I offer my own life to correct this rupture."

It was Rugen's turn again and *ce* appeared aloof and cold. "Your inaccuracies are many and careless, Belinda. I will not debate you about who died more often for The Cause; however, let's do talk about Gathos because it demonstrates who you truly are. I did not let you die on Gathos. You flaunted your assertions in the government's face. Your behavior was careless, just as it is now. Down through time, your most grievous sin was to speak before you should. Your impatience is legendary and your mouth is a vehicle for that same impatience. Look under your impatience Belinda and you will find your conceit, your belief that you can do no wrong."

"Why you childish little brat!"

The angry tone of Rugen's voice sounded like a threat. "I'm not finished."

"I am," I interrupted. I could not listen to another moment of this war of words. Belinda and Rugen would never convince anyone with their antagonistic tone. I arose from my chair as if I had a spring up my ass. "I refuse to sit here any longer and watch you two fuck each other with icicles. Listen to me Belinda, Rugen and I have decided that we want to go back in time with Hope. If she agrees to go with us, I ask you to step aside so we have an iota of a chance to succeed in this insane mission." I stalked out of the room and this time, Nova followed me.

****

I walked outside where it was cold and dark. When Nova caught up with me *le* said, "It took a lot of nerve to speak up as you just did. You're changing."

I was shaking with emotion and I kept walking—running away. "Why did you let it go so far? Why didn't you stop Rugen from making a fool out of *cim*self?"

"Did you expect me to stop *cim* with my will?"

I stopped and faced Nova, but the dark cut *lim* in half and turned *lim* into a handsome profile. "I guess I did."

"How could I do that when I have given most of my will to you?"

"Don't—say that."

"You know it's true." Nova came closer so that I could sense *üm* in every way. "Sante, let me give it all to you."

"Please Nova, don't—"

We held each other and *le* whispered, "I cannot help you from this perspective." We began to cry as equals, not trying to comfort each other— just crying because we knew the sacrifices we needed to make. "Let me return to our oversoul." I fell against *lim* softly hammering my head against *lis* shoulder. "From the oversoul, I can give you more than I can give you from here. I will wait until you leave. That way, it will be easier for you."

"I don't want easier—you should know that by now."

"Then let's find a place where we can be alone and we will create an unbreakable bond." *Le* took my arm and I felt as if *le* was dragging me as we went inside to find Rugen. *Ce* had left the library and gone to our room. We found *cim* sitting on the edge of our bed with *cis* head hanging low between *cis* knees. *Ce* looked terrible as if *cis* heart had exploded inside *cis* chest. "I'm so sorry," *ce* mouthed.

"What for?" asked Nova.

"For acting like an arrogant fool."

"You mean that silly debate with Belinda?" asked Nova. "You're right. She is careless and illogical. She had the power to turn Bejan into a raving lunatic at times and *ce* was one of the most patient people I have ever known. If Belinda had her way, she would have turned Bejan into a celebrity and spoiled the entire era of Regression enlightenment. You were correct in your observations of her."

"But I missed my chance to learn my lesson through her—didn't I?"

"Maybe not," said Nova. "Another chance to learn that same lesson may be right around the corner. Besides, the lesson could be a simple reminder such as, be compassionate in your assertions, especially when your assertions are true." Nova smiled and kissed Rugen on *cis* damp left cheek. "Who can say? It could be that Belinda was due for a strong rebuff and you were destined to be the one to give it to her. Anyway, I'm going to employ my puny psychic abilities and predict that by tomorrow morning, it will be as I say."

Rugen reached for my hands. "I'm so sorry, Sante."

"I'm sorry too," I said. "I was not very kind to you a few minutes ago. I'm not sure what happened back there, whether I abandoned you because I dislike debates or whether your logic cut me away. I do know we lost each other for a few minutes."

"It was my fault and you are both being too kind," insisted Rugen.

Nova chuckled. "That's because we both have missed the mark so many times ourselves."

****

Nova and I sat down with Rugen between us. "Do you feel brave tonight?" asked Nova.

Rugen laughed dryly. "No—"

"Good!" said Nova. "Bravery is fighting your fear. Instead, try to relax into it."

"That's the last thing I want to do," said Rugen. More tears came down from *cis* eyes.

Nova's voice held so much emotion at that moment. Every part of *lim* vibrated with refinement. "Please Rugen, collect your understanding and wrap it around me as you would a warm blanket. I desperately need your gifts tonight." Nova got up from the bed and knelt down in front of Rugen. Nova did it slowly, carefully, and deliberately. "See, I can make the consort gesture too." *Le* laid *lis* head in Rugen's lap and Rugen collapsed downward enfolding Nova into the middle of *cis* body.

"You can't complete this journey without my help," said Nova.

Rugen swore, "If you must die for us to succeed, then I will not go."

"You said it yourself. You have no choice. You must go."

"Screw going backward in time," said Rugen. "Let's do what Sante originally said. We can go away, together, just the three of us. We will go so far that no one will ever find us."

Nova grabbed Rugen by *cis* forearms and made *cim* sit up. "Look at me," Nova said. "I'm telling you plainly; you and Sante will not die. Do you understand? You will live—I swear." Nova shook Rugen as a breeze rustles a leaf. "Listen to me, Rugen. I'm asking for your trust. Will you give me your trust now?"

"Yes!" Rugen said. "Absolutely!"

"Then understand that I cannot give what I need to give to both of you. I can give it only to one of you and I have decided to give it to Sante. I ask that you respect my decision and in time, Sante will give you everything from me. This I swear. I am now going to ask you a favor bordering on impossible. I want you to say goodbye to me and leave this room."

"No—how in the name of heaven can I do such a thing?"

"I said it bordered on impossible. Rugen, my life's energy is waning. You know life lasts but a moment. If the slightest unfulfilled expression is left between us, I swear I will reincarnate and make it right between us." Nova needed to help Rugen stand and then *le* took *cim* to the door.

Rugen turned and stared at us both. *Ce* was stunned and *cis* eyes were on fire with fear. "At some point we are going to look back at this moment and realize we were crazy," *ce* said.

"Tell me you do not mean that," said Nova.

"If we could make love as we did on Sasaybin, it would convince me that I don't mean it. If once more, you could take me to that place of clarity between us, then I could find my courage and I might believe everything is going to be okay."

"I don't have the energy to make that kind of love anymore." Rugen kissed Nova and there were shreds of consort seduction in the kiss. Nova responded with equal passion because *lis* vulnerability was absolute. Rugen retracted *cis* energetic thrust for passion because of *cis* respect for Nova and then I had to look away. To watch them say goodbye was a torture I could not endure. "Come back in about an hour and help Sante separate from my body," Nova said. "Sante will need all the understanding and patience you can muster at that time. Go now," *le* said.

****

Nova closed the door and leaned against it. *Lis* eyes sought mine. "I'm cold," *le* said. "Stay with me; wait with me with your consciousness by the door. Will you warm me?"

Le knew I would so *le* turned off the lights. We got into bed together. "Please be gentle," *le* whispered and *lis* statement stopped me dead in my sexual mind tracks. "Be tender and show me your best love. Every time we think about these final moments together, it will bring us together—don't you see?"

It was not a question between us; Nova knew I belonged to *lim*. *Le* embraced me with one hand and laid the flat of *lis* other hand upon my midsection. I gasped in total astonishment, as *lis* hand slipped inside me and cradled my heart. I began to shutter and shake. *It's okay, it's okay,* *le* seemed to be saying and then I felt *lis* hand abruptly drop away.

I fumbled for *lis* pulse along *lis* neck, put my head to *lis* chest where I witnessed the last patient beat of *lis* physical heart. *Lis* death was quick and incomprehensible. *Lis* body immediately turned cold, as if this life was a momentary pause at a well where *le* stopped for a drink of water. I reached out as far as I could into the beyond, Ezek flying farther than ever before and nothing could change it, explain it, or return Nova to me. Still, I could not comprehend how to separate from *lis* body, which I loved beyond all description.

I began to scream—reeling, out of my mind with grief. Rugen was there. "No! No!" *ce* was sobbing in rhythm to my beating heart. My screaming brought others—servants, Ceff and Kayya, Bogwa and Belinda, and even Hope. They tried to help, but nothing worked. They struggled to separate me from the body and I felt as if they were tearing me in half. I was wanton, yet helpless as a newborn. Nothing in this universe mattered with Nova gone.

"Why?" everyone asked. "Why did Nova do such a thing? It was so unnecessary." They did not understand and I was too devastated to try to explain. Words were shadows that meant nothing. In a wordless oath, fired in the forge of my feelings, I swore that if any words asked me for expression, I would hurl them back into the darkness from whence they came. There, they could wander as the folly they forever will be.

****

Silly life demanded that Rugen and I respond. This time, it seemed an impossible chore. If it weren't for the intimacy between Rugen and me, I would have died of a broken heart.

The vitasphere was ready and we needed to leave as soon as possible. In truth, it was foolish to consider dallying since so many obstacles waited. Rugen and I insisted on one last bit of protocol before leaving. We accompanied the body that was Nova's home to the crematorium. People we think of as strangers did these final favors for us. I was so numb I possess no memory of who they were or what they said to us. I feel sorry about that. No words came to thank these strangers for the difficult chore they performed.

As Nova predicted, Hope would go with us. "I will establish a psychic link with Hope and Sante and give you as much help as I can," Belinda promised. "We left in early morning. Rugen and I had not slept one wink. We were terrified to get into bed together. What nightmare we might concoct between us was enough to keep us awake.

Ceff and Kayya planned to accompany us to the edge of the corridor. We said goodbye to Evose, Bogwa, and Belinda. Evose appeared so feeble he looked like Bogwa's grandfather. I had no pity for him. All I felt was distance and suspicion. The fact that Evose was alive and the perfect Nova was dead was crazier than any plot I ever invented in a book. We had beaten the empathy among us into submission. We stood together, but as separate islands of quiet grief.

****

Lifetimes of involvement ran through the minds of Rugen and *cis* mothers. Among the three, I picked up deep feelings of commitment, pride and love of the meticulous life. Bogwa embraced Hope several times, but so much confusion surrounded them, not even hope and possibility leapt out toward me. I decided I could not leave and never see Evose and Bogwa again without first asking them the only question worth asking. I walked over to their private circle and intruded. With the toe of his boot, Bogwa moved some dirt around on the ground. My eyes were already open and waiting for his great black wonders to meet mine. "Since Rugen and I are going to sacrifice our lives for this mission, I think we have a right to know who you are and why you are here?"

Bogwa opened his eyes to me and they were gentle as a passing glance. I hesitated because the experience of falling through Evose was still fresh in my mind. "Come," said Bogwa with a twist of his long fingers. I released Ezek and he was eager to tell me that Bogwa had an authentic soul, but his origins were not of this universe. This was no surprise, but what Bogwa communicated telepathically was—*we come from below, that place which you call Chaos. We have kept manifestation pristine on the surface of your dimension, performing miracles with nothing but sticks and stones to keep it right. I, personally, have ventured through the trial of death to manifest this life and the lives of Evose and Hope. Along the way, I have persuaded great souls to return to life to help transform the appalling pockets of ignorance that still hold sway over this dimension. I cannot do that anymore. Walking through the evidence of third-dimensional denial has its price for the truly compassionate. It's not something to be shaken off lightly. I have lost so many parts of myself along the way that karma now demands the life of my precious soul mate and son. I only have Hope left to give you. Use her wisely and not, as so many of you have done in the past, as blind optimism.*

Bogwa put a hand on my shoulder and I sensed more. His soul was a great demigod; yet, he was capable of putting a hand on my shoulder and creating a physical bond. "Great blessings upon the Janaforma and their future" he said.

"I love you," I said and he kissed me on the forehead.

Belinda came up behind me and put her arm through mine. "Let me talk to Sante for just a moment," she said to Bogwa. We walked off, a short distance away. "We will see each other again," she promised.

"Perhaps sooner than you think."

"As Iris, I will not remember you."

"If we get there, do you want me to help your previous incarnation remember you?"

"Don't do anything careless. Rugen said that lovers have a penchant for carelessness, taking the impossible leap. Perhaps *ce* is right."

"I need to know from you how to break the link between Evose and Iris."

She turned serious. "I thought that was obvious. With Evose unable to go, you'll need to take on a much bigger role in changing the past."

I was shocked because I saw what was in her mind. "You can forget about that. I'm not going to seduce Iris."

"I don't know of any other way of breaking the connection between Evose and Iris than for you to do it with your skills as a lover. You will need to take Iris on as a project, seduce her, and hold her interest so when Evose comes onto her like a warp-drive engine, she will have someone physical to hold onto."

"Once I seduce her, what are Rugen and I supposed to do with her?"

Belinda said, "We've discussed this problem and we do have options. We think the best plan is to get Iris out of the picture and bring her back to this time where we have better tools to handle this metaphysical problem."

I gazed into her eyes. "Are you trying to destroy my relationship with Rugen?"

"Why would I do that? I believe you complement each other."

"Why did you get into that silly debate with *cim*?"

"Because I still believe I should go. I did not realize then that Nova would be able to recover enough from *lis* grief of losing *lis* mates to give *lim*self to you as *le* has. Because of *lis* magnificent sacrifice, your evolvement will continue at an accelerated rate. If nothing else, I hope my debate with Rugen demonstrates that *ce* needs you to temper *cim*. Actually, I envy you and your new relationship with Rugen. *Ce* is a magnificent soul and always has been and *ce* is only going to get better with Regression and age."

"Just because you're in an old body doesn't mean you should allow your passion to die."

She glanced away. "All is not as it seems. I feel I need to resort to makeup and a sexy negligee to convince myself that I still have the fire."

"I understand why Bogwa, Sirushi and Mehiel are with you."

"You do? I don't."

"They're trying to learn about love from one of the greatest lovers alive. Hope and possibility need love to make the equation come out right."

"I agree with that," she said.

Rugen and I made the rounds of saying goodbye before boarding the shuttle. I took the remains of Nova's body with us into space. His physical beauty was now reduced to a small bag of gray-white ash that sat inside my coat pocket. The residue felt light for such a great soul, as if nothing at all was there. The feeling was different from what now lived inside me. Something new sat in me like a brilliant black diamond and I could not get rid of it if I tried. I could not piss or shit it away with irreverence; I could not fuck it away with my semen, vomit it up as grief in a toilet, or explain it away with words. When Rugen broke into the sleeproom a moment after I realized Nova was gone, I tried to explain. "Tell me!" Rugen demanded through blinding tears.

"It feels as if Nova has fed me the New Delphi Crystal," I said.

****

On the planet Hattonia, at the Ababa Space Museum, a mockup of a vitasphere is on display. Rugen tells me the mockup does not come close to the real thing. Not many people have seen an actual vitasphere because they're too fragile and impractical for regular space travel. *Vitaspheres* are made to traverse space between dimensions, without harming the fragile - threads. *Vitaspheres* are made of polymicroflex, a translucent, super-lightweight substance, the formula for which is a closely guarded secret. Polymicroflex possesses exceptional properties allowing seventy-five percent of the light waves intersecting the vitasphere to pass through without reflection. Much of the interior workings of vitaspheres—instrumentation, control panels, chairs and seat cushions, are constructed or coated with this same top-secret material. From a few meters distance, a vitasphere is undetectable by scanners.

Energetic waves, scientists call " threads," trail outward from the third dimension. Like the ends of long hair caught in a breeze, these time threads dangle and dance into hyperspace. Some of these threads go all the way to the *manatee* barrier. This "threaded space" is home to *graeymlins* that swim and weave through the lingering threads and whip them into a cosmic froth of confusion. When Tyrowsians first used rifter spacecraft, crewed with Ganat Cerribeame, neither Tyrowsians nor Ganats realized *graeymlins* were acutely sensitive to disturbances in these energetic waves. Shaped like a Chinese shuriken, or ninja star of death, rifters were capable of light-speed travel. The concave surface of a rifter acts as a powerful parabolic reflector causing damage to these delicate energy fields and excruciating pain to *graeymlins*. When *graeymlins* become agitated, they react violently. Shimmering and trembling, at just under the speed of light, whatever lies in the path of a *graeymlin* is annihilated. Many Ganats died in the corridor from *graeymlin* backlash. Some estimates put the number as high as ten million, some as low as two million. Whatever the truth, it's certain the agitated thrashing of a *graeymlin* tail killed many Ganat Cerribeame.

****

I flew in a vitasphere only once before and it was for a short jaunt for my eighteenth birthcycle. Nova took me out to show me the corridor in an up-close and personal way, yet all I could think about was getting back to *The Mother* and my friends. Nova brought up the subject of *graeymlins* while out in the corridor and I wondered why. "The word 'graeymlin' is a word construct to describe what's out here in the corridor," Nova explained. "It all started because the Cerribeame had no fear; but then learned from Tyrowsians that they should be fearful." Nova laughed with a hypothetical imagining. "Picture this, Sante: a rifter returns from the corridor after seeing its first *graeymlin*, and its Cerribeame captain is excited because she has observed a new phenomenon. She tells the Tyrowsian VIP in charge how a mysterious force knocked the rifter off-course. The VIP gets dramatic, and screams, 'Well, what was it? Was it big, small, green, or blue?'"

"What's your point?" I asked.

"*Graeymlins* began as an indescribable phenomenon and mutated in the minds of Tyrowsians until *graeymlins* became a problem. With absolutely no investigation, *graeymlins* were declared obstacles that must be eradicated."

"To call a *graeymlin* an obstacle is a gross understatement. I think something like saber-toothed leviathan seems a more apropos descriptor. *Graeymlins* are dangerous and responsible for millions of deaths."

"Not in the beginning. Ganat Cerribeame never started dying out in the corridor until they were gripped by a paralytic fear that made them rigid and unresponsive to the spontaneity of the situation."

"Are you suggesting the Cerribeame died because they did not know how to relax in the situation?"

"I think contagious fear has more to do with Cerribeame deaths in the corridor then we acknowledge."

I was more interested in the *manatees* on that trip. To me, they represented the elusive, especially since I never saw one. By the age of eighteen, Michael and Elay's tales about the fourth dimension had me hyped. "How did the *manatees* get their name?" I asked Nova.

"Have you read *The Odyssey* by Homer?"

"Yes, it's one of my favorites." This was a lie. At the time, *The Odyssey* offended me and I thought it was brutal and stupid. However, it was Nova's favorite book and I was trying to curry as much favor with *lim* as possible. I thought I could accomplish this by liking whatever *le* liked. At the same time, I resented and secretly blamed *lim* for my impasse. I was already causing Nova plenty of grief in my effort to garner *lis* attention.

Back then, I was sure Nova loved *The Odyssey* because Odysseus was a man of unshakable will, someone who never gave up, just like Nova. Now I think *lis* fascination with *The Odyssey* had more to do with Odysseus' ability to cut through illusion and maybe something about reclaiming soul fragments stranded out in the fourth dimension.

Nova began to explain about the *manatees*. "An actual marine creature, called a *manatee*, exists on several planets in the Orion Spur. On Earth, *manatees* belong to the scientific order, Sirenia. In Greek mythology, the word 'siren' was a term used for sea nymph or nyad. In ancient times, nyads had a reputation for luring sailors and their ships into treacherous rocks with their enchanting songs. A suspicion persists to this day that what sailors once thought were mermaids might have been *manatees*."

"So we named the creatures in the fourth dimension *manatees* because they had the ability to enchant and confuse?"

"Yes, but I think the truth goes deeper."

"In what way?"

"Do you remember the part in *The Odyssey* when Circe took Odysseus by the hand and told him what would come? She warns him that when he leaves the Aeaean Islands that he will be obligated to pass through the sirens. Circe tells Odysseus that if he imprudently draws too close and hears the sirens' song he will be mesmerized and so lost that he will never see his wife or children again. She advises Odysseus to stuff the ears of his men with wax so they can row safely beyond the enchanting songs. Finally, Circe says that if Odysseus cares to listen to the sirens that he must allow his men to tie him to the crosspiece of the mast so he cannot respond."

"So what's the warning?"

"Perhaps the warning is that illusion is the greatest seductress, a force we cannot expect to face unless we are tethered to a strong crosspiece."

"Maybe Odysseus was a masochist?"

"Why do you say that?"

"Because he suffered for no reason at all. He could have stuffed his ears with wax along with his men."

"Maybe he felt responsible to stand the watch."

"And maybe he wanted to get off with those sirens without sticking around afterward to pay the price."

"What is the price?" asked Nova.

"A full commitment to love," I said. By eighteen, I knew my driver. That cycle was the first time Nova suggested I take Regression. I cannot help wondering what our lives might have been like if I did. I do know, in retrospect, that Regression would have brought Nova and I together. At the very least, we would have had almost ten more years in greater honesty. In those ten years, maybe *le* could have transmitted what I needed to know without dying. Maybe *le* would be with me now, in the flesh, instead of sitting like a black diamond inside my chest.

****

The specially modified vitasphere for our trip was waiting at one of the space stations above Uropae. The vitasphere took up the entire cargo hold on a Pulsar 44 transport. Our plan was to allow the huge pulsar to take us to the edge of the corridor where Ceff and Kayya would launch the vitasphere. Because a vitasphere is unsuitable for third dimensional space travel, we needed a second vessel, something we could use to fly to the planet Earth. This second pulsar was mounted inside the vitasphere and hanging by its tail like a bat. Ceff had attempted to camouflage the pulsar with a fresh coat of polymicroflex and it was the best she could do with our three-day deadline.

From all my space travel, my internal time clock seemed permanently screwed up. I was exhausted, but still worried about nightmares. Rugen and I were like glue, never leaving each other's side. We even went to the toilet together. Hope was in her cabin and I did not see her. I kept thinking of her as our silent partner in this venture and expected that with time she would emerge and be a bit more companionable.

It took thirty-six hours to reach the corridor and I dozed off every few hours for an hour or two. Every time I was near waking, Nova drifted closer and whispered incomprehensible suggestions in my ears. It was as if *le* were communicating with that black diamond *le* left inside me. It was still too soon for me, something I could not get near without getting emotionally overwrought. Sometimes I would get up and take *lis* ashes out of my coat pocket. I would stand there staring at the bag of gray-white powder trying to convince myself that it was all that remained. One time, I took a pinch of ash and ate it. Rugen watched me do it. "It's a sacrament," I said. "I don't think Nova would mind. *Le* might even be flattered."

"*Le* might say you are still worshipping *lis* body. By the way, how does Nova taste?"

My viewpoint abruptly shifted and I knew my behavior was bizarre. I started to laugh as the tears rolled down my cheeks. I managed to say, "*Le* tastes gritty."

I worked on my book and it gave me comfort and a feeling of continuity. My writing was turning into a journal, a search for a reason within me as to why I would agree to this crazy exploit of trying to travel backward in time and change the past. I felt Nova's presence reminding me of so many lapsed memories, especially the part about my eighteenth birthcycle. Rugen helped me too with *cis* scholarship concerning vitasphere technology and *cis* historical knowledge of the corridor. I have almost twelve chapters complete and plan to give a copy to Ceff and Kayya and ask them to forward it to Senon on *The Mother*. Of course, the story is not all told. If we succeed in traversing time, it will be ironic to have the first half of the book in the future and the conclusion of the book in the past. Maybe that will make it a true backward epic. Or as I told Rugen, perhaps I am writing this book for myself and no one will ever know what happens beyond this final word.

****

We were almost to The Door. It looked like nothing but black space, but it was the one-way-in and the one-way-out. Taking into account the vast dimensions of our known universe, The Door to the fourth dimension was nothing more than a gain of sand on a beach. The proportions of The Door fluctuated and shifted at its extremities. At its center, or widest span, it remained roughly five by fifty kilometers. If The Door were visible with the naked eye, it would have appeared as an irregular, undulating line with a tear-shaped droplet in its middle.

Kayya was flying the transport and Rugen was urging her to, "push it." We were aware of the critical importance of timing, especially Rugen. The best time to launch our vitasphere was when the on-duty shift of the Vanguard was coming out of the corridor and the new shift was going in. If we did not make it to The Door in the next three hours, we would need to wait another exposed and dangerous ten hours for a comparable opportunity.

"We'll need to be super quick," Rugen stressed. "If we're lucky, the bridge on *The Mother* will think we are a shadow-blip. If not, I plan on being in and gone by the time the bridge staff can do anything about us." Rugen guaranteed that the presence of six other vitaspheres in the vicinity— involved in a maneuver the Vanguard called, "the bread-and-butter"— would offer us optimum opportunity for subterfuge.

"Being in and gone," sounded like loose strategy, but it was all we had. I had been flying by the seat of my pants ever since I hooked up with Miro Rugen, so I tried to believe. The being-in-and-gone strategy called for launching our vitasphere through the extreme left end of The Door. The portal was narrow on the left, but Rugen swore that *ce* could, "fly it through." My faith went this far: if anyone could "fly it through" unnoticed, Rugen was the one who could do it. *Ce* was excited in this stage of our strange backward adventure as if too much energy was pouring through *cim*. That energy made *cim* more animated than usual and I watched as *ce* explained the logistics of how we could avoid the Vanguard patrols. "Near the left end, we can idle with our nose parallel with The Door. We'll wait for the Vanguard to do the bread-and-butter exchange, shadow it, then slip into the corridor unnoticed."

****

We spent the last hour on the transport allowing Ceff to brief us about the century in Earth's history between the years 1950 through 2050. She told us that, "It was a turbulent time in Earth's history. Remnants of superstition and overblown egos regarded Community as a place rather than a commitment to the equity of the greater good." Once I heard that, I knew the Earthly definition of community would not make us welcome. I didn't need anymore bad news so I allowed Ceff's voice to go in one ear and out the other. Besides, I wanted to spend the last few hours in my native time with my private thoughts. Maybe it was a selfish or indulgent on my part, but I believed no amount of fancy gadgetry could bring me back to my original time once I went beyond The Door. Furthermore, I was convinced that no amount of preprogramming by Ceff could adequately brief us about the specific reality waiting in 2015.

I watched as Rugen checked the vitasphere and fired up its large Prime-I multidex. This vitasphere was new and elegant, a working prototype for next year's designs from Trans-Miro Technologies. The outside of the vitasphere was beautiful and appeared fragile, no more than a translucent bubble, so thin that one might think it could easily pop. Inside was mounted the pulsar. This pulsar was a reliable model, one we used on *La Ventana* for the last two years.

Ceff and Kayya spared no expense in the state-of-the art technology installed in these two crafts. Whatever Rugen asked for and Ceff and Kayya were able to obtain, was ours. Our pulsar was equipped with three interactive, yet independent Prime-I multidexes. Each one was capable of running a full-flight program for a trip to the edge of the Milky Way Galaxy and back to the Orion Spur. The piéce de résistance in software was a sealed cartridge Ceff emphasized as "vital," and she handed Rugen a container that was capable of withstanding the pressures of open space. "Inside are the latest prototypes on time travel and all the cartography available on the fourth dimension," she explained. "It will utilize most of the memory inside multidex two and three, so I did not install the program. Until you need them, the spools are safer inside this sealed cartridge. If you make it through the mission and want any chance to return to this time, you must dump everything but life-support, link multidexes two and three, so they can communicate and install these spools. Only these spools will allow you to have a chance to get back to this time."

Beyond technology, we had a few articles of clothing, which were appropriate reproductions for the time, and a full medical kit that contained a plentiful supply of Regression drug. "What's the Regression for?" asked Rugen.

"That's in case you forget who you are," explained Kayya.

"If I cannot remember who I am, how am I supposed to remember what Regression is used for?" asked Rugen.

Kayya sighed. "I hate it when you ask me questions such as that. Take it and allow me a few indulgences beyond logic. Besides, every inhalant has insert literature that describes its course of action."

"Here's another indulgence," said Ceff showing me two large canisters of green capsules. "I've included a few bottles of nutrient capsules because we're worried that you will not get proper food in the past." They were the same kind of capsules that Nova liked to consume.

Rugen's parents were thoughtful enough to give us five thousand dollars in the currency of the land appropriate for that time in history. "You don't need to worry about this money; it's not counterfeit," said Ceff. "We bought it from a museum." I was impressed with their ingenuity in thinking to buy money from a museum. We knew that if we made it to Earth in 2015 that we would need to use our cunning to survive. Whatever Rugen's parents gave us would not cover what we would need. Still, they were giving us their absolute best and we knew it.

****

"We're coming in range of The Door," announced Kayya. We all went forward and watched out the span of the cockpit window. I was waiting to see the profile of my precious *La Ventana* again, even if it was from a distance of fifty kilometers. Kayya was peering down at the control panel, not into space, when she announced, "Something's wrong, terribly wrong! *The Mother* is gone."

Hope's attention snapped to the window. Her eyelids narrowed and she seemed to scan along an invisible line. Rugen leaned over Kayya's shoulder and boosted the settings on the blue line of the space scanner, allowing it to fan its readings out into wider and wider spheres. We all watched breathlessly—eighty, one hundred, two hundred, a thousand, ten thousand, fifty thousand kilometers. "There's an android freighter out of Zenith at fifty-two thousand kilometers," announced Rugen. "Otherwise, space is empty all the way to Aeternus."

"*The Mother* wouldn't retreat to fifty thousand kilometers," half-screamed Kayya. "It's impossible to launch 'spheres into the corridor from that distance. I must be off course."

Rugen reiterated our flight coordinates into the navigational software of the multidex. We watched as the second coordinate superimposed over the first on the appropriate screen. "We're dead on course," Rugen announced. "There's nothing out there except—" suddenly, *ce* looked stunned. "The dimensions of The Door have widened to a thousand kilometers."

"*The Mother* was sucked through The Door!" declared Hope. "We have to rescue her."

It was very quiet among us until Rugen said, "No! *The Mother's* crew is capable of handling any crisis. Our job is to go back in time and attempt to heal this rupture if we can. We will launch into the corridor exactly as planned." Rugen stared at me and I knew *ce* needed my support.

"I agree with Rugen," I said, although, in my heart, I wanted to rescue *The Mother* too.

None of us talked about *The Mother* or the widening rupture, but I thought of Senon, that young soul that believed so much in life. I hoped that *le* was somewhere safe. I already had asked Kayya to send Senon a copy of my book. Now she asked me, "If I can't locate Senon, what do you want me to do with the manuscript of your latest book?"

"Send a copy to Una when you get a chance," I said. "She's on Delphi."

"I'll do that." Kayya put her arms around me and attempted to comfort me. "*The Mother* has adequate evacuation vessels aboard. I know that for sure."

TWELVE

We busied ourselves with getting the vitasphere into space. It was a quick operation, almost too quick now that nobody was there to stop us. We retreated to our private rooms to change into our spacesuits that would accommodate our bodily functions. This part had Hope worried. She did not know that no way existed to reproduce gravity or the comforts of home in the fourth dimension. Once we strapped ourselves into our chairs, we would not be getting up. That meant we had to catheterize ourselves. Hope asked a flurry of questions about how to accomplish this and I was all too happy to allow Rugen to do all the explaining.

Rugen was a typical Vanguard scout in these last moments. *Ce* was edgy, eager, and lost in a trance of *cis* personal thoughts. *Ce* wanted to get on with the mission. "Hope is taking a long time to get ready," *ce* fussed. "Maybe I should ask Kayya to help Hope with the catheter."

I tried to make *cim* smile with, "Sounds as if you want to launch a probe into the problem."

"Fuck off!" *ce* returned.

When Hope returned she said. "I feel as if I've lost my virginity," and she twisted her hips a bit. Questions appeared and darted around my mind like electrons. I let them go on their merry and mysterious way. Besides, I already decided that I, personally, was not going down the sexual road of Hope.

Ceff and Kayya were Janaforma in their previous lives; but in these last few moments with Rugen, they spoke Cuneate, telling *tham* that they incarnated more times as Tyrowsians than as any other species. Cuneate has no past or future tense and the language seemed apropos for our departure. Diehard Tyrowsians never acknowledge past or future by word of mouth, but certain hand movements always indicate what they are afraid to say. Tyrowsians spread two fingers into a v-shaped pattern and point to the right if they mean past or to the left if they mean future. These hand movements have emerged into art forms that are quite poignant expressions for Tyrowsians when they resort to using them.

Now, Ceff spread all the fingers of both her hands and pointed them toward each other—indicating the convergence of past and future in the unfolding moment. *"Haserod et turpa**",* she said, with her fingers trembling toward each other. She reverted to Mescale. "We will wait until you return. I know you will return in just a moment."

"Please go home," said Rugen. "Go on with your lives. If you stay here, you will only focus attention on this area of space. Besides, it's dangerous here. When I think of you—and that will be often—I want to think of you safe at Iona. Anyway, we have the pulsar and if we make it back to this time, we will use it to come home."

"Etnna (into) *hataeasta,"* said Kayya.

Ceff and Kayya stepped back and retreated behind the safety of the double doors. Their pale and tender faces pressed against the small window near the top while expressions of *watarie* filled their tear-stained eyes. Kayya raised her hands in front of her face, and made the symbol of the convergence of past and future on the unfolding moment—of *hataeasta*. We turned toward space then and activated our *vitaratthas*. I gazed out the rear of the transport and the vitasphere looked like a gigantic translucent egg waiting for us to step aboard.

A swoosh sound came through my ear receivers as Rugen shutdown the forcefield on the open end of the transport. "Let's do it," *ce* said through my receivers. It's the last thing Vanguard Scouts say before leaving on missions. Let's do it! It's a simple, direct statement of purpose. To all involved it says, "This is it, no turning back."

Hope, Rugen, and I stepped off the rear of the transport and hung in the suspension. I took the bag containing the remains of Nova's body and opened it. We watched in passive acceptance as space took the ashes at its own rate. The tiny particles formed waves that drifted off into the dark.

****

We crossed the few meters of open space to the vitasphere and went inside. Rugen took the pilot's chair and I sat next to *cim* in the co-pilot's position. Hope sat between us, but a little removed from the panel display. Ceff had removed the jump seat that usually sits in this position and installed a full-sized chair so Hope could be comfortable for the longest ride in the history of this universe.

I enjoyed a 360° view of space and kept twisting around and searching.

---

*"sound is dying," idiomatic for "words fail me."; language origin, Cuneate.

"What are you looking for?" asked Hope.

"Signs of life," I said. "It would be worth the added risk of sneaking around *La Ventana's* vitaspheres just to know she is safe." Senon's last words about wanting to stay on *The Mother*, "no matter what" was turning into an compulsive mantra in my head so I asked Rugen if I could do something to help.

"Will you get the inhalants out?" *ce* asked.

We needed to administer inhalants of what the Vanguard called, "Bounce." "Bounce," helps stabilize the physical senses—inner ear, stomach etc.—in prolonged zero gravity situations. Each of us inserted an ampoule up our nose and released .03 micrograms of the cocktail drug. It was odorless and the only smell came from its carrier, attar.

Rugen was busy. *Ce* put the equilibrium band around *cis* head and brought its left eyepiece into *cis* line of vision. *Ce* pulled down another visor in front of *cis* right eye that gave *cim* a twin view of the larger control panel in front of us without the necessity of moving *cis* head. Finally, *ce* slipped *cis* hands into the control gloves. "Watch it," *ce* warned. The automatic restraints jutted forward around our bodies and snuggled us into place. "Thirty seconds," said Rugen, but in *cis* heart, *ce* was telling me so much more.

"I'm ready," said Hope. Her voice sounded confident and this was a good sign. At just under the speed of light we shot forward. A crimson line along the horizon flashed from behind us like an eyelid blinking closed on a final sunset. We passed the event horizon and then we were in total darkness and I do mean total darkness. We experienced no sensation of movement.

"We're inside," announced Rugen. There was a slight zing-sound inside my ear receivers as the polymicroflex snapped-back on itself and the forcefield took hold. Now, nothing stood between the fourth dimension and us except the charged power of our *vitarattha* technology.

****

A vitasphere uses most of its energy breaching hyperspace, but little once inside the fourth dimension. The propulsion system works on the principle of allowing the undulating time threads to move the vitasphere, while the pilot uses the momentum to nudge the craft in the continuing correct trajectory. In order to negotiate the time threads, a pilot needs to be a cut above the regular space jockey. The vitasphere pilot navigates the craft with the left eye by looking into a tiny eyepiece screen in the direction that *ce* wants to go. Simultaneously, the right eye is scanning a wide range of possibilities coming from the multidex, which include several overlay screens, informing the pilot of critical functions within the vitasphere. To accomplish this feat, it requires incredible concentration and independent eye action. The job is so physically demanding the shift for vitasphere pilots is less than two hours and why Kayya told Rugen that to pilot a vitasphere for *cis* estimated twenty-two hours was an impossible feat. Only slightly less demanding for the pilot are the control gloves, which are the connection between the multidex and vitasphere. Of course, control gloves are standard technology and I used them three thousand years ago when flying *The Mother*. However, the difference between the control gloves I used then and the ones Rugen uses now is like the difference between counting on one's toes and quantum physics.

Success in the fourth dimension depends on a pilot's ability to become a spontaneous and intuitive presence, an interactive link among the multidex, the ship, and the fourth dimension itself. The essential pilot must encompass an incredible range of coping skills in a realm where guideposts are nonexistent and reliance on cause and effect logic can be a deadly error. From inside the fourth dimension, the blackness seems to loom. No known way exists to mark the position of The Door back to the third dimension because no way exists to anchor a fixed position inside a black void. Without reference points, instrumentation is useless. If the pilot has the misfortune of being alone, physical vision will suggest the vitasphere is not even moving. If two vitaspheres are present, the best the pilot can hope for is to know that the vitasphere is moving in relationship to the other vitasphere without knowing which ship is moving and to where.

One might ponder how any pilot could negotiate a realm as elusive as the fourth and survive. Obviously, pilots do it. Young hotshot pilots, such as Rugen, do it almost as a matter of course. *Vitasphere* pilots begin training as young as thirteen bio-years because, older than that, the physical mind becomes too rigid to adapt to the incredible demands of this alien dimension. Of course, it takes more than the flexibility of youth; it takes intrinsic talent that cannot be learned in one lifetime. Rugen admits freely, "I could not do this job if my great, great-grandparents were not genetically-modified beings. Only in this life, have I evolved into the biological creature that can do these sorts of tasks." Rugen was not being egotistical when *ce* said this; *ce* was telling the truth.

****

The darkness inside the fourth dimension was the darkest dark I ever witnessed. It was suspended everything, total deprivation. Faith was impossible, trust essential. The faint glow of the instrument panel was our hearth and communal comfort. Beyond the forcefield, my physical eyes were useless. I put myself into an open-eye mediation and waited for Ezek to feed me information. Slowly, as if my eyes were adjusting to a very gloomy sunrise, I began sensing the time threads streaming out through the seemingly endless black. Like the loose ends of a spider's web the threads waved toward the deeper unknown of the fourth dimension.

"I'm going to bring it around," said Rugen. Only the multidex could tell

183

us if our vitasphere was lateral or perpendicular to the concentration of time threads between dimensions. The vitasphere moved to the left bringing us into right angles with the threads. This was our one clue that we were on course. Rugen sighed. "From here on out, I'll need to concentrate on where we need to go, so I will not be communicating unless necessary."

The sudden, yet enduring, lack of physical stimulation caused me to fall into a meditative state. Sometime later, Rugen said, "Look sharp to our right; you might see something interesting." A screen on the console showed three amber lights that were hovering at a relative distance of three hundred kilometers from our vitasphere. They were *graeymlins*.

"They're coming closer," I announced.

"I can see them with my physical eyes," said Hope. I was about to say impossible, when I glanced up and saw them too.

"They look like enormous crystal fireflies," said Hope. "How do they do that here in the darkness? Do they charge-up somewhere and then fly around until their energy cells wear down?"

"Stay alert!" said Rugen. "They're closing in on us. They probably can sense the pulsar hanging there and are curious. I hope it's not going to be a problem."

No living creatures in our known third-dimensional universe are as large as *graeymlins*. To describe them, one always must resort to grand hyperbole, saying they are gargantuan, awesome, and beyond compare. They are reminders of all things impossible, which exist despite their unlikelihood. The largest of the three *graeymlins* was twice the size of *The Mother* and the smallest, about half that size. Their heads were enormous and their necks covered in thick manes that made them look as if they were wearing elaborate boas. Their manes contain sensitive feelers, which helped them negotiate the time threads. When their bodies undulated and swayed, I glimpsed flashes of silver as if they had fish scales. Here in their native space, they moved very fast and could pop up, out of the clear black, as if materializing out of nowhere. They do this quite often and I hear that it is terrifying to be on the opposite end of the surprise. These three *graeymlins* remained at a respectful distance of twenty kilometers and actually seemed to be cruising alongside us like the gray dolphins of Earth or the blue-nosed trossells of Hattonia. I was thrilled to see them this close. It was obvious that the littlest of the three *graeymlins* could have played with our vitasphere on the tip of its proboscis and swallowed us whole.

"Holy Mother of Creation!" exclaimed Hope. "I can see right down their throats and into their bellies!"

"Stay cool!" advised Rugen. "They can sense tension and excitement. That's what they do with the time threads; they play with its tensions and reverberations."

The three *graeymlins* stayed with us for what Hope thought was twenty minutes and what Rugen estimated to be an hour. The multidex recorded the same time as fifteen years. It was our first sampling of the illusions involved in the corridor. Rugen insisted that none of us had the right answer and the multidex was not to be trusted anymore than our personal judgment.

****

"How long do you think it will be until the first birth crisis arrives?" Hope asked. This was the first difficulty that Kayya mentioned concerning the corridor. The first time of probable crisis would be Rugen's birth— eighteen bio-years, then mine at twenty-seven bio-years and finally Hope's at thirty bio-years. Of course, if something happened to Rugen at the eighteen-year mark, we were doomed.

"Whatever happens, we need to stay calm and focused," said Rugen.

Seconds later, Ezek told me, *I hear a noise.*

"What's wrong?" asked Rugen.

"I thought I heard a noise," I said.

"It's probably feedback in your ear receivers," Rugen said.

"You're right." I removed my receivers to adjust them and that's when I realized the sound was coming from out in the corridor. "Hope? Did you hear that?"

She listened and then said, "I hear nothing at all."

The sound grew louder. "I have perfect pitch and it sounds like the toning of E-natural."

"E-natural on the musical scale?" Rugen questioned. "Trust me. It's an auditory illusion."

Then I saw a tiny blue-black spider marching across the top of the console panel. As if in normal gravity, it stopped and dropped a line. Ezek was already advising me, *don't look and it will disappear.* "Rugen? Do you ever get extraneous creatures walking around inside a vitasphere?"

"What do you see now?" *ce* asked.

"A spider."

"Spiders are the most ubiquitous creatures in all creation," chirped Hope. "I once read that wherever we are, a spider is somewhere within a meter of us."

I glanced at the console and the spider moved closer and spoke confidentially. *She means, I'm common*, it said. *That's right! Close your eyes and pretend I'm not here. Stuff your ears with wax. Did you expect me to communicate with you like some grand wizard or appear as a heavenly flash of light? There you sit tied to your crosspiece, struggling to face the great illusions. Look how silly Rugen looks.* I allowed my eyes to drift sideways. Rugen looked like an android trussed up inside *cis* equipment, acting as if *ce* knew what *ce* was doing. Fear sprang up inside me and I said, "What we're doing makes no sense at all."

"Hold steady," said Rugen.

"Sante is right," said Hope. "We should—" and then her voice trailed off into nothing.

"You're both starting to have a few problems with corridor distortions," said Rugen.

Watch cim *carefully,* urged the spider. *Any second now, Rugen is going to disappear right into* cis *false sense of security.* At that instant, Rugen winked out of existence. I think I screamed. *See! I told you so. Where is your great love of understanding when you understand so little? Eons of commitment to every illusion and now it's just primal will and—watch! I'm going to disappear next and then there will be—*

Vibrations of energy were armed with a deafening sound. The energy oscillated, searching for any connection within me. Traveling downward, from the crown of my head, the energy headed straight for the black diamond at my core.

Where am I? Sasaybin! I'm standing by No Name Lake. The colors are vivid—cosmic-tree greens, light-speed blues, transparent tans, gut-wrenching reds. I can see forever, yet my eyes seek only the tranquil loveliness of the clear water eddying around my feet. It's morning. The day is pristine and the rain lingers in the air like diamond dust.

Nova is walking toward me. "What took you so long to get here?" le *asks. Creation has spun* lis *hair from gold;* lis *eyes are living sapphires. Lis skin shimmers like white opals. Le is the jewel of creation.*

You're alive!

Forget old concepts of alive or dead and the limitations of time. We have eternity.

I'm not supposed to be here—am I? I'm supposed to be with Rugen in the vitasphere *helping* cim *go back in time.*

Rugen will understand. It's cis *job to understand. Cis understanding is infinite. Your job is to love me. Take the wax out of your ears and unbind yourself from the crosspiece. Consciousness is, therefore help yourself. Tell me what you want and it's yours.*

I want to help Rugen and Hope mend the rupture.

Then do it!

I was back in the vitasphere and everything was as it was. Rugen was sitting beside me and Hope was there too. "Holy Mother!" I exclaimed. "Something incredible just happened to me. I was all over the place. Did I pass out?"

"No, you just saw a *manatee*," declared Rugen. "You okay, Hope?"

"I thought I was home on Earth!" she said. "It was incredibly vivid!"

"Forget it," said Rugen. "We need to stay focused. I think I'm starting to experience my birth crisis. I'm starting to get an empty feeling as if I'm lonely or abandoned."

Ezek began to pick up the replay of Rugen's transitional reality into this life. I reached over and touched *cis* arm and *ce* jumped in surprise. "Rugen!" I said sternly. "*Snap out of it!*"

Ce started gritting *cis* teeth. "I'm okay," *ce* said with steely determination. "You will relive your birth trauma and the first few months of helplessness and that's all. I know now that it can't kill or stop us."

"I'm glad. I was worried," admitted Hope. "Thoughts of physical death bother me because I've never experienced it. Bogwa makes it seem horrible. Evose thinks our spirits might not know where they are supposed to go because we're in an alien dimension."

At that instant, my attention snapped backward and I knew my birth trauma was beginning to happen too. I held on, knowing I could not fall out of existence. *Tiny chimes rustle above my crib. I look up into familiar shapes and faces that are yet unclear to me. My adoring parents pass me around. Elay puts me to her breast while Bejan sings lullabies. For a moment, I fear that I may be separate, right after they cut the umbilical cord. I inhale my first breath of air. It is hard work being born, but I know how to do it because I've done it many times before. I am a fetal hotshot. Nova, Bejan, and Michael come as visiting envoys inside Elay where their spirits commune with mine. I decide to stay inside the fetus because an incredible love begins to bloom in me for the potential within this new life. Sometimes, I sleep inside the fetus to try it out, and sometimes I move around, go back to my oversoul, and move among my new parents. I know I possess freewill to go or stay. I travel through Nova and into Elay, into the Eden of her glory. I actually say, "Let's do it!" like the Vanguard Scout I was in my last life. Nova warns me that le is ready to climax and I must be ready. I help lim make love to Elay as le gives her lis life essence that will spark my new body. Nova allows me to watch as Bejan puts a pipette of the bio-engineered DNA, my genetic hardware, into Elay's uterus. I am inside Nova's body. Sometimes I move up into Nova's head and look out through lis eyes at Elay, Michael, or Bejan. I can move down and touch lis sex, move up and squeeze lis heart until le weeps with incredible love. Through me, Nova becomes a sexual poet. I fuel lis passion and lis mates are astonished over lis newfound sexual stamina. The light is orange, lovely, and dynamic, a place that etches my spirit with its gleaming receptivity of Nova's divine-will. I reside in lis communal dimension, inside lis energy school of great bliss. Nova has prepared a sacred place for me inside limself that sits like a cozy Ganat nest right below lis heart. I am hanging over Lemira Jha watching Nova participate in a sex ritual with Sirushi. Nova is calling me. I am one with my oversoul.*

I emerged from my rebirth and sat there in complete awe.

"Wow!" yelped Hope. I just relived my birth in reverse."

"Yeah, it was great," I agreed.

"Parts of it were not so good for me," admitted Rugen. "I was five weeks old when my biological parents died."

Hope leaned forward and put her hand on Rugen's shoulder to comfort *cim* before I could do it myself. "I'm so sorry," she said.

Ezek shouted, *Hope is falling in love with Rugen. Ce is beautiful, desirable, and non-threatening to her long held virginity. You need to see where this is going.*

No question existed in my mind that Rugen would not betray my trust, but this was much subtler. This had to do with honoring urges within the darkest corners of each other. I did not want Rugen to deny *cis* desire for

Hope. I wanted *cim* to feel fulfilled. I wanted to honor all *cis* desires as *ce* already honored mine with Nova. Rather than forget *cis* attraction for Hope, as I had thus far, I decided to bring the situation out in the open. "Hope? Are you attracted to Rugen?" I asked. She did not answer me at first. I turned and gave her a pointed stare.

"Pardon?" she asked. I repeated what I said and she appeared a bit flustered. "Well, of course, Rugen is an attractive consort—if that's what you mean?"

Rugen was insulted that we were talking about *cim* in the third person. "Sante! Don't be so—Human!" *ce* said. I could have turned it around and talked about simpering love as *ce* had, but I let it go. Clearly, this was different. Hope was brand new territory. I decided to blame Hibernia and hoped she would not mind. "Our mate in our last life was Human. She could be direct when the occasion called for it and she taught me how to be direct too."

"I guess you've figured out that I'm a virgin," said Hope.

Rugen was silent and I tried to sound surprised. "No kidding!"

"Yeah. I guess it sounds strange. I'm almost thirty-one. Bogwa told me that the Janaforma possess a strong sex drive because they need to contend with that extra step in procreation. When we came here in our last life, we were merely going to observe, but Bogwa involved himself in sex. Just a few minutes ago, when I was reliving my birth, I saw him having sex with Estrella. He seemed to be enjoying himself quite a bit. It made me curious about how it might feel to have sex with someone."

Rugen finally spoke up. "You merely felt curious?"

"Well, that's a start—isn't it? I was wondering—if we make it through this mission maybe you could introduce me to sex."

"What did you have in mind, a demonstration or participation?" I asked.

"Oh, definitely participation," said Hope.

"How do you feel about changing your name to Trust?" I asked.

Rugen sounded like a prude when *ce* said, "This is a ridiculous conversation. Sante and I don't have sex; we make love. A world of difference exists between those two things."

"Rugen can be a snob," I told her. "Of course we have sex. We have some of the wildest sex you could possibly imagine. *Ce* is merely suggesting that we take it seriously."

"We need to take this mission seriously too," said Rugen. "We should keep our minds on our purpose for being here, not on frivolity."

"Right Captain Rugen!" I said. I turned around and winked at Hope and she actually smiled at me for the first time. Miracles do abound.

****

The tiny blue-black spider returned, this time creeping along the edge of the console. "Do you see a small spider creeping along the edge of the auxiliary multidex screen?" I asked Hope.

She leaned forward and peered over my shoulder. "I think I do see something moving," she admitted.

Rugen raised *cis* eyepiece and demanded, "Where? Show me this damn spider you both believe is real." By then, the crafty spider had vanished. Rugen declared it, "contagious *manatee* delusion," before yanking down *cis* eyepiece and returning to guiding our vitasphere.

No sooner did Rugen leave me with my delusional self than the spider returned for its next performance. Despite no conscious memory of ever encountering anything frighteningly arachnid in nature, the spider remained alluringly real and exquisite in detail. *You are an illusion created by the manatee*, I told it. This time the spider did not speak, but dropped a silver thread from its spinnerets as if it were under the influence of a wonder drug that made it into a civil engineer. Its web was a genius of geometric construction and I knew that somewhere, sentient arachnids existed because they were logical and clever. Whatever the vision's purpose, the tiny spider took its time, excreting its woven wonder with sure and intricate skill. Its humor was not lost on me. The web began to take shape and was what some scientists postulate the third dimension looks like snuggled up against the fourth. The web had two perfect cradles, the second cupped inside the first. I observed no guide-wires, no elastic bands, and no cause-and-effect reality holding this web in place. As soon as the spider finished, it climbed inside its double cradle and sat motionless, waiting to sense a signal along its sensory-conscious threads.

Eye to eye and still and patient its compound eyes watched my many faces. A confluence of jumbled thoughts poured through me in this unfair encounter. I could read nothing from this particular spider, yet my conscious mind was forced back from psychic projections and into a deeper part of me. There, I found an internal interface, a literal conjunction point where my conscious and unconscious met. This is where the *manatee* was sucking meaning from the unresolved desires of my heart.

I have come so far, I pleaded. *Now that I am here, do not think I will falter either from my fear or your venom. I want access to the fourth dimension.*

In response, the *manatee* hesitated behind its spider façade and I heard its vesper tone, a deep, velvet purring as viscous as syrup. It said—*nothing*.

Tell me about nothing, I thought.

There is nothing to be said about nothing. Then the *manatee* dropped me like a hot coal and ran away. I fell into normal reality. For me, the moment only made me feel foolish. My mind did not produce any grand gesture or unique vista of truth or reality. My vision demonstrated my participation with my self-induced illusions. I was a common spider building a double-web of consciousness.

I closed my eyes and went away from the fourth dimensional darkness into the darkness inside my eyes. I sat in the temple of myself and called out to my beloved. *Do not leave me alone in this confusing darkness.*

Then I saw the spider differently because it had vanished and I was remembering it through the vehicle of memory. I saw the web vibrating, swinging back and forth as if the spider was lounging in a hammock. The vibration produced a lullaby of feminine softness as if someone was rocking me to sleep.

****

Hope tapped my arm and I opened my eyes. "Look!" she said and she pointed her chin toward the right side of the vitasphere. Tiny lights, like sleet, were deflecting off the outside of the forcefield. Rugen slid *cis* eyepiece away to take a quick peek. Hope and I waited for *cis* judgment on what it might be. "I think it's real," *ce* said after a few seconds. As soon as Rugen acknowledged the light's authenticity, the phenomenon grew stronger until it became a buffeting of minute flecks outside the forcefield. Within a heartbeat, a migraine headache threatened to split my head into two pieces. My hands flew up to clutch my throbbing temples. "What's wrong?" Rugen asked.

"It's Belinda," I managed to say. Then everything went black before my eyes and I was falling, plummeting downward. I stared up from inside a maelstrom and saw Rugen with *cis* arms extended toward me. *Ce* appeared terrified and confused and all the while, Belinda was pulling me down into the sea of herself. Drowning, I could taste the luscious brine of her watery embrace. Belinda lifted from the depths, her voice heard through dimensions as a roar from a seashell. *You are experiencing the collective nightmare of soul fragments*, she wailed. *Think only of the year 2015 or you're not going to make it.* Then, she took me as if I were a fish and tossed me up on the beach at Rugen's feet.

"I'm going to vomit!" I choked and I put my hand over my mouth.

I had extreme vertigo from my rapid shuttling between levels of consciousness. Rugen unlocked *cis* seat restraint and fast-floated to my assistance. A second later, *ce* snapped open an inhalant of Bounce from the medical kit and released its contents up my nose. "Hold onto me," said Rugen. "I will steady you."

Hope's voice filtered through my lingering nausea. "I heard what Belinda said and I disagree with her. We need to acknowledge these soul fragments."

"What did Belinda say?" asked Rugen.

I pointed to the insistent pelting light outside the vitasphere. "They're soul fragments. Belinda said we should not acknowledge them or we will be unable to get back to the year 2015."

"That makes absolutely no sense," declared Hope. "Can't you see that if we deny these soul fragments, then we will be in a state of denial too?"

The pelting outside the vitasphere increased and a confused expression gained strength on Rugen's face. "I'm unsure about what we should do," *ce* admitted.

Belinda responded by pressuring me more, which caused me excruciating pain between my eyes. I panicked and thought again that I might vomit. I had too many voices inside me, too many causes demanding attention and taking me in the wrong direction. Where was I in this chaos? I had cast my lot with Nova so long ago that I trusted only *lim* to cut a new path." I consciously turned toward the black diamond within myself. This time it seemed excruciatingly difficult, a veritable effort to swim against the current. Because of the outside pressures, it seemed to take an eternity to move my mind the few degrees necessary to see the faintest spark of divine-will within myself. Death had seized my beloved, taking *lim* to another shore. Now *le* was blipping out messages made of love-light and the black diamond within me was interpreter of *lis* will.

Hope was recalcitrant, yet she was biting her bottom lip as if she were reluctant to speak words her soul was asking her to tell. Her mouth suddenly relented to her truth. "The answer to mending the rupture is here in this moment, not in the past."

I said, "I'll join you. Together, we will go out to these soul fragments with our love."

"No!" Rugen said so loudly that I thought my head might shatter.

I assured *cim*, "I can do this."

Rugen appeared desperate. "Sante, we're soul mates on a definite mission. We're supposed to mend the rupture in the past, not stop here. I cannot do this without you. You know that."

I had a choice, although my choices seemed exceedingly few. I could have debated Rugen, although I'm positive that after *cis* fiasco with Belinda, on principle alone, *ce* would have let me win. I quickly vetoed debating. Besides, from *cis* perspective, Rugen was right. I did promise to go all the way back to 2015. "I'm sorry," I told Hope. "My allegiance is with Rugen."

She sighed in frustration. "Then, I'll go out to the soul fragments without you."

"No you're not!" snapped Rugen.

Hope grew more determined. "I know you think you're in charge, but you're only one-third of our team, our pilot, and nothing more. I've decided to stay here and you're honor bound to respect my decision."

Rugen turned as polarized as Hope. This scared me because I knew being stuck in the fourth dimension between two extremes could keep us there forever. "You're right," Rugen said much too calmly. "I'm merely the pilot on this mission. My duty is to get you to the year 2015 and your job is to mend the rupture when we arrive. Please allow me to remind you that you promised to undertake this expedition because Evose was unfit and unable to fulfill his part of the bargain. Your soul mates are primarily responsible for this rupture and it's your obligation to go the distance, not to get distracted along the way. Besides, Sante and I know zilch about how to fix dimensional ruptures."

I knew then that Hope was the will connection between her soul mates. Despite my support for Rugen, I tried to help Hope explain her point of view. "Divine-will cannot skip over misery," I said as gently as possible.

"Time is running out," insisted Rugen. "If we don't get back to 2015, the third-dimensional universe will cease to exist."

"Third dimensional time does not exist here in the fourth," said Hope.

"The problem is bigger than time," said Rugen. "This problem involves a dimensional rupture, which is on the verge of annihilating time."

"Okay," said Hope. "Then you and Sante go back to 2015 and I'll stay here in the fourth dimension and work from here."

"I can't let you do that," said Rugen. "These soul fragments will tear you to shreds."

Hope smiled. "That's not going to happen. I existed as a conscious being when your ancestors were monkeys swinging around in trees. Do you wish to see how resilient I can be?" Before we had a chance to answer yes or no, Hope began demonstrating her adaptability for her astounded audience of two. What I thought was her immutable physical body, she transformed before our eyes. She changed herself into a soft rose-colored sphere that bounced around the inside of the vitasphere like a delicate Ping-Pong ball. Hope actually possessed the ability to manipulate matter—her physical body—and she did it with her will.

"Holy shit!" Rugen said.

The light ball turned a deeper scarlet with green edges and grew very large. Then the ball exploded into the head of a dragon that roared in our faces and spit forth fire. I felt the heat. The energy slid back into a blade of light that fleshed out into the innocent Hope. "That's just one of the things you can do with evolved will," she declared.

"Holy shit!" Rugen exclaimed a second time.

"Super holy shit!" agreed Hope and she slid into another blade of light and morphed into an image of Nova. Then she leaned over and kissed me on the cheek. A second later, she squeezed herself into Hope again. "When I was Mehiel, I occupied Nova's body to keep it alive while Sirushi took Nova's spirit to Lemira Jha." She tapped the side of her cheek with her forefinger. "Once I've been inside a body, I remember it. When the Cerribeame prepared to strip Nova of *lis* mind, I scared the Heat out of them with a few antics such as my fire-breathing dragon. It was so real for the Ganat mind-strippers that I managed to singe the nap off their arms."

Rugen looked as if *cis* eyes were ready to pop out of *cis* head. "You're a shapeshifter!" *ce* said, as if it were a crime instead of a talent.

"Not exactly," returned Hope. "Shapeshifting is different. My talents are more in the area of total projection." She laughed again and said, "You both look so amazed. As I said before, I'll stay here and go out to the soul fragments and you two go back in time and mend the rupture. It's the comfortable solution for all involved." She managed to get in a small dig regarding masculinity saying, "Think of it as the traditional solution. Females stay behind and do the nursing while the masculine goes off on a quest."

A slight *varoom* sound interrupted our exchange and an enormous vision half-materialized on top of the console. The new vision was angelic. It appeared as a life-sized projection inside an arc of the palest blue light. Its hair was white and gleaming with intense fiber-optic beauty as if each hair was a conduit for radiance. The face appeared familiar, but I did not know the identity behind the form until it extended a delicate hand toward Hope. It was a stylized Estrella, an overlay of what Estrella looked like in life. Her face and shape kept changing, so I could see Estrella at many stages of her existence. The one tangible aspect to the apparition was its clothing. Layers and layers of blue and white fabric draped about her form as if she needed to swaddle herself against the cold of the fourth dimension or perhaps hide her blinding light from mortal eyes. "Take my hand, my darling child," she said.

Hope's voice filled with emotion. "*Mebrí*"

"Come with me," said Estrella.

Hope hesitated before the awesome vision and laid down her terms. "Only if you promise to stay and nurse the fragments with me."

"I have come for no other purpose. I will stay with you and together we will bind wounds and heal even ancient scars. Together, we will bring miracles to the needy."

Hope saw her goal and never hesitated. "As you can see, I must go," she said. "I'm sure a trip into the past with you would be exciting; but I have work to do here in the fourth dimension. If you're interested in spending a life with me, we could make a pledge to meet. It will happen if we want it enough."

Rugen and I stared at Hope until Rugen poked me and prompted me, "answer her Sante!"

"I'm sorry," I said. "Our souls have joined with Nova. We cannot make any lifelong commitments without *lim* agreeing to it."

"I understand," she said. "I only wish my soul mates had the same loyalty to me that you show Nova." She leaned over Rugen and said, "You are so beautiful. I see no gaps in your soul where denial oozes forth as shadows. That's why I thought sexual contact with you would be— enjoyable." Abruptly, her expression turned to sadness. If you see my soul mates before I do, please tell them I'm in the fourth dimension with my darling *mebr*. Tell them, I will wrap myself in blue and by my color they will know me." Hope narrowed and again turned into a blade of light and joined with the greater Estrella. Incredibly, the projection now appeared as a hybrid of Estrella and Hope. I swear, I even saw a bit of Mehiel in there at times.

"A segment of the angel's face glanced my way. "A large part of me wants to stay here and help," I told her.

A delicate hand reached out of the arc of light and touched my shoulder. "I took a bit of your love," she said. "I will hand it out like bread to beggars as we go about our work."

"I could do this work with you."

"You already are," said the united form and then they were gone. Outside the vitasphere, I heard a devilish giggle that made chills run up and down my spine. Then the flicking against our craft ceased.

THIRTEEN

Rugen and I sat alone in the perfect silence of the fourth dimension. Rugen's voice seemed to moan when *ce* said, "I'm so exhausted and afraid for our purpose. We don't know where we're going or what we're supposed to do if we ever get there. We can't turn ourselves into flashing lights as Hope just did. All we possess is a bit of technology. Without Hope, our mission is doomed. The shame of our failure is more than I can bear. I'm sorry, Sante—sorry that I dragged you into this mess. This time I was so sure the outcome would be different. Where do I keep going wrong?"

I took *cis* hand and placed it on the spot where the black diamond lived. It awoke and using me as its telepathic amplifier, Nova's voice came through loud and clear. *Through my own hunger to know, I brought you into being. I nourished you from love's own breast and declared you my miracle, my muse of eloquence and truth. I knew then that if anyone could rise above my wildest imagined potential, it would be you. You came to manifest my completion, my dream, my beloved Rugen. Without you, I am a forgotten dream.*

We knew we had no choice. Perhaps thousands of years prior we enjoyed some leeway, but no longer. We were at the bottom of our own funnel, conveying the conclusions of our millenniums of experiential wisdom. Rugen bared *cis* soul to me, not realizing how naked *ce* already was before me. "I have a confession to make," *ce* said. "I have been lost out here for what seems like the last three or four hours."

"I know."

"There's more. Some of the visions the *manatees* were manifesting for your benefit actually were mine. I was filtering my unresolved emotions through you. I was deluding myself with the rationalization that it was okay for me to put my denial on you because I was the one doing the physical

195

flying of this craft."

"I know that too."

"At first I did it unconsciously, but when I knew that I was doing it, I did not stop, at least not for a while. I'm sorry I used you that way, Sante."

"Rugen, you were only leaning on me a little. That's why I came along, so you would have somebody to lean on. Please forgive yourself, because forgiveness is not an issue between us."

"If you were not here with me, I would die," *ce* said. "That's how thin and used up I feel right now. Help me, Sante; help me with your psychic powers to find The Door to the third dimension. I know you can do it. You can do it just as you pulled the Wheel of Fortune card out of Belinda's deck."

"Every gift I have is yours, but I offer no guarantees because I don't consciously know how I do these types of things." What I did know was—the feeling came easily and I would release Ezek and he was hot on the case. This time, without precedent, nothing seemed easy. I had to go where it was difficult for me to go, to that place that held my trust, to the black diamond in my heart. When I took that leap of faith, Nova was already waiting for me.

Then I saw it! A huge *graeymlin* abruptly appeared in the distance and it was phosphorescing in luminous shades of the rainbow. "Nova is communicating with me," I told Rugen. *Le* is saying, 'Follow the *graeymlin*.'" The tail of the *graeymlin* began to move gently from side to side, like the tail of a fish. A moment later, a tunnel appeared outside the vitasphere illuminated by the magnificent colors of the graeymlin itself.

"I'm on it!" Rugen replied. The tunnel was molded of time threads that were gently parting to allow us access. Rugen nudged the vitasphere closer, toward the opening passageway, until the peristaltic action of the threads engulfed us. "I've just lost control of the vitasphere," said Rugen. "Whatever happens now, is beyond my control." Where were we bound? We knew not where. We had no fixed reference points, direction, or time, yet our faith in this tenuous connection kept us moving through that space of blackness with no direction or sense of movement, for the first time in creation.

****

Afterward, when Rugen and I discussed those moments of crisis in the fourth dimension, I thought the time lapse was about twenty minutes and *ce* thought we found The Door almost immediately. We both agreed, some amount of time passed before we saw the first visible clues of the portal back to the third dimension.

I glimpsed a small patch of stars many light years distance. They were quasars because they flashed like a bevy of sparklebugs. The time threads expelled us from the fourth and a few dangling threads near the end of the breach even gave us a gentle nudge. Steadily, the stars grew more focused and joined others until multitudes dominated a larger and larger frame. It took us another two hours to reach a point we could confidently call, "The Door." At one crucial moment, which lasted for about thirty seconds, there was sound, a sucking noise that reminded me of a gasp for air. I glanced over at Rugen and *ce* looked confident for the first time in hours.

"We're going to make it!" I exclaimed. We declared a two minute holiday, freed ourselves from our seats, embraced, and proclaimed our love for each other with as much enthusiasm as we could muster considering we had not slept for what we conjointly decided was thirty-four space hours. For two minutes, we bounced up and down in the weightlessness like two insane fools. "Rugen, do you realize what this means?"

Ce looked blank before venturing a guess. "It means we're still alive and have a chance to mend the rupture."

"It's bigger than that," I said. "It means that everything we previously imagined about historical time, things such as logical continuity, historical meaning, are all fluky! Knowing that, we know nothing at all!"

"You're right!" *ce* screamed with laughter. Despite our joy in finding our way back to the third dimension, many critical unknowns lay ahead, unknowns such as—what time were we in? Rugen began to perform the critical tests to determine our location. *Ce* sent out a sub-light probe and waited for the multidex to interpret the data. The function of the probe was to emit energy sensors capable of mapping the shape of The Door. Rugen was staring straight ahead into *cis* navigational eyepieces and I was staring out into space and searching for familiar star patterns. As soon as the multidex told *cim* its results, *ce* said, "The Door is smaller and not as deep, especially from the third-dimensional side."

A couple minutes later, we came into visual light range of the star Pegasus. The light was dim, but definitely Pegasus. We would have recognized Pegasus from any angle. Rugen turned our sensors toward the Orion sectors of space. The light magnitude from that reading would tell us approximately, what time we were in. In silence, we waited for the critical answer to flash on the appropriate screen. It took the multidex two minutes to take the readings and analyze the results. "Praise The Mother!" Rugen screamed. "The multidex says we're approximately three months early."

****

For added protection, Rugen caused the polymicroflex panels to snap open and encase the vitasphere. *Ce* pointed to a nearby moon a few hundred kilometers away. "Let's see if we can locate a suitable hiding place to put the vitasphere," *ce* said. Ten minutes later, we discovered a rogue asteroid that had escaped from the Kalalangla Asteroid Belt approximately ten thousand years earlier. We christened the asteroid Hope. Its orbit was stable and its calm surface was composed of cratered silica rock. One of these craters would serve as a perfect shelter for the vitasphere. We circumnavigated the asteroid a couple of times, flying at between two and eight kilometers altitude so we could check out the integrity of its mass. From this perspective, we could see ridges and escarpments along the surface caused by expansion and contraction of its surface, probably in the range of a million years old, but no major fractures that might make it unstable. "What do you think?" asked Rugen. "It appears cozy to me."

I agreed and Rugen set the vitasphere down in a narrow crater two kilometers deep. We pinned on a couple of *vitaratthas*, activated them, and allowed the ambiance controls inside the vitasphere to extract our breathable air mix. We spent the next two hours securing the vitasphere and disembarking the pulsar.

Most of the equipment for the next leg of the journey was already stowed aboard the pulsar. We said adieu to the vitasphere and went inside the pulsar for the first time. It was smaller, but more civilized. It contained a sleep space, shower, proper toilet, a tiny food center, and a couple of lounge chairs. Most importantly, the pulsar had a gravity simulator.

Together, we decided that the best plan was to hold our position for another cycle (approximately three Earth days). During that time, I would attempt to contact Belinda and get a bead on the present whereabouts of Iris. We could monitor Earth transmissions, and rest.

"I can't wait to get out of this suit," Rugen said. In the tiny bathroom, we disconnected our bodies from our spacesuits and plugged them into their separate cleaning units, showered, and put on comfortable clothing. "Are you hungry or tired yet?" *ce* asked.

I managed to make Rugen smile despite our exhaustion. "I'm hyped. This is the most exciting thing I've ever done that is not directly connected to making love."

"I was thinking of eating some solid food," *ce* said.

"I don't think I should try to eat until after I contact Belinda—just in case she feels the need to turn my stomach inside-out again."

"I'm trying, but her impulsiveness makes me not trust her. She ought to know better than to go around hurting people if she is so damn evolved. This time, if you agree, I'll sit close by while you conjure her, so I can help you absorb her radical impact."

"Thanks, I accept your offer. I will give you as much of the communication as I can."

We did nothing elaborate to contact Belinda because she was already on the alert for me. Rugen sat cross-legged in the middle of the floor and I marked out a circle around *cim* with my footsteps. Then I sat down with my back to *cis* chest. I felt safer with *cim* holding me in that position. "I have you," *ce* whispered in my ear.

I brought my energy up to my brow and waited with it, holding it in the color of indigo purple. To attract Belinda, I gave her an image to grab onto that would hold her attention. The scene was a memory from another life. *We're on the planet Jotta Shay and the setting is a small forest, where the New Delphi Order of Trinity Witches maintains a retreat lodge. The trail through the forest is narrow, winding, and steep. Belinda ambles down the sloping trail, in my direction. She is barefoot. Her hair is hanging loose and her blouse open to the waist. She has tucked a scarlet flower between her breasts.*

Good evening, sister; are the auroras up yet? I ask.

She stops and looks me up and down. Actually, she is doing more than looking; she is examining me both inside and out. It's difficult to say this time of year, she replies. Want to go to my special spot? We can watch the sky and see if the auroras appear.

My mind jumped and we were making love. I knew Belinda had fully arrived and she was adding her strength to the vision. Between Belinda and me, sex was our strongest connection. I had no notions of resisting her and was ready to climax within seconds. Then Rugen reached around and grabbed my penis, which caused a shield of *cis* energy to block an orgasm between Belinda and me. "How about we get on with the necessary communication," *ce* said.

Belinda retracted her sex energy and punished me by forcing me to look at her as a manifestation of a goddess. She was sitting nude, inside an egg of energy, her knees bent and the soles of her feet pressed together. She lit up her chakras with colored light; her breasts were cherry-pink, her shoulders powdery blue, and her clitoris a thick and scaly red-eyed snake. Her hair cascaded down her back as a thousand, white flower petals. She raised her arms and gestured upward, meaning that she was now ready to allow her energy to go all the way up through her head.

I did the same with mine.

Tragedy strikes everywhere, said her vision. *A few hours after you left, my precious Evose allowed his physical form to die. He was so despondent that he asked us to destroy his body as soon as he was gone, so he could not return to this dimension. Reluctantly, we agreed. I must admit that I was surprised that Hope insisted upon going out to the soul fragments. I did not think she had the courage to make that sacrifice. Estrella appeared to Bogwa and told him a vein of possibility was widening that Hope would disembark the* vitasphere. *She promised us that she would stay with Hope and protect her. That's when Evose decided that he must go and help them too. I respect all their decisions and hope their sacrifice will ease the flow of denial along the dimensional line. As much as I mourn the physical loss of my child, I cannot deny that Evose's great presence along with Estrella and Hope will ameliorate your own chances of succeeding. My spirit longs to go to the fourth, but I have promised to help you and I will stay alive as long as you need me to direct your attention toward Iris.*

How long have we been gone in your timeframe, I asked.

In Uropaen time, you've been gone sixteen days. La Ventana went missing ten days ago. A lackluster acknowledgement comes from the scientific community that the portal to *the fourth dimension has suffered, what the media is calling, 'another minor rupture.' The official stance is that the rupture is not serious because in relation to the size of this universe the rupture is insignificant."* Despite official denial from the Orion Spur Alliance, a desperate mayhem is gathering strength in Daleth Sector and parts of the Hattonian Hub. A cresting wave of denial from all time is causing a marked polarity in the behavior of people. The Spur has experienced a rash of grizzly and unexplained murders in the Hattonian Hub, hundreds of cases of mental breakdown among Tyrowsian populations, thousands of natural disasters on every planet. I'm proud to say that at the same time, heroism and spontaneous acts of compassion are up by fifty percent. I'm still on Uropae and not yet seen the effect on other planets. Bogwa and I are leaving for Delphi in a few hours where we will put our energy together with Una and the others to see if we can neutralize the impacting denial in this time.*

I'm sorry that our initial psychic link caused you discomfort, but I was desperate to get your attention. I had been psychically hailing you for days. When you finally recognized me, the backed up energy unleashed an energy surge. If you want my help, it's important that you keep an open link between us from now on. I know you trust Nova more than you trust me, so if you focus on that conscious spot where you hold his spirit, I will speak to him and he will relay my messages to you with absolute clarity. It makes no difference, which way we communicate, either directly or through Nova. The results will be identical.

We arrived three months early, I told her. *Can you give us an idea about when the optimum time might be to contact Iris?*

That's great news! she communicated. *The period of time that Evose and Iris were in psychic contact was short, not more than a collection of a few days in the months of October, November, and December in the Earth year 2015. If you are three months early, you have slack time to make appropriate plans. Of course, do not wait until the last minute to contact her. The sooner you get to know her, the more she will trust you at the critical time.*

What's the best way to gain her confidence?

Just as I am, Iris is a love emanation. She will not trust you unless you connect with her though love.

I told you before. I will not be coerced into seducing Iris.

I know no other way to win her over. As you already know, she is living on Earth in a community called Key West, Florida on the continent of North America. Her name is Iris A. Syriaca. A word of caution concerning her, do not allow her appearance of innocence or her unassuming social position to fool you. She is a powerful clairvoyant.

Could you please give me a clear vision of her physical appearance so I can recognize her? Belinda allowed her image to morph into the appearance of someone new. What I saw was a Human female between the ages of 30 and 40 bio-years old. Her shoulder length hair was dark and pulled back. Her eyes were dark brown and her lips full and red. Her features were refined and she certainly was fuckable. She was wearing a small cross around her neck, a symbol for the Christian religion. Her posture exuded self-confidence.

Whether the confidence was authentic, I could not tell. *Okay, I have it.*

That's it for now, said Belinda. *Once you get down to the planet, contact me, or Nova, for details.*

Belinda, I'm sorry about Evose. I understand about that kind of loss.

I know you do, Sante. We part now in the spirit of peace, love, and the hope that there will be a future.

I emerged from my communicative trance with Belinda and realized Rugen was still holding my crotch. "Stopping my energy in that way hurt," I said.

"Sorry!" *ce* replied.

I was annoyed and tired. "What's this vigilance you feel concerning my interactions with Belinda?"

"It's not what you're thinking."

"Okay, what is it?" My intense passion for Rugen wanted to cut *cim* slack, so just for starters, I sent *cim* a million megawatts of my love.

Ce thought for a moment about the best way to say it. "I don't know if we should trust Belinda. Her sexuality seems to be all over the place and she was getting very personal with you a moment ago. If you want to have sex with Belinda or her previous incarnation, I'll try to understand, but I'd like a heads-up on your honest feelings."

"I'm not going to do anything we haven't agreed upon beforehand. Having sex with Iris would not be a pleasure; it would be a chore. Besides, a thousand ways exist to become intimate with another person besides having sex."

"Maybe so, but let's face facts. Sex is your go-to solution for everything. I'm sorry, Sante, but I don't see me in the scenario Belinda is trying to put into your head." A tear flowed down Rugen's cheek from *cis* right eye. "Please tell me I'm wrong because my imagination is starting to run wild. I'm thinking that Nova left the black diamond in you because I've screwed up so many times that I can't be trusted anymore."

I was no longer annoyed, merely astonished that Rugen would entertain such preposterous misconceptions. "You're wrong," I declared rather firmly. "I have no hidden agenda. Rugen, my love, you need prove nothing to me for I knew your divine worth centuries ago. All you need to say is 'give me Nova' and I will.

Rugen had trouble saying it as simply as I needed to hear it. *Ce* backed up, just a tad. *Ce* reminded me, "We've not made love since our honeymoon. You haven't even tried to come near me since Nova left that piece of *lim*self inside you."

"Does that mean you're ready?" Rugen needed to give me a clear yes. No other way existed, despite my desire to make it easy for *cim*.

Ce backed up even more. "When you wanted to go out to the soul fragments in the fourth dimension, I was afraid you were going to abandon me."

"Why do you lump me with your abandoners? In our many lives together, have I ever deserted you? I wanted you to wait in the vitasphere while I went out to nurse the soul fragments. Don't you know by now that I would have returned merely to hold you in my arms? The truth is—I was a cosmic failure in the fourth dimension. My love for you rattled my sense of integrity. I made a commitment to accompany you on this mission and I will keep my promise; however, I'm no longer sure if our original mission is the best plan. We might have handled the denial when it was so close that it was raining on our vitasphere. Now we have bypassed the fourth dimension and come to this alien past. We've ended up here for innumerable reasons, but what I was, I still am." I kissed *cim* and wiped away *cis* tears.

"My fear paints a scenario where you might be afraid to tell Iris that I even exist."

"That's never ever going to happen, Rugen."

This time my softness did not sooth *cim* and *ce* pushed my hand away. "You intend to hold Iris' attention by fucking her."

"You tell me, Rugen. How are we going to break the connection? Should we debate her or try to convince her with a speech? I don't know anyway to break the connection except to use highly charged sexual energy. I cannot imagine the results if we did otherwise." I waited for Rugen's answer and was disappointed. I wanted *cim* to surprise me with some new and clever way to proceed so I could get around this new dilemma.

Rugen was rankled and *cis* face flushed red. It was a signal that *ce* was going to be brutally honest. "I admit it!" *ce* said. "My fatal flaw is you! I'm jealous, but not of Iris. I'm jealous that your commitment to love is greater than your commitment to me." Of all the things Rugen might have said, I never expected this. Zap! Truth jumped out of the time threads and stung me. *Cis* statement rocked the foundations of what I believed about myself. The ramifications of *cis* statement reached back into my ancient incarnations, especially ones with *cim*. In that instant, *cis* words—"Your commitment to love is greater than your commitment to me"—became a catalyst to an evolutionary jump for me. Like Belinda, love was my answer to everything wrong. Revelations continued to unfold and I realized that dispersion of passion was love's deadliest sin. Now I knew Rugen was right. I had deserted *cim* and *cis* past failures were partially my fault. I had left *cim* behind in the most crippling of ways. My love for *cim* was extravagant and deep, yet I put *cim* second. My loyalty to the vehicle was greater than my loyalty to *cim*. I was living as a fundamentalist—for a narrow concept. Rugen was asking me to change all that. *Ce* was suggesting, *let me use your love as if it were my own.* This realization so devastated me that I fell into a state of confusion. My mind churned and threw out a question that lay at my feet like a slippery silver fish. *Do you trust Rugen enough to surrender the purpose of your soul to cim?*

We became quieter with each other and embraced. Rugen's total devotion for me flooded me with the most exquisite longing and a compulsion to express my love with heroic gestures. I knew now that heroic gestures were not enough. What could I do that was commensurate with Rugen's devotion for me? This pledge emerged from my mouth. "I promise that I will not connect with Iris either dishonestly or without you. If we connect with Iris, it will be because we decide to do it together and it is the appropriate move for the three of us. We will leave no part of ourselves behind."

Rugen sighed with relief. "And I pledge that all my understanding will flow through you." Rugen was a genius in shifting moods and *ce* did it now. *Ce* invaded my space and touched my cheek. *Ce* started holding me with *cis* eyes and slowly my jagged concentration calmed. *Ce* ran *cis* fingers down the bridge of my nose so I could smell the scent on the palm of *cis* hand. "Give me Nova," *ce* said quite deliberately. The atmosphere already charged made Rugen turn dreamy-eyed and seductive with need. We kissed gently. After all our lifetimes together, *cis* vulnerability still filled me with amazement. Now I wanted to be just as vulnerable with *cim*. I could see all the way through *cim* and, just as Hope observed, *Rugen* had no obscure corners. We kissed deeper the second time and I sent all my passion back to *cim*.

What followed was the culmination of what we sought from this universe from the beginning of time. Eons ago, we came into existence to experience a greater love and understanding through the vehicle of conscious creation. The glory we experienced on Sasaybin was a breezy prelude compared to this triumphant moment. Nova had sacrificed *lis* physical body to allow this to happen. Now, *le* was a mouth inside me capable of swallowing us whole. That mouth was the eloquent poet, the bard of all creation. My blessing was to be the surrendering force among us, an altar for the worshiping Rugen. It was the most exquisite, profound, naked, transcendent, and humbling experience of any of my lives.

Our lovemaking had no side streets—no quasi emotions, ulterior motives, or fantasizing minds. We went to the sleep space on the pulsar and our clothes came off along the way, discarded as trees discard leaves in late autumn windstorms. I felt the Heat, like divine sex energy, oozing around and through me. It was the cosmic Nova. Rugen and I kissed, and we got lost in each other's hair as Nova's tongue wrapped around mine and sucked Rugen in. I began to taste things I never tasted before, tasting love in a new way. My lover tasted of comfort food, both sweet and salty. Our tongues wandered hills and valleys of living flesh leaving glittery trails of passion behind.

We came together and our energy danced. Rugen took everything *ce* wanted from me at *cis* own pace. I had experienced the kundalini energy many times before with Rugen. The kundalini is an eruption of harmonious energy that explodes through the top of the lover's heads as an effulgent offering to the godhead. This was different. New analogies need inventing to explain it. I can only call it a cosmic caduceus with our oversoul because it hints at the blessing, the absolute healing, that comes through divine-will. Ecstatically happy in the bliss of surrender, suddenly, Nova was rearranging our minds like furniture. No need existed to verbalize anything because I was part of Rugen's consciousness and the truth was obvious everywhere within us.

The exclusivity of our original minds remained in shock. It was more of a shock to Rugen because *ce* had not experienced Nova's constancy inside *cim* before. Now, I-ness was not a matter of shifting viewpoints between Rugen's mind or my own. We were both bodies; we were both minds. Our one minor separation came from the disincarnate Nova who possessed the ability to pull back and announce to both bodies and minds with complete practicality, "You were shattered by the divine. Now go to sleep and rest." As if someone turned off a switch inside our heads, we were sleeping.

Sometime later, I opened my eyes and blinked a few times. I was an unsteady bowl of jelly, but I was inside Sante's body and holding Rugen in my arms. Rugen's eyes were opening too. After a while, *ce* whispered, "You are everything to me." I knew exactly what *ce* meant because *cis* words came from the depths of my soul. Separate consciousness was a minute adjustment within our new panorama and it took a few minutes to realize our separateness was an illusion we needed to nurture in order to relate to third-dimensional reality. In our new unity, the predicament concerning how to deal with Iris no longer held the same weight. We absolutely could not disregard the truth of the other.

We got up and took a shower together. We possessed complete telepathy. We were in symbiotic union and could use each other's memories. I discovered that I possessed a new world of technical knowledge, about flying vitaspheres and space procedures that was unknown to me before. Rugen's childhood and *cis* years at the Cerribeame Academy were mine. As Rugen, I hid in a small dormitory closet and masturbated instead of taking a lover so I could devote myself exclusively to my education. Through Rugen, I believed it was the right thing to do. Poor Rugen had to suffer the slagheap of memories from my aborted love affairs, shameful memories of me indulging my vanity and pride. We did not linger in the past for that was another trap. The past was only one of the many useful tools that helped us negotiate the future. We had a new sense of divine timing that would help us overcome many of the difficulties we would encounter.

Rugen said, "I'm acutely sensitive as never before. I can feel Nova tickling around inside me."

Nova whispered cosmic secrets we heard in states of simultaneous bliss. *Le* told us, *We are projections from an oversoul capable of birthing thousands of souls from its womb. This oversoul is radically alive with one purpose, to disseminate love and understanding through as many incarnations as possible.*

Rugen spoke aloud. "Actual conversation seems superfluous, something we can indulge in for added emphasis." Our smiles mirrored and we were exquisite within each other. How could it be otherwise?

****

We ate and eating helped ground us. In order to function as the two bodies we still were, we decided to work on separate projects. Rugen went to the console on the pulsar and began to monitor transmissions from Earth while I opened the microdex that Senon entrusted to me. I set the microdex on one of the two lounge chairs and sat opposite. The hardware appeared ordinary—a beige case, about a quarter of a meter square and a few millimeters thick, with a hinged lid. Opening the lid, I discovered a typical keyboard with keys that could be programmed in several different languages. The microdex had a tiny speaker membrane for vocal communication and the lid was fitted with a small screen. I tapped the power button and waited. The microdex began to flash through some colorful introductory screens showing me that Senon had created and copyrighted the software. The screen went black for an instant and then an image of Senon's head and shoulders appeared. "Good morning, Sante" *le* said. "I realize this may be an inappropriate greeting for the time we're in now; however, life is relevant only when it is interactive."

Emotion filled my heart at seeing a facsimile of Senon's face. "Good morning," I said.

The eyes on the screen sought mine and performed a biometric eye scan. That's better," it said slipping into a more conversational tone. "Why don't you activate the holographic feature, then we can talk face to face?"

"Open hologram,' I said. I uttered the magic words and a holographic image appeared in the middle of the empty space between the lounge chairs and the console. The projection appeared real and was the same size as Senon—tall. What I mean by real is I saw no distortions around the edges of the projected form. Rugen stopped what *ce* was doing and remarked, "nice technology!"

So many amazing things had happened to Rugen and me that a high-quality holograph seemed merely impressive, not startling. However, what happened next went way beyond any holographic prestidigitation I ever witnessed before. Senon's image walked over to the lounge chair, picked up the microdex unit, which the image had projected itself from, and sat down in the chair. It nonchalantly crossed one long leg over the other in a manner so reminiscent of the actual Senon that it was uncanny. "Excuse me," it said. "Let me make a few adjustments to my internal timing." Then it typed

205

something on the keyboard of the microdex.

"Holy shit!" said Rugen.

I arose from my chair and approached the hologram that appeared to be sitting in the chair in front of me. I tried to penetrate the image with the tip of my forefinger, but discovered I could not. At the point where my finger touched the projection's chest, a silver glimmer appeared informing me that the form was not as real as it seemed.

"You both seemed nonplussed," it observed. Its expression was amused and tinged with a bit of obvious pride.

"How come you need to make changes to your programming on the keyboard?" asked Rugen. "Why don't you merely make the adjustments internally?"

"If you prefer, I can work that way too," offered the program. "I was merely showing off a little. I certainly did not mean to startle you."

I acknowledged our bewilderment. "We never saw a holograph capable of moving solid objects or projecting an image with such total clarity."

"My technical precision allows me to manipulate objects with a concentrated forcefield that I can focus toward any object," it explained. The hologram set the microdex down on the floor beside the chair. "Stand up," it directed. I stood up and so did the hologram. "Extend your right hand." I did and its projected hand shook mine. It was marvelous the way the fingers meshed with mine. Senon, whom I always surmised was a genius, actually was. To program a hologram to shake somebody's hand with the ease and elegance that this form did, was technology that could come only from a great mind. Then the hologram put its arms around me and gave me a gentle hug. It felt real, but did not have the warmth of a physical body.

"Your sophistication is incredible," exclaimed Rugen.

The hologram assumed a stance with one leg sleekly poised over the other. It pointed one of its toes toward the floor. Then it performed a brief soft-shoe dance around the area. It stopped and grinned with pride. "My sophistication goes way beyond the technical—don't you agree?"

Rugen and I stared at each other with our mouths open before we broke into laughter.

"How come Sante can't put *cis* hand through your projection?" asked Rugen. "Does that have something to do with your forcefield too?"

The hologram scratched its head for a moment. "I have an extension in that area of my programming. It must be a quirk in the physical Senon's personality because I cannot compute any logical reason for the barrier's existence. The physical Senon insisted that I not let others occupy my space at the same time. *Le* said that if extrinsic energy mingled with mine that it might corrupt the integrity of my systems. Does that make sense to you?"

Rugen and I were passing looks of amazement back and forth. In a way, this is exactly what was happening to Rugen and me. We were wallowing in each other's energy.

"Perhaps the physical Senon was right," Rugen said. "You need to trust someone before you open yourself to their energy."

"What do you want us to call you?" I asked.

It shrugged. "Let's keep it simple, call me Senon." Senon explained that *le* was at our disposal and wanted to know as much as possible about our mission. *Le* already knew that *le* had accompanied us backward in time to mend a rupture between the dimensions. *Lis* knowledge of even that much, told us Nova shared more with the physical Senon than we suspected. Senon's expression possessed a questioning quality. "Something vague about this mission disturbs me," *le* admitted.

"Rugen and I will deal with the vagaries, but we could use your help to perform a few specific tasks."

We sat down with Senon and attempted to explain the problem from our perspective. "We're here to find a Human female by the name of Iris Syriaca," I said. "She is a progenitor of Guise Belinda. If we can find Iris, a possibility exists that we can prevent the physical rupture between the third and fourth in our natural future."

"Is denial somehow involved in this crisis?" asked Senon.

"Yes!" I said. "The root of the problem has always been the denial that consciousness has stashed in the corridor."

"Don't look so glum," said Rugen. "We have a few clues about how we should proceed."

"Do you believe, as I do, that your destiny is to be here?" asked Senon.

Rugen gave me a candid glance before telling Senon, "I try to avoid grand thoughts about my destiny. What I'm thinking is we are very lucky to have made it this far."

"Since we agreed to this journey, Rugen and I have been through a great deal. We have stripped ourselves to the bone to be honest with each other so we can have a chance to make a difference. Belinda is guiding us with her suggestions, but we are double-checking everything she says through Nova."

"I deduce that you don't quite trust Belinda," said Senon.

"Belinda is not the problem she once was," said Rugen.

Senon was thoughtful. "I understand the historical perspective, that we are faced with an environmental crisis of apocalyptic proportions. I also understand how denial accumulates and contributes to actual cosmic events; however, I don't understand how two people, in two different times, possess the power to alter the timeline."

"We don't understand it either," said Rugen. "Sante and I don't even know if breaking the link between Evose and Iris is the right move."

"Is this Iris supposed to be an innocent victim or a deliberate progenitor fostering this rupture?"

"Iris is an unknown factor," I said. "Belinda claims she is innocent, yet savvy." I took the spool containing my book and popped it into the side of Senon's microdex. "Read this," I said. "Maybe it will help clear up some of your questions." Senon sucked *lim*self back inside *lis* box so that *le* could read the manuscript more efficiently. It took *lim* less than ten seconds to read. When *le* reappeared, *lis* expression had gone from blasé to sober. "Do you know if the physical Senon is dead?" *le* asked.

"I don't know," I admitted. "Cursory evidence indicates that *The Mother* went through The Door when it ruptured. *La Ventana* is a huge spaceship built for travel in third-dimensional space. She has her strengths, but I have no idea if she could hold together inside the fourth dimension."

Senon seemed to stare at the floor. "Tell me what I can do to help."

Rugen explained. "Earth culture is isolated in this time; therefore, we need to appear as natives so we can move around unencumbered. Each of us needs a plausible personal history consisting of a birth certificate and an item called a social security number. These two documents can help us pass as natives in the geographical area we are entering. If you can find a way to get these documents, it will be helpful. So far, we have a few pieces of clothing appropriate for the time and approximately five thousand credits in the currency of the land. We know this is not enough to sustain us, especially since we are three months early. We will need to live by our wits and we are prepared to do that. Right now, we need an inconspicuous ground base until we get our bearings."

"Such as?" asked Senon.

"A small and unobtrusive apartment within the vicinity of Key West will do," I said.

Senon thought for a couple of seconds. "We will need to reconfigure some of our multidex equipment so it can interface with the technology of this time. If they have telecommunication satellites, we could fly in close to one and our proximity will allow me to hack into the satellite's multidex. Once I get inside a multidex, I can travel anywhere."

"They have plenty of satellites," said Rugen. "Take your pick."

"What's our present position?" Senon asked.

"We're sitting on an asteroid seventeen cycles from Earth's orbit."

"Electronically speaking, it would be even more seamless if I could link my microdex to the pulsar's Prime I. I could work inside on analyzing the signal codes as we approach the satellites and store them in separate files. By the time we get into range, I would be ready to zip right in and start work." Rugen extended the Prime I's network to include Senon's microdex and next time we heard Senon's voice, it came from speakers on the console panel. "As long as I'm in here, do you want me to set the coordinates for Earth?" *le* asked.

"Sure!" said Rugen. Twenty minutes later, we launched off the asteroid, we named Hope, and headed for Earth.

FOURTEEN

"**D**o you mind if I work on my book?" I asked Rugen.

"Not at all," *ce* said. "Senon and I can handle the flying." The writing flowed as never before and I can only thank Rugen and Nova for their inspiration. We used the time on the way to Earth to repair our physical and mental bodies. I tried to contact Belinda several times, but drew a complete blank. Something was wrong. Had Belinda and Bogwa gone to Delphi as planned? If Belinda was on Delphi, the power of the New Delphi Crystal should have made communications easier between us. Lacking any connection with Belinda, I stopped calling out to her in my meditations; instead, I aimed all my meditations toward Nova and salved my conscience with the knowledge that Belinda told me that I could get all my guidance from Nova if I wanted to proceed in that direction. The only problem was the closer we drew to Earth, the more tenuous all my spiritual connections became. Sometimes in meditation, I was not sure if Nova was speaking or I was making up words for *lim*. We seemed to be in a dead zone and completely on our own.

I took responsibility for assembling the equipment we needed for Earth. We planned to leave the pulsar in shielded orbit and go down to the planet with *vitaratthas* and jetpaks. The largest item we were taking was a multidex capable of monitoring the physical integrity of the vitasphere on the asteroid Hope and the orbit of our pulsar. A second smaller and less powerful multidex we planned to modify to use as an interface with Earth systems. We had a few personal items, some clothing, and, thanks to Kayya and Ceff, a huge medical kit. When I had everything stacked in the forward compartment, it was obvious that it was going to be difficult to carry everything inside two *vitaratthas*. On Senon's suggestion, we decided to

210

allow *lim* to occupy a third *vitarattha* so *le* could assist us.

In the process of consolidating our belongings, I noticed my tarot cards inside the side pouch of my personal bag. I took them out and decided it was appropriate to select a card for Senon. I held *lim* in my thoughts for several minutes before selecting the card and realized that it was difficult for me to separate the software Senon from the physical Senon. I almost convinced myself that the flesh and blood Senon was the archetype Magician while the software Senon was the rabbit inside *lis* hat. I decided that I wanted a card exclusively for the software Senon, so drew the card with only *lim* in mind. The card I drew was the Two of Wands. "The Two of Wands is a compassionate, altruistic, and balanced individual. A person devoted to pure thought and honest desire; someone who is strong enough to wait for the greater plan to reach fruition; someone interested in science and future technology. It is a person possessing creative ability with the accompanying genius to express it." Maybe the Two of Wands was not The Magician; but it certainly was a magician in the making.

After I showed the card to Rugen, *ce* dubbed Senon, "our good luck charm."

****

Senon's expertise in programming coordinates reduced our flying time to Earth to twelve cycles. We orbited the blue and white planet twice to map the orbit of their satellites. From our space perspective, Earth's appearance reminded me of a beautiful clear eye. On the side facing its star, it was wide-awake and on the dark side, the eyelid had winked closed for a quick nap. The Earth of 2015 appeared much like the Earth in the sixth millennium except for coastal regions where rising sea levels were beginning to flood great swaths of coastland.

Rugen and Senon spent the next three hours debating the merits and disadvantages of several satellites before agreeing upon one. We approached the selected satellite on its space side and closed in to a range of three kilometers. The words "ATLAS CORPORATION" appeared on one side in large, black block letters and below were the words, "The United States of America." The satellite was a fragile silver-colored rectangle with several solar collection umbrellas. Rugen flashed the pulsar's photon beams and the umbrellas closest to us opened. Seconds later, Senon communicated, "I've found a way in."

"Do it!" Rugen replied.

Senon was already on *lis* way, but turned back to say, "If you could fly in closer, you could get some better pictures."

"Not with this pulsar," said Rugen. "Our energy dynamics might cause a power surge on a satellite that old."

"Better not then," agreed Senon. "I thought you might use the cameras on the pulsar to take some micro-range photos so I could study them later.

It is a hobby of mine. I collect interesting minutiae on antique satellites."

The way Senon projected *lim*self over to the satellite was simple. We sent out a tiny stream of directional light to the solar collectors on the satellite and Senon piggybacked the light to make the jump. Once he reached the satellite, *le* returned a stronger signal to us that we could use for communication. Senon's first expedition to the Atlas satellite was to make energy connections with other satellites and create accurate cartography so *le* could move around. *Le* estimated that mapping would take approximately ten minutes. *Le* shut down *lis* vocal hardware and went internal. We were able to communicate with *lim*, during *lis* absence, by typing additional questions and/or instructions on the small keyboard of *lis* microdex. Communications from us went into a separate file that *le* could access and check at *lis* convenience. As soon as *lis* mapping was complete, the hard drive on the Prime-I multidex began filling with new files. Rugen opened one to see what Senon was concocting as our new identities.

"Congratulations!" said Rugen. "Your new name is Sante Janaforma instead of Jana Sante. You were born in Miami, Florida on the Earth date, June 9, 1987. Now I'm your younger brother instead of your consort. My new name is Rugen Janaforma and I was born in Miami on February 2, 1996. Our parents are dead, killed in—a space accident? That's impossible!" Rugen shifted to the microdex keyboard and typed in, "Our parents cannot die in a space accident. You need to make their deaths appropriate to this time."

"I'll fix it," said Senon. "How about—your parents died in an automobile accident in 1996?" At that instant, I thought of Nova and *lis* dream that *le* killed Una and I in a land vehicle and a definite chill went up my spine.

"We better double check everything *le* is doing," said Rugen. "Just to make certain *le* does not give us two heads." We split the accumulating files between us and began to read what Senon was cooking up as our counterfeit identities. Senon used a code we call Pivot that is compact and efficient. Thankfully, through Rugen, I could now read Pivot as well as *ce* could.

The rest of Senon's fabrications seemed more plausible, although some, if checked, were going to provoke questions. Between Rugen and me, we attended several schools. Rugen's résumé, now part of Earth's permanent records claimed *ce* had worked as an airline pilot for British Air. Now *ce* was unemployed and searching for work. I was a writer and published several books. Senon used actual titles that I published in the future.

"Oh well!" shrugged Rugen. "Who is going to check this stuff?"

Senon returned two hours later and projected *lis* hologram for us. "They don't call a multidex a multidex in this time; they call them computers; and, I just discovered their Internet. It's slow, generic, and barely interactive, but

I can access maps and pictures, make reservations in hotels, do research, and eavesdrop on what's topical. I can also learn new idiomatic jargon and pass it along to you. For example, do you know what an omega scout is?"

Rugen and I looked blank.

"It's an eschatologist," said Senon. "There is a thriving legion of omega scouts down on Earth. The End is hot news! It's everywhere, in books, magazines, on the media and Internet."

"What else?" I asked.

"To say it like a real Earthling in 2015, 'I seeded the database, so you two wonks can pass as natives, but you'll need some activated plastic to stash in your jeans.' Earthlings say, 'Plastic is the only way to go.'"

Rugen asked Senon to interpret and then gently suggested that Senon put *lis* new vocabulary in a separate file. "I appreciate your new jargon, but it's important that we all remain clear with each other."

Senon said, "My research shows that Humans frequently lose or misplace important documents. Requesting duplicates is routine here. As soon as we have a permanent address, I will claim we need duplicates and ask the appropriate agencies to send documentation directly to us. I already put your birth certificates into the computer files at the Dade County Court House. I helped myself to two numbers from their Social Security Office in Washington D. C. and forged two driver's licenses. Your pictures already are on file at the Florida Division of Motor Vehicles."

"Hold on," said Rugen. "I don't know if we want pictures attached to official documents. That sounds risky."

"A driver's license is the most important document in the United States. You can't do anything without a driver's license, which requires a picture. Don't worry, I took the liberty of changing your appearances slightly so you look more in line with early twenty-first century males."

"Okay, let's see them," said Rugen.

Senon snapped *lis* holograph fingers for effect and two side-by-side pictures popped up of some very silly looking "wonks."

"Holy shit!" said Rugen for the tenth time.

In the picture of me, my hair was about thirty millimeters long and sticking straight up into the air. Around my ears, my hair was shaved close to my scalp. It was embarrassing. Rugen had short hair too, but a patch of longer hair ran straight down the middle of *lis* scalp. *Le* was wearing glasses and sporting a mustache. Rugen's face was as smooth as silk, so this seemed particularly ridiculous to me.

"I put the mustache on Rugen to make *cim* look older and manlier," explained Senon.

The sight of our altered selves was so absurd that Rugen broke down into uncontrollable peals of laughter. "I look like a squirrel!" *ce* managed to tell me.

"Well! I am not cutting my hair to match that picture," I declared.

Rugen wiped tears of laughter from *cis* eyes. "Why did you make us look so bizarre? We're trying to hide not get noticed."

Senon projected a sober expression as if we were ruining *lis* fun. *Le* hesitated and pretended *le* was scrambling for the right words. This was a ruse. Sentient multidex programs never fumble for words. "Your actual appearances are slightly inappropriate," *le* informed us.

"How slightly inappropriate?" I pressed.

"You know the old saying, 'a picture is worth a thousand words'?" *Le* popped back inside the multidex and oozed out ten seconds later sporting a new look *lim*self. *Lis* short hair made the crown of *lis* head look like a tabletop. *Le* was wearing a gray three-piece outfit that *le* explained was apropos male business attire for 2015. "This is vogue!" *le* said.

This time Rugen and I were too baffled to laugh.

Then Senon materialized a wand and pointed to a series of projections *le* caused to appear as a flat screen. "Please observe. Exhibit one is from a magazine called *GQ* or *Gentleman's Quarterly*." Senon showed us the cover with a picture of a sweaty-looking male wearing a fake acrimonious expression. The anger was on his lips, not in his eyes. His eyes were kind and I could tell by their drab bloodshot and lackluster appearance that he had a serious physical illness. Senon flipped through about forty pictures from inside the magazine to illustrate what *le* labeled, "The Look." Every man had a variation on the same-butchered hairdo, a hairdo I began to think of as, "the startled porcupine."

Personally, I'm attracted to all kinds of beauty in many different species, but these Human men went to great lengths to appear unattractive. Forced expressions of thirty-two and bored, thirty-five and efficient, eighteen and tough, Asian and sad, gave me no thrills. Men's casual or "sport clothing" was large and droopy as if they were ashamed of their bodies. Their business attire looked like a bad habit—uncomfortable and confining. Senon showed us another magazine—*Esquire*. A handsome man adorned the cover, but he sported the same tortured hairdo. Models looked like clones from the *GQ* library. Some actually were bald.

"Damn!" said Rugen shaking *cis* head in bewilderment. "It takes nerve to walk around with no hair. Can we see those pictures again?" *Ce* instructed Senon to back up a couple of frames to a previous screen. I jumped inside Rugen's mind and realized what *ce* wanted me to see.

Both magazines contained copious advertisements about how to grow hair and make hair beautiful, yet each model possessed hardly any hair at all. "Why?" I asked.

"Don't ask me to make sense of this place," Senon said. "I'm showing you what I found."

We glanced at some more pictures. Senon projected the cover of a new magazine, called *Cosmopolitan*. "He looks good," said Rugen.

"That's not a man!" barked Senon. "Can't you see the breasts?" It was clear what Senon was suggesting. Senon believed we looked more like females than males.

"Then let's go down to Earth as females," I said.

"That's going to take time to change!" Senon said. "You already are in two hundred different computer files as males. Besides, it's illegal to pass yourself off as a female when you're not a female. I saw that law when I sifted through the computer files in a place called the Bureau of Records in Miami, Florida."

"I don't care if it's illegal," said Rugen. "We need proper cover. The truth is we are no more male than we are female, especially me! Technically we are not even Human."

"True," conceded Senon. "If you need to be females, I'll try to make the changes."

"Wait a second," I said. "The important thing is we appear to be Human and I don't think we will have any problems doing that except for my Gathosian eyes."

"Did you bring enough adhesion lenses to hide your eyes?" asked Rugen.

"Not enough to last three months. I'll wear sunglasses," was my quick solution to the problem. Rugen suggested that we do some superficial hiding under hats and sunglasses before doing anything as drastic as cutting our hair. "Sounds reasonable to me," I quickly agreed.

"Let's get back to what's important," said Rugen. "Did you find us a place to live?"

"No luck in that department," said Senon, "unless you want to make reservations in a hotel. Cursory information suggests that it will be easier to go down physically and look for an apartment from there."

****

Senon's help was turning out to be essential. We asked *lim* to do one more chore before we went down to the planet's surface. "Could you do a search on a female named Iris A. Syriaca? Senon began *lis* search immediately and this time *le* was gone for nearly twenty minutes. The moment *le* returned, *le* said, "I was unable to find out much, but what I found is fascinating. Her full name is Iris Astarte Syriaca. She was born on December 25, 1979 in Philadelphia, Pennsylvania."

Rugen tapped *cis* temple with *cis* fingertips. "That name! That name! It sure rings a bell."

"Like a Belinda bell?" I asked.

Senon filled us in on the historical context of *Astarte Syriaca*. "It's the name of a Pre-Raphaelite painting by Dante Gabriel Rossetti, from the Earth year 1877. Senon flashed up a picture of the painting on the main console screen.

"Holy shit!" gasped Rugen. This time *ce* was speaking for us both. The picture was of Belinda and the most striking feature about it was the mysterious expression on her face. It was seductive, yet dead, as if she were a martyr imprisoned inside her great physical proportions. "The symbolism surrounding her appears a bit stylized," said Rugen.

Astarte Syriaca was pointing to her genitals and cupping her breasts or heart, showing us the way of the lover. Two female figures stood behind her, one to each side. They were paler and more beautiful than *Astarte Syriaca*. I was certain they were Belinda's soul mates looking up in divine bliss toward their oversoul. Their seductive expressions possessed a false edge. All three figures were swaddled in green fabric, the "rags" of the Trinity Witches.

Rugen stared at the painting with intense interest before telling me, "The painting has merit, but technically falls short of great art. What saves it is its obvious inspiration. If I were buying it, I would not pay top price and if I owned it, I would hang it as a gorgon inside my front door so the painting could inspect my guests as they arrived."

I jumped over into Rugen's mind and saw what *ce* meant.

"You're right," *ce* said crossing over into mine. "Belinda looks like a sacrifice, her oversoul's projection that put her into incarnation to satisfy its boredom."

We wondered about it together. "Why would Belinda allow herself to be painted that way?"

"Unknown," I said. "When we meet Iris again, maybe she'll help us figure it out."

"Those false expressions on her soul mates faces are worrisome," said Rugen.

"There's more," said Senon. "Maybe you know this already, but Astarte was the name of the ancient Phoenician moon goddess here on Earth."

"This is an authentic historical connection," I explained. "In a past life, Belinda and I were Astarte's temple prostitutes—we called ourselves handmaidens. In that life, we were Canaanites from Western Mesopotamia. Everyone else called us Phoenicians. We served in a Kition temple on the island of Cyprus. Cyprus was the crossroad of the continents during that time and our job, which we considered honorable, was to meet the ships and service the sailors. The gold we earned was dedicated to the greater glory of Astarte."

"Yeah, I can see the whole thing," moaned Rugen. "It still makes me blush."

"What else can you tell us about Iris?" I asked.

"She has grand aspirations," said Senon. "She considers herself an 'intuitive facilitator' and works with people for a fixed fee and conducts workshops on esoteric subjects such as Human potential and growth. The term "intuitive facilitator" must be an idiomatic expression in this time because I don't understand what an intuitive facilitator does. Of course, intuitive means, 'perceptive, judicious, and clear-eyed' and a facilitator is 'someone who knows how to move with dexterity and ease through problems,' but I'm having a difficult time putting those clues together into a legitimate profession, such as an engineer or dentist. I made a copy of a file she placed in the public domain. Want to see it?"

"Definitely," I said.

Senon displayed the information on the console screen and then we asked *lim* to magnify it so we could see it more clearly. This is a copy of what we saw:

♥ Iris Syraica ♥
Nationally known Psychic Facilitator of Well Being
In an effort to give you a clear and honest interpretation of your inner life experiences, Iris Syriaca will be available for a limited amount of time during the months of July and August for private psychic consultation.
July 10, 11 and 12 "Life Direction Class"
Fee: $250.
This gathering is designed to empower you with clarity about your life purpose and to create positive change in your life.
August 20, 21, and 22, "The Soul Mate Class"
Fee: $300.
Using universal principles, Iris will assist you in attracting a soul mate into your life.

Rugen chuckled. "Soul mate classes! That's going to be fascinating."

About an hour later, I attempted to contact Belinda to ask about the Astarte Syrica painting, and I still could not reach her. I turned to Nova and tried to contact *lim*. Again there was nothing.

"I'm worried," *ce* said. "For the first time, we seem to be on our own."

"What if the future no longer exists?" asked Senon.

"Then we'll be stuck here for the rest of our natural lives," I said.

****

In range of Earth, we settled into a flexible orbit to mimic the pattern of a small asteroid trapped inside the gravitational field of the planet. We held that elliptical trajectory for almost eight Earth hours to monitor atmospheric conditions and determine an optimum time-window for our descent. We gradually refined our orbit to coincide with Key West every six hours. Rugen and I made light of the fact that I could not establish a psychic link with either Belinda or Nova and concentrated on practical considerations. We worked together and began to stow gear that needed to remain aboard. Going through procedures involved in decontamination and shutdown aboard a spaceship was a well-worn groove within us, so this part was easy. Rugen became more pensive as we worked. I knew *ce* was feeling some tension again, a heroic feeling of responsibility about our mission. We reached the stage when the next logical step was to seal off the living area and confine our movements to the bridge alcove.

A bridge alcove on a pulsar measures roughly four meters square. Squashed inside these four meters is a full console decked out with an array of information screens and two large pilot chairs that can double as uncomfortable beds. We stacked all the gear going to Earth behind the two chairs. We were anxious to go, but a thunderstorm moved in from the Gulf of Mexico and for almost three hours, hung over Key West. The storm moved fast, hovered, moved again, and then tracked back on itself. After a while, it felt stuffy and hot in that small alcove. We turned off most of the lights and sat in the dark with only the essential panels flashing their data. The dull hiss of the ventilation system was cycling too quickly, trying to cool that tiny blocked space. As we sat there in the boredom and heat, I nodded off to sleep.

In a dream, *Rugen and I are children. We're inside one vitarattha and soaring through a brilliant cerulean sky. I know we are involved in a game of Hide and Seek because Rugen whispers in my ear, Let's hide behind this big fluffy cloud so Nova can't find us.*

I'm tired of playing this game, I complain and then I turn around and yell to all the other players, Folly, folly, frees for all! An incredible blue sky opens and multitudes of light-points emerge, coming toward us from every direction in space and time.

Then the physical Rugen was waking me. "Sante? The storm has cleared."

I felt disoriented because my dream was vivid compared to the dark cockpit. What woke me completely was the static coming off Rugen. *Ce* was getting more impatient about the delay. "How long was I asleep?" I asked.

Ce made me wait for an answer. It was just enough time for me to sense *cis* abandonment as my own. "Not long," *ce* said. "About ten minutes."

"We're going to be together, no matter what happens down there," I assured *cim*. I touched *cis* cheek and felt his anxiety. "Rugen, what's wrong?"

Ce hesitated again and I wondered if the ventilation system was giving us enough oxygen in the cramped cockpit. Reading my conscious projection, *ce* said, "Oxygen levels are inside acceptable margins, but we really should not stack gear in front of the air vents." I had a crick in my neck from falling asleep in an awkward position, so I sat up and slowly twisted my head and yawned. When I looked at Rugen the next time, *ce* was staring out the cockpit window involved in one of *cis* infinite stares. "I'm scared," *ce* admitted. "We seem to be alone and so far from home. I feel as if the future is a dream slipping away from us. Where's Nova? And why have our meditations turned so hollow?"

I went to *cim*, touched *cim,* and spoke words fired in the kiln of my passion so *ce* might know my love was real. "You can feel Nova through my love—I swear, Rugen. Love is like ground water; it seeks to fill the lowest levels. That's why Nova said, 'Love is in Hell too.' Love goes everywhere, can heal anything. Know that I am a river of love for you."

"The only evidence I have that Nova ever existed is when I gaze into your eyes," and *ce* leaned forward and relaxed *cis* forehead against my shoulder. I let my love seep into *cim*, letting it go where it needed to go. "While you were asleep, a past life memory surfaced within me." I allowed Rugen to explain with words instead of telepathy. *Ce* needed do it this way, to spit out the memory like a toxin. *Ce* moved away from me and stared out the window again.

"They came for me—six of them. They were tiny, a bit taller than my waist—dark figures attacking in dim light. They wore stunguns on their fingertips and struck the backs of my legs and groin causing me searing pain. Like fierce sharp-nailed harpies, they took me down and I knew my attackers were the Cerribeame Guard. Two sat on my chest and I found it difficult to breathe. Two others held my legs and the last two snapped a clamp around my head. The clamp burned my hair away, while the burning pain from their stunguns poured into my chest. I stopped breathing in the middle of my last scream." Rugen caught *cis* breath as *ce* remembered more. "I went to death's door, asked permission to go through to the other side. There, I met a voice—heard it ringing with urgency—begging me to go back to my body." *Ce* glanced up and *cis* eyes were glassy with tears. "I woke up shrieking, 'Please, don't hurt me. I'll do anything, say anything you want me to say.' The Cerribeame never answered—never uttered one single word. After that, I went into a state of paralytic shock—could not feel the pain, but could not escape it either. I was an unflinching eye watching a fiendish standoff inside me. I was a witness against myself at my own trial, yet I could not die or run away from the pain. My soul had to bear the torture and humiliation as I shit my pants." *Ce* wiped tears off *cis* cheek with *cis* fist. "Why, Sante? Why did our oversoul send me back to witness my own defeat?"

"I don't know my love."

We embraced again and I knew *cis* pain. "Your pain is real to me—so real that I would not arrogantly assume that I know what it means." I remembered an incident from one of my past lives and told Rugen about it. "Once, in my life with Merisi, he took a painter's trowel and smeared cobalt paint in the center of a blank canvas. Then he sat in his dirty painter's clothes, drank wine, and stared at the smudge for hours. 'What's that supposed to be?' I finally asked. 'The unexpected mark is as much art as planned symmetry,' he said. 'When you understand that, there is nothing else left to learn.'"

Rugen rubbed *cis* temples in an attempt to remove the memory of the scourging pain. "This unexpected mark put a gouge in my canvas," *ce* said.

We kissed and Rugen's tension flowed into me. *Ce* apologized for it, but could not arrest the outpouring of *cis* emotions. I told *cim*, "It's my greatest joy to know your every mood."

"I will be better once we get underway," *ce* promised. If Rugen were any better, *ce* would have melted away into perfection. I told *cim* that and it made *cim* smile. *Ce* struggled to control *cis* tension and it ruptured into compulsive behavior. *Ce* checked every detail on the final shutdown of the pulsar at least three times.

****

We stood inside the airlock and Rugen's eyes scanned along the console a final time. Two minutes later, we stepped out into space. There was no formation to our flying as in the Vanguard, no standard approach. Despite that, these were thrilling moments. My body was a genetically programmed organism created to live and work in space. For me, flying around in a *vitarattha* was a pleasurable experience. It would have been fun to soar for a couple of hours, but we were concerned about the weather. We dropped straight down until we were a few hundred meters over the dark water of the Atlantic Ocean.

Nothing impeded our smooth and rapid advance. Rugen and I each wore a microdex pulled down across a right eye; it was another way to stay in touch. The red arrow inside my microdex pointed to a spot two-kilometers ahead as our designated landing spot. Life-support on our *vitaratthas* was set on automatic and as we descended, more of the salty, ocean air mixed with our rarified blend. It was moonless and the impinging sounds of Earth seemed to spring up from vague points in the darkness. To the cursory observer, I knew we were invisible. The glow of our *vitaratthas* would appear as shimmering light across the water, a flying Dutchmen effect, or a million other gossamer imaginings.

Coming down over the deep dark water, ironies struck like counterfeit coins—vivid, grand, and completely absurd. I knew existence hung on a rickety chain of events that barely were real. My own likelihood seemed particularly problematic. It would be almost 3,000 years before Simon Forma created my great, great grandparents in a nativity vat on the planet Hattonia; yet, here I was probing a past that would declare me an impossible dream. Rugen and I had proven linear time was permeable, but only we knew the premise was true. A thousand different faces flashed before me, some were dead, some were not yet born, and some would never be. A mythological Astarte superimposed herself over Iris, as Belinda morphed into Bell, then back to Astarte again. All faces were absurd masks; yet, I was about to don one myself.

Communications cut between Rugen and me with the power of

thunderbolts and we mused between us, *Could absurdity be the masked expression on the faces of Astarte Syriaca's soul mates?*

Rugen took it a step further. *If it is, do you think absurdity so jaded them that they no longer sensed the anguish of the living?* It was easy to interpret life as absurd because of its vagaries; but Rugen and I knew it was real. Third dimensional reality was not a *manatee* projection formed from a remnant trapped inside our minds. The third dimension was deeply persistent and was the realest reality around. It was so real and persistent it had scared me to death many, many times.

We decided to come down in the environs, a few kilometers south-southwest of the Key West Airport. We hovered over some salt ponds and flew in closer to search for a suitable place to land. Rugen and I switched our microdex lenses to infrared to have a better look around. Senon continued to feed us some general information through our linked audio, pointing out interesting local flora—knurly-rooted mangroves, royal palms, saw grass, and the exotic epiphytes lounging along the branches of twiggy trees. Everything appeared eerie through the infrared. "It's too swampy to land," said Senon.

We made camp by linking *vitaratthas* and hanging in the air about twenty meters above the ground. The plan was for Senon to remain with the equipment while Rugen and I went into Key West to gain a more intimate view of the area. Senon wanted to know, "Are you going to shut me down?"

"No, we need you to stay alert while we're gone," said Rugen. "If anyone comes near, move away from them and contact us immediately and we'll return and help you move the gear."

Rugen and I changed from our lightweight spacesuits to our native wear that Kayya and Ceff provided. We put most of our hair under some caps. "Don't forget to shade your eyes," Rugen reminded me and I took out a pair of blue adhesion lenses and popped them into place. We each had, what I dubbed, two small "fool's wallets" containing a medical kit, our currency, some nutrient capsules, and our water for the day. Our *vitaratthas* hardware we attached under the edge of our collars. We stood side by side so Senon could inspect our masked appearance and Rugen asked, "What do you think?"

Senon said, "You'll pass."

Some of the clothing was too large and Rugen smirked, "Maybe Kayya thinks we're still growing," and we giggled like a couple of fools. I wore the wrisceptor that we would use to communicate with Senon because Rugen still hated restrictions on *cis* wrists. It was easy to hide under my too long sleeve.

"We'll check in with you every two hours to make sure everything is okay," I told Senon. "Stay as motionless as you can during the day. Moving around will cause light to reflect off the *vitarattha* and attract attention."

"I'll stay in the multidex," said Senon.

Rugen touched Senon's projected forearm making the light sparkle there. "We will return by night fall, no matter what," *ce* promised.

****

Kayya and Ceff had supplied us with a case of compact jetpacks that the Vanguard used inside the atmosphere of planets. The jetpacks were small enough to fit into a bag and when stowed in their case, they appeared to be a common flashlight. They were not as powerful as the jetpacks we used to come from the pulsar, but they were sufficient to give us enough lift, so we could fly into Key West. It was early morning and the date on Earth was Friday, June 9 (my fake birthday), 2015 when we set down in an alley behind a row of attached housing units. The moment I deactivated my *vitarattha*, strange exotic odors began assaulting my olfactory senses. The air smelled salty, with musty overtones of stale beer and wafting traces of fried foods. Large trash canisters, sitting invitingly open, were serving breakfast to a flock of scavenging seagulls. Our sudden landing startled the birds and they flushed and scattered.

We crept out of the alley, not sure what we might find. Our plan was to blend in as much as possible. We did some research and discovered that businesses did not open in Key West until nine, ten, and even eleven o'clock in the morning. No android shopkeepers existed in this time; shopkeepers were authentically biological and all Human. Shops along the main concourse of Duval Street sold clothing, trinkets, and shells stolen from the sea. Flowered and tie-dyed clothing and billboard shirts—the natives called tee shirts—seemed to be the fashion trend. Some stores sold nothing but tee shirts with rude and colorful logos printed on the fronts. "Kiss My Ass And Like It!" and "I May Have More Than I Can Handle, But I Can Never Have Enough!" and "Shut Up And Fuck Me!" kept us shocked and amused for almost three minutes.

The side streets were covered with dark green vegetation. Huge vines grew up some of the flower-covered trees. Buildings were small, one and two-story structures, weather-beaten from the constant assault of salty, ocean air. We stopped by two or three realtor's offices around ten o'clock to check for apartment rentals. They told us our "best bet" was to check the "free press." We followed their advice and found a variety of paper periodicals available in most coffee shops, restaurants, and right inside the front entrance of stores. Most were sell and trade journals. "Do you need a wedding dress with a six foot train?" asked Rugen. "It's a size 18 petite. Is that big or small? Whatever, the dress can be yours for $200. How about a dozen pairs of ladies platform shoes, circa 1976, size 13? They too can be yours for $45." People were advertising trailers, boats, refrigerators, and "night crawlers (worm bait for fishing)." Somebody wanted to trade "a gun case for antique guns." Rugen saw an ad for the grizzly art of taxidermy. "Listen to this one, Sante; '—award winning taxidermist, reasonable rates, all work guaranteed. Big game my specialty, telephone Ed.'"

It was around eleven in the morning and we had no leads in finding a place to rent through any free-press periodicals. In an attempt to sound upbeat, Rugen said, "At least we're learning our way around Key West." We already knew hotels were too expensive, but they appeared inviting with their potted palms and cool inviting lobbies. Most of them were displaying vacancy signs. "We could check into a hotel and hope we find a permanent place to stay in a few days." I was ready to agree despite our limited amount of cash. It was hot walking around in the sunlight. We stopped in a public courtyard and sat on a shaded bench to have a few sips of water. "It just occurred to me that we are authentically poor and can't do anything about it," Rugen said. "It's humbling."

A couple of minutes later, a man sat next to me on the bench and opened a brown paper bag. He took out a sandwich and can of beer. He appeared to be in his mid-thirties, swarthy, and sported a wiry mustache that hid his upper lip. He was wearing a tight tee shirt that said, "Nettle And Tate, We Lay 'em Straight." Faded black jeans hung snug on his hips and the top two fly buttons were unclasped. "Hot?" he said glancing my way.

"If you mean the weather, it is hot," I returned.

He took a shark's bite out of his sandwich, followed by a slug of beer to wash the mouthful down. The juice from the meat had bled into the bread making it bloody red. The sight made me feel queasy and I glanced away. "Here on vacation?" he asked.

"We're looking for an apartment to rent," said Rugen. My psychic gear suggested that we should not trust this man and I began pressing my leg against Rugen as a signal to be careful about what *ce* revealed. The man squinted and scanned his eyes around the courtyard before looking squarely at Rugen for the first time. Then his voice turned a lot friendlier. "Welcome to Paradise!" he said. "Where you from? Your accents sound—different." His eyes lingered longer and longer on Rugen. He told us his name was Ray and a short time later, he cast out the first lure. "I might be able to put you up for a few days and show you the ropes around the local scene."

"Thanks, but we're an exclusive team," I said.

He grinned at me in a conspiratorial way that suggested we were cohorts. "No offense," he said and he bumped his shoulder against mine. "I see you've already staked your claim." Then he went back to eating his bloody sandwich.

Was this type of casual conversation peculiar to Ray or did all Humans talk this way in this ancient time? As I sat there, I tried to proclaim myself above his insolence. Later, when I was writing the scene, I realized his awkward attempt at seducing Rugen reminded me of times when I too was cruising with an eye set for an easy connection.

"Say!" said Ray and he looked brighter. "I just remembered. I have a compadre who lives over on Catherine Street. He has a small pad over his garage that's empty right now. A nice clean couple just moved out about a week ago—went back to Minneapolis 'cause they couldn't stand the heat here in The Keys."

Ray tore a scrap of paper off the edge of his lunch bag. "Got a pen?" Rugen gave Ray a pen and he tried to write without blowing on the tip. I snatched the pen from his hand and blew on its point to make it work. "Is that one of those new astronaut space pens?" Ray asked.

"Yeah," I said.

Ray wrote down a telephone number and handed me the important scrap of paper. Then he tucked Rugen's pen into the breast pocket of his tee shirt. "Give Dennis a buzz and mention my name," he said getting up to go.

"My pen?" asked Rugen.

"Oh yeah!" said Ray and he winked at me. When Rugen reached out to reclaim *cis* pen, Ray playfully slapped at Rugen's hand. "You're a dish!" he said. "Call me when you're ready to dump your queen."

As the afternoon wore on, we began to feel more like fools than genetically engineered beings from the future. Everything took more energy to figure out in the past. One did not walk up to a public communicator, as one did on *The Mother*, and say, "Please connect me with Jana Sante on G deck." Here it took five minutes to obtain the proper coins to insert into a gadget called a telephone box and another five minutes to figure out how to use the actual instrument.

At the telephone number that Ray gave us, no one answered. A clunky-sounding answering machine, that blipped a half dozen times and then shrieked in my ear, instructed me to, "Leave a message and Dennis or Greg will get back to you in a Key West jiffy!" Senon was not there to explain the time involved in a "Key West jiffy" so the statement remained a mystery. Of course, we had no contact number to leave, so I left a simple message saying we were interested in the apartment and would call again.

We slipped into another alley to contact Senon and make sure *le* was secure and then stopped by an outdoor cafe called Take Five, to check for free-press periodicals. While there, we ordered two iced teas. We sat in the shade, nursed our iced teas, and watched the people amble past in their baggy shorts, billboard tee shirts, and porcupine hairdos. We both felt confused and Rugen began wondering, *Where is our divine guidance? I feel as if we walked into an illusion and it's on the verge of collapsing.*

"Do you want divine help in locating an apartment?" I asked *cim*.

"For starters, that would be extremely helpful," *ce* said. Halfway through our iced teas, Rugen started feeling sick to *cis* stomach; five minutes later, *ce* was vomiting in the alley where we first landed. I held *cis* head so *ce* did not fall over. "That tea tasted odd," *ce* claimed. "My head is starting to hurt too."

I touched the back of *cis* neck and *ce* felt warm on levels deeper than *cis* flesh. We found a bench and I made *cim* sit while I searched through my tiny medical kit and located an inhalant of Aquila Breeze, which is a mild remedy for upset stomach. It helped *cim* only slightly and I began to worry. Discreetly as possible, I put my hand on some spots on *cis* arms and neck to manipulate *cis* energy. "Let's go back to the ship until you feel better," I said. "We can let Senon work on the apartment problem through *lis* Internet connections."

"I don't want to backtrack now," Rugen insisted. "It's late afternoon and we've accomplished nothing." Rugen convinced me that we needed to try the number Ray gave us again before calling it quits for the day. *Ce* apologized several times for being what *ce* called, "a burden instead of a help."

When *ce* said that I realized that despite our merging the heroic part of Rugen was not going to go away. *Cis* hero was big and fragile and perhaps was *cis* potential omega god "You could never be a burden, especially to me," I assured *cim*. I went on to remind *cim* how *ce* rescued me numerous times, once as recently as when *ce* found me sitting in my own piss in the toilet next to Nova's sleeproom.

****

We searched for another telephone box. This one was different and it did not work like the first model. However, a miracle did happen. When the signal rang on the other end, a live person said, "Hello, this is Greg." I mentioned that Ray gave us the number and Greg said, "Oh! Crazy Ray! Sure!" The apartment was still available and Greg said we could drop by to see it in about an hour. The price was twelve hundred dollars a month and utilities were not included. Rugen sighed when I told *cim* the cost.

It was twilight now, so we could use our jetpacks and *vitaratthas*. Greg met us at his front door with a glass of white wine in one hand. He was in his early forties, short and chubby. His pudgy cheeks and small turned-up nose made him look like a large boy. His hair, while trimmed short like most Human men, was black underneath and burgundy red on top. He acted fidgety for a Human and I wondered if he was inebriated from the wine.

"Come on back?" he said, leading us toward the rear of his home. He was barefoot and his feet made flip-flop sounds on the wooden floor as we followed him around a staircase and through a short hall. We emerged into a large and attractive kitchen with polished copper pots and pans hanging from a rack over a stove. A wooden plaque on the wall proclaimed in

Italian, *Buon appetito!* "Care for a glass of Chardonnay?" he asked.

"No thank you," said Rugen. "We appreciate you letting us see the apartment on such short notice."

"Where you all from?" he asked. "Your accents sound British."

"Our parents educated us in Europe," I said.

"Oh! Excuse me. I guess you're like royalty or something." He gave us a sly smile. "Brothers or lovers?"

"Bothers," Rugen quickly replied.

"What's the gay scene like up in Miami?" Greg asked.

At that early stage, I did not understand the idiomatic meaning of gay, so I said, "As a child, I enjoyed the gaiety of my summers in Miami."

"Yeah," Greg replied. "Even as a kid you know what pops your cork." I knew I was off course because I had no idea what Greg and I were talking about. Greg took his wineglass with him as we followed him out his kitchen door. We walked down a short winding path and then up a wooden stairway starving for a fresh coat of paint. On the way, Greg said, "I hope you two are not into the party scene." Since Greg seemed to disapprove of parties, I assured him that we were not into them. "The apartment has been closed for the last couple of weeks," he said. It was stuffy inside and the moment the lights came up, I felt Rugen's heart sink. Greg went over to a large contraption protruding from under the window and switched on one of the two air coolers.

The apartment was gloomy, despite the fact that it had a cathedral ceiling, bright pink walls, and blue-flowered ceramic tile on the floor. It was devoid of furnishings and it was generous of Greg to refer to the apartment as, "two rooms and a bath." The eating area was as cramped as the cockpit alcove on our pulsar. Two large windows sat perpendicular to each other in one corner of the sitting area and a smaller window, with a colored-glass panel, looked out over the sink in the food preparation alcove. All the windows looked as if someone had whitewashed them with chalky paint and I asked, "Why are all the windows opaque?"

"Oh that! That was our previous tenant's cheap solution for curtains. Lance had the *savoir-faire* of a horseshoe crab. Clean the windows or paint the walls if you wish. I just ask that you choose some normal shade of paint this time. Personally, I think bubble gum pink should be limited to plastic flamingos in front yards." Conversation with Greg was getting thinner and thinner, so we continue to cover our ignorance with agreeable smiles.

The sleeproom was miniscule. The only natural light came from a skylight, again streaked with opaque whitewash. The sleeproom had a closet almost the size of the room itself. This was an advantage. Rugen and I were hoping to find a situation with private walled-off space where we could hide the two multidexes and our space paraphernalia. The toilet was in the same room with the bathtub and Rugen communicated that *ce* considered that, *borderline unacceptable.*

My smell receptors were shouting that the apartment was marginally clean. Lingering smells of rancid grease oozed out from around the cooktop and a large, dead bug was a legs-up mummy at the bottom of the sink. Greg noticed the dead bug too and assured us, "It's a common palmetto, not a cockroach." He flushed the sink with water, giving the bug no further testimonial. I was surprised to learn that bug discrimination on Earth in 2015, makes palmettos smug social climbers in a cockroach-infested world.

The small refrigerator in the corner rattled when its motor was running. Rugen and I did more telepathic dialoging and *ce* communicated, *It's three thousand years and fifteen light years from our native time; but I have a feeling we should rent this apartment so we can get on with our mission.*

I attempted to negotiate a month-to-month lease and Greg explained the lease was for an entire year. When I asked if he needed all the rent up-front, he let go a silly titter and called me, "honey," and further offered; "if you give me ten thousand bucks up-front, I'll guarantee to serve you Sunday morning breakfast, in the buff, for the entire year." My total lack of response made Greg turn abruptly serious. "Just give me a security check for a thousand dollars and two month's rent and the apartment is yours." We negotiated a bit more and I gave him five hundred dollars and promised to give him the remaining twenty-one hundred the following day. "Real cash!" he exclaimed and he waved it in the air and actually kissed it. Back in Greg's kitchen, he rooted around in a drawer until he found two metal keys dangling from a ring.

How quaint! Rugen thought.

"I will get the lease ready," Greg promised. "Oh! And by the way, I will need proper references."

"No problem," I told him. I knew Senon would enjoy creating references that would satisfy Greg.

Greg was friendly and asked us, "Would you like to stay for dinner? I'm making Dennis's favorite, meatloaf and mashed potatoes. We thanked him again and said we had dinner arrangements with an old friend.

By that time, it was dark. We lost no time in flying back to Senon at the salt ponds. Senon retracted *lis* holographic projection to save space and I took Rugen into my *vitarattha* so we could rest side by side. The next four days were difficult to the extreme.

FIFTEEN

That night, Rugen was violently ill. *Ce* vomited several times, had diarrhea, an elevated temperature, and rapid pulses. When I realized how sick *ce* truly was, *ce* was too sick to fly *cis vitarattha* up to the pulsar.

A *vitarattha* provides a perfect zero gravity space and in a pinch can serve as a temporary shelter on an alien world. If you happen to be inside a *vitarattha* with someone sick, the smell can be difficult to handle and the mess even dangerous. The problem is especially difficult for me because I'm living with bio-enhanced olfactory senses. I must confess that compared with my eyes and ears, my nose is a snob in what it considers pleasant experience. Aside from esthetics, I was scared. Worries over Rugen dying young still haunted me. Despite my sensitive nose, it was automatic for me to slip into my healer's mode when someone I loved was suffering. This time I was determined that Rugen would get better and I was not going to lose *cim* because I was cavalier about *cis* condition. I insisted that *ce* submit *cis* body for a careful head to toe examination. During the examination, I found an inflamed and swollen area on *cis* inner thigh. When I touched the affected area, it felt hot and hard and on closer examination, I could see a raised and watery-looking blister. Rugen said the spot felt tender and itched. I got some surgical paraphernalia out of the medical kit and took a biopsy. The bioscan installed in the lid of the medical kit informed me the tissue sample contained proteases, lipases, alkaline phophatases and hyaduronidase and sphingomyelinase D." I asked Senon, "Please see if you can obtain information on Earth's spiders local to this peninsula, especially spiders known to have a toxic bite."

Five minutes later, Senon came up with, "Emergency Management of Brown Recluse Spider Bites: A Review." I read the information and found a list of symptoms that fit Rugen's condition. "…local pruritis, pain, swelling, induration, erythema, and blister and pustule formation." I became more concerned as I read, "If the patient experiences symptoms within 48-96 hours after being bitten, necrosis in the affected area is more likely." I had no idea how long ago Rugen was bitten, but if it was recently and *ce* already was ill, Rugen was in trouble. My mind flipped back to Evose and the horrible necrosis I saw around his groin. The Internet article further reported, "The patient's immune response to the foreign antigens, found in the venom, might be responsible for the tissue necrosis." because, "The quality of cytotoxic proteins, in the venom, is inadequate to account for the degree of necrosis in any one patient." Since Rugen was already ill, to me this meant that Rugen's immune response was high.

I explained to Rugen what I wanted to do and told *cim* it might hurt. "This is another one of my medical decisions based upon my inability to do nothing," I explained.

"I trust you. Do whatever you believe is right."

I isolated the affected field and excised the area with a laser point. Then, I put a cool refrigerant pack on the wound to reduce swelling. The darkness, the next three nights out by the salt ponds, was filled with interminable flashbacks to my previous lives. I sat up the first night and held Rugen in my arms as if *ce* were my child. Sweat poured off *cim* when *ce* was not freezing and shaking with fever. *Ce* would fall asleep and wake up screaming. Once *ce* awoke and began weeping uncontrollably and telling me that the Cerribeame were burning *cim* alive. "I love you," I told *cim* as often as *ce* needed to hear it. On a deeper level, I knew my assertions were foolish thrusts of bravery, me attempting to wave a spear at the darkness and telling it to go away. I felt so practical in this latest crisis. One thing I knew for sure. If Rugen was going to die, *ce* was going to die as a Janaforma, out in space, not in the garbage heap of the past, hovering over a salt pond. I had time to plan a retreat and I began sorting through my options. I decided that if Rugen showed no improvement at the end of six hours, I would leave Senon here on Earth with all the equipment and take Rugen back up to the ship. From there, I could take care of *cim* in a clean environment. In my last life, as a doctor aboard *Aeternus One*, I often carried people inside my *vitarattha* from ground level all the way up to the ship. The carrying part did not worry me; but abandoning our equipment, and telling Senon that *le* must stay behind to protect it, did.

That night, my desperation turned to fear. I reached out to Nova to show me how to cope and I heard no answer, just the echo of my fear crying out for help. This time I did not blame the connection; I blamed Nova *lim*self. "Why have you deserted me?" I cried out to the empty indifference. A half-hour before my six-hour deadline, Rugen's fever broke.

The following morning, I asked Senon to use *lis* skills and figure a way to connect me with Greg's telephone service. It took *lim* about ten minutes to figure out how to make the proper connections, but *le* did it. Through the membrane on Senon's multidex, I heard the now familiar screeching of Greg's answering machine and I left a message, telling him that Rugen was ill and I would get in touch in a couple of days and give him the remainder of the money.

We stayed out by the salt ponds for three days and nobody noticed us or came near. After a while, I forgot about the world around us. I did not care if the rupture happened for I was doing the best I could. I poured all my love and attention into Rugen. Hourly, I performed my energy tricks to make *cim* well. I held *cim* and massaged *cis* body that *ce* complained, "hurt all over."

It was when Rugen was getting better that *ce* asked me, "Do you think we brought this spider with us from the fourth dimension?"

Cis question started me thinking and I asked in return, "Remember when I mentioned that Michael said the *manatees'* particular genius was exposing our will to the quintessential, aboriginal heart?"

Rugen appeared puzzled. "I remember, but my mind is still fuzzy. Have you figured out what Michael meant?"

"The *manatees* created the vision of the spider expressly for me, but the vision acts as a two-edged sword between illusion and reality. Even when everything seemed to disappear, my consciousness still was radically alive. I could not escape from my essential core, my essence. When the *manatees* realized they could not shake my faith in my continuation, they created the one thing that might seduce me. They wove an illusion of the resplendent Nova with a promise of an eternity of pleasure with *lim* in a honeymoon setting. If it wasn't for you, I still would be wallowing in my fictional Nova and be none the wiser."

"Excuse me," said Rugen. "I think I am a little slow on the uptake because of my illness and lack of sleep. What is the two-edged message?"

"When the *manatees* create an illusion from our unresolved desires, they encode those desires with the truth to give us a chance to escape."

Rugen was eager. "Tell me more."

"When I met Nova by No Name Lake, *le* said, 'conscious is, Sante. We can go anywhere we want at any moment in time.'"

"How?"

"By believing we can."

Rugen looked a bit terrified over that possibility. "Please don't tell me that this reality is an illusion that we conjured up between us and we're still lost."

"We are inside an illusion, but we certainly are here." Rugen glanced around as if reality might disappear with my declaration. "Don't you see? We are inside a collective illusion. We are lending our credibility to this illusion to keep it alive."

"What about the impending rupture?" Rugen asked.

"I don't know," I admitted. "I do know our job is to figure out our purpose here and make peace with our part in this collective illusion. When that happens, we will be free agents to stay and partake or move on."

"But where can we go? I hardly call the emptiness of the fourth dimension a place I would care to spend eternity."

I refused to allow the emptiness of my meditations to destroy my belief in Nova and for the first time in my life, I had to believe in something with nothing but my faith. "We are one with Nova. With Nova, we will create any reality we want."

"And what about this horrible spider bite on my inner thigh? Is that an illusion too?"

"You're the flower of Nova's creation; therefore, you bear the stigmata for the Janaforma denial."

"That is a fantastic projection," suggested Rugen.

Rugen turned out *cis* leg so I could see *cis* inner thigh again. The redness covered almost the entire area between *cis* knee and his crotch. "Do you want to see some magic, Rugen?"

"Yeah, I do."

I put the flat of my hand against the wound and declared, "Love is here to heal you." I took my hands away and Rugen and I watched the spot for perhaps thirty seconds as it rapidly disappeared. "It was real within this illusion," I presumed to explain. "It was so real, it could have killed you." Was I right to remove the affliction from Rugen's inner thigh? Just like Bogwa, I did not question what I had done.

****

Rugen's ordeal left *cim* exhausted. I encouraged *cim* to rest and on June 12, 2015, I flew into Key West alone to make final arrangements with Greg and give him the balance of the money for the apartment. Dennis was there this time. He was big and muscular, like Ray, and his voice was deep and manly. Dennis said he worked in construction, but did not say what he constructed. "Your boyfriend got AIDS?" he asked. "Lots of men come here, to Key West, to die."

Dennis looked relieved when I said, "Rugen is my brother and he was bitten by a brown recluse spider, but is getting better now."

That night, secure in the undercover of darkness, Senon and I moved our gear into the apartment on Catherine Street while Rugen stayed behind and rested at the salt ponds. It took Senon and I three trips to bring everything in because our belongings were more disorganized than when we came down from space. On the final trip, I fussed over Rugen like an over-protective parent. "I'm perfectly well to fly my *vitarattha*," *ce* assured me. *Ce* was, but my vigilance concerning *cis* bodily safety made me insist on linking our *vitaratthas* the entire way.

We had been unable to bathe or change clothing since we came down from the pulsar. I smelled of suppressed fear and old sweat and Rugen's hair was hanging in tangled clumps as if *ce* dunked *cis* head in a vat of oil. The tub in our new apartment was too dirty to bathe in and had no shield to keep the water from splashing out. We took turns sponge bathing and I helped Rugen wash *cis* hair. We spent our first night sleeping inside our *vitaratthas*, suspended a meter above the floor.

The following morning, the light through the dirty windows awoke us. "Yikes!" said Senon. "This joint is a designer's nightmare." I took our remaining twenty-five hundred dollars and tossed it in the middle of the floor. "That's our entire fortune. What do you suggest we do to make this place a bit more livable for the next few weeks?" The three of us had plenty of ideas.

Rugen and I went to a nearby supermarket called Winn-Dixie and bought $73.21 worth of cleaning supplies. On the way home, we stopped at a paint store and bought four gallons of pale yellow paint called, "Froth." We spent the entire day cleaning the apartment from top to bottom and painting. It was actually fun. After dark, we cheated and employed some of our future technology for practical purposes. Senon projected *lim*self outside and washed all the windows and the skylight clean. We rewarded ourselves that evening by taking a long, hot bath. I mixed up some aromatherapy from our medical kit of *tartan ratu*, rosewood, and camphor and put it into our bath water.

The next day when Sol came up, the ambiance of our apartment was pleasant and friendly for the first time. Rugen claimed that if *ce* had to spend another night with the refrigerator chattering away like a bird, *ce* was going to start building a nest. *Ce* and Senon promptly disassembled the refrigerator and its motor. This worried me and I wondered if they knew how to put a refrigerator back together. They did, and afterward it ran like a silent miracle. That afternoon, we went out and bought a $200 futon, a $10 shower curtain, a tiny secondhand table and two chairs for $50, votive candles, plastic dishes, utensils, and a teakettle for $80. It took us five trips; all taken in expensive taxi rides, to lug our purchases back to our new apartment. We were exhausted that night and fell asleep right after taking our bath.

On June 15, we went shopping for food. We had lived mostly on nutrient capsules for the last six days and decided it was time to take the plunge into real Earth food. At a "health food store" called Carrot Brazil, we bought dried rice, miso paste, fresh vegetables and fruit, a few herbs, bread, tea, and some yogurt. We decided to be mindful about everything we consumed so we treated all our water with a small purification system we brought with us.

Rugen looked at our remaining cash and declared, "We've got to find a way to generate credit." We decided to give ourselves three additional days to find a way to make money before considering contacting Iris. We tried to get employment, but our attempts were unsuccessful except for jobs, in what Humans call, "the fast food industry." Rugen and I could not abide doing that type of work because it meant handling dead animal meat. Our experiences were identical. We would go out separately and meet at our apartment every three or four hours to commiserate on our failures. The truth was, we did not have the proper credentials to get the jobs we were qualified do unless we allowed Senon to forge more phony documents. We had a limit to what we could claim through forged documents; besides, Rugen and I felt uncomfortable about lying.

Our situations were humbling. In my last life, I was a physician. I served on *Aeternus One*, the elite flagship of the Orion Arm Alliance, as one of its senior surgeons specializing in trauma. I preformed medical procedures that doctors in the early twenty-first century might consider impossible, yet here in the past I could not get a job as an orderly in a nursing home called Sunnybrook Farms. Rugen's problem was worse. *Ce* was too young to get many jobs. One of the flunky jobs *ce* tried to get was as a chauffeur, supposedly someone to drive people from the airport to their hotels. Problem was, the person needed to be at least twenty-five years old because of insurance purposes. Rugen used a Human expression that *ce* said *ce* learned from other people out looking for work. "I'm pissed. Nobody is ever going to believe I was a pilot for British Air. Anybody that takes a good look at my records will know we're lying. Maybe if I shaved my head, I would be accepted as an older Human male."

We stood in the middle of our empty apartment and held each other. I ran my fingers through my lover's hair to help *cim* calm down and asked, "What could I get lost in if you shaved your head?"

Rugen put *cis* head on my shoulder. "Sante?" *ce* whispered. "Do you realize how ridiculous our situation is? I am a vitasphere pilot, a Vanguard Scout. I just flew a vitasphere backward in time from SY5603 and I can't find employment as a chauffeur here."

Rugen and I gave Senon free reign to come and go whenever appropriate. *Le* appeared and made a sound as if clearing *lis* throat. "Excuse me," *le* said. "I think I know a slick way to generate some quick dough around here that can put us on Easy Street in a few days."

Again, I asked Senon to interpret. Senon believed *le* could create software programs and sell them over the Internet. These programs were obvious technological improvements to us because we were looking backward through the scope. It was important that we not introduce advanced technology before its proper time, even if it was as simple as a breath-activated pen. It was similar to what Hope suggested about proper alien involvement. We wanted to play by the rules of this time. Senon promised not to get our advanced multidex technology involved in *lis* scheme, so we gave *lim* permission to try *lis* idea. Still, Rugen and I were adamant that Senon not support us. We needed jobs not just for credit; but getting jobs would help us assimilate so we could pass as natives. If Senon succeeded in *lis* endeavor, it would cut us some slack until we could find the right jobs. Senon knew how to take the pressure off like a pro. Over the following week, Senon's new business earned a thousand dollars.

****

Friday, June 19. We've been on Earth for ten days but not found employment nor have we contacted Iris. We've spent sweltering days following leads and filling out job applications with vital statistics from our invented past. Days are long, sweaty, and unrewarding. Evenings with Rugen are intimate, fun, and restorative.

I find it difficult to sleep for more than an hour or two at a time. My genetic programming tells me it's normal to sleep in reduced gravity and that's what I've done most of my life. I found no way to duplicate weightlessness, here in the past, unless I sleep inside my *vitarattha*. At first, I lectured myself about playing by the rules, then, every three or four nights, I would break my vow and tuck myself away inside a *vitarattha* for a few hours of great sleep.

Sometimes in those in-between nights, when I refuse to give in to my urge to float, I work on this book. Writing has turned difficult. The syntax of every sentence reconstructs itself a dozen times. There seems to be no best way to say anything. I'm stammering with writer's block. It makes no difference that I am undergoing unique experiences in this past world with its rank smells and rambunctious crudities; life here does not inspire me. This mission does not call for heroic rescues of the Vanguard sort. My new challenge involves coping with the boring minutiae of trying to establish a survival base and keeping my mind and principles intact on an illusion-ridden world. How I might translate that into a book remains unclear. As much as I enjoyed reading my own words, I wanted bigger thrills than whining about how I couldn't find employment and couldn't sleep. I had three choices, stop writing and wait, junk it, or make up something to get the action going. After three days of stewing, I decided the experiment was not over and I would continue to write about what was happening, even if the events were mundane.

Monday, June 22, 2015. We keep our futon in the sitting area because it doubles as our sofa during the daytime. We made the tiny sleeproom into our *neipanin*. The room is empty except for a couple of inflatable cushions we brought from the pulsar and three votive candles sitting on an interesting piece of scrap wood that Rugen found in the garden. I feel deprived without a beautiful amulet or two to create a small meaningful altar. Yesterday, Rugen picked a couple of large leaves from the overgrown garden outside our door and arranged the leaves in an empty bottle. *Ce* placed the arrangement in balanced proximity with the candles and insisted, "It looks great! It's simple, clean, and honors The Mother of Creation."

Tuesday, June 23: The restrictive dualities and hollow meanings involved in language are more obvious in the Earth of 2015. The blind acceptance of inadequate and inferior expression is puzzling. Words compress unique perspectives into perverted forms while people speak, but do not understand their own minds. Polarizing words exist in all languages and sometimes Universal seems built upon the concept of opposites. As a soul moves toward integration, the perspective widens and polarized viewpoints lose their appeal. As Rugen and I merge, our telepathy grows increasingly intricate and refined. Will telepathy become our common language in the future? If telepathy outpaces the spoken word and makes speech into an outmoded tool, then, I guess, so be it. As a writer, I already consider the careful construction of thought, through the written word, an art form. I do not believe expression of this variety will die; nevertheless, language as a communicative tool is constrained, vague, and misleading, affording shields to those who wish to hide meaning and themselves. If telepathy actually succeeds in displacing language, perhaps the limitations involved in speech will finally vanish and language will move into the realm of passive amusement, something we experience such as a drama acted upon a stage. As surely as denial exists, part of that denial exists inside language, and inside the willful ignorance of duality thinking. In my opinion, the benefits of expanding language now, in 2015, might be the key to preventing the rupture we fear in 5603.

Wednesday, June 24: Every day we walk the hard concrete streets of Key West. A great deal of deliberate ugliness is stifling this place. Natural beauty lies trampled in what Ray calls, "Paradise." Nature is dying from neglect and no one seems to care or notice. Humans have paved over the natural and relegated nature to the trivial. Humans in this time seem unaware of the universal principle that conditions must be favorable for energy to incarnate into specific form. It's not as if one cannot see the natural beauty rupturing between the cracks of this contrived world, trying to reincarnate. Nevertheless, the easily disposable remains the focus. Advertising exaggerates the value of useless commodities with great enthusiasm, fanfare, and gift-wrapped expense. Worship is secular, contrived, and made from the very body and bones they scorn.

Thursday afternoon, June 25: It's obvious to us now that Ceff and Kayya provided us with a few costumes, a few articles of clothing capable of disguising our identities for a short time. Our costumes are starting to show wear. Every night, we wash socks and underwear. The shirts we dry on hangers look like wrinkled cardboard. It takes our socks two days to dry.

We resorted to draping socks over the air-cooling vents in our apartment to dry the heels and toes. "If I was allowed to give one gift to the past, it would be texoplex fabric."

Friday morning, June 26: We found a laundry called Fluff and Dry this morning. We met some interesting Humans from our neighborhood. Karl, a hairdresser, gave me a small white card that pictured a pair of open scissors cutting the words Karl's Kutery in two. He called it his, "business card." Karl's hair has that mean, wired, stay-away look that Human men favor in this time. "What's with the Rapunzel-look you two are sporting?" he asked me.

"We like it better than the porcupine-look," I said.

He laughed and told me, "You got style," just as Weegan Zu had. "You are a good-looking guy. Did you ever think of going into modeling?" I remembered the covers of *Esquire* and *Gentlemen's Quarterly* and told him that modeling was probably not for me. Then he came out with, "That hair color looks great on you too—almost real."

"It is real," I said, not mentioning my parents had selected genetic trait 201.34 so I could look like Nova.

"Whatever!" he said. "Come by my shop and I'll give you a proper cut."

"*Ouch!*" said my hair.

We also met Rose Katuto. When I told Rose my name was Sante Janaforma, she wanted to know if I was born in The States or in Cuba. She said she was 82, the same age as Belinda; but Rose Katuto looked as if she were 882. I tried to help her with her heavy laundry basket and she insisted, "I can do it myself, sonny. I have been doing it myself for the last sixty-two years." She also told us, "I sell flowers down on Duval Street during the tourist season to make ends meet. The rest of the time I consider myself retired." She had the whitest towels I've ever seen. Her "secret formula" for getting towels white was one cup of sudsy ammonia with every batch of white towels. Nova said, "Everything is important." Perhaps we came to the past for the secret formula for whitening towels.

****

Saturday morning, June 27: Rugen and I bought cell phones. It's helpful to be able to leave a number with potential employers. We also discovered the wonders of Target. We bought new clothing and a laundry basket to tote our laundry back and forth between home and Fluff and Dry.

June 28, early evening: Rugen and I are afraid to leave our apartment unless we cover our arms and legs, especially in the evenings when mosquitoes bite like hungry vampires. We have used the remaining insect repellent from our honeymoon on Sasaybin. Fortunately, at the Carrot Brazil, I was able to purchase the essential oils of lavender, pennyroyal, and geranium for a total of $17.98. We are using these oils in our bath and shampoo. I put several drops of pennyroyal in some generic powder we brought with us, and we are sprinkling the powder in our shoes. We have experienced no more problems with aggressive mosquitoes since then.

June 29: We have leads on jobs. Rugen's best bet is working in construction with Dennis or as a waiter in a restaurant called Hideaways. The construction job pays $15 an hour and the job as a waiter is strictly for tips; but the lecherous Ray works with Dennis and that is a definite minus. I'm hoping a local newspaper called *The Key West Advertiser and Liberty Times* will hire me. The position is for copy editor and only part time. I have neither the legitimate training nor the fake credentials to be a copy editor. A woman named Helen Mead granted me an interview. I showed her that I could do the work by editing a couple of articles for her and when she looked over my work, Ezek was reporting, *she's sexually attracted to you.* I was preparing to say, thank you for hiring me, when she asked, "Why did you capitalize Human in the sentence, 'The Human tendency to procrastinate is fatally endemic?'"

"Humans are a particular species—are they not?"

"I'll let you know," she said.

I knew what she meant, but was annoyed with my inability to find work so I asked, "What will you let me know—whether Humans are endemic procrastinators, a particular species, or if I have the job?" Oh well, maybe I won't get that job.

Tuesday, June 30: After the exhaustion of each day, Rugen and I take turns soaking in our tiny bathtub. While one of us bathes, the other one sits on the lid of the toilet; then we switch for a while. Our main topic always centers on how we might contact Iris and make it seem natural so we will not scare her away. Adhering to our plan for living honestly means creating as few fabrications as possible, especially with Iris. What we envision for the future is a situation where we can confide in her and make her our ally in whatever may lie ahead.

****

Wednesday afternoon, July 1: Greg saw me coming in from my day's search for work, popped out his kitchen door, and invited Rugen and me for dinner on Saturday evening. I told him, "We would love to come; but Rugen and I are being very conscious about our diets and are sticking to simple vegetarian food."

Greg threw me an open-hand gesture and said. "I make great vegetarian food. Do you eat salad?"

"Sure—"

"You and Rugen drop by about six on Saturday and we'll eat some Greek salad, drink a bottle of *Classico*, and share a couple of baguettes that I get right down the street in that sweet, little French shop on the corner."

Friday afternoon, July 3: This morning I stopped by the shop that Greg mentioned. At *Maison Du Fleur et Pain*, I bought some pink and white roses to take with us to dinner. Then on a whim, I bought Rugen three scarlet roses and a small cobalt blue vase to hold them. I presented the flowers to *cim* with a little flourish and said, "To my flower of manifestation." *Ce* put the roses on the tiny secondhand table and the whole room perked up and seemed to smile just because roses were present.

It was a fascinating evening with Greg and Dennis. They love each other despite some thorns between them that neither one has any notion how to remove. Their relationship does not have much energy going through it, but they seem to be committed to staying together. They ignored each other most of the time we were there; but fussed over Rugen and me as if we were their best friends. I thought the situation odd that they treated acquaintances better than they treated each other, especially since Ezek was telling me, *They're soul mates.*

I gave Greg the roses and his eyes lit up with joy before going teary. "They're beautiful!" he sniffed. "Dennis? Why don't you ever bring me roses?"

"I'm allergic to roses," said Dennis, in that deep rumbling voice of his.

Greg had mentioned that they were not into the "party scene," so Rugen asked, "What do you do for fun?"

Greg's face dropped into what appeared to be a practiced frown. "Not much," he admitted. "Dennis watches ESPN (a television channel that features sporting events) all the time and I read cookbooks."

"Did you ever think of doing some gardening together," I suggested. "A lovely spot could be developed in the center of the garden, near that old magnolia, that would be perfect for meditation."

"This is one queer who don't pick no pansies," Dennis said.

"Pardon?" Rugen asked.

"Fuck that!" said Dennis. "I slave all day in the Florida heat. I'm not going to pluck weeds when I get home. I gotta sit, let my ass spread out on the sofa, drink a couple of beers—know why?"

"Why?" Rugen asked.

"So I can do the same damn thing the next day." Dennis laughed and his right eye squinted. "You know what a Key Largo interlocking paver is?"

"Sorry, I don't know," we both admitted.

"Go down to the West End of town, have a look around. I laid all those bricks down there—worked on the fancy brickwork down on Mallory Dock too, way back in the Nineties when all those Mexican Indians started moving into the state. Finished the job right before the big two-triple-zero celebration." His tone turned confidential. "The Preservation Society wanted things shipshape for the big millennium shindig." At that point, one of Dennis and Greg's many exchanges of the evening began.

"You make it sound as if you laid all the bricks yourself," squawked Greg.

Dennis boomed. "So what! I worked on the goddamn job."

Greg reminded him, "But that was six years ago, Dennis."

Dennis' face flushed a brighter red. "Was it that long?" He apologized and appeared self-conscious. "Sometimes I get talking and get carried away." His sudden awkwardness made us all feel awkward.

Rugen attempted to smooth the conversation over by asking if we could have permission to tidy the garden between the house and the garage. "Do you know anything about gardening?" Greg asked.

"Personally, I don't," said Rugen. "However, Sante learned a great deal about gardening from our father." Rugen was referring to Bejan. "Dear old dad had a thriving business making one-of-a-kind perfumes. As a child, Sante helped by gathering flowers in the mornings from which the scents were extracted."

"Sounds as if you had an interesting childhood," said Greg. "Well, if you can do anything with that mess back there, I will be tinkled bright pink."

"Good!" said Rugen. *Ce* made the venture sound like fun instead of hard work. "We'll get creative tomorrow morning." Rugen's enthusiasm brought my attention to how much *ce* enjoyed initiating projects. *Cis* innocent charm was stirring up notions of romance in me. *We're going to have an opportunity to create something beautiful. I can see the garden already; it's going to look great!*

Greg decided, "I want to help too." He managed to appear redeemed. "Besides, I guess that proves—some queers do pick pansies!"

Greg was a wonderful cook. Dinner was tasty, well prepared, and arranged on the plate with meticulous care. He was a one-person cook in the kitchen and it made him fidgety when Rugen and I attempted to help. "I'm used to doing things my way," he explained. He sounded like Rose Katuto. Dennis sat with his back wedged against the wall and talked to us while Greg prepared the food. Dennis was drinking a yellow-colored beer called *Corona* with a twist of lime. By the time we began to eat, he had three empty beer bottles lined up in front of him with wedges of spent lime lingering at the bottom of each one.

The more Dennis drank, the more his voice took on a clever twang. The rhythm in his speech linked into fresh and startling idioms that came out sounding funny. He told us several amusing stories about his life in construction and about laying Key Largo interlocking pavers, that he explained, "—had to be laid just right, or the ground would bust right through, and crack 'em all to shit."

After telling Greg that we were particular about our diets, we did not have the brass to say we did not want to drink their wine. Greg poured us each a huge glass of wine and I found myself drinking it. It tasted good with the food. I had not drunk alcoholic beverages more than a dozen times in my life because of its deleterious effects on me; but in the last few weeks I drank with Evose, on my honeymoon, and now tonight. Rugen seemed to be no steadier drinker than I was and I noticed the wine affected *cim* too. As soon as Rugen became a little inebriated, *ce* turned careless. Carelessness put *cis* life into jeopardy in several past lives and could turn into a theme for *cim*. Tonight, *cis* carelessness merely took the lid off *cis* genius; therefore, I felt no urge to interfere in *cis* fun.

Dennis was at the end of one of his long stories. This one concerned the police catching him with his pants down when he was sixteen years old. "I'm an East Saint Louis boy," he said, settling into his plucky rhyme. "I'm nobody's fool. All those hackers were running like squirrels with their tails up. What was I supposed to do, pull up my pants and run like a squirrel too?"

Rugen thought this was hilarious and said, "What was I supposed to do, run like a squirrel too?" The problem was Rugen imitated Dennis's voice. It was a precise imitation and *ce* even managed to caricaturize Dennis for a few seconds.

Dennis and Greg were stunned and, of course, fascinated. "Can you do other voices?" Greg asked immediately.

"Can you do other voices?" mimicked Rugen, going up into the higher register where Greg's voice lived.

"That's amazing!" exclaimed Greg. "Can you do anybody famous? Can you do Barbara or The King?"

We did not know who Barbara or The King was, but Rugen bragged, "If I hear a voice, then I can imitate it." Greg played a song on his computer of Barbara Streisand singing, "People." Just when Rugen was about to do *cis* imitation, I gently reminded *cim, if you don't back off soon, you might be sorry tomorrow morning.*

From Greg and Dennis, we learned about Mallory Square Dock and the Sunset Ritual. "Where have you been—outer space?" Greg asked. Rugen and I glanced at each other and blinked. "Sunsets on Mallory Dock are essential Key West! To stand on the point of land where the Atlantic Ocean meets the Gulf of Mexico is like standing on the last male projection into the great womb of the sea. To be there at sunset is like witnessing The Mother falling asleep as she embraces her children. It shows our love for Earth when we go there to say goodnight."

Rugen and I stared at each other in amazement and Rugen asked, "Do you believe in planet consciousness?"

Greg said, "Sure, I do! Everything is alive. Isn't it Dennis?"

"If you say so. Want to go down to the docks tomorrow evening with Greg and me? Dennis reached across the table and held hands with Greg. "We go there all the time. Watching the sunset from Mallory Dock puts Greg in a poetic mood."

****

Early Sunday morning, July 5, 2015: I woke up with a headache that was an intense pressure between my eyes. I attributed the headache to drinking wine the night before, but grew suspicious as the day progressed and the headache refused to go away. When I first awoke, I ambled outside in my bare beet and undershorts to survey the tangled mess of vegetation that once was a garden. "Working in the garden today is going to be great fun," Rugen called from inside.

I went back indoors. *Ce* was leaning against the counter in our kitchen alcove making a cup of tea. "Your enthusiasm and innocence are refreshing to see in someone as ancient as you," I said.

"Tell me you love it," *ce* coaxed.

"I love you more, but Rugen—I don't want to get distracted. Don't you think we should be contacting Iris instead of doing this gardening work?"

"I haven't forgotten about Iris. In fact, I finally have an idea how we can meet her without appearing contrived. Let's sign up for one of her classes. I think Senon mentioned that her class on life direction starts on July 10. That's this coming Friday."

"That's a great idea, Rugen. We'll do it."

Now, let's have some fun." A few minutes later, as we began to trim back the dead wood in the garden, we found hidden patches of herbs in several spots. We discovered several varieties of ginger, onions, and bits of trailing thyme. There was fuchsia-colored bougainvillea, ferns, taro root, and plumeria. We used a pair of clippers from a tool kit we brought with us. Their actual purpose was to trim polyplex hosing, not to trim garden vines; but they worked. About ten o'clock, Greg came out and offered to help. "I have another pair of garden clippers somewhere," he said. We followed him to the garage under our apartment where we found the garage door jammed shut. Rugen managed to dislodge a garden rake that was wedged in the track. Once the door was open, I was surprised to see that the garage held a dusty hodgepodge of forgotten items.

"You've got a LV (land vehicle)!" Rugen exclaimed.

Greg explained, "Oh, you mean the car. It hasn't run for years. I think several things are wrong with it."

"Do you mind if I play around with it?" asked Rugen. "Maybe I could get it running."

Greg brightened. "You know how to fix cars too?"

"I know a little about cars," said Rugen. "Collecting old propulsion systems was my hobby when I was a child." Greg gave Rugen an odd look and I wondered if Rugen was being a little too forthright.

"It would be great to have a car again," Greg admitted. "We could all drive up the coast together. There's a super-fabulous fruit stand up in Homestead called Robert Is Here that sells great sweet corn. I'd loved to introduce you and Sante to their mamay and mango milkshakes." We knew what mangos were, but not mamay. Greg explained that a mamay looked like a huge brown potato on the outside, but had scarlet flesh inside and tasted like a sweet avocado. He patted his plump behind and told us, "Mamay shakes are fattening!" Greg's dream of having a working car gained momentum while I kept remembering Nova's dream. "I could shop for clothes again in Miami," Greg projected. His mind shot all the way up the North American coastline. "Maybe, Dennis and I could go see my baby sister in Baltimore. I haven't seen Louise in sixteen years."

"Don't get too excited," said Rugen. "I said I would try to fix it."

"I'm amazed that you have the courage to try." Greg glanced at Rugen as if trying to alter his perspective a bit. "Someone as smart as you should really go to college," said Greg. "You know you could make something out of your life." A moment later, he straightened himself and gave me a cold stare. "You should help your brother get an education," he said.

I immediately wanted to defend myself. It felt shameful to allow someone to believe that I was retarding Rugen's potential. I might have bragged that Rugen had earned an advanced degree from the Cerribeame Academy when ce was fifteen; but that would have opened doors to some astonishing facts that would have been impossible to explain. Rugen jumped to my defense with, "Sante supports everything I do," but it seemed, Greg barely listened because this particular conversation had nothing to do with us. This conversation was all about Greg.

As we continued to work in the garden, I explained the concept of projection. I asked Greg as casually as possible, "Do you believe Dennis stopped you from furthering your education?"

Greg shrugged. "I once had dreams of going to cooking school. I used to dream of owning my own restaurant too. Dennis never showed much enthusiasm for my passion in the kitchen."

The three of us worked on the garden project until almost noon. Dennis wandered out of the house around 11:30. He was shirtless and his shorts were hanging low around his hips. A fine spider web of black hair blanketed his chest and narrowed to an arrow that disappeared down his shorts. Obviously, he was missing Greg and wanted to join in the fun. Dennis did not know how to ease into the spirit of the game after his blunt statement about pansy pickers the night before. He stuck out his belly a bit and yawned to show how disinterested he still was in our project. "Need some help?" he asked, exaggerating his boredom. My flower of manifestation never missed a beat, putting Dennis to work hauling the accumulating pile of garden trimmings to the rear of the property. Every time Dennis returned for another armload, Rugen lectured him about recycling trimmings via a compost bin.

"I'll compost bin something!" Dennis grumbled. He had a difficult time maintaining his grumpy exterior in the face of Rugen's enthusiasm If nudged in the right direction, I felt, both Dennis and Greg were ready to flower, just like their garden.

SIXTEEN

Later, the four of us took a taxi down to Mallory Square and Dennis insisted on paying the entire fare. It was obvious he wanted us to view him as generous; instead, I saw him as stingy in his unwillingness to participate in the active life of his mate.

That evening, the light from Sol was burnt-orange and everything seemed to be soaking up the light. Even the Key West interlocking pavers seemed dusted with gold. We emerged from between some tourist shops on Duval Street onto Mallory Square. In our search for employment, we walked through this area several times, but had not realized its significance. People were pouring out of the converging streets with one purpose in mind, the Sunset Ritual. We fell in with these worshipers; caught up in their rhythm, we became a Community that moved as a mighty river to the sea.

Despite our persistent feelings of alienation since coming to this time and place, we felt a strange sense of belonging that night. It was not the feelings of oneness we felt with our family or the Janaforma people. In this awkward past, we knew we were a couple of Senon's odd socks. Waiting there, we felt camaraderie with every long-deserted argyle in the bottom drawer.

Mallory Dock was such an ordinary place—sun, sea, and the florid colors of the promenade. Behind the prosaic and tawdry, the Sunset Ritual was serene and authentic. People were perched along the dock with their feet dangling toward the water as they stared out to sea. As they sat there, I hoped some realized why they possessed such clarity of thought, such feelings of love and grace as they watched the setting sun. I hoped they knew that they were the ones pulling down the light with their love.

A slight breeze sailed in off the ocean and the clean air felt fabulous against my face. The warm breeze gave me déjà vu prickles, reminding me of other nights in other places, other beaches, and other crowds. We mingled and had a good time watching the interaction that varied only slightly on the ancient theme of Community. Venders with brightly painted carts dotted the scene—pedaling snack foods, folk crafts, and trinkets galore. Closer to the water were performers—a juggler, a bagpipe player, The Statue Man, The Shakespearean Bard, and an Iguana named Coach and his handler, Roach. Luscious smells of corn popping mixed with the odor of deep fried food. A gaunt man wearing a prickly, straw hat was cracking coconuts and selling them for a dollar apiece. In another life, I watched a crusty old Gathosian who owned a nettle-nut concession on the Southern tip of the Ivory Coast of Euterpe. For about a dollar, he would crack open nettle nuts with a blade and buyers would devour the soft green flesh on the spot.

A vigorous business was going on at Mallory Dock in the lemonade trade. A pretty woman in one stall was making conch fritters in a deep fry machine. Louis the Falafel man, was selling sandwiches advertised as, "falafel now, feel better later!" Accidental counterpoints of music drifted toward us from several separate locations. An African-looking man tapped out jazzy rhythms on three hide-covered drums. A placard sat in front of a guitar player that read "Jimmy Buffet selections upon request."

As on Wonder World, the fortunetellers and palm readers were plying their trade. A woman named Lola gazed into people's eyes and told them what she saw. Venders were selling amulets, crystals, and tiny charms. As a joke, I suggested, "Maybe we should set up a concession ourselves."

Rugen laughed and added, "You could read tarot and I could sing like Barbara or The King."

We left Greg and Dennis at the falafel stand where they decided to have a snack and planned to rejoin them a half-hour later. We watched The Shakespearean Bard do his Duke Orsino from *Twelfth Night*:

> If music be the food of love, play on;
> Give me excess of it, that surfeiting,
> The appetite may sicken, and so die,
> That strain again, it had a dying fall...

"Orsino had a Tyrowsian heart," said Rugen. "He knew how to sing the blues."

"Maybe Shakespeare was Tyrowsian," I joked.

We stopped at one of the carts and bought each other matching hand-braided friendship bracelets for a dollar each. For lifetimes, Rugen's incarnations hated to wear anything on *cis* wrists. *Ce* realized now that because *ce* refused to wear a wrisceptor, when *ce* was Cle, *ce* could not call me for help when the Cerribeame attacked. Now *ce* decided that *ce* wanted to wear one of these bracelets as a symbol of our new commitment to have all channels open between us. I tied one on *cis* wrist, and *ce* tied one on me. We kissed discreetly. Right after we kissed, I felt the pain between my eyes take a turn for the worse. "Are you all right?" *ce* whispered.

Reality turned eerie from my perspective. The air hummed and the quality of the light appeared altered or heavier. Then, I felt a preternatural wind blow against my arms and I grabbed Rugen and hung on while Ezek began screaming *PAY ATTENTION!*"

We both stopped dead in our tracks and waited. Then, the voice of The Shakespearean Bard pierced through the superficial noise of the crowd. His tone was the voice of a narrator nearing the end of a drama—eloquent, nostalgic, and a little removed. "Our revels now are ended," The Bard recited. Then the curtain began to glow with a transparency for me.

"'These our actors,
As I foretold you, were all spirits and
Are melted into air, into thin air:
And, like the baseless fabric of this vision,
The cloud-capp'd towers, the gorgeous palaces,
The solemn temples, the great globe itself,
Ye all which it inherit, shall dissolve
And, like this insubstantial pageant faded,
Leave not a rack behind. We are such stuff
As dreams are made on, and our little life
Is rounded with a sleep.'"

I heard some applause. *"The Tempest,* act I, scene I," The Bard said and the cosmic gear turned for Rugen and me.

I decided to get a better look at The Shakespearean Bard and we began to pick our way through the crowd. Then I noticed a huge crowd standing around another performer. "Wait!" I said. "We need to see who is standing inside this larger circle." Ezek's ruthless psychic instinct led me.

We moved toward the edge of the water to get a better view. What we saw was a small, thin man standing on a square mat. He was dressed in a straightjacket and draped in enough heavy chain to make him droop under the weight. Two other men were just now securing his chains with a large padlock that dangled behind his back. The man in question peered straight ahead and spoke from inside an altered state. His immediate magnetism pulled me in and I imagined myself standing with him inside his prison of chains.

His aura was vibrating with the blue-white light of transcendence. He told the crowd, "Sometimes I can get loose in as little as ten minutes and sometimes it takes me hours. It all depends on how well my assistants imprison me. While I'm struggling, if you see signs that I am progressing, please feel free to encourage me." Finally, he pointed to a box, and indicated that donations "were appreciated," if anyone thought his performance worth a reward.

"Holy shit!" Rugen whispered in my ear.

True, Rugen and I were strangers in a new land and we were failing at managing the subtleties of adaption; but one thing we knew for sure; this man wrapped in chains was not an Earthling. For starters, his skin was an eerie shade of blue. "Do you remember when we were on Wonder World in our last life?" I asked. "We saw a troop of acrobats from the planet Kulupa. They were jumping in and out of locked boxes and doing all sorts of weird stunts that seemed impossible."

Rugen snapped *cis* fingers. "That man is a Kulupan shadowman!" We watched the Kulupan for the next few minutes. During that time, he got down on his mat and actively struggled; but the struggle progressed by millimeters and seemed mostly internal until he found a critical new move that freed him a tiny bit more from his restraints. The shadowman was on Earth for an important reason, no doubt existed in my mind about that. Just for starters, he was reenacting the stance of the willing sacrifice before the mesmerized crowd. He was the martyred Christ, the conscious Buddha, and the active Baybairn in his struggle for freedom. His shadowman demonstration was heroic, archetypal, a moment on the stage. Slowly, very slowly, the first huge chain slipped off his shoulder and the crowd went wild with cheers.

Should we try to talk to him or go on pretending he's just another Human?" asked Rugen. At that moment, the strangeness got stranger and I glanced across the circle of the gathered crowd and spied a woman gazing into my eyes. As soon as I saw her, a bolt of energy shot through me as if she stuck me with lightening. Ezek laughed like a parrot when he squawked, *The future is here*!

****

"It's Iris," Rugen whispered. "Do something Sante!"

"What?" I whispered back.

"Go talk to her."

"What am I supposed to say?"

"You'll think of something charming. You always do." A hot flash of energy went through my heart. How could I be charming on cue? It was like asking me to get an erection on demand. Rugen kept urging me to move and I cautiously led us around the circle to the opposite side. By the time we got through the crowd, Iris had walked away. At first, I was relieved. "There she is!" Rugen seemed to shout in my ear.

Iris walked over to a small, square table, covered with a tie-dyed scarf, and sat down. A moment later, she turned a cardboard sign around to face the crowd to show that she was open for business. The sign read, "Tarot

Readings by Iris. Fifteen minutes for ten dollars, a half-hour for seventeen." Rugen was pushing me. "She is prettier in person," were the first words out of *cis* mouth. "She looks younger than 35 bio-years too. You have no idea how much I've been worrying about the age difference between us." Of course, Rugen could not hide *cis* thoughts from me and thoughts of connecting with Iris were already romping around inside *cis* libido. Strangely, the notion of connecting sexually with Iris still did not move me. I also felt events were moving too fast, just as they always do, when I plug into an energy vein that has my name written all over it. I wanted to plan our next move and Rugen kept urging me on with, "That's nonsense, Sante! We cannot plan the future in that much detail and we can't allow this opportunity to slip by without taking our best shot." We stared at each other. It was up to me, I knew that. Rugen would accept and support my decision whatever it was. "We should ask her to read our tarot," *ce* said.

"Cool it!" I replied. "My psychic agitation is in the danger zone." I kept flashing from the Kulupan shadowman to Iris and my head was throbbing with pain. Why do you think she was watching the Kulupan?" I wondered aloud.

"Maybe her psychic business is slow tonight."

"Do you think she was waiting for us? Suppose a readjustment in time has occurred because something terrible already happened in the future. Suppose Belinda is filling Iris' head with new dreams or Evose is connecting with her? We have no idea what's going on. We haven't heard from Belinda or Nova in over two weeks." I had to stand there, attempt to sort through my psychic insight, and separate it from my projected fears. I concentrated all my psychic vision toward Iris and tried to read what was coming through. I needed years, even lifetimes, to do it right, now all I had were a few seconds to decide. One thing I knew for sure, Iris was no stranger to me. It seemed impossible to isolate what was unique about her now. We had lived together, loved and worshiped together in several different bodies. Those memories now created a bias, a multi-layered façade that I could never be certain I had cleared away. Plus the face she wore in this lifetime looked so much like the faces she wore in other lives that I wondered what her oversoul loved about soft, dreamy-looking women who liked to wear green. Iris was younger than Belinda was. All her youthful dewiness was intact, but her core was essential Belinda. As always, her hair was luxuriant and black, the kind lovers need to tangle themselves inside. She was curvy with a dark complexion, sensuous lips, and sparkling, brown eyes.

Seeing Iris sitting there, she made me realize the different ways that will, understanding, and love incarnations carry personal denial. Will incarnations hide their denial under a guise of cool detachment; understanding people hide under the subterfuge of logic and debate while love people—me included—hide under masks of cynicism while trying to appear tough. Underneath Iris' tough façade, she was a sensitive lover who had felt the pain of playing the fool endless times. Like Hibernia, Iris' aura was orange. It even matched Hibernia in that dark spots appeared around the heart, like red wine stains. "If I go over there, you have to go with me," I said to Rugen.

"You can't believe that I would let you go alone." Rugen snatched my upper arm and gave me a gentle tug and we were on our way.

Iris' focus had shifted and now she was gazing out toward the sea, her awareness apart from the crowd. She seemed lost, lonely, and resolved in her loneliness. It was such a cold denial that I shivered. "Excuse me? Could you read our tarot?" I asked. She glanced up and her expression did not change one iota. Seeing me for the first time did not affect her, yet her gaze made the pain between my eyes explode into incredible pleasure. I felt dizzy from the sudden clearing and knew that it was from the polarities of our energies coming together.

Her perfume was not her usual Essence of Salamander, but the scent of mixed spices basking in heat. The way Rugen was leaning toward her, I felt as if *ce* were dragging me forward into her sphere of energy. "I saw you watching the escape artist," she said to Rugen. "I thought at the time, he will drag his lover over here in a few minutes and they will be my first customers of the night."

"We're brothers not lovers," said Rugen.

"How much do you want to bet?" she asked.

"Are you psychic?" I asked, taking care to make my voice sound normal.

She shrugged with indifference and gazed out toward the sea again. "It comes and goes. My common sense takes up the slack."

"What does your common sense tell you about us?"

She seemed surprised. "My clients usually are not interested in common sense; they're always looking for magic cures through the cards." She folded her hands on the table and I noticed the pinkie finger on her left hand was missing. "Common sense suggests that people who watch the escape artist always start asking themselves questions—questions like, 'What if I could get free too?' When that happens, they start searching for ways to do it. That usually leads them to me." She gave her tabletop a gentle pat.

"Do we look especially entangled?" asked Rugen.

"Merely confused, as if you suddenly woke up and found yourself in a new place. Sit down and we'll put the cards on your case." She gestured toward a couple of empty chairs that seemed to be waiting for us. "My professional name is The Eye of Iris," she explained. "Some people call me The Eye, or simply I." Rugen and I sat down. "Do you want the fifteen minute or half-hour reading?"

I took a twenty-dollar bill out of my pocket and put it on the table.

"Let's see how far this takes us. We can give you more if we need additional time."

"It's your money," she said as if we were negotiating the rules of a new game. She instructed us—"Each of you, give me one of your hands." She extended both hands and bowed her head to us. Rugen took her right hand and I took her left—the one with the missing pinkie—and together we sent a jolt of our combined energy up her arms. We did not plan it. It was spontaneous. Iris' head bobbed a little from our energy and that's all She remained with her head bowed for almost a minute while the noise buzzed around us. In those thirty seconds, the crowd cheered again for the Kulupan shadowman and the African drummer changed rhythms. My focus narrowed and everything except Iris and Rugen disappeared for me.

We told her our personal names.

As soon as she released our hands she announced, "You both have pure energy." She took the silk scarf off her cards and placed them on the table between us. This deck was the same deck Belinda was using, thirty-five hundreds years into the future. Iris fanned the cards out in front of us. "Each of you choose three cards," she said.

"Before we do, could Sante choose a card for you?" asked Rugen.

Iris came out of herself a little and appeared annoyed. "That's not how I do it."

"I like the idea," I piped up. "If we choose a card for you, it will give us an indication of the variables your personality puts into the reading."

"My personality does not get involved in a reading," she said with a certain amount of presumption. "My direction comes only from God."

Rugen put *cis* hand to *cis* temple imitating a fake swami in a sideshow. "I feel a great psychic need to have Sante pull this card."

Iris stopped playing our game. "Listen, you guys, if you don't want to take this reading seriously, you can take back your twenty dollars and be on your way."

Rugen, the consummate strategist, stopped playing games too. "Okay, let's forget the card reading and we can talk instead."

Iris backed up, unaware that we were prepared to win both ways. "What the hell!" she conceded. "If you want to waste your time and money by picking a card for me, go ahead." Then she fanned the deck out before me. I asked if I might hold the cards for a moment. She searched my eyes before handing them over. "Be careful," she warned. "This deck is my favorite."

I accepted her favorite deck in my hands and closed my eyes while gently shuffling for a few seconds to permeate the cards with my personal energy. In those few seconds, those cards revived vivid scenes of our past lives together. *Behave for me*, I told them. *Help me make this come out right for the three of us.* Then I extracted the Eight of Wands and placed it on the purple-draped table.

"The Eight of Wands—very interesting," and she assumed a shrewd expression. I knew she had not put the clues together concerning the Eight of Wands; however, she was hot on its symbolic trail. The first interpretation she offered was the lover's definition. "If I did not know better, I would suggest that you are trying to seduce me with this card." She stared into my eyes and her soul flirted with mine. Her hungry internal lover swooped forward and suggested it wanted to have sex with me. "You better watch yourself," she said. "I am curious about the narcissism of homosexual men." Obviously, we were playing games I was not aware we were playing, so I allowed her to believe whatever she wanted. "The card speaks of seduction—"

Rugen jumped in with, "What makes you suggest the Eight of Wands points toward seduction?"

Iris smirked. "All those wands pointing outward from inside the infinity symbol? How would you interpret the card?"

"The card also stands for sudden intuitive recognition," I said.

Still, she did not remember me and said, "Let's get serious with these cards." She ran off stage for a moment and made a quick costume change. When she returned, she was The Eye of Iris reading her own fortune. "The Eight of Wands tells us that the end of a long journey is near. Despite the card's feelings of completion, the situation holds energy, swift movement, and great possibility. A goal is at hand, a goal directed by the precise hand of the universe." Iris smiled and focused on me again. "Since you chose this card for me, I can only say 'thank you,' for the unexpected bounty. I have been waiting for the last sixteen years for good fortune to knock at my door. Now, let's choose some cards for you. Do you have a particular problem you want the cards to address?"

"We are having difficulty finding employment," said Rugen.

"So your question is—will any job opportunities be forthcoming?"

"That a tedious question to ask the cards," I said.

"It's a fine question," insisted Iris. She leaned forward and in a stage whisper told me. "It doesn't make any difference what we asked the cards. They are a pack of hunting dogs. They sniff out the highest sources and bring back what we need most."

Iris fanned out the cards before Rugen and then me. Rugen pulled the Four of Swords, the King of Wands, and The Universe. I pulled the Nine of Cups, the Eight of Pentacles, and The Moon.

Iris glanced at Rugen's cards and smiled. "You've always been a fortunate boy—haven't you?" She pointed to the Four of Swords and told us this card represented Rugen's fears. The Four of Swords depicted a Shardasko Warrior lying on top of a funeral bier inside a temple (the temple depicted was actually the Jade Temple next to the New Delphi Crystal).

One sword flanked the casket and three hung on the wall above the warrior's head. The warrior was in a state of deep meditation. "This card represents deliberate withdrawal, not death as it may appear," she said. "Sometimes we withdraw because of fear and other times because we need time to consider, meditate, and heal."

Rugen was candid. "I have experienced fear lately concerning death. Do you think it is because I once had a penchant for carelessness that always got me into trouble and now I must consider a measured approach?"

"Could be," said Iris. "This card presents a dilemma to someone whose liveliness reaches levels of carelessness. Careless souls want to treat the influence of this card as an omen of death by stagnation, but the true message of this card suggests patience is required. Notice the light coming through the stained-glass windows in the picture. Light through a window is always a symbolic reminder that we are never without spiritual guidance."

Rugen said, "This card reminds me of the sleeping beauty myth in that true love is the one thing that will awaken a soul to a new round of activity."

"So is Sante your true love?" she asked.

"Yes," said Rugen. "Sante is my true love."

"Good for you. Now let's look at your second card, the King of Wands, which represents the foundation of the matter, the greater reality, or the part you hold within your unconscious. The King of Wands is a court card, often chosen as a significator, like the significator you chose for me. This particular card represents the relationship between the one who has selected the card and significant others that have a deep influence on his life. The King of Wands represents the driving force behind your soul. It could represent you, or someone who has had a profound influence on your life."

"That's Nova!" said Rugen.

Iris questioned it. "Nova? You and the people around you have such strange sounding names." It was another opportunity to open the door to the truth. Rugen was pulling me, kicking and screaming toward revealing more; but Iris herself had just mentioned patience. "The King of Wands suggests authority and responsibility," she was saying. "After all, a king must be a king before all else, even before thoughts of himself. In the picture, the king contains great energy that he is ready to release when he decides to move and not before. The two prominent symbols on the card are the salamander and the lion. The salamander is an old symbol used by alchemists and therefore represents psychic forces and great passion. The lion is the symbol of authority, the king of manifestation."

It was obvious that if Rugen chose the card for Nova, then I had to be the psychic salamander and Rugen was The Lion of Manifestation.

Iris tapped The Universe card with her fingernail. "Finally, we have one of my favorite cards, The Universe. Notice how the figure dances encircled by a snake. The oval wreath represents nature's potential for rejuvenation, like the potential held within the ovum of an egg. The Universe card is an acknowledgement by our soul that we have surrendered our life to the Great Mother of Creation. The figure on this card is androgynous, but not sexless. It has feminine breasts and possesses the ability to nurture and be nurtured in kind and its hips belong to a man; they're ready to move and make manifest." Iris peered down and examined the card carefully. "You look very much like this figure to me."

"I agree," I said.

She smiled at Rugen and I caught her off guard. A dart shot across her mind that she didn't notice because she was concentrating on us. The dart left a trail through her conscious mind and told her, *Rugen looks like Tommy*, and I knew that Tommy was one of her adolescent sweethearts. She softened a little and I was able to penetrate all the way to the shore of her memories. There, I heard a musical quality, a wider, syncopated rhythm, not easily known, but easily recognizable. *Flute notes; plucked wires. Flashes came; scenes; ancient pictures of an elegant woman in another life. It's springtime and Iris sits under a magnificent chestnut tree. Wafting scents of daffodils perfume the air. She spreads her layers of green skirts out on the dry afternoon grass. Her costume is vivid finery and the jewelry on her ears and around her wrists is gold filigree. Her waist is slender and she wears a fancy belt of knotted twine laced with pieces of cut jade. Two escorts travel everywhere with her; they are always by her side. One is dark, pretty, and internal and plays the flute; the other is fair with pale hair. The pale one has wistful blue eyes and strums a mandolin. Her two musicians never make eye contact with the crowd; their function is to look askance and frame the woman's storytelling with music. Sometimes they lean closer and whisper secrets in her ears. The woman is a psychic and she goes from village to village to tell her stories about love. I hear her mention something about a pearl of great price. More, flute notes; plucked wires, and the vision drops away.*

****

Rugen's hand sought mine because *ce* was concerned for me. We held hands as *cis* attention went back to Iris. "So do the cards hold an answer to my simple question? Are any job opportunities at hand?"

"I guess the answer to your question is you possess all the talent and authority you need. The Universe is your oyster as are you its pearl."

Rugen wanted more from her and he pressed his need forward. "It would be nice if the cards could be more specific, something such as, tomorrow morning I'll receive a job offer."

"Very well," said Iris. "Tomorrow morning, you will receive a job offer. I promise."

Suddenly, it was my turn and Iris focused all her attention on me. She reminded me that the Nine of Cups represented my fears. She laughed softly to herself as if she possessed exclusive knowledge concerning the Nine of Cups. "At first, The Nine of Cups is a benign looking card, but it packs a hell of a wallop when carefully examined. Readers often interpret this card as a symbol of over indulgence because the corpulent man sits squarely in front of nine cups. He is dressed in luxurious animal skins and a velvet cap, as a symbol of his grounding in the good life. Notice how his arms fold before him that mimic the shape of the infinity symbol and how his feet stay planted firmly on the ground. He is a determined and conscious individual and he looks as if he intends to sit there and command those nine cups to come to him. The Suit of Cups relates to love, happiness, and emotions. Cups symbolize the feminine, the emotional, and the kingdom of the unconscious. These nine emotional cups sit behind on a draped, banquet table at the man's disposal. Eight is the symbolic number of completion; therefore, nine reins over eight as the unifying force of the universe. This card comes to us at the proper time to explain our connection to the highest sources—that is if we can balance and master the basic emotions held in each cup."

"What are these basic emotions?" I asked, thinking she could not name them.

"Fear, anger, grief, joy, nostalgia, desire, confusion and pain," she reeled off.

"That's only eight. You said there are nine."

"Love is the ninth emotion and the Nine of Cups tells us that every emotion must bow down before love because it is the unifying emotion of the universe." Her smile turned shrewd. "Besides, I told you. Tomorrow morning, Rugen will receive a job offer."

I glanced at Rugen and gave him a tender smile. *I'm with The Lion of Manifestation. You can do anything,* I sent *cim.*

Iris moved to my second card, The Eight of Pentacles, the card that represented— according to her—"the backbone of my situation."

"As you can see, in this card, a man sits at a workbench and is intent upon his creation. Eight, again, is the number of completion, yet this man works diligently and with total concentration, inspiration, and creativity. He cares about his work and does not notice the job is almost complete. Pentacles deal with material gain and the world of matter." She glanced up from the card. "Are you working on a project near completion?"

"I'm in the midst of writing a book."

"A writer! I'd like to read your book."

Rugen pushed his knee into my leg and communicated, *This is another opportunity. Tell her she can read it.*

Avoiding both their requests, I asked, "Could you tell me about my final card?"

"Certainly, The Moon card shows a crab crawling out of the water as a symbol of our beginning, our primitive self. The crab wears an exoskeleton, or façade, as a knight puts on armor before he begins a quest. Beyond the crab are a wolf and a dog howling at the moon. In the background lies a wide-open gate with golden towers and flowers strewn upon the ground. Above, The Moon shines with a lovely feminine face as the sun cradles the moon within the circle of completion. Teardrops, like heavenly manna, seem to be falling from the moon's eyes."

I decided to reveal a little more and feed her a bit of Tyrowsian mysticism. "It's a symbol of *watarie*," I said. Again, her expression was questioning. "It's the expression of longing for what can never be recreated. It's the longing from the shadows on either side of us as we move through the permeable web of time."

She turned thoughtful. "I've experienced those feelings." She began to ask what the permeable web of time was and I nipped the discussion in the bud by telling her that it was the title of my new book.

"I definitely want to read your book," she said.

"Tell me more about The Moon card," I countered. I sat back and enjoyed listening to the sound of her voice that sounded like *flute notes, plucked wires*.

"The Moon acts as Earth's subconscious and glows with the silvery truths that Sun's bright light obscures. The heroic crayfish, as you see, is destined to move between the wildness of the wolf and the domestication of the dog. As demonstrated in almost every tarot card, this card stresses the need to balance opposing forces within ourselves without destroying them. Once upon land, a crab is out of his native sphere. He moves sideways instead of forward. The crab may seem clumsy to us, yet it remains a symbol of movement within us that connects us to nature's cycles and logic greater than our conscious minds can fathom. The heroic crab makes a regressive journey, into his past, in order to come into the light of self-realization."

"What do you think that means in relationship to the personal me?" I asked.

"The Moon is the card of psychic energy. One who draws this card does not wait for knowledge to find him. He is an active player, at heart a witch, a witch that knows how to cook. He knows all the tricks of the trade. No doubt exists that this heroic little crab will complete his journey. All he has to do is move all the way back to his source.

"Then what?"

"Then he will descend quietly into the sea of the unconscious again. Only he will be the wiser. If the rest of us are lucky, we will see the trail he has left behind in the sand and follow."

****

"There you are!" Greg chirped and he nudged Dennis in the ribs. "Let's get our tarot read too."

Rugen sprung up from *cis* chair with a quick, "Sorry, we lost track of time."

Dennis's left shoulder twitched as if hiding a blushing heart. "No problem, I was enjoying myself, gazing out to sea."

"Come on! Let's get our tarot read," said Greg. "It'll be fun."

Dennis flipped a twenty-dollar bill out of his open wallet and laid it on Iris' table. "I aim to give my man everything he wants," he said.

"Well, this time your man will have to wait," Iris replied and she handed the twenty-dollar bill back to Dennis. "We'll be done here in about ten minutes."

Dennis began apologizing for interrupting and Rugen said, "It's okay. We're finished, at least for this evening. "Iris, is it possible to see you in private?" Rugen gestured toward the crowd, "what I mean is away from the atmosphere of this carnival-like setting."

Iris reached under the table and brought up a small black handbag. She rooted around inside that mysterious, feminine space until she found a red-leather card case. She wrote a telephone number on the card and handed it to Rugen. It read, "The Eye of Iris by appointment only." Iris said, "Call me."

****

We waited for Dennis and Greg by the edge of the dock with our feet dangling toward the water. My headache crept back and sat above my eyes. I watched Iris as she held hands with Dennis and Greg as she had held hands with us. Ezek wanted to eavesdrop on the three and tempted me by telling me the cards waiting for Greg and Dennis. *Greg will pull the Ace of Wands for his creativity and the Two of Pentacles for his equal poise within masculine and feminine. Finally, the Five of Pentacles will present itself as a symbol of the barren hunger inside his soul. Dennis's beleaguered subconscious will send him the Two of Cups as a plea for loving communion and the Two of Wands will assure him that hope is still alive. His final card will be the Eight of Swords as a reminder of his continued isolation and denial.*

I gazed out toward the waning sun. Its brilliance was blinding—out where its light-beams stretched up toward the zenith of darker sky. Mallory Dock was quieter now; most of the performers had gone away. It was too late to track down the Kulupan shadowman and ask why he was on Earth. The time was exactly 8:20 Eastern Daylight Savings Time, when Earth rolled over and fell asleep beside her star. The western sky remained streaked with milky purple for a fleeting moment and then faded to a dilute and insubstantial gray. "Do you still have a headache?" Rugen asked.

"It's manageable." I possessed just enough energy to fuss about the mundane irritations in our lives. I felt dirty, sweaty, poor, and ill dressed and could not sleep on a futon mattress. The frazzled and frustrated Ezek regurgitated a final projection before retiring to his nest in the watchtower. *I don't think the rupture is going to happen as one great, overt catastrophe,* Ezek thought. *It's going to be different from what Belinda and Evose are predicting.*

Rugen took my hand and held it. "However it happens, I don't think we have much time left. There's no point in continuing this charade with Iris; besides, she is even more perceptive than Belinda predicted. Iris can handle the truth if we have the courage to tell it to her."

I leaned over and kissed Rugen on the cheek. "I agree. Now tell me, in the name of virtue, which truth should we reveal first?" Rugen definitely wanted to think about that one.

When Dennis and Greg rejoined us, we all decided to walk home. Despite my headache and frustration, I was able to focus on ordinary reality long enough to appreciate that it was a lovely evening. Greg and Dennis held hands as we walked all the way down Duval Street until we came to Catherine. Somewhere near Truman Avenue, we saw the next surprise waiting in the window of a tee shirt shop. There, on a tee shirt was a picture of a Ganat with huge black eyes staring back at us. The picture was the official logo of the Ganat Cerribeame. Under the logo were the words, "THEY'RE HERE!"

By the time we arrived home, I was on the verge of physical illness from my psychic agitation. Rugen preformed some energy manipulation on me in an attempt to soothe my throbbing headache; but despite *cis* efforts, the pain felt as if it were cutting my head in two. Foreboding thoughts of the Ganat Cerribeame would not go away. I felt frazzled, exposed, and afraid to let down my guard. Four hours past midnight, I surrendered to my urge to rest minus gravity, and activated a *vitarattha* around me. I cut the gravity controls all the way up to sixty percent, so I was floating near the ceiling while Rugen attempted to sleep on the futon below. *Cis* sleep had been fitful for hours, but *ce* was more determined than I was about sleeping au naturel on a futon. Rugen woke me just as I was drifting off to sleep with, "Are you going to leave me down here alone?"

I went down in a flash, hovering in my *vitarattha* bubble. Nose to nose I said, "Let's go," and I snatched *cim* up as if I was kidnapping *cim*. Within five seconds, I had *cim* up near the ceiling and involved in a passionate kiss. I missed the mark of my evolved-self by a lifetime or two that night as I deliberately began stirring up the energy between us on a low level. The first thing I threw out the window was higher consciousness; then, one by one, I pulled all the tricks out of my closet and got involved in fucking Rugen as hard as I could. Rugen went along for the ride. My solitary climax cured my headache, but I had a guilty conscious about gypping Rugen. Regardless, I fell into a death sleep and later had a light-filled dream.

I'm in an Athens bathhouse where Candidus/Rugen and I are about to take a dip in a pool. He/Ce looks up at me from the edge of the pool and says, "We're dreaming Sante, and we are inside the same dream."

Socrates wades into the water with his hand bracing the small of his back. He is nude and I can see his body is hard and sense that his mind is erudite. When he speaks, his assertions cut like knife blades. "I have declared creations dead with mere diversions inside my mind," he booms. "You're not an accident or idle musing! You're not something I can forget, like a dream. I have collected volumes on you inside The Library of All Creation. The consideration I put into you is of a craftsman who takes ten years to carve one sandalwood box. Incarnations of my own thought went into making you. I am not ashamed that I care."

Candidus/Rugen paces up and down along the pool edge. His/Cis voice is higher, befitting his/cis youth. "Try to understand," he/ce begs. "This time, I was supposed to be wild. Being wild, I would know a freedom from you, a relief from your tidy perfectionism. That's why I created denial. Denial is my instrument and dispassionate tool. Lamentably, my denial began eroding like beach sand right after my first sentimental desire for you lodged in my heart." His/cis face turns strained with a new incredulous thought. "What happened between us? Why do I yearn for you so? Why do I erect monuments to your memory?"

Socrates is confident with a ready rebuttal. "I always search for patterns of progress within you, my child. If that is my 'tidy perfectionism'—as you want to ridicule it—then you have no concept of the transcendent thrills still waiting for you. You're as headstrong now as you were then. This time I attempted to fulfill your every wish, although I warned you beforehand that your forgetfulness was a foolish choice. If that makes me a sentimental old fool for indulging you, then I will wear that witless cap." Socrates smiles with an expression of secure knowing. "Besides, who are we fooling? Let's be honest with each other for once. Will you at least admit that I allowed you to tinker with yourself for eons?"

Candidus/Rugen hesitates, searching for hidden traps in Socrates' logic. "I concede that point," he/ce says.

"And will you concede that I made every attempt to camouflage your divinity, that thing you claimed prevented your wildness?"

"I will not concede that point," declares Candidus/Rugen. "I will not concede that point until you tell me what the experiment was supposed to be."

Socrates is generous, like a good father. "Is that all you want to know? Damn child! I would have asked for the keys to The Library if I were in your shoes. You might have gotten them too!" Socrates wades out of the water and walks up some steps as he wraps a wide girdle around his waist. He begins to leave and then turns back, his bare chest pink and plump from the hot water. He stands with arms akimbo. He is a man put together from odd pieces that do not match—arms too long and legs too short on that square Mediterranean frame. In the comfort of his oddness, he manages to appear graceful. "Long ago, there was a debate between us. You took the side that one needed to be wild in order to create and I took the side that one needed to be completely conscious to do it well."

Candidus/Rugen looks as if a multidex is computing inside his/cis head. "So my wildness is an illusion because I am forever a conscious part of you?"

Socrates bows with exaggerated courtesy. "It has taken us six thousand years to resolve this particular debate. The solution is easy when you truly remember. Do not forget! You remembered inside this dream."

SEVENTEEN

Senon was shouting. "Wake up!"

I squinted and saw an eerie glow emerging in the darkness below. The glow was chalk-white and for a second, I was certain soul fragments had ruptured through the time threads and were preparing to gobble us up. Then the Kulupan shadowman switched on the light by the outside door. He made an up and down gesture with his hand to indicate that he wanted us to descend to floor level. Rugen snatched the *vitarattha* remote floating near my head and deactivated it. *Ce* landed on *cis* feet while I fell flat on my bare ass on the cold ceramic floor. Rugen had to help me stand as we both started grabbing for clothes. "How did you get in here?" I demanded.

The Kulupan spoke to us via telepathy, his words arriving in my head with a precision that surpassed speech. *Chains are difficult restraints; walls are simply walls.*

"You startled us," said Rugen. "We're used to a bit more formality when it comes to respecting private space."

The Kulupan leaned into his thoughts, his eyes lively and his face and arms gesturing as if speaking with his mouth. *I find the notion of private space delusional, sometimes even psychotic. Get dressed; I will take you to meet the others.* He seemed different now, more ordinary. His superficial skin tones were the same shade as a dark Caucasian male. His blueness had sunk deep inside his flesh so that only the observant might perceive anything amiss. His hair was still an odd shade of gray giving off a mossy-green hue and his eyes were blue-black, almost like those of a Gathosian. Perhaps his Human clothing made him appear ordinary. Dressed in gray sweatpants and rubber-thong sandals he looked like everyone else in Key West. What intrigued me was his tee shirt imprinted with the words, "The Consortium of Dimensional

Travelers."

"How did you find us?" asked Rugen.

The Kulupan's right eye twitched and then his stance changed until he resembled the standing Buddha. *Your vitarattha energy is traceable.*

"We realize it's traceable," said Rugen; "however, in this case, we did not mean to use the *vitarattha* as an attractant."

The Kulupan spoke with his mouth for the first time. "Yet, after you saw me on Mallory Dock, you still used the *vitarattha.* Obviously, your conscious mind is unconscious of what your 'so called' unconscious mind is doing. Your shadows tell me your wish to contact me was stronger than your wish to hide."

Just as Rugen said to Socrates, Rugen now said, "I concede your point."

"We were using the *vitarattha* as a sleeping chamber," I confessed.

The Kulupan pointed at me. "So you're the psychic!" he said. "Psychics usually experience sleeping problems when they choose to come to this time and space. Tiltoenay told me, 'We might find the new Janaforma envoys by their psychic turmoil alone.' But your charged *vitarattha*, with its distinctive energy signature, made locating you very easy indeed."

"Tiltoenay?" Rugen questioned.

"In our consortium, Tiltoenay commands the widest spread as a dimensional traveler. Even now her voice dances through my head with tales about when she stood the watch with other Janaforma envoys." The Kulupan lost himself in a memory and smiled. "She related many stories to me about your Janaforma Wonder and said that Jana Una is a great psychic."

"Una is my sibling."

"I see!" exclaimed the shadowman. "Now I understand more about what's happening here. Tiltoenay predicted the Janaforma would send someone intense to help balance their enormous altruistic contingent working in the fourth. I'm honored to meet Una's sibling. Welcome! If you're as intense as Tiltoenay believes, I hope it will not interfere with doing some practical work for The Consortium. Actually, we need practical workers more than we need intensity."

I told him, "I don't know why you think we're here, but no one informed us that we came here to be Janaforma envoys."

The shadowman narrowed his gaze as if looking out from his third eye. "You came here seeking miracles—did you not? The miracle you seek is involvement in The Consortium." He began to read our deeper thoughts with incredible ease and allowed us to witness his personal reverie. *It seems so long ago that I was like you. I have forgotten about the doubt and confusion that goes along with arriving in strange new places. The confusion of new language in an alien terrain can be disconcerting to those just beginning to travel.* He called himself back and apologized for what he called his wandering mind. "I came here thinking of myself merely as your escort to The Consortium; now I see you will need a mentor." He glanced at his watch and then sat down cross-legged on the floor. We sat too.

"My mother named me Tymequillum-Moss," he said, "but you may call me Tyme." His communications slipped into telepathy again. *In a previous cycle, wisdom unchained me from my dimensional bonds. Despite my accumulated knowledge, I was naïve until Tiltoenay favored me and showed me how to jump dimensions with a simple change of thought. Since then, I've become her willing intimate as we go about our altruistic tasks.*

Rugen said, "In our last lifetime, we saw members of your native species. They called themselves Kulupan shadowmen."

Tyme smiled internally and it showed as a slight glimmer on his face. *My performance on Mallory Dock is a bit of shadow work. I use my talents and skills to add a bit of color to my existence; besides, I like to eat.* His smile grew broader. He raised his left hand and rubbed his thumb and middle finger together. The friction created a golden spark, a spark that exploded into a beautiful little star. He balanced it, for a moment, in the palm of his hand and then tossed it in the air. The star died slowly, disappearing like a miniature skyrocket. As children, *Kulupans learn this trick so we are never in the dark. We practice flexibility and learn to slip inside dimensions you do not know exist. Skills other species might consider prestidigitation, Kulupans know are every child's innate gift. Our mothers teach us to welcome the release hidden in the longest shadows. Watch, I'll do it again; this time watch the shadows instead of the light."* He performed the trick a second time and said, *my shadows are open for your inspection.* He stopped and apologized. "I'm sorry," he said aloud. "Yesterday morning, Tiltoenay told me I was long-winded and spoke too much. I apologize; are you able to go completely telepathic?"

Our telepathic abilities were in their infancy compared to Tyme. Nevertheless, we began to communicate with the skills we had. *It's more efficient than waiting for lips to form the appropriate words around our separate thoughts,* Tyme thought. *Let's speak openly from mind to mind and hold truth as a precious trust. Together, we will unshadow ourselves.*

Thoughts passed with light speed among us; and Rugen and I were mindful to limit our thoughts to those we wished to send. *My name is Miro Rugen and this is Jana Sante,* Rugen projected. *We come from the space year 5603. We arrived fourteen days ago by means of a* vitasphere *traveling through the corridor of the fourth dimension.*

"Congratulations!" Tyme exclaimed. "You did it through physical reality. That must have been an adventure."

"It was," Rugen admitted. Then *ce* attempted to relay most of our story through the vehicle of telepathy. *The Janaforma are involved with three individuals of doubtful origin. Nobody knows for sure who or what they are, but they presently call themselves Bogwa, Evose, and Hope?"*

"I never heard of Evose or Hope, but I certainly know Bogwa," Tyme acknowledged. A sudden sinking feeling hit the pit of my stomach that went right down to my toes. "Based on what I know about Bogwa and his two dimensional traveling companions, I would guess that Evose and Hope actually are Siruchi and Mehiel. Where did the Janaforma meet up with these three?"

"The starship *La Ventana* found them near the planet Cassiel, in the Triborian Star System, about seventy years ago," said Rugen. *These three possess powers we do not understand and a philosophy that seems transcendent compared with our simple Janaforma ideal of Community. We took them in and, on the surface, they appeared to be model citizens; while underneath, they were living according to their own rules. Over time, more of us have come to realize that Bogwa, Siruchi, and Mehiel are extra-dimensional beings. We never condemned them for being extra-dimensional and when Bogwa mated with two of our Janaforma lifebearers, no one said a word. Bogwa sired three children with these two lifebearers and we know for sure that two of these children are dimensional hybrids.*

"Are you suggesting they've found a way to reproduce third-dimensional bodies for themselves in this dimension?" asked Tyme.

"That's exactly what were suggesting," said Rugen. "Bogwa's children are none other than Mehiel and Siruchi."

I see a crisis looming in both your minds, said Tyme. *This crisis has driven you back to the Earth year 2015. Why?*

Rugen transmitted, "*Siruchi, aka Evose, told us the fourth dimension is a prison where life from this dimension abandons its denial.*"

That much is true, acknowledged Tyme.

Evose claims a crisis occurred when he and his Janaforma mebr *entered a meditative state and she connected with one of her previous incarnations. She and Evose were using this previous incarnation to reintegrate soul fragments and were having great success until a rush of soul fragments caused a rupture between the dimensions. Evose swears that soul fragments came pouring into the third from the fourth and some of these soul fragments pirated away the previous incarnation. He says the rupture is not minor, but starts here in the year 2015. In the future, we have a technical piece exacerbating the probability of a dimensional rupture too. The constant use of rifter spacecraft around The Door has weakened the fabric of space in that area. The fear in our time is that the rupture between now and the future will merge and tear this dimension inside out.*

"Thank you for that careful synopsis," said Tyme. *I managed to read a bit between your lines and see you are convinced that this rupture is a certainty.*

Not entirely, I interjected. *Una told us the rupture was a strong possibility. Only because I have faith in Una's judgment, did we agree to travel back to this time and attempt to break the connection. We hope that by doing this, we can buy enough time in the future to process the overload of denial abandoned in the fourth dimension.*

That's it? Tyme asked. *Now listen to me, both of you. You cannot mend ruptures between dimensions with wholesale remedies, but you can claim your own denial and then the rupture around you will heal just as a wound will heal once you remove the offending thorn. Furthermore, if a rupture did occur of the magnitude you are suggesting, this dimension would not turn inside out. The worst that could happen is everything between the third and sixth millennium would disappear."*

"I don't consider that an acceptable loss," I said.

"Actually I do," said Tyme. *Do you honestly believe that this is the first time the timeline has been on the verge of rupturing? It's actually happened and many times before. Your own sibling, Una, stood the last crisis with Tiltoenay and me. The three of us were on Earth when the five Cerribeame rifters permeated the membrane between the third and fourth dimension in the year SY5413. It created a mess we still haven't been able to clean up. The Cerribeame decided to slaughter a few hundred Graeymlin infants along the timeline and their mother came out of her cave and with one swat of her tail, swept the rifters from her queendom. Serendipity ruled and two rifters held together despite her swat and began ricocheting back and forth along the corridor of hyperspace, eventually slicing a hole between the dimensions and reemerging in the third dimension in the Earth's twentieth century. The Cerribeame were unaware they were in the past. One of the rifters was badly damaged so they began searching for a landing site they knew about in their own time. The landing site was on Earth in the state of Montana.*

"The Cerribeame Guard once had a breeding facility in Montana," Rugen said.

"Correct," said Tyme. *They were searching for that site run by one of Jana Revba's many clones. We understand from our Ganat sources that one of these rifters crashed near Roswell, New Mexico, which is a geographical location approximately two thousand miles west of here. The Earth date was July 2, 1947. Two Humans, a ranch-hand named William Brazel and his seven-year-old neighbor, Dee Proctor, found the crash site and notified local authorities. Rather than deal with the problem directly and openly, a bureau of the United States government—actually called the Counter Intelligence Corps—got involved and attempted a bungled cover-up. The Counter Intelligence Corps gathered up the crash evidence and concealed it, even threatened Mr. Brazel with imprisonment and death if he ever told the truth of what he observed.*

"Were there any survivors?" asked Rugen.

Humans discovered three dead Ganat bodies amid the wreckage, but so far, no one knows what happened to the second rifter or its crew. Since then, the truth, as Human's know it, remains mangled. Governmental denial has concealed most of the evidence for the last sixty-seven years.

It sounds as if you have little respect for the governments on this planet.

Why should I? The truth is difficult enough to ferret out when everyone heads in an honest direction. When forces seek to counter-intelligence the rest of us, we all become ignorant pawns, victims of denial; it drags us all down.

"That means Rugen and I navigated the same path created by the Cerribeame rifters."

Correct, by now a beaten trail exists along the timeline.

"You said before that if we removed the thorn, or the cause, then the rupture would heal," Rugen said. "We already know we have too many thorns to be removed and they all can't be removed with the same tool."

"That's right," said Tyme. *We need a multi-dimensional approach to healing, which involves conscious, spiritual, societal, physical, elemental, and definitely energetic aspects of reality. To state it simply, all levels of reality are reactive components in the problem. The rupture is endemic and the most pessimistic of us believe that this latest cycle was born with innate flaws that we'll be unable to fix. Experience has taught us that the most we can hope for is to reclaim our personal portion of the problem. If we can continue to reclaim our personal denial, at least we will have every element of ourselves in a cohesive family if a rupture does occur.*

"It sounds as if parts of you have given up hope," said Rugen.

I still believe in miracles because not a day passes without a profound miracle revealing itself to me. However, we must be practical, face our entrenched denial, and recognize the inertia it puts on every life in this dimension. Bottom line, despite our best efforts, since 1947, the rupture has widened until its spans far into the future.

"Do you have any insight into the innate flaws in this cycle of creation?" asked Rugen.

Tyme scratched his chin. "We have theories." *We know the rupture would prove that the second law of thermodynamics* is indeed a real factor, at least in this dimension. Once the fourth dimension was relatively empty compared to this universe; but when ruptures occur, the third dimension begins losing energy to the fourth; this gives whatever is in the fourth more power than ever before. Let me back up a bit to explain properly. Have you ever seen a bee's honeycomb? Dimensions fit together somewhat like endless honeycombs. In my eons of dimensional hopping, I've never found an edge or an end to what is. The Consortium believes the honeycomb of dimensions is endless.*

I interrupted with a question nagging scientists for generations. "Then, what is the shape of our universe?"

"Perhaps the best way for you to understand is for me to picture it so you can see my vision," he said inviting us to come closer into his mind.

"It looks like a tree!" exclaimed Rugen. It did. It resembled a tree with exposed roots on both ends.

Tyme attempted to elucidate with some more telepathic pictures. *The energy threads on the edge of each universe act as roots reaching into the next. The threads create an intricate system of interwoven stability between dimensions that make creation more stable throughout.*

> We know how universes come into existence.
> The centers and ends of universes are twisted and braided
> with incalculable force into the shape of Infinity.
> We merely do not know why;
> we know only that All is One.
> Beloved, Jana Michael, SY: 5552-5603, from *cis* 5602 address to the Jubilee Gathering.

---

*The second law of thermodynamics suggests the entropy of closed systems, in this case, the third dimensional universe, is increasing and its available energy is decreasing.

Rugen was excited. "Then the idea of dimensions must be erroneous! We truly are One."

Not exactly, communicated Tyme. *Some universes remain locked to us; therefore, we respect their seals and do not attempt to enter. Still, I have visited over ten thousand universes and Tiltoenay has been inside ten times ten thousand. That's plenty of multidimensional space to move around in and one might question why The Consortium puts so much effort into this particular dimension and time. I take personal responsibility for concentrating The Consortium's efforts on the here and now. When I reached my freedom, many cycles ago, I left my body and met Tiltoenay in what this universe thinks of as the fifth dimension. The fifth is a repository for those who live many lives in the third. Tiltoenay presented me with the choice as she came out to greet me on the edge. Either I could become a dimensional traveler or I could return as an incarnate being into this dimension. I already loved her from spending many lives with her in several past incarnations, so the choice was easy for me. I decided not to return for another life.*

"Yet you became a teacher despite your decision not to reincarnate and you appear to be inside a body too," Rugen said.

Indeed, I am a teacher, Tyme agreed. *My body, I put on and take off comparable to a suit of clothing. After the Cerribeame rifter crashed here on Earth, incarnate dimensional travelers, from many universes, began arriving. As they approach this universe, the bulk enters where the rent is largest, here in this time. Most incarnate travelers are curious tourists, some come to help with the denial, as you have, and others are self-serving oafs. Tiltoenay and I came right after the initial opening and since then have worn a variety of Human clothes. Our motivation concerning the third dimension is the simplest thing about us. We feel our roots as natives here and just as you do, that makes us care.*

What about the soul fragments? Rugen asked. *We encountered them as we came through the fourth. We know they're real.*

Unquestionably! The fourth dimension holds a mother lode of soul fragments. Even as we speak, they gain strength because of the energy leaking from this dimension.

Questions were jumping around in my mind and I reeled off a few. *Can you tell us the original purpose of the fourth dimension? Where goes our soul when it dies? And what dimension serves as home to our oversouls?*

Tyme smiled and bowed his head. He was quiet for almost a minute. I was eager and invaded him a bit deeper to determine what he might say. I saw he was communing with his oversoul for guidance in how to explain it to us. So, I backed off and waited. *It might take me awhile to explain,* Tyme began. *The Consortium planned to allow you to choose mentors among us, someone you feel comfortable with that could answer these questions within the context of your particular spiritual background. But if you feel comfortable with me, I will try to explain reality as I understand it.*

We are grateful for any mentoring you can offer, thought Rugen.

Please realize I am not presumptuously suggesting that I know the entire purpose of the honeycomb of creation or the problematic relationship between dimensions. I can tell you what I believe is true from my observations and travels and from my association within The Consortium. The third dimension was a sealed universe until 1947. Before that, the fourth dimension served as a womb to this dimension. Souls planning to enter closed universes usually approach a frontier surrounding its borders. Souls waiting in border dimensions immerse themselves in the mood of the womb as they negotiate for receptive bodies in which to live. Waiting souls become very receptive to opportunities for rebirth in that state. When the proper connection is prepared, a soul osmoses through the threads and becomes an incarnate being. This function is natural and holistic. It does no damage to dimensional walls and we have noticed that dimensions that entertain the most rebirthing activity have a healthier resiliency than quieter dimensions. The passing through happens on a very high frequency. The Consortium travels on this same frequency. To answer your second question, souls may go to many different dimensions when they die. Oversouls do not reside in one dimension, but are active and multi-conscious consortiums that move about freely. When healthy souls die, they reattach to their oversouls wherever they may be. If the connection is healthy, the way back is short; however, sometimes incarnations alienate themselves from their oversouls and use their freewill to exist in a state of denial. When they die in denial, they have no choice but to identify with their denial rather than with their oversouls.

I wondered if Tyme knew the whereabouts of my family. "You said before that a contingent of altruistic Janaforma was now working in the fourth dimension. I believe my biological family, in this life, might be part of that contingent. Do you know where they are?"

I do not know exactly where they are, but they would be easy to locate. The Consortium considers the Janaforma missionaries of the highest order. They took an oath before the consciousness of their oversouls that they will listen and sooth the wretches in denial with the appropriate salve. Resolve is coalescing everywhere in those that care. We cannot ignore the suffering and denial in the fourth dimension and we will no longer protect those incarnate soul fragments in the third dimension that seek to maintain a selfish and egotistical approach to existence. A great inter-dimensional contingent is coming together in an attempt to correct the inequities between the third and fourth dimensions. Every soul fragment trapped in the fourth soon will have a spiritual mentor. Our mission is to reunite as many fragments as possible with their appropriate souls. From this incarnate perspective, the climax of that work will occur between 2018 and 5750.

"We already realize that nothing gets better," I said. "Situations on planets deteriorate from this time until the Janaforma introduce the Regression drug."

You're looking at the problem through the narrow scope of physical reality, thought Tyme. *Try looking at it through the lens of a multi-dimensional future where enlightenment can be found through every vehicle of expression.*

Rugen and I appeared confused and Tyme shrugged his shoulders as if everything was obvious to him. *Every soul in this dimension maintains a tough shell of resistance so we must use many different techniques to get through to them. We use the unexpected to shake static visions of reality. Sometimes we begin to soften stubbornness with vivid dreams. Mental breakdowns are useful tools and we have much success with the use of near-death trauma. Occasionally, an evolved loved one within a soul's family dies as a willing sacrifice. That's an effective tool for Christians, because the Christ archetype brands their souls. Whatever it takes, we try to soften their shells.*

That sounds cruel, I thought.

"I'm a shadowman," he said aloud. *If you had any idea of the true suffering that lurks in shadows, you would not declare our methods cruel. We merely subject souls to periods of episodic discomfort to highlight the unending suffering of their fragments.*

"Do you think it's possible that the previous incarnation of this Janaforma lifebearer could be pirated away by soul fragments?" Rugen asked.

Perhaps, but what I honestly believe is you both were manipulated.

"No kidding," I said with my most cynical tone. "I've thought that since the beginning."

"Perhaps encouraged to make the journey is a better choice of words," said Tyme. *In a soul's development, there always comes a time to leave the nest. Some fledglings are eager to try their wings while others need a bit of encouragement to take flight. Perhaps you needed a small push. What a perfect enticement for two young positive energies to search for the disappearance of a beautiful young vessel that might hold them both.*

We did not say she is beautiful or young, said Rugen.

Tyme assumed an amused expression. *Then she is old and ugly?* We both were silent and I used all my talents to block him. *All right then! You both lived many lives as Humans; therefore, Human myths permeate your soul. The rescue of the maiden is an ancient archetypal pattern woven into the tapestry of your beings. I noticed that you both avoided mentioning the name of the Janaforma lifebearer involved in this situation, which leads me to believe that you want to protect her along with her previous incarnation. Perhaps the female you've come back to rescue is your soul mate.*

Rugen and I stared at each other as theories ricocheted between us. Evose told me that every soul divides itself into four parts, not three parts. Nova, Rugen, and I were one. I had assumed the fourth part was our oversoul, but if Tyme were telling the truth, could that fourth part be Iris?

****

Tyme saw my thoughts and now he knew her name. He grinned and put his fingertips to his forehead before speaking aloud. "Thanks for the confirmation," he said. "I guess I should mention that I've known Iris for almost fifteen years. She's a close friend and a lovely feminine soul. I can't imagine anyone who needs rescuing more than she does or deserves the humble interaction of her soul mates. I've often wondered why she's here instead of a billion other places that might welcome her as the queen she was meant to be." Tyme laughed and waved his arms around a bit. "Excuse me for surfing with the humor in this situation, but the thought of you two coming back to the past to rescue your soul mate is such a perfect delight to me. I cannot wait to tell Tiltoenay; she loves stories about heroes and maidens. Perhaps, your journey will serve as an example to all souls for I tell you plainly and truthfully, no soul can reach freedom without reclaiming all parts of itself.

"I don't believe Isis is our soul mate," I said.

"Why not?" Tyme asked.

"It feels wrong."

Tyme still seemed pleased. *Soul mates come and go, while the expectation of fulfillment in the other seems eternal. Iris is worthy of your attention whether she is your soul mate or not. I promise you that if you do not get involved with her, others will, and some of those others most likely will be Bogwa, Siruchi and Mehiel. If she chooses them over you, guaranteed, you will not see her for eons.*

"We're taking our time because we don't want to make any major mistakes," said Rugen.

"Okay, but don't linger," Tyme advised. "Do you have more general questions this morning?"

"I have dozens," said Rugen.

Tyme laughed and again glanced at his watch. "I imagine you do; however, I think you have enough to ponder for the time being. Of course, the situation is not as you expected to find it. If you pay minute attention to your continuing journey, you will discover that the frustration of detailed expectations is a persistent trend in this dimension. Once you arrive at your destination, the assumptions that launched your journey will be as faulty as a bucket filled with holes." Tyme glanced at his watch a final time. "Unfortunately, this first meeting took longer than expected. I wanted to take you to meet the members of The Consortium; but it's too late now for they have met and gone about their separate tasks. I promised Tiltoenay to meet her for a late breakfast, down near the water, and I do not want to be late. I will return for you in three days and take you to meet the others. Until then, go on with your lives here. Lamentably, all dimensional travelers need a cover to maintain themselves."

"We admired your demonstration on Mallory Dock," I said as he took our hands in farewell.

"Thank you," he said. "It's a cover, but not a trick." He kissed me on both sides of my forehead in the Janaforma fashion and then he did the same with Rugen. Tyme made a slight open gesture with his hands, explaining that it was an equivalent Kulupan gesture of saying goodbye. "Thank you for your trust and this opportunity to serve you," he said. He rubbed his fingers together and vanished into the light.

Rugen was quiet until *ce* was sure we were alone. "Do you think we should trust him?"

"I don't know about trust; however, I think we should accept his offer to join his Consortium. Maybe Tyme and his friends can help us with our mission." Just then, Rugen's cellphone rang for the first time. It was Monday morning and Hideaways was calling to tell *cim* that if *ce* wanted the job *ce* should report for work at 4:30 P.M. that same afternoon.

****

Rugen leaned over the sink in the bathroom and scrutinized *cis* face in the mirror at several critical angles. "Can I do anything to help you get ready for your new job?" I asked.

"I can handle it," *ce* tossed my way.

Rugen's focus was on *cis* appearance, not on my desire to enjoy *cis* companionship. Despite our intimacy, certain moods within Rugen still eluded me. My voice softened. I did it on purpose. I listened and that was intentional too. I never wanted the intimacy to go away between us, so I used a hot topic to get *cis* attention. "Your hair could use a trim. It took a beating when you were thrashing around with a fever."

Hair is a cherished part of any Janaforma's physical assets and we are never cavalier when it comes to the subject of haircutting. On *The Mother*, hairdressers were androids with ancient and refined databases, some with programming over three thousand years old. All have records of accomplishment concerning the handling of Janaforma hair. Haircutting is an especially sensitive subject with Rugen because *cis* trauma with the Cerribeame is not yet resolved. Rugen's voice went up an octave when *ce* asked, "What do you mean I could use a trim? Besides, who could accomplish such a delicate operation here in this barbaric past? That butcher Karl is not getting near my hair with his scissors."

"I could do it. Don't you remember? Once we enjoyed trimming each other's hair."

"Vaguely."

"You mean I can make love to your immortal soul, but I can't trim your hair?"

Finally, I had *cis* attention; but of course, now I wanted more than *cis* attention. I watched as *ce* jumped around from several radical perspectives before admitting, "Perhaps I'm overreacting a bit. I probably have an extra dose of hair jitters from Kayya and Ceff. Nothing is more important to a Tyrowsian female than her hair." Rugen said nothing about the past-life trauma with the Cerribeame. *Ce* pulled a few locks over *cis* shoulders and examined the ends. "Oh no! I do have split ends." Rugen adjusted the screw on *cis* "debater" down a micro-hair—down to *cis* "negotiator." "Okay Sante, you may cut my hair, but then you will have to allow me to cut yours."

"Absolutely; I'd love that."

"And if you fuck up my hair, you have to understand that I am going to be upset."

"I wouldn't blame you. I promise to be careful, as careful as when we first made love." Rugen insisted on examining the scissors I planned to use to make sure they were sharpened correctly. That was all right with me; the longer this game took, the better I liked it. *Ce* positioned *cim*self sideways on one of our two chairs with *cis* back poker straight. *Cis* hair draped over *cis* shoulder and ended in the delicate arch of *cis* back. I adored this view of *cim*. This was my space, the place I snuggled into when I waited for sleep to come.

"Hurry up and do it," *ce* snapped.

I was sexually excited and certainly did not want to rush my pleasure. "I need to study the situation before I start; besides, it will be easier if you relax and breathe." I tried to remember some tips Elay taught me about the esthetics of haircutting and I gave Rugen a conservative and careful trim.

Afterward, *ce* stood peering into a small hand mirror, adjusting it, to see *cis* rear view in the mirror over the sink. "You did a good job," *ce* said with considerable relief. "Just like the surgeon you used to be. You didn't cut the quick on even one hair. That's almost a miracle!" Only then, did I confess how the spontaneous ritual had given me a sexual rush. "I'll be home around midnight," *ce* said. "If you wait up, I'll trim your hair for you."

After *ce* dressed—dark pants and white shirt—*ce* allowed me to braid *cis* hair. While I exercised my fingers in *cis* sensuous extensions, our conversation flowed easily into telepathy. Once we got going, we were soaking in mutual bliss. Our game eventually would explode into the physical; my plan all along was that it would. Meanwhile, I immersed myself in the thrill of lacing *lis* hair with the attention of my heart. Our minds drifted in concert imaginings, each of us sacrificing a few projections to feed the hot flames. Before long, we had a blaze going between us. It was instinctive, fun, a romp in pleasure's woods. In the middle of our intimate frolic, *ce* spoke and *cis* vocal-gymnast changed tempo. "Make my hair tight," *ce* said. "I don't want loose hair to be a problem at work." The abrupt change startled me. My mood still was hanging on *cis* mood and then *ce* began to apologize and explain why *ce* deserted our game. "I have a few apprehensions about going out alone. Maybe I'm being silly; but I'm concerned that somebody might think my appearance odd or I will not understand the simple things everyone in this time takes for granted."

I meant to steady *cim* so I overstated the truth to make my point. "People are blind here. Look at Tyme. His skin is larkspur blue and no one seems to care. Who is that tiny Hindu saint that's blue?"

"Lord Krishna?"

"That's right! Tyme is the same shade of blue as Baby Krishna and no one seems to care."

"Maybe the simple fact that people avoid eye contact in this time will save me."

"You'll be fine, Rugen. We could alight from *vitaratthas* during the Sunset Ritual on Mallory Dock and no one would notice or care."

"Some would, a few might drop coins in our palms and leave us standing there, pondering if we had enough money to buy lunch."

I laughed and turned serious too. "I could stay in psychic touch with you while we are separated."

"I'll be okay. I know you want to write. I'll do the sensible thing and wear a wrisceptor." Offering to wear a wrisceptor was a big step for Rugen. When *ce* was Candidus, the guards that arrested him had locked manacles on *cis* arms and legs. They were not removed until we reached Mycenae Prison twenty-two days later. By that time, his wrists and ankles were raw and infected.

I finished braiding *cis* hair and we stared at ourselves in the mirror. "I'm trying to do the right thing; you know that—don't you, Sante? Sometimes, I feel as if I am a slow learner compared to you. You realized a long time before I did that this rupture did not rest completely on our shoulders; yet you never once called me a heroic fool."

"It's not your fault that everyone pressed their expectations on you."

"You never did. All you ever wanted to do was to weave flowers in my hair. Would you do me a favor?"

"Anything, you know that."

"If you notice me getting off course—falling into old patterns of behavior—let me know. Kayya had warnings about the obstacles of going back in time. We've proven some of them wrong, but I have a feeling she might be right about losing our souls if we died in this time. The notion has occurred to me that if that happened, I might have to live as Cle again. I couldn't handle that with my Regression memories."

"Nova promised that we are not going to die here. Like good Shardasko Warriors, we are going to take what we need and return to the future. After we're gone, nobody will ever know we were here."

****

Despite the intimacy between Rugen and me, I knew our direct experiences were different. The path of each soul is as circuitous and lonely as the road to Ithaca was for Odysseus. Whether Rugen and I could complete our journey and live to tell the tale was unknown. Many sirens were attempting to shape our journey; but tied to the mainsail of this latest commitment, all their songs sounded slightly over-rehearsed. I lacked the essential enthusiasm for success—belief. All my versions of truth only highlighted my existential loneliness. What did I, Jana Sante of *The Mother,* know for sure?

Sensing stagnation as a greater death, I had committed to a journey that tore me from family, home, and the comfort of my personal illusions. Here, in this alien time, sentient spiders, beautiful witches, and Kulupan shadowmen were preparing to test my Achilles heel. On the eve of confrontation, I was a nonstop shipwreck—out of time and out of luck, with no belief. I had drowned and knew I would drown again. My only prayer was that this time no one would notice my clumsy dying. Lost and so far from Ithaca, I could not remember why the future sent me to this alien realm as its envoy. I felt too much, but believed in nothing. My future existed only in my mind. The rigidity of the past did not understand me nor did the past care about the suffered injustices of the future. *If there be any light, lift me from this trial,* I wailed.

Who comes to sooth my wretchedness? Who keeps faith with me when all seems lost? Truth would not come, for truth already had its way with me; understanding would not come because it was hunkering down inside my fear. Only one dared descend into my darkness. I knew Love by its humility and inner brilliance. I knew love by the dirty gowns it wore and its ability to annihilate pain. Grasping, my needy finger left stains on the front of Love's gown along with all the other beggar's marks. Love alone salvages us no matter when we live. Love nurses us from its nipple of golden light, and only through Love's grace, do we levitate to higher ground. What did I know for sure? I knew love is not bound by time and love would take me into authentic experience anywhere I might care to go.

****

My telepathy with Rugen changed tempo. Energy danced with us, and we were whirling and snatching bits of gossamer thought with our joined minds. Rugen separated from me and flew off like an accomplished dancer. *Ce* was incredibly beautiful as pure thought and I loved *cim* best this way. Every time *ce* came out with something brilliant, it made me sexually excited. *You know what, love? ce* called out to me. *Despite all your doom and gloom about death and the wrenching journey, I still feel positive about us. We have struggled to maintain responsibility for our actions despite the fact that we do not know where we are going or what we are supposed to be doing. We've proven to ourselves that the experience itself has immeasurable value.*

Baybairn's image popped into Rugen's mind and *ce* came down into words to tell me this anecdote. "One time, when I sat with Baybairn and drank his goat milk and ate his jhap biscuits, he said, 'Rugen, my skinny little *yant*, if truth could be transmitted by mere inference, oversouls would have no reason to incarnate souls. We live because direct experience is the only way to verify the truth."

Rugen's energy rejoined mine and together we began searching for answers, which led us into a guessing game about members of our own family—about who knew what, and when. "Do you believe the people we love and trust above all others—Nova, Una, Ceff and Kayya—would send us here on false premises?" I asked.

"Absolutely not," said Rugen. "As far as Belinda and Bogwa are concerned, it's not that I think they are evil, but rather their judgment is askew. Whatever Tyme is or wherever he has been, his experience is different from ours. He believes we came back to this time on a heroic mission only to save Iris because that's what his experience tells him is true. My beliefs are my own, but I believe that my life is worth more when I serve others, as well as myself."

Despite Tyme's suggestion that Iris might be our missing soul mate, no real answers came. I was getting intensely curious about Iris and her role in this mystery. Ezek was begging to fly off to her house and take inventory. The total commitment of my love for Rugen meant I needed to wait until *ce* was ready and, of course, *ce* extended the same consideration to me. We had to fit perfectly into each other. The fit needed to be tight and genuine and intentions needed to be clear, as when Rugen said, "Give me Nova." My passion flushed with excitement when Rugen said the critical words that meant we could go forward. "Let's take a swim in the mystery of the Iris Sea and see where she takes us ashore," *ce* said.

Again, we agreed to swim only together. We had just enough time to telephone Iris before Rugen left for work. I was nervous as *ce* placed the call and waited for her to answer at the other end. An answering machine clicked on and Rugen left the message, "Sante and I would like to see you again and explore our future through the tarot. Please give us a call as soon as you have a chance."

EIGHTEEN

After Rugen left for work, I felt at loose ends knowing *ce* was starting a new adventure, which I could not share. Senon materialized and we talked about *lis* new Internet business. In two weeks, *le* had earned almost four thousand dollars. When *le* first appeared, *le* hugged me and said, "Don't worry about getting a job, Sante. My business is taking off."

I cautioned *lim* that I did not want *lim* spending more than a quarter of *lis* programming on *lis* Internet business because I didn't want *lim* to generate unnecessary credit. Too much credit was bound to bring unwanted attention to our doorstep and I did not want Senon's brain clogged with nonsense. I was already dreaming about going home. Psychic flashes suggested that if we ever wanted to take our physical bodies back to the future, Senon possessed the only sentient brain capable of mastering those spools that Ceff gave us. I asked Senon's opinion of Tyme since Senon was privy to Tyme's visit, but had chosen to stay inside *lis* box. "I think Tyme should have knocked on the door before barging in," Senon said.

"What did you think about what he said after he did barge in?"

Senon assumed a thoughtful expression. *Le* hesitated before answering and I wondered if *le* should do a diagnostic scan on *lim*self to make sure *le* had not picked up some kind of lethal bug. Playing around on the Internet was risky. Senon was a pure child of the future walking blithely through a plague infested past and expecting to come out uninfected on the other side. I mentioned some of my concerns and *le* assured me that *le* had a complete set of immunity programs in place to protect *lim* from danger. "Although I do feel Tyme might have overloaded my circuits in some areas," *le* finally admitted. "Of course, I am speaking metaphorically."

"Thanks for clarifying that."

"I'm accumulating a large file I've named, 'soul search.' Soon I will need to download these files or commit more programming to this subject."

"What's your difficulty?"

"After reading your book and allowing my sensors to monitor you and Rugen, it makes me wonder where my evolution lies. I'm hoping the physical Senon is one of my soul mates, but I'm afraid that I might be nothing more than one of *lis* fragments. I don't want to end up lost in the fourth dimension. What do you think, Sante?"

"I don't know if I can answer that question for you. You might need to decide for yourself about your relationship with the physical Senon."

"Can you get me back to *lim*?"

"Senon probably has a copy of you."

"Not with my experience."

"We all want to go home, Senon, but there are no guarantees for any of us."

"If you don't mind, I would like to devote a bit more of my capacity to the problem of my relationship with the physical Senon. How much capacity do you think I could safely open to the problem?"

I managed to surprise *lim* by saying, "one hundred percent."

"How can I maintain my Internet business, interact with you, and do everything else you expect me to do?"

"By studying your own feelings and behavior in whatever you may be doing."

"Oh!" *le* said slowly. "I think I get it. What an absolutely groovy idea." Then *le* disappeared without saying another word.

Five minutes later, my cellphone rang. I expected the call to be from Rugen, but it was Iris asking, "How are you, Sante?"

"You were right about Rugen getting a job offer today," I told her. "He left about an hour ago for Hideaways where he'll be working as a waiter."

I heard her laugh for the first time. It was soft and enticing, an exquisite bit of diminutive melody, the call of a mysterious siren. "I just know when a good thing is going to happen for somebody." I could not answer immediately because her laughter left ringing in my ears. *Flute notes, plucked wires!* "You're quiet," she said. "I noticed you were quiet last night."

"I'm listening to the sound of your voice; it has a musical quality."

"Don't flatter me," she said. "My psychic mirror cannot be influenced by vain praise."

Her sudden change of tone was jarring and she provoked a defensive feeling around my heart. I felt tongue-tied over what to say next, but told her, "You sell us both short if you believe I might employ flattery to find an advantage with you. Your voice and especially your laughter are haunting; besides, your psychic advice is merely one of your interesting talents. The truth is my psychic talents are quite well developed too."

"Then why did you pay me to read your tarot?"

"I saw your Internet site, that you offer classes in how to find soul mates. Rugen and I are searching for our soul mates."

"I think you are well beyond my soul mate classes. Besides, I'm certain Rugen is your soul mate."

"Rugen definitely is my soul mate; but Rugen and I are searching for other soul mates."

"Have you found anyone?"

"We have! Nova is our soul mate."

"Nova? That's the person Rugen called his mentor."

"Nova is my mentor too."

"Is your mentor one of those gurus invading this country of late?" She was mocking me and mocking Nova. Nova was my sacred refuge, my unexplainable god. I wanted to close down; but instead, I consciously attempted to become more vulnerable. "How many soul mates do you have?" she asked.

"I don't know, but I do know you're going to help Rugen and I figure that out. I knew that when I first saw you on Mallory Dock."

"Am I supposed to believe that you experienced one of those eerie *woo-woo* things when you first saw me?" She laughed and it left another ringing tone that faded *so* slowly. *Plucked wires!*

"Actually I did."

"You talk very funny for a man." The next logical step was to tell her I was a Janaforma lifegiver not a Human man, but I could say nothing more about sexual labels without Rugen present. "I would be a liar if I claimed you did not intrigue me," she said. "Can you come over to my house tomorrow about four in the afternoon?"

"It has to be earlier. Rugen needs to be at work at four-thirty."

"Then come around noon. We can have lunch together and talk. And by the way, you can bring lunch."

After we hung up, I worked on my book. I attempted to read between my own lines. I was not going to be a liar either; Iris intrigued me. One thing I knew for sure; two Irises existed. The inner Iris was a Trinity high priestess and she was doing weird and witchy tricks with my senses. She was causing sound to move through me in a new way. The sounds emanating from Iris kept repeating as a spontaneous mantra, an echo of passion from her dark place. I heard the lush beginnings of the Panansha Symphony by Dulce Cœur, "Bea-birtha, nei-michi," *Flute notes, plucked wires.*

****

It was half-past midnight when Rugen returned home. "Hideaways is the perfect name for that place," *ce* declared. "Denial is a popular item on their menu." *Ce* took two black garters off from around each of *cis* shirtsleeves and the string necktie from around *cis* neck and tossed the items on the table. *Ce* perched on a chair, straddling the back with *cis* legs. "Did you get any writing done?"

"Some. First, tell me all about Hideaways."

Ce looked sober. "I don't know if I can go back there. My job entails serving huge chunks of bloody flesh decorated with bits of wilted parsley tucked in around the charred bones. The manger instructed me to recommend the most expensive drinks and food on the menu. He said this approach would benefit not only Hideaways, but also me. I told the manager that I envisioned my job as serving whatever was available on the menu and doing it in a pleasant and efficient way."

"What did he say?"

"He made fun of me for using the word 'envisioned,' and followed up by calling me, 'son.'" Rugen imitated some stranger's voice, complete with facial tics and arm gestures. "'Son, you are going to be an asset to Hideaways; but first, you need to learn the rules of the game. Rule one: People never know what they want, so it's up to the shrewd to help them decide.' He evoked some negative feelings in me, made me realize I still have a long way to go to be as compassionate as you are. I wanted to tell him he was incredibly stupid and presumptuous about my naïveté and that he was one of the worst cases of perverted will I had ever encountered. Naturally, I said none of these things. I did tell him that I intend to act as his asset while working at Hideaways and treat everyone fairly and honestly.' I assured him that I would give him full credit for any virtue I accumulated in that area."

"Did it work?"

"Yeah, it actually did. He said, 'Okay, grab an apron and Maeve will show you what to do. '"

"It sounds as if you handled the situation well."

"I called out to you for help."

"I was calling out for your help at the same time. Iris called while you were away."

"And?" I gave Rugen the highlights and *ce* said, "Sounds as if the conversation picked up some sexual heat."

"It felt more like one of your debates. Whatever happens tomorrow, I don't want to get into a debate with Iris. Let's aim for dialogue. All my instincts tell me we should approach her as angelic suitors."

We made the evening last awhile longer. Rugen stood there and removed the clip from the end of *cis* long braid. *Ce* ran *cis* fingers through *cis* hair so it spilled out and draped over *cis* shoulders. "Let's leave meditating to the morning," *ce* sighed. "Tonight, let's pretend it is just you and me." We showered—Rugen to get the food smells off and I simply to be close to *cim*—and then, I let *cim* trim my hair. There was no break between the haircutting and the lovemaking.

****

The following morning we were up before dawn. We sat in meditation for three hours plus in preparation to meet Iris. The meditation turned into a grueling session, reminding me of how much denial Rugen and I still needed to integrate. The problem began when Rugen saw an image from *cis* past and *ce* grabbed me as a lifeline. Then *cis* mind jumped from the image of the wrisceptors, to the image of the Cerribeame, and my mind jumped inside Rugen's mind in an attempt to protect *cim. I cried out for you!* ce gasped. *It was the wail of ancient abandonment. You could not hear me because we communicated with only vocal chords and clunky technology. Yet, I did not honor even our limited consciousness. I lost contact with you because I refused to wear a wrisceptor.* I was amazed that Rugen still carried guilt over *cis* own demise.

Cle and Candidus were projections from the same soul. Rugen now, as witness, followed both Cle and Candidus into the breach. This process of witnessing, in meditation, is a practice Janaforma learn to do as children. The moment the witness, Rugen, encountered the memory of Cle and Candidus, their rationale and goals were identical. All three wanted to resolve their unexpressed pain.

Then the unexpected happened within me and it was more than empathy for Rugen's dilemma. Truth swatted my pretty-plaster icon of past lives off its pedestal and I saw the shadows of Cle and Candidus. Past-life memories flooded my mind and I struggled to witness and remain uninvolved. It was difficult. However successful or unsuccessful I was about acting as my witness, I cannot deny the life of a Babylonian freed slave, Victory, and the Greek citizen, Candidus, held an equal charge within me.

Ordinary reality continued to crumble. This time I neither panicked nor went off the deep end as I did so many times before when my reality collapsed. However, this time I knew Nova was right. I possessed real memories that were not experiential.

I heard The Lecturer, the voice that told me things I already knew. *Memories are not singular recollections. Memories are recycled programs. Biologically, they are mind contaminants; socially, memories are mostly illusions, certainly biased, self-staged nostalgia. Soulfully, memories are treasures, true communion with self.* I knew I was Cle and Candidus as well as Victory and Sante. *Damn!* Now my evolution would require that I reconsider even the validity of my Regression memories. It was confusing. As I waited for thunder and lightning to strike, truth stood still and demanded, *See Sante! I did not kill your past. I merely destroyed your plaster icons.*

In total confusion, I called out to Nova. I am split consciousness. I could see bits of me living inside other bodies. I-was-in-the-future-and-I-will-be-in-the-past. I am Nova. My existence spans other dimensions. Existence spreads me out into a thin layer of awareness. I hung onto my sense of self; it was all I had. I declared consciousness mine as I flung myself into greater darkness to find the parts of me that still were missing.

I Sante, not I Rugen, again made the choice, as all sentient life must do. This time I asked for forgiveness, for the call from the darkness was powerful, a growing urge within me to merge with my oversoul. *Forgive me for choosing this reality and my selfish concentration.* I was not as strong as Nova. I did not possess the courage to shatter those final icons to live in that black angelic space even with a beloved such as *le*. *Le* had held me with authentic physical arms, died so *le* might live through me. I could barely believe it happened; yet, if I could not understand *lis* ruthless love for me—who could?

In those moments, Rugen was afraid that *ce* might lose me so *ce* brought us down even more. For the time being, it felt safer to do it *cis* way. Besides, I already knew Rugen was my excuse, my way of avoiding this final call. *Love? ce* called me with the voice of a fragile bird. *Let's make certain we can always reach each other, especially when we are physically apart*, was *cis* plea.

As one, I promised again. In reality, I knew so many parts of me never were there for Rugen in the first place and I experienced a wave of shame. How could I make it right with Rugen as Nova made it right with me? I knew that I was so shallow that parts of me were walking right past *cim*, even as we meditated in complete intimacy. Rugen and I calmed together. *Nothing will change this moment, and this moment, and this moment,* we said ticking off time together.

After meditating, we bathed again. We were meticulous in our toilet and indecisive about our dress. We held no plan about how to approach Iris except to use all our intuitive skills. I had considered and reconsidered whether I should allow her to read the seventeen plus chapters of *The Permeable Web of Time*. When Rugen and I emerged from meditation, our decision was, "yes."

****

Iris lived in a small house with a tiny front porch. The house appeared old, but was painted a cheerful lime green. Shrubbery poked through the porch railings, making the porch appear smaller, while twiggy branches half-obscured the entrance and swatted people's legs as they climbed the stairs. As Rugen rang the bell, I thought, *another neglected garden.* She opened the door with a smile on her face. We were startled and Rugen asked, "Where'd you get that shirt?" Iris was wearing green tights and a tee shirt that said, "The Consortium of Dimensional Travelers."

"At a shop down on Duval," she said breezily. "It's clever—don't you think? She explained that tee shirts were like bumper stickers for the body, a way to advertise one's beliefs in a cute and interesting way. "Have you seen the shirt that comes only in women's sizes that says, 'I Left My Heart on Venus. He Left His Mind on Mars?'" She laughed and the sound immediately caused ringing in my ears.

Rugen and I laughed too; *cis* was full of steel and mine was full of nerves. Rugen lost no time in activating *cis* dialectic with, "Does that statement imply that the masculine is mindless?"

Iris giggled. "You said it, not me!"

Rugen got sneaky. "Have you seen the tee shirt that says, 'The Truth Is In There?'"

Iris smiled. "You mean 'The Truth Is Out There'—don't you?"

"I could have sworn the shirt said, 'The Truth Is In There.'"

"Don't play tricks on me!" she giggled. More, *flute notes, plucked wires!*

Rugen pushed a little harder. "Have you seen the shirt with the alien face that proclaims, 'They're Here?'"

"That's a spooky one," she agreed. "I saw a tee shirt the other day that said, 'I've Been Anally Probed by Aliens and Enjoyed It." Iris immediately began apologizing because she thought she had offended us. "Sorry," she said. "I meant no offense to you two personally."

At that point, I could hold Ezek back no longer. My invincible and vigilant hawk flushed from the dark between my eyes and began searching for clues. I was snooping in her refrigerator to see what she ate—*Umm . . . a container of tofu, three pears, soy sauce, ketchup, mango chutney, eggs, and bread."* Upstairs, hawk was checking out her bed—*sex, sweat, and traces of spicy perfume.* Psychic energy was opening her private drawers filled with bits of costume jewelry, some broken pearls that once belonged to her mother, clawing through shiny bits of gold, crystal, and beads, always fascinated with the glitter of possibility. In the bottom of one drawer was a wedge of fancy parchment paper smudged with drops of rancid perfume. Hawk snatched up the paper with its crumpled red ribbon and brought it to my curious eyes to read:

We Three

My love wanders rooms, melodious
flute notes, plucked wires,
full of a wine the Magi drank
on the way to Bethlehem

We are three. The moon comes
from its quiet corner, puts a pitcher of water
down in the center. The circle
of surface flames.

One of us kneels to kiss the threshold.
One drinks, with wine-flames playing over his face.
One watches the gathering,
and says to any cold onlookers,
This dance is the joy of existence.

I am filled with you.
Skin, blood, bone, brain, and soul.
There's no room for lack of trust, or trust.
Nothing in this existence but that existence.

Jelaluddin Rumi, 1207-1273; translation by Colman Barks, Human; *The Essential Rumi*

Chaotic energy circulated inside Iris' house and it was doing strange witchy things to my mind. In an attempt to calm myself, I brought my full awareness into the physical. I glanced around her place noticing only what was physically real. Her surroundings were typically Belinda, cluttered with too many possessions—knickknacks and dusty crystals, weary houseplants longing for light and rain. She owned a resin soaked incense burner and many books on the occult. Stacks of magazines concerning gardening, cooking, and, a mysterious 21st Century pursuit called, "housekeeping," littered several tables. For a Janaforma, this living space contained too much furniture. The disorganization that always surrounded this soul had annoyed me in several past lives; but if I truly believed that we all are one then I had to accept this new situation as my own.

Rugen and I gave Iris three red roses. She did not ask us why three red roses; so, we did not tell her the roses were a symbol of surrendering souls. She put the roses in a lovely crystal vase and placed the vase in the middle of a large Queen Anne style table, where the roses seemed lost among several stacks of magazines and her unopened mail. As always, roses reminded me of compassion and I wondered if roses were important to Iris as they were to me.

I kept the bookscreen folded and close to my side as I handed her the small shopping bag with the food for lunch. We had brought Greek feta, Ionian olives—I ate feta and Ionian olives in my life as Victory/Candidus—local mixed-greens made into a salad, kukicha tea from China. I drank twig tea in my life as Chwang in Northern China. I brought grapes from Chili. I had never been there. She took the bag from me and I offered to make tea. Iris said, "Tea can wait. First, let's sit in the sunroom and chat."

We stepped down a level and I noticed the sunroom smelled of feline urine. Thirteen pillows sat here and there on the furniture and my compulsion made me count them twice. I found a spot on the dark green sofa and moved three of the pillows to make room to sit. Rugen sat on the opposite end of the sofa while Iris sat across the room in a chair. As soon as we were comfortable in our respective corners, in strolled a black feline named Miranda and a slate gray feline named Meyou. Both felines were only vaguely present. They definitely were mediums for Iris' psychic gifts. Iris introduced them, but they ignored us and acted as if they did not care one whiff about us. Black Miranda eventually sprang up on Iris' lap and

Meyou leapt onto the chair back and put her pure-white paws over Iris' left shoulder in a protective gesture. Meyou's paws pointed to Iris's heart and the juxtaposition in all their poses reminded me of the Astarte Syriaca painting. "Nice pussycats," said Iris snuggling between her two psychic energy channels. "Do you like cats?" she asked us.

"I love all animals," I said.

"But do you prefer cats?" she pressed.

"I like birds," *they are the subtle essence of divine-will, the psychic eye.*

"I like dogs," said Rugen. "I like big shaggy dogs that are full of energy and like to play ball." *Dogs are the humble face of divinity in action.*

"Then you're not cat people?"

I hoped her "cat people" question was a joke, but she was serious. Our "chat" meandered along superficial lines while Rugen and I waited for the first opportunity to exploit our conversation into revelation.

"I mistrust people who dislike cats," she said.

I quickly added, "Felines are wonderful. They're intelligent, sentient, extremely meticulous, sensual, romantic, and truly affectionate." Then I set her up with, "But felines are abridged lovers, not very loyal."

"Miranda and Meyou are extremely loyal! They love only me."

"I bet you're wrong," challenged Rugen. "I'll wager that Sante and I can persuade Miranda and Meyou to come and sit on our laps in less than two minutes flat. With a bit more effort, I bet we could persuade Miranda and Meyou to go home with us when we leave."

"You might persuade them to sit on your laps if you bribed them with a piece of fish or a wedge of cheese, but they would never go home with you."

"Fish morsels and cheese wedges would be cheating," admitted Rugen. "I'm talking about a subtler trick. Sante and I can influence your felines to sit on our laps with our personal will."

"Let's see you do it," she challenged.

Rugen glanced my way and threw me a, *trust me, love.*

Rugen zeroed in on Meyou so I took on Miranda. It took us about twenty seconds to get the felines' attention on the energy level of the sixth chakra. We allowed a directional stream of energy to gently flow from between our eyes and travel toward the two animals. When the energy reached the felines, we merely began to retract the energy. Psychic energy attracts felines and some felines are psychic energy hogs. In less than one minute, I had Miranda trying to get comfortable on my lap and Meyou had hopped onto Rugen's lap and was gazing adoringly up into *cis* eyes. Obviously, Rugen fed Meyou a large dose of *cis* glory and now Meyou was definitely in love with Rugen.

What a break! my thoughts shouted to Rugen. *As soon as Meyou returns to Iris, she will influence her with your love.*

"I'm impressed," said Iris. "How did you do that?" Rugen told her exactly how we did it, but Iris did not believe *cim*.

Okay, Sante, thought Rugen. *It's your turn to try Hibernia's direct approach.*

I started out with, "Rugen and I have an important secret to tell you that might be difficult for you to comprehend; but we are not who or what you think we are." If I were writing this scene in one of my novels, I would have rewritten that scene until I got it right. Unfortunately, this is what I said along with, "Rugen and I are aliens."

Iris was confused and I heard Rugen sigh over my insipid beginning. "Not another pair of illegal aliens!" Isis exclaimed. "I have no interest in marrying an alien so he can obtain a Green Card. Where are you alien from anyway? I thought you said you were from a nice civilized place like England."

"We're not from England; we're from the future."

"Never heard of *few tour*," she said, imitating my accent. "Is that somewhere in Eastern Europe?"

Rugen snickered. "Go ahead, Sante. Tell her where future is located."

I thought for a couple of seconds and went with the statement, "Rugen and I are extra-terrestrials from the space year 5603.

Her laughter unleashed a multitude of bells inside my head and I could say nothing until my ears stopped ringing. Rugen jumped in to help. "A few weeks ago we boarded a spaceship called a vitasphere and entered the fourth dimension where we traveled backward to your present time."

"You think you're time travelers?"

"We don't think we're time travelers; we know we're time travelers," Rugen said.

Iris let go an unabashed laugh that I thought might shatter my eardrums. Her look was incredulous, worthy of the critical and questioning Cle. "I thought you two were serious about your spiritual growth, not UFO kooks?"

Do you think we are being too direct? I thought.

Suddenly, Iris was uneasy.

It was too late to start over, so Rugen fed her some more truth. "That tee shirt that says 'They're Here!' is real. Alien species are coming and going on this planet. The picture on that tee shirt that says, "They're here," is of a species known as Ganats. That picture is the official logo of their Cerribeame Guard." Iris' face dropped into confident boredom. We were dropping truths that would destroy her sense of reality, yet she was bored. I did not understand her reaction and decided we must be botching the job.

"I take my spirituality seriously," she lectured us. "I have no interest in tabloid nonsense or those who waste their energy in believing it. Wise up! The only way to higher consciousness is through God."

"We can prove everything we say," Rugen said.

"Poppycock! All you UFO kooks say you've seen flying saucers and tiny little men in silver suits. Some of you claim you've gone for joy rides in funky spacecraft. Others of your kind have enjoyed their anal probes; but none of you ever produces a lick of solid evidence, so the rest of us can believe too. Sorry, I do not consider a blurry snapshot of a disc hovering over Mount Fuji as evidence."

"Give her your book," said Rugen quite deliberately.

I pulled the bookscreen out from between my body and the arm of the sofa. "What's that?" she asked.

"We call it a bookscreen," I said. "It contains the manuscript of my book, *The Permeable Web of Time*. You said you wanted to read it."

Suspicion dripped from her face. "How does your bookscreen work?"

"Excuse me," I said to Miranda, forcing her to jump off my lap. Ceremoniously, I took the bookscreen to Iris and attempted to hand it to her. "Relax," I advised her. "You will be able to absorb it faster if you sink into the experience." I could feel her rigidity as a repellent force pushing the bookscreen and me away.

"I thought you had a real manuscript—words that I could read on a piece of paper."

"You can read much faster this way," I explained. "It's standard technology in the sixth millennium."

Iris put her hand up, in the way Humans communicate stop, with the palm facing outward. "I'll read it, but let's forget about all this UFO nonsense."

Physically, I was very close to Iris. I could smell her and I managed briefly to touch her hair as I showed her how to put the bookscreen membranes in both her ears. Rugen was sitting across the room looking as if *ce* wanted to get involved so I sent *cim* an invitation. *You are the physical consort here; would you care to do the honors instead?*

No! You're doing fine, ce thought.

Then I picked up Iris' thoughts. *Why should I trust them? They could be weirdoes or rapists. Angelic faces often are a trick.*

First, I thrust it toward her as a thought—lines from a poem she kept hidden upstairs in the bottom of her jewelry drawer.

I am filled with you.
Skin, blood, bone, brain, and soul.
There's no room for lack of trust, or trust.

She thought of the words, but did not know I brought them to her like Hermes. For good measure, Rugen recited them aloud.

"I am filled with you.
Skin, blood, bone, brain, and soul.
There's no room for lack of trust, or trust."

She abruptly glanced up, definitely spooked. "Jelaluddin Rumi," I told her. "Do you remember a life in Konya, Turkey as one of his students?"

She bolted a little, but it was mostly internal. She let a glimmer of that past life into her memory. It seemed almost a miracle and then her limited-mind glazed over the revelation with its pseudo logic of denial. "That poem sounds familiar," she admitted. "I know I've heard it somewhere."

Rugen smiled and softly bit *cis* bottom lip. *Let her absorb it slowly, ce* thought. *Set it for forty minutes.* Rugen was referring to the delivery rate on the bookscreen.

I switched the language to play in Universal. "Are you ready?" I asked.

"For what?" she asked.

"To read my book." She seemed confused. "You are in charge," I explained. "Whenever you are ready to begin reading, look into the screen and say, "Begin *The Permeable Web of Time*, chapter 1." I knew we were unsettling her ordinary reality because the bewilderment was evident on her face.

"Say the words," echoed Rugen.

"I will never forgive you if this is some kind of joke," her ego warned. With a bit of bravado, she said, "Okay! I can do this. Begin, *The Permeable Web of Time*, chapter 1." Then her lower jaw dropped until her mouth formed one large open circle. The moment her mouth opened, Rugen and I began pouring our energy into her exactly as we had done with the felines. Her mouth closed slowly and I watched her swallow our energy. Her eyes twitched as she followed the story like a dream that enters the mind in sleep. In an instant, I knew that she heard page one. She knew that once I sat in a garden with Elay. I hoped Iris was adept at reading between the lines and knew a bit of Elay's grace and beauty. Suddenly, Iris' jaw dropped. I was dancing with Rugen at The Quasar and soon I would be going home alone. She glanced up. "Stop this machine!" she exclaimed. The bookscreen did pause because by accident she uttered the word, "stop. It's very vivid!" she exclaimed. "Is this some kind of new technology from Japan?"

"Finish listening to chapter one," I said. "Go ahead. Tell it to continue."

She stared down at the bookscreen as if it were a snake coiled in her lap. It was! "Continue," she finally managed to say. She truly listened this time. She got quiet and closed her eyes for almost a minute. Her concentration was good. Rugen and I sat there and waited in mutual stasis as a sign of respect. Then Iris said, "I think it's finished. Is there anymore?"

"There's much more," I said. "The next chapter might be more difficult to handle because you're in it."

"Me? You mean another of my incarnations—don't you?"

"Not exactly" said Rugen. "Your other incarnations are in it too; but Sante means the flesh and blood Iris, the one sitting right here in this room with us. You play a pivotal role in *The Permeable Web of Time*."

I decided that I definitely needed to soften chapter 2 for her, so I explained, "You will meet Evose in the next chapter and he will confess his love for you. Don't be afraid. His assessment that you are in danger is flawed."

"What kind of danger?"

"Tell it to start chapter 2," Rugen encouraged her.

Iris told the machine to start and she listened again. It was dead quiet in that room for the next four minutes. When chapter 2 finished, she glanced up and said, "I don't believe one word of it. It's too—weird!"

She obviously was lying, but mostly to herself. "Keep reading," I told her. I helped her by telling the bookscreen to continue without her input. I almost thought she was going to bolt when I did it, but then something I was saying inside the context of the book caught her attention and she began to listen again. She listened to me describe the death of my family, my ordeal to keep Nova alive, my first sexual encounter with Rugen. She cried through that part. She got up once to get a tissue to wipe her eyes. In chapter 5 and 6, she met herself in the future as Belinda. That had to be weird, as she liked to say. At seventeen minutes, Iris was deep into chapter 7 when we left *The Mother*. It happened as it did the first time, only now Iris was leaving with us. Chapter 8, and Evose, the man who adores her, from a distance of almost thirty-five hundred years, is dying. She was distraught and glanced back and forth between Rugen and me for answers. "If I could believe you," she began so tentatively and then she stared off into empty space. I wanted to comfort her, but waited so not to abort what we were trying to accomplish. "Somewhere in the middle of chapter eight, she said, "I don't want to read anymore, not today." She picked the bookscreen off her lap and attempted to hand it back to me. "Maybe I'll read the rest later."

"You're upset," said Rugen.

With a raise in voice, she said, "I'm not upset! I never get upset."

I backed off. Iris was still uncomfortable with us so we told her only as much as she could handle. I believed that if we could bring Iris to the point where she was an equal and open partner with us, nothing could make her disappear, not Evose, not Bogwa, and not Belinda. "Could I sit closer to you?" I asked.

"Why?" Isis asked. She was so raw that this simple request made her suspicious.

"It's my book. I feel responsible for its effect on you. I thought perhaps I could hand you tissues as you needed to cry."

"I don't need to cry; besides, I don't trust you."

"That's obvious," I conceded. "However, if you read the remainder of chapter 8, the answer about trust is at the end of that chapter. I suffered for that insight and it was hard won. Now I give it to you gratis."

She was incredibly quiet when she finished chapter 8. "Iris?" said Rugen.

She did not answer, merely sat staring at the black screen. I got up and sat on the arm of her chair again. She glanced my way, not making eye contact. Before she could escape, I said, "Play chapters 9, 10, and 11." Iris went with us to Uropae, shared our honeymoon on *Sasaybin*, and then went back to Uropae again. In Chapter 10, she knows that Nova is dead. Incredibly, she sheds no tears for My Great One. I still cannot read my words about Nova's death without weeping. She sat up straighter before saying, "The real reason Nova committed suicide is that he was appalled over having a sexual relationship with his own child."

"Nova did not kill *lim*self," I said. "Nova went into our greater future to prepare a safe place for our becoming. Nova is will spirit, what Humans now call 'the higher self.' Will's function is to prepare a place for our evolvement. My soul incarnated itself into three separate bodies so we could become physical lovers. We did it of our own freewill. Granted, it was a very macho thing to do; we are heroic with middle age and wanted to see which one of us was the strongest in the experience of life. As you can see, I won, yet I lost my little Nova because *le* has plunged into the fire of my heart."

"You incarnated an entire lifetime, to be with Nova such a short time?" she questioned. "Then what about Rugen?"

"Rugen is Nova; Rugen is me and Rugen is *cim*self."

"Do you consider Rugen divine as you do Nova?"

"Oh yes!"

"That philosophy takes a lot of trust in a relationship."

I told Iris to read chapters 12, 13, and 14. When she did, she became so quiet that I wondered if she was shutting the words out of her conscious mind. On and on, she travels through the chapters not looking at either Rugen or me anymore. Listening for almost forty minutes, she is not finished. She is a slow reader, probably because the trauma is so devastating and the bookscreen is still alien technology to her.

****

The clock on the wall said it was almost 1:30 in the afternoon. I thought we needed a break and announced that I was going to make tea and put out the lunch. Iris glanced up from the bookscreen and told it, "stop." Her fear of the bookscreen, as a piece of alien gadgetry, had diminished. She took the membranes out of her ears without assistance and set the components on a nearby table.

Rugen and I invaded her kitchen like two hungry wolves because we had not eaten since early that morning. I found the tea things all scattered here and there—on the rear of the stove, in cupboards, in drawers. The teakettle was under the sink. Rugen retrieved the food we brought and divided it on three plates. "You didn't search for that teakettle," Iris told me. "You knew where I keep it."

"I can sense things when I concentrate in the right way," I told her. "Besides, in every one of your lives, you always kept your teakettle near your water source."

"Oh, that's right," she said and her voice had a sarcastic edge. "You knew me in several previous lives." Iris fell silent for a couple of minutes. Now that she was away from the bookscreen, her limited mind took every opportunity to intervene. Her inner wheels were spinning and some were jamming in an attempt to engage in new ways. "I don't believe any of your nonsense," she said after a minute. "Your book is an interesting read. It fits certain criteria I know to be true; but I don't believe it as fact. Besides, there are too many plot flaws in your story to make it believable."

Now Iris was attacking my baby, my creation. Like any mother, I became protective. "What are you talking about?" I insisted. "How can there be plot flaws in a non-fiction book? That's the way actual events unfolded."

"First of all, the characters you call Rugen and Sante are too goody-goody. Nobody is going to believe these two guys are real."

"But we are real! We're standing right here in front of you."

"I'm not talking about you; I'm talking about your characters, Sante and Rugen. No two people could love each other with the unabashed acceptance you describe. The book is obviously fiction, just like all books. In the end, every book is pure fiction, empty words of hope on a page."

My mouth was hanging open as my private assertions returned through Iris' mouth. I knew beyond all doubt that the collusion to bring me to this point was a monumental manipulation by the forces that brought me to the past. *Damn!* I felt as if I was being poked with a stick. I hung on and struggled to adjust as Iris buffeted me around in the chaos of her accusations. She went on tearing *The Permeable Web of Time* to shreds. "Where are the women in your science-fiction adventure? In most science fiction, women at least get a superficial nod. In your book, you show me an elusive vision of an angelic Elay; then, introduce a bitchy broad named Belinda that thinks it's okay if she makes a few mistakes like destroying this universe. Why do you portray the only strong woman in your novel as a flirty bitch? Finally, you give me the pathetic little mouse that you blatantly named Hope. Couldn't you have called her something more dynamic than Hope? God! Give me Durga or Kali or Demeter; but don't give me feeble little Hope."

"But Hope proved herself to be a powerful individual," I argued. "She possessed the courage to go out to the denial in the fourth dimension when I did not."

"Cut me a break! Miranda and Meyou have more emotional depth than your fictional Hope. A thirty-year-old virgin that is just beginning to get curious about sex is—nonsense! Who is going to believe that crap? You may be psychic about where my teapot lives, but you know zippo about real women and sex. Besides, that character you call Iris is nothing but an empty name, an undeveloped character. You may be a clever writer, but I'm not stupid about the way things can be fudged in writing and I know how computers work too. Right after we met, you went home and changed the name of that particular character to Iris. Before you met me, her name could have been Nancy, Carol, or Marie. Tell me! Is that what you did after I talked to you on the telephone last night? Did you change that character's name to Iris?"

"What purpose would it serve to go to such elaborate subterfuge? Do you feel I am here to steal your obvious poverty? Have I attempted to use you in a beguiling and selfish way?"

"How should I know? Anyway, your book proves nothing. Your book doesn't even exist as words on a page. It's a damn contraption that makes sound go through my ears and makes me have silly visions."

"You feel no affinity for Belinda?" asked Rugen.

"No! In my opinion, she is a narcissistic old bitty. Furthermore, I'm insulted that you equate me with her."

"How did you lose that missing finger on your left hand?" I asked.

"None of your damn business!" Iris responded. "And furthermore, I don't want to be part of your silly all-male science fiction novel."

"All male? The only males are Evose and Bogwa."

"Phooey! Your Janaforma lifegivers and consorts are all variations on a male theme. I want nothing to do with your book and forbid you to use my name and will consider it an invasion of my privacy."

I had battles with critics before, but this certainly was a new twist. Writing "non-fiction" was bizarre. It was like having one of my characters step out of the pages and tell me, "This book is shit! I refuse to be in it any longer."

I settled into the truth about my obvious shortcomings in writing *The Permeable Web of Time*. Later, when I sat completely within myself and remembered her accusations, I knew she was right about the lack of feminine involvement in my book. Why had lifebearers and females eluded me? Why had they become minor characters when they were so important to every scene and every moment of my life? What other reason could there be than I did not care enough about them to develop a greater understanding of the parts they played and include them in my story? I was smart enough to realize that Iris was going to help me figure out not only what was missing, but she was going to help me write the rest of the book.

****

Rugen told her, "It's only a matter of time."

"What do you mean?" Iris demanded.

How could the physical Iris understand time the way Rugen and I did?

To Iris, time was linear and inescapable. She sat in her narrow one life with her shroud of rationality wrapped around her. Only in forgotten dreams did she connect with her previous and future selves. Nevertheless, I could see the veins of her past and the probable arteries of her future. One future was ugly with a mouth pinched with grief and denial. Another was confused and unaware of its great psychic gifts. The third was ready to leap into the darkness with Evose and disappear without a trace. I saw a fourth alternative, and that was with Rugen and me. I turned specific with the concrete Iris. My feelings were swelling, almost spilling over for our mutual quandary. I wanted to save her, for her to be safe, no matter what she thought about my talents as a writer. "What will it take to convince you of our veracity?" I asked her.

Iris was on the verge of tears. "I don't know. Maybe something physical."

"You will barely allow us to touch you," I pointed out.

Incredibly, when I said that she retreated even more and told us, "That's right. I don't want either of you pawing me and thinking you can get your way just because you're good-looking. I find handsome men particularly bad medicine for me. Show me a homely man and I will show you someone I can trust."

"That's ridiculous!" said Rugen. Perhaps she knew innately that if we could touch her we could change her. I did not understand how many of the subtle and peripheral energies worked; but I knew psychic hawks sat inside each of us resting on our points of auric light. Those hawks circled and communicated, when their masters were lethargic or fell asleep. Ezek reached out to communicate with Iris' psychic bird while Rugen assured her, "Nobody is going to touch you until you are ready," *but we will touch you.*

Her eyes darted back and forth between Rugen and me. "You're communicating with each other telepathically—aren't you?"

"Yes," I told her. "You haven't read the chapter yet about how that begins to happen."

Rugen thought. *I bet if we took her for a ride in a vitarattha it would convince her fast enough.*

Then I remembered the physical evidence that would convince Iris. I leaned over and popped the blue adhesion lenses off my eyeballs. "Look at my eyes," I said. "Look deeply into my eyes and you will know the truth."

The pupils in her eyes dilated as she focused in my direction. She was stunned. "Oh my God! Oh my God!" she kept saying as she stared at me in disbelief and terror. My empathy became an energetic Ping-Pong ball bouncing back and forth between us. I felt her fear, but felt my ego slink away too. She was looking at me as if I were a monster. She struggled to speak and her voice caught in her paralyzed throat. She clutched the wall along the alcove as if she might fall—knees buckling. Rugen and I rushed to prop her up. Rugen helped her to sit on the floor for she still feared me and told me, "get away from me." I stepped back as she asked me to do. I retreated into her kitchen where the kettle was screaming with boiling water and I made tea.

Rugen began explaining, "Once you get used to them, Gathosian eyes are very beautiful."

Iris put her fear on me and now she needed someone as her ally. She quickly decided Rugen was handy and semi-okay. "Are your eyes weird too?" she asked.

"My eyes are blue, exactly as you see them now," *ce* assured her.

I brought the tea into the sunroom on a tray and fixed hers with milk and sweetener, the way she liked it. Rugen helped her sit in a chair and asked if she wanted *cim* to hold her teacup while she sipped it. I swear she said, "I haven't gone completely insane."

Ezek flew up from the periphery and perched on my shoulder with this clear advice. *Repeating your exact words is not an authentic synchronicity. She is using them because she read them in your book. She excerpted them from the second chapter when Rugen rescued you. The genuine link is that both your reactions are parallel.*

What is the bottom line? I asked.

The bottom line is that greater reality had occasion to shatter you both and you both withstood the destruction rather well. Ezek flew off, back to the watchtower screaming, *Truth is the One conscious pattern within The Permeable Web of Time.*

NINETEEN

Iris was too distraught to eat lunch. Rugen and I excused ourselves for indulging and while we ate, she asked us a variety of questions. Iris' main curiosity centered on alien species—what they looked like, what they thought, and how Humans were interacting with other species in the future. She asked, "In your time, are Humans still considered the good guys?" She was relieved when we told her that Humans still called themselves, "God's special creation." We did not mention that every other species felt the same way. Attempting to explain the legitimacy of the Orion Spur Alliance and the Council's views on fourth dimensional travel was particularly difficult for us. She asked a few broad questions such as "How long will it take Earthlings to finally acknowledge aliens are visiting Earth?" She wanted to know where we had traveled in the galaxy and, "What's the most amazing thing you ever saw out in space?" After her mind reached the outer limits of our universe, it turned around and asked, "What's it really feel like out there? I've seen pictures. Astronauts return and say things like, 'Space is awesome,' or, 'Earth looks like a big blue marble;' but I want to know how it feels to lay back in the arms of infinity and contemplate the whole thing."

"Why settle for our meager descriptions?" asked Rugen. "Why don't we take you up in a *vitarattha* so you can contemplate the whole thing for yourself?" I was a little surprised that Rugen would suggest this option so soon; but had no doubt that a short adventure in a *vitarattha* was the stimulus that would convince her that we were on the level. *What makes you so sure she's ready for space?* I mused.

Rugen was a breezy hotshot concerning space. *We'll be with her. What can happen?* I tickled Rugen's caution a bit and this prodded *cim* to add, "Of course, we should not attempt to go up until after dark." Rugen needed to explain why because Iris had not yet read chapters 15 and did not understand how light reflects off *vitaratthas* in daylight. "What time is it now?" Rugen asked. Iris pointed to the clock on the wall. It was two forty-five. "Maybe the ride should wait until tomorrow. I need to be at work shortly. Besides you look a tad overwhelmed."

Iris was disappointed. "Don't leave. You can't breeze in here and halfway convince me you're aliens from the future and then leave me with all my unanswered questions."

"Halfway convince? Eyes don't lie," I declared.

"Eyes are the biggest liars of all!" she declared right back. Then she began rooting around for more inconsistencies in our story. She supported her flagging reality with a new line of absurdity. "Who knows? You could be wearing a second pair of contact lenses under the first pair that you just took off. I saw a rerun of *Mission Impossible** recently and a man was wearing several layers of masks, one right on top of the other." She got more ridiculous with, "Besides, if you believe this rupture is going to happen, why don't you contact CNN (Cable News Network). You could land on the White House lawn and advise the President about how to handle the crisis?"

Ignoring these absurd ideas, we promised to return the following day. She still insisted, "You can't go; I have to read the rest of your book. I need to know what happens to me."

"And we need to go," said Rugen.

"Then at least leave the bookscreen. You can trust me. I won't tell anybody that you are extra-terrestrials. Even if I did, who would believe me?"

I tried to explain, "When you read the next chapters, I want to be close by to answer your questions."

"Why? Am I going to die?"

"I haven't written an ending, but I promise nothing terrible is going to happen to you. We've come all the way back from the sixth millennium to make sure you're safe."

"I don't believe you. You're going to leave and I'll never see either of you again."

"This is the test of trust," said Rugen. *Ce* opened *cis* arms to her and asked, "May I give you a hug?" When she hugged Rugen, I realized she had a great deal to learn about the art of hugging. Her hug was a quick

---

*Senon researched the reference and found that *Mission Impossible* was a television series popular during the years 1966-1973, which featured the exploits of a team of secret agents that would undertake hopeless missions against impossible evils. The team's exploits were supported by elaborate masks, costumes, and roll playing although they never tried to do anything as convoluted as going backward through time.

gratuitous squeeze. However incomplete her embrace, it was our first opportunity to hold her consciously. Ezek flew out as my courier with an urgent plea to Nova. *Dear Nova, she is so fragile. Teach us how to help her in the right way.*

I hugged her too and missed her when she broke away because she made me feel warm and complete in a new way. I felt her potential and wanted to connect with it in my typical sexual way. As we moved apart, I managed to captivate her eyes for a moment and therefore read her thoughts. The openness in her eyes was incredible because she did nothing to block me. It was as if she honestly did not know how to block another person. *Sante's eyes are like broken glass*, drifted through her mind. *If I look too closely, the gold in them pierces me with their sharp splinters.* Going deeper, into her desire, I respectfully, went no further. All I wanted was assurance that her desire was still alive.

"I have an idea," said Rugen. "Take this," *ce* said pushing up *cis* sleeve and removing *cis* wrisceptor. *Ce* snapped it around Iris' arm and showed her a few of its basic functions. "We'll leave an open channel between us so you never need to be afraid when we're not here."

"What are you going to use?" I asked.

"I have an extra wrisceptor at the apartment—honest!"

Iris appealed to me directly. "Stay? Just because Rugen needs to leave doesn't mean you need to go."

"I can't Iris. I can't be alone with you; not yet."

****

Rugen left our apartment around 4:00 and I sat down to write. I turned my wrisceptor connection with Iris up and my connection with Rugen down. It was noisy at Hideaways and quiet at Iris' house. If either of them needed me, they could give my wrisceptor a buzz. I said nothing to Iris, thinking she might need some private time after our volatile day. The wrisceptor felt hot on my arm so I finally removed it and placed it close by, on the table. Then, I focused on writing and hours passed unnoticed. Around 9:00 in the evening, Iris buzzed me and said, "Hi, I'm going to take a bath and go to bed."

"Have fun, and don't forget to wash behind your ears."

Despite her insistence that I could not use her in my book, I had just finished writing a great deal about her. The prospect of deleting that material was a frustrating expectation. I decided begging was in order and decided to use my skills in seduction to get my way. Iris obviously had put the wrisceptor near the bathtub because I could hear the splashing of water. "Are you still there?" I asked.

"Umm, I'm here."

"Will you allow me to use your warmth to round out my Iris character? If you say yes, I promise to treat you respectfully."

"So you finally are admitting that you put my name on that character after you met me yesterday?"

She made me laugh because she had spunk. "I swear Iris, that's not the way it happened."

I heard the sound of a soap bar plopping into water. "It's embarrassing, the thought of a bunch of nosy people peeking into my personal life."

I wanted to tell her the personal-life illusion could not survive the truth; but she was too fragile to hear it. "I plan to change the names of the major characters, so you're safe."

More splashing and then she opened the drain and the water made a slogging sound as it began to go down the drain. I heard the snap of a bath towel. "I think I understand Rugen, but I have a feeling I'm never going to understand you. It's more than your alien eyes and all that power hidden behind your angelic face. What you say scares me. Tell me the real reason you came back through time."

"If you are looking for hidden agendas than I can only swear that I have none in my conscious mind; beyond that, I cannot speak for what is real."

"If you could tell me something about yourself, something reassuring that I could finally believe, maybe I'll give you permission to use me in your book."

I glanced at the multidex screen and scrolled backward to what I wrote a few minutes earlier. It was fresh, a hot-off-the-press description of me.

"I cannot define myself; but I remember where I was born. Created in Love, I can never be other than Love. I fly far, yet I still am Love. I cannot fly out of Love or out of the spark that Love animates within me. My commitment is to what I am; and all my energy is in what I am. My allegiance to Love is so complete that if this universe denies me my full glory then I will seek ecstasy somewhere else."

"See!" said Iris. "It doesn't make any difference what I ask you, you give me more riddles."

"Sorry, but that's the best I can do for now." More silence. "Iris, are you there?"

"What?"

"*The Permeable Web of Time* has no ending without you."

"Okay, you may use me, but with stipulations. You must promise that you will allow me to read everything you write concerning me and if I don't like it, you will change it."

My emotional investment in this book was heavy. My foibles and intimacy with Nova and Rugen already were committed words along those revealing lines. Any notion of introducing an intentionally false picture, after the sacrifices I made for this book, was unconscionable. If I was going to write about Iris, it had to come from my unexpurgated perspective. "I promise to let you read everything I write," I said and she did not call me on the if-I-don't-like-it, you-will-change-it part.

"Okay, you have my permission" she agreed.

Yes! Conversation trailed off and I went back to writing. Now I possessed her quasi-consent, I fleshed out her character even more. An hour later, she buzzed me and said, "I'm going to bed now; maybe I'll read until I fall asleep."

My voice came out as a whisper. "Let me know when you get sleepy; I will come to you in a special way." She accepted that I could do it. Later, when she was feeling very sleepy, she asked, "What if Evose shows up tonight?"

Instinct bypassed consideration and I went to her in a flash and found myself hovering over her. "You're safe with me," I said. Breathing into her, I covered her face with my energetic kisses and whispered in her ear:

> "Between me and you no barriers
> Heart-to-heart talk, Eye-to-eye
> On the pillow
> Of Eternity."

"Rumi again?" she mumbled. She was floating now, floating in a dimension halfway to sleep.

****

As I write these new chapters, I feel an honest connection to my spiritual roots. Nova is not as a distant god, but an authentic internal force with me. No need exists for me to call out to *lim* because he is always there. I hear Bejan's voice when my passion awakes and spills over with *cis* colorful visions. Bejan has always possessed the genius to show me physical reality, both the exquisite and the obscene. *Cis* depth of feeling for the denial in the fourth dimension is incomprehensible to me; or more honestly put, *cis* depth of compassion for the denial frightens me and I am afraid to connect completely with what *ce* feels. *Cis* advice is always to surrender totally and love completely. I have not yet figured out how to accomplish this task and remain inside my body and inside my relationship with Rugen. I still feel shame that I did not go out to the soul fragments in the fourth dimension. *Ce* would have gone without question; I know that now. In retrospect, my denial is obvious. I gave in too easily to Rugen's demands and I sacrificed my integrity to remain in my comfort zone.

I thought about the criticism Iris made concerning my book—that I was misrepresenting and ignoring souls manifesting as females. The more I wrote, the more I realized I had dropped a few stitches in my feminine weaving. Despite this realization, I didn't know how to fix what I wrote. Souls manifesting as physical females and lifebearers had not said too much in the pages of this book. Why was Belinda's magnificence so elusive? Why was Hope so reclusive until she flew off and deserted us in the fourth dimension? Why had I ignored Una who had firsthand knowledge of The

Consortium of Dimensional Travelers? The missing parts nagged me. Balance is important to me. I would not have tolerated imbalance if writing fiction. I would have changed myself into a consort or changed Rugen into a lifebearer to maintain the creative tension among the sexes; but this book was not fiction; it was my lopsided attempt to reflect unfolding events, which were becoming more complex and chaotic as the story progressed.

My neglect of the feminine began all the way back in the first chapter when Elay and I were in the garden. Did it mean that I neglected the feminine in my real life? Only Iris, with her crazy logic, saw the truth and brought it to my attention. I knew Elay was distressed when we sat in the garden together. When she asked for my help, I acted like a selfish ass. Would the whole story be different if I had the courage to ask, "What can I do to help you, *mebr*?"

I thought of the times I incarnated as a female and through that experiential door, I could connect with the irritation Iris felt over the exclusion of physical women. Being female was difficult for me too. Inside, I knew nothing could define my soul, especially labels such as male, female, consort, lifegiver or lifebearer. I could empathize with all distinctions as they rose to the surface of my being. I honestly possessed no preference for one outward form over another because all forms offered me possibilities for love. Despite that, I decided to come down exclusively into my femininity to see what it might say.

I went into our *neipanin* and lit a stick of lavender incense—Elay's keyed scent—to set the mood. If any soul could help me understand, Elay, that strong and willful mystery between Michael and Bejan, could. I sat on a cushion and waited knowing that no one had fully communicated with me since Belinda weeks earlier. Now I called out to Elay for help. *Elay, I adore you. It is Sante. I am part of you as you are part of me, forever as One. Speak to me now.* After a short hesitation, I felt an incredible love settle around me. I was on fire and then cool. An energetic breeze blew against my arms and then the tingling of a thousand tiny fingers danced upon my face. A vision appeared with its arms held high above its head. It twirled around and around like a tiny ballerina inside an ovum of pink light. Elay was dressed in gossamer baggy pants and a scarf-draped blouse. She was no longer wearing her favorite shades of brown, blue, or green, but brilliant red. Several long strands of pearls hung from her neck and teardrop pearls dangled from her ears. Her hair was dark and shiny with the weight of resin soaked pollen. Her twirling slowed and her arms moved gracefully as if she were a fluttering moth. *I've been shopping,* she called out in her familiar and playful way. *Here, I can create paradise with the perfection of my thoughts. Since consciousness is malleable as it is persistent, Michael, Bejan, and I saw no reason why we should not indulge in a short holiday. Of course, I went shopping as soon as we arrived. I walked into a jewelry store and helped myself to a few precious gems—pearls of wisdom and such.*

She giggled and it trailed off leaving that familiar ringing in my ears. *The staff only materializes in order to tell customers how marvelous they look in their new treasures. Then they ask if they can gift-wrap your selections or if you want to wear the items yourself.*

You mean you don't pay?

I create my own reality here. Why would I create a reality where I have to pay? There are no strings here except the heartstrings our musicians play.

For me, your reality sounds like an illusion because I can't imagine what you're describing.

It's an illusion ten thousand times stronger than your puny reality inside the third dimension. Besides, you would not deny me a few new precious jewels—would you? After all, I am your mebr.

What have you selected so far?

The pearls that you see around my neck and a few new outfits I wear as perspectives. Michael and Bejan sometimes wear pearls too, when they appear as females. Her giggling echoed like the ringing of a crystal bowl and I wanted to linger in the sound waves. *Sometimes we attend Gatherings with more evolved souls and go wearing our new outfits. I enjoy these outings where we communicate with others unfamiliar to us by modulating our energy vibrations until we can dialogue with each other in exactly the same way I am communicating with you now.* She appeared amused. *You'll love this part, Sante. The amusements our oversouls create for us are endless. I know how addicted you are to feeling the bliss and our Gatherings can get quite energetic.*

Are you helping with the denial in the fourth dimension?

Oh yes, my cherub; I merely thought you would be more interested in how we have fun instead of all the work we do.

I'm interested in everything you do? I allowed time to pass and knew I needed to speak or I would lose her connection. *Will you forgive me for my ignorant behavior in the garden? I was selfish. I swear, Mebr, my journey into the past has made me humble. Please tell me what you know about the fourth dimension. I want to hear all your truth.*

Elay began to talk like the willful Vanguard Scout she was in her last triumphant life.

I go into the fourth dimension alone. We go alone because not enough of us exist to go as a team. I work exclusively with fragments that lived as Humans, Gathosians, and Tyrowsians because I am familiar with their spiritual customs that act as touch points to their souls. I attempt to cull out lost will fragments and interact with them as if the denial were my own. Every soul must do its own work, but if I offer my complete empathy, then my response usually hits the mark. She recited part of the Shardasko Credo,

"Truth is responsibility and karmic legacy
My disposition cooperates with me
I accept each new situation

I am at peace with myself."

It was quiet between us again. *May I quote all you told me in the book I am writing?*

She began dancing like a flame. *Of course, my cherub; but please play me lightly.*

What do you mean?

Show me with my pearls of possibility; show me finely dressed. I know your tendencies to follow everyone into their shadows. I am not faulting you, for I have enjoyed a peek with all the others. I'm asking you to love me and treat me as tenderly as Bejan and Michael always do. Allow me my dignity, show them my best angles, and please never show them that I am tired. Then her face turned to dust and blew away, leaving nothing but a pair of eyes. Two great owl eyes peered out toward me, like eyes that never sleep.

Behold the eyes of the fourth dimension, she said. *When we go into the fourth, we face battlegrounds. Soul fragments consumed in psychotic illusions swagger around in armor and carry weapons. Fragments wearing camouflage military outfits and brandishing knives are quite common too. You know the types; disguises vary, but all are stifling their omnipotence, the thing they want most. Like any new fool that has just cleared the third dimension, the first time I attempted to enter the fourth, I went wearing only my pearls. 'Damn!' I said when I got back here. 'Those folks are mean.' The second time, I wore my Shardasko common sense and put all my new pearls inside my shirt where they felt secure and cool against my breasts.*

Her eyes morphed out into a body again and she performed another quick spin. *No matter what metaphors we employ here, we all use the same approach. The best tools seem to be our conscious wit and our trust that we can sort illusion from truth. The strategy I find most effective is to cull out the least psychotic soul fragments and isolate them until they begin to communicate with me. Then I stay conscious with them until we make a breakthrough and they decide what they want to do next. Usually they want to go home. In the beginning, some fragments attempted to break away from me, even believing they were capable of injuring me; but of course, I merely jump to the fifth dimension. Some fragments try to run away and when this happens, I stand very still in their presence until they are ready to talk. Watching them carefully usually evokes their curiosity. Funny thing about soul fragments, even utter despair cannot destroy them. Our experts here, in all things esoteric, are postulating that curiosity is the impetus of all souls dedicated to will.*

Is your work in the fourth dimension helping us here in the third with our denial?

I can only report that our methods seem to be working here in the fourth dimension. However, every time we return to the fourth to cull out a new fragment, we need to go deeper and be more patient. The amazing thing is that some of the most resistant fragments are beginning to move quickly toward realignment. If their realignment coincides with incarnations in the third dimension, then those third dimensional incarnations must be ready to accept what comes knocking at their door.

Do you believe we could use your approach here in the third dimension to help us realign with soul fragments in denial?

Absolutely! This process is not a great cosmic secret that we know about in other dimensions, but are keeping from you in the third. Every encounter, with another soul, has an emotional charge that we must reclaim, soothe, and reconcile. The witness is the final illusion of the quiet mind. Realize that you never were a witness nor ever will be a witness to anything but the truth.

Denial is a stone we toss into the moving stream.
Know that we are the thrower, the hand, the water, and the stone.
Let us now accept that we also are the current of the stream.
Beloved, Jana Elay, SY: 5552-5603, from her 5602 address to the Jubilee Gathering.

I feel guilty, I told Elay. *I should have stayed in the fourth dimension and nursed the fragments with Hope and Estrella.*

You're heading in the wrong direction when you entertain guilt, which you therefore put upon Rugen, Nova, and even me. You made the decision to accompany Rugen backward through time. It was honorable and you did it for love. Your only sin is attaching yourself to guilt.

Have you seen Nova yet?

"*I have. We met* lim *at The Door when* le *came through. She looked sober and that made me scared. Le was exhausted and slept in Bejan's arms for a long while.*"

"*What is it?*" I demanded.

"*We offered* lim *shelter, but* le *refuses us because of you and Rugen. Le said* le *must be exclusive with you until you are again one. It is something souls of Nova's ilk do when major portions of them are still in incarnation. But never doubt that* lis *concentration on you is fierce. Sometimes* le *rests close to us because* le *does not want to be alone, but* le *refuses to dance or feel the bliss without you and Rugen here. Le told us that sometimes* le *goes to Lemira Jha to meditate or a small retreat on a moon called Sasaybin, where you honeymooned. Much of your love is now in* Nova *and it is difficult for* lim *to hold your passion so close, without you here. Nova weeps for you; so don't think all the yearning is strictly on your side. Despite* lis *loyalty to you, I do send* lim *my complete energetic compassion in everything I do and hope that it will help* lim *stay strong. Unfortunately, my charge is not cohesive with* lis *if* le *is not my willing partner. I believe it will help* lim *if you hold* lim *in your thoughts. Hold* lim *especially when you and Rugen meditate. Nova needs your bliss until your souls are again one.*"

I love you, mebr, I said.

And I love you, she returned. *By the way, I adore your new book; and confidentially, if you would have asked me these same questions in earlier chapters, I could not have told you what I told you now. For one thing, you would not have understood as you do now.*

Do you know how my book ends?

Yes, I even know how your life ends.

How does it end?

Write it and live it and you'll find out, she said in a mocking tone. Then the cool feminine breeze returned and took my precious Elay away.

$$****$$

I was writing furiously when Rugen arrived home at half-past midnight. "How's Iris doing?" *ce* asked.

"She's been asleep for about three hours. How was Hideaways?"

Rugen took the garters and necktie off exactly as *ce* had the night before and dropped them on the table. *Ce* was tired; after all, we both had been up from before dawn. "I thought it was crazy, but Mauve said it was a typical night at Hideaways. I must admit, in some ways, it was as exciting as being a vitasphere pilot."

"You must be kidding."

"Not really. Around 8:00 o'clock, two waiters got into an argument in front of the kitchen window over an identical order to two different tables. The food, they were arguing over, ended up on the floor. A short time later, Mauve confided to me that she had PMS, which she informed me stood for pre-menstrual syndrome. Have you ever heard of such a malady?"

"Yes, but it's non-existant in our time."

"She said her breasts ached with fullness and she felt like telling everyone exactly what she thought for a change. I urged her to do it, explaining that when the veneer comes off the female body, the soul inside get psychically direct. Then she kissed me on the cheek and called me 'doll.' During our break, we walked out in the alley behind the restaurant. She smoked a cigarette called a Camel and I stood around smelling the rotting banana peels in the trashcans. She asked me to feel her breasts while we were out there." Rugen imitated her voice. Mauve was prosaic coming out of Rugen's mouth. *Ce* cupped *cis* hands on *cis* chest showing me how she stood in front of *cim* saying, "Feel my tits."

"Did you?"

"Sure! I wasn't going to miss that opportunity. It was all very— biological. She asked, 'Don't they feel as if they are too heavy for their size?'"

"What did you say?"

"I told her the truth, that I could not give her a definitive answer until I weighed her breasts at several different and prescribed intervals. I warned her that her different clothing and undergarments might affect my judgment. When we were about to go back inside, we noticed a ginger-colored feline giving birth to two calico kittens behind the trash dumpster. By the way, I'm sure these three felines are soul mates. Anyway, Mauve called an agency called SPCA, which means Society for the Prevention of Cruelty to Animals. The SPCA could not take the felines until Friday morning, so Mauve took the mother and kittens home with her in a cheese crate she found in the kitchen. I would have offered to care for the felines, but did not want to take on the responsibility without you agreeing."

"That sounds like quite an evening."

"Actually there's more. Around 10:00 o'clock, a diner at one of Peggy's tables got a chunk of meat caught in his throat and she performed the Heimlich Maneuver on him. "Do you want to see how the Heimlich Maneuver works?"

"No thanks, I know about the Heimlich maneuver too."

"About twenty minutes later, the manager chased a beggar away from the kitchen door. As soon as the manager left, Terri, the entrée chief, made the beggar a meal that she called a "doggie bag," and took it out to him in the back alley. This doggie bag contained quiche Lorraine, Caesar Salad, chocolate cake with raspberry sauce and a split of Hideaways best champagne." Then Rugen took one hundred sixty-three dollars from *cis* pocket and laid it on the table.

"You made all that money tonight?"

"The other waiters told me that I was doing a great job. Sante, I think I can do this job," *ce* said with a bit of pride.

"What about the meat you're forced to serve?"

"I talked to Terri and asked her if she thought vegetarian entrées might sell if we offered them on the menu. She's a vegetarian herself and we decided that it would be reasonable to see if customers would be interested in well-prepared vegetarian entrées. All the waiters agreed to ask customers and allow them to decide. I know it's very minor, but I'm willing to put up with my own disgust if I can institute some positive change." Rugen sat down and faced me. "Did you get much writing done?"

I handed *cim* the bookscreen with chapters 18 and half of 19. "Read the part in nineteen about Nova first." Ten minutes later, *ce* had read the whole thing. *Ce* did not even mind that I turned up the heat with Iris and astrally projected to her side and held her until she fell asleep.

****

Senon awoke us with the reminder, "Tyme is coming up the stairs." Tyme arrived right before Earthly daybreak. His chalky aura made him appear as if he were a ghost that had survived the night. He was not noisy or flashy upon arrival, but still, he possessed a certain presence, a high-energy charge. Rugen and I were sleeping up near the ceiling. I had given up trying to sleep in heavy gravity and now was unabashedly indulging in eighty percent less gravity and sleeping soundly. We were not as startled as the first time; at least, I did not fall on my ass when I hit the floor. Still, we scrambled for clothing because Tyme announced, "Let's be quick! I'm here to take you to meet the other consortium members." This morning Tyme looked spiffy in his white pants and a red tee shirt that advertised, "Round trips to Paradise Cove $39.95." From Hope we learned how to bargain with greater spirits, so we told Tyme we needed a few extra minutes to shower.

We were quick and when we emerged, still damp in our clothing, we discovered that Tyme had made tea. He even insisted we had plenty of time.

Rugen asked, "What should we do about Iris? She expects us to be available this morning."

Senon materialized and suggested, "Maybe I can help."

"It's a pleasure to make your acquaintance," said Tyme bowing his head toward Senon.

"Hello," said Senon and then he ignored Tyme and said, "If you want, I can take the call from Iris."

"She's sleeping and will not awake for hours," said Tyme. "She has bouts of psychic agitation and sometimes needs to sleep late to make up for a sleepless night."

"How do you know that?" asked Senon.

"Iris and I are old friends," said Tyme.

I was curious about where we were going and Tyme said, "It's not far from here. See that shadow on the far side of the window. We'll use that as a portal; it is as good as any. You might feel dizzy because you're unaccustomed to rapid inter-dimensional travel so, each of you, hold one of my hands. I don't want to lose one of you in the void." Any suggestion of being lost in a void of inter-dimensional space was enough to make Rugen and I hold on tight.

****

We were on our way, but I experienced no cataclysmic sounds or visions, only a gentle "puff!" followed by a sensation of free fall that lasted about five seconds. The darkened space gradually gave way to an empty, desert landscape. The surrounding scene was glowing with a dim vermilion twilight that seemed to have no source. I observed a few unfamiliar dark trees and bushes that cast no shadows while the sky muted to a dusky violet blue. "Where are we?" Rugen asked.

"We call this place One World," said Tyme. "We create One World every time we meet; otherwise, it does not exist. Sit down, for it seems our enthusiasm has made us the first to arrive this morning. Others will arrive shortly." Tyme sat down on the dry dusty earth and hugged his knees with his arms. Rugen and I wandered around, felt some rocks, and touched some trees to make sure they were real.

A variety of soul creatures began arriving and Tyme introduced us to several groups. The more souls that arrived, the more One World gathered strength, light, substance, and detail. Everyone arrived by the same method and that was by merely popping into view. Many species were familiar, but others completely unknown. Colorful tee shirts seemed to be the de-rigueur fashion for inter-dimensional travel.

We communicated by means of telepathy and Tyme introduced us to three very green-looking individuals that he called Gobbins. Their hair was dark green and they stood about two meters tall. All three wore tee shirts with the enigmatic question, "Are the Pledged Perplexed or Perfidious?" Six individuals arrived a moment later— representatives from a species Tyme identified as Logtrites. Each Logtrite had three yellow eyes and they told us their names were One, Two and Three. Two was the friendliest, and confided that they were the last contingent to join the "dimensional hoppers." They wore brown tee shirts with the statement, "Original Cause: Our Archetypal Rationale." Gathosians dropped in slowly, like descending angels, holding their hands before their hearts. Already in meditation, they offered us a typical Mescale, "*afen*," which means peace. Their pale-blue tee shirts merely reiterated their *afen* message in bold blue lettering. There were hundreds of Ganats. Tyme made sure to introduce the Cerribeame separately from the others. All Ganats wore the same green tee shirts that said, "Heat," in bright red lettering. Two hundred Tyrowsians arrived soon afterward and it was impossible to meet more than a few. All Tyrowsians were in pale pink shirts with the message, "*Hataeasta.*" Humans were about seventy-five in number and dressed in tee shirts with the statement: "I am Divine Love." Over a hundred blonde and beautiful Loppolodians arrived in yellow-flowered shirts. Their statement tee shirt said, "Compassion Flowers Through Me." Two-dozen Damarians came outfitted in black shirts with the message, "Hope, Possibility & Love." Finally, ten Kulupans popped in, all in identical red tee shirts advertising, "Round trips to Paradise Cove $39.95."

Tyme made a special point to introduce his beloved Tiltoenay. She was mesmerizing and stunningly beautiful, very blue—bluer than Tyme was— with cobalt blue hair and refined chiseled features. She took Rugen's hand and kissed its palm and then she did the same with me. We each kissed her palm in return. "I am humbled that you accepted Tyme as your consortium mentor," she said. "Since Tyme and I are one, I will be working closely with you too."

"Thank you," Rugen told her. "We're humbled by your offer to join your altruistic cause."

The crowd was now over a thousand strong. The scene glowed with so much light and authority that it looked like a Gathering on *The Mother*. I felt slightly disappointed about no Janaforma being present. I had entertained hopes that I might see a familiar soul from *The Mother*. Rugen and I felt responsible, as if we were carrying the banner for all Janaforma at this meeting. As soon as Tyme picked up our feelings of responsibility, he recommended, *cool your delusions of grandeur and your feelings of inadequacy. Relax and accept whatever happens next.*

A few others arrived—latecomers. They were too far out on the periphery and I could not read their tee shirts. Finally, a sparkling appeared over our heads that illuminated the desert scene with brilliant light. The atmospheric color of One World was now a bright and lively pink.

Where is this newest light coming from? Rugen asked.

Tyme called them Quaid and explained, *Quaid are light entities from the seventh dimension. Sometimes they drop in to lend us more light.*

Our assembly now was about twelve hundred in number. What was our common purpose? I was unsure. I expected someone to organize our energy with appropriate expectations, such as, "Today we will cure all denial on Earth and this evening a potluck dinner will be held to celebrate our success." No one rose to speak and no one gave any indication that we should sit; but almost in unity, and as if on cue, everyone sat down in the desert dust and we were knee to knee. Then I realized that participants were modulating their personal energy and connecting it so that we were an energetic pattern of greater magnitude. Rugen and I sat close and were knee to knee too. Just to make sure, we linked our arms at the elbows. Tiltoenay and Tyme sat right behind us. Tiltoenay leaned between Rugen and me and whispered, "You're going to love this part. I know you both are surrendering kindness; but just remember to always share."

Then, I heard a sound like Iris's voice, the sound of "flute notes, plucked wires." The sound was etching deeper and deeper into my surrender. The sound became a choir of alien tongues as one prolonged, "Aaaaaaahhhhhhh," swept over us. This energy was microscopic conscious, pliable, and filled with light. Held in the power of The Consortium, the bliss enveloped me in a sweet cloud of love. I foolishly assumed, up to now, that to bask in this much bliss I would need to be dead. Only I was not dead, I felt extremely alive. Later, when we all stood to go our separate ways, I knew both the peace and the power of my singular love. New light was shining from Rugen's face as we held hands. "You're glowing," *ce* told me. I glanced around at the others, at Tyme and Tiltoenay, and everyone was afire with new light. On some, the effect was so powerful, one needed to strain to see their original forms beneath.

The crowd began to thin out quickly and I noticed as more souls departed, One World began to lose its vibrancy. We lingered a bit longer as a few new souls—ones we missed meeting earlier—came by to say, "Hello." A Human named Remo Klugman introduced himself and gave us his business card, telling us that he owned a tee shirt shop on Duval Street in Key West. "Stop by and get an apropos tee shirt that you can wear when we all meet," he suggested.

****

Foolish me, the newcomer! I thought Tyme would escort us safely home until Tiltoenay explained, "It's time to go to work and discharge our collective light to those that need us most. We will take you out with us the first few times, but after you learn how to project your energy, you and

Rugen must go alone. As you can see, there are not enough of us that we can afford to always go in groups of four."

"Wherever you are going this morning, we can't go," I attempted to explain. "We promised to meet someone and it's important that we keep our promise."

"We are outside time," Tiltoenay said. "We have not used more than a few seconds between when we arrived and now."

"If we're not going home, where are we going?" asked Rugen.

"We always go where we are needed most," said Tiltoenay. The four of us joined hands in a special way that Tiltoenay showed us, so that our left hands were palms upward and our right hands were with their palms facing downward.

We stood in a circle and Tyme said, "Let's go!" Again, I heard a gentle "puff" and a feeling of free fall inside the void. We emerged in an alien place; its energetic contrast to One World was as darkness was to midday. The setting was third dimensional physical reality, but I questioned if it was real because of its diminished light. We were standing by the side of a muddy road with a stream of water gushing down the center. Torrential rain was falling and it seemed as if we stepped backward in time. By squinting, I could discern a few squat mud-brick shacks scattered around the dim landscape. The countryside beyond was flat with a few scrubby trees and weedy plants. Despite the cleansing rain, horrible smells assaulted my nose. It was the stench of excrement mingling with the choking odor of smoky fires and rotting vegetation. The smells were so noxious that Rugen immediately asked if I was going to be sick.

I put my palm over my nose and mouth and mumbled, "I'll try to handle it."

"Where are we?" asked Rugen.

Tiltoenay asked, "If I tell you, will you pin this depravity upon others? Let us approach each new situation as a coming home to ourselves. Move out now, as we too will be doing. Follow your instincts to those who need help most. We will meet you, at dawn, at the other end of the village." Tyme and Tiltoenay left us standing there, in the dark and malodor, to find our way through this nightmare.

Rugen and I were afraid. My psychic senses emerged like a headlight on my forehead to lead the way. We stepped lightly, believing we could keep our feet dry as we attempted to pick our way down the muddy, rut-filled road. It got darker as we walked into the murkiness of the village. The houses were hovels, made from sun-dried clay and their doors were nonexistent. A few filthy rags hung over the door openings in a futile attempt to hide the view. The rain muted sound, but I could hear the vague life-chatter beyond and a dog barking endlessly in the distance. "Where did Tyme and Tiltoenay go?" whispered Rugen. No signs of them were anywhere.

A flickering, yellow candle seemed to beckon us, and we instinctively moved toward the light when a dark figure ran diagonally across our path and then slipped behind a curtained doorway. We went to the same doorway and heard cries and moans inside. It was someone's private dwelling. Desperate to escape the sharp pelting of the rain, we stepped beyond the muddy rain-soaked drape. Immediately, an ancient woman flew up and set upon us from that interior space. I knew her! She was the old woman Cle and I encountered on Sutcay Tay, the one *ce* gave our only spare *vitarattha* to. She was still the old woman I wanted to ignore. I told Rugen telepathically who she was and just like Cle, Rugen said, "We need to help her."

She was wretched. Time was twisting and I no longer was certain when events were happening. The only thing I knew for sure was this was the second time I met this soul. This time she was dressed in a dark red garment with a vibrant green scarf draped around her head. The bright colors of her apparel were a shocking contrast to the drab squalor of her world. Everything, especially her face, was an assault to my senses—her gaunt expression suggested starvation. The folds of the wrinkled parchment that she wore as skin featured owl eyes, like Elay's eyes. The old woman attacked us and began clawing at my arm, dragging us deeper into the dark. She was speaking excitedly in a language I did not understand; but Rugen relayed to me that the woman was speaking a regional Earth dialect.

"She thinks we're gods who have come to help her," said Rugen over her desperate chattering. "She says her granddaughter is trying to give birth, but Kali is waiting to steal the unborn infant away."

Rugen spoke to the woman in her own language and tried to pacify her and then she led us into a darker darkness. There, in a corner, on a damp and revoltingly dirty mattress was the indistinct form of an adolescent girl large with child. "Holy Mother!" Rugen whispered. "A birth in Hell!"

"Get me better light," I ordered.

Rugen began communicating with the grandmother and she found a candle and lit it. She handed the burning candle to Rugen who held it high so I could see a little better. "Give me the light," I said, and Rugen handed it over and I brought it closer to the girl's face. Her eyes were wide open and staring into the dark. I searched desperately for her pulses. There were none, but she was still warm. "She's dead," I whispered. Perhaps, as we entered this dwelling, uninvited, she was severing her last fragile connection to her hellish life. *Was her hold so tenuous that we scared her completely away?* My hands quickly trailed down the body to hover above the mound of stomach. "The fetus may yet be alive."

Rugen told the grandmother the facts and she began to shriek and moan hysterically. As always, I reverted to my opposite in the crisis. I became methodical. "Ask her if she has a clean towel and knife."

Rugen began begging the old woman to help us and she kept shaking her head in confusing ways. "She says to let the unborn die now rather than later," translated Rugen. "No way exists to care for a newborn without the mother." Then, the grandmother ran away and left us kneeling there in the filth and muck with her dead granddaughter and the fetus trapped inside the dead body. Rugen got up to stop her. "Let her go," I said. "Find Tiltoenay."

"Hang on," *ce* said tapping me on the shoulder. I sent Ezek with Rugen for guidance and protection as *ce* went out into the dark. Without my psychic insight, I sat there with the dead and the unborn and was afraid to move. Rugen was gone only a few seconds. I do not know how *ce* managed to find Tiltoenay so quickly; but my hero performed the miracle and brought her swiftly to my side.

Tiltoenay fell to her knees beside me. "I understand," she said quietly. "But we must hurry; the moonflowers are closing." She rubbed her hands together as Tyme did the first time we met and produced a silver scalpel. When it appeared in her hand, the knife caught the candlelight and the blade gleamed with its precious power of liberation. Then Rugen held our one candle as I literally cut open the dead mother and released the fetus from her womb.

"I'm sorry, I can't watch," said Rugen halfway through and *ce* turned away. I do not deny that it was gruesome. The bloody potential I pulled from that womb was pale blue and very quiet. When I saw that small bundle of flesh, great doubt seized me that what I was doing was appropriate or sane. I cut the cord in order to separate the potential from that heavy deadness waiting to consume it. If the mother were alive, I would not have cut the umbilical cord. In the Janaforma tradition, the mother is the one person with the right to cut the cord and release the child to life.

"The infant's body has no soul and therefore is not alive," said Tiltoenay. "Only if we vow to mentor this potential, will life enter this body."

I was on automatic pilot. "Will you care for this child with me?" I asked Rugen.

I cannot think of that moment without weeping with gratitude and wonder. Praise Rugen! No finer soul exists in creation than Miro Rugen. I vow to spend eternity writing love poetry to this great soul. *Ce* did not hesitate for a moment—as I might have. "I will," *ce* said, and then the three of us breathed the light The Consortium gave us into that potential, which immediately began to cry.

The grandmother did not return. If she had, no way would I have handed the infant over to her. As far as I was concerned, the child now belonged to Rugen and me, for the soul came into the body at our behest. Blood covered my shirt and arms and I was soaking wet and covered with mud up to my waist. Rugen stripped off *cis* shirt and wrapped it around the infant to give it warmth. Exhausted, the three of us made our way to the opposite end of the village where Tyme was waiting.

TWENTY

"**I**t's imperative to get the baby to warmth and safety," explained Tiltoenay. "We can discuss details on the other end. For the third time, with a "puff" and feelings of free fall, we emerged in our Key West apartment. Tiltoenay offered to take the babe from my arms and I handed her the child as I dashed off to the bathroom to grab a clean towel. "Tyme and I will see this child gets to safety," she offered.

"This baby is ours!" said Rugen. "Sante and I will raise it as our own."

"That's impossible," declared Tyme. "You are not prepared for a challenge of this magnitude. This child will be a magnet for soul fragments. This child will not thrive unless you open yourself up to the fourth dimension so that the parts of it not here, can find the courage to join in this infant's life."

"Sante and I will do whatever is necessary," said Rugen.

Tyme hesitated and studied Rugen with a careful eye. "You do not realize what you are asking for," he cautioned.

"I'm committed, both to Sante and now this child," said Rugen.

Tyme turned to me. "What about you?"

"This child belongs with Rugen and me," I declared with equal passion.

It was quiet in that room for about ten seconds. "Okay," Tyme said slowly. "Tiltoenay and I will be your conduits to the soul fragments. Realize, right now, that this situation will be difficult no matter how much help Tiltoenay and I give you."

"Thank you," I said. "We are not so foolish to believe that reclaiming this child's fragments would be an easy chore."

"Would you like me to nurse the infant for you?" Tiltoenay offered.

"Yes, if you could do that, it would help us tremendously," I said.

"Clean the child of the blood and I will put it to my breast," she offered.

Rugen and I washed the infant in the kitchen sink and wrapped it in a clean dry towel. Its tiny mouth was already making sucking movements. "It will be just a moment," I whispered. I took the infant back to Tiltoenay who opened her bodice and put it to her breast. Her breasts were lovely with nipples the color of indigo blue, just like her lips. She gently rubbed one against the infant's cheek until it turned and latched on.

The baby fell asleep after a few minutes and I took it and gently suspended it inside a *vitarattha*, so it could sleep in total comfort. I watched this new life as it slept peacefully and was filled with infant trust. The child brought my compassion to the surface. I already loved it madly and completely. I loved this child just as I loved the fetus my parents created to house my potential life. I loved this child as myself; I loved it with the knowledge that love cannot desert what love adores unconditionally. All those old feelings from my last life, my unconsummated desire for children came forth to claim me and declare triumphant over me. My quiet desires had never died. I had suppressed them, but failed.

Rugen and I lit a candle for the child's biological mother that we feared had fled to the fourth dimension. *Help her Elay,* we prayed. *Help this lost mother and we will help her child.*

Tiltoenay put her hand on my shoulder as I stood before our makeshift altar. "You will need clothing for this child," she reminded me. "We can help you get whatever you need. I will be in touch later today."

"Thank you," I told her again.

"You both look exhausted," she noticed. "Try to get some rest. Tyme is right. It's never easy to raise a child and it's especially difficult to undertake the nurturing of a child that is a soul fragment. My best advice to you both is spend as much time as you can with this infant, especially in states of deep meditation. The sooner you can urge the fragments to join in this incarnation's life, the better. Wait too long and the child's body and mind will harden and refuse your love and understanding."

"Take care," said Tyme. "Don't forget that in three days The Consortium will be meeting again. I will see you later today so we can talk." Then they both flashed away.

We went to bathe and put on clean clothing. We were so exhausted that it felt as if it were the end of a cycle rather than the beginning. Senon crept out of *lis* box and told us that everything was completely silent on the Iris front. *Le* was curious and wanted to see the child too. We followed *lim* into the *neipanin* so *le* could have a peek. "It's an extremely beautiful child," *le* said with a sigh of reverence. "Is it male or female?"

Rugen and I stared at each other in total stupidity. "Holy Mother!" I exclaimed. "We forgot to check."

Rugen went over and poked *lis* hand inside the *vitarattha*. "It's a female," *ce* announced. Shortly afterward, I declared the only appropriate name for our child was Lotus Blossom.

****

As dawn's moments waned, Rugen and I enjoyed a cup of tea. Despite the trapped denial in the fourth dimension and the impeding rupture, I knew joy with *cim* that morning. Our windows were open and we could hear birds courting outside with their sweetest songs. My heart was open and I sensed the tantalizing expectation of fulfillment in this alien time. I felt clean and reverent, no facades. Rugen and I tapped teacups before sipping a second time. We reached for each other across the table and held hands. Morning's sweet innocence lingered, sleeping on as a child in our *neipanin.*

"Happiness," drifted through Rugen as a peaceful emotion and *ce* set out our blessings as a child arranges *cis* favored toys. "What more could we want?" *ce* asked me. "Lotus Blossom is ours to have and to hold; Tyme and Tiltoenay are wise and understanding mentors; and The Consortium is a source of light and communal bliss. Maybe we can even convince Iris of our veracity."

"That's asking a lot," I remarked.

Behind our easy laughter, I could hear the clatter of the trash handler's truck coming down the alley to the rear of our apartment and the sounds of shouting men. Then I caught the noxious wafting that went along with their passing. Rugen's cellphone rang then and the day's tempo picked up. It was Iris. She had switched off her wrisceptor and could not figure out how to switch it on again. She was suspicious when Rugen asked her to come to our place instead of us going to hers. Rugen responded to her doubts by setting a blaze of new information before her. It was clearly half act and half *cis* genius at work. Like a history teacher announcing, "This morning we need to cover all of Ancient Greece and this afternoon we will have the final exam," Rugen advised Iris to "mind her P's and Q's" (sustain her prejudice and hold her questions) and get over to our apartment. "Forget about your lipstick and bra," *ce* advised. "Just lash your mind on straight so we can plunge ahead. Don't you realize that the future is outpacing us? You are still reading chapter 14 and Sante is plucking chapter 20 from thin air. Do you have any concept of what has happened since chapter 14, any notion at all? Two hours ago, Sante and I became the proud parents of a newborn baby girl." Rugen paused and Iris recited a new litany of questions fueled by her doubts. "Come and see for yourself, if you do not believe me," *ce* said. "This time the truth is simple. Sante and I need to be practical and wise in Lotus Blossom's care. Oh! I forgot—we named her Lotus Blossom about an hour ago. Anyway, we must protect her dignity. She came to us so recently that she is still indisposed—her only clothing being a towel. Forget about your silly pride, because I tell you Lotus Blossom is

313

here dressed only in her authentic physical body. Hurry, because Sante and I need your help meditating, so we can encourage Lotus Blossom's soul fragments to join in her new life."

Iris promised to come in about an hour; but arrived promptly twelve minutes later. I opened the door and our eyes met in a brief dance. My unmasked eyes still had the power to cause energy surges in her. Just when I was feeling good about my ability to spike her energy, she called attention to my nakedness, which made me want to pull back. She said, "You should cover your eyes when you answer the door. You could scare someone." Her comment let me know that my narcissism was still alive. I was accustomed only to the deepest flattery concerning my eyes.

This morning, Iris was dressed in crisp green shorts and a fresh white tee shirt. The message printed on her shirt suggested, "Theta Waves Are the Choice of Geniuses." Her crispness and freshness of dress were distractions and the blue-black shadows under her eyes were not noticed until a second glance—another set of owl eyes, the eyes of my mother, the eyes of the psychic visionary having trouble sleeping through the stress. "I laid awake most of the night, thinking about Belinda and the future," Iris said. "No matter what you write or say about her, I picture her as frivolous, someone I do not wish to become."

Iris' safe boundaries were down considerably and she admitted, "I think I could use a hug." She hugged us separately and we gave her as much energy as she would allow us to give. Despite her exhaustion, we began to nudge her along toward greater revelation. It was counterproductive to relax the pace since we had such enormous ground to cover. Actually, her exhaustion was a good sign, a clue that she was close to a breakthrough into a greater conscious state that hopefully would include Rugen and me.

We respected her vulnerability and kept it light, easy, and fun. Besides Lotus Blossom was sleeping in the *neipanin* and we did not want to wake her with loud words or violent emotions. Iris glanced around at our sparsely furnished apartment and asked, "Where's this new baby that Rugen insisted is here?" I took Iris by the hand and led her off to the *neipanin*. The awe of seeing an activated *vitarattha* froze her in her tracks and she asked, "Is that one of your vitaspheres?"

Rugen reminded her, "*Vitaspheres* are the vehicles we use for fourth dimensional travel. This is a *vitarattha*—similar technology, but a smaller device."

It looks fragile, she thought.

She did not notice we were reading her mind when Rugen assured her, "It's quite sturdy. Go ahead and touch it."

On tiptoe, Iris edged closer and then she spied Lotus Blossom inside. "You do have a baby!" Iris slowly closed the distance with her right hand outstretched for contact. Tentatively, she touched the *vitarattha* with her fingertips making the periphery sparkle with little bits of pink light. "It tickles my fingers," she smiled. Her hand leaned into the forcefield a little harder so the energy gelled out around her wrist. *"It feels like touching a soft vibrating balloon,"* she thought. Lotus Blossom stirred and made tiny bubbling sounds with her mouth. "Hello there," Iris said. "Where did you come from? She's so tiny! Her nose is no bigger than the tip of my little finger."

"The baby's biological mother was a mere child herself," I explained.

"Where's her mother?" Iris asked.

Rugen touched my arm as a caution to go slow. "Why don't we go out in the sitting area and have a cup of tea and we will attempt to explain everything to you," *ce* said.

Because we needed diapers and infant formula, Rugen offered to take the seven-block hike to Target while I stayed with Iris to respond to all her questions. Rugen and I already decided that the best solution was to allow Iris to read the remainder of my book so that information would dovetail into the subject of Lotus Blossom. Iris graciously accepted doing it our way with the stipulation that we explain the presence of Lotus Blossom immediately afterward. I made tea and Iris started right in on Chapter 15.

My attention kept switching between Lotus Blossom and Iris, wondering which one might need me first. Our Lotus slept on peacefully; but I knew that once she awoke her needs were going to be close to the bone—essential. I was anxious to sit down and enter meditation with her tucked in between Rugen and me so we could determine how much of her soul was still in the fourth dimension. I was willing to postpone that venture a bit longer to help Iris, but not for long.

Iris glanced up from the bookscreen. She had just read the part in Chapter 14 when I activated Senon's programming. "What does Senon look like?" she asked.

Senon, of course, heard and responded by half-materializing *lis* standard hologram. "Nice to finally meet you in the flesh," *le* bowed like a gallant Shardasko Warrior. Then *le* did something rather cute. *Le* created a perfect red rose and held it out to her. Iris attempted to take the rose, but it could not hold its form once it left Senon's hand. "It's the thought that counts," Senon reminded her.

"Oh!" she said, as the rose vanished and her hand held empty space. "It's nice to meet you in the flesh." She was unsure of the courtesies extended to sentient multidex programs and she tried to correct herself. "But you are not flesh—are you? Sorry, I meant no offense."

"No offense taken," Senon assured her. "I've got a question though that has cut a minor glitch in my programming since I researched you on the web. Why do you call yourself an intuitive facilitator and how do you facilitate intuitively?"

"My intuitive facilitating days may be over," Iris confessed. "I'm not sure who I am anymore or if I'll ever be able to intuitively facilitate again. I'm supposed to lead a seminar on soul mates in a few weeks, but I'm beginning to realize I know as much about soul mates as I do about the dark side of the moon." She stared at me. "I am going to cancel my seminar."

"I'm sorry," said Senon. "I did not mean to upset you."

Sitting down on the futon, I gently slipped my arm around her shoulder. "Don't cancel it," I advised her. "What you do is important work; besides, your psychic skills will return."

I glanced up at Senon and *le* was biting *lis* bottom lip as Nova used to do. "Would you go into the *neipanin* and monitor Lotus Blossom's vital functions so I can concentrate on Iris."

"Definitely, right away," *le* responded.

"Let me know if even slight fluctuations occur," I called after *lim*.

"Righto!" *le* promised.

****

I encouraged Iris to begin reading again. She stopped when she got to the part about our first night on Mallory Dock. She asked me a dozen questions about Tyme. She verified that she had known Tyme for almost fifteen years. I was curious. "How come you never noticed that he is blue?"

"He does look a bit odd. But his complexion is only slightly blue. Once Tyme told me that he was probably a one-of-a-kind creation—said his father was half-Greek and half-Polynesian and his mother was half-French and half-Indian."

"How did you meet?"

"We met up in Philly; I'm from that area. My father was a jazz musician and Tyme used to play guitar in my father's band. Tyme would drop by our house for my mother's Sunday afternoon spaghetti dinners. I remember Tyme and Dad spent lots of time together. When I moved down here to The Keys, seven years ago, Tyme was already here and he helped me find a place to live. We've been friends ever since. When my life goes into crisis, he's always there to help me. When my parents were killed in an automobile accident, he drove me up to Philadelphia and stayed with me the entire time."

"Your parents were killed in an automobile accident?"

Iris' eyes immediately got glassy with tears. "I need to tell you something, Sante. It has to do with that part in your book when Nova tells you the dream about crossed-signals." She stopped and blew her nose on a wad of tissues she held clenched in her hands. "My father and Uncle Steve went to Atlantic City to play a gig and my mother went along for the ride. It was after two in the morning, when they were driving back to Philly. Uncle Steve was behind the wheel and Dad was sitting next to him; Mom was sleeping in the back seat. You probably don't realize this yet, but at that time of night, many outlying traffic signals merely flash warnings instead of cycling from red to green. The intersection where the accident occurred had faulty traffic signals."

Taking Iris' hands, I held them as she moved into some difficult questions that I could not answer. "If reincarnation is not linear, as Nova suggested to you, was Uncle Steve a split off of Nova or was my father a split off of you?"

"I don't know. I do know that as the veneer of limited self becomes thinner, we are able to see that consciousness is not a singular perspective."

"I feel like a pawn being moved around on a chessboard."

"Sometimes, I feel the same way," I admitted.

Iris had read most of chapter 17. It was perfectly apparent to her that Rugen and I were contemplating a sexual relationship, yet she had not given either of us one word of encouragement in that direction. Nor had she mentioned the conflict that Rugen and I experienced over connecting with her. I thought this was odd for a love emanation because expressions of love were always the first thing that caught my interest and the first thing I wanted to explore. Iris seemed calm, so I decided to take a bigger chance and see if she would respond to a few words of direct love. "Knowing that the watching is constant means that greater spirits are aware of our slightest lies," I told her.

"That's a scary thought," she said.

"In full view of all watchers, I would like to confess that my imaginings of late are running toward scenes of the three of us together in a loving relationship. What do you think about my projection? Do you bless my imaginings with any projections of your own?"

"Truthfully, there were hints my whole life that you were coming to claim me," she confessed. She began to tell me about her synchronistic hints that started all the way back when she was a mere three years old. "When I was three, I began having a reoccurring dream." She described what she called, "a man." She knew a lot about this "man" considering she met him only in her dreams. She described him as square-shouldered and saintly. "His humor was great and his agility and strength seemed limitless. His hair drew the light to it and was the same color as yours." Iris was describing Nova. Then she startled me by saying that I was the man in her dreams. "I see you sitting on the back of a hay wagon being pulled down a road by a team of horses. I run after you and you give me your hand and pull me up alongside you. We are both laughing and feelings are happy and carefree between us. Sometimes we kiss or we just sit there and hold each other as we watch the road disappear."

"Is there anymore to your dream?"

"No, that's it. It's the act of you giving me a hand up into the hay wagon and wonderful feelings between us and then sleep." Iris stared at me. "The dream became such a familiar part of my routine that when I would go to bed each night, I could conjure you up. You never failed me; you always came to take me away with you into restorative sleep. Once I even drew your picture; but, of course, I thought I was drawing a picture of the man in my dreams. I still have the picture and will show it to you the next time you come to my house. It's of you with your long, flame-gold hair, your angelic power face, and your little square chin. The picture is of you, Sante—I swear." She laughed a little and it still possessed the power to make my ears ring. "You know what? I could never get the eyes right on that damn picture? I have been involved with projections of that dream man my whole life. What if you are one more illusion that mimics my dream man?"

I offered her my hands as I imagined the man in the hay wagon did and tried to explain the honesty of my intentions. "The three of us started at different times and entertained separate journeys until now; but here we are together in the Earth year of 2015, purpose to purpose, and face to face. Let's go forward together. Let's imagine that we are the Magi in Rumi's poem, seeking to worship at the altar of our greater selves. We have traveled far. Our intentions are not empty for we each have real gifts to offer each other. Rugen brings *cis* perfect understanding, while Nova brings the true sentience of our soul. Through Nova's grace, I do guarantee that Rugen and I have come to offer you the fullest gift of our love."

"I am not sure I understand."

"It's an invitation to bond with Rugen and I."

"What does bonding with you and Rugen mean beyond having sex with you?"

"It means recommitting to each other through acts of love; it means dying into Nova when this life wanes; it means an open journey beyond that."

She touched my cheek with her hand. "You are so handsome. Every man I ever fell in love with has looked like you in some way. When I saw you standing across the circle the other night at Mallory Dock, I thought, he looks like my dream man, only my jealousy immediately got in the way because I knew full well that Rugen was your lover."

My desires were to hold her until all her rough edges dissolved and we enfolded into each other. Of course, the physical Rugen was now at Target; but *cis* consciousness was intimate with mine and *ce* was helping me with Iris. "Do you have any dreams or memories of Rugen?" I asked her.

"Not a one," she claimed.

"You will when you take Regression."

She appeared slightly shocked. "I'm too scared to take Regression."

"Yes, it's too early for that."

She nodded her head a few times. "I understand that you and Rugen are inseparable, but I am not attracted to Rugen the way I am attracted to you. Rugen is—young."

In many ways, Rugen was ancient compared to Iris. I reminded her, "My commitment with Rugen is absolute; the love has to include Rugen in every way."

"I know!" she said. "But please keep in mind that I have been living as a barbarian with other barbarians for a long time and I can't change into an accepting butterfly in two days."

Her analogy made me smile and I kissed her lightly on both cheeks. That turned the heat up between us and I knew I needed to back off. I persuaded her to begin reading again and she stopped about two minutes later and verified that the tarot cards that Greg and Dennis pulled were indeed the ones Ezek claimed they were. She went back to reading and her eyes got big. I peeked over her shoulder to see what was scrolling up through the bookscreen. She was reading the part in Chapter 18 about Tyme appearing in our apartment for the first time. She stopped long enough to ask, "Why have I never met Tiltoenay?"

I shrugged. "You will have to ask Tyme or Tiltoenay."

The part about the Cerribeame crash-landing in the New Mexico desert in 1947 really fired her excitement. She said, "My mother was a young girl when it happened. Mom said there was lots of media hullabaloo over the notion that Earth was no longer an isolated world. Then, a day or two later, the government claimed the object found was not a space ship, but merely the tattered remnants of a weather balloon." It took her three minutes more to read through to the middle of chapter 19 where Elay appeared and explained her work in the fourth dimension. Iris glanced up and smiled this time. "I like this part about Elay. Thank you for putting more in your book about women, or as you Janaforma call them, lifebearers."

"You were absolutely right," I told her. "My book needs the contribution of physical females."

****

My promise to Rugen was that we would tell Iris together about how Lotus Blossom came into our life and I had to plead to make Iris wait. Rugen returned about ten minutes later lugging two large brown bags. Sweat was trickling down *cis* face and *cis* long hair was wet around *cis* neck from the heat outside. "I rushed," *ce* said. I jumped up to help *cim* set the bags down and *ce* started saying how great it would be to have a car so that we could drive instead of walk. You can bet that I put a bookmark on the car topic. "Is our Lotus Blossom awake yet?" *ce* asked.

"No. Senon is monitoring her vitals; but I'm getting concerned because she should be hungry by now. She has been asleep for almost three hours. That's unusual for a newborn child."

We decided to take Lotus Blossom out of the *vitarattha* and see to her needs. "The towel is wet with urine," Rugen proclaimed as if Lotus Blossom was very clever to have done that. "It's a good sign that her plumbing is working correctly—don't you agree?"

Rugen was so eager and full of optimistic energy holding our newborn Bud. *Thank you*, I thought. My gratitude encompassed *cis* trudging all the way to Target and back in the heat and went as far as when *ce* was Candidus and bought my freedom for too many *drachmae*.

Rugen took our Lotus Blossom to the sink and rinsed her carefully with warm water while I prepared the soy formula according to the directions on the package. Iris pitched in and we had, what I considered, a fun time playing family. Lotus Blossom was a good sport about our incompetence and did not cry one bit. The diapers Rugen bought were too large and went around her tiny body almost twice. She was a good sport about her ill-fitting clothing. The job of feeding fell to me since Rugen claimed that it was the lifegiver's privilege to have the first honors in that area. I tried to feed her, but she did not like the plastic nipple as much as Tiltoenay's breast. One of the problems was that it was too large for her tiny mouth. I began to imagine that Iris might solve our problem if she would agree to nurse Lotus Blossom; but I did not have the nerve to ask. While I attempted to get a few drops of formula inside Lotus Blossom, Rugen and I launched into the story of the events of the last few hours. Iris began crying again, especially when I told her how I took the baby from the dead mother. This time her tears were as copious as the torrential rains of Sutcay Tay.

Rugen was by her side in a flash and a new revelation came spilling out of her mouth. "Early this morning, I had a vivid nightmare," she sobbed. "I'm searching for my family and running out of time. I seem to be in the past standing on the outskirts of an ancient village that is hidden in darkness. I knew I had been there before—had this dream before. Rain is drenching me and covering the entire landscape and it's so dark that I can barely see. I try to walk, trip, and fall facedown in the mud that smells like shit. I struggle to get up, but the suction will not allow me to escape. I look up and see writing scribbled along a wall. Then, out of the darkness, I see a person slip from a door and come toward me. She is running and nearly trips over me, as I am lying there in the mud unable to move. She is angry and shouts at me in a foreign tongue I can't understand, yet I understand her perfectly."

"What did she say?" Rugen asked.

"She says, 'Run you fool! Soul fragments are coming to dine on your soul!'"

Rugen put *cis* arms around Iris and she wept against *cis* chest. "You are safe with us," *ce* told her.

"I was wringing wet when I woke up."

"Bond with us?" whispered Rugen. "Bond with us and we will keep you safe—I swear."

Since I was trying to feed Lotus Blossom and she was almost off to sleep again, I did not want to move and risk waking her. It was difficult to stay put. Seeing Rugen with *cis* arms wrapped around Iris stimulated my lifegiver instincts and made me want to join their fold. Only Janaforma lifegivers will truly know what I mean; but my attention was on Rugen and *cis* attention was on Iris. The missing link was that Iris' did not have her attention on me to close the energy loop. If I could have gotten closer to them physically, it would have been a different story. Now, the embrace was going on across the room and the split in Iris's attention between Rugen and me was cleaving her energy in two.

Out of the loop, my imagination intervened and began creating scenes to satisfy my inexhaustible lust. I was content to drift off on those images and then Ezek interrupted my reverie by flushing forth from his nest. Rugen and I were attentive as Ezek announced with prosaic confidence that *dreams are an important key in this rupture puzzle.*

This time I demanded, *speak!*

During sleep, the mind and body rest, but consciousness never sleeps. During deepest sleep, consciousness soars as it charts the evolutionary direction ahead for the soul. The dream emerges when the energy vibrations of the soul resonate with other energy vibrations under the concept of like attraction. When the sleeper moves back toward awaking, the soul passes through the energetic stages of feeling. It is in the realm of feeling that emotional blocks of denial manifest both personal and cosmic denial. I explained to Iris what Ezek said. "That's bad news for me," she decided. "If Evose and Belinda get my attention while I'm asleep, I will disappear into the fourth dimension."

****

Tiltoenay popped in around ten o'clock wearing a bright red tee shirt that said, "Motherhood Ain't For Sissies!" She looked happy and almost breathless as if caught up in a flurry of creative activity. She was an incredibly beautiful creature and she reminded me of Santa Claus with her blue skin and bright red tee shirt. She was holding two large, brown parcels, which contributed to her Santa Claus facade. Rugen and I rushed to help her set down her burdens. "Oh! Thank you," she puffed a bit. "Objects are so heavy to bring through the void! Twenty lively souls are lighter than two inert grocery bags of baby clothing." Her smile was grand. Her attention breezed right past the amazed and reality-shattered Iris with a simple, "Hi Iris! Isn't it a beautiful morning?" Tiltoenay told us, "Tyme and I just spent the last two hours at Fluff and Dry washing these clothes. The clothing is all used, donated by Consortium members when they heard about your needs."

Rugen and I thanked her profusely knowing profuse thanking was inadequate.

Without us saying anything, Tiltoenay was already at work reading our concerns. She put her arms around Rugen before announcing, "In the last couple of hours, I've conferred with the most enlightened members of our Consortium; our consensus is Lotus Blossom is going to live if we all do our parts. Tyme and I plan on doing as much as we can to help and have decided to put ourselves at your disposal until your situation stabilizes." Tiltoenay smiled and her teeth looked very white between her dark blue lips. "I, personally, have decided to make my divine nectar available to Lotus Blossom anytime she is hungry."

"Your generosity is immense," said Rugen and *ce* gave Tiltoenay a spontaneous embrace.

"It is!" she agreed and she smiled grandly again. "But my love is so big that it needs immense space."

I was overwhelmed with gratitude. Her gift to Lotus Blossom meant more than physical nourishment to an infant plucked from the arms of death. Tiltoenay's offering meant the exchange of energy, an infusion of divine brilliance into our child. I felt Tiltoenay's divine presence most strongly and never, in any of my lives, had I ever encountered a soul more incredibly alive with love. She was a jewel box of compassion. Her focus was direct, absolute, and she knew how to love.

She went into the *neipanin* to fetch Lotus Blossom. We dressed her in some of her new clothing, which consisted of, what else, a tee shirt. Lotus Blossom's tee shirt said nothing, but it had tiny pink flowers around the neck. We watched with delight as she awoke so naturally to take nourishment from the blue nipple of Tiltoenay's love.

Tyme popped in a short time later wearing the same red tee shirt as Tiltoenay. "Iris!" he cried and he went to greet her.

"Why didn't you tell me that you were an extra-terrestrial?" Iris demanded.

Rugen and I did not wait around for Tyme's explanation and instead slipped into the pocket of our kitchen alcove to make more tea for everyone. "I'm so happy," Rugen whispered. "For the first time since we've arrived here, I think we are on the right track."

Rugen and I were experiencing community with a capital C. As Lotus Blossom helped herself to Tiltoenay's milk, we drank tea. Tyme told us, "It's important we begin meditating as soon as possible to bring Lotus Blossom's denial into this dimension." Rugen and I were anxious to get started so we dragged the futon off its frame and put it on the floor in the middle of the *neipanin*. As soon as Lotus Blossom was satisfied and falling off to sleep, we placed her in the center of the futon and the five of us arranged ourselves around her, sitting cross-legged in a tight circle.

****

"The idea is to agitate the denial enough so it will arise with all its sticky needs and cling to us," said Tyme. "The denial will head for the one of us that it can relate to best. It's our job to accept, soothe, and nurture the denial until it feels cleansed enough to fuse with Lotus Blossom. Don't try to force anything. You will know the purification has happened by the spontaneous fusion that will occur between Lotus Blossom and the denial. If you cannot accomplish this cleansing, with what is clinging to you, ask the denial to wait for you in a space of convalescence, which we will create with our energy. Try to get the unresolved denial to wait in that space rather than retreating to the fourth dimension and agree on a word or thought connection so we can find it quickly. Then, when we emerge from meditation, we will share our collective experiences, especially our failures." Tyme smiled and it seemed as great and generous as Tiltoenay's smile. "I promise that in the sharing, we will find the answers to Lotus Blossom's unresolved denial."

Up front, this sounded easy, but Tyme was right, and Rugen and I were unprepared for what waited in the fourth dimension to destroy Lotus Blossom. We joined hands for a moment as Tiltoenay spoke in prayer. "Great Goddess of Love and Wealth, grant the blessing of a full life on this humble child."

I leaned toward Iris, who was sitting between Tyme and me and whispered, "If this mediation gets too scary for you, just give my hand a squeeze."

Then it began and I felt the concern of gods and goddess at our disposal and the shuttling of their collective energy around me. I waited alone in the meditative dark for something to happen. A vision started. I saw the old woman of Sutcay Tay. As she began running down the muddy path toward me, she changed into Lotus Blossom's grandmother. It was raining; it was always raining whenever this hag and I met. She ran down the same muddy road a dozen times without noticing me. I projected myself into the scene and stood in the middle of the road, waiting for the old woman's curiosity to arise. The pelting rain was annoying and I declared it should "stop!" My control extended only over my reality so, it still was raining everywhere except over my head. I struggled with all my might to limit our mutual space and then the old woman began running right through my body. It was so damn real that I could feel the cold clamminess of her filthy rags and the flabby flesh of her sagging skin as she brushed through me. She repeated this new compulsion a dozen times until my frustrating presence caused her to snarl, *get out of my way you arrogant fool!*

My persistence projected me into whatever illusion she created. Her illusions were all rather mundane: storms, wind, mud, and darkness. Finally, her game seemed too tedious to continue and I sat down on a rock and waited for her to race by a few more times. My sitting in the light and sunshine finally attracted her attention and she slowed down. Each time she whisked past, she ran slower until she stopped directly in front of me and put her hands on her hips. *Oh! I might have known it was you*, she said. *You are the arrogant son-of-a-bitch that sits in the light while I suffer in the rain.*

Why do you call me arrogant?

What else would I call you but arrogant?

Would you come and sit with me in the sunshine and tell me why you think I'm arrogant?

You and your arrogance should come and sit in the rain with me.

I got up off my rock and joined her in her rain. *Now what?* I asked.

Now your arrogance takes you down, she declared, and with that, she disappeared.

I feel different now, know I am different and I stare down as my hands spread out before me. They're small, a child's hands and dirt cakes under my fingernails. I finger my clothing and feel its threadbare vulnerability and my calloused bare feet. An excruciating pain in my head tells me I have a fever. My throat is raw with resignation and my guts rumble with cosmic emptiness.

An angry voice, half hidden in the darkness, comes out to destroy my world. Large rough hands, disembodied hands like mindless instruments, emerge from the dark and rip away my meager rags that dissolve like tissue paper. I am naked and shiver in fear and sickness; yet I see my clothing has not torn from around my neck. I still wear a yoke of rags dangling from my shoulders. The light comes up. Everything appears yellowish-green and with the greater light, I see the face behind the hands, the owner of the angry voice. The face is vile. Too terrified to scream or cry, I hold my breath. "You filthy little tramp! I will teach you not to disobey." It snatches my yoke of rags and pummels me with angry mitts. At first, the pain is sharp and then a blessed paralysis sets in. I cannot feel, yet a part of me knows my neck is broken and my child's jaw is broken too. Too weak to fight, the terror is on top of me, pinning me with diseased weight on my tiny chest. I cannot breathe, yet I can smell its revolting stink. I am choking, choking on vomit and germs from its terrible discharge. Then comes the death snap.

Only after the snap do I realize I am Sante again. My eyes open spontaneously like spring-loaded shutters and I desperately need to escape. I attempt to withdraw from the circle and Tiltoenay touches my arm telling me telepathically that I must stay. I bury my face in my hands so as not to disturb the others, but it is useless. I desperately need to breathe, to escape to some place clean. I jump up and bolt for the door, sure that if I do not get fresh air at that instant that I am going to suffocate.

****

Rugen found me outside in the garden. *Ce* startled me when *ce* touched my shoulder and I realized only then that a vertebra in my neck was dislocated. "My love, let me help you?" *ce* said. I was in an acute state of denial and unable to admit to even Rugen what happened. "Whatever it is; you know I'm on your side," *ce* said.

We went back inside and Iris asked, "What happened, Sante? I was just getting into the meditation when I saw the same old woman that I saw last night in my dream. Then I heard you making some kind of strange noise and I could not get any deeper."

"Give Sante a chance to catch *lis* breath," advised Tiltoenay.

"I need help," I said. "I have a serious block in my body that has dislocated a vertebra in my neck. I feel partially paralyzed on my left side."

"This could be serious," said Tiltoenay. "Let me suspended Lotus Blossom in the *vitarattha* so she will be out of the sphere of the negative energy. Rugen held me in *cis* arms while the others dragged the futon mattress back out in the sitting area so I could lie down. I did not want anyone except Rugen to touch me, so *ce* had to fix my neck by *cim*self. My neck made a loud snap as it went back into place. Even afterward, I was unable to sit up. I lay there and wept as I told them how the old woman had deceived me.

"Why did she persist in calling you arrogant?" asked Tyme.

"I don't know."

"You know!" insisted Tyme and he got very explicit with me. "Let me tell you something, Sante. I have done this kind of work for eons and never have I left The Consortium and gone out to disburse my light and come home with an infant in my arms. Now, tell us. Why did you take that child from the dead mother on your first excursion out for The Consortium?"

I finally managed to sit up. "Be careful of your neck," Rugen advised.

"Answer me!" demanded Tyme.

"The potential for life was there and I wanted to give it a chance to survive."

"At what cost?" Tyme demanded.

"I helped Sante bring the child to life," offered Tiltoenay.

"So did I," added Rugen.

"But who made the initial decision to save the child?"

I stared into Tyme's accusing face. "Me," I admitted.

His tone turned softer. "Why did you do it?"

"I've always wanted to have a child."

"It's just as I said. You took the child to serve yourself. Tell me Sante, how many times has your arrogance challenged death to get what you wanted?"

The answer was, "countless times." This wrestling with death was an old theme down through my lives; after all, I had been a doctor many times. I thought of Nova and realized that I had violated even my soul mate, not allowing *lim* to die when *le* wanted to go. Shame took me down into the truth and showed me how I had used my power to get what I wanted.

Rugen tried to soothe me, but Tyme said, "You must face every last bit of your denial before you can help Lotus Blossom. Our job is to heal through soothing, not to impose our needs on the weak and suffering."

Tiltoenay spoke up and her voice was a soothing balm compared to Tyme's. "What happened after you encountered the old woman?" she asked.

"Nothing," I said. The scene of the cancerous old man started to replay in my head and I knew Rugen, Tyme, and Tiltoenay could see everything that happened to me and it was useless to hide.

Rugen was my righteous defender. *Ce* was angry with Tyme and Tiltoenay saying, "You are supposed to be our mentors, to protect us. Why did you allow Sante's innocence to be beaten and raped by that filth?"

"Sante is responsible for what happened," Tyme returned.

"What happened?" asked Iris.

"Tell Iris the truth!" demanded Tyme. "Come down off your holier-than-thou pedestal and realize that you are an ancient spirit capable of great metaphysical powers; you were not only the child in your vision. You brought that horror up from the depths of the fourth dimension. Admit it! You cannot help anyone until you acknowledge the truth. You may be able to fool Rugen and Iris with your beautiful face, but you cannot fool Tiltoenay and me. Let me tell you something, Sante. You were that cancerous old man raping that child as well as the child."

"No!"

"You molested that child—admit it!"

"No!"

"Now I see it!" Iris said. She put her hands over her face. "My God! I see the whole thing."

"Say it!" said Tyme.

Rugen held me and I could not stop crying. I knew the truth, but it took several more minutes for me to confess my culpability aloud to the others. It was quiet in that room as they waited for me to admit, "I played both the abuser and the abused."

"Yes you did," agreed Tyme. "As do we all. We are one in the shadows as well as in the light. Our oneness does not cease because it gets difficult." Tyme leaned forward and patted me on the head as if were a dog. "Did you ask the denial to wait in the space of convalescence?"

"I'm sorry; I forgot. I didn't even remember who I was until I opened my eyes."

"It's okay," he said. "We'll find that denial again. The grotesque is always easy to spot. Anyway, Tiltoenay or I will go with you the next time."

"I have to know something," I said. "Was it real or merely a vision I conjured up to bring my denial out of hiding?"

"Sorry," said Tyme. "Your experience was about as real as this reality can handle. It needed to be real to awaken you to the full ugliness just beyond your conscious mind. Actually, you are very lucky. Think of the souls who incarnate here and live their whole lives playing out that drama. We are not involved in a game here. If we continue in our denial, that vision will become the experienced norm. Look at me, Sante." I stared into Tyme's eyes, into the eyes of truth. "Any enlightenment is false unless the individual can freely acknowledge and take full responsibility for the vilest horrors inside this creation."

TWENTY-ONE

Silence persisted among us and I began to wonder what happened to Rugen if my experience was so devastating. "It was terrible," Rugen admitted; "but it wasn't like Sante's experience at all."

"Tell us about it," said Tiltoenay.

Rugen shifted *cis* position a little and wrapped *cis* arms around *cis* knees in a protective gesture. I wanted to support *cim*, as *ce* did me, but could barely move with the physical pain in my shoulder and neck. "I did not get involved, as Sante did, in what was happening. I remained the witness to everything going on in my vision."

"Why do you think you remained the witness?" asked Tiltoenay.

"Maybe I was afraid to get involved."

"Perhaps," she granted. "Tell us, dear, what did you witness?"

"I was in the dark too and then suddenly I was standing in the middle of a vast emptiness that was stippled in shades of sepia. It's difficult to explain what it actually looked like because I was overwhelmed with a need to fill the emptiness with something familiar—houses or gardens, something beautiful and comforting."

"Were you able to do that?" asked Tiltoenay.

"No. The emptiness persisted and with all my skills in meditative visualization, I could not make the familiar take hold. It was as if I was attempting to paint a picture on a slick canvas where everything kept sliding off."

"So what did it feel like in the middle of your emptiness?"

Rugen did not answer right away. *Ce* thought about it, digging deeper inside *cim*self for the truth. "I was exposed and had no protection. I felt abandoned as if fate left me there and only I could turn it around and make the situation better. Nobody was going to come and rescue me. All I had were my wits. Then I saw a horizon tinged with red and knew it was dawn. I thought, 'Red sky in the morning, sailors take warning.' Then a vast collection of children came pouring over the red horizon. Millions upon millions of them came toward me, until they seemed as copious as stars. At first, I thought, this is not real. Then I reasoned—they're so faraway I'll finish this meditation before they ever reach me."

"What was your fear in them reaching you?" asked Tyme.

Rugen glanced up. "That they would overcome me with their need."

Tiltoenay leaned closer to Rugen and asked, "Who was whispering in your ear?"

"It claimed that it was an advisor, but I did not believe it. I had no empathy with it."

"What did the adviser recommend?" she asked.

"It's shameful. The advisor said, 'They are not children. They are the shiftless and infected with their culture of poverty and dependence. They are deadbeats, criminals; they are the demons climbing out of the holocaust of our future'"

"What else?" Tiltoenay asked.

"There wasn't anything else. I was filled with an urgent need to escape and that time was running out."

"That's pretty damn bleak," said Tyme. "You two know how to go to the bottom line." A dreadful silence sat among us for several seconds and I wondered if Rugen and I were about to become Consortium dropouts.

"Did you ask the voice to wait for you in the dimension of convalescence?" asked Tiltoenay.

"Yes," said Rugen. "We decided on the password, 'cohort.' Aren't you going to scrutinize my behavior as you did with Sante?" questioned Rugen.

"What for?" asked Tyme. "You're the Janaforma whiz kid. You don't need me to tell you that your denial is so cowardly that it had to step outside you and whisper in your ear."

"I do not believe that whispering voice," said Rugen. "I know it was wrong."

"Of course you do," said Tiltoenay. "You are an honorable soul. Both you and Sante are honorable souls. That's why we're here to help you. Your problem is no different than many others. You've been in the light for so long that the darkness within you has taken you by surprise. However, you need to know the potential demons, which you carry around inside you. Believe me, you have no reason for fear and panic because together, we will face your denial and put things right for Lotus Blossom's sake."

"Understand this," added Tyme. "The denial that arose within each of you highlights conjunction points between you and Lotus Blossom. These difficulties may not have presented themselves to you for many more lifetimes without her contribution. These issues represent her physical reality, what she suffers each time she is born."

"Holy Mother!" said Rugen. "Lotus Blossom is carrying these horrible realities inside her?"

"That's why Tyme and I told you that it was going to be difficult to help her," said Tiltoenay. "Lotus Blossom did not become a soul fragment in one lost lifetime. She is the incarnation of centuries of denial and abuse."

Iris demanded of Tyme, "So what happened in your meditation?"

"Yes dear," said Tiltoenay. "Please, tell us what happened to you so that these fine young souls can feel better about themselves."

Tyme cleared his voice and sat up straighter. He looked then as I first saw him with those heavy chains wrapped around him on Mallory Dock. "I approached the darkness exactly as the rest of you did only I felt great anger within myself. I would call it cosmic anger, the kind of anger that causes gods to destroy worlds."

"That has always been your special problem," said Tiltoenay sweetly. "Are you sure you were connecting with the proper conjunction points in Lotus Blossom."

"I went into the meditation using her name as a mantra and I felt her anger and my anger come together as a perfect storm. Anyway, I saw the whole thing just as I always do when I do these types of meditations. I saw creation from the beginning of time to the end spread out like a great rolling ocean with my consciousness trying to stay afloat in the indifference. I saw the chains of my karmic impulses pulling me down. Great turbulence attempted to take me under and I fought my anger with nothing but a speck of love inside me. I had no choice, just as I never have a choice, so I allowed the water to swallow me. The action began to grind me up as the churning of the sea pulverizes shells into common sand. In the grinding, I did feel the love of the ocean, its great peace infusing me and I knew my commonality with all other grains of sand. In those moments of surrender, the choice finally came and the God of Indifference gave me the honor of bestowing my love in any direction I chose. I gave all my love to Lotus Blossom and her future and was filled with great peace."

"That's wonderful!" said Tiltoenay. "I think we are making real progress. Now, please allow me to tell you my meditation experience." Tiltoenay leaned in closer and almost whispered. "In the darkness, I found myself sitting inside a seed. By will alone, I burst forth and found that I was not one, but many. I was as common as dust and as extravagant as the seeds of a dandelion. As always, my inclination was to fall prey to a type of beautiful nostalgia, so much so that I wept for the passing of every single form. Then, as always, I attempted to nurture each one, to preserve each moment, but found I could not because I am mere emptiness. In my confusion and love, I decided that I needed to choose. I was able to choose because remembering that I am Tiltoenay, I was able to will my dissolution for a greater purpose. There in the chaos, I chose Lotus Blossom and took her to my breast with great love."

"That's it?" asked Iris.

Tiltoenay appeared startled. "What more could there be?"

"It sounds as if you are wallowing in some self-denial yourself."

"Why do you say such a thing?" asked Tiltoenay.

"It sounds like too much sweetness and perfect surrender. Where was your struggle? You did not suffer like Sante or Rugen."

"I did suffer," said Tiltoenay. "I have been suffering for eons; I simply do not mention it anymore."

Tyme put his hand on Iris' shoulder before asking, "When you began this mediation, where did you find yourself?"

"In the middle of the road, just like Sante."

"Why do you think you could progress no farther?"

"Take it easy on her," I warned Tyme.

He gave me a quick glance and went right back to Iris. "Why was your vision analogous to Sante's?"

"Why don't you tell me," she snapped. "You and Tiltoenay seem to be the evolved experts around here."

"Your energy vibrations match Sante's vibrations," said Tyme. "You are a love emanation exactly as he is. Think about it, Iris. There's only one reason your meditation went no farther and that's because Sante absorbed the sting for you."

"I did not consciously do that," I said.

Tyme shrugged. "Iris, what did Sante whisper to you just as we began this meditation?"

"Sante told me that if the mediation became too scary all I needed to do was squeeze his hand."

"Did you squeeze Sante's hand?" asked Tiltoenay.

"I don't remember," said Iris.

"Neither do I," I added.

"Have it your own way," said Tyme. "I stick to my original statement. Sante absorbed the sting of the meditation for you. You felt nothing and *le* felt everything; *le* took the full impact of your denial, Lotus Blossom's denial, along with *lis* own. The pattern is clear in these types of mediations. Love emanations are going to experience the full spectrum of love's possibilities and that includes all perversions of love's possibilities. That will continue to happen until their love flows clear and without impediment."

"What about understanding creations?" Rugen asked.

"Sorry," said Tyme. "I did not mean to leave you out of the equation. Your denial is going to be the intellectualization of suffering."

Ezek grabbed me by the throat and swore that he was going to eat my heart, unless I spoke up for love. I had no idea what I was going to say, but Rugen would tell me later that my facial expression was one of defiance. "I no longer believe in the division of incarnate purpose," I said. "It may be a way to understand personal motivation, but it does not explain our fundamental natures. Tyme, your personal meditation comes off sounding like something a will emanation might experience; but your surrender was a climax into none other than love. Tiltoenay, your meditation sounds as if you are a goddess, but your nurturing was an act of personal love for something you favored over all creation, which is Lotus Blossom. We are all love emanations because our souls know that will and understanding are trifling compared to the power of love. We could sit here forever and we would find that the only thing that can ever embrace the glory of love is Truth. My own personal god bows down before love. I know Rugen. We are intimate lovers and I tell you *cis* love equals mine in all things. Rugen often flabbergasts me with *cis* commitment to the highest aspects of love."

"Okay!" declared Tiltoenay, and she applauded Ezek's little speech. Her applause seemed to mock me and I felt embarrassed. "This time we have a live one on the hook," she said.

I apologized. "I did not mean to sound pedantic."

"It's all right," said Tyme. "We're here to learn from you too."

Tiltoenay added, "Perhaps the most honest thing we can say is that the refined self reflects all aspects of incarnate purpose with equal clarity."

"That sounds right," I conceded.

It was only 11:30 in the morning and I already felt as if this was turning into one of the longest days of my life. The five of us took a break and decided that it was appropriate to eat lunch. I was in terrible physical shape, despite the fact that I felt obliged to speak up for the sovereignty of Love. My shoulder and chest ached; and I could barely move my left arm. Rugen searched our refrigerator and took stock of our dry foods and we could not figure out how to put any of these foodstuffs together to make lunch for five people.

"Let's order out," suggested Tiltoenay. "It will be much simpler."

Tyme and Iris immediately decided that they wanted to introduce Rugen and I to Earth food. In our cruising around Key West, Rugen and I saw advertisements for pizza. We knew it was a popular Earth food, but had not tried it. While Tiltoenay nursed Lotus Blossom, Iris called a pizzeria around the corner called *Viva La Pizza*. She ordered two large pies with mushrooms, black olives, spinach, broccoli and three kinds of cheese. About a half-hour later, someone brought the pizzas to our door. They were still red hot because the delivery person brought them sealed inside insulated bags. I must confess that I was impressed. We never thought of this innovation on *The Mother*, having hot food brought directly to our front doors. The luxury was not cheap. The two pizzas cost nearly forty dollars.

Tyme advised us to eat lightly because he wanted us to do another meditation as soon as we finished eating. "We can't let that old woman get too far away," he winked at me.

"I agree," said Tiltoenay. "She is one of the major keys to this whole situation for Lotus Blossom."

"I don't mean to seem ungrateful," I said. "But I'm exhausted and my powers of concentrations are starting to wane. I don't know if I can do another meditation so soon."

"Be brave," advised Tyme. "You can rest tomorrow."

****

For the morning meditation, Rugen and I had dragged the futon mattress into our *neipanin* because we considered the space sanctified. We had cleansed the room in special ways according to Janaforma tradition. Tiltoenay insisted that one space was as sacred as the next; and on a greater level, we realized that she was right. The afternoon meditation we conducted in our sitting area where there was more room, light, and air.

Lotus Blossom was holding up well and I was beginning to think she was the best infant in all creation. She never cried, nursed patiently, and managed to look radiantly beautiful as she slept. Again, we placed her in the center of the futon and the five of us sat around her in a closed circle. Tiltoenay was sitting to my left and she leaned closer and whispered in my ear. "Don't be afraid, Sante. I am going with you this time."

"I'm with you too," said several of my internal voices.

This time out, I felt intrepid and knew my immortal connections. "I have some ideas that I want to explore," I explained. "Don't interfere unless I ask you to—okay?"

Tiltoenay promised to stay in the background and to come forth only if I needed her help. I faced the darkness again and waited. *The energy came and again I was standing in the middle of the road with the rain pouring down upon my head. Here she comes, I think. Then sure enough, the old woman comes running down the road toward me.*

"Back again so soon?" she asked as she breezed past me at full tilt.

I start running with her and am amazed that one so old and feeble cam run so fast. "May I run alongside you?" I ask.

"You've been running alongside me for eons and only now has it occurred to you to ask my permission. Do you usually live this way, ass-backwards?

"I want to talk."

She stopped dead in her tracks and faced me. "After all these centuries of me begging for your attention, now you want to talk?"

This was the closest I had been to her while she was standing still and more light was upon the scene than ever before. She was much shorter than I was, thin and haggard. Grimy dirt filled the creases of her face and she appeared to be one of the most neglected creatures I ever encountered. I wanted to take pity upon her, but none came up from my depths. *I had plenty of disgust and repulsion in me, yet I pushed onward knowing what I needed to do. "This time, let's face each other in complete honesty," I said.*

"Okay," she said. "You can start by telling me how you like being raped by the cancer of time?"

"I did not like it any better than you did."

"Good! Maybe we do have something in common." She stared at me—hard.

"I'm your mirror as you are mine," I assured her.

"I'm old, neglected, and doomed and you are beautiful and filled with light,"
I promised, "I can make you as light-filled as I am."

"How?"

"If we embrace in complete love, we will become one and you will share my reality from this moment forward."

"You have that kind of power?"

"I do. I've heard of late that I am an ancient spirit capable of great metaphysical powers."

"I don't sleep around. I may be old and ugly, but I have my pride."

"Would you sleep with Love?"

"I would if I believed Love were real."

"Know yourself in me." I held out my arms and embraced her. It was so completely easy that it was incredible. No other words were necessary between us. We embraced and I felt her come into me and become me. We were one. The child and the old man did not manifest and I came out of the meditation and cried some more. The old woman did not heal instantly. She had been too long lingering in neglect. Over the next few weeks, every time I glanced sideways in the mirror I could see her lurking out of me as one of my shadows.

****

Rugen had no clue about how to handle *cis* denial the second time. I offered to accompany *cim* into *cis* "vast emptiness" where children poured over the horizon and *ce* insisted that I should not strain myself anymore that day. Tyme and Tiltoenay agreed that I needed to rest. I was too exhausted to argue so I went and sat at the table while the rest of them closed the gap around Lotus Blossom.

Despite my exhaustion, it was difficult not to get Ezek involved. The four of them sat there in silence for almost forty minutes. Then Rugen broke *cis* pose and rubbed *cis* face and hands and turned around so *ce* could stretch *cis* legs as *ce* often did after meditation.

Iris said, "You were great, Rugen! I was there and saw the whole thing. Thank you," she told Tyme and Tiltoenay. "Thank you for including me this time." Iris looked and sounded different. Her face was relaxed and when she said, "Rugen," and "thank you," her voice gushed with goodwill.

"Don't thank us," said Tyme. "You were present by your own authority."

"Tell me everything," I said.

"There is not much to tell," said Rugen. "The children came pouring over the horizon and, again, the voice came and whispered in my ear; only this time, Tyme was whispering in my other ear, telling me that I had the internal resources to make the situation right and that everything was going to be okay. I decided to allow the children to descend upon me. They came down a rise—thousands and thousands surrounding me, pressing in on me with their demands. They wanted things, told me their needs and despite the fact that the last time I could not manifest anything, now I was able to do certain things to help."

"Like what?" I asked.

"I seemed to be able to manifest whatever they wanted simply with the power of my mind."

"What did you manifest?"

"Nothing elaborate. They were hungry and they wanted bread, so I gave them bread."

Tiltoenay leaned over and gave Rugen a big kiss on the cheek. "Iris is right," she said. "You were great!"

****

It was after two o'clock in the afternoon when they finished Rugen's meditation. Tyme said he needed time to prepare for his act on Mallory Dock, but would return the following morning to escort us to The Consortium; Tiltoenay promised to return to nurse Lotus Blossom whenever needed. As soon as they left, Iris said, "It's been a long day; I need to shove off too."

Rugen was holding Lotus Blossom in *cis* arms and light streamed through the corner windows and illuminated their faces. Memory took another indelible picture of Rugen holding our new child. No matter how time might change them, I wanted to remember them like this—Rugen; blonde, spirited, and heroically handsome; Lotus Blossom; tiny, fragile, with little tufts of dark hair sticking straight up from her head.

Rugen attempted to change Iris' mind about leaving by using a few innocent consort lures. Every Janaforma consort has an innate gift for seduction, which has nothing to do with affectation. The way the faculty exhibits itself is highly personal in each consort; but when the will to connect arises in a consort, *cis* demeanor will change in characteristic ways. The expression on *cis* face will instinctively know how to ooze with sensuality until *cis* aura charges up with exuberant light. Rugen's sense of dignity usually suppressed *cis* consort moods in all but our most private trysts; however, the expression on *cis* face, at that moment, was definitely something out of one of our sleeproom scenes. "Please reconsider," *ce* pleaded with Iris. "I was hoping I might have the pleasure of finding you here when I arrived home tonight. We've made great strides in the last few days. Am I being too presumptuous to imagine a small celebration might be in order?" Despite Rugen's urging, Iris began glancing toward the door.

"What kind of celebration did you have in mind?" she asked.

Rugen turned up the heat a few degrees. "Whatever you think is appropriate. Janaforma celebrations usually feature happy feelings of Community, special foods, singing, dancing, and even romance. We own few material possessions in this time, but are rich in spirit; and, this is Lotus Blossom's actual birthday. What do you say, Iris? We're eager to learn and share in your honored traditions."

Iris began to look stoical and a faraway expression clouded her face. "We did not mean to pressure you," I assured her. "Rugen merely is asking if there's something special that you like to do for fun. Now that the truth is out between us, we have a real opportunity to get to know each other on a more intimate level."

Iris' shoulders pulled forward and her chin dropped. Then out of her dark insecurities came this ridiculous thought marching right into her conscious mind. *They're perfect and I'm too fat. I'll need to lose at least five pounds before I can let them see me naked.*

Rugen's zeal for making a connection with Iris was greater than *cis* etiquette over the fact that *ce* was able to read her thoughts and *ce* said, "Sante and I don't give two hoots about the extra five pounds on your hips."

Iris shut down even more. "I consider it an invasion of my privacy for you to be constantly reading my mind." Rugen apologized and explained that *ce* could not help it when her inner voice was shouting in *cis* ears. The shouting was from her ego that was getting loud and obvious as a brass band. Her ego was responding by acting tyrannical and stingy in the pleasure it would allow her to enjoy. Rugen and I were about to discover that Iris was one of the most variable individuals we would ever encounter. We could not reason with her, second-guess her, flatter her, humor her, or pacify her. She was stubborn and proud of it, as if the trait were an asset instead of a liability. Once she made up her mind, her thinking always became entrenched. When we thought she was going to be tender, she would become resolute and even nasty. When we assumed that she was going to be inflexible, she would turn charming and innocent as a small child. No wonder she had chewed up a novice like Evose.

Her voice was shrill now. "You both are acting as if all this sex stuff is easy. Well, it is not easy for me. My religion says it's wrong to sleep with two men at once; anyway, Rugen is—young and I am almost thirty (she was thirty-five)."

Wait until she takes Regression and remembers her life as a temple prostitute, Rugen thought. "What's your religion?" *ce* asked.

"I don't follow any religion, not anymore, but I got Catholic programming still in my head. The problem is—well, I'm unsure what my problem is, but something feels weird about this situation. Too many unanswered questions are still bothering me."

Bless Rugen. *Ce* was steady with determination. "We're always going to encounter unanswered questions," *ce* said. "Unanswered questions still exist between Sante and me. If you need more time to decide whether you want to take a chance with us, we'll try to understand. We arrived early and have the luxury of a few weeks; but time is never going to change the fact that we are different physical ages. If you're concerned about your physical appearance, I already find you attractive. I think you could be beautiful if you relaxed and embraced your own sexuality. If you're worried about us judging you in a superficial ways, it's not going to happen. I don't know what intimate experiences you've experienced thus far, but I guarantee, intimacy with a Janaforma consort and lifegiver will be different."

"Sante has hinted that you are different, but how different are you?"

Rugen looked at me and I communicated, *she doesn't want a philosophical explanation concerning transcendent states that occur during passion; she wants nuts-and-bolts. She wants to see our genitals. Do you want to be the explainer or the one to take off your pants?*

Rugen started toying with *cis* hair in sexual frustration. "I'll keep it simple," *ce* said with determination. "As you already know, the Janaforma have three sexes, a lifebearer, a lifegiver, and a consort. Sante is a lifegiver and the closest Janaforma sex to a male while the lifebearer is the closest Janaforma sex to a female. I'm a consort, a true hermaphrodite."

"You poor thing," Iris said.

"I'm not an accident," Rugen said. "I'm a genetically engineered miracle. Sante and I can enjoy sex is innumerable ways, just as Humans do; however, for natural conception to occur, it's a bit more tricky for us."

"How tricky?" she asked.

Rugen gave me a quick look of desperation, so I decided to jump in and help. "It's takes timing and coordination and three sexually aroused Janaforma to complete the act. I must penetrate Rugen through *cis abiltona*, which is similar to your vagina and located just below *cis* penis. When I experience an orgasm inside *cis abiltona*, it triggers an orgasm in Rugen that carries active sperm into the lifebearer. It varies, but usually we have only a short time to get the viable sperm into the lifebearer. Once the Janaforma obtained Simon Forma's genetic records, we knew that the highest success rate for triads attempting to reproduce naturally was for the lifegiver and consort to penetrate the lifebearer at the same time."

"That certainly doesn't sound natural to me," said Iris. "Plus I still don't understand how you are different."

Rugen managed to appear confused and perturbed at the same time. *I told you so*, I communicated to *cim* and now I was hot to prove my point.

"Iris, I'm prepared to disrobe for your inspection if you would like to see my genitals."

Her eyes dilated and her face flushed red. She put her hands up and said, "Stop. This conversation is definitely getting out of control."

"I thought it was finally getting interesting," said Rugen. "Sante and I understand that complete intimacy takes time. Our emotional closeness could begin with simply agreeing to be in each other's presence in a mindful way. We could immerse ourselves in a mood of generosity—some simple embracing."

Iris appeared relieved and her shoulders relaxed. "I still need to go. Miranda and Meyou need dinner and then I must go down to Mallory Dock so I can attempt to earn my rent money for this month. I'm not rich like you are in the future; I have to work."

Rugen ignored her dig and told her, "If you need money, we will help you pay your rent."

Our interactions turned stranger and Iris became annoyed over the suggestion that we wanted to help her financially. "Let's get something straight. I pay my own way wherever I go. I know what happens to women when they depend on men. When a woman lets down her guard, a man steps in with a bunch of phony sweet-talk and the first thing a woman finds is she is barefoot, pregnant, and stuck. You asked me before about my honored traditions; well, my honored tradition is I never ask a man for one red dime."

"We have no desire to abridge your independence," said Rugen. "We want to help you toward greater independence."

Her voice took on an impatient edge and her ego clamped down harder. The harder her ego clamped, the more desperate and illogical her assertions became. It was as if her ego was hiding in a bunker and popped up every few seconds with a grenade it needed to throw. Since Rugen and I refused definition as men, her argument made an erratic jump and she began attacking extra-terrestrials. "I'm not one of these nut cases waiting around for extra-terrestrials to land so they can solve all my problems. You know why? Extra-terrestrials are not Human and never will be Human. Extra-terrestrials know nothing about the Human experience."

"People on other planets and other times contend with the same core issues that you endure here," I said. "We may be extra-terrestrials, but since we've arrived, we've attempted to live as Humans of this time. It really does not matter who you are, life can be difficult."

"Baloney! You've been here less than three weeks and have jobs, a beautiful baby, and spiritual mentors. You're genetically engineered beings with all the answers. Well, hip, hip, hooray for you! You don't understand my life or me and you can't make my pain go away with a few kind words. I'm like that old woman in the meditation. I refuse to be appeased with a simple embrace. I'm a Human being, not one of your goddamn soul fragments that you can absorb with a hug. For years I've suffered here and I am not going to say—so what! Forget it! Let's have a sex party!"

Rugen sighed again. "Why to you take everything we say down to its lowest common denominator?"

She could not answer *cim* so her mind made another dodge and this time she went all the way back to her childhood. "For your information, while you were soaking in your familial bliss, my childhood was bleak, morose, and rootless. When I was seven years old, one of my father's musician friends molested me. My father was a small-minded man with crazy dreams who never got beyond the struggling musician stage. His ambitions, for what he called 'the easy life,' destroyed my mother's life. He got her pregnant when she was sixteen and she dropped out of high school and followed him around Jersey and Pennsylvania so he could act like a hotshot musician for the next twenty years of their lives. After a while, my mother took a job working in a factory— assembling toys for other people's children, toys she could not afford to buy for me. She worked in that fucking factory for twenty years until it moved to China. When I was seventeen, she got breast cancer and had a nervous breakdown all at the same time while my father worked sporadically. After her breakdown, she actually considered herself fortunate to get a job as a daycare worker with children. Just when it seemed everything might be okay in their lives, they both died in that damn automobile accident."

Rugen patted Iris on the shoulder before telling her, "Good or bad, you should be grateful that you had a chance to know your physical parents. They held a universe of unique knowledge, which you had a chance to observe and weigh against your own inner truths. I lost my biological parents when I was a mere five weeks old and have no conscious memory of them, yet I still miss them and sometimes wonder what they might do when I'm stuck for answers. My adoptive parents are exceptionally good parents and I always feel lucky that they are part of my life. They have encouraged me to define and refine my own dream; to live my life with intention and to remake myself anytime I choose. That's why I can tell you—if you don't like who you are, change yourself."

"My father believed my psychic abilities came from the devil. The pious child-molester, Father Mahoney, was advising Dad that I should undergo exorcism to get rid of my demons while Mom was telling me to keep my psychic abilities under wraps because they would lead me astray."

"When did you realize you were psychic?" I asked.

"I knew early that I was different. By the time that I was thirteen, my psychic abilities were nearly out of control. In the place where you come from, people might honor psychic insight, but not here. Most people laugh at us and think of us as tricksters and devil worshipers. I can't get an ordinary job by putting down on my resume that I am psychic; people would laugh. How would you feel if you knew your greatest gift was a joke to the rest of society?"

"Psychic skills are special connections to our oversoul and in the future, we do not use them for employment," said Rugen.

"Then you must think my tarot reading is a perversion of my psychic talents."

"I didn't say that—"

"But you were thinking it—weren't you?"

"No! I wasn't thinking it," said Rugen. "Perhaps your psychic abilities are not as good as you believe if you are misconstruing my honest intentions."

"It doesn't matter," she said. "You don't need to worry about me perverting my psychic skills because they've vanished."

"Your psychic skills will return," I said. "They always return. Mine often seem to disappear. Psychic skills sense our confusion and become our envoys into the unknown. There, they attempt to assemble fresh clues to help us toward greater evolution."

"Maybe you feel secure about your psychic talents. After all, you're a famous writer in the future. Who am I? I'm a nobody." She started to sob.

"What about your common sense?" Rugen questioned. "When we first met you down on Mallory Dock, you told us that you were replete with common sense. I rely on my common sense above any psychic abilities Sante sends my way."

"You don't understand," she sobbed. "I relied on my psychic abilities to read tarot for people. The cards were merely my facilitators. If my skills never come back, how am I supposed to survive?"

Rugen went completely spontaneous with, "How would you like to return to the future with us?"

I haven't agreed to that possibility, I shot *cis* way.

Rugen's suggestion trumped Iris and she quieted down considerably. She sniffed and sobbed for a few seconds. "I thought you were committed to staying here."

"Quite the opposite," said Rugen. "We're committed to going home. Sante can't hide *lis* Gathosian eyes for the rest of *lis* life."

She glanced toward the door again. "I still need to go. I have to feed my cats."

Personally, I was ready to give up, at least for the time being. "Go!" I said. "We'll be here if you need us for anything at all." Rugen made sure her wrisceptor was working, so with nothing more than a stingy little hug for each of us, she scooted out the door and left us behind.

"Will you please do me one favor, Rugen? The next time Iris says she needs to go, let her go. And why did you suggest that we might take her with us when we leave? We don't understand the ramifications of doing that yet."

"I apologize," *ce* said. "We should have discussed it first. I thought if we could get her out of this barbaric time, then we might have a chance to change her mind. We can't leave her here. You know I'm right."

"Let's give her a day or two to think our proposal over."

Rugen leaned against the inside of the door and said, "Iris sure is nothing like Hibernia. She was always there for us. She was my lover, my teacher, even my *mebr*, whatever I needed, she miraculously became."

"I'm sorry, Rugen. I know it's difficult to think of connecting with Iris after spending a whole lifetime with someone as rich and warm as Hibernia."

"I probably should not try to compare them," *ce* said. "I choose to believe that Iris is going to be all right. Subjecting her to all this fourth dimensional denial, so soon, is making her slightly crazy."

"You're right, Rugen. Iris was completely normal when we first met her."

The comforting image of Hibernia lingered in our joined minds. I realized then what an art it was for any incarnation to keep its soul intact. As the day progressed, more images of Hibernia drifted through Rugen's mind. *The three of us were very hot together*, *ce* thought. "How did Rumi phrase it in the poem Iris tucked away in her jewelry box?"

I repeated the end of Rumi's poem. "'One of us kneels to kiss the threshold. One drinks, with wine-flames over his face. One watches the gathering and says to any cold onlookers, I am filled with you. Skin, blood, bone, brain, and soul. There's no room for lack of trust, or trust. Nothing in this existence but that existence.'"

****

As time approached for Rugen to leave for work, a new mood overtook me. I felt anxious and knew I did not want to be alone. "Aren't you too tired to go to work?" I asked *cim*. "We were up since before dawn again."

Rugen assured me, "I'm fine. Does your shoulder and neck still hurt?"

"A little."

"Meditation is a rough sport," *ce* smiled. "Why don't you go to bed early and try to get some rest? You don't need to wait up tonight."

"No, I intend to wait up every night with my wrisceptor on full alert."

"Nothing is going to happen to me, my love. The Consortium has tamed all the Cerribeame in this time."

"I could never sleep unless I have you wrapped safely in my arms." Before Rugen walked out the door, I insisted that we indulge in a prolonged kiss. "I have to go; I don't want to be late," *ce* said breaking away.

After *ce* was gone, a fresh past-life memory returned and I knew the Regression drug was still doing its work inside me too. After all these weeks, it was still peeling back my resistance to deeply suppressed memories. I saw myself sleeping next to Hibernia. She woke me, told me that Cle was late, and wanted me to get up and search for *cim*. Bleary eyed, I struggled out of bed and threw on some clothing before combing the entire building complex, in which we lived. Hibernia got up and helped me search. It took us about an hour to find the first horrible evidence that something had happened to Cle. We found *cis* burned-off hair in a trashcan in the hairdressing salon in the lobby. The Cerribeame, in their utter savagery, had left *cis* hair for us to find, as if to brag that they kidnapped Cle from under our noses. The events of that long ago Aeternus cycle still carried a potent sting. The memory whipped up greater agitation inside me. I fought an urge to go to Hideaways and make sure Rugen was safe. I signaled *cim* on *cis* wrisceptor and it took *cim* ninety seconds to answer because *ce* needed to find a private spot so *ce* could talk. "Are you okay?" I asked.

"I'm fine," *ce* whispered. "What's the matter, love?"

"Nothing's wrong; I miss you. Hurry home."

"I'll be home around 12:30," *ce* promised.

Just like Rugen, I carried guilt over Cle's demise. Mine was for my lack of vigilance and allowing the Cerribeame the opportunity to swoop down and kidnap *cim* from the very building in which we lived. My agitation seemed to increase and it felt like a scribbling hand, an uncontrollable impetus to eradicate the past and change what already was. I was aware of my karmic twists, yet I did not know how to reconcile what happened with who I was now. My natural impulse was to act as a rescuer and when my rescuing fell short, I fractured into guilt, shame, and greater vigilance, which caused me to become more controlling. A deluge of questions poured into my mind. Chief among them was why The Consortium was righteous in their plans to change the future, but I was arrogant in my wishes to accomplish the same deed. What was the difference? I could not answer my question so I resolved to ask Tyme the next time I saw him.

Again, I wanted to call Rugen. Instead, I went and plucked Lotus Blossom from her *vitarattha* and held her in my arms. Merely holding her brought me calm. She was beyond beautiful to me; she was gorgeous. How all this beauty could be brought forth from poverty, despair, and death was beyond common comprehension. I held her infant fragility in my arms and the two of us declared together that genetic engineering was a silly pomposity that scientists invented in the future, a rational that we were improving our collective species. Genetic manipulation was doing nothing more than changing the vehicle and making it more cumbersome for souls to be born. Another deluge of unanswerable questions poured forth from my curious brain. All these questions were frazzled coils spoiling the picture of who I thought I was. Why had Simon Forma split the masculine in two and created a consort and a lifegiver? Janaforma reproduction was clumsy compared to direct Human methods of reproduction. With all the genetic manipulation my parents employed in my creation, how was I better than Lotus Blossom? If I was better, it was only because my parents loved me totally and fostered my potential with loving-kindness.

As Lotus Blossom lay nestled in my arms, she was an epiphany for me. Rugen and I loved her and would give her every advantage. Her potential for greatness would be equal to anyone who ever lived. The only obstacle standing between Lotus Blossom and her fulfillment was the part of her still cowering in the darkness of denial.

My fondness for spontaneous ritual wanted to make this special moment into a ceremony, so I took her into the *neipanin* and lit two candles, one for her biological mother and one for Lotus Blossom herself. "I dedicate my life to the fulfillment of your potential," I whispered to her. I told her a secret. "You know what my infant wonder? I'm psychic and can sense that not only are you going to be the smartest child who ever lived, but you are going to be the most beautiful child who ever lived too."

I sat on the floor in a meditative posture with her body across my lap. Holding her tiny head in the palm of my hand, I gave her my complete love in the form of energy. She opened her eyes, but was unable to focus on my face. "You are a complete miracle," I whispered to her. "You can hear me—can't you?" I held her against my heart so she could feel its beating and I could synchronize my rhythm to hers. I told her things, knowing her greater consciousness could hear. *Let us be Now in this stillness together. We can sit inside alien chaos, our Buddha nature seeking the preeminence of a forgotten home. We have passed through unknowable darkness, not knowing how we arrived with nothing but questions pursed upon our lips. So far from home, what can we know of this place or ourselves? Who will share our vision and be our intimates?*

Nova spoke clearly through the black diamond *le* left inside me. *Life is a gift. Gifts are for opening, sharing, and remembering. Open your gifts so this child might see that she is truly blessed. Give her your treasures of love and your rich legacy of intricate passion. Prove to her that she is an honored guest at a banquet prepared expressly for her. Demonstrate how to love from inside direct experience and how to fuel the flame inside her heart. Show her these experiences are precious and sacred and that our gods travel with us. Let her know that love is active and effusive, that it dances and leaps for joy, can move in unexpected ways, and can soak her in ecstatic bliss. Show her that love is ruthless, forever curious, and that passion loves truth above all else. Give her the tools to connect with truth in the most empathic way she can. Explain that to connect with truth empathetically is to connect with it on every level of consciousness, from the sub-atomic level to the stillness at The Source. Do all that my love and Lotus Blossom will fulfill herself.*

TWENTY-TWO

I was floating when I felt a gentle feminine hand on my shoulder. At first, it felt like a nudge, a reminder of Elay when she woke me from meditation in the garden. I opened my eyes and saw the beautiful blue face of Tiltoenay. "Is it Lotus Blossom's feeding time?" I asked.

She blinked, her eyes nodding "yes" and she sat down on the floor and rested her back against the wall. I glanced at the wrisceptor on my arm and it was 10:00 o'clock. "It would be nice if you and Rugen could manage to get a few more pieces of furniture," she said.

"Janaforma usually do not put furniture in a *neipanin*. Would you care to go out to the other room and sit on the futon?"

"I like the energy in this room, although it's hot," and she casually slipped off her red tee shirt that said, "Motherhood Ain't For Sissies," and tossed it on the floor.

She sat before me naked from the waist up. In the candlelight, her full ripe breasts glowed like two luminous eggplants and refused to be ignored. She extended her arms to take the sleeping Lotus Blossom and after handing her over, I had the notion to be helpful. I retrieved a cushion and attempted to tuck it under Tiltoenay's right elbow so she would be more comfortable. As I was doing this, my hand brushed the side of her breast. In stark reaction to our physical contact, I became so hot that beads of sweat formed across my forehead. It happened so quickly that I could not think, was afraid to think, and frankly, did not want to think.

"You're right; it's hot in here," I said. "I hate to run the air coolers because they're noisy." Tiltoenay said nothing; she already was involved in nursing Lotus Blossom. "I'll go turn them on and cool the place down." As I closed the windows out in the sitting area, I began to feel strange and attempted to take several breaths of fresh air to ground myself. Where was Ezek to advise me? He was unusually quiet and I was alone. I peeked around the doorjamb of the *neipanin* and whispered, "While you're nursing Lotus Blossom, I'm going to wash the dirty dishes in the kitchen sink."

"Don't go," said Tiltoenay. "Come, sit with me and we'll talk." Her greater will seemed to glue me to the spot. "Does your shoulder and neck still hurt?"

I touched my left shoulder with my hand. "It's feels much better, thank you."

"Come, sit, I want to talk to you." This time it sounded like a command. "When I'm finished feeling Lotus Blossom I'll do some energy work on you, that is if you don't mind me touching you."

"Why do you think I would have an objection to you touching me?"

"You didn't want anyone but Rugen to touch you this morning."

"This morning I felt vulnerable."

"If you would have let me touch you, you would not be standing there now all confused about me and my godly powers."

My strange feeling turned stranger. "You definitely have powers I do not understand. You seem able to slip from the shackles of your physicality with ease. I can't do that, at least not yet. Rugen tells me some Vanguard Scouts are learning to negotiate the microfibers of the time threads and can use this knowledge to move beyond the range of normal physical vision. If that's true, then your powers are not so godly, but a learned skill that we'll all be doing in time. You, however, intrigue me on many, many levels. I know you possess knowledge I've longed for, but I will not compromise my integrity to get it."

"The Janaforma call the sex act connecting—don't they?"

"Yes, what do Kulupans call it?"

She smiled and showed me her white teeth. "All Kulupans call it *pa!*" When she said the word *pa*, it came out like a passionate explosion of air from her mouth. "Every form of *pa* is powerful. Kulupans think of *pa* as the primal force that first created this universe."

Each time she said, "*pa*" the urge became stronger within me until she convinced me that *pa* was it's original and correct name. I wanted to know all about her kind of *pa*. I wanted to experience this primal force that created everything, but to know it, I needed someone as evolved as Tiltoenay.

****

It was then that I remembered that I was wearing my wrisceptor with an open channel to Rugen and Iris. Of course, my connection to Rugen was turned down, but I was not sure about Iris and I was afraid to take my eyes off Tiltoenay to check the wrisceptor setting. I pointed to my right wrist and Tiltoenay shrugged. "Why are you ashamed of your feelings for me? You extended your love to that old woman in your meditation so easily— why not me? You and Rugen want a complete relationship with a feminine soul again—do you not?"

"It's something we've entertained."

"Why do you think Iris has so many doubts concerning you and Rugen, despite the fact that you are everything she ever hoped to find?"

"I don't know."

"Don't be willfully ignorant," said Tiltoenay. "How do you feel about me and how do you feel about Iris?" Tiltoenay released her grip on me, just a little, and allowed me to think. Truth began to unfurl like a big red flag and I began to sink down into myself where I realized the passion I felt so easily for Tiltoenay, I needed to struggle to feel for Iris. "Would you go and get me a wash cloth so I can wipe the milk from the corners of Lotus Blossom's mouth?" she asked. The sound of her voice startled me and I jumped up to do her bidding. Returning with the cloth she assured me, "Nothing is written in stone. It's entirely up to you and, of course, up to me; but if we *pa*, I promise you will become one with me. Through me, you will learn to travel through every dimension open to me and I will teach you to manifest realities with a snap of the fingers. Beyond that, I invite you and Rugen into my fertile darkness, my own raw possibility where we can create the future together. With me, if you have any trace of fear or shame, any perversion of spirit, I will heal it."

"That's an extremely generous offer. Am I to assume that the lust I'm feeling at this moment is also yours?

"Absolutely!" she smiled. "I want you to teach me what you know about love. I'm not like Iris. I'm a ready and willing learner. I want to *pa* with you with great abandon for I guarantee I have no inhibitions as she does. I accept all my shadows and everything I am offers me bliss.

"Why me? Love must constantly pursue one as beautiful and evolved as you."

"I want you because I'm impressed with your arrogant magnanimity. As great as The Consortium is in its purpose of dispersion of light, never has a member brought back a soul fragment to rear as its own child. Not only did you do this; you did it the first time out. That kind of loving courage, I want to know as completely as I can."

"If we *pa* what would happen to my commitments to Rugen, Lotus Blossom, and Iris?

"Rugen and you are life mates and soul mates. *Ce* did not hesitate when you ask *cim* to share the responsibility of Lotus Blossom. I'm eager to know *cim* on the level of *pa* too. Iris can go with Evose and his soul mates or go with you and Rugen back to the future. It makes no difference to me. I really don't care who you have a relationship with as long as you are mine when we decide to come together."

"May I ask what will happen to Tyme if Rugen and I accepted your offer?"

I am one with Tyme and always will be. Through me, you will know Tyme as you know me."

"And Nova?"

"Nova is your god?"

"Nova is my divine-will, my connection to our oversoul."

Now that I know you, I definitely want to know Nova's magnificence too. Le is undoubtedly a resident of the fifth dimension and will be extremely easy for us to find. I will take you there and we can pa *with Nova until your heart is content.*

At that moment, I was ready to throw everything away and go. I wanted to climb inside her, live inside her, drown my desire in her blue passionate depths, yet I could not understand why or what about this blue goddess enslaved me. Nothing I can say, write or convey can describe the dark beauty of her soul. I knew this magnificent blue lady less than one full Earth day, yet I desired her beyond all description. If I had not pledged that all my love would flow through Rugen, I would have flown away with her without a backward thought. "I have great passion for you," I admitted, which was an understatement to say the least. "I will not put my feelings for this *pa* experience into denial any longer, but my commitment to my soul mates is as sacred as my integrity and I cannot promise anything until Rugen and I speak."

"I appreciate your clarity with me. Take your time; in fact take all the time you need. Please understand that time does not rule me. My word, once spoken, is law within me; and therefore, my offer stands. It stands until we decide together that we are fulfilled in each other. Now take our child and put her in her *vitarattha* and I will heal your shoulder and neck."

****

When Rugen arrived home, *ce* was tired. I knew *ce* would want to shower and do nothing more than relax. The first thing *ce* said after coming through the door was, "All evening, I was worried about you." *Ce* took off that silly, string necktie, the garters, and wrisceptor and laid everything on the table. I took my wrisceptor off too and put it next to *cis*, making sure both were deactivated.

"What if Iris needs us?" *ce* asked.

"We need a bit of privacy."

"Is Lotus Blossom okay?"

"She's fine." Rugen went to check, but did not pick her up because *ce* wanted to bathe before touching her. I followed *cim* into the bathroom and sat on the toilet cover as *ce* undressed and began to run water in the tub. "Do you remember when we were doing the rescue work on Sutcay Tay and the exhaustion we felt? That's how tired I feel after all we've been through today."

"I'm tired too. I had a difficult time at work and earned only thirty-six dollars in tips. The manager was punishing me and only seated customers in my section when all other sections were filled."

"Why did he do that?"

"Each evening, before the restaurant opens, the staff gathers in the kitchen and the manager explains about specials not on the menu. Tonight he said, 'A certain new waiter thinks he knows more about the restaurant business than I do. He thinks we should be serving vegetarian entrées. If this new waiter doesn't mind his own business, he is going to find himself minus a job.' Everyone knew he was talking about me so I spoke up and tried to explain why at least one vegetarian entrée was a good idea. The manager immediately interrupted me and said, 'I don't give two shits about your vegetarian ideas, just serve what's on the menu and keep your opinions to yourself.' I felt humiliated, especially when the other waiters walked away and left me standing there like a pariah."

"Your friend Mauve didn't stand up for you?"

"It was her night off."

"I'm sorry, Rugen. You don't need to work there. Senon is making plenty of money."

"Let me try for a few more days. I refuse to lose completely. I would like to recoup a bit of my dignity before leaving that place." Rugen pulled *cis* long hair up in a knot on the top of *cis* head and climbed into the filling tub. *Ce* slid down into the steamy water before gazing up into my eyes. "What's going on with you, love? I am not able to read you as I usually can."

"That's because I want to tell you this with words, especially because I'm not sure what it means or why it happened." I told Rugen everything that Tiltoenay said.

"Tiltoenay's offer is tempting," Rugen admitted. "The three of us—together! Can you imagine what we might learn from a blue, Kulupan goddess?"

"I was half-afraid you would be angry with me, angry the my passions were surging."

"My love, forgiveness is not an issue between us. Where Tiltoenay is concerned, I trust you more than I trust myself."

****

I shut the air coolers off and the silence was a relief. We carefully moved Lotus Blossom out to the sitting area so our two *vitaratthas* could float side by side. It felt heavenly, the quiet, the floating womb-like comfort inside the *vitarattha*, and Rugen and I embracing like two spoons.

I heard Tiltoenay arrive later to feed Lotus Blossom. I picked up my head and she said, "Go back to sleep, dear." I immediately went back to sleep and then she woke me again to say, "I'm leaving; but I think you should know that Iris is on her way over here because she just experienced a bad dream. If my calculations are correct, and they always are, she will be here in four minutes."

"What time is it?" I asked.

"3:22 a.m." said Tiltoenay and she rubbed her fingers together and disappeared.

I touched Rugen's shoulder. "Did you hear what Tiltoenay just said?"

"I hoped I was dreaming," *ce* mumbled. Then we heard an almost frantic rapping at our door. Rugen tapped the down button on the *vitarattha* and we each grabbed pants. "Just a minute," *ce* yelled, which startled Lotus Blossom, and she began to cry. "If you get the door, I'll get Lotus Blossom," *ce* offered.

Iris burst into the room and she was almost breathless with excitement. "I had a nightmare," she said. "You have to listen—right away."

"Shush," I whispered, but my voice sounded like an angry hiss.

"Sorry!" Iris said. She seemed unaware that her chaotic energy was frightening Lotus Blossom. "In this dream, I'm hungry so I go out to the refrigerator for a snack. When I open the door, a burglar is sitting inside my refrigerator. He jumps out and says, 'You think you are going to eat me; but I am going to eat you.' I woke up screaming. Do you think he was a soul fragment? Maybe it was Evose trying to make first contact."

It was difficult to think over the noise and I felt a sudden desperate urge to escape. "Whether you realize it you not, it's 3:30 in the morning," I said.

Iris appeared startled and offended. "You said I could call you anytime, day or night. Now you're offering me the stupid excuse that you're tired."

"I did say you might call me at anytime, but I didn't think you would abuse my offer by waking me at 3:30 in the morning to interpret a frivolous dream."

"You're not as genetically superior as you pretend."

"You're right, Iris. Keep whittling me down and soon you can report me for being just another jokester from the future. It seems to mean nothing to you that Rugen and I gave up our lives to get here. We took on the chore of mending a rupture that you and Evose perpetuated. Now that we're here, I find myself asking, why should we save an undeserving ignoramus, when so many have fallen through the web of time? With no trouble at all, I could find a million people more deserving than you." I snatched the *vitarattha* off the floor, activated it around myself before saying, "The man in your refrigerator was telling you to stop eating ice cream and you'll lose those extra five pounds on your hips." Then I left her standing in the middle of our sitting area staring up at me with her mouth hanging open. Rugen was stuck not only dealing with Lotus Blossom, but Iris.

"You're welcome to sleep on the futon," *ce* said. Iris stood there sulking for almost a minute, trying to decide what to do next. Then she kicked off her shoes, which went in opposite directions, and sat down on the futon with her elbows on her knees.

"Do you have anything remotely like a pillow or a blanket?" she asked.

Rugen gave her a blanket and the two pillows from the *neipanin*. She put one pillow under her head and clutched the other one to her chest as she tried to make herself comfortable on the futon. After a minute, I could hear her stifled sobs over the fussing Lotus Blossom. My damn guilty conscience, which I was getting sick of accommodating, would not allow me to sleep. I tapped the *vitarattha* and came down to the floor. I went over and patted Iris on the shoulder. "I'm sorry I was short with you. We will talk more about your dream tomorrow morning."

"Go back to bed," Rugen advised me."

"I'm going to make a bottle for Lotus Blossom," I insisted and I plodded out to the alcove like a zombie. Of course, when the bottle was prepared, Lotus Blossom did not want it; she wanted Tiltoenay's breast.

We need some feminine help Rugen projected my way. *I'm going to ask Iris to nurse the baby.*

She is not going to do it I projected right back. *Haven't you noticed she has not even asked to hold Lotus Blossom?*

For Lotus Blossom's sake, I have to try, ce thought; so Rugen plunged ahead with *cis* decision. "Iris, would you consider helping us? As you can see, we are in a bind. Would you offer Lotus Blossom the comfort of your breast so she could get back to sleep?"

Iris had curled up on the futon with her back turned toward us. Her voice sounded muffled when she said, "You must be joking."

"Why would I joke about something so serious?" asked Rugen. "A little motherly compassion from you would be much appreciated, plus it would be a way for you to bond with Lotus Blossom."

Iris hit the pillow under her head with her fist and declared, "I am not that child's mother. Get Tiltoenay to feed her. She's the one acting like the Great Earth Mother around here."

Now I was angry. My anger was not explosive, but surgical and extremely mean. "You and Evose deserve each other," I said. "Your passion is distant and cold, just like his. You're becoming the very person you were afraid of becoming."

"Sante!" Rugen warned me. The new authority in *cis* voice startled me. "You've said quite enough. You're making matters worse." Actually, I had said very little compared with what I was thinking and Rugen knew it was true because *ce* was reading my every thought.

Iris got up and began searching for her shoes. "Fuck you both! I'm out of here! It's obvious you care more about your little street urchin than you care about me disappearing forever."

"Please stop your shouting," said Rugen. "You're upsetting Lotus Blossom and you're upsetting me too."

Iris ignored Rugen and continued to pelt us with her illusions. "Tyme was right about you two. He warned me there were uncertainties involving you. I defended you, told him you were different—evolved! Now I can see Tyme was right. You're just like all the other men I've ever known—selfish and self-absorbed! All you care about is getting me into bed and having me take care of your little brat. You both disgust me. You can take your phony tenderness and put it where the sun never shines, which I'm sure is your preference anyway."

I foolishly assumed "where the sun never shines," meant the fourth dimension so I replied, "That's exactly where you are going to end up, where the sun never shines."

Lotus Blossom was full out crying again and Tiltoenay did appear. "I could hear shouting from outside," she said. "It's not good to expose a newborn to anger, especially this newborn. Give her to me," she ordered. Rugen handed Lotus Blossom over and Tiltoenay immediately put her to her breast. In an instant, there was a miracle of perfect silence.

Nevertheless, I still was shaking with rage. It took great effort to tell Iris, "Believe whatever you want and do whatever you want; I'm done accommodating your crazy moods and unfair suspicions."

"All of you go to bed," ordered Tiltoenay. "We will discuss this matter when you are all less psychotic."

"I'm leaving," declared Iris.

"No you're not," said Tiltoenay. "Lie down on that futon and go to sleep or I will think of an appropriate punishment for you."

"You can't make me," challenged Iris.

"You want to bet?" asked Tiltoenay. "Now go lie down on that futon, before I put a big ugly wart, right on the end of your cute little nose." Tiltoenay rubbed her fingers together a couple of times and Iris felt compelled to lie down as Tiltoenay instructed.

I grabbed a *vitarattha* and Rugen and I went up into our private world.

"I'll stick around for a while," said Tiltoenay. "Just to make sure you all behave." She rubbed her fingers together again and the lights went out.

I was bleary eyed with exhaustion, but so upset that it still took me almost an hour to fall asleep. Every few minutes, I would glance down and see Tiltoenay sitting there like a great blue Buddha with Lotus Blossom enclosed inside her huge, pale-white aura. I was filled only with awe.

****

Tyme arrived soon after dawn. I woke up a little more and realized how exhausted I still felt. I tried to open my eyes and my eyelids were half-glued shut. I tried to focus and saw Tiltoenay sitting in the exact same position with Lotus Blossom in her arms. Tyme was sitting before Tiltoenay as if she were his altar. "Isn't The Consortium meeting tomorrow morning?" I asked him.

"Yes," he whispered. "Don't you remember? I told you that I would come this morning to teach you how to maneuver the void. Tiltoenay has explained the problems you're having, so we will postpone the lesson. Go back to sleep." I immediately fell into a half-sleep and felt a secure peace as if I was a child and my parents were happy in the next room. After a while, I could hear Tyme and Tiltoenay moving around, and heard the puff of the gas flame being lit on the kitchen stove.

Rugen and I got up and went to the bathroom together. *Ce* locked the door and we did our usual morning rituals. It was a painful experience to insert adhesion lenses over my tired eyes. "I can't make it through today without some help," I told *cim*. "Do we have any aminoply in the medical kit?"

"You know we do."

"I feel depressed," I told *cim*. "All I want to do is go home to the future."

"Let's adjust our mission statement," said Rugen. "Do you still want to take Iris back to the future?"

"I'm more sold on the idea than when Belinda first mentioned it. Besides, it would be just punishment for Belinda to see what a pain in the ass she was in her previous life."

I went into the closet off the *neipanin* and shut the door. I opened the medical kit and rooted around in the dim light of the closet until I found what I wanted. I pulled out an inhalant of aminoply and shot the drug up my nose. Immediately, I felt alert, bright, and optimistic despite the fact that I had no logical reason to feel that way. "Okay," Rugen told me. As soon as she agrees, let's get the hell outta here."

Iris lifted her head off the futon when she saw us. A moment later, she headed for the bathroom without speaking to anyone. Tiltoenay made breakfast for us and told me to sit down and eat the eggs and toast she made. "I'm not hungry," I told her and I grabbed a cup of tea and went outside to get a breath of fresh air before the day turned unbearably hot. Outside, the new foliage was covering over the rough edges where we had trimmed the branches back. *Thank you*, I told the garden. *Thank you for your beauty in this mean and suspicious world.* I stuck my head back inside and told everyone, "I need some private time. I'm going to walk down to the Carrot Brazil for food supplies and go to Target for more diapers. Do we need any other supplies, Rugen?"

"That should do it," *ce* said.

"I'll be back in about an hour."

****

When I returned two hours later, the last few steps seemed the hardest. I hesitated at the door, listened, and sent Ezek to check out the scene. Everything seemed exceptionally peaceful on the other side of the door and that alone raised my suspicion. All I sensed was the activity of a meditative mind. I went inside and found Rugen sitting in the middle of the futon holding Lotus Blossom and feeding her a bottle of milk. "How did you accomplish this miracle?" I asked.

"Just like every other miracle I ever accomplished," said Rugen, "through perseverance and patience."

"Why isn't Tiltoenay feeding Lotus Blossom?"

"She still is, in a way. She gave me a huge jar of her concentrated breast milk. All we need to do is mix the concentrate with cooled sterilized water. Lotus Blossom loves it! Tiltoenay promised to return, but not as often. She said that she wanted to give us space to settle our problems with Iris. Now Lotus Blossom and I are enjoying the wonderful silence. How are you doing?"

"I'm okay."

"You're talking to me, my love."

I revised my statement to, "If you can put up with Hideaways then I can put up with Iris and her nonsense. I'm sorry about my behavior last night."

"No longer will I be putting up with Hideaways. The manager called about twenty minutes ago to inform me that my services were no longer required."

"I'm sorry, Rugen."

"I'm not; I'm relieved." *Ce* got up and took Lotus Blossom into the *neipanin* where *ce* tucked her into her *vitarattha*. When *ce* came back *ce* said, "We need to talk, Sante, seriously."

"Okay, I'll put on the tea kettle."

"As soon as everyone cleared out of here I had a visit from two apparitions. They came as visible manifestations, comparable to Estrella when she appeared before us in the fourth dimension. They helped me and after they were gone it was as if a tremendous dark cloud lifted from my head."

"Did you have any sense of who they might be?"

"Oh yes! I knew them. It was Socrates and Nova. Socrates appeared first and paced back and forth in front of me reminding me of lessons he taught me thousands of years ago. He advised me that I needed to pull back a little from your complete-love-and-acceptance approach when dealing with unknown situations and people and to question everything that was happening to us. He said that I needed to rely on my innate tools of logic to put the obvious clues together that he claimed were staring me smack in the face. Then, Nova came—"

"How did *le* look? Was *le* okay?"

"*Le* looked ethereal, glowing, just like Estrella, only *le* was dressed in regular clothing. *Le* spoke quietly and was very poignant. *Le* actually held Lotus Blossom in *lis* arms and told me that she reminded *lim* of Una when she was an infant. Nova said, and I quote *lim* exactly, 'You and Sante are in the final phase of your journey into the past.' Then he kissed Lotus

Blossom on both sides of the forehead and handed her back to me. *Le* kissed me on the lips and said, "No matter what, Number One, I will see you on the other side of life." Rugen's eyes filled with tears and *ce* pursed *cis* lips to prevent *cim*self from crying as I already was doing. "I think I have said this before, Sante; but this time I mean it. I'm afraid that we are going to do the wrong thing and screw everything up for Nova."

I sat down on the floor and cried. All I could think was that Nova appeared and I missed seeing *lim*. "If I can't go home soon, then I am going to die of homesickness."

"Take it easy," said Rugen. "I have a plan that starts with us going into our *neipanin* and doing what each of us does best. I want you to use your psychic skills; I will use my understanding; and together, we will decide our next move."

I went over to the stove and turned off the flame under the teakettle. "Let's go," I said. "Let's do it before I collapse from exhaustion."

"Do you remember the story of Buddha sitting under a bodhi tree and what he swore?" asked Rugen.

"He swore that he would not get up until he reached enlightenment?"

"Exactly, and that is what we must do."

I was sweaty and smelly from my walk in the heat; despite that, we circumvented the niceties of ceremonial bathing. I turned off both our wrisceptors and instructed Senon to stop anyone who attempted to enter our apartment and not to interrupt us until we emerged from the *neipanin*. Just like my sibling Senon, the multidex Senon agreed to, "hold down the fort."

"This is it," Rugen announced and we sat down facing each other. "If we fall short this time, we are going to fall into a deep pit of indecision. I understand that better now than I ever understood it before." We sat with our knees touching as we both quieted and centered our minds. It was extremely difficult to do and my head hurt intensely. Rugen advised me to, "Do the best you can." My job was to remain as open as possible for clues that I would relate to Rugen, who would then attempt to put the clues together into meaning. Rugen's pressure was open and inclusive as if *ce* were a hungry mouth waiting to be fed. *Ce* asked the first question and it was the most difficult of all. "Who is Iris besides being Belinda's previous incarnation?"

Astoundingly, the answer came immediately and was more than either of us bargained for. "Iris carries the alpha denial of The Janaforma as Lotus Blossom carries the omega denial," came slipping out of my mouth.

There was a short pause and Rugen asked, "Who are Tyme and Tiltoenay?"

"Tyme and Tiltoenay are highly evolved beings as are all Consortium members. Their oversoul dominates the farthest realms of the fourth dimension is one we think of as the *manatees*."

"Holy shit!" Rugen mumbled. "What is the purpose of our interactions with The Consortium?"

"You cannot reach completion without facing the full picture of yourself. Their job is to present the ultimate challenge both personally and universally."

"Did you hear what you just said?" Rugen asked me.

"Of course I heard what I said. Why don't you tell me what I mean?"

Rugen let go a deep sigh and buried *cis* face in *cis* hands. When *ce* looked up, *cis* face lit up with realization. "If Iris reflects the alpha or original denial and Lotus Blossom reflects the omega or completed denial, then they are a continuum, essentially one. If The Consortium is an emanation from the *manatee*, then again, they are one, a continuum. We've witnessed their behavior. Both the *manatee* and The Consortium are dedicated to redemption of denial. We came here promoting our own illusions, which were fueled by your promiscuous history and my rambunctious exuberance. We convinced ourselves that we were stuck and needed to take Iris as our mate; but the only thing we ever agreed to do was attempt to prevent the rupture. If Iris is the true progenitor of the rupture then removing her from this time should do the trick. I'm prepared to commit to this theory and gamble that we are right. To me, this means we're still on track. Let's not break this continuum now. Let's take Iris back to the future and allow Belinda to deal with Iris."

"Look at me," said Rugen. I gazed into *cis* two pools of lake-blue. "When Buddha sat under his bodhi tree, he was not confronted with terror, pain, or any of those horrible things we might imagine. He already experienced the spectrum of anguish through his many incarnations, just as we have. What Buddha experienced was an invitation from the *manatee* to join in their eternal bliss. He experienced it just as you did last night when Tiltoenay came to you with her incredible offer."

"I would have gone with her if it was not for you."

"You know what, Sante? Your instincts are still on target. The future is calling us and it's time to go home. I purpose that we go see Iris and give it to her straight. We cannot undermine her freewill; but we can give her the facts and allow her to decide if she wants to come into the future with us."

"Every time we attempt to give Iris the facts, we get bogged down in her doubts and anger."

"I purpose that we act with the will Nova put into us; furthermore, I think we should act immediately. What's stopping us, Sante? Let's move our belongings—tonight, as soon as it's dark—and then we can go over to Iris' house and tell her this is her one chance to go for a ride in a *vitarattha*. I have a strong hunch that she is going to see reality differently from the perspective of space."

When we emerged from the *neipanin*, it was five o'clock in the afternoon. We had refined our plan a bit, but essentially our goal had not changed. We were determined to leave Earth that very night. We couldn't make a move until nightfall and that wouldn't happen for another three hours. I was excited over the thought that we might be going home. It was enough to give me hope and I held on, believing in Rugen and trusting our shaky plan.

We attempted to tie up a few loose ends and were grateful we did not accumulate more possessions. We informed Senon of our decision and told *lim* to close any outstanding accounts connected with *lis* Internet business. *Le* complained a bit that we were not giving *lim* enough time. At around 5:30, *le* informed us that we had seventeen thousand dollars profit in a Swiss bank account from *lis* business that *le* did not know how to liquidate. Rugen and I quickly decided that we would give the money to Greg and Dennis to fulfill our lease agreement.

I made two brief telephone calls. First, I called Iris and left a message telling her we would be at her place at exactly 9:30 because the three of us needed to talk and make some decisions. "If you want to talk before then, give us a call. We'll be here." She never called and Rugen and I were worried, but still determined. We had no guarantees that our assumptions were correct, only a fervent trust in our combined skills that we were doing the best we could under the circumstances. When the phone did ring, I picked it up hoping it might be Iris. It was Mauve, asking for Rugen.

Rugen smiled afterward telling me. "Mauve said the manager announced to the waiters before dinner that he was adding three new vegetarian items to the permanent menu. I feel redeemed. That's all I wanted," he said.

Because we would need to carry Lotus Blossom, her necessities, and maybe Iris in our *vitaratthas*, we decided to leave everything we accumulated on Earth behind. The one sentimental exception was the small inexpensive blue cobalt vase I gave Rugen. *Ce* wrapped it up carefully in *cis* shirt and tucked it away in *cis* personal bag.

****

Our plan was to retreat almost exactly as we arrived. We would return to the salt ponds and leave Senon there with Lotus Blossom and our belongings while we contacted Iris and attempted to convince her to go for a ride.

Around seven o'clock, we heard a knock at our door. The knock spooked us and Rugen nodded toward me that I should do my psychic tricks. What Ezek sensed was an unknown problem waiting on the other side. I slipped into the bathroom and popped a pair of adhesion lenses in place and when I reemerged, I found two strange men standing there talking to Rugen. They definitely were *Gentlemen's Quarterly* subscribers. One was carrying a small and expensive looking attaché. Something about their appearance appeared official as they stood there sweating in their dark business suits. They were formally polite and identified themselves as Agents Daryl Bluff and John O'Neal. Bluff told us, "An anonymous complaint was lodged with local welfare authorities and passed along to the FBI about a child in your care."

Panic-stricken, my mind shot to Iris and I wondered if she had betrayed us. I was almost unable to speak so Rugen took charge and told them, "I can't imagine what you are talking about. We have no children. We are two simple homosexual men that have just moved here from Miami."

Obviously, they thought Rugen's statement bizarre and we were not sure why; but Agent Bluff appeared stern and countered, "I did not ask nor do I care about your sexual orientation." His upper lip curled giving him a crooked smile. I already hated him and wanted to say that genetic engineering had eliminated asymmetrical smiles in the future. Then he asked if he could have a look around our premises. They both opened their wallets and flashed official looking cards with some poker-faced pictures of themselves. The cards identified them as agents of The Federal Bureau of Investigation, United States of America.

I began to explain, "We were just leaving, planning to go out for the evening—"

"This won't take long," said O'Neal. Most reluctantly, we agreed to let them search our apartment. Something was menacing about them and their dark presence filled the room. Their suit jackets bulged where they hid weapons. Neither of these men remembered their past lives nor believed in past lives. They did not remember seeing individuals die as I had. Death was remote and as unreal to them as their flat-screen media entertainment. Yet, they were itching to experience violence and their minds were brimming with heroic notions of the 2015 variety. We certainly did not want our last day on Earth to climax in an inauspicious brawl with two Human barbarians. Rugen and I were sending telepathic messages back and forth and we were advising each other to stay calm and think fast. "Where's your furniture?" asked O'Neal.

I glanced toward the kitchen alcove and spied Lotus Blossom's bottle sitting near the sink so I moved my body slightly to block the alcove view. "We sold most of our furniture in Miami before moving here," I said. "We expect delivery of our new furniture early next week."

"What's in the other room?" asked Bluff.

"It's empty!" said Rugen quickly. "We're sleeping here on the futon until our new furniture arrives."

"Do you mind if we have a look around?"

I was praying and sending telepathic messages to Senon too, hoping *le* could invent an impromptu subterfuge to hide Lotus Blossom from their prying eyes. Rugen tensed and this filled me with dread. Rugen would never allow these two men to take Lotus Blossom from us. *Remember, we agreed not to do anything foolish. If you kill them, you will add to Lotus Blossom's denial.*

Rugen walked over to the *neipanin* and looked inside *cim*self. "Go ahead, have a look," *ce* offered. "You will see; we have nothing to hide."

Then I saw O'Neal put his hand inside his coat and touch his gun. This was disgusting to me. His gesture reminded me of perverted men who touch their genitals in front of children. When these two men walked into our *neipanin*, I thought, *that room is contaminated.* It was fortunate we were leaving because I swore I would never be able to meditate inside that room after knowing they stood inside it with their violent minds. The *neipanin* appeared empty to them and it was obvious Senon had moved Lotus Blossom somewhere. "What's in there?" asked Bluff and he pointed toward the closet.

"It's an empty closet," Rugen said.

Bluff went over and opened the closet door. What he saw was a space almost one quarter its original size. Senon had created an impromptu closet wall to hide everything from their view. When the four of us walked out into the sitting area again, I noticed that the baby bottle was gone. Senon had projected *lim*self out there and done a rapid cleanup while we were in the *neipanin*. It was then that Bluff and O'Neal got down to why they actually were there. Bluff opened his attaché, took out a twenty-dollar bill in United States currency, and handed it to Rugen. "Does this look familiar to you?" he asked.

Rugen took the bill, turned it over a couple of times, and examined both sides. "It looks like an ordinary twenty-dollar bill," *ce* said.

"Look at the date," instructed Bluff.

Rugen examined the bill more closely and then handed it to me. The twenty-dollar bill was one we brought with us from the future. Unfortunately, the bill carried the mint date of the year 2016. O'Neal glared at Rugen and said, "Yesterday, a man fitting your description bought a box of Pampers and a container of infant formula at a local Target and paid the clerk with this twenty dollar bill."

Rugen was quick. "I got several twenty dollar bills from a man in Miami right before we left. We sold him our furniture and he paid in cash. This could be one of those bills."

"How much cash was involved?"

"Five hundred dollars."

"What was the man's name?"

Rugen pretended to think. "His name was John—like yours. John Smith!"

Bluff looked disgusted. "What did John Smith look like?"

"Sort of like you," said Rugen using *cis* most innocent and amenable voice. "About six foot tall, chopped off brown hair and a dark business suit. I thought his clothing was odd because he seemed uncomfortably hot. In retrospect, it does seem that he might have been hiding something because his eyes kept shifting around."

"We're very interested in tracing the source of these bills," said O'Neal. "Your John Smith was no casual counterfeiter. Everything is authentic about these bills, the paper and even the ink. The only incongruity is the date. Your John Smith seems like a counterfeiter with a very eccentric sense of humor."

Rugen attempted to appear confident and forthright. "He is not my John Smith, merely a stranger who stopped by our garage sale and bought a sofa and some bedroom furniture from us."

Bluff's disgust for us was growing. "Do you mind telling me why you were at Target yesterday buying diapers and infant formula?"

"Is it illegal to buy these items?" asked Rugen.

They both managed to look embarrassed for us and then they prepared to leave reminding us that counterfeiting was a federal crime. "We'll be in touch," promised Bluff. "On Monday morning, I want you both to come down to the local FBI office and look at some pictures. Maybe you'll recognize a picture of your John Smith." As soon as they were gone, if there was any doubt before, we knew we needed to leave Earth as soon as possible.

TWENTY-THREE

We waited for darkness as one waits for a good friend, yet our impatience grew and felt impossible to shake. We waited with a rare hyper-vigilance helped along by generous doses of aminoply while realizing no technology ever invented could make the darkness and our future arrive before its appointed time. Our aminoply induced energy translated into a compulsion to clean our apartment in microscopic detail. In case the FBI decided to return and do some scanning themselves, we used the DNA scanner on our secondary multidex to check for minute particles of hair and tissue. We decided to take our trash with us, to incinerate in space and I told Rugen, "Elay always said, "Leave a place cleaner than you found it."

The one questionable decision we made was to slip a note under Greg's kitchen door that told him a seventeen thousand-dollar bank check would be arriving in his mailbox in the next few days. I explained to Greg, "Rugen and I are giving you this money in hopes that it will help you return to school or open your own restaurant if that's something you still want to do. We will never forget you and will think of you often. Thank you for your hospitality. Peace and Love, Rugen and Sante."

****

Shortly after 9:00 o'clock, we lifted off for the salt ponds. It felt like the old days; our *vitaratthas* were overloaded and it was questionable whether we could make space. Out at the salt ponds, Senon would stand guard over our gear while holding Lotus Blossom in *lis* forcefield arms. Senon knew it was a huge responsibility and we promised to return as soon as possible. Rugen and I then flew over to Iris' to make our final plea. We landed across the street and when we approached her front door, we heard the soft and relaxing sounds of music playing inside and Rugen remarked, "I hope the music means that she in a better mood than last night."

I rang the bell and Iris opened the door and appeared startled to see us. "You both are looking stiff and official—what's up?" she asked. We went inside and were amazed to see that Iris was riding a wave of transformational energy. Everything was orderly inside Iris' house. I was not relieved, merely suspicious. Never had any of Iris' incarnations shown any interest in orderliness. "I decided to tidy up a bit," she said. "How does it look—so far?"

"It looks beautiful," said Rugen.

"I'm extremely embarrassed about my behavior last night. I don't know what came over me. You might find this difficult to believe, but I'm usually the cool and rational one in any crisis." She was right about one thing; that was difficult to believe. She went on to say, "Around 1:00 o'clock today (around the same time Socrates and Nova appeared to Rugen), I started feeling better—clearer. I felt as if a cloud lifted from my mind and I could think again. A few of my psychic skills returned, along with the realization that I am lucky to have friends as loyal as you."

"I too apologize for my anger last night," I said and she was making me into a believer. "In the future, I will be more patient. Being tired is a poor excuse for nasty behavior."

"Truce," she decreed. "I thought I might do something altruistic and feminine like cook dinner for you both; but I guess it's too late for dinner now. Time got away from me, but I did get your message. I called both your cellphones about a dozen times to invite you to dinner, but they always went directly to voice mail."

"Have you seen Tyme or Tiltoenay since this morning?" asked Rugen.

"No and Tyme didn't perform during the Sunset Ritual this evening. Say, where's Lotus Blossom?"

"Senon is caring for her."

"Can a computer program be trusted to care for an infant?"

"Much more than some bios," I said.

Rugen took Iris by the shoulders and said, "Listen carefully to me, Iris; another variable has been thrown into our equation. A few hours ago, two investigators from the Federal Bureau of Investigation paid us a visit. They told us an anonymous complaint had been lodged with local welfare authorities concerning a child in our care."

"That's the most insane thing I've ever heard," said Iris. "Neither of you is capable of hurting a flea. Wait a second, why would the FBI be interested in child abuse? Oh my God! They must suspect you're extra-terrestrials."

Rugen assured her, "It's not quite that dramatic. Unfortunately, we didn't notice the money my mothers supplied was printed in the year 2016. Two FBI agents were tracing the source of the premature money we spent over the past few weeks and came to our door about three hours ago to ask questions."

"They actually came to your house? Well, you'll have to move, lose them. Once the FBI starts hounding you, you're chickenfeed!"

"We've decided to return to our own time," I said.

"We're leaving tonight," Rugen added.

The pupils in Iris' eyes dilated. "No! Not tonight—not now! Can't you hide in your *vitaratthas* for a while or—what about your spaceship? You're both smart; outwitting the FBI will be easy for you."

"We're leaving tonight," Rugen said more firmly.

Iris started to breakdown again. "You're using the FBI as an excuse; you're leaving because of me—giving up on me. I tell you the fog has lifted. If you're so evolved, you must be capable of compassion. Think of the pressure I'm under. Okay, I admit all my stubbornness. I do accept truths today that only yesterday I did not realize were possible. Please, give me another chance."

"The fog has lifted for us too," I admitted. "One thing we realize is the agitation you experienced over the past few days was an intense pressure put on you from The Consortium to resolve your denial. We know who and what The Consortium is now. The Consortium is consciousness from the fourth dimension, the ones we call *manatee*. Because you've not experienced the Regression drug, you don't realize how important you are, but in incarnation after incarnation, you've chosen to become a Trinity Witch. If you consent to come with us, come into the future, then we believe you will see the clear light of your own potential for the first time in any of your lives."

"What about the rupture and all that?"

"We don't know if the rupture is going to happen or not," said Rugen. "But if you come with us then no chance exists that the rupture could be anchored to this time through you."

Iris looked slightly terrified. "You mean give up life here on Earth, in 2015, and simply go into the sixth millennium with you?"

"That's right," said Rugen. "Come with us, now, tonight. I swear we will not put pressure on you to connect sexually with us. Sante and I realize it was *his* passion and my youthful enthusiasm that envisioned this scenario. It was wrong of us to assume that you would respond in kind. It will not happen again."

"This is our proposal," I said. "Come with us tonight and if you decide that you want to return to Earth between now and the time we reach the vitasphere, we will bring you back—no questions asked."

"Certainly we could not return once we entered the fourth dimension," she said.

"That's true," agreed Rugen. "It will take us about twelve to fifteen Earth days to reach the asteroid where we hid the vitasphere. We promise that if you change your mind during that time, we will bring you back to Earth."

Her distraught showed in the tension in her face. "This is so different from what I expected would happen."

Rugen took her hands and held them. "We don't have the power or knowledge to mend or control this rupture; but we can take responsibility for our personal denial that contributes to the rupture."

"What if I tell you I will not go?" she asked.

"We're leaving tonight," I said. "We are committed to our personal survival and to the survival of Lotus Blossom. It's our sacred duty to make sure she lives and thrives." Iris put her fingers to her forehead as if a psychic pain was attacking her. "Our minds are firm," I added. I gave her my hardest look so she might sense my resolve. It was difficult for me to appear hard because I wanted to be soft with everyone.

She stared at me and said, "I have to bring my cats."

My eyes shifted to Rugen. "Is that a yes?" *ce* asked her.

"It's a yes if I can bring Miranda and Meyou."

I immediately wanted to know, "How are felines going to manage in zero gravity?"

And Rugen cut me short with— "We'll figure that out later."

I glanced at my thumbnail watch and informed Iris that she had one hour to decide what she wanted to bring besides Miranda and Meyou. Luckily, she owned a feline carrier equipped with a sturdy handle. We helped her pack what I considered a large and bulky suitcase.

It's fascinating what's important to a person in a crunch. Iris reminded me of Senon when we were children and *le* was packing for a family holiday. Senon had packed three multidexes; a bag of marbles; *lis* pet turtle and, naturally, turtle food; one pair of underwear; and an extra pair of socks. Now, Iris was taking her jewelry box, a photo album, some personal letters, and a few articles of clothing—all green in color, a bag of feline food, and her favorite book of Rumi poetry. Her precious tarot cards she tucked into the breast pocket of her jacket. She wanted to bring a kitty litter box and litter but Rugen told her it was not necessary because *ce* already had the toilet facilities for the felines figured out. I probed Rugen's mind on the feline problem and the truth was that *ce* did not have the foggiest notion how to handle felines in space.

Despite our promise—that we would bring Iris back to Earth if she wanted to return—it seemed clear that she was determined to go the entire way. I was impressed with her resolve and newborn efficiency. She packed and was ready to go in slightly under thirty minutes. She stood glancing around her sitting area afraid to set down her suitcase for even a minute. "I'm never going to see these rooms again," she announced.

"Regardless, our original offer stands," promised Rugen. "If you change your mind, we will return you to Earth."

She swore, "I will not change my mind."

Rugen took her two felines with *cim* in *cis vitarattha* and I took Iris in mine. It was quite an experience for her. As she stepped inside my *vitarattha*, she admitted she had flown in an airplane only once before in her life. As we took off from the ground, she experienced a moment of panic and a few expletives escaped from her mouth starting with "Oh my God!" and ending with "Holy Mother of God!" I held her around the waist and she was clutching at my neck as if she could fall out of the *vitarattha*. "It's thrilling but I'm really scared," she whispered in my ear.

I took her in my arms and she buried her face against my neck. She smelled wonderful. She wrapped her legs around mine for extra security and she felt hot, soft, and feminine. I could not help but enjoy the sensation of her clinging to me for dear life.

It took us approximately two minutes to fly back to the salt ponds. Fortune seemed to be smiling upon us for the first time in days. The weather was perfect for flying and Senon assured us that Lotus Blossom slept the entire time we were gone. We still had to make last minute adjustments and Rugen and I, like good Vanguard Scouts, checked all our equipment carefully. Despite Iris' protests, we took her belongings, split them among the three *vitaratthas*, and put the trash in her large, bulky suitcase.

I persuaded her to allow me to give Miranda and Meyou a mild tranquilizer in case they decided to get actively terrified inside their carrier while going up to the ship. Senon calculated the reduced dosage they would need and I took two inhalants, from our medical kit, and emptied them except for the last few drams of tranquilizer. "Please be gentle," said Iris. While Iris held each feline's head, I made a hand funnel around each their noses. Then Rugen sprayed the drug into the opening between my hands. Both cats jerked a little as I held my hand there for a moment to make sure they inhaled a good whiff. We watched the felines carefully for the next ten minutes and they seemed to be subdued, exactly the way we wanted them to be. Iris wrapped their carrier in a thermal bag to keep them warm.

We changed Lotus Blossom's diaper a final time and wrapped her in a thermal bag too. She looked cute with nothing but her little button nose sticking out. Finally, we put on our spacesuits and got a new one out for Iris. "Be careful with your spacesuit," Rugen warned her. "We are fresh out of spares."

The last ten minutes we sat in the darkness and listened to the sound of croaking frogs. When Rugen announced, "Let's do it!" *ce* startled me out of my hyper-vigilant daze. *Ce* handed me Lotus Blossom. During the waiting, a bit of telepathic negotiating had gone on between us and we decided Iris needed to go with Rugen. Our promise was not to put any pressure on Iris to connect and Rugen was helping me keep my promise.

As we lifted off from the salt ponds, Iris buried her head against Rugen's chest. The higher up we went, the braver she became until she managed to peek out every now and then. We were carrying so much gear that going up was slow until we cleared the lower atmospheres. Three kilometers, straight up from the ground, Rugen ejected the suitcase full of trash and incinerated it with one well-placed rephazer blast. We reached our rendezvous point with only twenty-nine minutes to spare.

We joined *vitaratthas* and waited in almost complete silence until Senon announced, "Here comes the pulsar, right on schedule."

Rugen used the remote to slow and maneuver the pulsar into optimum range. When we opened the door and went inside, I was ecstatic with joy. Finally and again, something from my time held me. My compassion arose for Iris because I better understood the sacrifice she was making. She was giving up her home, all she knew, in order to take a chance with us. She stood by the narrow window on the pulsar staring back at Earth and I told her, "I honestly admire your courage."

"It's real!" she said. "I finally can see Earth with my own physical eyes and I know it's real!"

****

We broke orbit immediately, allowing Senon to do the piloting. The two felines were groggy and did not emerge from their drug-induced stupor for another hour. Once they began to explore, we knew they were okay. I thought they were wise to explore their new situation thoroughly. They were not hungry.

I held Lotus Blossom and fed her a bottle while Rugen made each of us a bowl of soup from our extravagant food stocks aboard the pulsar. Iris asked what the soup was and Rugen told her, "gramlick chowder." A gramlick is a small white tuber, similar to a potato, which is a popular food staple in Gathosian cultures.

Iris tasted the soup and declared it, "delicious!" She made Rugen and I laugh. "It tastes like my mother's potato stew," she said. "I always suspected mom was an extra-terrestrial."

She wanted to retrieve her belongings that we split among the three *vitaratthas*. She particularly wanted to find her photo album. I understood why when she located it. She produced the drawing that she told me about two days before. The picture was of her, "dream man." It was a startling likeness. I immediately went to the multidex and requested, "Display a picture collage of Jana Nova." The multidex showed some pictures of Nova across the screen. "My God! I'm more psychic than I ever realized," she exclaimed. Her drawing was a picture of Nova, not of me.

****

Aboard a spaceship, the captain is the ultimate decision-maker. The captain's authority over the crew can be either tyrannical or tender as an intimate friend. In my two lives as a Janaforma, I have experienced the spectrum of captain possibilities. Rugen was the kind of captain that could make veteran spacemen, like Commander Solange, refuse a promotion. No doubt existed in my mind that Rugen was our captain; but Iris certainly did not understand this. She resented anyone and anything that smacked of authority, so Rugen kept it extremely light with a few brief lectures. "On a spaceship everything has its place and everything must be put back in that place after we use it," Rugen declared.

My captain is a genius in all things great and small and this is how Rugen solved our cats-in-space crisis: On the side of every spaceship are retractable arms with pincers on the ends. These pincers are useful when landing on moons and asteroids to retrieve soil samples for scientific analysis. As we passed through the asteroid belt in the Jupiter orbit, we made a brief stop and Rugen used one of the retractable arms to snatch a small asteroid bit floating nearby. Then *ce* took an empty food tray, which our freeze-dried food came packed inside, set it in the trash-disposal airlock, brought the asteroid bit inside the airlock and programmed the disposal to sterilize and pulverize the bit into millimeter chunks. Voila! Kitty litter. Rugen subjected Iris to more captaining, explaining that she needed to clean the litter box every time either Meyou or Miranda used it. "Not cleaning it is comparable to one of us not flushing the toilet," *ce* explained.

Rugen and I set up the sleeping alcove with some thermal sacks and allowed Iris to experience reduced gravity for the first time. "It's womb-like," she said, trying to bounce around in the suspension. I gave her a microdex for her personal use. On it, she could access books, films, games, etc. She could keep a journal if she wanted to write, but she spent most of her time staring out the window, which was a show in itself.

Rugen and I then retired and despite the fact that we had not slept in several days, we could not sleep. It was partly the excitement and partly that we still had aminoply in our systems. We began drinking liters of water to flush ourselves clean.

The three of us floated in the suspension for a while and it was very quiet and relaxing. We watched the felines play. They were curious about the reduced gravity and they reached out with their paws and touched the space as if it might bite them. Iris encouraged them to join us. It took the felines a few hours to decide the reduced gravity field was safe. When they did, they could not get enough reduced gravity time and when they tried to walk through it, their toes would spread. After awhile, they felt at home sleeping suspended in space. Miranda groomed Meyou and herself and afterward Meyou purred with happiness. I enjoyed the relaxing sound of the purring. The only thing I did not enjoy was their loose fur, which drifted around and got in my eyes, nose, and mouth.

Iris floated near the narrow window and I knew she was watching her Solar System get smaller and smaller. "You know what?" she asked. "This is the first time in my life that I have felt privileged and blessed." She was quiet for several minutes after that. When she spoke the next time, it was as if no time had passed. "That's not exactly right," she said. "What I meant to say is the first time I believe that God truly loves me."

****

It took us three hundred Earth hours (approximately nine cycles) to reach the asteroid where we hid the vitasphere. The hours were extremely uneventful and that was fine with me. The first three cycles, I did nothing but sleep and putter around. Rugen and I meditated with Lotus Blossom and we all played with the felines. The next six cycles, I devoted myself to working on *The Permeable Web of Time*.

The most exciting thing that happened was that Meyou, who was in love with Rugen, decided to sleep with *cim*. We all were asleep for hours when, all of a sudden, Rugen was up and scrambling to get free of *cis* thermal bag. Meyou had crawled inside with *cim* and was settling in against Rugen's chest when her whiskers barely touched *cis* chest. Meyou was more startled than Rugen when *ce* started yelping. Iris and I enjoyed a good laugh at Rugen's expense. Rugen laughed too, but much later. "I thought it was a spider," *ce* confessed. "Bookmark spiders for our next meditation, Sante."

When we reached the asteroid, which we had christened Hope, we found our vitasphere completely buried by dusty silt. Rugen needed to use the starboard ramjets on the pulsar to blow most of the dust off the vitasphere. When it was clearly visible, Iris marveled over its beauty. "It looks like a giant aura," she decided. This was Iris' last chance to change her mind and Rugen and I anticipated a bit of last minute obstinacy from her; but when I asked her if she was sure, she said, "Once I make up my mind about something, that's it."

It was finally time to break open the sealed space cartridge that Kayya and Ceff gave us. We were only slightly amazed to see the spools were made of platinum. We needed to dump all the programming from the main multidex on the vitasphere to make room for the information on these spools, but it felt like an irrational act of suicide. We broke the news to Senon that we wanted *lim* to act as the coordinator between the multidex and the vitasphere. For the first time, Senon was authentically unsure of something we asked *lim* to do. *Le* was not shy about explaining *lis* problem. "I will need to dump all the new programming I have acquired on Earth," *le* explained. "I've accumulated a huge database on the probability of my soul. A few more calculations and I can prove scientifically that all sentient programmed creations have a soul."

Not enough memory existed on the second multidex to accommodate all *lis* new data and our life-support systems too. The reality was that for us to have a chance to survive, Senon would need to revert to *lis* base programming. The dangers were real. The huge multidex could strip *lim* of *lis* memories. Senon was a sentience equal to any sentience alive. *Le* possessed rights. We would have foundered many times without *lis* altruistic help and I considered *lim* a Janaforma dedicated to the highest principles. It was extremely difficult to ask *lim* to make another sacrifice. The only reason we did ask was we believed *le* was the only one capable of doing the job. *Le* was stoical, like a soldier going to war who had calculated the odds. Never had we sat down with Senon and meditated and Rugen and I were ashamed we never thought to include *lim*. Now Senon asked us, "If we have time, I would like to meditate with you before I go."

"We will make time," decided Captain Miro.

We did it right, with full ceremony. We bathed, put on fresh clothing, and lit our last stick of incense. Iris, Rugen, and I sat down knee-to-knee and Senon projected *lis* hologram into our center. "I have found a way to override the programming the physical Senon put into my systems to protect me from contamination," *le* said. "You may touch me, but be careful. I am an electric virgin."

We offered prayers on Senon's behalf, prayers to Nova, to our oversoul, and to my sibling, Senon *lim*self. Our mutual prayer was, *If there be any denial in any of us that would impede this mission, show us now so that we might face our insufficiencies.* When we arose from our meditation, we had confidence in our path of action.

One last time, Senon appeared before us dressed as a Vanguard Scout. Rugen told Senon to change *lis* appearance slightly and display a Ribbon of Valor on *lis* collar. "I am honored to obey my captain," said Senon. Rugen kissed Senon on both sides of *lis* forehead and then Senon turned into a white mini-typhoon and took one last sweep around the area before disappearing into *lis* original multidex. A moment later, a question box came up on the screen asking, "Are you sure you want to delete the folder entitled, 'soul search?'"

"You will need to do the final honors," said Senon from inside *lis* box.

I went over and pressed the delete button manually. I had just committed murder and I knew it. Thirty seconds later, the main multidex on the vitasphere responded and informed us the link with Senon was complete. Rugen promptly uploaded the information from the platinum spools. "Upload complete," said the generic voice of the multidex.

****

Rugen and I tranquilized the felines again. Rugen came up with another bizarre solution to the urine and waste problem that definitely would be a major problem in the zero gravity of the fourth dimension. We decided to put a diaper on each feline. We anesthetized them again because they would have torn off their diapers. Felines sense of humor does not extend to themselves. The only chore left was to put on our own suits. I probably was already assuming too much, never thinking a minor necessity like inserting a catheter would be a problem for Iris as it was for Hope. Iris retired to the toilet cubicle and was in there for a good half-hour. When she did not reemerge in a reasonable amount of time, I knew she had a problem. *No one is here to help her except one of us*, Rugen thought.

Shortly afterward, she came out of the toilet and made the announcement, "I can't do it."

"Did you use the lubricant I gave you?" I asked.

"Yes, but I still can't get the front one—you know—in." I attempted to give her additional verbal instruction and she returned to the toilet to try again. "I can't do it," she yelled from behind the closed door. "You might as well take me back to Earth."

I panicked, but tried to sound assuring and normal. "I would be glad to help."

"No way!" she shouted.

"I can be clinical. I was a physician in my last life."

"Well you are a lecher in this one!"

"I'll help you," Rugen said.

A long silence followed and I could almost hear her thinking on the other side of the door. "Okay," she said. Rugen went into the toilet and helped her. "You're hurting me," I heard her say twice.

"I'm sorry, but you've irritated the tissue in that area," *ce* lectured her.

I went to the medical kit, pulled out an anesthetic spray, and passed it in through the small opening in the door. It was very quiet on the other side for the next couple of minutes. When they both emerged, Iris looked as stoical as Senon had. "Good job!" I said. "Ribbons of Valor for you both."

"You are really pushing it!" Iris glared. "With all your damn advanced technology, way can't you invent something simpler than me sticking a tube up my—up my whatever?"

****

A short time later, we retracted our gravity in the pulsar and it took Rugen about twenty minutes to maneuver the pulsar up inside the vitasphere and complete the locking process. While *ce* was doing that, I changed Lotus Blossom's diaper a final time and snuggled her inside a thermal bag. We had converted a drawer from the pulsar into a makeshift bassinet that I lashed between the two center seats. We attached the feline carrier to the rear of the center seat, where Iris would be sitting so they would not float around. The last thing we did before leaving the third dimension of 2015 was to drink plenty of water.

Just like when we were leaving the third dimension of the future, we sat down in our seats and Rugen announced, "twenty seconds." The seat restraints came up and I felt a slight ignition. I turned around to check on

Iris and she was squeezing her eyes closed again. She was missing the lovely crimson sunset, the last view of her universe, in the year 2015.

"Excuse my arrogance," said Rugen. "But the data I'm collecting indicates that the rupture has shrunk in this time." I glanced down at the screen where Rugen was pointing and saw the evidence for myself.

"I thought Tyme was so sure that the rupture could not be mended," said Iris.

"It's even going to be tight when we go through," said Rugen.

For the second time, we approached the blacker than black darkness, the void of the fourth. Rugen put on *cis* eye gear only now. This was more of a monitoring precaution because we had no idea which way was home. We were strangers in an alien universe with no fixed reference points and only a few clues. Rugen leaned forward and *cis* voice got intimate with *cis* beloved technology. "Take us home, Senon. Take us back to *The Mother* in the year 5603."

"Something is wrong," said Iris. "Nothing is happening."

"Nothing is wrong," Rugen assured her. "This is the way it is in the fourth—nothing to see, hear, or feel except one's illusions. If you have no illusions, you don't even have those to entertain you."

We sat there for what we all agreed was about thirty minutes and Iris said, "This is getting boring," yet the multidex was feeding us the most fantastic information, telling us that thirty-five hundred years elapsed in that tiny amount of time. "People say the trip home always seems to go faster, but this is ridiculous." I said.

"There is a single object, dead ahead," said Rugen. "It looks like a *graeymlin*. Either it is not moving or we're not moving." Just in case we were the one moving, Rugen told the Prime-I to slow the vitasphere and give *cim* manual control. Rugen raised *cis* eye screen and peered out at the total darkness beyond. "It's not phosphorescing. Maybe it's dead."

"Turn on the outside beams," I said.

"If this *graeymlin* is merely sleeping and we wake it up, we might be destroyed," Rugen reminded me.

"It's not a *graeymlin*." Rugen was reading my suspicions and *ce* turned on the lights to see if I was right. We found ourselves up against a white surface. I could read the letters "ANA," high above us. "We've found her!" I screamed. Rugen pulled the vitasphere back and concentrated the light. Then we all could see *LA VENTANA* displayed prominently across *The Mother*'s hull.

"My God! She's a monster, a world!" exclaimed Iris.

"It may be an illusion," Rugen said carefully. "Although this would be a big one."

"*The Mother* is not an illusion," I swore and Ezek was screaming, *tell it like it is!*

"Let me do some calculating," said the careful Captain Miro, and *ce* pulled down *cis* eye gear and we circumvented *The Mother's* hull. It was quiet inside that vitasphere for the next ten minutes. When Rugen took off *cis* eye gear the next time, *ce* said, "Not only is it the authentic *La Ventana*, we are in our own time. The Door is straight ahead."

"We need to take *The Mother* back with us, back to the third," I said.

"How?" Rugen asked.

"We'll go aboard and fly her back."

"I don't know how to fly a starship."

"I do."

"You were afraid to fly that little cruiser back on Uropae.

"But I flew it, and I can fly *The Mother*. Besides, leaving *The Mother* in the fourth is leaving her in denial and that's not an option for me."

"I think you should listen to Rugen," said Iris. "You're acting irrationally again."

"I'm not interested in your critique on my mental health," I said. My sarcasm was enough to set Iris off again. She was on the attack and let out a string of expletives calling me a, "narcissistic asshole."

"Enough!" boomed Rugen and *ce* startled me with *cis* voice-of-god tone. Ten seconds of total silence followed. "Let's do it!" Rugen said. "Let's take *The Mother* home if we can do it."

Iris lowered her voice when she said, "You're going to be sorry."

Rugen turned around and stared at her for several seconds before saying, "I don't mean to be rude, Iris, but would you please be quiet for the next few minutes. Thank you," *ce* added a few moments later.

****

Getting inside *The Mother* was easy. We approached her aft at the inner curve between port and starboard sides. This is where the vitaspheres went in and out. The first code Rugen tried did the trick opening the lens door. "*The Mother* must have been taken quickly," *ce* said. "Controls on the bridge automatically change door codes in most exigency situations. It's incredible that none of them worked." We docked inside the vitasphere cove taking our choice of the thirty-three empty gasket cups that served as vitasphere pedestals.

We had full life-support aboard *The Mother*. Rugen carried Lotus Blossom and I took the felines inside their carrier. Iris stayed between Rugen and me, hanging onto Rugen's arm for dear life. She said the place felt, "ghostly." This time I shared her evaluation. In the past, the vitasphere cove was a high-security area, replete with alert security guards. It was easier to walk onto the bridge than it was to walk into the vitasphere cove. Now, it was silent, deserted, and eerie.

"Let's go up to the bridge," I said. "From there, we can sweep for life signs."

"I also have an idea I want to try," said Rugen. "Let's interface the multidex on our vitasphere with *The Mother's* Prime-I multidex. Then we can download whatever is left of Senon and see if *The Mother's* multidexes can reconfigure what's left of *lim* into another workable program." We went back inside the vitasphere and Rugen set the codes. My sentimental captain whispered into the multidex, "Hang on Senon, you're going for a ride up *to The Mother's* bridge."

It's impossible for me to remember everything that Iris said as we made our way through the empty byways and up the nineteen levels toward the bridge because she was chattering the entire way. I do remember that she was impressed with *The Mother's* size and beauty. My own memories were imbued with incredible *watarie*. Now that I had returned to *The Mother*, I saw her grandeur and beauty with new eyes. Everything was intact inside her. The sprinklers were watering the orange trees along the main promenade and many oranges were ripe and ready for harvest. We walked a little farther and heard some music playing, and I hoped to find an android had weathered the storm and could tell us what happened. We went inside a hair salon and discovered a small multidex stuck on play. I shut it off. As we expected, the bridge was empty. We scanned the entire ship for life signs and found no sentient life aboard except ourselves. On the bridge, I sat down at the console. More or less, three thousand years before, in my life as Sante The First, I complained that I felt glued to this console as we pointed *The Mother's* nose directly toward the great Pegasus constellation. Then, there was great emphasis in the Gatherings for everyone to procreate so we could fill the emptiness of *The Mother* with new life. The situation was different now.

Rugen sat down at the console too and tabbed a series of major touchpads. "Save all data in all codes and reconfigure," Rugen said to *The Mother's* Prime-I multidex. Some lights began to play on the console. It lasted for about two minutes and then the multidex announced, "reconfiguration complete. Do you wish to open the program?" It took Senon about forty seconds to stabilize *lis* holographic projection. Rugen told *The Mother's* multidex, "assist program to stabilize its holographic capacity."

Ten seconds later, Senon asked, "What are you waiting for? Go ahead and push the delete button."

Rugen and I were so delighted that we jumped up and down for joy. Even Iris was happy that Senon was still alive. We made so much noise that Lotus Blossom woke up startled. I was laughing and crying with relief. Senon was staring at us as if we were crazy because *le* did not know what happened. We told *lim* everything. "It's not critical, but we were wondering if any of your 'soul search' files survived your transfer," I asked.

Senon went internal for a moment. "No," *le* said quite confidently. Then *le* looked disturbed. "I hope I did not lose something important to you."

"No! It's all right," I assured *lim*. "We can reconstruct that data in no time at all. After all, you're an enlightened Vanguard Scout. A recipient of the Ribbon of Valor." Senon managed to appear as proud as one of Iris' felines.

****

This was my moment and I knew it. With all Rugen's skills as a pilot, *ce* never flew *The Mother*. Of course, *ce* was not completely ignorant of her workings. If I had ten thousand hotshot pilots lined up as my co-pilot, you can bet your Ribbon of Valor I would choose Miro Rugen every time. The first thing I decided to do was abort the two remaining annex sections still attached to *The Mother's* midsection, which made her look like an overweight cow. It took me about forty-five minutes to accomplish this task. "Ah!" I proclaimed afterward. "I can almost feel the physical relief. *The Mother* is talking to me," I told Iris and Rugen. "She is telling me she feels sleek and ready for a race." I decided that since everyone from the sixth millennium backward in time had declared me arrogant, this certainly was no time for me to revert to the humble waif. "I can do this," I said with considerable bravado and I slipped on *The Mother's* control gloves and drove her through The Door. An hour later, we were completely home in the year 5603.

As soon as we emerged in the third dimension, Rugen said, "I knew you could do it."

"I didn't," I admitted.

Iris asked, "Now what?"

"Now we go home to Uropae," said Rugen.

"It's going to take The Orion Alliance a few days to realize *The Mother* is back in space," I said. "When they do, you can bet they'll have a salvage team handy to start dividing The Mother's booty. Before they arrive, I am going to take a few things myself."

"Like what?" Rugen asked.

"Personal things from my apartment and a few things from the ship's museum." What I had in mind from the museum were two paintings by Jana Markette who had worked as a holographic reimager on *The Mother.* When Jana Markette took the Regression drug, she remembered being the Human Sandro Botticelli in another life. Botticelli was an Italian Renaissance painter of *Primavera* and *The Birth of Venus.* Jana Markette had repainted these two exquisite works of art and they hung in *La Ventana's* museum. Many people, who saw the originals—still hanging in the *Galleria degli Uffizi* in Florence, Italy on Earth—thought that Jana Markette's work surpassed Botticelli's. I wanted those two painting because every time I saw them they gave me a rush. No way was I was going to leave them on *The Mother* for a salvage crew to find.

****

We went to my apartment and I packed, what I considered, a few essential items and Iris chided me with, "You allowed me one tiny suitcase—now you are taking all this shit?"

Iris was right; I was pathetic. I packed all my socks, whether they had mates or not "It's a symbolic gesture," I explained. "My brother Senon might still be alive somewhere and we promised to get our unmatched socks together to see if we can make some pairs." We stopped by Rugen's place and the only thing *ce* wanted were *cis* New Delphi Crystals still sitting on *cis* altar and *cis* clothes. "Let's go get those paintings and get out of here," I said. I felt as uneasy as Iris did. It was a vague fear that everything had become too easy and another test was waiting around the next corner.

On the way to the museum, Iris was the one who noticed something amiss. "The emptiness of this place must be getting to me," she said. "I thought I saw somebody walk around that pillar a moment ago."

The sensation I experienced that night on Mallory Dock came to reclaim me and Ezek decreed with cosmic authority, "PAY ATTENTION, SANTE!" I stopped dead in my tracks and announced, "We're no longer alone."

Rugen stopped too. "Okay, should we check it out or vamoose immediately?"

"Let's check it out," I said.

"Are you kidding?" screamed Iris. "Let's get out of here!"

"We're going to check it out," said Rugen.

"Damn you!" Iris shouted. "Every time I say white, one of you says black. You are the most exasperating people I've ever met." Rugen started walking toward the pillar in question. "Wait for me!" Iris screamed.

I felt no fear as Iris did; but I did feel intense curiosity and I thought of Elay's comments about the soul fragments and that their curiosity was indestructible. Ezek led me and I merely followed, as did Iris and Rugen. Where we ended up was The Pavilion, where Rugen's Gathering was held. As we drew near, we could hear the undercurrent of soft conversation coming from a waiting crowd. The double doors were standing wide open. "Holy shit!" said Rugen in a sinking voice filled with inevitability.

I peeked around one of the doors. It was a Gathering, not of the living, but of flimsy spirits so ephemeral, they looked like a grisaille painting— chalky, blue-white, and thin. "Welcome back," said a voice in a broad Universal drawl. My attention shot to the right and there hung Evose suspended in midair. I knew the corporeal Evose was dead, but this was almost an exact memorial copy of the original. He appeared real, as real as any good hologram. He was more handsome that he was in life and glowed with the light of his oversoul that was supporting his ability to manifest before us. "You succeeded in finding her," said Evose. "Plus you convinced her to come into the future. That's more than I ever considered possible.

Hello," Evose said to Iris. "I love you. I suppose you already know that. Sante has probably pinned me to a board and explained to you all about my feelings."

Iris was terrified and I could feel her shivering with fright next to me. "It's him—isn't it? Go away!" she shouted toward Evose. "I am not going anywhere with you—you ghost from Hell!"

Evose was hurt and I said, "Iris is rather high strung. In the long run, it wouldn't have worked out between you two."

"We will not allow you to take her," said Rugen. "She is pre-Regression and unaware as a child."

"That's right!" said Iris. "I don't know my head from a hole in the ground. I'm so stupid I could not possibly be of any value to you." Iris began tugging on my arm. "Let's go."

"We have nothing to fear from the dead," I assured her. "Nothing and nobody can abridge incarnate freewill."

"Obviously, you never saw *The Night of The Living Dead*," she said.

"Who are all these other spirits?" I asked.

"Let's go inside," said Evose. "I'll introduce you."

It was quiet as we walked through the open doors and the Gathering gained clarity, life, and substance, just as One World had. It was a packed house filled with soul fragments. "Did we drag you with us from the fourth dimension or did you merely pop in to scare us back into denial?" My sarcasm set off a buzz and they actually laughed as if I was the opening act sent out to warm-up the crowd.

From the moment Evose first saw Iris, he had gazed longingly toward her and his gaze now intensified. It was the look of yearning from an unrequited lover. The gallery of soul fragments was feeding off his energy; and in a few cases, I heard their insincere swoons and sighs. It was offensive because they were rollicking in Evose's unfulfilled love for Iris, enjoying his quandary. "Have you no pity for me?" Evose asked Iris. "The Mother of all creation sent me to you. She sent me to help you free your soul."

Iris was as cold as a stone when she told him, "If you believe that then I feel sorry for you."

Evose fell to his knees and looked at Iris as if she had stabbed him through the heart. He gazed up at her and tears filled his eyes. Evose could tolerate almost anything, but he could not abide her pity. "I cannot believe you did this to me!" he exclaimed. "I died for you, yet you live on in your denial of me. You're a cruel and self-centered woman, unworthy of my love."

The soul fragments wept with empathy and something in all their faces reminded me of the Astarte Syriaca painting by Rossetti. Their faces were the faces of Astarte's soul mates, perfectly beautiful and yet jaded and racked with boredom. It was obvious that none of them had felt anything firsthand in eons. I was still arrogant and I raised my fist at the fragments and declared, "Why don't you go experience a life firsthand."

They started shouting, telling me, "shut up!" and "mind my own business!" Rugen advised me to watch myself because I was dealing with a hoard of crazy soul fragments. At that instant, there was a flash of light. It was as if someone ignited a tray of flash powder because, for an instant, the brightness blinded me.

When my vision returned, Nova was there. The fragments were silent before *lim*, perhaps even afraid. *Le* floated over to Evose and sat down next to him on the stairs. It's time to go home," *le* said softly "Don't be afraid. Your oversoul thinks of you as a great saint and a party is waiting for you. Please come before all the food gets cold."

"I've forgotten how to make the jump," said Evose.

"Just let go and a Gathering of your loved ones will escort you home."

"Are you sure?" asked Evose.

"I'm very sure," said Nova.

Evose still appeared a bit uncertain, but he stood up and took one last look at Iris. "This was a hard lesson for me," he told her. "Other lessons await—I'm sure; but I will not experience you again." Then his oversoul took him. It felt the same as that night Nova died, a cold wind came and then Evose was no more.

****

The crowd of soul fragments groaned and I heard some catcalling. Nova looked up and said, "Be gone with you! Get a life!" Then as if someone blew out an entire stand of candles, the fragments began disappearing one by one until no one was there except Nova, Rugen, Lotus Blossom, Iris, the felines, and me.

Nova approached Iris and she recognized *lim* as the "man" of her dreams. "My lady," *le* said, and *le* produced a single piece of straw and handed it to her with great ceremony. *Le* extended a hand saying, "Could I give you a hand into the future?"

"Where have I been going my entire life?" she asked Nova.

"Why to this moment," *le* said. "Welcome to your own future. Enlightenment is available to everyone; but it is not a gift freely given. Great honor is involved and I expect complete respect from you from this moment forward. Do you understand?"

"Yes," she said without hesitation.

"Good," *le* said. "My oldest child Una and Belinda are docking on *The Mother*, even as we speak."

"Belinda?" she questioned. "That's me in the future—right? Won't I disappear if we come face to face?"

"No," said Nova. "Communion with your future will educate you like

376

never before. I want you to accompany Belinda and Una to New Delphi where they will help you toward your own enlightenment. Make your oversoul proud. I will visit you often and be your spiritual connection from this moment forward. Do you understand?"

"Yes," she said again and I was amazed to see that with Nova she was meek as a lamb.

"Excellent," said Nova. "You are already showing yourself to be a willing student. Now go sit down over there and wait for Una and Belinda. Allow me to have a bit of intimate time with my soul mates because I definitely am on borrowed time." We walked off with Nova and out into the hall. "Stay available," *le* told us. "Iris will need friends when she begins to remember. When she dies into her oversoul, there will be a great feast upon her consciousness. In her completion, her oversoul will know great fulfillment. She will remember you then and you will share in the glory of that feast. Nova hesitated and said, "Enough about Iris, enough about what will be. Let's talk about now. I want you to finish this life, which you have already begun. Tell me you will do it willingly—for me?" Like Tantalus with his grapes, Nova kept us moving in the right direction and *le* said, "We are so close now. Keep faith. We have incredible power together and our separation is an illusion. I am always with you, now, forever, as one." Nova began to fade for our oversoul was calling *lim* home. I knew *le* was still right there, yet the visible was so powerful for me that I felt the absence of *lis* form immediately. After *le* was gone, Rugen and I held onto each other and cried.

A Ganat ship called the *Zephyr* docked a short time later and aboard was Belinda and Una. "Did Senon make it off *The Mother*?" I asked them immediately.

"Senon is alive and on New Delphi with *lis* mates," said Una and it finally seemed as if she was learning to smile. Una confirmed that she had dealt with The Consortium right before her last life. "They did call me the Janaforma Wonder," she acknowledged.

Belinda told me that she felt, "charged with new energy. I might stick around for another thirty or forty years merely to see what happens next."

When Iris met Una and Belinda, she dropped Rugen and I like two hot potatoes. While they were gone, Rugen and I got our pulsar out of the vitasphere and readied her for flight. We dumped the entire programming from the main multidex for a second time and transferred the Senon programming back to the pulsar. We organized our belongings and wrapped the two paintings from the museum so they would not be damaged during flight.

Rugen and I met the three women in the landing bay two hours later. They were waiting for a shuttlecraft that would take them to Delphi. They were all indescribably themselves; Una, the stoic saint; Iris, the fuming firecracker; and Belinda, the flirty bitch, each one, one by one, kissed us goodbye. No tears came from Iris. She was the least sentimental person I ever met. She did tell us, "thank you. I understand I get a vacation in six months, maybe I can come to Uropae and see you." Then she looked down at Lotus Blossom in my arms and kissed her on the forehead. It was the first time she had ever touched her. "She's a cutie," Iris said. "I know you'll take good care of her."

After they left, life seemed too easy. I indulged and took my time writing what I knew were the last few pages of this book. I still cannot decide whether to release it for publication or not. It definitely is revealing. Maybe I'll hold onto it for a while and see.

Senon told us that *le* was talking to *The Mother* too and she told *lim,* "Now that I'm back in the third dimension, I want a little time to meditate on what happened while I was in the fourth."

Senon decided to help *The Mother* avoid the salvage crews by reprogramming her orbit so it encompassed a larger ellipse than before. "She won't be around this way for another five space years," *le* explained.

On the third cycle I awoke and said to Rugen, "Lotus Blossom and I are yearning for some fresh air. I want to fly home to Uropae. I bet you have a rowboat somewhere on your property. I think it would be neat to sit back, allow you to row us around Iona, and show us the sites. Besides, I'd love to see your pecs and biceps gleaming with sweat."

"Is that right?" asked Rugen. "What will you be doing while I row you two around?"

"Lotus Blossom will be growing into her potential and I will be gazing into your eyes and checking to see if they are the same color as the water."

"Then what?"

"Then, we can fly to Sasaybin and see Baybairn again, eat his jhap biscuits, and visit my statue. Maybe I will write a few more books. Yes, I definitely will do that."

"Then what?"

"Then, maybe we can plant a rose garden in that spot behind the library and stick around to actually smell the roses when they bloom."

Rugen eagerly suggested, "We could go to the beaches during Conjunction. That's something I dream of doing with you."

"Then what?"

"Then we will race home and make wild and passionate love."

"Let's do it!" I said.

"*Ejesay epay,*" said Rugen surrendering to all permutations of my love.

ABOUT THE AUTHOR

Martha Fawcett was born in Tiffin, Ohio. As a child, her dad stoked her imagination with talk of future inventions, space travel, and meeting alien species. In addition to writing science fiction, she now takes delight in the protocols and absurdity of politics, a June garden in the morning, highly polished gemstones, and the beautiful flow of life. She enjoys time with her husband Bill and their two children, Penelope and Adam.

www.ingramcontent.com/pod-product-compliance
Lightning Source LLC
Chambersburg PA
CBHW050907250626
47155CB00001B/134